ABOUT THE AUTHOR: Father Herman B. Kramer was born in Petersburg, Iowa, March 24, 1884. He lived all his early life in Iowa, attending parish schools in the Diocese of Sioux City. He graduated from business college at the age of 21 with a degree in accounting. A year later, he entered St. Lawrence College (now Seminary) at Mt. Calvary, Wisconsin, completing a course in philosophy in five years. He studied theology at Innsbruck, Austria for one year. Ill health forced him to return to America, and he completed his studies at St. Paul Seminary, St. Paul, Minnesota, where he was ordained a priest in 1914.

He served as a priest in the Diocese of Sioux City for 40 years in various capacities, including a two-year term as chancellor and 37 years as a pastor. He is presently retired (1975) and residing in Oakland, California. Father Kramer learned to read and write seven languages. He became interested in the *Apocalypse* after reading it as a student in the seminary, and it later became a life-time study. His world famous *Book of Destiny* took 30 years to complete and is the result of these years of study.

The Book of Destiny

An Open Statement of the
Authentic and Inspired Prophecies of the
Old and New Testament

By

HERMAN BERNARD F. LEONARD KRAMER

TAN Books
Charlotte, North Carolina

NIHIL OBSTAT: J. S. Considine, O.P.
Censor Deputatus

IMPRIMATUR: ✠ John M. Mueller, D.D.
Bishop of Sioux City, Iowa
January 26, 1956

Originally published in 1955 by Buechler Publishing Company, Belleville, Illinois. Reprinted in 1972 by Apostolate of Christian Action, Fresno, California using entirely new type set under the author's supervision, from which this printing has been made.

Library of Congress Catalog Number: 75-13556

ISBN: 978-0-89555-046-0

Cover art by Peter Massari.

Printed and bound in India

TAN Books
Charlotte, North Carolina
www.TANBooks.com

2012

DEDICATION

This work is dedicated to the LITTLE LAMB, who is the ROOT OF DAVID, the HEAD of the Church, the MASTER and CENTRAL FIGURE OF HISTORY, the RULER over the kings of the earth, the KING of kings and the VICTOR over all evil powers, and who has been shaping the destiny of the world in His own Mysterious Manner since His Sacrificial Death on the Cross.

FOREWORD

The title chosen for this book sets forth the contents of the inspired message revealed to St. John, the Apostle. It is a summing up of the prophetical work in the Bible by the Holy Spirit and a revelation of the Great Causes shaping future history which will constitute the destiny of mankind. This destiny will be created and developed by man's free will. It is the *Book of Destiny,* because it shows forth the destiny of the whole human race. It is building up now and will grow until the Day of Judgment. This building up began with the renewed persecution of the Christians by Trajan after the benign lull under the Emperor Nerva.

The Apocalypse received its name from the first word of these revelations. Whether St. John gave it this name or not cannot be established. The secrets of the future written in this book have mystified and intrigued the minds of the most inquisitive for nineteen hundred years. St. Vincent Ferrer five hundred years ago and St. Bernardine of Siena a half a century later threatened their hearers with the judgments enumerated in the Apocalypse, but their words were not well heeded. Yet the FIRST WOE was averted from the countries which they envangelized. For a hundred years now the secrets have been quite openly expressed and written about, though with some uncertainty and misgivings, but have not been noticed by the world. In the meantime events have succeeded with increasing speed and growth towards a denouement of the secrets of the GREAT WORLD DRAMA so long wrapped up in mysterious visions. Any day may flash upon the consciousness of men the DESTINY towards which mankind is hastening.

THE AUTHOR

I.

INTRODUCTION

THE APOCALYPSE A PROPHETICAL BOOK

The word PROPHET, derived from the Greek, orginally meant the same as the Hebrew word 'NABI', an interpreter or mouthpiece of God. (Exod. VII. 1-2). The prophet in the Old Testament was commonly called "a man of God", being His spokesman, the inspired deliverer of His revelations and the interpreter of His Will and His Designs with the people of Israel. When Samuel was the great leader about 1000 B.C., the prophets were a permanent institution and formed communities or schools, in which young men were educated and trained for their calling to praise God in psalms and hymns, especially when moved by the Holy Spirit (1 Kings X. 5-12). Throughout the history of His people, God chose by an extraordinary act those whom He desired for special manifestations of His Will and Power to Israel. Thus He chose Samuel, Elias, Eliseus, Isaias, Ezechiel and others.

The prophets are divided into two classes: The older prophets, who delivered God's message orally, many of whom were mighty in power and deed; the younger prophets, who appeared later in time and committed their message to writing, although they also preached to people and rulers. All the great prophets envisioned future events and evolutions of history. And therefore the word, PROPHET, eventually came to mean only one who foretells the future. St. Paul (1 Cor. XIV. 24-25) does not use the word exclusively for one who foretells the future but includes those who reveal present secrets. In the Apocalypse, prophecy denotes both a revelation of present secrets and of future facts.

In the Old Testament, the prophets wrote seventeen books during the course of about four hundred years, from 800 to 400 B.C. Thereafter the voice of prophecy became silent. All prophets were held in highest esteem by the Israelites. They exercised far-reaching authority both before and after the Babylonian Captivity. And later, when even the priesthood was in perplexity and doubt, deliberating what course to pursue, they waited "till there should come a prophet" (1 Macc. IV. 46). But the spirit of prophecy remained dormant in Israel up to the time of our Lord, who is the Prophet of prophets.

Then Mary and Zachary, Simeon and Anne prophesied (Lc. I. 46, 67; II. 29). And our Lord called John the Baptist the greatest of all the prophets, because he held the office of Precursor (Lc. VII. 28).

Jesus Christ was soon recognized as a "great prophet". He came into the world endowed with the prophetic dignity, and He exercised this office during His whole public ministry. Even before this, when but twelve years old, He manifested this prerogative (Lc. II. 46). When outlining His mission to the world, He promised His hearers prophets who should reveal new truths as well as interpret the old (Mt. XIII. 52; XXIII. 34). But He obviously had the apostles in mind not the charismatic prophets who appeared later among the gifts of the Holy Spirit. Not our Lord, but the Holy Spirit sent them. The Apostles had the gift of prophecy in a more eminent degree than those who were mere prophets; the prophetical office promised by our Lord was embodied in the apostolate, embracing the power to teach, rule and sanctify the Church, for He made those whom He appointed apostles His spokesmen and the bearers of His message. He conferred the OFFICE of the apostolate on His chosen and appointed ones; while the Holy Spirit, by the graces and charismata He infused into them, endowed them with the ability to carry out the threefold office of the apostolate. Our Lord called and ordained the original apostles for OFFICIAL positions in the Church, and these in turn appointed their successors, the college of bishops. But the GIFT of the apostolate was given by the Holy Spirit to other men not appointed official apostles by the Lord, to those who together with them were gifted to do apostolic work, to preach the Gospel and establish churches. These other apostles received the charismata of the Spirit. There is therefore a distinction to be made between this charismatic gift and the office of the apostolate.

There is likewise a distinction to be made between the gift of prophecy and the office of prophet. The gift of prophecy was a grace of the Spirit, in the light of which wonderful, secret and future things hidden even from the official apostles were revealed to the recipients (Acts XX. 22; XXI. 11). All the charismatic gifts were particular endowments of the Spirit for particular works in the Church. The charismatic prophets were gifted to edify, exhort and console the faithful, as the doctors were to instruct them in their faith. These prophets were not like the prophets of Israel, appointed to hold any jurisdiction in the Church. Such jurisdiction was reserved for the bishops appointed and ordained by the Apostles (Acts XX. 28; Titus 1. 5). In choosing bishops to rule the Church and to continue the work of the apostolate, the Apostles may have considered only those whom the Holy Spirit had endowed with the gift of prophecy, because the grace of prophecy was an efficacious help in the work of the apostolate and ranked next in order to the grace of the apostolate (I. Cor. XII. 28). But that the Apostles gave preference for the episcopate to those who were thus endowed cannot be proven from Scripture.

On Pentecost, St. Peter in his first sermon announced to the world the conferring of the gift of prophecy by the Holy Spirit. But neither his explanation nor our Lord's promise means that a hierarchical order of prophets would be instituted in the Church. St. Peter merely explained that the astounding miracle witnessed by the multitude manifested the presence of the Holy Spirit. St. Paul enumerates prophecy as one of the charismata of the Spirit (1 Cor. XII. 28; XIII. 2; XIV. 3; Eph. III. 5; IV. 11). Greater than the gift of prophecy is charity (1 Cor. XIII. 1 ff). Prophecy is not called an order; it gave no authority to rule; it was but a special gift to extend the power and influence of the Church after the Apostles had established it to bring new converts into it and to edify, exhort and console the believers (1 Cor. XIV. 3, 24).

In his letter to the Ephesians, St. Paul makes the apostles and prophets the foundation of the Church and Christ the cornerstone. The reference there is clearly to the prophets of the Old Testament. The church pre-existed in the Old Testament, and the prophets were the teachers officially appointed by Jahve as were the Apostles by Jesus Christ, so that the Church of the Old Testament was prophetic in character as that of the New is apostolic. Both the teachings of the prophets and apostles constitute the foundation of the Church, and the revelations of the charismatic prophets are not part of that foundation.

The Apocalypse is a prophetical book (IV. 1), and it ranks St. John with the prophets of the Old Testament (X. 11). The "mystery of God" had been declared by His "servants the prophets" (X. 7), and that prediction promised the complete victory of Christ. No records exist of the charismatic prophets making any such predictions. The Apocalypse is so largely a restatement of the Old Testament prophecies, that some have called it a mere compilation. Where the "prophets and saints" are mentioned (XI. 18), the reference is to the Two Witnesses and the martyrs who shall suffer and die under Antichrist. And the same significance is attached to "the blood of saints and prophets" (XVI. 6), which calls for the seven last plagues; and the same motive is given for the rejoicing over the fall of Babylon (XIX. 2), the capital of the False Prophet, from which shall issue the edicts of persecution and bloodshed meriting the vengeance of Heaven (XVIII. 24). The ancient prophets had pronounced the judgment upon Old Babylon, and St. John was inspired to pronounce it upon the new. And perhaps the blood of all Old Testament prophets as well as of all martyrs of the Church shall be avenged in the destruction of this city of sin as it was in the destruction of old Jerusalem (Mt. XXIII. 35).

The Apocalypse is not the work of the charismatic prophets but the work of an apostle who is endowed with the gift of prophecy. The Christian prophets contributed no literature to the treasury of the Church as did the prophets of old. The charismata in the Church may have disappeared before the Apocalypse was written, for St. Ignatius mentions no prophets in the churches at the time of his martyrdom. With him the all-important offices are the ranks of the hierarchy, those of bishop, priest and deacon. The prophets he makes reference to are those of the Old Testament (Magn. VIII. 2; Phil. V. 2, 9). Obviously therefore the Christian prophets of apostolic times were an ephemeral product of the Holy Spirit called to convince unbelievers of the divine origin of the Church and never intended to be a permanent teaching force. The Apocalypse does not appear to make any reference to the prophets and other charismatic men so numerous in the days of St. Paul. Chapters I. II. III. IV. treat of the hierarchy as the life-giving principle within the Church, through which the destiny of the Church and the world is to be shaped, and the final enduring victory for Christ and mankind is to be won.

Use Of The Old Testament

The author of the Apocalypse uses the Old Testament

extensively. He not only adapts the symbolism and imagery of the prophets to his needs but gives out a new edition of many prophecies. Whole passages are verbally taken from the Septuagint. Other passages are re-stated and are the substance of prophecies as contained in the Hebrew text. St. John does not make formal quotations from the prophets and does not appeal to their authority, because he writes in the strength of his own apostolic authority, which excells that of the prophets. His verbal extracts from the prophets must then be understood to be interpretations of the obscure Old Testament prophecies. Some coincidences of language, of words and phrases with those of the Greek Septuagint, are no doubt accidental. The common commercial or conversational Greek was adopted in the composition of the Apocalypse, the same as used in the Septuagint. In that simple Greek style, a deep student of the Septuagint would readily use the same words to describe the same visions. For these and other reasons many passages of the Apocalypse are verbally the same as those found in the voluminous contents of the Old Testament. However, from the contents of the Apocalypse, it is perfectly plain, that St. John verbally copied many passages from the O.T. to give them fuller expression and to put them in a context where their true meaning can be easily understood. Such use of the prophets appears decisively intentional in many instances. Many prophecies of the Old Testament are just fragments, are mere glimpses of the future empire of the Messias. St. John takes these fragments and pieces them together and shows the full import of each prophetic glimpse. His work is not a compilation of those prophecies but is as concise as possible a statement of the revelations made to him. Since those revelations were the completed visions, the glimpses of the Old Testament prophecies fit in here and there without an apparent conscious effort by the Apocalyptist.

The apocalyptic visions gave the prophets ages in advance the materials for their prophetical descriptions. In our interpretation, St. John is not supposed to have borrowed any ideas from the Old Testament other than similes and figures of speech by which he gives more vivid expression to some of the descriptions and narratives. The materials of the Apocalypse, where they are the same or similar to those of the Old Testament, are always handled in an original way. So this is not the work of a mere poet who combines ideas and forms of older poets into new forms and new ideas but is a new creation of the prophetic mind. No poet could have taken the prophecies of the Old Testament and made our Apocalypse out of them by his own unaided poetic genius. Whatever St. John borrowed from the Old Testament, he always modified to suit his purpose making the detailed descriptions of the visions sometimes approach nearer to those of the Hebrew version, sometimes to those of the Septuagint. It is claimed that he refers to the book of Daniel in forty-five places. Isaias, Ezechiel and Zacharias are next most frequently in evidence. And the book of Psalms has a large share in his attention. With all that, the book is not a compilation but a logical unity from beginning to end. The logical sequence lies in the text and will be demonstrated in this interpretation. The unity of authorship is also so evident in the text itself, that even without the unvarying external evidence from Christian antiquity, no serious student of the book could find any difficulty in admitting it.

The Author Of The Apocalypse

The genuineness of the authorship of the Apocalypse is solidly established from both the internal and external evidence. St. Clement of Rome seems to quote it (Ad. Cor. 34). St Justin quotes it (Dial 81) and according to Eusebius attributes it to St. John (Eus. Hist. Eccl. XVIII. 8). Irenaeus writes a commentary on it and ascribes the book to St. John, the Apostle (Adv. Haer. V. 25-30). Hippolytus writes a large treatise on Antichrist explaining the apocalyptic description about him. Theophilus, Cyprian, Tertullian, Clement of Alexandria, Origin and Victorin all attribute the book to St. John, the Apostle. The Apocalypse was in the Itala and in the Sahidic and Bohairic versions of the Bible. It is also enumerated as Scripture in the Muratorian Fragment.

The internal evidence is so decisive especially when combined with the external historical testimony, that no doubt can remain about the authorship. The contents clearly delineate the character of St. John, the beloved disciple. Some of the so called super-critics have tried to overthrow the internal evidence by making a distinction between the Apostle John and the beloved disciple and even another John called the Presbyter. For the deeper and more thorough student of the gospel and epistles of St. John and of the Apocalypse, the same mind and character is prominent in all these documents. Hence those critics realizing the strength of the evidence have tried to ascribe even the gospel to some one else not the Apostle. In the Apocalypse he mentions his name as the author and as a servant of Christ. He writes in the name of Christ with apostolic authority to the seven churches and to all the world. The Apocalypse simply states that it is "John" who wrote the book. That simple mentioning of his name clinches the argument of his authorship. The name "John" was a sufficient guarantee of the writer's authority to gain a respectful hearing or reception for the book. He received the revelations on the Island of Patmos. Irregularities of grammar in the composition of the Apocalypse are no proof that the author is not the same one who wrote the gospel. It may have been written by one or more secretaries under St. John's dictation. Or St. John may in his last years have lost some hold on the Greek language, or he may not have taken the time to correct the Greek of his original notes.

The Time of Composition

The time of its composition is very definitely stated by Irenaeus to have been towards the end of Domitian's reign (V. 30, 3). Irenaeus writes that he met and tarried with Polycarp, the disciple of St. John. The testimony of Eusebius agrees with that of Irenaeus.

From the internal evidence we glean a respite from persecution during which the Apocalypse was written, but Asia might soon expect the arrival of the "great tribulation". There were martyrs long ago, as the letters suggest (II. 3, 13), and many of them in the Empire (VI. 10). Now the first persecution was begun by Nero, A.D. 64. The next one was towards the end of Domitian's reign. The Apocalypse quite clearly suggests the reign of Domitian, during which emperor-worship was at a high pitch (II. 13; VI. 2; XIII. 4, 15) reaching its culmination towards the end of his life. The letters reveal that the faith had long been planted in the cities addressed and that some of the people had lost the apostolic fervor, which would suppose that a second generation had grown up, and thirty years or more had passed since the establishment of these congregations. This would bring the composition of the book after the year 90 A.D. Furthermore, St. John could not have interfered in the administration of the churches during the lifetime of St. Paul. But the letters indicate a long acquaintanceship with the churches and a comprehensive knowledge of their spiritual and temporal condition. The mentioning of the Temple in the Apocalypse on the other hand is no proof if its existence, because the Temple mentioned is an *ideal* temple, like that of Ezechiel.

The so-called HIGHER critics claim the first three verses to be spurious and the work of a later editor or compiler. Only their prejudice could prompt them to thus contradict the internal evidence. For the language of these verses including grammatical irregularities is that of St. John. The first three verses are a suitable introduction. To begin the book with verse four would make it begin like an ordinary epistle. It would be just as logical to reject the first eight verses as the first three and following out the same kind of logic reject the first nine chapters. In the present interpretation, we take the verdict of the true critics and accept the whole received text as genuine. The work of determining the true and authentic text has been completed by the archeologists, commentators, exegetes and textual critics. Such research is therefore superfluous at present and does not come within the scope of our interpretation. Ours is but an attempt to establish and prove some fundamental principles, which seem to be the key to the revelations, and interpret the whole book by adhering to and following out those principles from beginning to end. And the received Greek text makes such an attempt possible. Each word in the text has its rightful place of importance and no word is superfluous. There are some differences in the ancient manuscripts as well as in the quotations of the Fathers, but the textual critics are in agreement on the original text and have adopted the manuscripts that have always been held nearest the original. The Apocalypse has received the same careful study in this regard as all the other books of the New Testament, so that at present there is little disagreement on the true Greek text among Catholic, Protestant and Orthodox scholars.

Purpose of the Apocalypse

The immediate purpose of the Apocalypse is quite evident in many statements. It is plainly to CONSOLE the Christian congregations in the hardships of a virtuous life and in the dangers of practicing their religion with persecutions facing them. Their rights as citizens were jeopardized; their possessions were made evanescent. There was danger that the present persecution begun by Domitian would be extended to Asia. The Christians were viewed with suspicion, because they would have nothing to do with the worship of the gods or the worship of Caesar and kept aloof from many public functions. St. Paul, their spiritual father, had been martyred long ago. This was not the generation which St. Paul had converted but one that had grown up since his martyrdom. They had learned the promises of the Apostle from hearsay. The Parousia of which he had often spoken had not materialized, and therefore a new revelation was necessary to bolster up the courage of the Christians and steady them in their faith. Likewise was such a revelation needed to clear from the churches abuses and relapses into superstitious practices. A revelation that assured judgment upon the enemies of Christ, the speedy Parousia and the final triumph of the kingdom of God was of immediate and constant practical use. So the Apocalypse was of inestimable value to the Church upon its publication. The letters in the second and third chapters explain the dangers existing in the several congregations after each is ex-rayed by the Spirit. In that divine light material prosperity is seen to be far more dangerous than persecution. Each congregation has particular perils to face, and each is in turn specifically directed how to combat these perils.

The Apocalypse is also a book of consolations for all time to come, because the Church will at all times have many trials and persecutions to bear. The most insistent need of consolations shall be during the greatest crisis of its history in the days of Antichrist. The Apocalypse reveals the outcome of all attacks on the Church and the final victory of Christ. Not only does an eternal crown await the martyrs but also the triumph of Christ in the world through their constancy. And not only in the letters but throughout the book, the Christians are warned against drifting with the maelstrom of sin (XIV. 9) and are urged to keep themselves unsullied (XVI. 15) and to hold out until death against persecution (XIII. 10; XIV. 13). The book thus becomes a book of consolations for all times.

In the inspired outlook of St. John, the book was to reach a wide circulation down to the farthest horizons of future generations (XXII. 18). It would, like all other inspired writings be a book for all times, because it is the recital of the victories and the final grand triumph of his beloved Master. St. John recognized both his own gift of prophecy and the revelations as a prophecy (IV. 1-2), and he ranks this book with the other inspired Scriptures (Deut. IV. 2; XII. 32). In the most emphatic language possible, he promises the fullfillment of all prophecies in it.

The Apocalypse not only revealed the triumphs of Christ but of necessity also the sufferings of His Church, His mystical body. The growth and activities of the forces that caused these sufferings had to be revealed too. Thus the Apocalypse re-iterated the statements of Christ in the gospels, that His Church will suffer hatred and persecution but through this persecution will be purified and will win the victory over sin, over the world and over Satan.

The Apocalypse was needed at the time of its appearance for another reason. From the time in which prophecy ceased in Israel until the birth of our Lord, the chosen people had experienced many dire calamities. Those calamities moved many to decide that a prophecy was needed to bolster up the courage of the people and to revive their hope in the ultimate triumph of their nation over their oppressors. Many false prophets then took to writing apocalypses of various kinds. They produced the many aprocryphal apocalypses of pre-Christian and early Christian times. The book of Enoch is the most important of pre-Christian days, while after the destruction of Jerusalem, the apocalypse of Baruch and the IV. book of Esdras appeared. With the destruction of Jerusalem, the hope of that Israel that rejected Christ collapsed. Then, like the false prophets in the days of Jeremias, the false apocalyptists tried to keep alive the false hopes of the antichristian Jews. The revelations made to St. John appeared in the midst of this flood of false apocalypses to save the Christians of Jewish origin from being misled and to reveal the true destiny of God's people.

The text is similar to some passages of the aprocryphal apocalypses, but not because St. John made use of those books. Those books are very largely plagiaristic and had been verbally copied from the apocalyptic prophesies. Hence St. John, in restating the Old Testament prophecies, comes very near to the diction of the apocryphal books. He probably knew of the existance of these books, but there is no evidence to prove that they furnished him any material for his Apocalypse. His revelations are real and true, and his book is only the recital of what was revealed to him. His apocalypse bears his own name, while the apocryphal ones all bear the name of some older prophet. That St. John might have used current words and phrases often on the lips of people such as the word "logos" in the Gospel is not impossible

It was not necessary that the prophecies be understood at once. In fact, if they could have been interpreted as covering thousands of years of Church history, they would not have been so pithy. The Christians were not all of such heroic calibre and of such unwavering constancy as to be willing to lay down their lives, and more, suffer the most excruciating torments for an unseen reward, when those who denied their faith and saved their lives could have the good things of life, repent at leisure and be forgiven before they died. Had they known the true meaning of the prophecies, they might have apostatized during persecution. But the thought that the judgments upon the wicked were to begin at once, and they were to be wiped from the face of the earth, and only the good were to remain to inherit all things was a strong inducement to risk everything on the side on which the only hope of winning existed. Hence the book of the "seven seals" was a closed book, and when the seals were opened, events were revealed in such mysterious language and symbols, that they could not be understood or interpreted until after their happening. But the revelations contained in the open "booklet" are not so figurative and might be understood in advance. There is in it a far more minute description of events to come than in the seven seals and the first six trumpets. This is all-important for those who shall be on earth during the greatest crisis of history, the days of Antichrist.

The Imagery of the Apocalypse

St. John cannot be reasonably supposed to have been versed in all the literature and mythologies of the Greeks and Latins and all other ancient pagan peoples. It might even be going too far to credit him with a knowledge of all apocryphal books of the Jews. Before his call to the apostolate, he surely was not conversant in pagan lore or in spurious Jewish scriptures, and after his call he was the constant companion of our Lord and drank deeply at the divine fount of learning. After the Ascension began the incessant labors of the apostolate. To master the Greek "Koiné" language, to study the Septuagint version of the Old Testament and to preach the Gospel and establish churches was enough to fill up a human life. Added to that were the wearisome journeys of the apostolic life, during which there could be little time for study, and the all-absorbing attention to the churches established and to the Christians converted. In the light of all this, it seems unreasonable to consider an apostle as having time to study pagan literature so thoroughly as would enable him to adopt its phraseology and imagery spontaneously when writing an inspired book.

In our interpretation all borrowing from pagan sources and all allusions to mythology are rejected, and the traditional view is held that the visions are true and real, and that St. John labored to depict them as exactly and concisely as was possible with his knowledge of the Greek language. The Holy Spirit, as appears throughout the Old and New Testaments, accommodates Himself to the imagination, mind, will, temperament, attainments and experience of the one He inspires. In conveying to the writer the truths to be revealed, He excites those images that most naturally shape themselves in the seer's mind, higher or lower in the intellectual scale, consonant with his natural and acquired gifts. And He arouses those emotions that are most exactly expressive of the writer's character and temperament. The Prophet Amos, being a shepherd, uses pastoral similes and symbols to illustrate his message. Daniel, who spent most of his days at court, receives revelations concerning kingdoms and empires. Ezechiel, who was of priestly family, is ever solicitous about the Temple and the worship of the Deity and traces out the consequences of false worship. And St. John in the Gospel and epistles manifests a character of the highest spiritual tone. He begins the Gospel with the loftiest flight of imagination and theology and during the whole narrative maintains the same spiritual elevation of thought. The Apocalypse presents the same mind and heart, the same imaginative power, emotions and temperament as the Gospel and the epistles?

In the composition of the Apocalypse, which treats of a subject very different from that of the epistles and Gospel, St. John necessarily exhibited with prominence those faculties of the mind that were in the background in the other writings and relegated to the background those faculties that were in evidence in the Gospel composition. The Gospel was more subjective in tone, while the Apocalypse is more objective. The mind, heart and character of St. John were eminently qualified to receive these revelations. The great prophets of the Old Testament had received only glimpses of these and similar visions. But since St. John was spiritually and morally far superior to the ancient prophets, his qualifications made him worthy of receiving the complete revelations which the prophets received only in fragments.

The imagery of the Apocalypse is either entirely new or supplementary of the revelations partially made to the prophets. The Old Testament prophecies are thus interpreted and made clear. The Apocalypse is the finish, completion and summing up of all revelation. It was not neecessary that the imagery be drawn from the apocrypha or still less from pagan mythology. All that could be drawn from the apocrypha is contained in the inspired books, because the apocrypha are largely plagiarisms. They take the imagery of the prophetical books and embellish them with apt imaginings, but they reveal nothing new and clarify nothing. To suppose that St. John borrowed visions from spurious sources or even from pagan poetry or mythology would be supposing that his words were not true, for he represents all the visions as true and real. They could therefore have no affinity to the fancies of pagan poets. The revelations in the Apocalypse are likewise totally different from those received by the other Christian prophets of St. Paul's time. Theirs were only glimpses, flashes of divine light, and their purpose was edification or consolation for the time and place in which they were received without any obligation to record them. What visions they had cannot be known, because they were not recorded. The revelations of the Apocalypse were intended for all times.

St. John draws his imagery from all parts of creation and from all conditions of human life. The heavens lend a touch of sublimity to many truths revealed. The sun enwraps the Woman, the moon serves as her pedestal and stars encircle her head for a crown. At other times the sun is dimmed with mystery, the moon turns to the color of blood and stars fall from heaven. A meteor sweeps across the sky; lightnings and thunders terrify the peoples; winds and hail flay the earth. And the sea appears now and then with its fish, ships and mariners. Mountains and islands move away or sink into the sea, and into it is tumbled a volcano. Also a crystal sea appears. Earthquakes rock the earth; caves and dens furnish hiding places for the wicked; deserts, fertile fields, trees, orchards and vineyards, rivers and fountains adorn the descriptions.

All phases of human life appear. Agriculture furnishes its symbols of trees, vines, herbs and grass; the harvest and vintage pass review. Commerce with its freighter ships illustrates prosperity; business methods are hinted at; the opulence of the rich and the squalor of the poor come into view. Occasions of joy, the wedding feast, and occasions of mourning and weeping at the plagues of the destroying angels; The sensual pleasures of the lustful, and the spiritual joys of the virgins: All these are seen in turn. Priests appear in priestly robes and penitents in sackcloth. The patience of the saints, the benedictions pronounced upon them, the praises and adoration they offer the Deity exalt the mind of the reader; whilst the wailings and despair and blasphemous ravings of the inpenitent worshippers of the Beast and his sinful proposals instill a wholesome fear and dread. The ravages of raiding warriors or barbarian hordes and vast armies, despotic kings and world-controlling powers are depicted shedding the blood of defenseless victims. All classes of men: the kings of the earth, merchants, sailors, soldiers, musicians, craftsmen, slaves and free citizens cross the stage.

The powers of darkness are depicted battling the spirits of light; and the kings of the earth submitting to the direction of the dragon, the king of darkness, are drawn up in battle array against the King of kings and His armies of light. The happiness of the virtuous on earth in the midst of all turmoil encouraged by promises of everlasting bliss is contrasted with the sordid satisfaction of the servers of sin who are confronted with nothing but prospects of endless torments in the pool of fire.

The animal kingdom likewise furnishes many symbols. The living creatures, the wild beast and other beasts, a lion, a lamb, a calf, a leopard, a bear, an eagle, horses, locusts, scorpions, frogs, vultures and birds of the air appear and vivify the scenery. The elements, fire and water, personifications of death and sin, the underworld and the pool of fire and a bottomless abyss form settings for parts of the world-wide drama.

A very large part of the imagery is identical with that of the Old Testament, in employing which, St. John gives a new or fuller interpretation to its symbolism. Other symbols are taken from the Old Testament to represent new developments in the history of the Church. Symbolic names of Old Testament personages appear in the Apocalypse, such as the lion of the Tribe of Juda or the root of David. The tree of life, the water of life and the book of life are given a clearer meaning and add a halo of sublimity to the narrative. Famous places, such as Babylon, Sodom, Egypt come before us, and a New Jerusalem takes the place of the old. Many symbolic numbers are employed: 2, 3, 3½, 4, 5, 6, 7, 10, 12, 24, 42, 144, 666, 1,000 1260, 1600, 7,000 and 200,000,000. Of all of these numbers SEVEN is the most frequent. It is the sacred number of completion. The mystic number, the number of the Blessed Trinity, is combined with many numbers to compose the others. FOUR is the number of universality, and this multiplied by three gives the perfect number, 12, God's number. The world's number of perfection is TEN.

The last Judgment with the Great White Throne is the final scene toward which the whole action of the Great Drama converges. Glimpses of this judgment are flashed on the canvass as a background for intermediate judgments and to keep the final summing-up of all events before the mind of the reader.

THE INTERPRETATION OF THE APOCALYPSE

Our interpretation treats the Apocalypse as an inspired book, because the Infallible Church has spoken, has placed this book on the canon and proclaimed its inspiration. This is no longer an open question. As an inspired book the Apocalypse could not contain errors in matters of faith or morals. The INTERPRETATION of the Apocalypse is, however, an open question, and the odium theologicum could not attach to one which contains no teaching in conflict with the dogmas or moral doctrines of the Church.

Verbal dictation by the Holy Spirit is not held throughout, for in the ordinary narrative and in the descriptions of the visions, St. John chooses his own words. Verbal dictation is held where Christ or His representatives are directly quoted. The letters to the seven churches are a verbal dictation from Christ, and the choice of those churches are Christ's.

Divine inspiration would also preclude all possibility of images from pagan mythology, idolatry or astrology, because those things are unrealities, superstitions and abominations and could not condignly become vehicles of thought or expressions of divine revelation. Such use would seem repugnant to the Spirit of Truth and to human reason. However, the mentioning of superstitious practices and errors in doctrine, in order to refute and condemn them would not seem repugnant to the dignity of an inspired book. But it does not seem reasonable that the Seer would have drawn illustrations from aprocryphal sources. Divine inspiration deals with realities, past, present and future.

In accommodating Himself to a human mind for the purpose of making new revelations or of completing or re-stating old ones, the Holy Spirit evidently leaves His instrument intact with all his natural and supernatural equipment of mind and will; He leaves grace, intellect, will, memory, imagination, temperament, education and experience true to the owner. And it may be held He raises all these endowments and acquisitions to a higher plane for keener and more perfect use. He then rouses in the mind of the inspired one thoughts and images and brings before his senses visions which he will be most apt to understand clearly in all their relationships to the revelations to be made, so that he may easily and most naturally record every part and particle of the revelations truthfully. He may draw his words, images, symbols, figures of diction, allusions and amplifications from every source of human knowledge with which he is familiar; he may draw from the revelations formerly made through any and all inspired writers, from the revelations made by Jesus Christ Himself, from the organization of the Church, from her liturgy, laws, worship, doctrines; he may depict the revelations on a background of political, social, economical, moral or spiritual conditions in the world; he may use current literary expressions to attach new and higher meanings to them; he may allude to figures of speech in common use in particular communities to which he addresses his message; he may take cognizance of the moral and spiritual as well as social and political status of his readers: All this would not detract from the dignity of an inspired message. But to admit mythology or idolatry or any other abomination into the composition of an inspired book would seem like blasphemy to the Spirit of Truth and Holiness.

Accepting the above premise, we reject as unworthy of consideration many accretions to the text as contained in the commentaries on the Apocalypse after so many centuries of study. As is evident from the Gospel, St. John must have learned the Greek language very well. His diction, however, is not the classical but the conversational Greek. In this simple parlance, there would be many classical expressions from mythology having a practical meaning as in all our modern languages. But he would not by using the words and idioms allude to all the mythologies from which the words were derived. When therefore the philologists trace up the origin of these terms and read into the text the mythologies and astrologies for which they were coined, they "add unto" the prophecy.

In our interpretation, all definitions have been drawn from the Old and New Testaments. Many scenes and visions have been cleared up by the study of history, because a large part of the prophecies seem already past history. Studies on the constitution of the Church and on apostolic Tradition, as well as studies into the spiritual, moral, social, political, educational, economic and cultural conditions of the times have shed a great deal of light on the obscure symbolism of the Apocalypse. Using all this as a working basis, our interpretation has been worked out logically from beginning to end. It was written and re-written before commentaries of many sorts were searched for further light.

In the knowledge of St. John, the Church surely possessed of divine truth all she possesses today though in a less developed form. Hence for an interpretation, no one is restricted to the words of the text alone but may take the Apocalypse as a poetic description of many truths written down later in the traditional writings of the great Fathers and Doctors. If therefore an interpretation, which holds the doctrines of the Church of today to have been clearly outlined in the mind of the Sacred Writer and which understands these doctrines as portrayed in the historico-prophetical visions of the Apocalypse to be the same as those contained in the crystallized expressions of theology, will work out logically from beginning to end, such an intepretation should be justifiable. And surely St. John had a clear knowledge of the doctrines which in later ages were crystallized by the church, and he might express them in symbolic language such as makes up the Apocalypse. But he may not have understood the manner nor seen the perspective of time in all details in which the events revealed to him would go into fulfillment.

The Apocalypse can have no multiple literal sense any more than any other part of the Scriptures. But to discover the exact literal sense with certainty in the Apocalypse is more difficult than in any other book of Holy Writ. Our interpretation is written in a hypothetical strain throughout, because being a prophetical book and as mysterious as it is, the Apocalypse could not be affirmed to have absolutely such and such a meaning anywhere, even in the part that is commonly considered to be past history and that is held as such here. Prophecies can never be interpreted in advance with positive certainty, unless God gives the revelation of their exact meaning. Therefore it cannot be stated with certainty how much of the Apocalypse is fulfilled in our day. And the application of the visions to past historical events must always be made with reservations, no matter how true they may seem. All the more can the unfulfilled part of the Apocalypse be only a probability however convincing the text is. But it did not seem necessary to use the phrases, "probably this is the meaning", "possibly this will happen", or "maybe this and maybe that" on every page or in every paragraph. It has intentionally been worked out to appear as probable or plausible as possible.

The Beast

The Apocalypse is a vivid portrayal of St. John's knowledge of the struggle between the Church and the anti-Christian world-power in Asia. The Empire was the representative of that world-power that had continually existed for many ages and had led the nations and peoples of the earth into idolatry and emperor-worship by the military forces of an organized government and now silently and openly counteracted the influence of the Church. It is not so remarkable that St. John uses the word "Beast" and not the word "Antichrist", because he writes a prophetical book, and by using the same term used by Daniel, he puts this book in the same category. St. John, as Daniel did, presents the world-power under a figure that would arouse the reader's resentment and would heighten his trust in God to defend His Church against its malevolent might. Had he used the word "Antichrist", he would have restricted the prophecies to the man of sin, who according to both St. John and St. Paul was a person destined to gather all the evil forces in the world and unite and co-ordinate them under his dominion for the last desperate attack on the Church of Jesus Christ. By using the word "Beast", he could unite his empire of evil and his person of evil in one single term and include under it the anti-Christian world-power of his own time and unify their efforts against Christ and God by the mind and power of Satan. He thus aptly portrays the evil world-power of all times in the form of a bloodthirsty beast.

St. John presents Antichrist in a two-fold role, personal and political. He depicts the first in chapter XIII. and the second in chapter XVII. His idea of Antichrist is exactly that of St. Paul, that he is not on impersonal power but a man. "Little children, it is the last hour: and as you have heard that Antichrist cometh, even now there are become many antichrists" (1 Jo. II. 18, 22; IV. 3). St. Paul had expressed the same view: "unless there come a revolt first and the man of sin be revealed . . . etc." (2 Thess. II.), leaving no doubt of its being a man. St. John gives another view of Antichrist, that he not only "cometh," but is already in the world and his presence is in the form of a power or organization, and it manifested itself in the doctrines of the Docetae (1 Jo. IV. 3, 33; 2 Jo. 7). Irenaeus and Hippolytus apply the name to a person only not to an organization. The former identifies the "beast" with Antichrist. (Adv. Haer. V. xxvi, 1).

According to St. John's view so clearly revealed in the Apocalypse, before Antichrist appears, the beast is non-existent for a time. "The beast that was and is not and yet shall be" (XVII. 8) is the anti-Christian world-power. This sentence has mystified many interpreters. St. Jerome left the last clause out of his translation, probably because he considered it a contradiction. However, the beast in chapter XVII. is the empire of Antichrist though not entirely differentiated from his person. This anti-Christian empire existed in former times for a long course of ages but then ceased to exist for a time.

The Apocalypse demonstrates very clearly that the victory of the Lamb over all the forces of evil including the author of evil will be achieved by human agents. The more unwavering the loyalty and the truer the spirit of sacrifice with which the human actors play their roles, the more decisive and far-reaching will the victory be. If all the hierarchy labored with the zeal and perseverance of St. Francis Xavier and in them were found none of the vices of the pharisees, the heresies and schisms which will finally usher in the reign of Antichrist would not be established, nor would the apostasy before Antichrist come about, nor evil grow to the enormities it shall attain during his reign. After having redeemed mankind and endowed His Church with all power needed to convert the world, Christ left it free to mold its own destiny. Man's perverse will has produced all the evil that has grown side by side with good in the same field. God left men's will free. The Apocalypse might be called the Book of Destiny, because it clearly outlines the evolution of the world's destiny to the end and shows the forces acting to create it.

The Apocalypse seems to point obscurely and guardedly to Domitian as the present embodiment of the beast. St. Paul does not in his epistles take this view of either the empire or the emperor. Although in the epistles of St. John, the Docetae are antichrists, in the Apocalypse, the reigning emperor is the persecutor of the Church (Apoc. VI. 2). Still, the Seer does not identify him with Antichrist, although he desired to be called "Lord and God". This blasphemy made Domitian in his own time the representative or type of Antichrist but not Antichrist himself, because the numbers 666 or 616 do not fit his name. Emperor-worship was in St. John's estimation the greatest sin, for it made the city that practiced it the "seat of Satan" (Apoc. II. 13) and will make Antichrist "the man of sin" (2 Thess. II. 3-4). The term "Beast" was for St. John therefore the most felicitous and most expressive term for all purposes he had in mind.

Another evil force were the Jews in attacking and persecuting the Church. St. John calls them "the synagogue of Satan". They are thus classed with the emperor-worshippers for denying Christ His rightful honor. Connected with emperor-worship was the worship of Askulepius in Thiatira, of Artemis in Ephesus and of Dionysus and Zeus in Pergamum. Then there were the heresies of the Nicolaites (II.6), of the partakers of sacrificial meats in the pagan temples (II.14) and of compromisers with magicians and soothsayers (II. 20 ff.). All of these abominations indicated that the empire of the coming Antichrist was under construction. St. Paul had stated that "the mystery of iniquity already worketh" (2 Thess. II. 7), and St. John stated the same, "he is now already in the world" (1 Jo. IV. 3). In the Apocalypse, the Seer outlines the preparation of his empire in the first nine chapters and thereafter its growth to maturity under the personal direction of Antichrist and then its destruction. Emperor-worship, idolatry, magic, Judaism, heresy, schism, agnosticism, infidelity, liberalism, atheism, compromise with error or unbelief, persecution of the Church, hypocrisy and other vices are the roots out of which the enormities of Antichrist's reign will grow until they will overshadow the world.

The Defeats of Satan

The Apocalypse might be crowned by the caption of "The Book of Victories", for it depicts the victories of Jesus Christ, which culminate in His grand final triumph over Satan and all enemies. It would be more accurate to say that it depicts the last phase of the final victory over the archenemy. Throughout the sacred writings, he stands exposed as a constant loser in his war on God. Every new seeming victory brought him a more humiliating and crushing defeat. Had he stopped warring on God after his dethronement in the first instance, his degradation would have been at the hands of the Almighty. Not satisfied with that first verdict, he allured man to his side against God. That earned him a stinging humiliation in the elevation of human nature to union with God in one divine person for the purpose of redemption. Human nature united to that divine Person overpowered him then and began to destroy his kingdom in the world. He then contrived to have that Person put to death. This forever frustrated his initial design of keeping man from obtaining the glory which he and his angels had lost. And it brought a more humiliating defeat upon him than any former one in that the Church renews the death of Christ in a mystical way and through that mystical sacrifice shall ultimately root up his empire altogether. Thus in trying to destroy Christ and His work, he brought the greatest defeat and humiliation of all upon himself and lost everything he had apparently gained in Paradise. With man redeemed and heaven re-opened, Satan's kingdom in the world has been dismembered ever more and more, not so much by an almighty act of God or by an almighty word of the God-man, as by the words of mere man pronounced at the Consecration of the Mass. Man is here empowered to overthrow the kingdom of Satan and drive him out of the world. Christ is now triumphant over Satan in the humble and lifeless appearance of the eucharistic species. This is the last phase of the final and hopeless defeat and utmost humiliation of the archenemy of God and man. St. John describes in epic splendors this last act of the grand drama of Redemption with its series of victories for Jesus Christ and mankind and its consequent defeats for Satan.

Christ entrusted the power to renew His bloody death on the Cross in an unbloody mystic manner to the priests of His Church elevating man thereby to God-likeness and defeating forever the designs of Satan with the utmost humiliation to himself. So much has man been exalted and Satan's pride humiliated, that he who was far lower than the angels in natural gifts now rises in the power of grace to defeat his enemy and stand forth triumphant. The judgments executed by the eucharistic Lamb upon Satan shall involve the whole world not to destroy but to chasten it and wrest it from the hands of Satan liberating the human race from his sordid servitude.

The firm belief of the faithful of the Church in this sacred mystery, in the Reality of the Great Presence, in the truth and effectiveness of Christ's words at the Last Supper, just as the Church has explained and believed it through all ages, undoes the unbelief of the head of the human race in Paradise. This is the "victory that overcomes the world" and the empire of Satan with all its earthly and unearthly forces, *THIS FIRM FAITH*. In and through the Eucharistic Mystery, the power with which Christ endowed His priesthood, distinguishing it thereby from all other priesthoods of history, and the unshakable belief in the words of Christ by the faithful of the Church, Paradise will be regained, and the honor refused God by Adam through the intrigue and deception of Satan will be restored to Him. The Apocalypse reveals the fruits of the victory gained by the Mystic Presence in the restoration of more than paradisiac conditions on earth. Satan is thus exposed in the complete and finished defeats brought upon by himself by his own pride in presuming to measure his strength and excellence with that of his Creator.

SYNOPSIS

BOOK I

In the first three chapters of the Apocalypse, we have the principles out of which good and evil will evolve. The churches are warned against the existing evils in them, the harbingers of disaster, and are commended for their good qualities through which Christ shall renew the world. In chapters IV. and V., the constitution and organization of the Church are outlined and the Lamb is introduced. He will direct all future history, will foster the growth of all good and establish His everlasting kingdom through a decisive victory. In chapter VI., the judgment begins upon those who oppose Christ and adhere to false doctrines and principles. God's judgments will emanate out of the evils present in the world and will again check those evils and give all that is good a fair chance to grow. In chapter VII., there is a pause in the action of the world-drama to review the fruits of the Lamb's activities and of His victories so far won. The first scene in chapter VIII. presents an institution in the Church and in the world that will hurry the human race onwards to the destinies foreseen in prophetic light and prepare it for both the culmination of the "mystery of iniquity" and the revelation of the "mystery of God". Chapter nine reveals the last stages of this preparation, when evil will go unchecked and will welcome the advent of Antichrist.

BOOK II

An open booklet is presented to the Seer by an angel. It contains the judgments from this point to the end, and it begins with the judgment of the Church indicating the complete separation of the good from the wicked. This is immediately followed by the reign of Antichrist. Chapter X. is an interlude to introduce the action that follows upon IX. 21-22. Chapter XI. describes the work of the Two Witnesses, who labor to restore all things in Christ, combat the power of Antichrist and make the final victory possible and complete. Chapter XII. depicts the judgment at the headquarters of the Church, intimated in XI. 1, and her success in ridding herself of all evils and reproach. The dragon thus loses his last opportunity of destroying the Church from within. He then attacks her from without but to no avail. Chapter XIII. reveals the full license given Satan to do his utmost against the Church, and he establishes the universal reign of evil. He operates through the two beasts, the first of which is Antichrist and the second his prophet. The character of Antichrist, his method of attack against the Church, or rather against the faithful, and his campaign to gain universal world-dominion is described in this chapter. Chapter XIV. in various visions depicts the struggle, the first fruits of the victory for Christ and gives a glimpse of the final results of the whole contest, the defeat of Antichrist and end of all the wicked. Chapter XV. introduces the preparation for the third woe and the final judgment on the wicked. Chapter XVI. describes the execution of this judgment and the preparation for the last battle to destroy the forces of evil that have corrupted the earth. Chapter XVII. gives the political aspect of the powers of evil that rule the world through the Evil City. Chapter XVIII. describes much in detail the judgment upon this evil city and her complete annihilation, never to be rebuilt. In the first part of chapter XIX., the Church rejoices over the victory of Christ in the end of the evil city and celebrates in advance His final decisive victory over the two beasts in the last battle which has not yet been fought. Thereafter the triumphant advance of the armies of heaven against Antichrist, the False Prophet and their followers is reviewed and the result of the battle is briefly stated. Chapter XX. relates the expulsion of Satan from the world for 1,000 years, the last uprising against the Church by Gog and Magog and the Last Judgment. This should be the end of the Apocalypse. But chapters XXI. and XXII. are added to reveal the blessed state of the Church and the near paradisiac conditions in the world when Christ holds universal sway and brings all good to full maturity during the thousand years after the destruction of Antichrist. The book ends these revelations with the promise of the positive realization of all prophecies narrated on its pages and with a solemn threat against all who will not heed them or who will try to falsify the text.

DIVISION AND CONTENTS

The Apocalypse has been divided into partitions of various kinds, shapes and sizes of shapes according to the intentions and purposes of the interpreters. In this present work there are two main divisions: the Sealed Book, which is Book I., and the Open Booklet, which is Book II. The first three chapters are the introduction of Book I. and chapter ten is the introduction of Book II. The Apocalypse is then divided as follows.

BOOK I

THE BOOK OF THE SEVEN SEALS

I. INTRODUCTION

A

The Author, Purpose And Commission

1. Prologue: Chapter I., Verses 1-3.
2. Address to the Churches. Verses 4-9.
3. The Commission. Preparatory Vision of the Glorified Christ. Verses 9 - end.

B

Messages To The Angels Of The Seven Churches

1. To the Angel of the Church of Ephesus. Chapter II. Verses 1-7
2. To the Angel of the Church of Smyrna. Verses 8-11.
3. To the Angel of the Church of Pergamum. Verses 12-17.
4. To the Angel of the Church of Thyatira. Verses 18-to end.
5. To the Angel of the Church of Sardis. Chapter III. Verses 1-6.
6. To the Angel of the Church of Philadelphia. Verses 7-13.
7. To the Angel of the Church of Laodicea. Verses 14-end.

II. ADORATION OF GOD AND LAMB

A

The Glories Of The Church

1. The Vision of God. Chapter IV. Verses 1-3.
2. The Twenty-four Ancients. Verses 4-5.

3. The Crystal Sea. Verse 6.
4. The Four Living Beings. Verses 7-end.

B

THE BOOK OF THE SEVEN SEALS

1. The Sealed Book. Chapter V. Verses 1-5.
2. The Vision of the Lamb. Verses 6-7.
3. The Adoration of the Lamb. Verses 8-end.

III. THE SEALS

A

OPENING OF THE FIRST SIX SEALS

1. The First Seal. The White Horse. Chapter VI. Verses 1-2
2. The Second Seal. The Red Horse. Verses 3-4.
3. The Third Seal. The Black Horse. Verses 5-6.
4. The Fourth Seal. The Green Horse. Verses 7-8.
5. The Fifth Seal. The Souls of the Martyrs. Verses 9-12.
6. The Sixth Seal. The Powers of Heaven are moved. 12-end.

B

THE ESTABLISHMENT OF THE CHURCH

1. The Vision of the Four Angels holding the Winds. Chapter VII. Verse 1.
2. The Vision of the Angel from the Rising of the Sun. Verses 2-3.
3. The Sealing of the 144,000 from the Tribes of Israel. Verses 4-8.
4. Countless Multitudes also are signed. Verses 9-end.

IV. THE SEVEN TRUMPETS

A

PREPARATORY VISIONS

1. The Seventh Seal. Half Hour's Silence. Chapter VIII. Verse 1.
2. The Seven Angels with the Seven Trumpets. Verse 2.
3. The Second Vision. The Angel with the Golden Censer. Verses 3-5.

B

The Four Winds

1. The First Trumpet. The Plague of Hail. Verses 6-7.
2. The Second Trumpet. The Burning Mountain. Verses 8-9.
3. The Third Trumpet. The Star, Wormwood. Verses 10-11.
4. The Fourth Trumpet. The Lights of Heaven Dimmed. Verse 12.

V. THE WOES

1. The Eagle in Mid-heaven announces three Woes. Verse 13.
2. The Fifth Trumpet. The First Woe. Vision of the Locusts. Chapter IX. Verses 1-11.
3. The Sixth Trumpet. The Second Woe. Vision of 200,000,000 Horsemen. Verses 12-end.

BOOK II

THE OPEN BOOKLET

I. INTRODUCTION

1. The Mighty Angel with the Open Booklet. Seven Thunders. Oath. Chapter X. 1-7.
2. St. John takes and eats the Booklet. Verses 8-10.
3. He must prophesy again. Verse 11.

II. CONTINUATION OF SECOND WOE

1. St. John Measures the Temple. Chapter XI. Verses 1-2.
2. The Testimony of the Two Witnesses. Verses 3-13.
3. Seventh Trumpet. Third Woe and Victory of Christ announced. Verses 14-end.

III. BATTLE BETWEEN THE CHURCH AND THE DRAGON

1. Vision of the Woman. Chapter XII. Verses 1-2.
2. Vision of the Dragon. Verses 3-4.
3. Delivery of the Woman. Her Flight. Verses 5-6.
4. Battle in Heaven. Verses 7-12.
5. Malice of the Dragon against the Woman and her Children. Verses 13-end.

IV. DESCRIPTION OF THE TWO BEASTS

1. The Beast out of the Sea. Chapter XIII. Verses 1-4.
2. The Works of the Beast. Verses 5-8.
3. Warnings and Consolations. Verses 9-10.
4. The Beast out of the Earth. Verses 11-15.
5. The Character of the First Beast. Verses 16-end.

V. SOUNDS OF VICTORY

1. The Vision of the Virgins. Chapter XIV. Verses 1-5.
2. The Three Announcing Angels:
   A. Warning against Beast-worship. Verses 6-7.
   B. Second Angel announces Fall of Babylon. Verse 8.
   C. Third Angel threatens Punishments of Beast worshippers. Verses 9-11.
3. Consolations for the Martyrs. Verses 12-13.
4. The Harvest of the Good. Verses 14-16.
5. The Vintage of the Wicked. 17-end.

VI. THE THIRD WOE

1. Preparation for Third Woe. Seven Angels and the Crystal Sea. Chapter XV. Verses 1-4.
2. The Open Sanctuary and Seven Angels receiving Seven Vials. Verses 5-end.
3. The Seven Last Plagues. Chapter XVI. Verses 1-end.
   First Plague: Ulcer on Followers of Antichrist. Verses 1-2.
   Second Plague: The Sea becomes Blood. Verse 3.
   Third Plague: The Rivers and Fountains become blood. Verse 4.
   Pronouncement of the Angel of the Waters. Verses 5-7.
   Fourth Plague: Excessive Heat. Verses 8-9.
   Fifth Plague: Darkness settles on Capital of Antichrist. Verses 10-11.
   Sixth Plague: Euphrates is dried up. Armies from East. Evil Spirits gather all Antichrist's Followers. Verses 12-16.
   Seventh Plague: Final Judgements of God on Wicked reviewed. Verses 17-end.

VII. THE GREAT HARLOT AND THE BEAST

1. Description of Babylon, the Great Harlot. Chapter XVII. Verses 1-6.
2. Symbolic Meaning of the Beast. Verses 7-17.
3. Symbolic Meaning of the Harlot. Verse 18.

VIII. DESTRUCTION OF BABYLON

1. Announcement of Her Fall. Chapter XVIII. Verses 1-4.
2. Reasons for Her Fall. Verses 5-8.
3. Lamentations over Her Fall. Verses 9-19.
4. Rejoicings over Her Fall. Verse 20.
5. Demonstration of Her Fall. Verses 21-end.

IX. THE LAST BATTLE

1. General Rejoicings:

   Thanksgiving for the Fall of Babylon. Chapter XIX. Verses 1-6.
2. The Wedding Feast of the Lamb. Verses 7-10.
3. The Warrior on the White Horse. Armies of Heaven. Verses 11-16.
4. Invitation to the Supper of the Beast. Verses 17-18.
5. The Defeat of the Beast. Verses 19-end.

X. LAST JUDGMENTS

1. The Fruits of the Victory:

   A

   Satan is Bound for a Thousand Years. Chapter XX. Verses 1-3.

   B

   The Martyrs shall reign a Thousand Years. Verses 4-6.
2. The Last War of Gog and Magog Verses 7-8.
3. Satan's Final Destiny. Verses 9-10.
4. The Last Judgment. Verses 11-end.

XI. THE NEW CITY AND THE NEW WORLD

1. The New Jerusalem. Chapter XXI. Verses 1-2.
2. Diverse Promises to the Faithful. Verses 3-8.
3. The New Jerusalem described. Verses 9-end.
4. Paradise Re-established:

A

The Water of Life. Chapter XXII. Verses 1-2.

B

The Tree of Life. Verses 2-5.

XII. CONCLUSION

1. The Testimony of the Angel. Verses 6-11.
2. The Warning of our Lord. Verses 12-15.
3. Final Attestation. Verses 16-end.

BIBLIOGRAPHY

Arndt-Allioli Ausgabe der Heiligan Schrift Des Alten und Neuen Testamentes in drei Banden, mit dem Urtext der Vulgata. Herausgegeben von Augustin Arndt, S.J. Die Vulgata ubersetzt und mit erklarenden Anmerkungen versehen. Funfte Auflage, 1910. Druck von Friederich Pustet.
The Apocalypse is explained with extensive footnotes. These explanations are taken largely from the Fathers and Doctors of the Church, from Irenaeus to St. Thomas.

A Lapide, Cornelius, S.J. Commentarius in Apocalypsin Sancti Joannie, Apostoli. Feb. 18, 1626. ,

Allo, P.E.B.,O.P. Professeur a l'Universite de Fribourg Suisse. Deuxieme Edition. Etudes Biblique . . . Saint Jean L'Apocalypse.
Paris, Libraire Victor Le Coffre, J.Gabalda, Editeur . . . 1921.
This a complete and uptodate commentary on the Apocalypse, and takes in review all interpretations from the most ancient Fathers to the modern scripturists and biblical critics. It gives a synopsis of all the most noted interpretations and schools of interpretation. His synopsis covers the whole range from St. Justin to modern times.

Ante-Nicene Fathers. Ancient Fathers and Ecclesiastical Writers.
The English translation quoted is the edition of Charles Scribners & Sons, 1926, re-editing that of the Rev. Alexander Roberts, and James Donaldson and is finally the American re-print of the Edinburgh Edition in 10 volumes.

Justin, Saint, Martyr. d. 167 A.D. Dialogue with Triphon.

Irenaeus, Saint, Martyr. d. 202 A.D. Adversus Haereses, Book V.

Hippolytus, d. 236 A.D. Treatise on Christ and Antichrist. Fragments from Commentaries on Daniel.

Methodius. d. 312. The Banquet of the Ten Virgins: Discourse V. Chap. vi., viii., Discourse VIII. Chap. vi., x., xi., xiii.

Victorinus, Martyr about 305. Commentary on the Apocalypse of the Blessed John.

Melito of Sardis. d. 180 A. D. Treatise on the devil and the Apocalypse of St. John.

Catholic Encyclopedea. Special Edition 1914.

Cornely, Rudolph, S.J.: Introduction to Sacred Scriptures, sixth edition, emended by Martin Hagen, S.J. Parisiis Sumptibus P. Lethielleux, Editoris . . . 1909.

Eaton, Rev. Robert. Sands & Co., London & Edinburgh. Imprimatur May 26, 1930 Preface by Rev. E.T. Bird, D.D., Ph. D. Professor of Sacred Scripture at Oscott College.

Eyzaguirre, Rev. Raphale A., Apocalypseos Interpretatio Literalis; Romae 1911.

Gallois, R.P.M. Aug., des Freres Precheurs.
L'Apocalypse de St. Jean. Paris, P. Lethielleux, Libraire-Editeur . . . 1895. A short essay on the allegorical and prophetical visions of this book (Apocalypse).

Hogan, Fr. Stanislaus M., O.P.: Life of St. Vincent Ferrer., O.P. Longmans Greene & Co. 1911.

Honert, Wilhelm Herman. PROPHETEN STIMMEN 3te verbesserte Auflage. Regensburg. 1922. Verlagsanstatt vorm. G.J. Manz, Buch-U-Kunsdruckerei.

Kohlhofer, Dr. Mathis. Die Einheit Der Apokalypse. Herdershe Ver lags handlung, 1902. It is a refutation of the latest hypotheses of bibical criticism, which deny the inspiration of the book and the reality of the visions. It refutes most strikingly the theories of Eberhard Vischer, Otto Pfleiderer, Fr. Spitta, H. Bousset, Heinrich Holzman, Adolf Julicher, Hilgenfeld and others who were the representatives of the rationalistic critics.

Swete, Henry Barclay, D.D., F.B.C., . . . Third Edition, MacMillan & Co. 1922. A very learned and complete commentary on the Apocalypse, based on the Greek text. His studies comprise the Greek commentaries from Melito, Bishop of Sardis, under Marcus Aurelius, to Arethus who died about 900 A.D., Syrian commentaries, Latin commentaries from the third to the sixteenth centuries, and modern commentaries in Latin, French, German, English, the works of Catholics and heretics of the early centuries and of Catholics and Protestants in modern times. It reviews The ancient manuscripts which contain the Apocalypse, such as the Codex Vaticanus, Sinaiticus, Alexandrinus, Ephraemi and many miniscules. It makes comparisons of the ancient Itala and Vulgata in Latin and the Syrian, Armenian, Egyptian and Ethiopic texts. It follows the Greek text received by the scholars and critics as genuine, but shows throughout the book text diversities of the ancient codices of both uncials and minuscules.

Thureau-Dangin, Paul. S. Bernardine de Siene. Paris, 1896.
Life of St. Bernardine of Sienna. The best one ever written.

Westminster version of the Sacred Scriptures. Longmans Green & Co., 1915 Edition.

The commentaries and interpretations of the great Doctors of the fourth and later centuries and of the theologians of the Middle Ages have been skipped, because they gave the interpretation of the Apocalypse a purely "spiritual" direction, even before St. Augustine. Only modern scholars and theologians and scripturists have searched more deeply into the writings of ancient Fathers and into the prophetical books and fragments of prophecies of the Old Testament. They have come nearer to the true meaning of the prophetical visions and words of the Apocalypse than the doctors and theologians of the Middle Ages.

Many other modern commentaries, Catholic and Protestant, have been read and analysed carefully, and in all of them many parts have been found that agree exactly with the interpretation presented here. But many swerve off from the logical sequence in too many places to make a clear picture and narrative possible. Through many of them our interpretation might be said to run like a red line. How near it is to the truth, the advent of future facts of history must reveal.

After these many years of study on this wonderful book, the Apocalypse seems to be perfectly clear in all its visions. The same terms cannot be given the same meaning every time they return, nor can similar visions be always given the same significance. It depends on the setting in which they appear. The words and phrases also depend for their meaning on the context in which they appear.

CHAPTER I

Westminster Version

The Revelation of Jesus Christ which 1. God gave to him, that he
might disclose to his servants what must speedily befall. And he signified it
by a message of his angel to his servant John, who 2 bore witness to the
word of God and to the testimony of Jesus Christ, even to whatever things
he saw. Blessed is he 3 that readeth and they that hear the words of this
prophecy, and keep the things written in it: for the time is near. John to
the seven Churches 4 which are in Asia: grace and peace from him who
is and who was and who cometh, and from the seven spirits who are
before his throne, and from Jesus Christ, 5 the faithful witness, the first-
born of the dead, and the ruler of the kings of the earth. To him who
loveth us and hath loosed us from our sins in his blood, and made us to
be a kingdom, priests to 6 God and his Father – to him be the glory
and the might for ever and ever: Amen!

Behold he cometh with the clouds, and every eye shall see him,
even they 7 who pierced him, and all the tribes of the earth shall wail
because of him. Yea, Amen! 'I am the Alpha and the Omega,' 8. saith the
Lord God, 'who is and who was and who is to come, the Almighty One.'

I John, your brother and copartner 9. in Jesus in the tribulation and in
the kingdom and in the patience, came to be in the island which is called
Patmos, for the sake of the word of God and my witness to Jesus. I was
(rapt) 10. in the spirit on the Lord's day, and I heard behind me a great
voice as of a trumpet, saying: 'What thou beholdest, 11. write in a book,
and send to the seven Churches, to Ephesus, and to Smyrna, and to Pergamum, and to Thyatira, and to Sardis, and to Philadelphia, and to
Laodicea."

And I turned to see what voice it 12. was that spoke to me; and
having turned, I beheld seven golden lamps, and in the midst of the lamps,
one like to a 13. son of man, clothed with along robe and girt around at the
breasts with a golden girdle. But his head and his hair 14. were white as
white wool, as snow, and his eyes were like a flame of fire; his feet were
like bright bronze, as when 15. refined in a furnace, and his voice was as the
voice of many waters. In his right hand he had seven stars, and out of his
mouth issued a sharp two-edged sword, and his countenance was as the sun
shining in its power.

And when I beheld him, I fell at his 17 feet as dead; and he laid his
right hand upon me, saying, 'Fear not! I am the first and the last, and
he who liveth; I died, 18 and behold, I am living forever and ever; and
I have the keys of Death and Hell. Write therefore the things which thou 19
has seen, and the things which are, and the things which are to befall
after these, the mystery of the seven 20 stars which thou sawest upon
my right hand, and the seven golden lamps: the seven stars are the angels
of the seven churches, and the seven lamps are the seven churches.

Book I

BOOK I

THE BOOK OF THE SEVEN SEALS

I. INTRODUCTION

A

AUTHOR, PURPOSE AND COMMISSION

1. PROLOGUE, Chapter I. Verses 1-3.

Verse 1

The name Apocalypse is naturally the title of the book because it begins with that word, and it goes by that title in the Canon of the Church and in the oldest Greek manuscripts. St. Irenaeus uses the term "apocalyptic vision" in commenting on its revelations. (V. 30, 3.). The word means "revelation," and rightly so, because the book reveals truths heretofore unknown to man.

In the New Testament, the word "apocalypse" nearly always signifies a revelation that goes forth directly from God the Father, Jesus Christ or the Holy Spirit (Rom. XVI. 25); (1 Cor. I. 7; Gal. I. 12; Eph. III. 3; 2 Thess. I. 7; 1 Peter I. 7, 13). It stands for the unveiling of hidden truths which remain shrouded in mystery even after the revelation has been made. In substance those visions are a revelation but a revelation clothed in a mysterious garb. They are wrapped in prophetical light, and their content is mostly of an eschatological nature. The word therefore denotes a mystery revealed but not fully unveiled until the Church comes face to face with the facts concerned. St. Paul suggests that all such revelations are difficult of interpretation (1 Cor. XIV. 26). These revelations should then be expected to remain mysterious until their fulfillment.

The genitive complement to the word "Apocalypse" gives precision to its meaning. If Jesus Christ is the source of the revelation, the word has a different meaning than if He is the object. The former is evidently here intended, because the context of the verse seems to make Jesus Christ the Cause and Subject, since God gave these revelations to Him to make them known to His servants. Christ speaks in person many times, and He dictates the seven letters. Chapter V. throws considerable light upon this view, because there the ἀρνίον *"Little Lamb,"* is the Revealer and Executor of the revelations (V. 9). He paid the price of man's redemption in His Bloody Sacrifice, acquired for His human nature all divine prerogatives, and in His Unbloody Oblation, He continues, extends and completes His priestly triumphs. He is the Head of the Church, the Master and central figure of history, the King of kings and the Victor over all evil powers. As such He reveals Himself in this prophecy. Yet it is true that the revelations concern themselves with Jesus Christ and His guidance of the Church and the world. And the "mystery of God" (X. 7) and the "great day of Almighty God" mentioned often by the prophets concern Christ no less than the Father. Hence Jesus Christ is also the object of these revelations, which portray Him in His glorious Parousia. The book is therefore a revelation of Jesus Christ and by Jesus Christ.

By virtue of His Hypostatic Union, He acquired as man the right to have all divine knowledge necessary for the mediatorship between God and man and to bring the fruits of the Redemption to all men. He possesses the foreknowledge of everything that pertains to the guidance and destiny of the world. The purpose of this foreknowledge is here to make known whatever will bring safety and consolation to the Christian communities and to the individual Christian, in the dire visitations that are soon to afflict the universal Church. This book is therefore intended to be a message of consolation for all generations by showing what triumphs Christ will win through His Church in the loyalty of His faithful servants.

The "Mystery of God" revealed herein "must befall". It is not the effect of blind fate but a part of God's design. It can befall, because Jesus Christ has been slain making a perpetual oblation in the Church possible, through the mystery of which He will carry to completion all the decrees of God. The victory is so positive a certainty, that in this first age of the Church, He reveals as actually happening the successive events which will lead to His full and final triumph.

These revelations were urgently necessary at this time, for the Christians might after the death of the last Apostles lose courage when compelled to face the fierce persecutions impending. The fulfillment of these prophecies was to begin shortly, but the interval of time separating the many events would be a future revelation. The words ἐν τάχει, do not promise a completion of the whole prophecy at once but a beginning of its enactment very soon. It was not necessary for St. John to have the perspective of time for its accomplishment. It needed only to be clear as was called for in any critical epoch. The Seer demonstrates that he understood the delay in the full realization of the prophecy, when he admonishes the Christians to await the designs of God (XIII. 10; XIV. 12). The events related would become actuality in God's own time, in their proper order and in the way best fitted to reach the fulfillment of His intentions without frustation, for which the Christians must trust in His wisdom and power.

Sending the angel to St. John puts the seal of truth and reliability upon the recorded prophecies and on the promises to the faithful. The angel is to assist him in receiving the revelations entirely, to explain all unclear and unintelligible parts and guide him in recording all of them correctly. This makes it evident that he did not begin the composition of the book until after he had received all the revelations.

The book is in every sense a prophecy. St. John is called a servant of Christ as the prophets were called the servants of God. The revelations place him in the ranks of the prophets, for as God's spokesman he writes down many exhortations and predictions. He adds his name to the introduction to inform the reader that he who is the author of a gospel is the one who has received these revelations. Such mention was not necessary for the Evangelist John; for the Seer John, however, it was necessary, because there were no human witnesses to the reception of the prophecies. Whether the angel was a visible witness cannot be determined from the text. The first verse only briefly states that the Revelation originated in the mind of God, that Christ is the efficient cause of its disclosure and that its scope is to divulge the mysteries of the future. The witnesses are God, who gave the revelations to Jesus Christ and sent His Angel to assist St. John in receiving and making known the truths to the Christian communities.

Verse 2

St. John had borne witness to the word of God in various ways and on many occasions during a long and active life.

The clause may have one of several meanings. As an Apostle, he had preached the word of Christ and God for almost three quarters of a century. He may have written the three epistles before the Apocalypse. And there is not wanting in the Apocalypse itself an indication that he had written the gospel first. In chapter nineteen he calls Christ THE WORD OF GOD giving no definition of that appellation, as he does in the first chapter of the gospel. This may be the testimony he means. He had also borne witness to the "testimony" of Jesus Christ: he had borne witness to the words, miracles and prophecies by which Christ had testified to His own divinity, and he had written a gospel which has for its specific purpose to prove that divinity. And because he had witnessed the proofs given by Christ Himself, he was able to testify to the truth of his Master's revelations. "Seeing" the testimony means also "hearing" it. He had indeed given testimony by preaching the word of God. But this verse, if viewed in the light of the title given Christ in chapter nineteen, seems to refer to the gospel as the specific "testimony" which he claims. St. John may use the word here to convey the same meaning which it commonly conveyed in later times, that he had given testimony by deed as well as by word, by martydrom as well as by preaching and writing. He was cast into a caldron of boiling oil in Rome but being miraculously preserved from death or harm was banished to Patmos. By his martydrom he had given the most emphatic testimony of his faith in Christ and of his sincerity in all he had written and preached.

Verse 3

St. John speaks with our Lord's own words when he pronounces blessed whoever reads this prophecy and likewise whoever hears it read. But only then are they blessed if they ponder it in their hearts and regulate their lives by its doctrines. The Vulgate does not follow the Greek text closely. The text connotes the obligation for those to whom the revelations were addressed to read them publicly in the churches as part of the divine liturgy. Both readers and hearers in such congregations are pronounced blessed if they all persevere. This indicates that terrifying trials are drawing near, so that temptation to surrender and apostatize shall be very insistent. But those who take the admonitions seriously and are ready to lose all will persevere.

The modernists hold the Apocalypse to be a book of mere consolations, but St. John calls it a prophecy and thereby makes it rank among the prophecies of the Old Testament, as in truth it completes and sums up all prophecy. It does more than this – it interprets the obscure prophecies scattered through the Old Testament.

"For the time is near" does not mean that all the predictions in the book are imminent, but that the beginning of the judgments is at the door. These words add special significance to what the first verse stated by **ἐν τάχει**, "at once".

Some "critics" imagine the first three verses to have been added later by some follower of St. John. However, the words, ideas and style are too eminently Joannine to be anything but genuine. They bear such wonderful resemblance to verses 6 and 16 of the last chapter that they are surely the product of the same mind. St. John probably added them as a brief introduction, after he had finished the whole book, for introductions are ordinarily written last. These verses were certainly written with the contents of the whole book in mind.

2. ADDRESS TO THE CHURCHES.

Verses 4-9.

Verse 4

The whole book is addressed to the Seven Churches in Asia. Asia in apostolic times meant proconsular Asia, a part of what is now known as Asia Minor. Many different reasons why the Lord chose those particular churches to receive the revelations at first hand have been advanced. The most probable and natural reason will be stated in verse eleven. Seven is the sacred number in the dealings of Almighty God with men to express perfection and universality. It is the sum of 3 plus 4, the number of the Blessed Trinity plus the number of visible creation. It comprises the activity of God manifesting Himself through visible creation, which He finished in six days or periods of time. In the seventh day its purpose was actualized, for man, the crown of visible creation, appeared. This purpose shall continue in fulfillment until all is consummated. The sacred number SEVEN thus sums up all God's revelations. This book, which is to show the completion of God's purposes in revelation, is addressed to SEVEN bishops or SEVEN congregations, and the contents of the whole book are apportioned among a series of SEVENS.

The Seven Churches represent Christ's kingdom on earth, as the Temple visibly embodied the Old Testament theocracy. These churches are the "place of rest" of the Blessed Trinity, as the Jewish Temple was Jahve's "place of rest", (Isa. XI. 10; LXVI. 1). In the Old Testament, the "place of rest" was located only in one city, the city of the chosen people, while in the New Testament all peoples are chosen to have resting places of the Lord. Hence the book is not addressed to ONE people or city or nation but to a number that represents the whole world, the number of perfection and universality. The signification of these numbers grows clearer as the revelations progress. Satan, Antichrist and the city of the False Prophet also bear the number SEVEN in derision of the Sacred number. The number of the Holy Spirit is likewise SEVEN. This is found to be the sacred number throughout the Old and the New Testaments, possibly to indicate that both are the work of the Holy Spirit, for through the operations of the Seven Gifts, He leads the world to its consummation and final destiny. So then the book in being addressed to these seven churches is addressed to the whole Catholic Church.

In all his letters, except in that to the Hebrews, St. Paul expresses his affections for his followers by wishing them grace and peace. St. Peter too has this salutation in his two letters, and St. John has it in his second letter. The Apocalypse is a prophetical letter and should bear a resemblance to both the prophetical books of the Old Testament and the apostolic letters. The word grace is found only here and in the last chapter. "Peace" bears an ominous significance in view of the terrifying revelations to be made in this prophetical missive.

God is called "He that is, and was, and is to come", which is His stereotype name throughout the Apocalypse. In Exodus (III. 14) God revealed the first part of his name as His own. That title is here given to the Father alone. The addition to the Old Testament title, "He that is to come", points to the future events recorded in this book. As the Father was the Creator and Preserver in the past and the Ruler at present, so will He be the Director of all evolutions of history and the Guide of future ages, although the Lamb is the Executor of His Will.

The "seven spirits" here, as in III. 1, is the Holy Spirit, who in IV. 5 appears as the "seven lamps" and in V. 6 as the "seven eyes" of the Lamb. Those forms denote His diversified external activity in the Church or mission in the world, and therefore the "seven spirits" are before the throne of God. He obscurely revealed Himself in Isaias (XI. 2) as the "seven gifts" of the Messias and in Zacharias (IV. 10) as the "seven eyes". His relationship to the seven churches is here hinted at, because He abides with the Church and will direct and guide it till the consummation. The seven golden lampstands represent the seven churches and the Church Universal. The Father and the Holy Spirit are not named in this verse, are merely given these descriptive titles as a token of their relationship to the Church and their guidance of its destinies.

Verse 5

Grace flows from Jesus Christ as it does from the Father and the Holy Spirit. The divinity of Jesus Christ is thus implied in this new expression of the threefold personality in one God. The symbols of "grace" in the gospel and epistles of St. John and elsewhere in this prophetic epistle are "light" and "life" and "love" and the figures of speech corresponding to those words. St. John employes the definite article when writing "to THE seven churches", as if there were no more churches in Asia. But these churches chosen by Christ are in His intentions the models of all churches in Asia and of the Universal or Catholic Church. This entire message to be sent to each of the seven churches as to ONE reveals the mind of the Apostle and excludes a multiplicity of churches.

Jesus Christ is "the witness, the faithful one", who came "to give testimony to the truth" (John XVIII. 37). These words recall those of St. Paul to Timothy (1 Tim. VI. 13). Christ has until death given testimony of the truth by His word, His works and His martyrdom; and the Christians can rest assured that what He shall here reveal is pure truth. The characteristic trait of Christ as being the faithful one is set forth to signify that he will not only reveal in this book the future designs of God but will watch over His followers and lead them from grace to grace and to the final grand triumph. The purpose and result of this new revelation is to give absolute assurance of final "peace" to the Church.

This attribute of "the faithful witness" who assures peace but truth suggests the fact that follows, His Resurrection. He is the "first-born of the dead" (Coll. I. 18), for death gave birth to His immortal life. And since He is the first-born to the glorious life of the body, others who are faithful shall follow in this glorious birth. This new birth is the pattern and cause of all others (Thom) and is a consolation in all persecutions and an encouragement to perseverance until death. In the confident hope of his faithfulness, the Christians shall have peace. Such peace he procured for Himself by his death, wherefrom follows the succeeding idea that by His self-abnegation He overcame the world in a perfect victory (Jo. XVI. 33).

By His victory over the world and over death, Christ has won the right to a name that is above all names (Heb. I. 2-6) and to be the "ruler of the kings of the earth, King of kings and Lord of lords" (Apoc. XIX. 16). Thus the Apostle represents Him in His threefold Messianic dignity as Prophet, Priest and King, who preached the word of God, offered Himself in a sacrificial death and thereby became King of Kings.

The felicitous results from His triple dignity for the Apostle and the bishops to whom he wrote this book are wrapped in words that form a doxology of praise to Christ, namely (1) "who has loved us", (2) "and washed us from our sins in His blood", (3) "and has made us a kingdom, priests to God and His Father". The love of Christ as expressed in that doxology was His human love, the natural affection of His heart made divine by the union of the divine with the human nature in one person. In the strength of that human love He said: "Greater love than this no *man* has, than that a man lay down his life for his friends" (Jo. XV. 13). From clause number one above follows the other happy effect, that Christ by His voluntary death has washed them from their sins by his Blood. What keen, ecstatic joy must the pure, virgin-Apostle have felt in giving utterance to this thought. It expresses the fine enthusiasm of the lofty mind. He is clean because his beloved by a pure act of love washed him clean in His blood. And he owes it to no one but his beloved Lord and Savior, and to Him alone he wished the glory of it, and his wish is fulfilled.

Verse 6

The third and still greater result from the triple dignity

of Christ for the apostles is the establishment of an eternal kingdom in which they are the kings and also priests. The elders express this again in V. 10. In the apex of the doxology, St. John places the priesthood above royalty, elevating it to the feet of God by the phrase, "priests to God and His Father". He thereby reminds the bishops of their participation in the royal and priestly dignity of Jesus Christ (Heb. IX. 11-12). The last word, "His Father", recalls the other words of St. John spoken by our Lord at the Last Supper (Jo. XIV. 23). Through the redeeming blood of Christ, St. John and the bishops were cleansed and made priests acceptable to the Father. The priesthood of Jesus Christ connotes the Eucharistic Sacrifice. Overcome by so much love, he simply adds: "to Him be glory and empire forever and ever". The only two members in this doxology are, "glory and empire". But they comprehend and sum up all the Seer could express. And he closes the doxology with "so be it ever". A creature giving himself unreservedly to God can offer Him only praise and thanksgiving, yet it expresses love and submission, which is all that God demands. The two words embrace all creation. St. John desires for Christ "all glory", which is the homage due Him as God, and "empire", which is the submission to Him as Man of all peoples and kingdoms of this world. This is only just and fair to Him and would be the greatest blessing for the world. St. John in this passage places himself in equal rank with the bishops of the seven churches, because he and they are priests of God and through the priesthood kings and rulers in the kingdom of Christ.

The prevailing ideas of the Apocalypse are contained in the words: "He who is to come – the Prince and Ruler – the Kingdom – and the Priesthood". The order, which is consistent throughout the Apocalypse, is the same as in the last three verses. As here each succeeding idea emanates from the foregoing one naturally and necessarily, so each succeeding chapter evolves out of the foregoing theme naturally and with necessary sequence. This order holds out till the epilogue. No repetition, reduplication or parallelism is conceded in our interpretation, because it does not seem to exist in the text. After the action of the grand drama begins there is a constant development and unchecked onward movement.

Verse 7

Like the prophets of the Old Testament, St. John now loses

sight of the perspective of time and points to the final consummation, towards which all the prophecies to be recorded converge. The final Parousia will complete the triumphs of his Lord. And all those who receive the prophecies and take the warnings contained in them to heart will rejoice at the COMING of the Lord in the clouds of Heaven. St. John voices this rejoicing so long pent up in his heart in a cry of exultation. The vision is modelled after Daniel (VII. 13) and St. Matthew (XXIV. 30; XXVI. 64) and St. Mark (XIV. 62). Clouds body forth His divinity and the myriads of angels at His service. "Every eye shall see Him" contains the doctrine of the resurrection of all flesh. "They also that pierced Him" points to the gospel of St. John (XIX. 34) – St. John has before his mind the whole scene of the passion ending with the thrust of the lance into the Savior's side. This scene described by St. John himself (Jo. XIX. 34) brings in that of Zacharias (XII. 10) as also that of Daniel. It indicates that he wrote the gospel prior to the Apocalypse. Does he want to say that Christ will appear with His cross? Probably yes, because our Lord seems to say so (Mt. XXIV. 30). SS. Cyprian, Chrysostom and Jerome drew the conclusion here that His five wounds will be visible marks of glory. Those who "pierced" Him are not only the crucifiers but all the indifferent, the scoffers and other enemies of the cross. These words are a warning not to grow unfaithful when the "great tribulation" shall begin.

The main topic of the book is expressed in this last verse. The whole book deals with Christ's coming as Judge. He executes His judgments upon the Church and the world again and again during the course of ages, but comparatively few understand the events as judgments. In the end, however, all shall see Him. Then shall the wicked bewail themselves, not their sins, because they did not heed His other judgments, which were only acts of mercy urging them to repent and do penance. This verse seems to presage an apostasy of whole tribes and perhaps nations when Christ shall come for the final judgment, and they shall bewail the end of their career of sin which they enjoyed so much.

The fundamental antithesis running like a red line through the book is here announced in the introduction. The good and the bad are assembled in the two camps which compose the Church on the one hand and the "gates of hell" on the other.

The judgments will separate them ever more from each other until the separation is complete. Throughout the book, the adherents of the enemy, schismatics, heretics, infidels and followers of Antichrist are "of the earth". The faithful are in "heaven", are those who "dwell in heaven" and are the "saints". The mentality of the two groups is contradictory. The wails of the wicked at the coming of Christ are contrasted with the rejoicing of the faithful.

The verse ends with the double affirmation in Greek "to be sure" and Hebrew "amen", "so be it". It gives the proper solemnity to the grand theme and points to Christ as the "Amen". It is solemn confirmation by the Seer himself of what the verse contains, which is equivalent to a corroboration by the Holy Spirit under whose guidance St. John writes. It is a double assurance of a fulfillment of all that shall be recorded in the book.

Verse 8

Not satisfied with the voicing of his own solemn conviction and the testimony of the "Faithful Witness," St. John adds the testimony of the Father. He is the source of all created things and the end for whom all were created; He is the Alpha and the Omega, the first and last letter of all that is decreed to happen; He is eternal, all-knowing and almighty, the Ruler of all: And therefore events do not begin to exist in His mind but were known to Him from all eternity and do not outgrow His control. He knew the outcome from all eternity, because He is Irresistible Power, who will be able to accomplish His decrees, and nothing can frustrate them. Thus by the triumph of His Son Jesus Christ, so the Father assures us, shall all creation be brought to its final destiny.

This coming in the clouds of heaven alludes to the "Shekhina" of the Old Testament and concedes to the Son equality with the Father; and the testimony of the Father confirms that truth. St. John thus christianizes the symbol of the shekhina as he christianized the Gnostic word "logos". The text alludes clearly to Isaias (XLI. 4; XLIV. 6; XLVIII. 12), where the prophet writes down the ultimate restoration of Israel after its preservation in the Captivity. At that time the same solemn assurance was necessary to convince the Jews of the undoubtable fulfillment of the prophecy. The Seer uses the Greek alphabet because the book was intended for Greek readers. The Alpha and Omega appear again in XXI. XXII.

3. THE COMMISSION

Preparatory Vision Of The Glorified Christ. 9-End.

Verse 9

Verse nine begins the narration of the visions that compose the whole book. St. John mentions himself again as the recipient of the Revelations. In the Gospel such mention was not necessary because he related historical facts witnessed by thousands of competent witnesses, who had long ago testified to their belief in the veracity of the gospels by dying for them. Now he is about to relate something whereof he is the sole witness. He mentions his name as does Daniel (VIII. 1; IX. 2; X. 2.) emphasizing thereby the reality of the revelations and the authenticity of their authorship. This man should stand for truth and reliability. He adds "your brother and your partner in the tribulation" to place himself in the ranks of the bishops and call attention to their apostolic dignity and power and participation with him in the priestly gifts and to some degree in ecclesiastical jurisdiction. The word "partner" expresses very weakly the sense of the Greek text, which really signifies that he is a common fellow-sufferer in THE tribulation. The "tribulation" is the great Roman persecution which was soon to break forth with renewed fury.

The bishops are his brethren because they share with him the inheritance of the spiritual kingdom of Christ, possessing its powers and prerogatives on earth and expecting to be entitled to the kingdom of glory with Him in Heaven. The "kingdom" is the Church, as it was often so designated by the Lord Himself. St. John then reminds the bishops of his own "patience" in persecution, in which he is a shining example to them. His example points out the way to bear up under the persecution. Patience really means constancy in enduring the tribulation as he had endured it for the sake of Jesus. He suggests to them the Eight Beatitudes and all other promises of reward made by our Lord.

He mentions his place of exile, to reveal the place of the reception of the revelations. It reminds the bishops of his martyrdom in Rome, in which he had miraculously escaped death. He came to Patmos an exile, a prisoner of the Lord, for "the word of God and for the testimony of Jesus". Eusebius (III. 18) says that under Domitian, St. John was cast into a cauldron of boiling oil at Rome but being saved by divine power was banished to Patmos. It is a small island in the Aegean Sea, southwest of Ephesus, between Naxos and Samos. The island is barren and unhealthy. Pliny (Natural History IV. 12-13) says that it was a common place of exile. It was the last stopping place from Rome to Ephesus. The island is shaped like a crescent with the horns pointing east.

Verse 10

St. John here begins the narration of the revelations. He was "in the spirit on the Lord's day". The clause rather states that he became rapt in the spirit or elevated to a state of ecstasy or inspiration. He was inspired by the Holy Spirit and he knew it. In this state the senses are either shut off or elevated to a supernatural perfection enabling them to behold scenes hidden from the natural eye (Aug.). The events about to unravel themselves to the vision of the Apostle are in the mental order (Council of Ancyra). He was in communication with the spirit of prophecy. The visions came on the Lord's day, the first day of the week, on which the Christians from apostolic times were wont to assemble for the "breaking of the bread" as is mentioned in the Acts (XX. 7). This rule of assembling for sacrifice on the first day of the week is mentioned by St. Paul (1 Cor. XVI. 2). It is explained in the Didache and by St. Ignatius. St. John on this day was not privileged to offer the Holy Sacrifice but was transported by the Lord in spirit to see its reality, which lies beyond the reach of the senses.

He hears behind him a "great voice", which he hears frequently in the course of the revelations. A clear distinction is always made between the "voice as it were thunder" and the "great voice". This voice announces the beginning of the revelations. It may be the voice of the angel of verse one or the voice of Christ. His likening it to a trumpet expresses its strength and musical tone. It alludes to Joel (II. 1), where the priests are commanded to blow the trumpet to announce the coming of God's judgments. It also alludes to St. Paul's letter to the Thessalonians (IV. 16). It is not a trumpet but a voice that has some likeness to the sound of a trumpet.

Verse 11

The trumpet voice enjoins on St. John the command to write in a book whatever shall be revealed to him and to send a copy of it to each of the churches named. Since the seven churches are represented by the seven golden lamps; and since this number corresponds with the seven gifts of the Holy Spirit who directs the Universal Church; and since it symbolizes universality: These seven churches stand for the whole Catholic Church. The book is thus addressed to all Christians.

The seven cities named were situated in the west and center of proconsular Asia, which comprised the ancient kingdom of Pergamus. From Ephesus, evangelized by St. Paul, the Church spread along the valleys of the Meander and the Lycus to the other Phrygian cities, Hierapolis, Laodicea and Colossae. Smyrna, Pergamus, Thyatira and Philadelphia received the faith about the same time including Troas from St. Paul himself. Cysicus, the most important port of Bithynia, was likely also a Christian center (1 Peter, I. 1). Tralles and Magnesia received letters from St. Ignatius some 10 or 15 years later and were then important Christian centers and populous cities. All were in the neighborhood of Ephesus. Why did St. John at the command of Christ select the seven cities named for his message?

That he should choose SEVEN cities is quite intelligible, because it is God's sacred number and the fundamental number of the Apocalypse. And if his words are literally true, it was the number stipulated by the Lord Himself, and His was the choice of these particular churches. Perhaps St. John was better acquainted with those congregations or they were larger at that time. Ephesus was the great seaport, and from there the Roman highway ran north to Smyrna and Pergamus. Sardis and Laodicea were district capitals or seats of Roman government (Conventus). But Thyatira and Philadelphia were unimportant cities. Many another city among those mentioned above could have been chosen. The cities did not correspond to geographical divisions either.

A seemingly natural explanation is obtained from the studies of Ramsay. The seven cities are all situated on the grand circular route that connects up the richest, most influential and most populous provinces of Asia. If a messenger left Patmos, he would disembark at Ephesus and take the Roman highway northward to Smyrna and Pergamus along the imperial mail-route, which thence ran southeast to Thyatira, Sardis, Philadelphia and Laodicea. Thence he would return by the central route of Asia Minor along the valleys of the Cayster and Meander and reach Ephesus. But why should he omit Hierapolis, Tralles and Magnesia, more important cities than Philadelphia or Thyatira? Ramsay supposes each of the seven cities being a distributing point for mail, that the whole of Asia Minor could be reached from these points, if the messenger left a copy of the Revelations at each church with the instruction that copies be made and transmitted to the neighboring churches. "They were the best points on the circuit to serve as centers of communication with seven districts: Pergamus for the North", including Troas and Cysicus . . ; "Thyatira for an inland district on the Northeast and East; Sardis for the whole middle valley of the Hermus; Philadelphia for upper Lydia and North Phrygia; Laodicea for the Lycus valley and for central Phrygia; Ephesus for the Cayster and lower Meander valley and coasts; Smyrna for the lower Hermus valley and north Ionian coast". "Planted at these seven centers, the Apocalypse would spread through their neighborhoods and from thence to the rest of the province".

This ingenious explanation does not explain everything. For practical reasons the seven cities may have been well situated to spread the message throughout the whole of *proconsular* Asia. But if it were the purpose to spread the Revelations as far and as fast as possible to all Christian communities in Asia, why not also send copies to the cities in Galatia and Greece, which had equally important Christian churches? And why not send copies to the most important churches of all, Jerusalem, Antioch and Rome? Surely those Christians needed to be warned as much as those of proconsular Asia. The Apocalypse itself being inspired and written at the command of Christ states positively that the Lord chose those churches and dictated each letter. Would not St. John prevaricate, when he states that he was commanded to write to the churches named, if the Lord left the choice to him? Our Lord states particular reasons in each letter for which he orders St. John to write.

The following explanation is therefore ventured, because our Lord would more probably select the churches most suitable to receive his message for *supernatural* than for natural reasons. These seven churches and bishops may have been guilty to such a marked degree of the defects, faults and vices stated in the letters, that they would most likely admit their wrongdoing, if their attention were called to them. Such faults would court spiritual disaster in any persecution. All Christian communities, the whole Church, would at all times profit by a warning against them. They were conspicuous in the churches chosen and for that reason above all others, these seven churches were singled out to receive the message of Christ. On the other hand, they may have been pre-eminent for virtues, which would be the strength and glory of any congregation or Christian and would uphold him in the hour of trial. The seven churches were thus proposed as examples of highly reprehensible faults as well as patterns of divinely commendable virtues; and through them, all congregations of the world would receive a much needed warning against evils and encouragement for fearlessness in virtue.

Verse 12

At the sound of the voice, St. John slowly turned to see the one who spoke. And he saw seven golden lamps, seven separate lamps. The prophet Zacharias describes the vision of the golden lamp with seven arms. That lamp was the Synagogue or Temple. The seven flames fed by olive oil symbolized the seven-fold activity of the Holy Spirit (Zach. IV. 6). But here the seven lamps are the seven churches in Asia, to which St. John is to send the revelations. The lamps are all alike, but each one does its own work in serving God. They are golden lamps, because they are permeated with the grace of God and are therefore His precious possessions. The light of each one enlightens heathendom in its own way. The flames allude to the tongues of fire that appeared on Pentecost and to the eyes of the Lamb (V. 6) (See Zach. IV.). The churches are able to enlighten the world, because the Spirit of God is within them and operates through them. Each gift of the Holy Ghost manifests itself in the Church and in the lives of Christians, and therefore although consisting of but one element they are seven separate flames. Furthermore these seven lamps reveal the kinship of the Catholic Church to the Holy Spirit and visibly manifest His varied influences and activities.

Verse 13

St. John saw Someone standing in the midst of the seven

lamps. He does not say how these lamps were arranged nor where the figure stood. The lamps may have stood in a circle as in the vision of chapter five, where the Lamb occupies the central place, or they may have stood in a row and the figure behind them. The Someone did not hover in the air above the flames but stood on His feet. He looked like a "son of man". These words are the very words of Daniel (VII. 13), where they shadowed forth the figure of Christ. So this is evidently the Lord Himself. The name St. John gives Him was not taken from Daniel, for Christ assumed it Himself in almost every chapter of the Gospel. St. John beholds Him in His transfigured humanity and with the attributes He manifests later in action. (II. III. XIX.). Again this description is not picked by St. John from the Old Testament nor from apocryphal writings, which are only fiction, but from an original vision of Christ as He appeared then and there.

A white linen garment flows down to His feet. It is the emblem of His priesthood and calls to mind the Ephod of the high priest. The white linen also symbolizes sanctifying grace and the eminent holiness of Christ. Moreover it is the emblem of victory foreshadowing the holiness of Christ as the cause of victory. The girdle worn by the high priests indicated their continency. Christ wears it around His breast indicating the immunity of His human nature from all carnal as well as sinful desires. The golden girdle is also a symbol of His royalty, because in ancient times gold was presented only to kings and worn by kings. King Alexander presented a golden buckler to Jonathan (1 Macc. X. 89) as an acknowledgement of his royalty. Gold is lastly a symbol of wisdom and here of the divine wisdom of Christ's human mind. Thus the name "son of man" designates Christ as a prophet, the white garment a priest and the golden buckler a king.

Verse 14

In this verse St. John begins to set forth those attributes of Christ that will exert their power in the Apocalypse. "His head and His hairs were white as white wool and as snow". His head means His forehead and the roots of His hair and they are white showing forth His eternity and divine wisdom and His ability to guide the Church aright. For His hair St. John uses the plural, which is not the oridinary use in Greek any more than in English. He thus calls attention to every individual hair and may wish to refer to His manifold activity and to elaborate at the same time the details of His plan in the Church and in the world. The whole description recalls that of God, "the Ancient of Days". (Dan. VII. 9).

His eyes "were like a flame of fire". Those flaming eyes beam with omniscience. They know the deeds of the wicked, and they flame with wrath towards all wickedness. With such eyes He appears again to the Bishop of Thyatira, as the "one who searches the reins and hearts" (II. 23) and in XIX. 12 to judge and fight with justice and to destroy the wicked. But for good and faithful, those eyes beam with love. The power of His eyes was noticed by His disciples (Mc. III. 5; X. 21; Lc. XXII. 61) during His mortal life. How much more now did the gaze of those eyes reveal His divinity!

Verse 15

His feet were like bronze glowing in a furnace. Many attempts have been made to describe the meaning of the bronze or mixture of metal meant by the Greek word, χαλκολιβάνῳ but no one is satisfied with his own explanation. It must have been some mixture of metals that had an awe-inspiring glow when in a molten state. The glowing feet harmonize well with the flaming eyes. The feet are the symbol of stability and of destructive power. He will tread upon everything unholy and will consume it with fire. This vision contrasts the irresistible power of Christ with that of the world-empires which Nabuchodonosor saw in the form of a huge statue that had feet of iron mixed with clay (Dan. II. 33). These glowing feet menace all who give way to false teachings, false moral standards, hypocrisy and apostasy. The Latin translation, "Aurichalcum", for the Greek term points to very fine and precious brass resembling burnished gold. That would be ever emblematic of Christ's justice and purity of intention in treading upon evil.

The voice which the Seer heard was like the roar of the Aegean Sea, euphonic with sublime music for the good but terrifying for the wicked. Like fire, water is another beneficial element as well as a powerful instrument of vengeance. Christ's voice threatens and warns the wicked and defends and encourages the good. He announces His decrees to His Church and halts the attacks of the enemies. The waters symbolize the peoples of the earth. His voice is re-echoed among all peoples, and by it He subjects them all to Himself. (Greg. Bede).

Verse 16

The meaning of the SEVEN STARS which Christ holds in His right hand is given in verse 20. In the Old Testament, stars denoted various offices of God's people; In Numbers (XXIV. 17) and Isaias (XIV. 12) kings and in Daniel (XII. 3) teachers. The seven stars here represent the bishops of the seven churches. Bishops are the official teachers of Christ's doctrine. In their official capacity, they are the light of the world and like the stars in the firmament should light the faithful over the stormy waves of time. Christ holds them in His hand betokening whence they have their commission, authority and direction, their protection and all weapons with which to represent Him ably and valiantly.

The sharp two-edged sword issueing from His mouth bodies forth the power of His word, its truth and punitive authority. It will pierce the hearts of the sinners (Heb. IV. 12) and bring everlasting death to those who resist it. The word of Christ will make the wicked feel the justice of His judgments (XIX. 11), before which all His enemies will come to grief (Bede). The sword is the large Thracian sword foreboding judgment and symbolizing authority and the punitive power of the Church, which Christ will uphold in truth and justice.

His countenance shone as the noon-day sun radiating the divine knowledge and spiritual life with which He animates those who accept His full revelations and submit to His sway. It will sear the conscience of those whose faith and piety is rooted in worldliness and temporal hopes. Those who are not rooted in the love of Christ, which engenders the spirit of sacrifice and penance, will wither in the brightness of His presence in the Church and will fall away.

Verse 17

Moses (Exod. III. 6) and Daniel (VIII. 17) were terrified at the presence of God, and the seraphim veil their faces (Isa. VI. 2) before His Majesty. St. John likewise falls down before the transfigured Christ as he had done on Mt. Tabor. But our Lord touched His beloved disciple, as He did after the Transfiguration, and calmed His fears. After the Resurrection He was the same as now, only His divinity was hidden. Still He is the same yesterday and today without change and is no more terrifying now to those who love Him than when He taught and worked on earth. The text uses the word ὡς , which means here as elsewhere "a likeness to". He appeared dead. The hand that touched him was the same one that held the seven stars. This is then a mere symbolical action. The words, "fear not", were quite familiar to the ears of the apostles. Our Lord again testifies to His divinity by using the words which in the Old Testament referred only to God: "I am the First and the Last". He is the Creator, and through Him all things will be renewed (Isa. XLI. 4; XLIV. 6; XLVIII. 12; Apoc. XXI. 5; XXII. 13).

Verse 18

This whole vision represents Christ as the bearer of life; He is "the life" or "the Living One". It attributes the Apocalypse to the author of the fourth gospel (John V. 26), where Christ claims to "have life in Himself". It is another divine title and corresponds to many texts in the Old Testament (Jos. III. 10; Ps. XLI. 3; Dan. XII. 7). This life, which is His essence, is in sharp contrast with the inanimate gods of paganism. It is not the mortal life which He led before His death, for that life is dead, but it is the immortal life which He possesses forever after His Resurrection. As to His human nature, He WAS dead and now has entered into everlasting life and is therefore actually living His perfected human life. Death was only a transient phenomenon with Him, and though a real death then, it is no longer a reality now. Hence His assurance to St. John when He said "fear not" had double force. He had experienced real death, while St. John was only scared into apparent death. The life that was now visible in Him was not that of divinity but of His re-vivified humanity yet real and everlasting and linked inseparably with His divine life in the Hypostatic Union.

In consequence of this life, which is His by right of conquest, He holds the keys of death. He walked through the gates of death and took from the hands of Death his keys. He is now the Master of Death. "Death shall no more have dominion over Him". He also has the keys of Hades. He has then dominion and untrammelled authority both over the domain of Death and of Hades. He thus declares Himself the Prophet and the Judge, the One who proclaims the message of life and who will enforce its acceptance through all the moral forces to be described in this book. The message has special reference to the Four Living Beings (IV. 6). And the prerogatives He reveals here will through them become active in shaping the destiny of the Church and of the human race. He lives for those who love His Coming and will bring them life, and they need not fear Him. In Isaias (XXXVIII. 10) and in the gospel of St. Matthew (XVI. 18), the underworld is described as having gates. In Psalm IX. 15, Death is given a domain secured by gates. Since His Resurrection, Christ possesses the keys of both, which is the emblem of His ruling power over them.

Verse 19

As in verse eleven where the invisible voice first spoke to him, St. John is ordered to write what he has seen and heard, i.e. the vision of the glorified Christ, the Victor. Christ emphasizes His command with the "therefore", which points to the conclusion that follows from His authority as Creator and Last End of creation and as Victor over Death and Hades. The things he is to write about are further explained to him. In the first place it is the condition of the churches as will be revealed in chapters II. and III. and secondly the future events as will be revealed in chapters IV. to XXII.

Verse 20

Christ now explains two items of the "Mystery"; He explains the meaning of the seven stars and of the seven golden lamps. The grammatical construction of the Greek text presents difficulties, because there are two accusatives without a verb to govern them. But they may be governed by the preposition εἰς omitted but to be understood. 'As for the secret of the seven stars, and as for the seven lamps' might be the rendition of it in English.

The seven stars are the seven bishops of the churches to whom St. John is to write. The stars are like planets receiving from Christ, who is their sun, their light and heat. They depend absolutely on Him for instruction, protection, chastisement and reward. In Malachias (II. 7) the priest is called an angel. Such use of the word in the Old Testament gives us the interpretation of the figurative language and of the visions in the Apocalypse. This explanation of our Lord stamps the whole book an allegory.

And the language must be considered metaphorical unless the context argues for the literal sense. According to our Lord's words, "angel" means a bishop or priest throughout the Apocalypse, unless the context clearly shows him to be a celestial or evil spirit. Protestant interpreters do not like to admit that the "angels" are bishops of the churches, because they contend that there were no monarchical bishops over the churches at this time. But it is clear from Scripture and Tradition, that a bishop presided over the church by apostolic institution in every city. That these angels should be celestial spirits is unacceptable, because one of them is pronounced spiritually "dead" (III. 1) and another "lukewarm" (III. 16). An angel who is spiritually dead is a devil. Christ does not write to devils or make them the heads of His churches. These angels are obviously the bishops of the seven churches, and therefore they receive the blame for whatever is wrong with the congregations.

The seven lamps are the seven churches to which St. John is directed to send the revelations. Stars are heavenly bodies, and lamps are earthly vessels. The pastor is the heavenly representative of divine light, of doctrine and grace; the congregation is the visible reflection of that doctrine and grace. The pastor is the source and origin of divine light; his church is the visible society of faithful upon whom that light falls and whom it enlightens. But not alone the pastor enlightens the world as far as he is known by his teaching and example, the congregation also diffuses its light over the world in its own way and measure.

CHAPTER II

Westminster Version

To the angel of the church of Ephesus 1. write: Thus saith he who holdeth the seven stars in his right hand, he who walketh in the midst of the seven golden lamps.

I know thy works, and thy labor and thy 2. patience, and that thou canst not bear evil men, and thou didst try those who call themselves apostles and are not, and didst find them liars. And thou hast 3. patience, and thou didst bear for my name and hast not grown weary.

But I have against thee that thou hast 4. left thy first love. Remember therefore 5. whence thou hast fallen, and repent and do the former works: but if not, I will come to thee, and will move thy lamp out of its place, unless thou repent. How be it 6. this thou hast, that thou hatest the works of the Nicolaites, which I also hate.

He that hath an ear, let him hear what 7. the Spirit saith to the churches!

To him that conquereth, I will give to eat of the tree of life, which is in the paradise of God.

And to the angel of the church in 8. Smyrna write: Thus saith the first and the last, who died and came to life.

I know thine affliction and thy poverty 9. – but thou art rich – and the slander uttered by those that say that they are Jews and are not, but are a synagogue of Satan.

Fear not the things which thou art 10. about to suffer. Behold the devil is about to cast some of you into prison that ye may be tried, and ye shall have tribulation ten days. Be faithful unto death, and I will give thee the crown of life.

He that hath an ear, let him hear what the Spirit saith to the churches!
11. He that conquereth shall not be harmed by the second death.

And to the angel of the Church in Pergamum write: Thus saith he who hath the sharp two-edged sword: I know where 13. thou dwellest – where the throne of Satan is – and thou holdest fast my name, and didst not deny my faith, even in the days of Antipas, my witness, my faithful one, who was killed among you, where Satan dwelleth. But I have 14. against thee a few things: thou hast some there holding fast the doctrine of Balaam who taught Balac to cast a stumbling-block before the children of Israel, the eating of idol-offerings and the committing of impurity.

Even so, thou too hast some people 15. holding fast the doctrine of the Nicolaites in the same way. Repent therefore! But if not, I will come to thee quickly, 16. and I will war against them with the sword of my mouth. He that hath an ear 17. let him hear what the Spirit saith to the churches! To him that conquereth, I will give of the hidden manna, and I will give a white stone, and upon the stone a new name written, which no man knoweth, except him that receiveth it.

And to the angel of the Church in 18. Thyatira write: Thus saith the Son of God he who hath eyes as a flame of fire, and whose feet are

like bright bronze. I 19. know thy works, thy charity, thy faith, thy service
thy patience, and thy last works more numerous than the first.
But I 20. have this against thee, that thou dost tolerate the woman Jezabel,
who, calling herself a prophetess, teacheth and leadeth astray my servants
to commit impurity and to eat idol-offerings. And I gave 21. her time
that she should repent and she willeth not to repent of her impurity.
Behold, I cast her upon a bed, and the 22. companions of her adultery
into great tribulations, unless they shall repent of her works; and her
children I will 23. strike with death. And all the churches shall know that
I am he who searcheth reins and hearts; and I will give to each of you
according to your works. But to you I say, to the rest in Thyatira – 24.
whosoever do not hold this doctrine, such as have not (in their phrase),
"known the deep things of Satan" – I cast not upon you any other burden.
Only hold fast 25. what you have, until I come. As for him 26. that
conquereth and that keepeth my works till the end, I will give him power
over the nations, and he will rule them 27. with a rod of iron, as when
earthen vessels are broken in pieces, even as I myself 28. have received
from my Father; and I will give him the morning star. He that hath
an ear, let him 29. hear what the spirit saith to the churches.

B.

MESSAGE TO THE ANGELS OF THE SEVEN CHURCHES

1. To The Angel Of The Church Of Ephesus.

Chapter II. Verses 1-7.

Verse 1

The first letter is addressed to the Bishop of Ephesus. Ephesus was the most important Christian metropolis in Asia Minor, the most important city on the seaboard and the place of disembarkation from the Mediterranean Sea. St. John may have written or dictated the Apocaplyse at Ephesus from notes taken at the time of the revelation. Whether he did this or wrote the Revelations on the Island of Patmos, Ephesus would logically be the first church to address.

Ephesus was the most important seaport of international communication with Greece, Italy, Marseilles, Egypt, Antioch and the rest of the east Mediterranean coast. The great trade route through southern Asia Minor brought business from the Euphrates and possibly from India and China to the port of Ephesus. For a time its position as a seaport was in danger, because the alluvial deposits of the Cayster filled up the bay and pushed the shore away from the city. But this was arrested in 65 A.D.

Its political importance was not inferior to that of its commerce. It was the head of a "conventus", a judgment seat and a seat of proconsular government. In a series of inscriptions found at Ayasaluk near the ancient site of Ephesus is proven the renown it possessed of being "the first and greatest metropolis of Asia". The Acts (XIX. 31-40) state that the rulers of Ephesus were called the "rulers of Asia" and the "town clerks".

The culture and pagan refinement of its people was equal to its political and maritime importance. It boasted of many philosophers and rhetoricians and schools of painting and sculpture. It was the home of the philosopher Heraclitus, who was the first in history to speak of the divine Logos. The geographer Artemidorus and the historian and essayist Xenophon were born there. Architecture was also highly developed. Ephesus possessed an architectural gem, the temple of Diana, which was numbered among the wonders of the ancient world and which was a religious gem reflecting on Ephesus the renown of a religious metropolis. This temple had been destroyed and rebuilt several times. It was 400 feet long, 200 feet wide and had pillars 60 feet high. Tradition claimed a span of 120 years for its construction.

On his second missionary journey, St. Paul made a brief stop at Ephesus and preached in the synagogue (Acts XVIII. 19). Apollo, a disciple of John the Baptist, arrived later and was converted by Aquila and Priscilla. On a second visit, St. Paul remained two years at Ephesus and converted all the disciples of St. John. He taught in the lecture-hall of Tyrannus, the rhetorician, and firmly established the Church in Ephesus. Because of its rapid growth and the weakening of idolatry and consequent lessening of business for the silversmiths, Demetrius started a tumult against St. Paul forcing him for the sake of peace to leave the city. Later he ordered the clergy to meet him at Miletus (Acts XX. 17). He appointed Timothy, then a very young man from Lystra, Bishop of Ephesus.

The residence and death of St. John in Ephesus are not mentioned in the Scripture but are attested by early tradition (Iren. III. iii. 4). St. John wrote the Gospel there and possibly also the Apocalypse. The first letter to the Bishop of Ephesus contains indications that Timothy was the bishop. In 2 Timothy (IV. 1-5), St. Paul admonishes him with a touch of severity, which indicates that he was of a lenient and gentle disposition; and 1 Timothy (V. 23) shows that he was not of robust health. Verses 4 and 5 suggest the same qualities, an inclination to ease. St. Paul informs us that Timothy was liberated from prison (Heb. XIII. 23). Apparently St. Timothy lacked firmness with the indifferent priests and those who sought to get by with bluff and a pretense of doing their duty.

To each of the seven churches, Christ exhibits one or several characteristic titles He bears, which will manifest themselves in inflicting judgment upon that church or its bishop being always the attribute most applicable to the congregation and pastor addressed. The clause "who holdeth the seven stars" should read "who RULES" . . . It reminds the bishop of the Master's supreme authority over him and of his own total dependence on Christ's favor and grace, for He might do with each star what He will. The right hand symbolizes the power to execute justice. The right hand will also protect the stars against evil and mete out to them their reward.

"Who walks in the midst of the seven golden lampstands" points to verse five. The words addressed to the congregation make them aware of the presence of the overseer, the Lord, who patrols the ground and is found where He is needed. The terms used in this verse are stronger than those used in I. 13-16: There He stood, here He walks in the midst of the lampstands; there He held, here He rules the seven stars.

His words and actions reveal how His knowledge reviews the character and history of the bishop and every fault and good quality of the people. The reminder of these two facts, that He rules the stars and walks amidst the lamps, is a general admonition to all the churches, because Ephesus is representative of the whole province, and the Ephesian church is the pattern for all the Asian churches. It emphasizes the admonitions of St. Paul to Timothy of how important it was for the Bishop of Ephesus to have a firm grasp on the congregation and maintain a wide-awake vigilance in safeguarding its faith.

Verse 2

The first word of our Lord's message is, "I know". In Greek the word expresses more than mere acquaintanceship, it implies perfect knowledge. In that perfect knowledge He is able to give just and perfect praise and blame without danger of error.

The bishop receives commendation for tireless labor, for patience and constancy and faithful perseverance in the true morality of Christ. He has preserved his flock from heretics and chided the false brethren who stubbornly and maliciously resisted the truth or clung to heretical doctrines and strove to justify their evil ways. The bishop has not overlooked or condoned their evil deeds; he has obeyed St. Paul to "charge some not to teach otherwise". What horror the Apostolic Church felt for any sort of heresy is forcefully expressed by St. Irenaeus. (III. iii. 4).

The Bishop furthermore has tested the claims of itinerant teachers who posed as apostles or prophets in a wider sense without carrying commendatory letters and has proven them not to be self-deceived but malicious deceivers. Our Lord had given the norm of this test: "by their fruits you shall know them" (Mt. VII. 16). Their own reports of what they had heard or seen of the Lord told against them and exposed them as liars. In this watchfulness his flock had been of the same mind with him and had not been deceived or misled. The bishop receives credit for it all.

Verse 3

The bishop has borne the cross of Christ in all constancy, has not wearied of watching and exposing the pretenders or of striving to convert them, has born their jibes and sneers and has firmly upheld the truth and testified to the divinity of Christ. This kind of persecution must have lasted a long time and caused some to grow weary from spiritual exhaustion, for he receives special recognition for not wearying under the ordeal.

Verse 4

Patience, perseverance and untiring labor is not all that Christ demands. The bishop's love should have *grown* apace. But that first consuming love has cooled. He has not continued to make headway towards perfection in all his labor and endurance. He has overlooked this most necessary virtue, and therefore his zeal and enthusiasm has waned. Greek commentators point to a growing neglect of the poor in the congregation. The first generation of converts had passed away, and the Christians had grown tepid and selfish again. Their first fervor was shown by the burning of their books of magic at St. Paul's preaching (Acts XIX. 19) and by the grief of the clergy at his departure (Acts XX. 37). The bishop deserves the blame for the decrease in love and fervor, when his example should have lighted the way to its continuance and growth. He, however, has begun to walk the ways of the priests in ancient Israel. The verse faintly alludes to Jeremias (II. 2) and Ezechiel. (XVI. 8).

Verse 5

With divine authority Christ calls on the bishop to remember his state of mind and heart during his first love and how far he has wandered from his first ideals. He is not accused of sin but of laziness and torpor, or perhaps not even this, perhaps only of a weakened fervor and zeal. Yet of this he must repent and return to his first love. As a soul co-operates with grace it grows to greater capacity for more abundant and finer graces, and the growing zeal will urge it to finer and more perfect works. But this bishop has been content to remain on the same plane. His fall then consists in not having risen to the spiritual height to which he should have ascended.

If he does not heed the warning, Christ will punish him. The verb in the present tense does not denote the future judgments upon the world but a special visitation from Christ. The punishment is the removal of the lamp out of its place. This alludes to VI. 14, where the mountains and islands are moved out of their places. The congregation, like a lamp, will be a beacon guiding to the harbor of truth all who see it and who are tossed about on the waves of unbelief and passion. It shall by its renewed fervor and zeal give unending glory to God. If, however love for Christ does not grow in intensity from its present lowness, they will lose their relationship to Him and their place of honor before God and the world. The penalty will be a temporal one. The Greek word *κινήσω* intimates not a sudden and violent extermination of the church but a movement which will banish it from its place of spiritual distinction; heresies and apostasies will grow among them, and another congregation will receive their place of spiritual leadership. If they repent, the threat of extinction will not be carried out. They seem to have heeded the warning, for St. Ignatius calls the church "deservedly most happy" and "blessed in the greatness and fullness of God the Father." (Prol. to Eph). After the 11th century, the line of bishops became extinct.

Verse 6

Our Lord does not omit any praiseworthy deed. He does not want to crush their hope by unmitigated rigor of judgment but desires their sincere repentance. Hence He adds one more reason for their conversion, and that is their having taken an unfavorable attitude towards the Nicolaite heresy. They hate the evil deeds of those people not the people themselves and this accords with the mind of Christ. The bishop has consented to no compromise. This state of mind, to hold firmly to the true doctrine, will call down the grace of conversion. But that grace will be effective only if they repent. (2 Tim. II. 25-26). Hatred of evil is a divine attribute. The concordance of the Ephesians with the mind of Christ will gain for them the grace of conversion and pardon for other faults and imperfections. Heresy must be a grave crime against Christ, if He would thus express the divine hatred for it.

In verse four our Lord charges the bishop with having lost his first love; but his hatred and that of his congregation for the deeds of the heretics tempers that charge. Ancient writers (Iren. I. xxvi. 3) express the opinion that "the Nicolaites were founded by Nicolas, one of the seven deacons ordained by the apostles (Acts. VI. 5). Victorinus says that "the Nicolaites were false and troublesome men, who as ministers under the name of Nicolas had made for themselves a heresy, to the effect that what had been offered to idols might be exorcised and eaten and that whoever should have committed fornication might receive peace on the eighth day." In Pergamus there were Nicolaites (II. 15), and their tactics were akin to that of Balaam. In Thyatira they were connected with the Gnostics (II. 24). Modern commentators do not agree with St. Irenaeus for the origin of the sect and do not know whence they came.

Verse 7

The exclamation used here is common to the Synoptics (Mt. XI. 15). He uses the singular to individualize the readers and hearers. The promises to the victors *follow* the admonition to hear in the first three letters; in the last four the admonitions follow the promises. To have an ear is a willingness to give heed to the words of warning. The admonition is addressed to the faithful only, because they alone have proven to have an ear for the truths of God by accepting them. Heathens and heretics have no ear for truth.

In this book the Spirit speaks to the churches, because He inspires all sacred writers. Though the voice of Christ speaks to St. John, it is His Spirit who guides the hand of the writer to deliver the message he hears from the lips of Christ.

The churches are plural in number, because there are seven congregations. Every member of these or any other congregations who has an "ear" to receive the message must receive it entirely, whether he lives in Asia or elsewhere, and whether he lives in St. John's time or shall live in future ages.

To the victor who overcomes his lethargy and laziness is promised the permission to eat of the tree of life. He who heeds the message will be victorious. Victory and the victor are frequently in evidence in the Apocalypse. The whole book is a prophetical record of victories to be won by Christ and His Church. Through faith and the practice of it we win the victory (1 Jo. V. 4). At the Last Supper Christ assured the Apostles that He had already overcome the world (Jo. XVI. 33). Satan too shall be overcome.

The desire for the restoration of an earthly kingdom was a strong tradition among the Jews. It was in their hopes the culminating bliss which the Messias was to bring. Christ gives this desire a spiritual direction by promising the restoration of the Tree of Life to those who free themselves from attachment to this world, for the Tree of Life is "in the paradise of my God." Christ had explained this in the Gospel: "I am the bread of life... He who eats this bread shall live forever" (Jo. VI. 48-59). The "paradise of God" here mentioned is a spiritual paradise as contrasted with the earthly paradise of Genesis. This spiritual paradise is the Church, and the Tree of Life is the Holy Eucharist. To the Bishop and congregation of Ephesus is given this one promise, to eat of that tree. Only those who overcome temptations will be admitted to that tree and will partake of the purest joys that Christ can instill into the heart.

2. To The Angel Of The Church Of Smyrna.
Verses 8-11.

Verse 8

Smyrna rose like an amphitheatre or crown on the Gulf of Smyrna. It was about 55 miles north of Ephesus at the foot of Mt. Thmolus. It was called on ancient medals "the first for beauty" and "fresh as a bouquet". The height half surrounding it on the North, East and West was covered with flowers and was known as the "Crown of Smyrna". This natural floral display gave the city a very rich appearance.

Smyrna was founded by colonists from Lesbos about 1000 B.C. It was destroyed about 580 B.C. and was rebuilt around the year 300. In 133 B.C. it became Roman property. The Romans built a judiciary conventus and a mint there. It held the title of metropolis with other cities of Asia. The "concilium festivum" was celebrated there, at which the olympic games were an important feature. The victors were crowned with a garland of myrtle or ivy (Paus. VI. 14. 3). It was also distinguished by a temple to the emperor erected during the reign of Tiberius. Caesar Augustus had conceded the right to possess the temple in preference to Ephesus. (Tacitus IV. 15). The people had formerly made an alliance with Rome against the Seleucidae, which long endured. On that account it received from the Romans the title of "the faithful city", a title in which the citizens prided themselves very much. This faithfulness to

Rome later introduced the cult of emperor-worship. It was therefore called the "first in Asia" by its inhabitants and disputed with Ephesus the place and honor of first metropolis.

Smyrna had an export trade nearly equal to that of Ephesus, as it was situated at the terminal of a fine interior trade-route which drew from the rich Hermus valley, and on the other hand it had a safe harbor, which was entered by a long gulf.

Who established the church at Smyrna cannot be learned from the New Testament. The document, "Life of Polycarp", states that St. Paul visited Smyrna perhaps as reported in Acts XIX. 1 on his way to Ephesus and found disciples there as at Ephesus. Christianity must have begun in the synagogue. In the martyrdom of Polycarp, the Jews were the chief actors. The martyrdom took place at the concilium festivum in honor of the emperor. The Christians of Smyrna were wretchedly poor due probably to the persecution of the Jews and the pillaging of their property by the Jewish mobs, who incited the pagans against them.

Christ reminds the Smyrnan Christians of His titles of "the First and the Last", to encourage them in the persistent persecutions and to console them for the spoliation of their property by the Jewish and Pagan mobs. He would have them remember that all life comes from Him, and that all creation tends towards Him as its last end; and hence, if for His sake they are deprived of the very necessities of life to say nothing of all comforts and enjoyments, and even of life itself, He can and will repay them a thousand-fold. He will pronounce the final word of judgment upon all rational creatures. If they are now in abject poverty through the hatred and injustice of their enemies, they shall become rich hereafter.

The words "who became dead and lives" encourage to martyrdom. Christ preceded them; He was the First Martyr. **The Greek word ἔζησεν means the fullness and vigorous** freshness of life and being in the aorist tense calls attention to His Resurrection. In I. 18, He merely stated that He is the LIVING ONE. But here he reminds them of His martyrdom and of His Resurrection, which is the pattern of their own glorious resurrection, if they die for His sake. The word "dead" is against the Gnostics who taught He had a phantom body. The word "became alive" is against Simon Magus and others who denied His Resurrection. He deserves fidelity because He died for us and by His Resurrection gives assurance of our resurrection. The following words make clear what the titles mean to the church of Smyrna.

Verse 9

The abrupt change of construction in Greek here expresses the Lord's solicitude for the bishop and his congregation since He knows what they have endured. The bishop shares poverty with the people. He has borne the hatred of the enemies and has patiently suffered persecution from them. But he must not grieve over this, because he is spiritually rich. All this reechoes the Gospel (Lc. XII. 21). There is a contrast between the church of Smyrna and that of Laodicea in worldly possessions. The faithful of Smyrna are actually in need. But they are spiritually rich; while at Laodicea more than poor, they are "wretched".

The words, "who say they are Jews", indicate the source of the tribulation and poverty. The "Martyrdom of Polycarp" says (XIII.): "The Jews especially, according to custom eagerly assisting them in it". They pursued a campaign of slander and calumny against the bishop and the Christians. They were only "so-called" Jews. St. John with our Lord's words calls them the "synagogue of satan". They were the adversaries of Christ.

Wherever St. Paul preached, the rich and powerful Jews persecuted him (Acts XIII. 50; XIV. 2, 19; XVII. 5; XX. 3; XXI. 27). If the Jews could not personally injure the Christians, they would excite the pagan authorities against them by slanders and calumny (Acts. XIII. 45; XVIII. 6). The Jews at Smyrna may have been sincere in their belief, yet as elsewhere, they could not have been sinless if they slandered and blasphemed. The appellation, "Synagogue of Satan", stands in contrast with the title, "synagogue of God" (Num. XX. 4) given it in the Old Testament. The synagogue belongs to Satan, because he inspires it and through it incites men to blaspheme the Church (XII. 10, 15; XIII. 6). The Christians are the true descendants of Abraham, because they accept the prophecies of the Old Testament made to Abraham and his posterity and believe them to have been fulfilled in Christ.

Verse 10

More words of encouragement and consolation for the bishop follow. Though persecution shall be added to slander and blasphemy, he must not fear. This is a promise of sufficient grace in the moment of need to withstand all attacks. Confidence in Christ's support will make him victorious. The "synagogue of satan" will devise ways and means to cast some of the congregation into prison. Only the civil authorities have the right and power to arrest anyone. They will therefore be the acting persecutors. The "Martyrdom of Polycarp" (III.) and many other writings of the Fathers designate the devil as the instigator of the persecutions. Satan would try the whole Church as he tried the Apostles, not thinking that the victory of the Church over him would thus be vastly augmented.

In the opinion of some commentators, the "10 days" mean the ten persecutions decreed by the Roman Emperors. Others say the figure has been inspired by Daniel (I. 14). The 10 days *may* indeed mean ten separate persecutions. But it may be only a definite number for an indefinite one, and it suggests a limited number of persecutions and may stand for the world's number of completeness. Twelve is God's number of completeness. The Church has a crown of twelve stars, while the Beast has ten horns. It probably portends a severe and thorough trial for the Church of Smyrna inflicted by the Jewish and Pagan persecutors during a limited time. When St. Polycarp was martyred about 168 A. D., the Christians were still subject to molestations from the Pagans and Jews, and there were martyrdoms now and then.

"Be thou faithful until death" is probably an allusion to the reputed faithfulness of the city to Rome. A Christian can prove himself a patriot as well as a pagan can by dying for his country. Instancing this patriotic duty, our Lord demands equal faithfulness to Himself. This again forebodes the coming of bloody persecutions. But whilst the patriot who gives his life for his country will receive no personal reward, since he is beyond its reach, the soldier of Christ will receive the "crown of life." The phrases "faithful until death" and the "crown of life" show that St. John was in touch with present realities, for they seem clear allusions to popular slogans known to all.

The "crown of life" may allude to the garland of flowers with which the fairest city of Asia was surrounded. Or it may refer to the Olympic games, for which Smyrna was famous at the Concilium Festivum (Paus. VI. 14, 3). The crown which the successful competitors received was placed on their heads by the civil rulers and was an earthly crown. But Christ Himself will crown His faithful soldiers who fight to the death for Him not with a corruptible crown but with an incorruptible one. This crown which the victors in the games received was not a diadem but an emblem of victory and festivity otherwise worthless. The crown that Christ confers is the very life of glory and joy with Him. The same phrase, "the crown of life", is found in St. James (I. 12). Elsewhere in Scripture other figures are used. "The wreath" and "Crown of immortality" is in the "Martyrdom of Polycarp".

Verse 11

This message too is for all the churches of the world, for the Universal or Catholic Church. It differs from the message to Ephesus in this, that it imputes no fault to the bishop or congregation at Smyrna. If they had faults, they had atoned for them by their faithfulness to Christ in poverty and persecution. But all the faithful of the world must take to heart this message also.

Again a promise is made to those who "shall overcome". And this time the promise contains a warning of approaching martyrdoms. The promise carries immunity from the "second death". The same immunity is predicted for those who suffer death in the persecution of Antichrist (XX. 6). The reference of our Lord to Himself, "who died and came to life", calls attention to this promise. The "second death" has no resurrection. This is defined in XX. 14; it is condemnation to the "pool of fire". The above texts clearly prove that the Apocalypse is a unified composition written by one man. They also prove in St. John a consciousness of possessing the gift of prophecy and assert the fulfillment of all prophecies contained in the book.

3. To The Angel Of The Church Of Pergamos.

Verses 12 to 17.

Verse 12

Ancient Pergamos was situated where the present city of Bergama with a population of 20,000 stands. The name indicates a city of refuge, for Pergamos means citadel. It was captured by Xenophon in 399 B.C. (Anab. VII. viii. 8) but was immediately re-captured by the Persians. Being re-occupied by the Greeks, it reached its highest prosperity under Eumenios (197-159 B.C.). In honor of his exploits he erected a marble altar to Zeus, which was adorned by the "Battle of the Giants". The Kingdom had been established by Attalus I. (241 B.C.). Hence it was known as the Kingdom of the Attalides afterwards the kingdom of Mysia. Attalus III. bequeathed it to Rome in 133 B.C. Aristonicos tried to restore the monarchy but was captured in 129 B.C., and the kingdom was again annexed to Rome and was from that time on known as "Asia Propria". Present-day historians hold that it was the seat of a Roman proconsul rather than Ephesus, and that it held a hegemony over the whole of Asia Minor.

Pergamos nestled on a rock that towered about 900 feet above the valley of the Caicos facing the chain of the Hermos. The road ran along the coast from Smyrna for 40 miles and then turned northeastward up the Caicos valley for 15 miles more. The situation of the city gave it the appearance and character of force and majesty. The hill whose slope was adorned by the great altar to Zeus bore for a crown a temple in honor of Athena, which claimed for Pergamos a religious hegemony over Mysia. Rome must have attributed great importance to the city because the first temple of the imperial cult in Asia was erected there in 29 B.C. There was also a temple of Aeskulepios-serpent there with a school of medicine attached. Numerous pilgrimages sought this temple as also that of Dionysus and the Bull. In the former was practiced incubation, or a sort of trance in which miraculous cures were reported; in the latter pagan mysteries were practiced known as the Eleusinian mysteries. This practice was widespread among the Greeks and deteriorated into the Bacchanalian orgies. The Bull of Dionysus and the serpent of Aeskulepios were fraternized by the priests of these two cults, and it was said that "the bull was father of the serpent and the serpent was father of the bull". The mysticism of Dionysus might be alluded to by the description of the "second beast" (Apoc. XIII. 11) with its seeming miraculous powers; while the emperor-worship is indirectly alluded to in the description of the "first beast", Antichrist. These temples with their several cults and the Altar of Zeus visible far and wide through the plains won for Pergamos unrivalled religious pre-eminence. An Ionic temple for the worship of the Attalide kings has recently been unearthed at Pergamos. This reveals the antecedents of the imperial cult in that city. All these institutions combined with the Roman political importance shed on Pergamos an incomparable religious splendor and merited for it the same "Seat of Satan". In so strong a center of paganism, the Church was confronted with extraordinary difficulties. Obviously it was the place where the persecutions had begun in Asia.

"The sharp two-edged sword" is flashed before the eyes of the Bishop of Pergamos. This sword is the word of God and is the emblem of absolute supreme authority over all creatures and of the power over eternal life and death as opposed to the "jus gladii" of Caesar and his pro-consul. At the same time it points against the great altar of Zeus with its ornamentation of the "battle of the Giants". Christ is the Giant of giants. The Greek text states that the sword is the "two-edged one, the sharp one". It will be sharp enough to sever the soul from the body and will strike great gaping wounds unto death when it begins its work. The sword also points against the "Beast" in the background (XIII. 3) which has the death-wound by the power of the sword.

Verse 13

Christ knows the environment of the Church of Pergamos. Satan has his throne there, because Pergamos was the seat of a Roman superior court. The Roman judge could cite before his tribunal anyone who was accused of being a Christian and could command him to sacrifice to those gods whose temples stood there or to Caesar, that is to Satan. Since the edicts of Domition were in force, the power of Satan was enthroned there. The word *θρόνος* in the New Testament is the seat of a judge or king (Mt. XIX. 28; Lc. I. 32, 52) or of God or Christ (Mt. V. 34; XXV. 31). The phrase probably has specific meaning for the emperor-worship established here. This worship had a firmer hold on these people than elsewhere, because it was the continuation of the ancient king-worship of this city. In the "Martyrdom of Polycarp" are these words; "They seated themselves beside him, and endeavored to persuade him, saying 'what harm is there in saying, Lord Caesar, and in sacrificing with the other ceremonies observed on such occasions and so make sure of safety" (Mart. Polc. VIII.). The term "seat of Satan" was as pertinent here as "synagogue of Satan" at Smyrna. Such an appeal must have been dangerous to many Christians, for there was no escape from it, because the members of the Church were native inhabitants and could not migrate in a body. They must simply hold fast and defy all danger under the protection of the Lord of lords.

The bishop has remained steadfast. He has not bowed to the Lord Caesar but only to the Lord Jesus (1 Cor. XII. 3; Mart Polyc. IX.). As Christ holds the seven stars (II. 1), so does the bishop and his congregation hold to the name of Jesus securely and tenaciously without wavering or compromise. And in all temptations he and his faithful flock had not denied their belief in Jesus. They had not even submitted to anything paramount to denial such as eating meats sacrificed to idols or visiting the temple of Aeskulepios, of Athena or of the emperor. Not enough with that, they had remained firm when Antipas was martyred there. Our Lord gives Antipas the same title St. John gives Him, and which our Lord assumes Himself (III. 14), for as He was obedient and faithful unto death, so was Antipas. Who this Antipas was, no historian tells, but Simon Metaphrastes relates that he was a bishop and was roasted alive in an iron bull during the reign of Domitian. If this is true, he may have been martyred because he refused to participate in the mysteries of Dionysus. But the phrase, "where Satan dwells", is repeated. This seems to say that he refused to worship Caesar, whose pro-counsul was there and was likely to enforce the edicts of Caesar and compel everyone to acknowledge his divinity.

Verse 14

Although the bishop has held out faithfully in the face of great odds, he is not as blameless as the Bishop of Smyrna. He is culpable in a few things. The "few" things must not be deemed trivial. The term is carefully chosen so as not to weaken the recognition of the afore-mentioned virtues and to style the culpable things as exceptions to the otherwise blameless life of the bishop.

The sin of which some in the congregation are guilty is like that of the Israelites. According to the explanation given here, Balaam advised Balak, king of the Moabites, to lead the Israelites into ruin by a sly device (Numbers XXV. 2. ff). The Madianite and Moabite princesses were to bring meats which were not ritually pure to the princes of Israel after first inviting them to commit fornication with them. These were meats sacrificed to Beelphegor, the god of lust. They ate of those meats and then adored the god and consecrated themselves to him by committing further fornication. God then sent a plague among them in which 24,000 perished, until Phinees took a dagger and stabbed Zambri in his sin and thus ended the plague. Balak was powerless against Israel with the sword, but through the scheme suggested by Balaam, he caused God to send a destructive plague upon His people. This reference seems to show that some of the congregation took part in pagan feasts. They may have been poor who rarely had meat for their meals, or they may have given way to lust or partaken of the mysteries of Dionysus and Aeskulepios or been allured into communication with pagan rites for business reasons. The bishop faithfully resisted emperor-worship, thus overcoming Satan; but Satan slyly led some of the congregation into the grosser sins of indulging their passions.

Verse 15

Likewise in this congregation some members hold the doctrines of the Nicolaites. The Nicolaites probably did not keep the decrees of the Council of Jerusalem, rejected the apostolic traditions and restrictions, lapsed into moral laxity and compromised with pagans (Acts. XV. 29). St. Paul condemned lax practices in the corrupt city of Corinth, because they gave scandal to weak brethren and implied communication with evil spirits. (1 Cor. X. 20). Those who would eat such food could not partake of the Holy Eucharist. The blame for it all is placed upon the bishop, because he has been too lenient with his congregation and has not enforced the apostolic decrees.

Verse 16

In spite of his defiance against emperor-worship, the bishop is responsible for his passive toleration of the doctrine of Balaam and of the Nicolaites, by which some of his parish had fallen into grave sin, and he therefore stands in need of repentance and penance. If they do not repent, Christ will come in judgment very speedily. He will fight the evil-doers with the sword of His word. His decree will bring on persecution. When it breaks forth, the two-edged sword will separate the good from the bad and bring bloodshed, grief and tears of repentance. Those who can still be saved will die in martydrom, and the others will be cut off from the saving Church. The bishop, too, will share in the punishment indirectly. The lives of the faithful will be endangered, if the judgment begins against the wicked, and many may be sacrificed. Christ deftly intimates that the church had not accepted the doctrines of the heretics, when He says that

He will fight against "them", but some of the members had compromised by attending their meetings and listening to their propositions. The Divine Warrior will keep His Church pure, for in that state alone will she be able to save her members and convert the world. That God is a man of war, appears first in Exodus (XV. 3). If the bishop excommunicates the heretics by enforcing the apostolic decrees, the church will be spared the intervention of Christ and will remain under His protection.

Verse 17

This message to the Bishop of Pergamos is not for him alone but for all the churches and for every Christian. Christ will give the "hidden manna" to the one who overcomes his sensual appetites, fear of death and earthly attachments and avoids the allurements of sin. This "hidden manna" is variously explained. Victorinus says it is "immortality". Origen says it is the understanding of the sweet and hidden word of God. But Arethus points out the fitness of a reference to the Holy Eucharist in this mystic phrase at the end of a message which condemns participation in heathen feasts. Verse fourteen evidently takes the same stand that St. Paul took in his message to the Corinthians (X. 14 ff). St. John surely was familiar with that letter. In the light of that letter, the promise of the "hidden manna" is an undeniable appreciation of the Holy Eucharist. What is hidden there is the Sacred Humanity and Divinity of Christ. By communicating this to the faithful victor, He communicates His own divine life and with it a foretaste of the bliss of the Beatific Vision. Those who satisfy their sensual appetites cannot participate in this spiritual refreshment, for according to St. Paul, they partake of devil-worship and become associates of devils. The "hidden manna" is thus contrasted with the trance in the temple of Aeskulepios, in which the votaries experienced sensual pleasures and pretended to participate in the imagined divine life of Dionysos.

Many explanations are offered for the meaning of the "white stone" and the "new name" on the stone. No explanation seems satisfactory. The new name fits the white stone, because it is inscribed on it. The idea seems to refer to the Greek practice of casting a vote. The ballots were cast in a criminal case. A black ballot meant "guilty", whilst a white one, or "Athenian counter", acquittal of crime. White expresses victory (VI. 2; XIX. 11, 14). Christ Himself will bear a new name (XIX. 12), and

He will write new names on those who overcome (III. 12). In the light of XIV. 1, where the virgins bear the name of Christ on their foreheads, the "new name" may mean as much as the "white stone". He who receives the new name will have knowledge of his personal merits acquired by his own works. There may be a promise in it for those who had sinned by participation in idolatry, that if they repented and overcame their passions, they will receive full acquittal of all guilt, a clean conscience and a new state of mind with the old inclination to sin gone. No one except the one who experienced it would know that he had become a new man. In Isaias too we have a promise of a new name for Jerusalem and the elect (LXII. 2; LXV. 15). The one who overcomes sensuality and lust will receive a verdict from Christ that will acquit him of all faults and lesser sins. As he will sense the secret joys conveyed by Holy Communion, so he shall have the testimony of a blameless conscience and may be preserved from too severe tempations against chastity.

The text may hint at the superstitious practice of carrying amulettes, little stones with mystic inscriptions. This kind of magic was very largely in vogue among all pagan peoples of antiquity. Those amulettes were believed to protect against disease. A pointed allusion is possibly intended here to the imagined secret revelatons of Dionysos or to the imagined mysterious powers of Aeskulepios, as the foregoing phrase, "the hidden manna", pointed to the sacrificial meats offered to Zeus.

There seems to have been no necessity of warning the bishop and his congregation against caesar-worship, because they had all held fast to the Sacred Name and had not denied their faith by giving homage to Caesar. Some of the congregation had committed fornication, i.e. taken part in idolatrous worship and eaten of the meats sacrificed to Zeus. If they will spurn superstition, belief in the secret mysteries and the trust in amulettes, they shall receive a white stone and a name inscribed on it which is proof against all dangers. It will give them a truly divine estimation of life. "The Divine magic which inscribes on the human character and life the name of God and Christ is placed in contrast with the poor imitations that enthralled pagan society". (Swete).

4. TO THE ANGEL OF THE CHURCH OF THYATIRA.

Verses 18 to the end.

Verse 18

Thyatira is at present called Ak-Hissar and has a population of about 22,000. It was between 50 and 60 miles southeast of Pergamos and on a direct road to Sardis. It was named thus by the Seleucidae. It had originally been a Greek colony. Situated in the valley between the River Caicus and the Hermos Mountains, it was within the confines of Lydia but was sometimes counted a Mysian city. The Romans took it about 190 B.C. That fact developed a most thriving trade, although the city had otherwise not the importance of Ephesus, Smyrna and Pergamos. It had many trade guilds, such as bakers, dyers, tanners, clothiers, potters, linen-workers, wool-workers, shoemakers, coppersmiths, brass-workers etc. The Acts (XVI. 14) name a dealer in purples called Lydia.

There was no caesar-worship in Thyatira, but there was a temple there of the Turimnaean Apollo and one of Artemis and a shrine of Sambathe, an oriental Sibyl. St. Epiphanius states that at the beginning of the third century almost all of Thyatira was Christian (Adv. Haer. LI. 33), but that it had become a stronghold of Montanism. The Church of Thyatira may not have been large but was firm. Neither Jews nor Pagans caused any trouble. But they suffered trouble within the fold as the letter shows, from heresies and the vices of paganism or idolatry.

Christ reminds the bishop of His title of Son of God, which embraces all divine attributes. It prepares the reader for a severe tone in the letter. He speaks with divine authority as One who has the power to make good His threats. He has eyes like a flame of fire recalling I. 14 and intimating His Omniscience. It alludes to Ezechiel (VIII. 2) and the abominations of idolatry secretly practiced in the Temple, where God also appeared to the prophet's eyes in the likeness of fire. It asserts that what is mentioned in verse 20 is done secretly and is kept from the knowledge of the Bishop who is not watchful enough. Nothing is hidden from the all-seeing eyes of Christ. His eyes flame with righteous wrath against all profanations in His Church, and His feet of glowing bronze will stamp out this congregation. His knowledge will bring to light all religious frauds and expose those who are attached to sin in their hearts.

He will penetrate the secret recesses in which Jesabel practices her abominations and will sound the "depths of Satan" (II. 24).

Verse 19

He enumerates four praiseworthy deeds of the bishop and his congregation: Faith, charity, ministry and constancy. His strong faith is the motive of his activity, and it gives a supernatural reason and tone to all his great works. And thereby his last works have become "more numerous than the former". In contrast with the works of the Bishop of Ephesus, here is real progress. The Bishop of Thyatira has practiced self-denial.

Charity is the highest expression of anyone's faith. And the bishop receives unstinted praise for it. His love has urged him to work for the conversion of the community. It has expressed itself in service to the needy and in administering the income of the church for the relief of the poor and in enlightening and instructing those within and without the fold. He has been patient with the erring and with those who are weak in the faith and not a credit to the flock. He has labored tirelessly. The word "patience" literally means "patient toil". In consequence of all this, he has progressed in grace and has therefore been able to do ever greater works, as his capacity for grace grew and he worked with a purer intention. So in every sense are his present works greater.

Verse 20

The Bishop of Thyatira, however, has made himself gravely culpable by permitting a woman, called Jesabel, to belong to the Church, pose as a prophetess and mislead members of the congregation. The name alludes to the Old Testament (3 Kings, XVI. 31). King Achab married a Sidonian woman, named Jesabel, for whose sake he built an altar and temple to Baal and adored that idol. Here the woman, called Jesabel, who styled herself a prophetess, had gained admission into the Church. She may have held the office of deaconess and won a strong influence and following. The bishop may have feared an open schism, if he excommunicated her. He may therefore have tolerated her belonging to the Church and holding an office of teaching and leading the women astray, perhaps by sacrificing at the shrine of the Chaldean Sybil, Sambathe, and eating of the meats dedicated to the idol. She may have entered the Church like Simon Magus for gain.

This Jesabel worked under the guise of a prophetess. Perhaps the bishop was deceived and not fully aware of her abominations. The attention called to His flaming eyes by our Lord would indicate secrecy. It was in effect apostasy from worshipping at the Eucharistic Sacrifice and from Communion. Christ's flaming eyes will bring it to light and make it known publicly. No one may be an idolater and a member of the Church.

Verse 21

The Greek word ἔδωκα is in the aorist tense suggesting that she had not been left in ignorance of a coming judgment. She, however, remained obstinate. And those who adhered to her knew the admonitions and thus made themselves as guilty as her because her work had continued for some time. The prophets and prophetesses were usually itinerant teachers. So this woman may have tried her nefarious work elsewhere but was not tolerated and then found admittance at Thyatira (See Didache. 11, ff). God did not punish her immediately giving her time to repent, but the bishop had no right to let her teach. She abused the long-suffering of Christ, and being successful in her proselytising refused to do penance or leave off from her work.

Verse 22

The bed mentioned is disease, which is contrasted with the bed of luxury provided at those pagan feasts. This disease is but a symbol of the "great tribulation" that shall come upon those who follow this false prophetess. The "great tribulation" is a stereotyped phrase used often in the Apocalypse and elsewhere in the New Testament (Mt. XXIV. 21) for the Roman persecutions. (See VII. 14). By her pretended revelations, this Jesabel will bring the judgments of God upon her followers. "Adultery" is a prophetical term meaning unfaithfulness to Christ. The partaking of the sacrificial meats was spiritual adultery, because it is unfaithfulness to the Eucharistic Christ, the Bridegroom of the soul. In the prophetic writings of the Old Testament, Juda and Israel are called adulteresses because they practiced idolatry. King Achab did severe penance after Elias threatened him with the judgments of God for the murder of Naboth, and the sentence was deferred but not annulled. And so these who have followed this Jesabel into spiritual death may still redeem themselves, if they do penance.

Verse 23

As Elias threatened extinction to the posterity of Achab (3 Kings XXI. 21), so the plague shall strike the spiritual progeny of this new Jesabel. It will be a manifest punishment like the judgments upon the followers of the Beast (XV.), and the attribute of the "eyes like to a flame of fire" will become manifest to all the churches. These abominations practiced secretly will give Christ the opportunity of proving that nothing is hidden from Him and that He guides the destinies of the Church. In the Old Testament the heart was imagined to be the source of thoughts and the reins or kidneys the source of affections. Before the all-seeing eyes of Christ, thoughts and affections are clear, and all attachments to sin appear in their full hideousness. He attributes to Himself divinity by claiming the same knowledge of all secrets as Jahve in the Old Testament (Jer. XVII. 10). The words he speaks are almost verbatim those of Jeremias.

Besides His omniscience, our Lord puts forth His power and right as Judge to render to every man according to his works. Those who practice the teachings of this Jesabel shall reap the fruits of their works and shall admit, when the plague strikes them, that they have known what would follow and have wilfully courted "death".

Verse 24

Our Lord says to the bishop and to the "rest" who are not polluted with this doctrine, that from them He will demand nothing more than to keep aloof and remain faithful. "The rest" may mean the heathens here, as elsewhere in the Apocalypse and in St. Paul's letters (IX. 20; XIX. 21), as well as the faithful who have not been contaminated with the practices of the false prophetess.

Those who have known the "depths of Satan" were the Gnostic sects, who boasted of their depths of knowledge. Those sectaries pretended to have knowledge of divine depths which the faithful did not have. The "depths" of which they have knowledge, our Lord tells them, are not the "deep things of God" (1 Cor. II. 10) but are the "depths of Satan". They are merely the devices by which Satan deceives them into imagining that they have a deeper knowledge of divine mysteries than the faithful. Their claims were what St. Irenaeus calls "frauds". They "give forth profound and unspeakable mysteries to itching ears" (Adv. Haer. II. 21, 2) "affirming that they have found out the mysteries of God" (II. 22, 3). Tertullian says that they concealed what they preached, and if in good faith you ask them what they mean, they say "it is too deep" and feign to commiserate those who are in ignorance of their secrets. They know the "depths of Satan" because they oppose the true theology and mysteries and mislead their dupes into an illusory knowledge and mysticism.

The words of our Lord, that He will put no other burden upon them, seem to point to the apostolic decrees (Acts XV. 28) enjoined by the Council of Jerusalem. The clause may, however, be only an accidental correspondence of terms with that of the Acts. It might only mean that the Christians at Thyatira have led so exemplary a life, that they need only to keep themselves away from the desecrations of the Jezabellites to fulfill all our Lord's expectations.

Verse 25

Our Lord is not as exacting in His demands on His followers as were the Pharisees (Mt. XXIII. 4), and therefore He does not urge the believers of Thyatira to refute and combat the heresy of the laxists but only to hold fast to the pure and true doctrine, till He shall decide to come in judgment. His coming, according to the text, is not imminent but shall occur at His appointed time. Thus He considers those who have kept themselves free from the contamination of Jezabel's doctrines above reproach.

Verse 26

In this verse our Lord begins to enumerate various rewards for those who will overcome the temptation to forbidden things and will do the works He commands. The works are those just mentioned in the foregoing verses to the churches.

The "authority over the nations" does not mean bloody vengeance on the heathens, who are the enemies of God or citizens of the city of Satan, but the spiritual triumph of the Church. The promise fulfills itself in the influence which the Church imperceptibly gains over the world; and those who remain true receive the credit and reward for it. The Church is the greatest factor in the world to mold national character; and every member exerts an influence for the subjugation of the world to Christ in proportion to his loyalty. This authority promised by Christ is contrasted with what Satan will endow the Beast (XIII. 2). Christ, the Son of God, will impart to His followers, if they prove their right to the adopted sonship of God by the victory over temptations, His own authority over the nations. They will be spiritual leaders of the nations under their General, Christ. He thus represents the Church as supranational. He in this manner alludes to Psalm II. 8, 9 and to Apocalypse XX. 4 (See Mt. XXV. 21, 29; 1 Cor. VI. 2). Christ's faithful one will not be able to claim for himself "deep knowledge" of mysteries, which is a lie anyway, but will have far more than this – he will have "power" or "authority" to change the world and with Christ to "make all things new" (XXI. 5; Lc. XIX. 15 ff).

Verse 27

The one who is faithful will together with Christ rule the future nations with a rod of iron. The "rod of iron" symbolizes that judgment by which the elect are separated from the reprobate. He who is true to Christ will by his example keep the just from mingling with the wicked. This hints at the wicked in the Church of Thyatira. The example of the true believer will restrain those who are inclined to yield to temptations from yielding and prompt those who are resolved to do forbidden things to withdraw themselves from him and separate from the church of which he is a member. The wicked ever dislike the ways of the good, and this saves the good from the contamination of their social and moral standards. Therefore the example given by the good at the beginning of the Church's career will assert itself in future ages and will help to keep the church pure and segregated from the world that serves Satan.

Before that new order can be firmly established, the old order must be broken. If the potter breaks productions of his art, he does it because they are imperfect or worthless due to the materials, and he has in mind to reconstruct and fashion things without a flaw. So the Divine Potter will break the old social order and destroy the old moral standards and through the Church inaugurate a better social order and a more refined national existence. This clearly refers to Psalm II. 8-9. The true Christian will be a rod of iron in the hand of Christ to bring about this change and to renew the face of the earth. This points to XII. 5, where the Church shall be reformed and molded perfectly according to the ideals of Christ. The divine element in the Church will need no perfecting, but the human element will need to be reformed. The true believers can be fit instruments in the hand of the Divine Potter only if they will obey the Church.

Verse 28

Christ will give the last mentioned prerogatives to His followers as He received them from His Father. And besides that, He will give them another distinction, the "morning star". He is the morning star of the eternal day that will follow the Parousia (XXII). "Christus est stella matutina, qui nocte saeculi transacta lucem vitae sanctis promittit et pandet aeternum" (St. Bede). The morning star is the brightest star in the heavens, receives its light from the sun and is the sure harbinger of the sun's rising. The faithful soul will also be the harbinger of the full light of God that will enlighten the world, when the thousand years of Christ begin. The union with Christ by grace in this life is the harbinger of the full light of the Sun that is to bring the Eternal Day to each one in the Beatific Vision. In St. John's day the world was still in the darkness of paganism. Every congregation was a lamp in the midst of this darkness. And every Christian who risked everything and remained faithful in avoiding the abominations of paganism and in living the teachings of Christ was a prophetic light or star that heralded the coming of the great day of God.

Verse 29

What Christ promised the church of Ephesus under the figure of the "tree of life", the church of Smyrna in "the crown of life" and the church of Pergamos in "the hidden manna", He promises here in the "morning star". He promises the same to Sardis in the "white garments", to Philadelphia in being "a pillar in the temple" and to Laodicea to "sup with Him". These are temporal promises, promises of what the true Christian will gain for this life as compared with what the pagans gain by their life of sin. These promises fulfilled in this life are the pledge of the much greater rewards that will be meted out to the faithful in the Eternal Kingdom of God.

CHAPTER III.

Westminister Version

And to the angel of the Church of 1. Sardis write: Thus saith he who
hath the seven spirits of God, and the seven stars. I know thy works: thou
hast the name of being alive, and thou art dead. Be watchful and strengthen
what 2. still abideth, yet is about to die; for I have not found thy works
complete before my God. Remember therefore 3. what thou hast received
and heard, and keep it and repent. If, therefore, thou do not watch, I will
come as a thief, and thou shalt not know at what hour I will come upon
thee. Howbeit, thou 4. hast a few names in Sardis that have not defiled
their garments, and they shall walk with me in white, for they are worthy.
He that conquereth shall 5. be clad thus in white garments: and I will
not efface his name from the book of life, and I will confess his name
before my Father and before his holy angels. He that hath an ear, 6. let
him hear what the Spirit saith to the churches.

And to the angel of the church of 7. Philadelphia write: Thus saith the
holy one, the true one, he who hath the key of David, he who openeth
and no one shall shut, and shutteth and no one openeth. I know thy works –
behold, I 8. have set before thee a door opened, which no one is able
to shut – that thou hast but little power, and yet hast kept my word and
hast not denied my name. Behold I give thee some of the 9. synagogue of
Satan, that say that they are Jews and are not, but do lie – behold, I will
make them to come and to prostrate themselves before thy feet, and to
know that I have loved thee. Because thou hast kept fast the lesson 10.
of my patience, I also will keep thee from the hour of trial, which is about
to come upon the whole world, to try those that dwell upon the earth.

I am coming quickly; hold fast what 11. thou hast, in order that no
one seize thy crown. He that conquereth, I will make 12. him a pillar in the
sanctuary of my God, and never more shall he go out of it; and I will
write upon him the name of my God and the name of the city of my
God, – the new Jerusalem, which cometh down out of heaven from my
God, – and my new name. He that hath an ear, let him hear what 13.
the Spirit saith to the churches!

And to the angel of the church of 14. Laodicea write: Thus saith
the Amen, the faithful and true witness, the beginning of the creation of God. I know 15. thy works; thou art neither cold nor hot. Would
that thou hadst been cold or hot! As it is, because thou art lukewarm and
16. neither cold nor hot, I am about to vomit thee out of my mouth.
Thou sayest 17. 'I am rich, and have grown wealthy, and have need of
nothing', and knowest not that thou art the wretched and pitiable and
poor and blind and naked one. Therefore I counsel thee to buy of me
18. refined gold out of the fire, and thou mayest be made rich; and white
garments, that thou mayest be clothed withal, and that the shame of thy

nakedness be not made manifest; and eyesalve to annoint thine eyes, that
thou mayest see. Whom so 19. I love, I rebuke and chastise; be earnest
therefore, and repent.

Behold I stand at the door and knock. 20. If any man hear my voice
and open the door, I will come in to him, and I will sup with him, and
he with me.

As for him that conquereth, I will 21. give him to sit with me upon
my throne, as I myself conquered, and sat down with my Father on his
throne.

He that hath an ear, let him hear 22. what the Spirit saith to the
churches!

5. TO THE ANGEL OF THE CHURCH OF SARDES.

Chapter III. Verses 1-6.

Verse 1

Sardes was possibly named after the Shardani, a people said to be mentioned in cuneiform inscriptions as inhabiting this region. At an early period it was the capital of the Lydians under a dynasty which reigned from 766 to 687 B.C. The celebrated King Kroesos, the last of the next dynasty, was dethroned 546 B.C. by Cyrus, who took the city by surprise. Thenceforth it was the residence of Persian Satraps. It capitulated to Alexander the Great in 334 B.C. and after him belonged to Antigonos until 301 B.C., when it fell into the hands of the Seleucidae. The Romans took it 190 B.C. and incorporated it into the Kingdom of Pergamos and made it the capital of the province of Lydia. It was shattered by an earthquake in 17 A.D. but with the help of Tiberius was soon rebuilt. It became a large city again and was famous for its woolen manufactures and dyeing industries. It had been a city of great luxuries and of loose morals.

Sardes was situated on the Pactolos River at the foot of Mount Tmolos about 40 miles southeast of Thyatira. It commanded the great valley of the Hermos, being located where the roads from Thyatira, Smyrna and Laodicea and the River Lycos converged. It was built on a mountain detached from the Tmolos range and was accessible only from the South. Antiochus the Great had scaled the abrupt rocks and had taken the city by surprise like a thief in the night.

Sardes is at present a small village called Sart. The Church never played a distinguished part during its history. Nothing is known of the establishment of the Christian congregation there. St. Melito, who died about 171-180, was one of its bishops. He was an apologist. And there were some other martyrs. In the seventh century, Sardes ranked 6th in the hierarchy of Lydia and had 27 suffragans. The town was destroyed by the Turks at the beginning of the fourteenth century.

Verse 1

In the first words of his message to the Bishop of Sardes, Christ announces His possession of the Seven Spirits of God. These "seven spirits" are "sent forth into all the earth" (V. 6).

Their mission is to search the hearts of all men, to awaken the conscience of everyone and make him realize his spiritual condition. That is the mission and activity of the Holy Spirit. "Seven Spirits" is thus a symbol of the Holy Spirit. As Christ is One with the Father, so He is One with the Holy Spirit. Because He is one substance and one mind with the Holy Spirit, He knows not only the works but the conscience of everyone and the most secret recesses of his heart.

He also has the "seven stars" mentioned in I. 16, 20, and having them in His hand has absolute control over them. Possessing these two prerogatives, Christ can speak with infallible divine authority to the Bishop of Sardes. Because He enlightens the conscience of everyone by the Holy Spirit, each one knows His guilt and can advance no excuse for sin.

The Lydians had a bad reputation for luxury and its companion, immorality (Herod. I. 59). Sardes was prosperous since its re-construction. It had the business of central Asia, which made it very active and enterprising. The worship of Aphrodite promoted loose living.

In contrast with the ill-fame of the Lydians, the Bishop of Sardes has a GOOD reputation. However, Christ does not judge anyone by his reputation or popularity or external works but by his conscience. Being one in substance with the Holy Spirit, Christ knows every shade of guilt in the bishop's conscience, towit, that though he appears to be alive and has the name of being such, he is spiritually dead. He knows him to be a very active man, who can show "works" of his activity and is no doubt very popular on account of it; nevertheless he is dead. He may have advertised his works to get a "name" for the results. Thus he may have received his reward for them and has no merits with God.

The reminder that Christ has the "seven spirits" of God may hint at the sin against the Holy Spirit in the bishop. He may have been deaf to admonitions living on in complete indifference, self-justification and self-confidence. That sin is founded on pride. Hypocrisy, bluff and pretense is *one* manifestation of it. The hyprocrite is spiritually dead and was likened by our Lord to a sepulchre full of dead men's bones and rottenness. The hypocrite tries to keep up appearances. If he makes a blunder, he will not admit a mistake but will try to cover it up or will deny having made it, no matter what injustice he will inflict thereby. This bishop has not given way to the immoral life of the Lydians, for that sin cannot remain a secret. But the Holy Spirit has been driven out of his soul by other greater sins which are mortal in a bishop. The Holy Spirit is the spirit of life and the guide of the congregation; but because He has been quenched in the soul of the bishop, spiritual death has entered. The Holy Spirit is the sanctifier of souls but for the opposition offered, He cannot be such to this bishop. The bishop is thus not as good as his reputation, while the Lydians are probably not as bad as their ill-fame.

Expediency and diplomacy may be his special "virtues" and may have been inculcated by him in his priests and people instead of apostolic simplicity, candor and uprightness. A great Doctor of the Church says of this: "quia ab eis haec eadem duplicitatis iniquitas, nomine palliata, diligitur, dum mentis perversitas, urbanitas vocatur" (St. Gregory, Pope, Lib. X. Cap. 16 in cap. 12 on Job). By his example, he may have encouraged in his priests pretense and sanctimonious words. Thus he may have thirsted for flattery and recognition of his "works", while he pretended to despise it. Cardinal Newman says of such: "It detests *gross* adulation; not that it tends at all to the eradiction of the appetite to which the flatterer ministers, but it sees the absurdity of indulging it, . . . it demands great subtlety and art in the preparation".

Perhaps he proved his resentment and malice against priests who were truthful and candid with him and abused his sacred authority to satisfy his spite and revengefulness against them or against some deacon or members of his flock. Perhaps he even misrepresented and slandered some priest and gave condemnatory judgments against him on false assumptions; or perhaps he crushed down the truth by bluff or pretense or calumniated some priest whom he disliked or crushed down any self-defense against his slanders and injustices, thereby evading his duty to uphold law and order. He may have been in the habit of deciding in matters of importance according to his whims and fancies and thrown all consistency to the winds. Or he may have readily listened to some favorite who was an evil adviser among his clergy. He may have been of Jewish blood and favored his own nationality among the clergy. Hence his works not being disinterested were mere human works. He surely did not waste his time travelling, for that entailed hardships and danger in those days.

He may have been perfected in hypocrisy to such a degree as to feel himself satisfied with having done his duty when he avoided trouble or anything disagreeable, or when from human motive he overthrew principle and law, so that there was a grave contradiction between his sanctimonious words and unprincipled example. He evidently neglected upholding the apostolic decrees, which were of prime importance in those days to safeguard the Christians from returning to superstitious practices. He would thus make concessions to avoid conflict. St. Jerome (Lib. IV. comment. in cap. 23 Mt) says of hypocritical bishops of his time "vae vobis miseris, ad quos pharisaeorum vitia transierunt".

In harmony with his character, he was obviously not a man of prayer and contemplation. He would hardly be dead from the sin of Sloth, for he has the name of being alive. But he probably practiced laxism, not appreciating zeal in his priests, chiding those who demanded the fullness of apostolic sacrifices and works of penance from the people, condemning the denunciation of evils and non-observance of the laws of God and the Church and persecuting the courage to defend truth and justice. Most probably he did not labor to advance the faithful to higher spirituality but commended lax priests who were easy with the people in matters of piety and the study of their religion, so that piety and apostolic asceticism deteriorated and died. The succeeding verse suggests this. Together with this he would favor priests who cultivated his good graces and ignore or ill-treat those who faithfully did their duties and had no time for eye-service or flattery. The bishop has probably become worldly and appreciates earthly advancement above spiritual gains and has set up false standards. Christ has taken him and the congregation out of the state of spiritual death by the call to the faith and has given His Spirit to the members, that they might be zealous for God and for their own sanctification, but they are cold and indifferent. The bishop has brought this about by his own sins, hypocrisy, worldliness and lack of fervor.

Verse 2

Christ gives the bishop an ominous warning. Twice during its history, the city had fallen into the hands of the enemy for want of watchfulness, and so the warning had a threatening allusion. If persecution should suddenly confront the congregation it would surely fall, because its spiritual life is almost extinct. The people have not strength enough left to defend their faith or sacrifice their lives for it.

It is not enough to be vigilant and tell the people what to do; the bishop must cling to principle and strictly uphold the law and not let the people break away when they take a notion. He must revive and re-establish the faith in the whole congregation, for it is at the door of death. This is a decaying branch of the Church. And as it is wherever the faith has deteriorated, it will require very arduous labor to strengthen the people again in their religion, their piety and good works and to bring them up once more to apostolic expectations. The aorist tense used in the text expresses the fact that the worst will soon be past, since the decay is not complete. Some were on the verge of spiritual death, are enlivened again and can be saved, if the bishop fulfills his pastoral duties. The "things that remain" are the members of the congregation who have retained the practices of their religion in spite of the laxism of their bishop (Primasius). So there are still vestiges of spiritual life in the parish.

The bishop has earned the reputation of being alive by doing some good works, but they lacked the completeness that would make them acceptable to God; they had no spiritual quality. Works are "complete" only, when they are performed in the state of grace and with the supernatural motive and intention.

There are no Nicolaites in Sardes. This is a warning in itself. There is less danger to the faithful from heresies than from obtuseness of conscience towards neglect of serious duties. The congregations of Smyrna and Philadelphia have heresies to combat but are not in such spiritual plight as that of Sardes, where the Christians are unmolested, but where they overlook or wink at vices more dangerous than those occasioned by heresy. This has often been verified. And people and priests who come from Catholic countries are often swayed by earthly motives, hypocrisy and temporal gains. Because the bishops are blind to such things, they become national vices.

Verse 3

The bishop has received freely the fullness of the seven gifts of the Holy Spirit; and the Holy Spirit gives life in abundance. He received the sublime gifts joyfully and was zealous, just and truthful after his consecration. He had been dead in sin before, was raised to life but now has fallen back into death. He has kept "what" he has received, the faith, but has not preserved the "manner" in which he received it, the alacrity and zeal that awoke in his soul at the reception of the divine gifts. *Faith* has not yet departed from him, but *love* which accompanied it has fled.

The bishop must awaken from his torpor and lethargy, be watchful and do penance to save what may still be saved, lest all follow him into death. The priest is a watchman. "If he sees the sword coming and sounds not the trumpet, and the people look not to themselves, and the sword come and cut off a soul from among them; he indeed is taken away in his iniquity, but I will require his blood at the hand of the watchman". (Ezech. XXXIII. 6-9). The soul that is lost through the neglect of the pastor bears his own responsibility, but the Judge will hold the neglectful pastor responsible likewise. If however, the pastor has warned by word and example, he will have no responsibility. The Bishop of Sardes has grown indifferent about spreading the knowledge of the faith outside the fold. He must now return to his first zeal.

If he will not watch and guard against the inroads of the enemy, Christ will come stealthily and suddenly in judgment. The Greek word used alludes to the unexpected capture of the city in past centuries. It also alludes to the language used by the prophets (Jer. LI. 8; Joel II. 9) and to the warnings of our Lord (Mt. XXIV. 43; Lc. XII. 39). All this points to the approaching persecution. Those who are dead in sin will not sacrifice everything to save their souls. This admonition to watchfulness alludes to XVI. 15.

Verse 4

In Holy Scripture, defiled garments commonly represent the state of sin (Isa. LXIV. 6). The Greek word used for "defilement" probably points to the worship of Aphrodite and Dionysos or perhaps only to hypocrisy and worldliness. Taking advantage of the bishop's laxism, the people have allowed themselves every license, and very few are left who have not become defiled. Their defilement may have included the use of blood and the ignoring of the apostolic decrees in general.

The garments are sanctifying grace received in Baptism. Elsewhere in this book, the priests wear white robes and clean linens. Those who have kept themselves undefiled in the midst of the worldliness, license and general laxism shall be rewarded in a befitting way by this public acknowledgment of Christ. The walking with Him possibly alludes to His travels through Palestine constantly accompanied by his disciples. Those who have not consented to the attractions of luxury and hypocrisy are worthy to be in the company of the saints. The meaning of the word "worthy" is "deserving" and is not the same as in other passages, where it is conceded only to God and the Lamb.

Verse 5

In conclusion three distinctions are promised those who overcome the temptations to luxury, hypocrisy and worldliness: Their investiture in white garments of unspotted sanctity, the preservation of their names in the book of life and their presentation to the Father and His angels. The promise to the faithful one in Sardes is thus extended to the whole Church.

The "Book of Life" is first mentioned in the Old Testament (Ps. LXVIII. 29; Isa. IV. 3; Dan. XII. 1). It is really eternal, and the names of the elect are written there indelibly (Apoc. XIII. 8). The entering of one's name into the book does not interfere with his liberty, as this phrase indicates the possibility of having it effaced. St. Augustine says that no name inscribed there will be blotted out, while St. Thomas says that through justification the name is conditionally recorded but becomes indelible through perseverance and the entrance into eternal glory. It may allude to the baptismal register. The statement is rather hard to explain, because God foreknowing who will persevere will not blot out the name of anyone in the book. God's foreknowledge of final perseverance composes this book. Christ told His apostles that their names were written in heaven (Lc. X. 20). Re-calling to his mind the book of "life" carries an ominous message for the Bishop of Sardes, who is "dead" spiritually and whose name will not be in the book without repentance.

The third distinction promised the faithful one is the confession of his name before the Father and "before His angels" (Lc. XII. 8), and is the same as recorded in the gospel of Mt. X. 32. This promise will be fulfilled before the Last

Judgment, for then He will confess them before the whole world. If anyone receives this honorable distinction of being introduced by name to the Father and to the princes of Heaven from our Lord Himself, all other recognition and popularity would seem to be of no account. These last words are pure encouragement and hope for those who repent and persevere, otherwise Christ might have added what He added in the Gospel (Mt. X. 33). The glory of the risen body may enter into the promise of the "white garments".

Verse 6

The message concludes as all the others urging each individual Christian to accept in a good heart whatever is written to all the churches. In this message is the special warning against surrendering to temptations to a life of luxury, sensuality, self-indulgence and self-confidence, loss of horror for sin, hypocrisy, bluff, insincerity, injustice, pretended piety and worldly motives or crude selfishness.

6. To The Angel Of The Church Of Philadelphia.

Verses 7-13.

Verse 7

Philadelphia was founded by Attalus Philadelphus, king of Pergamos, between 159 and 138 B.C. For commercial purposes it was built in a strategic position on the left bank of the Colgamos River about 35 miles southeast of Sardes, where the present city of Ala Shehr is located. North and northeast was a rich agricultural region, the surface of which was strewn with volcanic rock. The city was subject to earthquakes and therefore was never very large, the citizens, from fear of the earthquakes, preferred to live in the surrounding country. It was a great wine-growing district, and so Dionysus, the Greek equivalent for Bacchus, was worshipped there. It became a Roman possession in 133 B.C. In the earthquake of 17 A.D., it was destroyed but was quickly rebuilt and became an important commercial center again. The commerce of all eastern and northeastern Asia Minor naturally passed to or through the city, and hence it prospered in spite of earthquakes. Its situation on the borders of Mysia, Lydia and Phrygia gave it the greatest opportunity of opening the door of the Church to all the eastern country. This was a natural gift.

According to the "Apostolic Constitutions" (VII. 46), the first bishop, Demetrius, was appointed by St. John. St. Ignatius addressed one of his seven letters to this church warning them against the Jews. The Church of Philadelphia has a long, faithful Christian history.

Verse 7

Christ introduces Himself to the Bishop of Philadelphia and the congregation as the Holy One, the True One, and the One who has the key of David. God is often called the "Holy One of Israel" (Isa. XII. 6; LX. 25). Christ presents Himself to the congregation under this title to proclaim Himself One with God the Father and to reprove the wicked Jews. Isaias when condemning their perfidy reminds the Jews of this attribute of God. By attributing to Himself this same infinite perfection, Christ encourages the Philadelphians in their unwavering faithfulness to Him and confronts the perverse Jews with a menacing tone for their perfidy and the persecution of His followers. As the Holy One, He will compel some of these Jews to acknowledge the service that His followers at Philadelphia have rendered them (V. 9). He is absolute sanctity Itself, the All-perfect, and therefore His word is all-perfect. Because He is the Holy One, the faithful must find a thrilling consolation and encouragement in His being satisfied with them and must desire still higher sanctity.

He is more than the *verax*, He is the Verus, the ὅ ὢν of the Old Testament, the only one who really, truly and substantially IS of necessity. This reminds the obstinate Jews of their perjury against God, who revealed Himself in this attribute to Moses from the burning bush. If they truly believe in Moses and are loyal to Jahve, the Holy and True One, they perjure themselves by not accepting the One whom Jahve sent as His Only Begotten Son. It is a joyful assurance to the congregation, that they are in the right in keeping His word and not denying His name, and that the blasphemous malice of the Jews will be brought to naught. In clinging to Him, they have clung to the True One.

He is likewise the son of David, the heir to that great king's everlasting kingdom; He is the King of Sion. This reference to David recalls the whole series of prophetic hopes now fulfilled in the exaltation of Christ. The text is borrowed from Isaias

(XXII. 22). Eliacim, the son of Helcias, is promised the key of David, which is the symbol of his power, while here the right to possess this key is claimed by the Antitype. David as head of the theocracy was only the prototype of the Lord and His eternal kingdom.

In I. 18, He explains that the keys bear with them the ruling power over the kingdom of Death and Hades. It comprehends all creation (Mt. XXVIII. 18; Rom. XIV. 9). The power and authority He conferred upon Peter is less comprehensive than His own. Peter was promised the supreme power over the Church on earth, supreme legislative, judicial and executive, magisterial and ministerial power; still, though he is the visible Vicar of Christ, and though the exercise of his power will be infallibly ratified in Heaven, his authority did not extend to the next world. Christ alone is the unlimited and supreme Head of the Church, which is the kingdom of David; and His power comprehends both time and eternity. He has the key of David so that He can open the kingdom to anyone He wills, i.e. no one can enter the Church unless Christ gives him the grace. In this sense He is also the Holy One and the True One, because He is the author of grace and sanctification. He can shut the door to anyone by denying him the grace of entrance, and no power in Heaven or earth can grant that man this grace. He can extend special favors of grace to one congregation and bishop, which He does not extend to another. He may also grant extraordinary grace to one and only ordinary grace to another.

Verse 8

As in all the letters, our Lord declares first that He knows the bishop's works and every phase of them. This is here equivalent to an unqualified approval. He has given the bishop and congregation an open door, which no power on earth can close. It alludes to the commercial position of the city. Christ has unlocked it with the key of David, which denotes the extension of His kingdom. The figure of the open door was used quite often by Christ and the apostles. In the Gospel, Christ is the "door" admitting into His Church by grace (Jo. X. 8, 9); in the Acts (XIV. 26), the "door of faith" is opened to the Gentiles; a "great door" was opened to St. Paul (1 Cor. XVI. 9) to convert many to the faith. In the letter to the Colossians, the figure meant the opportunity to preach (Col. IV.

3). The faithfulness of the bishop and congregation of Philadelphia has won for them these greater opportunities to extend the kingdom of Christ. Hence it has become a missionary city. It was so located that the whole eastern country of Lydia and even Phrygia was open to the Church in this place, and the loyalty of the Philadelphians to Christ in the face of opposition had obtained a special grace from Him, and they had been active to seize the favor proffered them. Christ assures the bishop of the continuance of this natural gift as a consideration for his faithfulness in using the "little strength" that had been conferred upon him. This order Christ will follow in His Church. When a congregation has advanced so far in spirituality and has persevered so tirelessly and dauntlessly in virtue that it satisfies the Lord, He will bring others into the fold through that congregation. When the members of a congregation compromise with pagans and heretics, they have no hope of converting others. The virtue of faith is developed by obedience to the Church and by holding out firmly in the face of taunts, sarcasm and persecution.

The next clause intimates some real tests endured by the church of Philadelphia. They had shown a little strength, possibly only a "little", because the flock was small and poor. But this little strength was irresistible and made of Philadelphia an influential congregation. Thereby they had gained a standing before God that surpassed the congregations in the metropolis and made them worthy missionaries to carry the light of faith to the regions of darkness around them. They are likened to a country parish not having the position to shine before the world but shining more brightly before God than those in a worldly-advantageous location. Through them Christ will do greater works than through the prominent parishes.

The enemy had put the Philadelphians to the test but could not terrify them into denying Christ's name or move them from His teachings. The rich and powerful Jews must have forbidden them, as the next verse suggests, to profess their belief in Christ and proclaim Him the Messias. They may have tempted them to worship Caesar and to profess him their lord and God. After the city was rebuilt following the earthquake of 17 A.D., it was named Neocaesarea, and it bears that name on the coins of the 1st century. Although the name did not cling to the city, the inhabitants may have introduced in it the caesar-cult. Not denying the "name" of Christ possibly means that they did not worship the lord Caesar. They had withstood with unbending determination the Judaizers, who ignored the apostolic decrees and wanted to impose on them circumcision and other Jewish superstitions, and they had held firmly to the ordinances of the apostles.

Verse 9

In the first sentence, Christ shows the contrast between Himself, who is the True One, and the "synagogue of Satan", who claim to be Jews but are false Jews and liars. They persecuted the Church at Philadelphia as at Smyrna. By doing so they persecute Christ. The Church is the Israel of God; and as they did in the days of St. Paul, so these false Jews still continue their hatred against Christ and His Church.

The expression "adore before thy feet" describes the attitude of a defeated enemy. These persecutors will receive the grace to see how wrong they were and will be converted through the Christians at Philadelphia, to whom they will then give the credit for their conversion making them co-saviors with Christ for themselves. These converts will understand what special love Christ showered upon the Philadelphian Christians. The Jews who shall be converted are those in good faith, who viewed the Christians as apostates from the theocracy. This predicted conversion is not the same as that promised by St. Paul (Rom. XI. 15, 25). His prophecy points to their general conversion, which is still a future event. The last part of this verse alludes to many texts in Isaias (Isa. XXXVII. 20; XLIII. 4; XLV. 3, 14; XLIX. 23; LX. 14; Zach. VIII. 20). These texts and the aorist tense used here manifest the love of God for the true believers to have been the same in the Old as in the New Testament and from all eternity, for from all eternity He foreknew who would love and serve Him, and these He loved with an eternal love.

Verse 10

Because the bishop has persevered in his first zeal, and the congregation has been fervent, Christ will protect them in the time of persecution and keep them firm. This takes in view the near approach of THE GREAT TRIBULATION, the Roman persecutions, and likewise presages who will hold out in the persecution of Antichrist in the distant future. At all times, those who live their faith, remain fervent, co-operate with the grace granted them and overcome the common temptations of life will persevere to the end. The verse again expresses the fore-shortened view taken by the apostles of future days up to the appearance of Antichrist. In St. John's outlook, however, the end of the world could not have been included in the "hour of temptation", because a thousand years must intervene between the days of Antichrist and the end of the world. Perhaps in this verse, the persecution under Antichrist is not clearly distinguished from the imperial persecutions, which had already begun. "Patience" means what the apostles express by constancy in duty to Christ and God (2 Thess. III. 5). The idea is more fully explained by St. Paul (Heb. XII. 1 ff). The patience of the saints is an image of the patience of Christ and connotes suffering (XIII. 10; XIV. 12). The promise to keep them in the hour of trial is not a pledge to ward off all persecution but a promise of sufficient strength to persevere. It foreshows the lot of the virgins in chapter XIV. and gives assurance of victory. Martyrdom is not considered an evil in the Apocalypse; the only thing held to be an absolute evil is sin and apostasy. Jeremias stated that every good seed shall be saved in the day of trial that shall come upon the whole world. The Church of Philadelphia held out longer against the Mohammedan Turk than any other that dates back to apostolic times. Those "who dwell upon the earth" is a phrase coined by St. John to differentiate from the faithful all who do not belong to the true Church.

Verse 11

Christ will come to assist in battle, to free in trial and to crown the victor (Thom.). In the first three letters He did not mention His coming; in that to Thyatira, He mentions it as a distant event; in that to Sardes, He states it to be unexpected, and here to be quick and sudden.

The next admonition is to the bishop personally: "Hold fast what thou hast", "be strong and firm in perseverance and in keeping from evil all those whom I have entrusted to thee". The "crown", in accord with the context, does not mean eternal life but the place of honor and pre-eminence retained by this church in the estimation of our Lord. That is the import of His promise to keep the congregation in the "hour of trial".

His coming then means His arrival with various visitations to perfect the church.

Verse 12

The promises point to the last chapters of the Apocalypse. Christ is now in the act of building His Church. The New Jerusalem is the Church after He shall have won the victory over all His enemies and re-constructed the world according to His own plans and specifications. The Temple is the symbol and visible representation of His Church. The old Temple was in ruins. This is the Temple of Christ's God not the old Temple of Jahve, though Jahve was only another name for the One Eternal God.

The promises are not for the Bishop of Philadelphia alone; they are for all faithful bishops, priests and people. The word "pillar" might allude to various things in the Old Testament but is used in a purely allegorical sense in the New. The apostles are pillars (Gal. II. 9); the Church itself is a pillar (1 Tim. III. 15). St. Clement employs the same metaphor (Clem. V.) when writing of the "greatest and most righteous pillars", which seem to be SS. Peter and Paul. A pillar is built into the church and remains an irremovable and integral part of the building giving it stability and beauty. The building of Christ's Church will go on until it stands finished during the thousand years that follow the reign of Antichrist. If anyone is made a pillar in the Church, he will remain there as long as the Church stands.

With His own hand, Christ will inscribe on each pillar in His Temple the name of God, the name of the New Jerusalem and His own new name. The one who will overcome the temptations can remain faithful only by the grace of God and co-operation with it, will enhance God's glory and will deserve to be decorated by Him as having rendered heroic service. He shall deserve to be distinguished by the name of the New Jerusalem, because his firmness will make the building of that city possible in the distant future. He shall deserve to bear the new mysterious name by which Christ will be honored after His victory over Anti-Christ. And he shall be an officer in the army of Christ and a co-victor with Him. Inscribing the name of God on the victor consecrates him in a special way to God. Such victors make up the true Israel as distinguished from the Jews who are the synagogue of Satan.

In the new Jerusalem there shall be no Temple as in olden times. The communion of the faithful will constitute the temple of which each congregation and each pastor is a pillar. The individual members are living stones. (1 Peter II. 5). St. Paul uses the same metaphor to show how all members compose the temple of God. (Eph. II. 19 ff). The name of the new Jerusalem will confer on the receiver the rights and privileges of citizenship in the Kingdom of Christ. What these rights amounted to could not be fully understood during the ages of persecution, when the Church was despised and oppressed and her members dispossessed of Roman privileges. After the pagan order shall have been wiped out and the political order of Christ and God been inaugurated in a divine democracy, the members of the Church shall have citizenship rights that excel all Roman rights. Those rights will not end with this world but will assure of admittance to eternal rights and privileges. If the congregation of Philadelphia remains faithful, each member shall participate in all the victories and glories which the Church shall ever win upon earth, because they hold citizenship in a Jerusalem which is from above and which shall stand forever. This hints at the Jerusalem which no longer existed. It also points to chapters XXI. and XXII. when the church shall rule unhindered and supreme.

The word used to denote the "new" Jerusalem and the "new" name of Christ betokens something strange, mysterious and unknown. In XIX. 12, His new name is mentioned again, and it is known to Christ alone. It will evidently be some glorious new title that shall be revealed in its time, when He comes to destroy Antichrist. Both Christ and the true believers who triumph with Him shall receive that new title and shall appear in a new glory. It may allude to the name of Neocaesarea, which Philadelphia assumed for a time in honor of Tiberius. The "new" Jerusalem may also refer to the rebuilding of Philadelphia after the earthquake of 17 A.D. And it refers to the destruction of the Temple of Jerusalem by the prediction that Christ will build an indestructible one.

Verse 13

The Christians are again called on everywhere to heed all the admonitions to all churches. In the present instance the whole message is one of consolation and encouragement, and it reminds all of how glorious a privilege it is to be a citizen of the Kingdom of Christ, of His One True Church.

7. To The Angel Of The Church Of Laodicea.

Verses 14 to end.

Verse 14

Laodicea was situated on the Lycos River 40 miles southeast of Philadelphia at the junction of the Roman roads from Sardes and from Ephesus. The city stood on a spur of Mt. Salbacos one mile from the left bank of the Lycos. It is said to have been called originally Diospolis and Rhoas. Antiochus Theos colonized it between 261-246 B.C. and gave it the name of Laodice, his wife. In 220 B.C., it formed part of the kingdom of Pergamos. It suffered severely in the war with Mithridates but recovered its prosperity under Roman rule. Near the beginning of the Christian era, it was one of the principal cities of Asia Minor for industries, commerce and banking. Cicero repaired to it for monetary transactions. It specialized in the manufacture of woolen goods, sandals and eyesalve. The Laodiceans developed a spirit of independence through their wealth, so that at the time of the great earthquake in 60 A.D., they rejected the imperial help to rebuild the city. It was rebuilt and embellished with beautiful monuments by the wealthy citizens. It had acquired from Rome the title of *free city* and had become the center of a conventus juridicus.

The city had a school of medicine. The inhabitants worshipped Zeus, Aeskulepios, Apollo and the emperors. Besides the indigenous inhabitants of Hellenized Syrians, it had Greeks, Romans and a large Jewish colony. Antiochus III. had transplanted 2000 Jews to Asia Minor, mostly to Phrygia and Lydia, a large percent of whom probably settled in this city. A Roman magistrate received a letter from authorities of Rome not to molest the Jews in their religious observances and customs. These Jews sent regularly to Jerusalem a tribute of 20 pounds of gold per year.

It was quite natural that the Christians of Laodicea shared the self-sufficiency of their fellow citizens and thought, felt and acted overconfidently in their relations with God. The commercial importance of the city and of the Jews warded off persecution from the Christians, but it brought a decline in their spiritual life. This decline was also shared by Colossae and Hierapolis.

There is much uncertainty about the founding of the Church in Laodicea, but Archippos seems to have been the first bishop (Col. IV. 17). St. Paul had not visited this part of the Lycos valley when he wrote his letter to the Colossians while a prisoner in Rome (Col. II. 1), but he knew some of the faithful by name (Col. IV. 15). It is quite certain that Epaphras labored to spread the Gospel at Laodicea (Col. IV. 12). The last bishop mentioned in history ruled about 1450 A.D., the time of the conquest of Constantinople by the Soliman Turks.

St. Paul ordered that his letter to Colossae be read in Laodicea, and that the letter to Laodicea be read in Colossae (IV. 16). St. Paul's letters clearly show that the Christians were unmolested and secure in the three cities Laodicea, Colossae and Hierapolis. The liberty enjoyed by them and the wealth of the city is also clearly set forth in our letter to the Bishop of Laodicea.

For the meaning of the word "Amen", commentators refer to Isaias (LXV. 16-17), who predicts the renewal of all things. It would apply very aptly under that meaning, since the following verses express lucidly the urgent need of reform and renewal in zeal and virtue of the bishop's mind and heart, before God will bear with him and his congregation. The *Amen* was quite familiar to all readers of the Gospel, because our Lord used it forcefully and eloquently day in and day out. It was an emphatic avowal of His eternal and infallible authority to speak the truth. He is TRUTH ITSELF, who makes real His ideals and never falls short. No saying of His can be assailed by doubt. Especially whenever He uses that solemn way of announcing a truth may no one gainsay Him; and no matter what the world may say, His word prevails over all. By this Hebrew idiom, He stresses the absolute certainty of what He has to say to the Church of Laodicea to rouse the bishop and people out of their self-confident lethargy. It is an accusation, an advice, a threat and a promise. It is equivalent to a divine Oath for He is the Oath; He can swear only by Himself.

Because He is the Amen, He is by His very nature the most faithful and truthful witness of the truth. He is more than this; He is simply the "faithful and true" witness, the only one who could be called "the Faithful and True One" without reserve.

He is also "the beginning of the creation of God". He is not the first of God's actual creation, but the one through whom it was begun, and who is the model and exemplar, the conception and Prime Cause of creation and its beginning (Clem. Alex. Theoph.). This passage alludes to Colossians (I. 15-18, 20) and was therefore known to the congregation at Laodicea. According to the theology of St. Paul, Christ in His personality is the uncreated principle of creation, and all creation is subjected to Him (Heb. II. 8). He has therefore uncontrovertible authority to accuse, advise and threaten. These titles now in evidence apply with precision and forceful persuasiveness to this proud and self-satisfied congregation.

Verses 15 and 16

The Amen, the faithful Witness and Cause of all creation, knows the spiritual condition of the Church at Laodicea. The bishop is free from the troubles and weaknesses of other churches. There are no Nicolaites or Jezabels here. He has no heresy among his people. Nevertheless the solemnity of the address prepares him for searching criticism. There is in him something very dangerous and disastrous to spiritual life, and that is TEPIDITY. He is neither icy cold nor burning hot (See Acts XVIII. 25; Rom. XII. 11), he is not fervent in spirit. The sinner is cold and the saint is hot. The icy cold is enmity and opposition (Ambrose, Bede). One who is cold, as Saul was before his conversion, is more easily convinced of his sorry plight and can be converted more readily. The lukewarm one deceives himself, thinking that he is virtuous enough and that to strive higher would be fanaticism. All admonitions are insipid and tasteless to a man of tepid heart, because he cannot feel that anything is wanting to him. He is sure of a reserved seat in Heaven. Through his own fault, he is in a state of pride and spiritual blindness. But he thinks he is a paragon of perfection for others, for he is so perfectly balanced and does not overdo anything. He feels resentment against any suggestion that he may have slighted his duty, or that he could add to his sanctity. The highest positions in the Church should be open to him, hence God can do nothing for him or with him. He has no spiritual zeal.

There is here an allusion to the hot springs of Hierapolis, which while flowing over the plateau became lukewarm and falling over the cliff opposite Laodicea could be seen for a long distance, owing to the white incrustation of lime which they deposited on the face of the cliff. (Strabo. 903). It was only six miles across the valley from one city to the other. The allusion is all the more insistent, because the letter to Laodicea was intended for all the cities of the Lycus Valley. (Ramsay, Cities of Asia, II. p. 85 ff.).

Lukewarm water provokes nausea, and a lukewarm pastor is nauseous to Christ. Religious indifference is disgustful to Christ. He prefers the consciousness of sin or the ignorance of heathenism which His grace has not enlightened or thawed. He speaks a threat against Laodicea more frightful than that against the Bishop of Sardes, who has the name of being alive but is dead. He will expel the tepid bishop from the Church unless he repents and does penance.

Verse 17

In the quotation attributed to the bishop there is a climax. He says: 'I am rich in what I have received, I have acquired more riches by my own exertions, my wealth has grown to such proportions that I am satisfied with it.' In this prosperous city the Christians may have brought the pride over their wealth into their spiritual life. The bishop may have engaged in business so as to become wealthy and have gained all the comforts and luxuries of the rich and is living at his ease. In those days the rich did not seek their enjoyment in travel or sight-seeing. But some interpreters (Bede, Gregory) think that spiritual riches are meant. The bishop may be keenly aware of having received the spiritual riches of the Church in his consecration and so has become arrogant and overbearing towards his priests and flock and self-satisfied with his work in the ministry and with the added spiritual wealth he has acquired. But he is careful not to exceed his good comfort or to do what might disturb his ease. He does not rebuke abuses for fear of arousing resentment either within the fold or without. If the strict persuance of his duties is bothersome, he will tone it down. He is satisfied with what he now possesses and makes no more advancement in sanctity. But he is not rich spiritually, for then he would not speak in so haughty a tone.

Christ heaps up epithets to give the greatest possible emphasis to His words. The bishop is in darkness, so that his mind, from a spiritual viewpoint, does not function reasonably. He does not know that he is wretched, suffering the hardships of slavery; that he is pitiable, arousing the commiseration of the One who beholds his plight, and that he is so poor as to be destitute of the most urgent necessities. Because he is in the most spiritual poverty, he is sold into slavery and is there reduced to such wretchedness as to bring tears of pity to the eyes of the inspired Seer. Then he is blind, too blind to see his own wretchedness. He is naked stripped of all meritorious works and therefore will be put to shame on the day of judgment. Because he is deprived of every necessity of life—food, house, clothing, and is blind and reduced to slavery – he is absolutely helpless. This description is taken from the ideas of the wealthy, for it is an enumeration of the very things the rich and well-to-do fear. In ancient times, a man who was reduced to such a pitiable state found no sympathy among his fellow-men. He could be of no use to anyone, and so no one would waste a copper coin on him. He became an outcast, and his only relief was death.

Verse 18

Our Lord merciful and kind directs the bishop how to alleviate his spiritual poverty. He counsels him to buy gold that is tried and refined in the fire, pure and true gold from Him, the value of which is far above that of the earthly wealth of the Laodiceans. With the imagined wealth in which they trust, the Laodicean Christians must come to Christ. The idea of gold suggests the idea of purchase. It suggests self-denial and sacrifice of their wealth in works of Christian charity conformable with the advice of Christ: "Make unto yourselves friends of the mammon of iniquity". They must give up their arrogance, self-confidence and self-adulation thereby securing the priceless riches Christ offers them.

As the reward for this change of heart, they shall be clothed in the white garments of sanctifying grace. The spiritual significance of white garments is contrasted with the black cloaks manufactured in Laodicea from the glossy black wool of the sheep of that region. This concrete example is to impress on the mind of the bishop and people, that only if they are roused from their torpor and become zealous in works of charity shall they obtain from Christ the gold with which to purchase the white garments of justification and no longer appear naked in the sight of God. Nakedness in the Apocalypse means being stripped of all meritorious works. The order of ideas is this: First the bishop must awaken from his self-complacency – the admonitions will move him if he heeds them. Then he must stir up his parish; both he and they must do penance. When he has atoned for this indifference, the fuller enlightment of his conscience by the Holy Spirit will enable him to see and become aware of the dangerous condition in which he was before the message came to him. The reference to eye-salve is an allusion to the school of medicine attached to the temple of Aeskulepios and to the eye-powder used by the physicians.

The epithets heaped up by our Lord in the last two verses seem to intimate that this extreme state of tepidity is a state of mortal sin, but the bishop's conscience is not aware of it. To have lived in ease and enjoyments thus has been for him only material sin, although he was culpable for not scrutinizing his conscience enough to understand the true condition of his soul. The Bishop of Sardes was conscious of his state of spiritual death. This letter will make the Bishop of Laodicea aware of the danger in which he hovered.

Verse 19

Here is an assurance of the undying love of Christ for His Church and for all who belong to it. He rebukes and chastises only to heal and save. In Greek the distinction between the two words employed is very fine and suggestive. The first word ἐλέγχω conveys the thought that Christ will convince of wrongdoing those whom He loves, and the word παιδεύω, that by afflictions, He will educate them to correct their ways. Let the bishop now do penance and be zealous to become worthy of such love of Christ. St. Thomas enumerates five reasons for the chastisements of God: To try and test, to preserve humility, to purify, to give glory to God and to punish the wicked.

Verse 20

In the first letter Christ speaks of "coming" to judge; in the third letter He threatens to come "quickly"; in the fifth letter He will "come as a thief", and in this last letter He stands "at the door". He expressed the same thought in the Gospel (Mt. XXIV. 33; Mc. XIII. 34). He does not come unexpectedly but announces His presence by knocking at the door.

Christ knocks at the door as a friend. He does not come as a destitute beggar to be a burden to the one who receives Him. He speaks while knocking, so there can be no mistaking the visitor. His children hear His voice and admit Him joyfully. And He will abide with His own in an inseparable union (Jo. XIV. 23) in the eucharistic banquet. Christ comes to minister to His host and to delight him with heavenly refreshment. The condition sine qua non is to accept this warning, to ponder it seriously and translate it into action with fear and humility.

Christ's knocking at the door has been interpreted consistently to mean that His coming in judgment is imminent. It also intimates no reception by this proud, self-satisfied and self-justified bishop. He is standing outside the door knocking and calling as a friend to be re-admitted in order to save this parish. All can easily recognize His voice in the words He speaks, because they are an echo of the Gospel. Though He pointedly calls to their attention the awful danger in which they hover and utters words of ominous import nay even threats of certain destruction, yet withal He speaks in pleading tones holding out promises of endless delights, if they grant Him entrance. He promises in this verse to feast them after His own fashion. It will be a banquet like the one at Emmaus. He Himself, the guest, will provide the banquet. The union of a household is most truly represented by the partaking of the common table. The ancients considered the sacrificial banquet a partaking with the deity; This undoubtedly indicates the Holy Eucharist; and in the eucharistic union, He gives the pledge of inseparable union with Him in His Kingdom. And it clearly indicates a neglect of frequent communion by the Christians in Laodicea and of daily Mass by the bishop, in whose estimation wealth, luxuries and sensual enjoyments ranked higher.

Verse 21

The further promise made in this verse sums up all the promises made in the SEVEN LETTERS. He had promised diverse rewards to those who overcome; but this is the promise of the final consummation, the promise to share in the prerogatives of His divinity. Now what did He overcome? He overcame the whole world, the flesh and the devil. He who would triumph with Him must renounce world-empire, sensual enjoyments and the gifts of Satan. The reward of all this is elevation to the throne of Christ, not only to sit with Him but to share the rights of His throne and to rule with Him. To fully gain the right for His Humanity to rule, He had died on the Cross. Without this sacrificial death, the Eucharist could not have become a reality and communion with His divinity would not have been so intimate.

The sitting with Him on His throne does not necessarily mean sharing the prerogatives of His divinity in Heaven. The context of this and the foregoing verse recalls other words of the New Testament. St. Paul writes to the Ephesians (II.6), as if they are already sitting in the heavenly places with Christ. And our Blessed Lord at the Last Supper certainly points to His Church and the eucharistic banquet, when He promises His disciples a place at His table (Lc. XXII. 29). They are to decide whom to admit into the Church and to the sacred Table. The elders express this very thought in chapter V. (V. 10). They as priests rule the world with Christ, because they have dominion over His Eucharistic Body, through which He rules the destinies of the Church and the world. As He won the victory over the world by His death and made His ever-abiding presence in the Eucharist possible; as He is inseparably united with the Father and the Holy Spirit under the eucharistic veil thence ruling the world as the KING OF KINGS: so will He grant the privilege of ruling the world with Him to those who overcome the world as He overcame it. This promise points directly to the Bishop of Laodicea and his priestly prerogatives. The seven letters are easily seen and universally admitted to be a perfect unity, and these last verses are an integral part of the whole Apocalypse. In his letter to the Corinthians (1 Cor. VI. 2, 3), St. Paul tells that they shall judge the world nay even the angels. The devils may have apostatized from God, because they would not adore the Sacred Humanity of Christ much less His Eucharistic Body and therefore those who believe and worship Him shall judge all apostates. The Greek text here implies a participation of the priests in the power and glory of Christ's triumphant humanity. But the rewards of victory are not the same in the disciple as in Christ, for He is σύνθρονος with the Father, while the disciple is not σύνθρονος with Christ.

Nowhere in the Old or New Testament does any inspired writer attempt to describe the bliss of Heaven. St. Paul was elevated to the Third Heaven but was not allowed to reveal what he had seen and heard. So it would be logical to hold that St. John does not attempt to describe the life with God but only the glories, struggles and triumphs of the Church. The promises for faithfulness in these seven letters are promises of rewards in the Church, temporal-spiritual rewards with the prospect of unending and ineffable bliss in Heaven, of which the spiritual advancement in the Church are the earnest.

Verse 22

The last words are the same as those addressed to each of the seven churches, but they have a wider import. They are an admonition not only to take to heart what is written to the Bishop of Laodicea and his congregation but to ponder and follow all warnings to all of them. The Seven Churches represent the Universal or Catholic Church. They emphasize the vices and neglects which bring disaster wherever they appear. They are an admonition to prepare for the judgment that is to begin soon but shall not reach its culmination till under Antichrist and its completion on the Last Day.

Chapter five will demonstrate with greater clearness the logical context of the last three verses above, the sequence of the succeeding chapters from the foregoing and will give the key to the interpretation of the whole Apocalypse and to the manner and scope of the victory to be won.

CHAPTER IV.

Westminster Version

After these things, I beheld and lo! 1. a door set open in heaven,
and the former voice which I had heard, as of a trumpet speaking to me
said: 'Come up hither, and I will show thee the things which must befall
hereafter.'

Immediately I was (rapt) in the 2. spirit; and behold a throne stood in
heaven, and upon the throne one seated. And he that sat was in appearance
3. like to a jasper and a cornelian; and the throne was encircled by a rainbow, in appearance like to an emerald. Round about the throne were
twenty-four 4. thrones and upon these thrones twenty-four elders were
sitting, clothed in white garments, with golden crowns on their heads.

Out of the throne go forth lightnings 5. and voices and thunder-peals,
and seven lighted lamps burn before the throne; which are the seven
spirits of God. In front of the throne there is as it 6. were a sea of glass,
like unto crystal. Within the space before the throne and round the throne
are four living beings, full of eyes in front and behind.

The first living being is like a 7. lion; the second like a calf; the
third hath a face like that of a man; and the fourth is like an eagle
flying.

The four living beings have each 8. of them six wings; they are full of
eyes all around and within; and they cease not day and night to say:
'Holy, holy, holy the Lord God almighty, who was and who is and who
is to come.'

And as often as these living beings 9. shall give glory and honor and
thanks to him who sitteth upon the throne, to him who liveth forever and
ever, the 10. twenty-four elders shall fall down before him who sitteth
upon the throne and shall adore him who liveth forever and ever, and
they shall cast down their crowns before the throne, saying:

'Worthy art thou, our Lord and our 11. God, to receive glory and
honor and power, for thou didst create all things and because of thy
will they were and they were created.'

II.

ADORATION OF GOD AND THE LAMB

A.

THE GLORIES OF THE CHURCH.

1. The Vision Of God.

Chapter IV. Verses 1-3.

Verse 1

The first clause of this verse suggests a lapse of some time between the last words of the foregoing chapter and the beginning of the new revelations. After noting down the last dictation, St. John looked up, and he saw a door set open before him, and it was the door of heaven, of the house of God. The same words occur again in VII. 1 demarcating each passage as the introduction to an important division in the revelations. The door had been opened awaiting his approach. Through it he looked, as it were, into heaven and saw the throne of God before him. The veil was lifted from the invisible, and he beheld the glory of God, as it is present in the Church, and as Ezechiel had seen it in the Temple (X. 4).

In the book of Daniel (VIII. 10), the Holy City is called the "strength of heaven"; In the Hebrew text, it is the "army of heaven"; Thus the church of the Old Testament is called "heaven". Our Blessed Lord called His Church "the kingdom of heaven". In chapter I. of this book, St. John calls it "the kingdom". In the present chapter and in many other places, he calls it simply "heaven" (VIII. 10; IX. 1; XIII. 6; XIX. 14; XXI. 1). For a further corroboration of this use of the term, we might turn to Isaias (XXXIV. 5). God said to the prophet that His sword had been "Inebriated in heaven", meaning that it was drunk with the blood of the Jews. It had wreaked vengeance on the theocracy and would now turn on the enemies of the Jews. The simple word "heaven" thus designates the Church of both the Old and the New Testament. In the Apocalypse, "heaven" is the Church, except where the context clearly shows it to mean the celestial dwellings.

As in spirit he enters the Church, St. John again hears the first voice speaking like a trumpet, telling him to put himself on the viewpoint of the speaker. It was not the voice of Christ that called him to receive the new revelations. As an angel assisted Daniel to see and understand the visions correctly, so an angel will assist St. John to see, to comprehend and to interpret in their true meaning the visions to be shown him. This sentence like that of the first chapter (I. 19) expresses the purpose of the revelations, that it is to show the future not of Heaven but of the Church and of the world and to relate in prophetic visions and in true order the events of history. In the first vision, the Seer was told to write "the things which ARE and which must be done hereafter", but now it is only "the things which must be done HEREAFTER". So the book from this place is future history, real prophecy. And the key to the visions is that all revelations contained in this prophecy will constitute the future history of the Church and also of the world, in as far as it is connected with the Church or exerts an influence on her destiny. That was the scope of the Old Testament prophecies. The prophets predicted God's judgments upon those nations only that exerted some influence on the destiny of the chosen people. The view of those interpreters who are modernistically inclined and assert that the Apocalypse is a book of mere consolations and was never intended to reveal intelligible prophecies must be rejected.

The things contained in the book "MUST" be done. They will be decrees of God, events that shall be subsequent to the receiving of the visions and the writing of the book. The starting point of the prophecies is the time of their reception. According to the best historical evidence, it was in the days of emperor Domitian in the last decade of the first century. The prophecies of the Apocalypse will concern themselves with those nations and peoples, kingdoms and empires that shall influence the growth, mission and destiny of the Church. However, no kingdom or empire is mentioned by name as was done in the prophecies of the Old Testament. The reason is obvious: The chosen people of the Old Testament were set apart from the rest of the nations, whilst the elect are a part of every nation on earth.

The things that "must be done" are not happenings or events determined by the free will of man alone but are decrees of God consequent upon man's free acts. As in the Old

Testament, so in the New God's judgments will fall upon the nations for their disobedience, schisms, heresies, apostasies, infidelity and pride; for their hating and persecuting the true believers and for leading them into vice. The Old Testament contains prophecies against Egypt and Assyria for their pride, against Babylon and Greece for their cruelty and oppression, against the Philistines, Moabites, Ammonites and others for their hatred and persecution of the Chosen People; for leading them into witchcrafts, fornication, apostasy, idolatry and other abominations and for exulting over the punishments which God inflicted upon them. All revelations will concern themselves directly with the work of Jesus Christ, the work of Redemption, and will be depicted as seen from God's viewpoint.

Verse 2

After manifesting his willingness to obey the speaker, St. John is immediately "in the spirit"; he and his work are inspired. The Greek text states that he *became* inspired, He *knows* that he is inspired and is writing under that influence. The first verse contains one of the elements of inspiration, the invitation to receive the revelations, and the second verse states his consciousness of being inspired to understand the coming messages fully and to write them infallibly. In the first vision he had received the command to write (I. 19). In that vision he was "in the spirit", that his eyes might see and his ears might hear. In that first vision the force of inspiration assisted his experience and human knowledge of the condition of the Seven Churches; but from now on his knowledge will depend entirely on the revelations. New and strange facts will be revealed to him making the force of inspiration wider in its scope.

The invisible becomes visible. The vision he beholds shows him a throne set in heaven, in the Church. The facts that the throne was "set" in heaven indicates it to be not the eternal throne of God but that of a divine institution. God occupies the throne. As Daniel saw Him coming in judgment (VII. 9-10) seated upon the throne of His power and majesty and surrounded by angels, so does St. John behold Him on His throne in the Church surrounded by the hierarchy. Daniel saw Him in human form, as also Ezechiel had seen Him in the likeness of a man at the River Chobar and again in the Temple, when He began judgment at His House (Ezech. I. 26; IX. 3; X. 1).

St. John's conception of God being of a loftier order than that of the other prophets, he does not mention any form.

As the judgments of God began at the Temple in the Old Testament, so will they begin here at the Church. St. Peter had stated this long before, saying "For time is that judgment should begin at the house of God" (1 Pet. IV. 17). That prophecy was fulfilled under Nero.

Verse 3

God appears to St. John like the color and luster of the jasper and the sardine-stone. The former is most probably our diamond, and the sardine-stone or carnelian being scarlet-colored is a species of ruby. The jasper symbolizes the holiness of God, and the sardine-stone His justice; the former turning towards the just and the latter menacing the wicked. The jasper is mentioned *first* here as in the twelve foundation stones of the New Jerusalem (XXI. 19). while in the breastplate of the high priest, the sardine-stone and emerald were in the first row and the jasper in the second (Exod. XXVIII. 17). Under the symbolic colors of the precious stones, God reveals Himself as the Judge who rewards the good and punishes the wicked. All judgments aim at purifying and sanctifying mankind.

Blending the two colors signifies the essential oneness of God's holiness and justice. These two colors blended are the color of fire. God appeared in a flame of fire to Moses (Ex. III. 2) and in the midst of fire to Ezechiel (I. 4) and Daniel (VII. 9). In his relationship to the Church, He appears in a less terrifying form and more clearly in His attributes as precious stones. The blending of His justice and holiness signifies too, that His guidance of the Church is always in accord with His infinite perfections.

The rainbow around the throne is the symbol of mercy. It is not a rainbow proper for it is emerald colored. The ἶρις is a Homeric term for rainbow. In the Septuagint the word τόξον is used. God appears infinitely just and holy in all that He decrees or permits to befall His Church. His perfections reflect mercy under the guise of an emerald-colored halo. Emerald is the symbol of faith which reflects the hope of salvation. "Faith is the substance of the things to be hoped for" (Heb. XI. 1). Thus will God reveal Himself throughout the history of the Church as the all-just and all-holy Guide, from whose guidance is reflected the hope of salvation.

2. The Twenty-Four Elders.

Verses 4-5.

Verse 4

St. John relates the details in this vision in a round-about way. The elders are the most important figures in this description of the scene and should catch the eye first. But the Seer mentions the thrones first. He thereby may want to emphasize their royal dignity. These thrones are similar to the central throne on which the Divine Majesty is seated, and by mentioning them first, St. John shows the occupants as participating in the sovereignty of God. Many interpreters have considered these elders to be the twelve apostles and the twelve patriarchs or the twelve lesser prophets. This is only a co-incidence of numbers. If the number means anything, there is in it a much nearer reference to the institution and regulation of the divine worship in the tabernacle of the Old Testament. David arranged the services of the priests in twenty-four courses. The chief men of the descendants of Aaron headed these courses, each in turn serving in the sanctuary, offering the morning and evening holocausts and the incense in the Holy of Holies (1 Para. XXIV. 1-19). These elders most probably represent the priesthood of the Church continually serving God and working out His ordinances (See V. 10). The word "priest" is derived from the Greek word πρεσβύτερος which is translated in the Apocalypse with the word "elder". These elders then represent the priesthood of the Christian Churches and are the spiritual heads of all the children of God, Jews and Gentiles, offering the Deity and the Lamb the adoration and oblations of all humanity. There is no distinction among them, just as there is no distinction between the nations and races of the elect before God (See Titus 1. 5; James V. 14-15).

The elders are not σύνθρονοι with the Deity, they are not in the midst of the throne, but sit on thrones apart from the central throne; they hold a subordinate position. Yet in the Church, the priesthood represents Christ and participates with Him in its spiritual government. This is symbolized in the vision by the insignia of royalty; namely, the sitting upon thrones and wearing golden crowns. The priests therefore belong to the hierarchy. (Council of Trent. Sess. XXIII. 965. Cap. 6). Golden crowns also symbolize divine wisdom. Crowned with wisdom, the priests of the Church will exercise their regal office. The gold of the crowns glitters with a manifold symbolism. Above all it proclaims as genuine and divine the authority of the wearers to rule Christ's people, as directed or enlightened by godly wisdom, as being pure and unselfish in their service and as a complete sacrifice. (Lc. XXII. 29)

Verse 5

In verse 5, God's holiness manifests itself in a twofold guidance of the Church: The first is through the endowments conferred upon His Church bodied forth in the lightnings, voices and thunders, which are the prerogatives enabling her to spread the Gospel; the second is through the divine assistance or activity of the Holy Spirit in the Church symbolized by the seven lamps before the throne, which denote the seven gifts of the Holy Spirit guiding and helping her in the spread of the Gospel. The lightnings are the charismata, the power of miracles and the powers of the ministerial office, which is a de condigno right of the Church, because she is in the supernatural order and needs supernatural means to fulfill her mission. The charismatic gifts were necessary in the beginning to spread the Gospel and establish the Church. The voices proceeding from the throne are the natural gift of eloquence in the Church to preach the revealed truth and are expressive of all external activity of the pastoral office, all of which has a sacred character and divine authority. Those voices find an echo among the peoples and nations that becomes a sound of jubilation and victory from those who have accepted the Gospel. The thunders are the voice of supreme authority in the Church issuing decrees, dogmas, laws, condemning idolatry and heresy and expressing anathemas and warnings against all who resist the truth and persist in sin. The seven lamps are lights like torches. In Greek the word λαμπάδες is used, which points to the lights on the lampstands. In I. 12 they were λυχνίαι and meant the Churches. The lighted lamps are not in this vision the seven churches. They symbolize the external mission and activity of the Holy Spirit enlightening, guiding and sanctifying the Church, comforting her in the trials endured and protecting her against danger. They also suggest His internal activity dealing out His gifts to individual souls enlightening, sanctifying, strengthening and consoling them. Through her prerogatives and the Divine Assistance, the Church is enabled to enlighten all members and the world.

This vision recalls the one depicted in Exodus (XIX. 6, 16) and Ezechiel (I. 13). In the books of Jeremias (XXV. 30-31) and Joel (III. 16) and Amos (I. 2), God has revealed that He will roar forth His judgments, His anathemas from the Temple, the center of the theocracy. In the same order can He be expected to execute judgment on the world in the New Testament through His Church and for the sake of His Church. Only those who belong to His Church and are faithful to it will escape the thunderbolts of His judgments.

3. The Crystal Sea.

Verse 6.

Verse 6

In the language of the prophets, the human race is often depicted as a sea. (Dan. VII. 2). The Crystal Sea now mentioned is composed of the lay members of the Church. It is like crystal, because it is pellucid with the light of God's presence; and this distinguishes it from the sea in which the Beast will reign, which is the world (XIII. 1; XVII. 15; Isa. LVII. 20). There is nothing dark or hidden within the Church, nothing secret about her doctrines or practices, because the light of God's truth and grace pervades it. In the visions of Ezechiel, the throne of God has different details and surroundings. The firmament is crystal and is over the heads of the living beings (Ezech. I. 22-28). And there is no crystal sea in that vision. This intimates a much higher perfection and a more sublime order for the New than for the Old Testament, because the hierarchy administer the sacraments that give the graces which transfuse the Church with crystal glory. And therefore this Crystal Sea is placed beneath their feet in the vision.

4. The Four Living Beings.

Verses 7-end.

Verse 7-8

In the last place St. John mentions the presence of FOUR

LIVING BEINGS in the vision and he describes them. The Four Living Beings are within the space before the throne and surround it. They are σύνθρονοι sharing the throne with the Deity and the Lamb. They must therefore possess prerogatives and powers which God has Himself conferred. Why does the Seer mention them last, whilst he first mentioned the One who occupied the throne? Probably because the beginning and end of a sentence or paragraph are the strongest positions. These Living Beings would therefore rank next in importance to the Deity. Their description sharing the throne with the Deity is similar to that in Isaias (VI. 2-3) and Ezechiel (I. 10). The prophets identify the living beings with the cherubim and seraphim. In those prophecies it represents the presence of God in the Holy of Holies. Later Ezechiel (X. 19) beholds the Presence departing from the Temple, when the judgment was breaking in upon Jerusalem. St. John does not, as Isaias and Ezechiel do, identify the living beings with the cherubim and seraphim. The symbol employed by him is obviously of much more elevated and sublime a character than that in the Old Testament and must be interpreted independently of the texts of the prophets. The living beings of the Apocalypse have not that mysterious unity which the figures have in the book of Ezechiel. They are distinct organisms.

St. Jerome (Lib. I. Contra Jov.) applies the forms of the four living beings to the four evangelists. He probably followed the ideas of St. Irenaeus (III. xi. 8). According to him, St. Matthew is represented by the human face, because he opens the gospel narrative with the human geneology of Christ; St. Mark introduces John the Baptist with the "voice of one crying in the wilderness" and therefore aptly presents him as a lion; St. Luke begins his narrative with the priest, Zachary, sacrificing in the Temple, and therefore has for his emblem the calf or ox; and St. John soars to the very nature and being of God in his introductory sentences and throughout his gospel treatise keeps in mind the divinity of Christ and exhibits the most striking proofs for it, for which reasons he is identified with the figure of the flying eagle. These explanations have been accepted by the majority of theologians without comment. Some divines have also tried to accommodate the forms of the living beings to the prophets of the Old Testament but have not found so apt and easy an application there as in the case of the evangelists. And the application or accommodation of the figures to the prophets is far-fetched.

The application of the "Living Beings" to the evangelists can be made only in an accommodated sense. For if they represented the four evangelists in the literal sense, and if the twenty-four elders represent the twelve lesser prophets and the twelve apostles, it would be necessary to number St. Paul and St. Barnabas among the apostles. Otherwise St. Matthew and St. John would be present in two places at the same time in the vision, among the four living beings and among the twenty-four elders. St. Paul was truly an apostle, but St. Barnabas was not an apostle proper. Again the Apostles would be of a lower order in God's dispensation than the two secretaries of the apostles, Mark and Luke. Furthermore. the twenty-four elders would represent twenty-four persons, twelve prophets and twelve apostles, whilst the FOUR living beings would represent EIGHT persons, four prophets and four evangelists. The apostles were of equal rank, with the exception of St. Peter, and all of the 16 or 17 prophets were of equal rank, differing among themselves only by the size of the volume which they wrote. Another consideration is that the vision in the Old Testament represented the presence of God in the Temple. That vision was similar to this one depicted by St. John. To this can be added other considerations which show the application of this text to the evangelists to be only in an *accommodated sense.* The interpretation of St. Jerome has been rather unfortunate for the exegesis of the Apocalypse.

The liturgical actions of the living beings in V. 8 are strictly the functions of the ministering body, the episcopate and priesthood of the Church, not of an evangelist as such. The highest function of the hierarchy is worshipping God and offering the worship of the entire membership to Him. And this duty is assigned to the living beings and the elders throughout the Apocalypse and also to the golden altar.

In chapter XIX. 4, the elders are the first of the hierarchy to pay public worship and thanksgiving to God for the reasons stated in the interpretation of that part of the revelations. But the entire hierarchy, the priesthood and the episcopate altogether, worship God the Victor, when the decisive victory is at the door.

At all times the living beings make the final pronouncement, put the seal of approval upon the worship of all creatures (V. 14). This is properly the right and role of the episcopate. The living beings exercise supreme authority not only in the liturgical worship of the Church but in all pastoral functions of guidance and direction. This is very evident in chapter VI. 1-8, where the living beings voice supreme authority at the opening of each seal. And here the impossibility of their being the evangelists is obvious. If the fourth living being were St. John, he would be on the scene in two places and in two roles at the same time (VI. 7, 8): One as a living being speaking to the other self, the seer, ordering him to come and contemplate the vision; the other obeying the living being, himself, and writing down the vision whilst contemplating it. This is plainly absurd and impossible. The living beings are in chapter VI. surely not the evangelists.

The voice of authority is heard coming from the Church in X. 4, 8. Most probably the "voices in heaven" are the voices of the living beings (XI. 15), for the elders as elsewhere immediately obey and worship God when they hear those voices. The "loud voice" in the next chapter (XII. 10) would also be that of a living being. Thereafter the living beings do not appear anymore until XV. 7, and the voice of authority is hushed until XVI. 1. This silence is explained by the text of the intervening chapters and is made necessary in the 42 months of greatest peril for the Church during which the old world is suffering its death agony. During that time the Two Witnesses take over the leadership in the Church. When that time has passed, a living being appears again in the rôle of authority (XV. 7) and by a symbolic action confers upon the seven angels from the sanctuary the power to inflict the seven last plagues. And the "voice" of supreme authority from the "sanctuary" orders the pouring out of the plagues. The voice is evidently the lion's.

The golden altar also speaks with authority in its proper place and rôle (IX. 13, 14). In chapter fourteen (7-11), three angels appear with messages to the faithful and the wicked, but they exercise no authority.

The logical conclusion from all the above facts is that the living beings represent not the evangelists but the episcopal office, dignity and authority in the Church.

The living beings share the throne with the Deity and the Lamb; they rule with God in the Church. And probably on that account, St. John describes them last returning then to the central throne which he depicted first. Thereafter he continues the theme which he had in mind from the beginning by describing the action that is to follow when the living beings take the leadership in directing the whole worship and adoration of the Deity and in working out God's plans and judgments in the world. The living beings are four in number, which is the number of catholicity. One has the appearance of a lion, another of a calf, the third of a man and the fourth of an eagle flying. In biblical language the lion is the symbol of royalty, of the right and power to rule, the calf or ox of sacrifice and patient toil, the man's face of reason and prudence, of guiding and directing power, and the flying eagle of contemplation. Now these duties and prerogatives belong to the episcopal office in the Church. The FOUR LIVING BEINGS therefore symbolize something else than the celestial spirits around the throne of God in Heaven; they represent the EPISCOPATE around the throne of God and Christ in the Church. In this vision the episcopal office and dignity is represented by the highest spirits in Heaven, and these appear in the forms of the highest types of life on earth, because the episcopacy is the highest office and dignity in the Church. The episcopacy comprises the complete apostolic office. It embodies the supreme ruling power in the Papacy, since the Pope is the bishop of bishops, and his emblem is therefore the lion; The episcopacy includes the priestly power of offering sacrifices and administering the sacraments, and those in that office have the duty of laboring with untiring zeal for the glory of God and the salvation of souls (7 letters), the emblem of which is the ox or calf; the episcopacy embraces the duty of preaching the Gospel, of guiding souls, of directing and administering the temporal affairs of the Church, all of which demands reason and prudence, the gift of eloquence and other natural endowments. For these reasons the Church aims to choose for the episcopate those who are eminently enriched with natural gifts by Almighty God, and this is emblematized by the face of a man; finally the episcopate must exemplify the contemplative life, the life of study, prayer and recollection, of which the flying eagle is the emblem. (St. Paul's letters to Timothy and Titus). The Episcopacy is thus represented as the PERFECT STATE in the vision.

The eyes of the four living beings are symbols of the knowledge of divine revelation possessed by the episcopacy. The eyes in front signify contemplation. With them the living beings behold God intently always, are able to penetrate the inner and true meaning of His revelation so as to be errorless in defining them. The episcopate has not individually but as a united body universal knowledge of God's revelations in both testaments and knows His will in all things pertaining to the guidance of the faithful unto eternal life. The figures have eyes behind signifying the ability of the episcopacy to make true application of God's truth to all mankind.

Each of the living beings has six wings as the Seraphim have in Isaias (VI. 2). But nothing is said of their covering the face or feet before the divine Majesty. This may denote a more intimate communion of the divinely constituted authority in the Church of Christ with the Deity than in the Old Testament, because it is in a higher degree of sanctity than even the prophets of the Ancient Covenant. The Synagogue could not look up to God without feeling its impurity (Isa. VI. 5) and its unworthiness, whilst in the Church all impurity is washed away in the blood of the Lamb.

A new feature in this vision not found in that of the prophets are the eyes within and all around the wings. The wings symbolize the power of the Church to fly speedily over the whole earth. And the eyes within the wings denote the knowledge which the Church has of all human achievements and developments, that like the Holy Spirit she may be on the lookout for all souls that can be saved. The eyes round about the wings denote the insight of the Church into natural revelation and her watchfulness to detect all dangerous tendencies and growths. Those eyes watch the progress of history, education and culture, the change of governments and the discoveries and inventions of science enabling the episcopate to put its imprimatur upon all the commendable works of man. Those eyes view all activity in the world from God's viewpoint; hence their knowledge of applying God's revelations to man is universal or catholic suited to all times and all places.

These living beings are mentioned and connected with the crystal sea in verse six by the ordinary conjunction. This intimates the close bond between the episcopate and the crystal sea. The meaning of the symbolism is quite clearly evident, since the episcopacy was instituted for the faithful.

The living beings keep on repeating incessantly the anthem of the Seraphim of Isaias (VI. 3): "Holy, holy, holy, Lord God Almighty, who was and who is and who is to come". The words are somewhat different and have a different meaning from those in Isaias. The living beings pronounce God all-holy and all-just in His judgment upon the world, past, present and future. They have a special reason for this anthem of adoration: The all-holy, all-just and almighty Lord who was the cause and origin of all things is also the author of grace. And He has bestowed the episcopal dignity and power upon them to represent Him and be nearest His throne. And in His justice, holiness and almighty power, he will execute His judgments and consummate His loving purposes for the salvation of the world. They are so overawed by the stupendous grace of the divine dignity they possess in the episcopacy, that they can utter only these words but in them voice all creation's worship.

The living beings are not in Heaven but in the Church on earth, for in Heaven there is no night. They never rest from divine worship "day and night" uttering and enacting the divine praises somewhere in the world incessantly. The Church is ever vigilant and solicitous about the praise and adoration due God from the whole world, assimilates all knowledge and accomplishments of the human race dedicating and consecrating them to the glory of God; she is the voice of creation, interprets the worship of all visible creatures and offers it to God in an acceptable and filial way.

Verse 9-11

The grammatical contruction in the last three verses of this chapter is significant. It uses the future instead of the present or past tense. This intimates the prophetical character of the vision. Whenever the voice of authority shall speak in the Church to give God honor, glory and thanksgiving, the priesthood shall obey quickly and joyfully with heart and soul. The Church gives glory, adoration and thanksgiving to God day and night. The words "honor and glory" have respect to the divine attributes, while the word εὐχαριστία a word not used in the Septuagint, points to the gifts of revelation to the Church, primarily to the eucharistic Presence, before which the living beings and elders are bowing in adoration and thanksgiving. The next chapters clarify this. The eucharistic body of Christ being inseparably united with His divinity and personality in the sacred species makes the words refer to the Divinity.

The living beings direct their adoration to "him who sitteth upon the throne", because He is the Creator and Lord, Guide and Disposer of all things. They have a personal motive for worshipping Him, for in His providence He has clothed them with divine prerogatives and disposed everything towards choosing them to be His representatives. He is the life of all living things, because He has eternal life within Himself. The same thought that inspires the living beings moves the elders to adoration and thanksgiving. They take up the canticle which the episcopate intoned and offer God the worship of all creatures, because He, the Creator, the Lord and Preserver, has chosen them for special love and adorned them with the dignity that is theirs.

In both instances, that of the living beings and of the elders, the act of worship is the same and the reason for it is the same. They worship Him as the *Life Giver,* the source particularly of SPIRITUAL LIFE. For that reason they emphasize and repeat the phrase "who liveth forever and ever". The Four are called LIVING BEINGS, because they share this life-giving power with the Deity possessing all the sources of spiritual life that God has entrusted to His Church; They are therefore in an eminent degree an image of God, "who liveth forever and ever", because the spiritual life of the world can be derived only from them, the sources of which they have received in the priestly ordination and episcopal consecration. As God gives life to whom He will, so these beings are able to communicate LIFE to whomever they choose and therefore are aptly called "LIVING BEINGS". They received this power to give life from Christ (Jo. V. 26). The elders are of a subordinate station yet share this life-giving power with the living beings; hence they also worship the Possessor of eternal life, who "liveth forever and ever". They do not possess the fullness of the sources of life as do the "living beings"; therefore they are not given that attribute.

In this allegory the episcopate is portrayed with its divine endowments. The theme of their act of worship is "holy, holy, holy", because the holiness of God is the source of all life to His creatures. The farther anyone advances in holiness, the more abundant is his own life. The episcopate possess all means of holiness personally. They have been entrusted with the life-giving doctrine of Christ, and they herald it without fear of error. They have the pastoral officc to lead their followers with security along the way of eternal life, because the seven lights of the Holy Spirit enlighten and guide them. They possess the fountain-heads of life in the seven sacraments and they have the power of inspiring by blessings and other external aids to piety and a religious life. And they have the power to confer all these active gifts on others. Also the elders repeat the significant words "who liveth forever and ever" in their act of worship, for they participate with the living beings in their divine endowments. The living beings voice the most effusive gratitude for this inestimable gift and power of dispensing LIFE to all rational creatures; and being so closely united with the source of Life, they become σύνθρονοι with God. And therefore because they animate all rational creatures on earth and bring into existence the new creation, the new heaven and the new earth, they are called the LIVING BEINGS.

The elders cast their crowns before the feet of God to betoken that the spiritual power they possess is from Him, and that they wear the crowns and rule in His name. Their crowns are not diadems but στεφάνοι, symbols of victory, wisdom and spiritual life. All human and divine wisdom possessed by the priests is as nothing in the presence of God. No one may wear a crown in the Church as of his own right, for all power is derived from God, and all honor and majesty belong to Him.

In verse 11, the last word of the elders is "power", while in verse 9, the final word of the living beings is "thanksgiving". The episcopate having intoned the Lord's Prayer, "Our Father who art in heaven", expressed in the words "holy, holy, holy", conclude their adoration with the word thanksgiving to utter their gratitude for the power received over the eucharistic Lord, which is the crown of all divine gifts and may be called its sum total. The priesthood, in the word "power", continues the Lord's prayer, "Thy kingdom come, thy will be done on earth as it is in Heaven" begging God to exercise His power to make this world His own by putting an end to the reign of evil.

In this vision including the next chapter, the inspired writer has drawn a vivid picture of the constitution and organization of the Church, as it functions today. This demonstrates clearly that the Church was fully organized under the direction of the apostles. It embodied everything essential, everything unchangeable. The episcopacy is shown in the figures of the LIVING BEINGS, because it embodies all the means of spiritual life personally. The priesthood is a distinct body, and the being represented as such reveals its distinctive importance.

The phrase "who liveth forever and ever" may be an allusion to the inanimate gods of paganism or to the mortality of Caesar, especially to Domitian, who wanted to be styled "Lord and God".

The divine character of the Church is portrayed in this and the next chapter. Her human character subject to suffering is depicted in chapter XII. The Church has a dual nature, the one human and the other divine, so she may aptly be the mystical body of Christ and carry on the work of salvation. In the prophetical books, Israel is sometimes called the servant of Jahve; in the New Testament, the Church is not a servant but a personification of Christ Himself mystically embodied in a living and functioning organism. When the Church suffers, the cause of Christ suffers; when the Church is triumphant, Christ is triumphant. In the Apocalypse, heaven means the Church under the aspect of her divine origin and endowments; the Temple whenever mentioned is the visible representation of the Church, for there the throne of God is "set"; the court of the Temple is the world.

CHAPTER V.

Westminster Version

And I beheld on the right hand of 1. him who sitteth upon the throne, a scroll with writing both on the face and on the back, and sealed down with seven souls. And I saw a strong angel proclaiming 2. with a mighty voice: 'who is worthy to open the scroll and to break the seals?' And no one in heaven or on 3. earth or under the earth was able to open the scroll or to behold it. And 4. I wept much, because no one was found worthy to open the volume or to behold it. Then saith one of the elders to me 5. 'Weep not; behold, the lion who is from the tribe of Judah, the root of David, hath conquered, so that he can open the scroll and its seven seals'.

And within the space between the throne 6. and the four living beings, and in the midst of the elders, I saw a Lamb standing, as it were sacrificed; he had seven horns, and seven eyes, which are the seven spirits of God, sent forth unto all the earth. He came and took the volume out 7. of the right hand of him who sitteth upon the throne. And when he had taken 8. the volume, the four living beings and the twenty-four elders fell down before the Lamb, each holding a harp and golden vials full of incense, which are the prayers of the saints. And they sing 9. a new canticle, saying: 'Worthy art thou to take the volume and to open its seals, for thou wast sacrificed, and didst redeem to God through thy blood men from every tribe and tongue and people and nation, and 10. hast made them a kingdom and priests to our God, and they shall reign upon the earth!'

Then I beheld, and I heard around the 11. throne and the living beings and the elders the voice of many angels, and their number was myriads of myriads and thousands of thousands, and they 12. said with a loud voice:

"Worthy is the Lamb who was sacrificed to receive power and riches and wisdom and might and honour and glory and blessing!"

And every creature which is in heaven 13. and on earth and under the earth and in the sea, and all things in them, I heard saying: 'To him who sitteth upon the throne and to the Lamb be blessing and honour and glory and might for ever and ever!'

And the four living beings said, 14. 'Amen', and the elders fell down and worshipped.

B.

THE BOOK OF THE SEVEN SEALS.

1. The Sealed Book. Chapter V.

Verses 1-5.

Verse 1

More and greater revelations come to the notice of the Seer in this vision. He beholds a scroll on the right side of the One sitting upon the throne. A scroll of parchment or papyrus was usually written only on the inner side. This scroll, however, was written within and without and was sealed with seven seals instead of the usual ONE. This might attribute a great depth of meaning to every word. Or there was no vacant space left on the parchment, because God's revelation is herewith ended and completed. Again it might be the summing up of all the revelations in the Old and New Testaments or an interpretation of all that was revealed but remained obscure and unintelligible and was a fuller statement of what was partially revealed and begun in the Old and was to be fulfilled in the New Testament and fulfilled in the manner related in this book. Or it might finally mean that the new prophecies are written on the inside and the old ones on the outside; they were thus secured against a clear understanding of them or their scope by the seals, or they could be clearly understood only when the seals are broken. The purpose for God's revelations and the designs of His Providence were begun and gradually elaborated in the Old Testament and will be completed in the New; and this book will narrate the manner and order of their completion.

The *seven* seals put the stamp of sacredness and completeness on the book and the revelations contained therein. Clement of Alexandria quotes Homer and Callimachus, who hold SEVEN to be the sacred number. In Babylonian literature, it is held in the same estimation.

Since this book was to reveal future happenings, it will contain the history of the Church from the time St. John received the revelations till the Last Judgment. The seven seals denote a closed book with contents that shall remain a secret until they shall become historical facts or be in the course of fulfillment. The seals contrast this book with the "little booklet" of chapter X., which is open in the hand of the angel making possible an understanding and interpretation of it and its content before their fulfillment. This book is sealed and remains closed, even after the seals are opened (VI. 1 ff) intimating an intentional mysteriousness in God's designs, when he reveals the future destiny of the world and yet does not reveal it. His purpose obviously was to keep the *time* and also the *manner* of fulfillment veiled in mystery.

It is noteworthy again that St. John avoids any anthropomorphism in speaking of God. The Greek text does not say that the book is "in the right hand" of Him who sits upon the throne but simply "at the right". When the Lamb takes the book, the Seer comes nearest to an anthropomorphism but again he took the book "from the right" of Him upon the throne.

It is difficult to explain the opening of the book. Is there only one piece of parchment or are there seven? The Vulgate states that the Lamb "opened the book", while the Greek text says he "*took*" it. In chapter six, He opens only the seals. The Greek text is therefore the logical one. There may be seven pieces of parchment rolled up into one roll each one sealed down with its own seal the outer one covering the ones yet remaining unopened. However, if there was but one piece of parchment, it could be explained to be sealed with seven seals at the outer edge. The contents are actually revealed by opening the seven seals only not the book. Yet the whole narrative has an allegorical meaning and is accommodated to human understanding. The successive events in the future history of the Church will be visibly represented to the Seer under allegorical figures, which might be easily remembered but left to the future for an interpretation. Hence the seals are opened in the next chapter, but the book remains closed.

Verses 2 and 3

A strong angel appears on the scene now and with a sonorous voice heard throughout creation asks, who of all God's creatures would be worthy of opening the book. Only a powerful angel armed with a divine commission might address and challenge all creation. It may be St. Michael. No creature offers to open the book, for none was found worthy of the divine task. The one who will loose the seals and open the book must be able to bring the revelations contained therein to fulfillment.

To loose the seals means to make known or reveal the contents of the book, and to open the book means to know their import and to direct all human affairs to fulfill the divine plan. He must have the worthiness, the knowledge, the wisdom and the power to bring to pass all secrets of the book through the instrumentality of free agents and enable the Church to accomplish the purposes of her existence.

No one was found worthy to even look at the book, because it contained revelations written on the outside. Neither angels nor men know the revelations, and how then could they direct all secrets towards their fulfillment? The hope of revealing the secrets dwindles to the vanishing point. In the last negative particle, the Greek language brings this out with a finesse. The threefold division of creation given here was a common way of classifying all creatures both in the Old Testament and in the writings and preachings of the Apostles. (Phil. II. 10).

Verse 4

Quite some time must have elapsed without any further action, because St. John wept "much". During the almost audible silence, he lost heart, when no one offers to open the seals. He weeps not from lack of confidence in the words of our Lord (I. 19) or the promise of the other voice (IV. 1) but from fear lest no one be found worthy of opening the seals to reveal the mysteries of the future. Though his grief is entirely needless, arising from the appearance of things and insufficient knowledge, he fears that the world would remain steeped in misery, if the hopes of the prophets would be doomed to disappointment.

Verse 5

The elder who re-assures St. John was not a mere interlocutor but one who had experienced the victory of Christ and who was convinced of its certain actualization for the world. He solves the difficulty by saying:: "The lion of the tribe of Juda will be able to open the book and break the seals".

Jacob called his son Juda a lion's whelp (Gen. XLIX. 9). In connection with this title, he prophesied concerning Christ. His words addressed to Juda under that title have a greater meaning in the typical sense when they point to Christ. In many passages of the Old Testament Christ is compared with a lion, and God is also given that name. In Jeremias (II. 15), the hostile kings are dubbed lions attacking Juda. The lion is ever the figure of royalty and supreme ruling power in voice and strength. By human descent, Christ is of the tribe of Juda, the noblest scion of that tribe, and he therefore eminently deserves to be styled the lion. He will overpower the enemy of man and will rule. He will even in His human nature be worthy to take the book and break the seals, to reveal its hidden contents and to direct all future evolutions of history, so that the "will of the Lord shall be prosperous in His hand" (Isa. LIII. 10), for He is "the Father of the world to come".

The opening of the scroll now recedes into the background, and the elder dwells at length on the titles of the Victor. It seems his definite intention to interpert in its true meaning the text of Isaias (XI. 1-10). Christ is there called the "root of Jesse", and here the "root of David". The latter is to emphasize His royal descent and His right and worthiness to rule and direct the whole future world. The elder using the words of Isaias to show their application and import substitutes the name of David for that of his father Jesse. This substantiates Christ's right to the other titles: "Father of the world to come, the Prince of Peace" and his right to occupy the throne of David. Isaias says of him directly: "He shall sit upon the throne of David, and upon his kingdom" (Is. IX. 6-7). The archangel Gabriel also declared this: "And the Lord God shall give unto Him the throne of David His father; and He shall rule in the house of Jacob forever. And of His kingdom there shall be no end" (Lc. I. 32-33). He has overcome the world; therefore He has the right and power to direct and carry it to its final consummation (Jo. XVI. 33). In this reference to the prophecies of Isaias is also an allusion to the second book of kings. The purpose of that book is clearly shown on its pages to relate the establishment of David's kingdom and to represent it as everlasting.

2. The Vision Of The Lamb.

Verses 6-7.

Verse 6

After the elder had conjured up in St. John's mind the titles and prerogatives of the lion of the tribe of Juda, the Seer suddenly beholds a Lamb before the throne standing in the space between the living creatures and the Deity, sharing the throne with the Deity and ranking thus above all other creatures. From the context it appears that He was not visible before, but St. John recognizes Him at once. The Baptist had named Him "lamb of God", and the Evangelist was a witness of this and recorded it in the Gospel.

St. John had used the word ἀμνὸς in the Gospel for the title, "Lamb of God". Elsewhere in the New Testament, as well as in the Septuagint, the same name, ἀμνὸς is a title of Christ. But the word does not occur in the Apocalypse. Again the word ἀρνίον used here, does not occur in the rest of the New Testament to mean Christ. St. John uses it in the Gospel to designate the little ones of the flock (XXI. 15). But even St. John calls Christ the ἀμνὸς in the Gospel (I. 29). This bespeaks a different role for Christ in each place, the Gospel and the Apocalypse. The word τὸ ἀρνίον translated is "the Little Lamb" and is used 29 times in 12 chapters. This is very significant. It appears to be intentionally used to attach a totally different meaning to the title "lamb" in the Apocalypse than in the Old Testament or elsewhere in the New. The allusion in our text to Isaias (XI. 10) and to Psalm 109 will help to get the reason for using τὸ ἀρνίον as a title for Christ in the Apocalypse.

The position of the Lamb is in the center of the tableau, on the throne of God. This throne is immediately surrounded by the four living beings, who are the σύνθρονοι and in a wider circle by the elders. The angels and the crystal sea are not mentioned now. The position which the Little Lamb occupies in the center of the tableau is as significant as the title. The position is that of the priest offering sacrifice (Heb. X. 11-14) and represents the Lamb as the victim and the priest.

The allusion to St. Paul's letter calls in review Psalm 109. In that Psalm the Royal Prophet very significantly links the victory of Christ over His enemies on the day of His strength and the day of His wrath (Apoc. XIX. 15) with His eucharistic priesthood. It is as a priest according to the order of Melchisedech that He shall be victorious, shall crush and wipe out the enemies.

The reason for His worthiness to open the scroll and break the seals is because He is "as it were sacrificed". The word σφάζω means immolated or sacrificed in divine worship. The word is not used for the death of Christ. It is used only in the

Apocalypse to denote His sacrifice. It might mean the same as the Latin word "jugulatus", which connotes the idea of immolation in divine worship, as the animals were sacrificed in the Temple. But it is not used for the sacrifice of the cross anywhere in the New Testament. This again, as every term connecting sacrifice with the Lamb of the Apocalypse, is very significant. It makes a distinction in the manner of offering between this and that of the sacrifice of the Cross.

The text does not say that He appears with wounds, as it does of the Beast (XIII. 3), who has a "death's wound", nor as Isaias says of the ἀμνὸς (LIII. 7), who is led to the slaughter, to a bloody death to atone for the sins of the world, which He bears under the divine will. Although He is the same Christ, the ἀρνίον as sacrificed has a different role in the scheme of Redemption than the ἀμνὸς who died a bloody death.

The words would remain very mystifying, if verse five did not refer to Isaias. The eleventh chapter of the great prophet points to a solution and shows the significance of the "Lamb standing as it were sacrificed". The original Hebrew text of Isaias, as well as the Septuagint, (XI. 10), does not read as our Vulgate: "HIS SEPULCHRE shall be glorious"; it reads: "HIS REST shall be glorious". All modern interpreters agree that St. Jerome gave his own private interpretation to this clause when he translated it into Latin. Its real meaning becomes evident when it is compared with other texts of Isaias (LXVI. 1), and with other passages of the Septuagint (Ps. 131). In the literal sense, it could not mean the SEPULCHRE of Christ. Isaias says (LXVI. 1): "thus saith the Lord . . . what kind of a house will you build me? and of what kind the place of my rest?". Psalm 131. 8 has the same meaning. Interpreters almost universally hold now that St. Jerome should have translated the first text of Isaias with the same meaning. The above passages UNMISTAKABLY point to the "place of rest" of the Lord in the Holy of Holies, the throne of God above the Ark of the Covenant. The text in the Septuagint (Isa. XI. 10) reads: "And there shall be in that day a root of Jesse . . . in him the Gentiles shall trust, and his rest shall be glorious". This text is Messianic and indicates Christ's "place of rest" in the Church. The elder when introducing the Lamb to the Seer calls Him the "root of David" for the reasons explained above.

But he thereby calls attention to the prophecy of Isaias. The "place of rest" of the "ROOT OF JESSE". They shall put their trust in the "root of Jesse" at His place of rest, and He shall rule them as a king rules His warriors and vassals. This can mean nothing but the REAL PRESENCE, the EUCHARISTIC CHRIST.

God's presence in the Temple was of a shadowy form, the Shekhina in the holy of holies; in the tabernacles of the New Law, He is really present in a constantly visible form. This is the Holy Eucharist which makes every church a temple and every tabernacle a throne of God. Verse five of this chapter points directly to Isaias when it uses the title ROOT OF DAVID for the Lamb. The new rendition of the old text lays stress on the royalty of Christ and demonstrates His kingship in His eucharistic throne over all creation and makes Him King of kings and Lord of lords. He will through the power of this sacred mystery "make all things new", create the new heaven and the new earth, to which Isaias points and which Christ asserts both in the introduction and peroration of this prophecy.

The new title of Christ, the peculiar phrase "as it were sacrificed" and the intentional reference to the eleventh chapter of Isaias; the position which Christ holds as a sacrificing priest in this tableau together with the allusion to St. Paul's letter to the Hebrews including Psalm 109: All these significant facts show that the "Little Lamb" is the EUCHARISTIC CHRIST.

The temple of Christ is every Catholic Church, where He dwells in the eucharistic mystery. The Sacrifice of the Mass is the sacred mystery, in which Christ is "as if sacrificed", is truly and mystically slain or immolated. The sacrifice is inseparably united with the bloody sacrifice of the Cross, because it represents and renews it. Through the sacrifice of the Mass, Christ becomes present, establishes His throne in the Church and extends the effects of His death on the Cross and carries out the purposes of God to completion. To outward appearance He is dead in the Eucharist, so there He rests "as if immolated". But the Holy Eucharist is the throne of God through the inseparable union of Christ with the Father and the Holy Spirit. St. John makes it easier to visualize this by avoiding all anthropomorphisms of the Godhead.

The Real Presence of Christ has been the shrine at which

the nations of the world have worshipped, and for which they have fought. It has been the standard for the armies of Christ. His soldiers, the martyrs, confessors and virgins have ever fought and bled for the altar and the cross. The prediction of Isaias is fulfilled in Christ's place of rest, His Eucharistic Presence. The reason then why St. John chose the word, "Little Lamb", for the sacrificial Lamb of the Apocalypse appears evident, to distinguish this mystery from the mystery of the Incarnation. By his presence in this mystery, He will unlock the secrets of the future and be the Master and Director of history and the world's final destiny.

Isaias explains, and Psalm 109 avers that Christ will execute judgment upon the world. After this will be the gathering of the Jews "the second time" and their conversion. In and through His power in the eucharist Christ will effect this judgment. And then the millenium, the days of endless peace will dawn upon the world.

St. John records in the Gospel (XII. 31) the words of our Lord, stating that the judgment of the world and of Satan is near: "Now is the judgment of the world: now shall the prince of this world be cast out". After He instituted the Sacred Mystery at the Last Supper, He announces that the judgment upon the "prince of this world" is pronounced, that he is already judged (Jo. XVI. 11). Satan was judged in Heaven as the leader of the rebellious host and was condemned; but as prince of the world, he was not judged until the Holy Sacrifice was offered at the Last Supper by Christ and the power to continue it conferred upon His Apostles. When Christ instituted the Sacred Mystery, the judgment on the prince of the world was pronounced, though the execution of the decree was not carried out till He died on the Cross. He dethroned Satan when He died. Yet the empire of Satan was still existing. The judgment of Satan as prince of the world was to be completed throughout the world and down the ages by the destruction of his empire. Christ's death on the Cross was not to be a mere memory of history but a living reality which would constantly manifest itself through the Holy Eucharist. The "Little Lamb" will continue the destruction of the empire of evil through the centuries. The work of overthrowing this empire of evil had been going on quietly and invisibly after the Last Supper until now, but soon after the reception of these revelations its break-up was to be enacted more visibly and manifestly. Christ's judgment will strike all who will not accept this mystery but choose to adhere to the empire of Satan. The recital of the judgment begins with chapter six.

The Lamb has seven horns and seven eyes, which are the seven Spirits of God. The relative pronoun, "which", in the masculine gender refers to the last word. It would be unnecessary redundancy to have the two terms, "horns" and "eyes", stand for the same thing. Only the eyes are the seven spirits of God. These seven spirits are the seven gifts of the Holy Spirit according to Isaias (XI. 2). They symbolically represent the union of the Holy Spirit with the Lamb. He had stated before when appearing in human form (II. 18), that He "has eyes like to a flame of fire" and "has the seven spirits of God" (III. 1). The eucharistic Lamb also has the seven spirits of God. Before the throne of God, these seven spirits abide in one form (IV. 5); but as the eyes of the Lamb, they have a mission to all the world. The Holy Spirit is thus revealed as proceeding from the Father and the Son. This symbol of the Holy Spirit as the eyes of the Lamb also demonstrates Christ's omniscience in the Holy Eucharist and His supervision over all rational creatures. Through the activity of the Holy Spirit, He searches out all souls who can be saved and participates with His human nature under the eucharistic species in all the works of the Spirit, enlightening, sanctifying and guiding the Church. He has in this mystery knowledge of the past, present and future, knowing the plan and end of God's whole revelation.

The seven eyes allude to Zacharias (III. 9), where the theocracy to be reconstructed is represented before Jesus, the highpriest, as a rock. Upon this rock the prophet sees seven eyes. These seven eyes as in our text here are emblems of the presence of the Holy Spirit, who watches over and guides events by His comprehensive knowledge to the end of developing and perfecting the re-established theocracy after the Babylonian Captivity. The highpriest, however, could not accomplish this, for he had neither the knowledge nor the power to chisel the theocracy into perfect form. The servent of God, the ORIENT (Zach. III. 8), will accomplish it. The restored theocracy is then the foundation upon which the perfect Messianic Empire shall be built. The eucharistic Lamb will complete that everlasting empire. In His omniscience, He will watch over the destiny of the Church, will direct and bring to reality the will and plan of God in creation and revelation.

Horns in prophetical language are emblems of power, strength or armies, and of glory, honor and brightness. Horns also represent kings and kingdoms. The seven horns of the Lamb evidently mean the seven sacraments. The sacraments are all connected with the mystical death of Christ in the sacrifice of the Mass. They are the weapons with which the eucharistic Lamb will destroy the kingdom of Satan. They are moreover the glory of the Church, because through them souls are cleansed, saints sanctified and made glorious with grace even in this world. Each of the seven sacraments constitutes a spiritual kingdom of its own, elevating men to a different rank in the kingdom of God and in the course of ages peopling Heaven with so many armies or kingdoms of elect.

Verse 7

The two different tenses used in the text makes the description very vivid. "He went and he has taken (it)". He does not receive but takes the scroll. This reveals His equality with the Father. Both His divinity and humanity are present in the Eucharist by virtue of His Hypostatic Union giving him the right to assume the role of Judge over all creatures, as He is "the Father of the world to come". St. John fails to explain how a Lamb could take a book and open it. So the symbolism must not be pressed too far. It is all shrouded in mystery, and in this sacred mystery Christ will bring to light the things still hidden in the plans of God. By inspiring His faithful followers through the eucharistic mystery with his own divine life, zeal and courage, He will use them as willing agents to achieve the victory over the enemy.

3. The Adoration Of The Lamb.

Verses 8 to end.

Verse 8

According to the context here, the four living beings and the elders bow down in adoration before the Lamb. The episcopate gives the example and the priesthood follows. Although the living beings are nowhere described as having hands, they and the elders seem to hold harps and patens filled with incense.

Incense was used in the earliest times during the celebration of Mass. The Apostolic Canons recognize it as a lawful symbol of adoration to be proffered the eucharistic Christ. The incense are the prayers of the worshippers. In these symbolic acts, the living beings and the elders offer the worship of the believers and submit their own minds to the mysterious Presence, in which Christ will direct the free actions of man and will rule and bring into actuality God's purpose for the sanctification and happiness of all mankind. For that reason the whole Church adores Him.

Harps are musical instruments used for exalted praise, worship and thanksgiving. They indicate that the Church will conduct the cult of the Eucharist with hymns and canticles. The peoples will no longer worship idols but the living presence of their God in the Eucharist.

Verses 9-10

The "new canticle" which the living beings and the elders sang was not a mere ode for a festive occasion, such as was often composed for a special festival in the Old Testament (Ps. XXXII. 3; XXXIX. 4). In the new order of life and worship inaugurated by Christ, a new canticle was called for. But the present canticle was more and presages more. The Lamb will take charge of future history; He will open the book of destiny and will renew all creation (XXI. 5). The Church celebrates the new order not by a mere new canticle but by a complete new liturgy, one that rises to vastly higher heights of expressiveness in worship than the liturgy of Old. It includes the eucharistic Lamb in Jahve's worship offering a purer love and filial devotion, since the shadows have passed away and the Great Reality dwells among men. The specific reason for the whole Church to pronounce Him worthy of taking charge of human destiny is that He "was immolated". And since for this reason he has merited to assume the government of the world, it behooved that a new worship be instituted to give divine honors in the new Holy of Holies. This new liturgy is in accord with the other things renewed, the new name (II. 17), the new Jerusalem (III. 12) and the new earth (XXI. 1).

And since the Little Lamb renews the sacrifice of the Cross, of the ἀμνὸς, the "new canticle" is all the more pertinent, because the Church understands that He will give new life to all things and actualize all that God has planned for the renovation of the human race and for its felicity.

When the Israelites had passed through the Red Sea, they sang a new canticle of thanksgiving and exultation for their deliverance from the domination of Pharaoh. Now the ruling and ministering body of the Church sings a canticle to commemorate the victory of Christ and to exult in His sacrifice, in consequence of which He has delivered them from sin and slavery and endowed them with a dignity far above that of Moses. They have an extraordinary reason for pronouncing Him worthy to take the scroll and open its seals, because His blood has not been shed in vain for them, since they have been washed in its cleansing flood. The Little Lamb has proven His power by selecting them out of every tribe and tongue and people and nation regenerating and sanctifying them. Though the ἀμνὸς shed His blood and rendered satisfaction to God for all mankind, the effects of His sacrifice did not reach all as yet. The Little Lamb has selected those who now thank Him for the election and through them is bringing the fruits of His bloody death to those still in the shadow of death. For these reasons and because the Church is a visible proof of His power and worthiness, they pronounce Him worthy to take charge of the future world.

Another reason why the episcopate and the priesthood find the Little Lamb worthy to direct the future world is that He has ordained them priests and has disposed to them a kingdom, so they may share in working out His redemption and ruling His followers. Their internal dignity is the priesthood (Thomas) and their office in the world is to rule. This is a clear definition of the meaning of the word πρεσβύτερος. That word was adopted by the apostles to designate the priesthood of the Church and distinguish it from the Jewish priesthood. As is clearly stated here and in chapter one (I. 6), the word means "priest", one who has the power and right to offer sacrifice.

The Vulgate reads: "Et fecisti nos Deo nostro regnum, et sacerdotes". "Thou hast made us to God a kingdom and priests", whilst the Greek text might be translated, "and hast made them a kingdom and priests". But the context makes the meaning the same, and the Vulgate translation is therefore correct and agrees with other parts of the New Testament. This verse agrees with what our Lord said to the apostles at the Last Supper: "I dispose to you as my Father has disposed to me a kingdom; that you may eat and drink at my table in my kingdom: and that you may sit upon thrones, judging the twelve tribes of Israel". These words obviously take in view the Holy Eucharist and call attention to the thrones of the elders. By instituting the Eucharist, Christ has sacrificed Himself in this mystic manner and founded a spiritual empire, in which those who are ordained and appointed to rule have the priestly dignity. His empire is much more sublime in its scope than any earthly empire, because it rules the souls of men. Its power is in the spiritual order and its jurisdiction pervades the whole temporal order of the world. The presbyteroi proclaim the eucharistic Lamb worthy to take the scroll and break its seals for having ordained and elevated them to His priesthood, conferring on them a power more intensive and extensive than that of any worldy officials and enabling them to participate in His sovereignty over the world, who Himself is King of kings.

The four words "out of every tribe and tongue and people and nation" signify the universality of adoration that will be given at the shrine of the eucharistic Lamb and connote the catholicity of the Church. The bishops and priests are selected by the "seven eyes" of the Lamb from all nations to offer up the prayers and worship of the elect. This alludes to the prophecy: "From the rising of the sun even to the going down, my name is great among the Gentiles, and in every place there is sacrifice and there is offered to my name a clean oblation". (Mal. I. 11). Those words bring to mind the development of the eucharistic cult, the great eucharistic congresses, perpetual adoration, forty hours' devotion, Corpus Christi processions, Benediction of the Blessed Sacrament, frequent and daily communions and many other acts of worship. These developments give a glimpse of the future, when the Lamb shall have won the victory over all nations, and all shall serve Him.

The Crystal Sea is not mentioned in this chapter, which deals with the position and dignity of the Eucharistic Lamb in the Church. He is the central figure. The four living beings, the episcopate, form the inner circle around the Lamb; the twenty-four elders, the priesthood, the outer circle. The priests also minister to Christ and deal directly with Him. The crystal sea, the lay members of the Church, who are ruled and guided by the elders, are united with the eucharistic Lamb only indirectly the priesthood and episcopate offering Him their prayers and good works. They are a "royal priesthood", like the kings of the Old Testament, not permitted to offer sacrifice (1 Peter, II. 9), though their dignity is far above that of the Old Testament kings. They rule upon the earth, because they are winning the victory over the world, the flesh and the devil; and in heaven they will share the kingdom with Christ.

Verses 11 and 12

The strong angel (v. 2) was the only one mentioned in this chapter, but now the vision grows larger, and St. John hears a countless number of angels taking up the refrain. Though they do not participate in the work of redemption, they exult in the fulfillment of God's plans, which will ultimately annihilate the power of His adversary. The angelic host has its position before the eucharistic throne outside the circle of the elders between them and the crystal sea. This puts the dignity of the priesthood in the Church above that of the angels (Heb. II. 5 etc.). The four living beings and the elders had proclaimed the Lamb worthy to loose the seals and to open the book of destiny. And now the angels in one accord with a great voice proclaim Him worthy of all the honors due God the Father, and again because "He is immolated". The Church proffers the Lamb all praise and honor in FOUR terms, denoting the universality of worship that shall be given the Lamb, after He shall be victorious over the earth. The angels express their homage of Him in the Sacred Mystery in SEVEN terms, in the sacred number. They add to the words of the Church "power and riches and wisdom" and substitute "strength" for the word "might". "Strength" calls special attention to the seeming weakness of the Little Lamb. The angels have no lyres nor incense bowls; they express their hymn only by the voice; they use the definite article only before the first word, "power", to combine all seven in a symphonic unity; they proclaim Christ in the Eucharist deserving all adoration and possessing all power and riches and wisdom and strength and honor and glory and benediction. This figure of speech, employing the conjunction before each word of worship, reveals the adoration of the angels to be not a succession of ideas but a simultaneous simple thought. These seven words sum up all worship due the Deity. The number of angels in the Greek text is myriads of myriads and thousands of thousands. These indefinite numbers denote that the hosts of angels hovering around the Eucharistic Mystery is countless.

Verses 13 and 14

All creation joins in glorifying the Lamb, because He will be the redemption of all. (See Rom. VIII. 21). St. John hears the voice of creation worshipping Christ in the eucharistic species, through which He will work out universal redemption. The earth, the sea, the underworld and heaven are standard divisions of creation and express the universality of worship accorded the Lamb as much as the Father. Rational and irrational creation thus join in one choir to swell the harmony of worship that shall rise to the altar. The worship of all creatures except that of the Church and the angelic host is but an echo of the higher form of worship given by those who know what they worship. (See Irenaeus. III. xi. 8).

Verse 14

The Four Living Beings pronounce the "AMEN". Some commentators hold that the eucharistic sacrifice had always been ended with this "Amen" at Ephesus and elesewhere in Asia Minor. "The whole passage is highly suggestive of the devotional attitude of the Asiatic Church in the time of Domitian towards the person of Christ. It conforms to Pliny's report '(Christianos) carmen Christo quasi deo dicere secum invicem' and the statement in Eusebius, H. E. v. 28 ψαλμοὶ δὲ ὅσοι καὶ ᾠδαὶ ἀδελφῶν ἀπ' ἀρχῆς ὑπὸ πιστῶν γραφεῖσαι τὸν λόγον τοῦ θεοῦ τον χριστὸν ὑμνοῦσι θεολογοῦντες. ' (H. B. Swete).

The voice of authority in the Church began the worship of the Lamb; the priesthood took it up; the angels gave Him the perfection of worship, and all creatures echoed the refrain and made it universal. The Church then says "Amen", and the priesthood forever continues to renew this acknowledgment of the supreme dominion of the Lamb, the King of kings. St. Justin writes that the people pronounced "Amen" after the consecration (Birkhauser p. 116).

In this chapter the sacrifice of the Mass is depicted in a symbolic vision. Because Christ offered Himself in a bloody manner on the Cross as a complete satisfication to God for all the sins of men, the sacrifice of the Eucharist and the Real Presence are possible. The Mass is an unceasing renewal and representation of the sacrifice of the Cross. In the Mass Christ is "as it were immolated". Through this mystic sacrifice He exercises the power merited in the bloody sacrifice to destroy the empire of Satan. All worship of the Church is centered around the Mass; from it flow all saving effects of His bloody death; and the power to administer the sacraments is transmitted in and through this sacrifice. These are the reasons for the acknowledgment Christ receives in His eucharistic presence from the episcopate and priesthood of the Church, the angels in Heaven and all creatures. In the preface of the Mass this is expressed. Before the sacrificial act is performed, the priest sings the praises of God and Christ and joins his canticle with the choirs of angels in language very similar to that spoken by the elders. All creatures, except the reprobates, join with the priesthood of the Church in giving the eucharistic Lamb the adoration due Him.

CHAPTER VI.

Westminster Version

And I beheld when the Lamb opened one 1. of the seven seals,
and I heard one of the four living beings say, as with a voice of thunder,
'Come!' And I saw, and behold, 2. a white horse, and he that sat thereon
had a bow and there was given him a crown, and he went forth conquering and to conquer. And when he opened the second 3. seal, I heard
the second living being say, 'Come!' And there went forth a second a
red horse, and to him that sat thereon 4. it was given to take peace from
off the earth, and to cause men to slay one another and there was given
him a great sword. And when he opened the third seal, I 5. heard the
third living being say 'Come!' And I saw, and behold a black horse, and
he that sat thereon had a balance in his hand. And I heard as it were a
voice 6. in the midst of the four living beings say: 'A quart of wheat for
a shilling, and three quarts of barley for a shilling; but harm not the oil
and the wine!' And when he opened the fourth seal, 7. I heard the voice
of the fourth living being say, 'Come!' And I saw, and 8. behold, a pale
horse, and he who sat thereon — his name was 'Death', and Hell followed
him, and there was given them power over the fourth part of the earth,
to kill with the sword and with famine and with the plague, and by the
wild beasts of the earth.

And when he opened the fifth seal, 9. I beheld under the altar
the soul of those who had been slain for the word of God, and for the
witness they bore.

And they cried with a loud voice, 10. saying; 'How long, O Sovereign
Lord, holy and true, dost thou delay to judge and avenge our blood
upon them that dwell upon the earth?'

Then there was given to each of them 11. a white robe, and they
were told that they should rest yet a little while, until the number should
be complete of their fellow-servants and their brethren, who are about
to be killed even as they.

And I beheld when he opened the sixth 12. seal, and there was a
great earthquake and the sun became black as haircloth, and the full moon
became as blood, and the 13. stars of heaven fell on earth, as casteth the figtree her winter fruit when shaken by a strong wind; and the heaven passed
14. away like a scroll that is rolled up, and all the mountains and islands
were removed from their places. And the kings 15. of the earth, and the
great men, and the generals, and the rich, and the strong, and every man,
slave and free, hid themselves in the caves and rocks of the mountains, and
they say to the mountains and to 16. the rocks: 'Fall upon us, and hide us
from the face of him who sitteth upon the throne, and from the wrath
of the Lamb, for the great day of their wrath 17. hath come, and who
can stand?'

III.
THE SEALS

A.
OPENING OF THE FIRST SIX SEALS

1. The First Seal. The White Horse.

CHAPTER VI
Verses 1-2.

Introduction.

The Church laboring to liberate the human race from the domination of Satan must discredit some widely accepted principles, standards of so-called virtues, which afflict the world. And her aims will not be reached and the peace of God established until those principles have been outlawed. The opening of the seals shall reveal those false ideals and the price which the world must pay for liberation from them, after it had freely accepted them and submitted to the despotic domination of Satan. The awfulness of the cost should not appall us, as it is only just that man should suffer the temporal consequences for his submission to Satan.

The first of these satanic doctrines is that victory by force is glorious, that "might makes right" regardless of the destruction it showers upon fellow-creatures. Throughout the ages, Satan founded and spread his dominion by his arrogated right to subjugate men and nations. It differs from the ideals of Christ, which invite acceptance of His standards by free choice and which bring safety and salvation by the abolition of false dogmas and the propagation of truth, justice and charity. Christ does not ride about killing His adversaries. But Satan will fight to the last ditch shedding blood to maintain his principles and compelling acceptance of them. The various phases of this conflict between the Church and Satan will be revealed in the opening of the seals, the blowing of the trumpets, the emptying of the bowls upon the world and the final victory of Christ. Conquest, considered glorious by pagan man, necessarily entails war, which produces bloodshed, famine and pestilence. But the world is regenerated by suffering. Satan then defeats himself, and Christ wins the victory through the persecutions which His followers must endure. The White Horse coming first on the scene is an allegorical figure of Conquest and of apparent victory over the Church.

Verse 1

The Lamb opened one of the seals whilst all creatures in the vision were bowed in adoration before Him. St. John saw the accomplished fact. One of the four living beings calls on him in a voice of thunder to come and see. It is an invitation to note all the details of the vision. The voice of thunder is the voice of the lion. According to ancient interpreters, the lion is the emblem of St. Mark, the secretary of St. Peter. But since the four living beings are the episcopate, the lion being the emblem of royalty represents the papacy. With the voice of authority that reverberates around the world, the supreme bishop commands all people to receive these revelations.

Verse 2

After the voice of the lion has died away, a WHITE HORSE appears in the vision. Where it is seen is not stated. The horse carries a rider who has a bow. A crown is given the rider. It is the figure of conquest. "Conquering that he might conquer" is a Hebrewism meaning a state of affairs or continuous action that would go on a long time.

In Roman times, the white horse was a symbol of victory won by the help of the gods and was thought to have some relationship with the supreme or imperial power. Roman historians in describing the "Triumphs" celebrated by victorious generals on entering Rome say that they rode in chariots drawn by white horses (Dio Cassius, H. R. XLIII. 14) (H. B. Swete, p. 86). Suetonius reports that Domitian accompanied his father and brother during the Judean war riding a white horse (Dom. II). This rider on the white horse would then allude to Domitian.

The extension of the Roman power to Asia is foretold in the Third Sibylline book (v. 175-178):

Mais lorsque viendra le commencement d'un autre empire,
Blanc et beaucoup de tetes, de la mer occidentale,
Qui dominera bien despays, en fer trembler beaucoup,
Et excitera la crainte chez tous les roi, etc. (P. E. B. Allo, p. 49).

White symbolized imperial domination of the conquering emperors of Rome. Ramsey (Letters p. 338) observes that the imperial solemnites in Asia were modelled after the "Triumphs" at Rome. Among the Persians, white was the sacred color, the color of the gods. Emperor-worship reached its full development under Domitian, who loved to hear himself styled "the divine", "the deity" etc. The fact of Domitian's accompanying his father and brother on a white horse in the re-conquest of Palestine was so noteworthy that historians make special mention of it. And because in pagan belief the color associated the rider with the gods, St. John probably found this description of the vision a clear intimation to the Christians, as to whom the white horse and its rider represented, that he did not give any further explanations of its significance. The clause "he went forth conquering and to conquer" shows him to be a mighty conqueror who conquers for conquest' sake. In St. John's day it could be none other than the Roman Emperor.

Some interpreters hold that the rider on the white horse is Christ Himself, (Iren. IV. 21/3; Victorinus and Andreas followed his opinion) and they remind us of chapter XIX. 12, where Christ appears riding on a white horse. Others hold that the white horse symbolizes the victorious Gospel, and the rider represents the preachers of the Gospel throughout the world.

The rider has a bow in his hand when he appears. This signifies not a speedy inauguration of conquest but an actual fact. He either had it by his own right and strength, or it was given him on an earlier occasion. He may have used the bow for a long time prior to this appearance and inflicted many wounds with it. The crown of victory is given him as St. John looks on.

The crown given the rider refers pointedly to his character. It calls to mind the words of Christ before Pilate: "Thou shouldst not have any power against me, unless it were GIVEN thee from above" (Jo. XIX. 11). Until Christ surrendered Himself into the Roman power, no one could injure Him. The words, "there was given him a crown", also allude to what is said of the beast in chapter XIII. verses 5 and 7, namely that he can persecute the Church only as long as it shall be GIVEN HIM to do so. The inference is that the rider on the white horse is an enemy of the Church. For just as the empire could have no power over Christ unless God gave it, so it could have no power over the Church unless God gave it. The word used for "crown" is στεφάνος, which might be a myrtle wreath, a perishable wreath denoting victory. But the Hebrewism in the sentence indicates a long and continuous victory, that it is a violent and often-renewed persecution of the Church.

When God appears in chapter IV., He appears under the symbolic colors of judgment as actually judging the Church and the world. With the opening of the seals begins the narration of these judgments, of which St. Peter had written: "For time is, that judgment should begin at the house of God" (1 Peter IV. 17). The voice of thunder inviting St. John to come and see is from the head of the Church. Judgment will begin where the lion, the papacy, resides. Some Christian writers say that the first persecution raged throughout the empire, but others are not so positive whether it raged in Rome or not. Thus persecution under Nero must have spread to the provinces, because Antipas was martyred (II. 13) quite some time before these revelations were written. The second general persecution was under Domitian A.D. 95 and was confined to Rome. St. John was banished to Patmos during this persecution. Domitian was assassinated soon after he began the persecution, which lasted about a year. Nerva, who succeeded him 96-98 A.D., was kind to the Christians. St. Timothy, however, was slain in 97 A.D. during a popular outbreak. Trajan decreed the third persecution and made it general and extended it to Asia Minor. Giving the crown would then point to Trajan and his successors, who enacted laws placing the penalty of death upon adherence to Christ and Christianity and branding the refusal to worship the emperor high treason.

The use of a bow for a weapon signifies the infliction of wounds on the Church but not destruction. The sword is the symbol of complete destruction as is evident in chapter XIX. 20, where it is decreed for the followers of the beast. Although the bow is far-reaching, it can only single out individuals for death. The persecutions did not end until the spring of 312 A.D., when Constantine won the victory over the army of Maxentius. Julian, the apostate, during the 18 months of his reign revived persecution in the form of severe penal laws and ridicule but also made a few martyrs. (See Ps. X. 3). The Christian religion was declared the religion of the empire by Theodosius in 392 A.D., and pagan worship was condemned as high treason.

To make Christ the rider on the white horse would not be very logical. Such an interpretation would destroy the unity of the scene. It would have Christ opening the seals under the form of a Little Lamb and at the same time and in the same place riding forth under the form of a man as a mighty conqueror. This is absurd. Besides, making this rider Christ would be an affront to His majesty and be entirely unworthy of Him. Everywhere in the Apocalypse He is portrayed as the King of kings, whose commands are obeyed and adored by heaven and earth. To represent Him with a bow killing whom He can hit would be to put Him on a level with the three other horsemen, who symbolize the scourges with which God will afflict the world. Christ is nowhere in Scripture a scourge. His Person and role in the scheme of revelation is too sacred and sublime to be cast in the guise of a killer, and no inspired writer assigns such a role to Him. The sword with which He will destroy the wicked is His word, His command. Again He wears many diadems (XIX. 12), while this rider wears only a crown or wreath.

It seems equally illogical to consider the rider the victorious Gospel or the Church conquering the world. If the Gospel were a warlike conqueror, it would be a death-dealing rather than a joyous message. Zacharias (IX. 10) shows that the Gospel of Christ or His Church does not go forth as a warrior, for "the bow of the warrior shall be broken". That prophecy may point directly to the figure of this "conqueror". The Church actually did break his bow. This scene rather recalls the words of Jeremias (L. 9-14) describing a victorious world-empire going forth to kill.

The above considerations make it appear at least logical that the rider is an enemy of the Church. The words, "a crown was given him", seem to dispel all doubt about it. It is an enemy of the Church who will persecute her and inflict death on many of her adherents. And since he is a great conqueror who rides a white horse, it designates the Roman Empire. He may, of course, be said to be the associate of the succeeding horsemen and simply represent "Victory" over the Jews and all other rebellious subjects, but it would again be the Roman Empire.

2. The Second Seal. The Red Horse.

Verses 3 and 4

The second living being now calls the Seer to watch the opening of the second seal. The voice is not like thunder but that of the figure which symbolizes sacrifice and bloodshed. A Red Horse, the symbol of war, appears. The rider receives the power to take peace from the earth and start slaughter and bloodshed. In addition to this, a "great sword" is given him. The calf, representing sacrifice and the priesthood of the Church announces this vision. The Greek text uses the word σφάξουσιν, which specifies the act of killing one another a sacrificial act giving God supreme adoration.

God calls the destruction of the Jews by the Babylonians a victim or holocaust (Soph. I. 7; Isa. XXXIV. 6), and Jeremias calls the destruction of the Egyptian hosts "a sacrifice to the Lord" (Jer. XLVI. 10). As in the Old Testament, so it would mean here the defeat and annihilation of armies, enemies of God who are either apostates or heathens. The "great sword" reminds us of the sword of Jahve in Isaias (XXXIV. 6).

The words "to take peace from the earth" and "that they should kill one another" denote insurrections and revolutions within the empire. The Roman Empire was at peace when Christ was born. But after the Crucifixion, those who refused to accept Christ as the Messias grew more fanatically nationalistic and finally rose in rebellion against the Roman government, which ended disastrously for them in the destruction of the Temple and the city of Jerusalem in A. D. 70. But Titus, the Roman general, had avoided as much bloodshed as possible. Hence, excepting strongly fortified cities, he left the nation intact. The Jews however, after the rejection of Jesus Christ, were easily misled by false prophets who advised rebellion against Rome. In the second century there were furious uprisings in Cyrenaica, Egypt and Cyprus with much bloodshed everywhere. Hadrian, the emperor, decided to build a heathen city on the ruins of Jerusalem. This exasperated the Jews and incited them to a general uprising under Bar Cochba, who claimed to be the Messias and was acknowledged as such by Rabbi Akiba. Hadrian then resolved to destroy the whole nation. The destruction is symbolized by the "great sword" given the rider on the red horse. Hadrian in a war that lasted five years from 131 A. D. to 135 A. D. devasted the whole country and put an end to the Jewish national existence. The inhabitants were either massacred or sold into slavery. The ruin of the nation was complete and final. Fifty cities and a thousand villages and 480 synagogues were wiped out. The Christian population did not take part in that rebellion and was not molested. After the fall of Jerusalem, they had lived largely beyond the Jordan. Some time after this war, Hadrian built Aelia Capitolina on the site of Jerusalem, in which only Christians of Gentile origin might reside. Caesarea became the Christian metropolis of Palestine.

This extinction of the Jewish nation was of vast importance to the Church. It proved the divinity of its Founder, for He had predicted this ruin. And this holocaust gave public divine honor to Jesus Christ and His words. It brought about the abolition of the Jewish rites and sacrifices and ended the distinction between Jew and Gentile Christians. The word of our text, *σφάξουσιν*, fits this destruction with precision.

The rider on the red horse is not an envoy of peace but a messenger of war. At first the Church was at peace. After she had grown strong enough, first the Jews, then the Romans were permitted to persecute her. By the year 131 A. D., the Jewish nation unified in its opposition to Christ presented a solid front against any more conversions. Then the nation was extirpated, and the surviving remnants were dispersed among the Gentiles. This freed the Church from Jewish influence.

The vision of the Red Horse calls to mind that of Zacharias (I. 8), wherein a red horse appears with a rider. Many interpreters consider this rider to be St. Michael. Other riders appear and report to the first one that the earth is at peace. The angel then begs God that while the world is in that state to consolidate the chosen people after the captivity, before greater upheavals in human society should come. In VI. 6, black horses appear, which are understood to be the Medes and Persians, who go to subjugate Babylon; and Victory (white horses) follows them. Babylon had oppressed God's people and was therefore doomed. The similarity of these visions in the Apocalypse with those in Zacharias suggests the opinion that the three horsemen are sent forth to exterminate the Jews, the first persecutors of the Church.

The possessor of the "great sword" is a figure of War and is again the Roman Empire under the aspect of a destructive force. The great sword is not a dagger for self-defense but the great weapon of destruction in the hands of War. The sword is given the rider to exterminate the obstinate Jewish nation. He, the Wielder of it, is God's agent and uses the sword to work out God's purposes. Thus the Church won the victory over Judaism without a special effort, as Isaias indicated (XLIX. 26), the enemy eating its own flesh. And although the Roman Empire was itself an enemy of the Church, it put an end to the first enemies and persecutors of Christ and His Church, as the Babylonians had put an end to the unfaithful Jewish nation in their time. And in this order, with one enemy destroying the other, the Church became victorious.

3. The Third Seal. The Black Horse.

Verses 5 and 6.

Verses 5-6

The third living being who has the face of a man calls St. John to see the vision of the Third Seal. A Black Horse appears. The description fits the personification of famine. Famine with exorbitant prices for food follows in the wake of war. Food is rationed and weighed during war. St. John hears a voice from the midst of the four living beings announcing the price of food. It is a 'denarion' for a quart of wheat and the same for three quarts of barley, and the voice adds, "and do not harm the oil or the wine". The common coin for a day's wages was a denarion. And the measure given is in Greek a χοῖνιξ which is about 1½ lbs. of wheat, or 2 lbs. according to some authorities. The rations fixed and the prices stipulated make it possible for a laborer to support his life. Wheat was the food of the rich. Ordinarily twelve such measures could be bought for a denarion. Three times as much barley could be bought for the same coin. Barley was mainly the food of the poor. And so the price fixed for barley made it possible for a hardened laborer to support a family in this time of famine.

The voice that announces all this remains invisible, but is probably that of the third living being, or may be the voice of all four living beings. The whole episcopate would be interested in providing for the temporalities of the Church and for the materials of sacrifice and the sacraments, oil and wine. In the designs of God, the Church exercises a restraining influence on the forces of destruction and will permit the avenging agencies to weild only such power as will not be disastrous to her interests or unbearable to the faithful (Mt. XXIV. 22). The voice is the authoritative and prophetical voice of the Church. She is directly interested in this scourge, because there are many faithful Christians in Palestine. They are not in danger from the "great sword", because they had not rebelled against the empire. They must be specially provided for and not included in the scourge of famine, which will follow the war and be more universal in its effects than the sword. The check upon the black horse and its rider is such that, though he may cause the Christians some hardships, he may not dare to bring them to starvation or deprive them of the Sacrifice or the sacraments, he may not harm the oil and the wine at all. During a protracted war, the occupations of peace and the crops that depend on annual seeding and cultivation are neglected. Yet on them mankind mainly depends for sustenance. In this instance the Church intervened and provided for her members.

Not to "harm the oil and the wine" has been interpreted to mean that God does not desire the utter ruin or extermination of any people that can still be converted but purifies it by suffering; hence He tempers His chastisements with mercy. Again it has been explained to mean that fruits gathered from permanent plantings, such as grapes and olives, will still continue to grow if they are not wantonly cut down. The prophetical books give another view. These and the historical books in many passages exhibit wheat, barley, oil and wine as the principal crops of Palestine. Whenever the prophets promise God's blessings to the people for faithful service, they hold out to them an abundance of wheat, oil and wine (Joel II. 24). In a long war the wheat would dwindle down. But the command to leave the oil and wine intact points directly to Palestine. Oil and wine were the principal export crops. They were to be left for the benefit of the Christians who shall inherit the land after the wicked Jews were exterminated or expelled (See Jer. XXXI. 5; Osee II. 22). The neglect of raising field crops during the war will make the Christians dependent on the permanent olive groves and vineyards. Since the Christians were but a fraction of the population these export crops will enable them to procure wheat and barley in return to sustain their lives. When the whole population was dependent on the production of the soil, it would starve on oil and wine alone.

The limit on the curtailment of food or its exorbitant price directed by the authority of the Church, shows her solicitude for the temporal well-being of her members, that they have a sufficiency not an abundance and that those who want to eat must work. The rich commercial Jews shall now feel the sting of poverty which they have inflicted on the Christians by persecution. The Christians being reared in poverty and self-denial will be able to support themselves and their families in the hard times to come, whilst of the rich Jews, whose money will dwindle away in financing the war, only those who are hardened by toil shall be able to earn a living and survive.

4. The Fourth Seal. The Green Horse.

Verses 7-8.

Verses 7-8

When the Fourth Seal is opened, the EAGLE invites St. John to come and see the figure. A horse of so strange a color appears, that the Seer calls it a "Green Horse". The color suggests to the mind a body decaying with pestilence. Death rides the horse. This personification of death presages utter depopulation or DEATH for this "FOURTH PART" of the earth. He is to use as his means the four great plagues of mankind enumerated in the prophets, the sword, famine, pestilence and the beasts of the earth. The last word, "death", stands for pestilence, while the name of the figure stands for "extermination". The other figures of the second and third scourges are at his service; and besides that, he has pestilence and the wild beasts to aid him in his sweeping job of destruction.

The figure itself has often been interpreted to mean "pestilence". But that would not be logical. It would be strange reasoning, if Pestilence were imagined to kill with war, famine and pestilence. The language of the Apocalypse is very often extraordinary but never ridiculous. It is always dignified and worthy of an inspired book. Therefore the figure is simply what the text says, a personification of Death (See Exod. XII. 23). The text recalls Jeremias (XV. 2-3) and Ezechiel (XIV. 21), where such utter annihilation is predicted, that those who flee from one form of violent death shall be met by another, until all the wicked are consumed. Violent death is a punishment for apostasy.

Hell follows or accompanies the figure of Death. This "hell" in our translation is the underworld, the world of the dead. The underworld receives all who fall into the hands of Death.

This clause reiterates the significance of the fourth figure, that a whole nation shall enter the realm of death. It suggests also the eternal punishments that shall be meted out to the persecutors of the Church.

The Vulgate says: "And power was given him over the four parts of the earth"; the Greek text has the "FOURTH PART" of the earth. The Greek text is the original and makes the context logical. It points clearly to the Jews for the reason that the same scourges named by Jeremias and Ezechiel were meant for them. Those plagues put an end to the Jewish nation under Hadrian, as they had done under Nabuchodonosor. The Jews were punished in both instances for unfaithfulness to God: in the first suppression and captivity the reason was idolatry and apostasy; in the final destruction, it was adherence to superstition, the refusal to heed the call of grace to the true Church of the Messias and persecution of the members. The scourges being the same would reasonably in both instances apply to the same nation. The FOURTH PART of the earth, as the original text has it, takes in only a small portion of the known world and thus unmistakably points to a small country such as Palestine. It is a smaller part of the earth than that effected by any ONE of all the following judgments. The clause "and power was given him" likewise agrees better with the Greek text, because it sets limits to the ravages of Death. If he had been given unlimited authority over the FOUR PARTS of the earth, it would have been equivalent to the extermination of the human race. If the human race was to survive, the sweeping concessions made to Death had to be restricted to a small part of the earth.

In the Old Testament, all nations that led the chosen people into apostasy and idolatry were punished by a world-power, and if that world-power oppressed God's people it was in turn punished by another. The Jews strove to enslave the Church at its beginning by imposing Jewish practices on her. Many fell into the snares of the Judaisers; and those sectaries gave the Church no little concern. They hindered her work everywhere and instigated persecutions. Some of the letters reveal this (II. 9). But all was stopped when the expedition under Hadrian ended the Jewish nation and scattered the remnants among the peoples of the earth.

The beasts of the earth are mentioned as one of the plagues;

and in fact lions became quite numerous in Palestine or any subtropical country when they were depopulated. Man is superior to those beasts only when well armed and sufficiently numerous to cope with their superior physical strength. When the able-bodied men had fallen in battle, the feeble and old, the women and children could not defend themselves against the attacks of wild beasts. However, at no time in history have large numbers of men fallen victim to beasts of prey, and they are mentioned here in the last place to intimate how complete the extirpation of the deicide Jewish nation should be. After the strong ones of the nation had been killed by the other three plagues, the weak remnants should be eaten by the beasts (Ezech V. 12; XXXIII. 27).

5. The Fifth Seal. The Souls Of The Martyrs.

Verses 9 to 11.

Verses 9-11

When the Lamb opened the Fifth Seal, no living being intervened. At the opening of the other four seals, the Church militant was vitally interested, and St. John saw in the visions such events depicted as were intimately bound up with her fate on earth. But the present vision is of the next world, and the Seer beholds it as it appears. He sees the altar of burnt offering, the altar affording God the highest act of worship in the Levitical Law. Under that altar are the souls of those who had been sacrificed for the word of God, for their constant faith and for their open profession of it before the authorities of the empire. This vision is timed after the destruction of the Jewish nation in 135 A. D. Trajan's bloody persecution spread through the empire is over, and new events are foreshadowed in this vision.

The Temple of the Old Testament and the ceremonies of worship prefigured the *real* worship of the New Testament. Hence the revelations in the Apocalypse are repeatedly made under the forms of the Levitical worship. The altar of burnt offering stood near the entrance of the Tabernacle or Temple (Lev. XVII. 6). The soul was thought to be in the blood of the victim (Lev. XVII. 11). And its blood was to be poured out at the foot of the altar of holocausts (Lev. IV. 7). That altar prefigured the altar of the New Testament, the Cross. The martyrs were God's most precious holocaust; their lives were given for Him in the highest act of worship and were a propitiation for the sins of the world and a plea for its conversion. Their blood was shed at the foot of the altar, the Cross. It was always the custom of the Church to keep holy relics of the martyrs under the altars and also to offer the Sacrifice of the Mass upon the tomb or relics of martyrs. It has long since been a positive law of the Church to offer no Mass except upon holy relics. In chapter IV., no altar is mentioned, but it is implied. God appears seated upon the altar, His seat of judgment; and the Lamb appears there also in chapter V.

The reason why these martyrs were sacrificed was because they accepted the word of God and believed in it. They testified to their belief in divine revelation before the world. They believed in One True God, rejected polytheism, caesar-worship and the worship of his statues. In the place of Caesar, they adored Jesus Christ and proclaimed Him their Lord, because He is the King of kings. His Real Presence was their sacred shrine. St. John guards the secret of the Divine Presence here, too, as elsewhere. The testimony of these martyrs put God's word and law above the laws and decrees of Caesar. For this and for refusing worship to the gods of Rome, they were "sacrificed".

This scene may be timed shortly after the end of the Jewish wars, because the souls of the martyrs call for just retribution upon their persecutors, who have gone unpunished. They suffered death under Nero, Domitian, Trajan and the pagan mobs. They have seen full justice meted out to the persecuting Jews and now deem the time ripe for the avenging of their own death. They waited for a continuation of the judgment that struck the Jews; but it seems to have come to a standstill. Now they venture the question.

The question they put to God is "quousque tandem", 'to what extent, Lord', wilt Thou permit Thy enemies to triumph? In their zeal for God's honor, they call for a manifestation of His justice and holiness to the Romans as well as the Jews. Otherwise The Jews might seem to have been punished only for rebellion against Rome not for contempt of Christ. But if God executes judgment upon Rome, His justice and holiness will be manifest to Jew and Roman, and He will vindicate the truth of His Word before the whole world. The prophets of Old frequently address God in like manner by their prayers. When they are to announce the destruction of Israel for its wickedness, they remind God of the jeers of His enemies, who in their proud and malicious attempt to overthrow Him by the subjugation of His chosen people boast that their gods are stronger than the God of Israel. And God replies that He will sanctify His name when He will inflict just penalties upon the persecutors of His people. The souls find the defilement of God's honor hard to bear and likewise the derision and defiance flung into His face by the victory of the enemy over His Church. The triumph of the wicked seems to show that God is not the Lord of the world. They know how the faithful are being slaughtered and God's kingdom diminished instead of extended. His holiness therefore cannot suffer the wicked to go unpunished nor His faithfulness to let His promises be nullified. Besides, the martyrs have made their sacrifice, have shed their blood in vain, as it appears, if no fruits of victory are made visible. For such reasons the souls call upon God for judgment not for hatred or thirst of revenge. Their words are but desires made audible by their blood.

Verse 11

The souls had to appear in a visible form that their reward immediately after death might be shown. Each one receives a white robe as a token of innocence, glory and happiness until the Day of Judgment. Their eternal happiness is secure as soon as they are with Christ, and they receive the fruits of their sacrifice in the joys and rest of the eternal kingdom and the Beatific Vision. But they must submit to the divine Will. They begged for a hastening of the day of judgment to vindicate God, but are told that He will direct events to His greater glory and that of His faithful followers, for there are still others who must have time to work out their destiny. They will be avenged in a little while. From God's viewpoint, centuries and thousands of years are but "as a day", but "a little while"; from an earthly viewpoint, however, the "short time" in which Antichrist shall be permitted to reign is not centuries; and in that place the context calls for an earthly measure. The souls of the martyrs do not wear crowns, because their full reward will not be theirs until after the Resurrection, when all the fruits of their sacrifice shall have been gathered.

The same consolation is given to the martyrs of Antichrist — that they are to rest from their labors, and their works shall follow them (XIV; 13). This vision reveals that God's judgments do not begin until those are converted and secured in grace and sanctity who have the will to be saved. No one shall be cut off at an inopportune time so as to lose his chance of salvation.

6. The Sixth Seal. The Powers Of Heaven Are Moved.

Verses 12 to the end.

Though the following verses describe future happenings somewhat as our Lord describes the end of the world, they would seem a useless repetition of the Gospel narratives, if they meant nothing else. That is consistent with the whole theme of this book. However, the events narrated here may be the type of events that shall be fulfilled near the end of the world and refer to them in an accommodated sense but are as described the mystical garb of past history, which was prophecy in St. John's time.

Verse 12

The key to the first part of this verse is furnished by St. Paul (Heb. XII. 26): "Now he promiseth, saying: 'Yet once more, and I will move not only the earth, but heaven also . . .'. Therefore receiving an immovable kingdom, we have grace". In that statement is involved a spiritual earthquake, for not only the earth but also heaven is moved, and it therefore is an omen of more than disturbances in civil society. It imports a spiritual or religious revolution. The same thing appears in similar language in the prophets (Agg. II. 22-24; Isa. XXIV. 17-23), where the overthrow of empires has a higher meaning than a mere earthly change. Some have interpreted this passage to mean upheavals in the Roman Empire that preceded and prepared its overthrow. Several emperors ruling at the same time instigated a civil war and each fought for the supremacy. This civil war met its decision at Rome, when Constantine defeated Maxentius and became sole emperor. The external unity of the empire was restored, but its strength was shaken to its foundations. Then Constantine in 330 A. D., moved the seat of empire to Constantinople, and Rome lost its prestige and world-dominion. But since the earthquake in the prophecies of Aggeus means the re-establishment of the theocracy, the earthquake in our text might mean the overthrow of paganism.

The Lamb would be interested far more in directing world-evolutions towards a spiritual change than a political one. And although the civil wars resulted in the victory of Constantine and eventually the transfer of world-dominion to Constantinople, the concomitant result of the civil war was the inauguration of religious liberty. This made the Church triumphant after the most bloody of all persecutions, that of Diocletian. Christ had now overthrown the pagan order in the world. This would seem a theme worthy of record in an inspired book and be of first and keenest interest to the Lamb, when He opened this seal. It was a social and religious earthquake ending the domination of paganism, emperor-worship and the tyranny of Satan. Now the Church would have an even chance with him in world-conquest. Heretofore she was at a disadvantage, the whole world-controlling power of the empire being leagued against her and aimed at her destruction. Although this was connected with the civil wars, the political change was only a minor detail. Religious liberty for the empire and freedom for the Church put the civilized world in a different status. Paganism had held undisputed sway since before the days of Abraham; Satan had had his way with the world: but now his empire was shaken; and he beheld his battlements tumbling down, his idols falling from the pedestals, his temples turned into sanctuaries of the eucharistic Lamb or demolished by the zeal of the Christians, and his philosophies discarded or purified and employed to prepare men's minds for the theology of Christ. The work was done rapidly and thoroughly as soon as the Church had an even chance with the enemy. By 392 A. D. the Catholic Religion was proclaimed the religion of the empire, and paganism was branded high treason. This is probably what the earthquake means. God had promised such an earthquake at the birth of His son (Agg. II. 7, 8). The "great" earthquake in this verse was then not a shake-up of the earth in diverse places in the first century nor a political or social upheaval and overthrow of governments or transfer of its seat but the victory of the Lamb over paganism and the establishment of Christianity in its place.

The darkening of the sun and moon and the falling of the

stars points to the Church as the object of this vision. The lights of heaven are darkened and fall. Christ said to His apostles: "You are the light of the world". Here the sun symbolizes the greatest light in the Church, the divinity of Christ giving force to her teaching authority. If the prophecies in the second chapter of Joel (II. 31) are written in chronological order, this vision would seem to mean the same, that the blackening of the sun to make it resemble the sackcloth woven from the hair of the black goat would represent the authority of the Church though still existent faded in its influence. The divinity of Christ enables the Church to enlighten the world with the knowledge of truth and warm it with love of God. And the ability of the Church to effect this fades in the proportion in which she recedes from this overshadowing power. Whatever portion of the Church loses this doctrine and belief loses its energy to enlighten the world (1 Jo. I. 1-7; I. 9).

The moon symbolizes the changeable elements in the Church, which derive their right from her divine teaching and ruling authority. The blood-color of the moon would signify disobedience, which instigated by the heresies engenders hatred and persecution within the Church to the point of bloodshed. In the Old Testament, a bloody moon foreboded war and bloodshed. Heresies in the Church have been very prolific of hatred, distrust, envies, vainglory, murders and war.

This description points to the Arian heresy. That heresy was put on foot immediately after the overthrow of paganism, in 318 A. D. Arius, a priest in Alexandria, began publicly to deny the divinity of Christ. That denial, if universally accepted, (which God will not permit), would ultimately extinguish the light of the Church and of the world. When in the Old Testament the synagogue lost the presence of God, the true worship disappeared, and the nation was enslaved and dispersed. The Prophet Jeremias wrote in the Lamentations (II. 1): "How has the Lord covered with thick darkness the daughter of Sion in His wrath". Ezechiel called the day on which it began a day of darkness (XXXIV. 12; Joel II. 2). The authority which God had conferred upon the chosen nation had been withdrawn, and it was ejected into the darkness outside. The symbols of the prophets were adopted by St. John and served to express similar revelations. Many heresies were rampant in the world at the birth of Arianism, some of which denied the divinity of the

Holy Spirit, who guides, enlightens and strengthens the Church. But Arianism almost engulfed the world in complete darkness. How heinous a sin heresy is may be learned from the apostolic Fathers. Irenaeus says of the heretics, when relating the meeting of Polycarp with Marcion, "such was the horror which the apostles and their disciples had against holding even verbal communication with any corruption of the truth" (Iren. III. iii. 4).

Verse 13

Stars in the Apocalypse (I. 20) are the bishops and priests of the Church. This falling of the stars then forebodes a great apostasy of bishops and priests. The stars fall as do green figs torn from the tree by a violent wind, by physical force. These figs are the ὀλύνθοι and grow in winter, most of which are of a poor quality and fall off in spring without ripening. It may denote those bishops and priests who are worldly-minded, unworthy ministers, having entered the priesthood from worldly motives. And for that reason they do not grow to maturity but are blown off the living tree, the Church, in the storms of heresy that sweep over the earth. Storms and winds in prophetic language represent rebellions, revolutions and invading armies.

The falling of the stars from heaven describes graphically the defection of apostates from the supernatural state of grace into the state of sin. And their falling as thickly as figs, when a loaded tree is shaken by a violent gust of wind, describes nothing more precisely than the apostasy of the clergy into Arianism during the fourth century. Great numbers of bishops apostatized, and they intrigued to have the orthodox ones deposed and banished. Tearing the figs from the tree by violence probably indicates that many bishops and priests did not consent to Arianism but were driven into it by the emperors or by wicked and scheming aspirants to the episcopate. The emperor Constantius banished all bishops who did not communicate with the Arians. Half of the bishops of the Church became Arians. In the Council of Rimini, 359 A. D., the hypocrisy of the Arians and the threats of the emperor induced nearly all bishops present, 400 in number of whom but 80 were Arians, to sign a semi-Arian creed. By fraud and open violence the Catholic truth was torn from their hands.

This vision alludes to various parts of the Old Testament.

In Lamentations (II. 1), the Holy City is said to have fallen from heaven. It had fallen from the state of being the center of the theocracy, to which dignity God had elevated it. The figure of the figtree adopted here alludes to Nahum (III. 12). There the falling figs meant the forts and strongholds of Assyria. Bishops and priests are the strongholds of the Church and should be forts of strength to protect the spiritual life of the members and keep them secure. This allegory fits the ravages of Arianism and other heresies of the time perfectly.

Verse 14

The first part of this verse depicts in a few words the result of what is stated in verses 12 and 13. The apostasy from the Church was so extensive under Arianism and the other heresies of this time, that the Church may be aptly represented as a volume rolled up. From the viewpoint of the laity, the true Church must have been hardly discernible. The teachings of the Arians were loudly broadcast, and the true doctrine was suppressed and hushed up by the emperors and fanatical Arian bishops and became hidden in a maze of Arianism and semi-Arianism. After 355 A. D., the Arians were everywhere triumphant. St. Jerome is reported to have exclaimed that after the Council of Rimini "the whole world groaned to find itself Arian". This, hyperbole though it was, had some justification, as modern Church-historical research has proven.

In Isaias is the identical figure (Is. XXXIV. 4-5). It there presages the judgments to come upon Israel and Juda and after them upon all nations that led them into idolatry. These judgments began in 725 B. C., when the Kingdom of Israel was extinguished and the remnants of the people were led into the Assyrian Captivity. And they were completed in 586 B. C., when Nabuchodonosor led the remains of the Kingdom of Juda into the Babylonian Captivity. The theocracy then became "folded together as a book", almost disappearing. Jeremias verifies the almost complete extermination of the chosen people by counting 4600 souls, who were led captive into Babylon (Jer. LII. 30). In verse 5 of the above chapter of Isaias, the sword of God executing judgment upon the Jews "is inebriated in heaven", meaning that the judgment began at the theocracy, and the sword of God wielded by the Assyrians and Babylonians was drunk with the blood of the

Jews; and then it turned in a drunken fury upon Idumea and extinguished that nation.

The second part of verse 14 points to the overthrow of the Roman Empire proper. The narrative connects it so closely with the first part of this verse, which reveals the greatest reduction of the true Church in its history, to show how the heresies of this time shall occasion the downfall of the empire as cause and effect. Not the persecutions called down the wrath of God, because the Church had overcome paganism and established a Christian empire in its place; but the heresies, the division of Christianity and corruption of the true faith, called for punishment. The fall of the empire followed speedily upon the spread of the heresies that shattered the Church.

In prophetical symbolism, mountains stand for kingdoms and empires (Is. XIII. 2; XLI. 15-16; Apoc. XVII. 9), independent states; whilst islands are dependencies, colonies, provinces and principalities. The mountains may in this instance also represent bishoprics. The penalty decreed upon the empire for heresy shall wrest from its jurisdiction the kingdoms, provinces and principalities of which it was composed. And the governors, tribunes and other magistrates who promoted heresy shall lose their positions. The Byzantine Empire had become heir to the Roman Empire, and it became the principal promoter of heresy, for which it lost the whole western part of the empire including Africa. The punishment came before the true faith was too far lost or the faithful too small in number to establish the Church among the immigrating barbarians. The prophesy was fulfilled by the inroads of these wild hordes during the fifth century. They overturned the seats of government within the empire and founded other kingdoms and principalities in other cities.

Verses 15-17

The effects of the barbarian invasions on all classes in the empire are briefly related in the final verses of this chapter. Seven classes who represent the Roman population are enumerated to describe vividly the total subversion of the Roman order. The sacred number SEVEN betokens the judgment of God and of the Lamb. It falls upon all Roman inhabitants: Upon the kings who rule under the suzerainty of Rome; upon the proconsuls who ruled the provinces; upon the officers of the army; upon the wealthy whose riches will only increase their danger; upon the strong warriors whose physical strength will avail them nothing because God is coming against them; upon the slaves who lived from the riches and luxuries of the Romans and upon the free citizens who enjoyed the prerogatives of Romans. All class distinction shall be wiped out, and all men shall be brought down to the same level of misery. One class of men shall have no more chance of escape than another, and those who do escape shall escape with their bare lives. They all flee for safety and hunt for any hiding-place they can find.

In threatening punishment upon the proud and the idolaters, Isaias uses language and paints a picture of the terrors of war against the Jews similar to the description in our text (Is. II. 10, 19, 21; III). When the Philistines came with innumerable warriors the Israelites hid in caves and dens (1 Kings, XIII. 6). In every instance where similar language is used in the Old Testament, the people hid from fear of an oncoming enemy. Our Lord advises the same thing when Jerusalem should be besieged (Mt. XXIV. 16-18) (Osee X. 8). The language of verses 16 and 17 also alludes to St. Luke (XXIII. 30). The words of our Lord do not take in view the end of the world but the destruction of Jerusalem. The inference from the similarity of diction in the various texts is that the end of the world is not considered here. In speaking of that event our Lord says: "The sun shall be darkened and the moon shall not give her light". If in the prophecy here the sun became black with smoke or volcanic ashes, the moon would no longer be visible. And since the whole chapter is couched in figurative language, these verses must also be taken figuratively. The last verses possibly give a glimpse of the end of the world as the final results of the judgments, which began at the house of God and then exterminated the Jewish nation and later the heretics in the Roman Empire. These verses are a pre-vision of the oncoming judgment not a statement of its actual arrival in this part of the Apocalypse.

The Romans might well desire the mountains to fall upon them and hide them from the barbarians, because all, except the Burgundians, were savage and bloodthirsty. They put to death all warriors and officials who fell into their hands. It was done with God's permission to wipe from the earth those Romans who were infected with moral and physical corruption resultant from the spiritual leprosy, HERESY. In all revolutions, God will protect his Church. In the barbarian invasions the Church was miraculously spared, and for the sake of the Church the city of Rome was spared. Attila and Genseric turned back and spared the city at the solicitations of Pope St. Leo. The Church then came in touch with and converted the barbarians, and these new Romans replaced the ancient people.

In the opinion of the Fathers of the Church, the end of the world was due soon after the revolt of the nations from the Roman Empire. The "revolt" mentioned by St. Paul (2 Thess. II. 3) was understood to mean the overthrow of the empire. This interpretation has long ago been discarded. The "revolt" pointed out by St. Paul means probably more than an apostasy from the Church rather a revolt against God altogether. The overthrow of the Roman Empire does prove the coming fulfillment of all prophecies in the Apocalypse including the Last Judgment. How far in time the successive acts of the judgment shall be separated can never be predicted in advance. The prophets relate in successive verses future happenings that are many centuries apart in actual time at fulfillment, and they give no indication of the long intervals that shall separate the events.

Not the true believers dread the judgments of God but the heretics and hypocrites who live an earthly life and are of the earth. The Arian bishops and priests sought the honors and income of the Catholic Church for their enjoyment and aggrandizement and accepted their appointments from the emperors. They denied the divinity of Christ. This implicitly denied the belief in the Real Presence of Christ in the Eucharist. The Lamb now comes upon them in judgment. Hence they fear His wrath. Before the invasions they spread Arianism among the barbarians. But in the turmoil of the invasions, Arianism almost disappeared. The Vandals adhered to it, but their kingdom was destroyed by the Greeks, and the nation later vanished under Saracen conquest. The Visigoths clung to it for a while but also fell under the sway of the Saracens for seven hundred years. Arianism was thus rooted out by the barbarian invasions and Mohammedanism, and the unity of Christendom was saved until the sixteenth century.

The words, "their wrath", attribute to the Eucharistic Lamb the same divine power and honor as to the Father. The "great day" of Almighty God mentioned often by the prophets means literally the final triumph of Christ over the world at the dethronement and damnation of Antichrist. It is the day on which the domination of the wicked shall end, and on which Christ shall begin to reign unhindered. The heretics and wicked of all classes in Roman times are filled with dread of the Little Lamb, because the day of judgment seems at hand. In the knowledge of their guilt, their troubled conscience antedates the judgment and its terrors. Error and lust cannot stand to face God's visitations. He "who enlighteneth every man who cometh into this world" will throw a searchlight upon those in sin and heresy and cause them in spite of their pretended security to tremble with fear and insecurity. The inspired Seer thus depicts the effects of the approaching barbarian invasions on the consciences and hearts of the Romans who suspect that it is the judgment of God.

CHAPTER VII.

Westminster Version

After this, I beheld four angels 1. standing at the four corners of the
earth, holding fast the four winds of the earth, in order that no wind
should blow on earth or sea, or against any tree. And I saw another angel
coming 2. up from the rising of the sun, holding the seal of the living
God, and he cried with a loud voice to the four angels to whom it was
given to harm earth and sea, saying, 'Harm not earth 3. or sea or trees,
until we have sealed the servants of our God on their foreheads'. And
I heard the number of 4. those that were sealed, a hundred and forty-
four thousand sealed out of every tribe of the sons of Israel: of the tribe
of Judah, twelve thousand 5. sealed; of the tribe of Ruben twelve thous-
and; of the tribe of Gad twelve thousand; of the tribe of Asher, twelve 6.
thousand; of the tribe of Nephthali, twelve thousand; of the tribe of Man-
asseh, twelve thousand; of the tribe 7. of Simeon, twelve thousand; of the
tribe of Levi, twelve thousand; of the tribe of Issachar, twelve thousand;
of the tribe of Zebulon, twelve 8. thousand; of the tribe of Joseph, twelve
thousand; of the tribe of Benjamin twelve thousand sealed.

After these things, I beheld, and lo! 9. a great multitude which no
man could number, from every nation, and all tribes and peoples and
tongues, standing before the throne and before the Lamb, clothed in white
robes, and with palms in their hands. And they cry 10. with a loud voice,
saying: Salvation belongeth to our God who sitteth upon the throne, and
to the Lamb!

And all the angels stood round the throne and round the elders and
the four 11. living beings; and they fell before the throne on their faces
and worshipped God, saying: 'Amen! Blessing and glory 12. and wisdom
and thanksgiving and honour and power and might be to our God for
ever and ever. Amen!'

Then one of the elders addressed me 13. saying, 'These that are
clothed in white robes, who are they, and whence have they come?'
I said to him, 'My lord, thou 14. knowest.' And he said to me, 'These are
they that have come out of the great tribulation; they have washed their
robes and have made them white in the blood of the Lamb. Therefore
they are 15. before the throne of God, and minister to him day and night
in his sanctuary, and he who sitteth upon the throne shall come and dwell
with them. They shall 16. hunger no more, nor any more thirst; the sun
shall not oppress them, nor any heat; for the Lamb who standeth 17. in
the space before the throne shall be their shepherd, and shall guide them
to the fountains of the waters of life, and God shall wipe away every tear
from their eyes'.

B.

THE ESTABLISHMENT OF THE CHURCH

1. The Vision Of The Four Angels Holding The Winds.

Chapter VII. Verse 1.

The first six seals narrated the destruction of the old order in the world. The Little Lamb, the eucharistic Christ, accomplished this. Judaism and paganism were overthrown by His direction of world affairs. But Satan was not fully vanquished. Hardly had the Church triumphed over the two great enemies, when Satan, working *within* the Church misled many bishops and priests into the heresies of Arianism, Monophysitism, Nestorianism and other religious vagaries. But the Lamb was not to be defeated. He summoned the barbarians to wipe out the sectaries and then called these instruments of His providence into the fold. After He had depicted the corruption, the punishments of the false prophets necessarily fitted into the same scene. So the inspired writer finished that part of the drama, as it was revealed to him, by portraying the fall of the Roman Empire. But before he can describe the further development of the world, of the Church and of the growth of both good and evil, he must go back and show another phase of the conflict, the preparedness of the Church to meet the barbarians and survive the fall of the empire. So the Seventh Seal foreshadows the new order that Christ planted in the world and its growth up to the appearance of the barbarians. Then the trumpets will announce the further machinations and attacks of Satan against the Church. And they will reveal the growth of his empire. The next two chapters give an epitomized history of the Church and of the world for a thousand years. They show how human perversity mutilated the greatest gift of God, His revealed truth. They describe the punishments that come upon those who disobey the Church, and they depict the gradual growth of evil up to the proximate preparation for the establishment of the empire of Antichrist. The Jews are ignored until they are gathered at Jerusalem to await their hoped-for "Messias", Antichrist.

Verse 1.

Before the seventh seal is opened, the providence of the Lamb directing events is manifested in two visions that bring the blessings of the Gospel to all men. The first vision shows the approach of the richly deserved judgment. But this judgment is delayed until the Church has won such influence, that through her all men who will may take them as blessings and derive eternal gain from them. However, these judgments are intended to destroy sin and not the sinner unless he clings to sin. The second vision shows the Church in the exercise of her hard-won influence with so much strength and wisdom taking over the direction of public affairs and radiating the divine light of truth through all the world, that the nations accept her leadership. The last chapter ended with the words: "who shall be able to stand" (Joel II. 11). And the present chapter answers that question with the response: "those whom the Lamb shall rule".

The four angels appearing collaborate with the winds that shall be permitted to blow upon the earth. They may be the guardians of the various nations, because the angel who restrains them says: "until we have signed the servants of OUR God". They have control of the four winds, north, south, east, west. This metaphor is used by Zacharias (VI. 5), where the four winds appear in the form of charioteers the horses drawing the chariots having the same colors as those of chapter six. Chariots are more terrifying instruments of destruction than horsemen. In the foregoing chapter, the horsemen brought the judgments of God upon ONE FOURTH of the earth, whereas these winds are universal. Zacharias stated that God's anger against the heathen nations is appeased by the chariot which the black horses drew, and which turned northward to Babylon followed by the white horses. The black horses symbolized destruction for Babylon and the white God's victory over this enemy of His people. Those charioteers represented the Medes and Persians, through whom God destroyed Babylon. The four winds in our text will also represent invaders.

These FOUR WINDS come upon the scene under new forms in the next chapter and are not called "winds" any more. The scourges represented by them are clothed in this metaphor to intimate their prophetical character. In the prophets, winds represent revolutions in human society (Dan. VIII. 2) or invading armies. In the vision of Daniel, the four winds blowing upon the Mediterranean Sea brought forth the four successive world-empires one destroying the other. In Jeremias (XLIX. 36), they mean great slaughter of the good and bad, extirpation of a nation; and a whirlwind signifies revolutions from nation to nation, invasions and the overturning of kingdoms (XXV. 32). The figure borrowed from the prophets retains its original meaning, but the winds blow for the benefit of the Church not for the extermination of nations. The four winds are let loose at the sound of the trumpets in chapter eight and afflict all peoples to whom the Church was known. These winnow the wheat and blow the chaff out of the Church. During this process there is great suffering for the nations. There is danger that the good might be blown away with the wicked. Therefore the angel announces something to console the faithful.

Holding the four winds presages a time of peace until the Church is ready to benefit by the new evolutions in the world. The Greek word means that the holding angels have power to "Rule" the winds. This is possible only with rational beings. The figure is extended and the trees are included as objects of special protection. They stand for the prominent people in society, those who will be struck with greater force in a revolution. But in the general overthrow brought about by the winds, all people shall suffer.

2. The Vision Of The Angel From The Rising Of The Sun.

Verses 2-3.

Verse 2

The angel who ascends from the rising of the sun has the seal of the "living God". This alludes to the FOUR LIVING BEINGS and represents him as a bishop, probably the Bishop of Caesarea. He resides in the East and gives his orders to the spirits of the winds to hold their execution of the judgments until the appointed time. That a bishop or the Head of the Church can stay God's visitations is quite clear from St. Paul (2 Thess. II. 7.). That this is the Bishop of Palestine is quite logical, for the following verses reveal that he needs some time to convert the remnants of Israel. After the destruction of the nation the scattered remains of the Jews were no longer so obstinate against the Church.

From St. Paul it is learned (2 Cor. I. 21, 22), that Confirmation was conferred by anointing and sealing besides the imposition of hands; probably just as it is now conferred. Confirmation presupposes Baptism. The above was meant by "sealing" in post-apostolic writings (Hermas sim. IX. 16; Clem. Alex., quis dives 42). As verse 1 alludes to Zacharias (VI. 5), so verse 2 alludes to the same prophet (VI. 12). The angel has the sign of the living God, the sign of the cross, and he comes from the East. He therefore comes in the name of Christ and with His authority. Zacharias called Him the ORIENT. Since he comes in the name of Christ, this bishop has the authority to stay off the judgments until the Church is ready for them. The four guardian spirits of some nations were already holding the winds when they appeared in the vision, but now the Seer learns the reason: Christ through his angel ordered them to hold until the judgments would bring about the intended results. The virtue of Ezechías was able to delay the oncoming judgment, the destruction of Jerusalem, but not avert it entirely since it had been decreed unconditionally (Is. XXXIX. 8).

The purpose of delaying the onrush of the four winds is to give time to sign the foreheads of God's servants. The scene calls to mind the order received by Ezechiel (IX. 4) to mark a "Thau" on the foreheads of the faithful Jews; and this Thau in ancient Hebrew had the form of a cross. This points to the Jews still unconverted in Palestine and to the Roman Empire in general allowing time for the conversion of all who would respond to the invitation of grace. Then the winds may begin to blow. The earth, the sea and the trees are named to make the description more graphic. The ruin and devastation of the revolution will strike all who set their hopes on things terrestrial instead of spiritual, symbolized by the "earth" and human society in general called "the sea" and the military and civil officials of the government represented by the "trees". No harm is permitted to come to anything until the Church has completed her work of preparing adequately all who can be trained into faithful servants of God. The voluptuous and heretical worldlings will be struck unawares whilst the Church is ready to meet all visitations of God.

In chapter XIII. 16, the followers of the Beast are signed on the forehead or in the right hand. They have the seal of the Beast in contrast with these who have the seal of the Spirit on their foreheads and in their hearts. Here the mark will preserve from harm these who bear it, whilst there the plagues of God (XIV. 9; XVI. 2; XX. 4) will single out for destruction those who are marked.

3. Sealing The 144,000 From The Tribes Of Israel.

Verses 4-8.

Verses 4-8

St. John does not see the actual signing, but he hears the number signed. It is 12 x 12,000, the number of completion. This definite number stands for a remnant of the Jews who will be converted, whilst the number of Gentiles is uncountable. Every tribe of Israel furnishes its quota of converts, except that of Dan, which is never enumerated after the Babylonian Captivity. Perhaps this tribe was the most anti-Christian in the days of the Apostles. In its place we have the two half-tribes, Manasses and Joseph. Joseph stands for Ephraim. The latter is left out, because in the time of the great prophets, Ephraim represented the apostate kingdom of Israel. Since the dispersion of the Jewish nation in the second century, the tribes have lost their identity. This was not so in the time of St. John. The true Israel are those who are converted to Christ, which is demonstrated by leaving out the tribes of Dan and Ephraim and by making the enumeration clearly symbolical. The Jews were converted in larger numbers especially after the miracles which occurred at Jerusalem, when Julian, the Apostate, tried to rebuild the Temple.

The census begins with Juda, because Christ is of that tribe. In our enumeration, Ruben, the eldest son of Jacob, follows Juda, and Joseph and Benjamin are last. The enumeration is not in the geographical order of the ancient allotment of territory. The principal reason for counting only the tribes of Israel by name may be that St. John being of the Jewish nation wishes to impress on the well-disposed of his own people that God waits for them, that His mercy towards them is not exhausted, and His long-suffering favors His own nation so that not a single one might lose the chance of salvation. And when their conversion has numbered all those of good will, the winds may begin to blow regardless of developments among Gentile nations. These nations were ripe for punishment, when the apostasy from

Catholicism into Arianism was at its height around the year 360 A. D., while Julian the Apostate ruled. He aimed at re-establishing paganism. When in his attempt to rebuild the Temple the work was frustrated by miracles, he and his Jewish co-laborers abandoned it. This may be the opportunity which the angel "from the rising of the sun" seized to stay off the judgments. Throughout the course of apocalyptical history the same thing is done for the sake of the Church. The judgments often wait until she is fully prepared to profit most from them.

4. Countless Multitudes Also Signed.

Verses 9 to end.

Verse 9

After the signing of the 144,000, the vision grows wider. The Crystal Sea of chapter IV. includes countless numbers of adorers before the throne of God and the Lamb. During the sealing of the Twelve Tribes, the Church was busy in all parts of the world bringing into the fold large numbers "of all nations, and tribes, and peoples, and tongues". Every nation furnished its converts, and these were joined with the Jews and composed the Crystal Sea before the throne of God and the Lamb. The catholicity of the Church and the equality before God of all nations is evident in this vision. The promise made to Abraham is at last fulfilled. The number of his posterity is countless.

The divinity of the Lamb is again asserted in this vision. The vast multitude is the property of the Lamb as well as of God. Their whole life is an open book to Christ, for He in the eucharistic mystery has searched the depths of their minds and wills and made them what they are. They stand with open eyes before Him. There is no guile or deceit in those who dare to approach the eucharistic Lamb, no hypocrisy, no selfish desires.

They are of one mind with the Church. Her interests are most vital to them, and her honor is their business. Therefore they are in the benignant sight of the Lamb and are known to the world, for they visibly bear the palm of victory in their daily lives.

These who stand before the throne of God and the Lamb wear white raiment, the robe of innocence, which they received in Baptism. The souls of the martyrs were given white robes, while here the "peoples" of many nations are clothed in such. Nations and races exist only in this world and are distinguished by bodily differences. There were martyrs in Heaven from all nations, but no distinction was noticed among the souls. So this vast throng before the throne of God and the Lamb is not the saints in Heaven but the faithful Christians who serve God on earth. They carry the palm of victory, because they have overcome pride, the desire of the flesh and the allurements of the world having always remained true to their baptismal vows. They are the descendants of the first Christians and martyrs who endured the great tribulation, and their numbers have grown to uncountable throngs. They have saved the fruits of ancient civilization and brought the benedictions of the chosen people of old and the attainments of all heathen nations to God's future people for the peace and beatitude of all ages. The seven eyes of the Lamb have sought out those white-robed worshippers from all peoples and nations of the earth.

Verse 10

The Roman persecutions officially decreed are over. The emperors are Christians. The Church comes forth from the catacombs and publicly worships God through a growing and developing liturgy in worthy temples and grand basilicas. The sacrifice of the eucharistic Lamb is no longer a covert act, a discipline of the secret; the doctrine is openly proclaimed before the world. The Church is gathered before the eucharistic throne. The laity rejoice in the possession of religious liberty and the right to follow their conscience, to worship God as they please and to receive communion daily. They are no longer trodden upon or hunted down to be dragged before judges and magistrates for their belief in God and Christ. And St. John hears the thanksgiving of this un-numbered congregation in a concord of sweet and holy words, a deep and ready harmony of many voices, as if it were a single voice. The order here is the reverse of that in chapter five, and logically so. The worship and acknowledgement now comes from the converted 144,000 and the nations who are members of the Church, because their happy state has been brought about by God, the Creator, and the eucharistic Lamb, who gave strength and endurance to His own to win the victory. In chapter five, the hierarchy began the worship and thanksgiving to the Lamb who had chosen and raised them to their rank; here the people converted and regenerated begin the hymn of exultation and thanksgiving.

The grammatical construction in verse nine is quite broken in keeping with the ecstasy that must have taken possession of the Seer at the sight of the great victory of the Lamb. In verse ten the language is smoother again. The phrase, "OUR God", as in verse three, can be rightly claimed for themselves only by the Christians, because God is the Father of Jesus Christ, who is not only their Lord but also their brother. The word "Salvation" stands for a great deal. It expresses the pent-up exultation and thanksgiving of the happy throng standing before the throne. They give God and the Lamb the glory for their prospective salvation. Their election also assures the same grace for all who yearn for it. Hence in their exultation they pray that this salvation may come to all eager souls. How could it be otherwise? God "sits upon the throne" as the Ruler, whose purposes will be attained without fail. However, His universal dominion will be gained only through the activity and direction of the Lamb. Therefore the same divine honor and glory is due Him. The word "Salvation" alludes to the deeply rooted conviction in Asia of seeing this prerogative in the emperor. The epistles of St. Paul to Timothy and Titus attribute the title "Savior" to Christ very frequently probably with the intention of correcting the misuse of that attribute by the heathens.

Verses 11 and 12

In chapter five, the act of worship and thanksgiving proceeds from the four living beings and is then taken up by the elders and the angels. Here it is the reverse. The uncountable multitude voices its thanksgiving and desire, and then the angels, the elders and the four living beings complete and perfect it. The laity can express their transports only in half articulate language as infants, when thrilled with the understanding of what God and Christ have accomplished. Then the Church in her sublime liturgical and symbolic language gives full expression to the spontaneous outburst of the infants, emphasizes each word of theirs and voices it as eloquently as they would wish to express it and composing it into a worship worthy of herself.

The phrase "all the angels" probably comprises only the

guardian spirits of the bishops, priests and people who are present at the eucharistic sacrifice. Before the eucharistic throne, they take their place of worship, not locally but condignly, to offer the Lamb and God through the priesthood the adoration of the Church.

The grammatical construction leaves in doubt whether the elders and the four living beings fall down on their faces to adore, but it seems proper for them to join in with the angels. And altogether they pronounce the "AMEN", so be it. With unbounded satisfaction the guardian angels hear their charges sing their sentiments, and in jubilant language and with one great voice they wish unbending victory to God and Christ. The highest and purest proof of love and devotion to Christ is given when the creature forgets himself and looks to Him and is interested only in His triumph. And so the angels adore God in ecstasy at seeing the peoples and nations under their tutelage in uncountable numbers thinking only of Christ and desiring only His honor and glory.

Naturally the priests and bishops should be as overwhelmed as the angels by the same ecstactic thought and feeling at seeing their labors and sacrifices rewarded to so large an extent. The Church has grown into a vast empire, and the priests and bishops rule over it as kings by divine right. It is not an empire established by military power, by assaults from without by subduing the bodies; it is a spiritual empire upheld by soundless spiritual forces, by an inward influence, "bringing into captivity every understanding unto the obedience of Christ"; It is therefore indestructible.

Every word of the doxology is preceded by the definite article emphasizing each word and declaring this to be the fitting and worthy praise to express the worship of God and of the Lamb. The word "thanksgiving" replaces "divinity" of chapter V., because thanksgiving is due the Lamb for His victory so exceedingly great. The Greek text has "riches" in chapter V., but this meaning supernatural riches is well translated with "divinity". In chapter V., the power and "divinity" of the Lamb had to be asserted, because He alone was able to open the seals and direct the future world by His divine right. No mere creature could undertake so divine a task.

In this period the Church labors to consolidate her gains,

to solidify her institutions and to develop her literature, liturgy, music and art. It is the age of the Great Fathers and Doctors, both East and West, both Latin and Greek. The Church is being fortified for the onrush of the barbarians and the coming upheavals in society. The heresies of the time stimulated to stronger and more sustained effort within the Church to express her doctrines clearly and more comprehensively, to develop and foster loyalty for the papacy and elicit from all a filial devotion to Christ. They determined her to stand her ground immovably in upholding the strictness and fullness of the apostolic traditions and in opposing all who rejected the divine ordinances. The state of freedom which the Church gained for all to follow Christ will continue. And because the Spirit animates the internal life of her members and inspires them to sacrifice everything for spiritual gains, the Church will labor to convert the world until all who are to be signed are signed. The prophecy of Malachias is in the process of fulfillment: "From the rising of the sun to the going down, my name is great among the Gentiles, and in every place there is SACRIFICE, and there is offered to my name a clean oblation: for my name is great among the Gentiles, says the Lord of Hosts" (Mal. I. 11).

Verse 13

St. Bede says of the elder's question, "interrogat ut doceat" He put the question to St. John to whet his desire for the knowledge to be imparted to him. Although St. John did not voice the question he had in mind, the elder knew it and spoke for him. It is not a rhetorical figure but a revelation. It intimates the importance of the information desired to understand the significance of the vision and to record it.

Verse 14

St. John's humble answer is that not he but the elder knows; he, however, reveals his eagerness for the information. And the elder answers that these wearing the white robes have come through THE GREAT TRIBULATION. The definite article used refers to something which had been mentioned before and was presumed to be known. In chapter I. 9 and II. 10, St. John states it and warns the Christians in Asia of its coming. He calls it the "hour of temptation" in III. 10. It is bloody persecution. In this verse, the stress placed on "the great one" points to the imperial persecutions, especially to the last one under Diocletian. This scene is then in the fourth century, when the Roman persecutions had been abolished. "The great tribulation" had passed away to return no more, and since then the Church had grown to grand proportions. These white-robed worshippers have been faithful, have faced the horrors of the tribulation and have merited the palm of victory.

They have furthermore washed their robes in the blood of the Lamb till they were shining white. Such paradoxical statements are not unusual in the Apocalypse. This blessed result for the believers is not accredited to the gory death of Christ on the cross, rather to the bloodless sacrifice of the eucharistic Lamb. By His death on the cross, Christ did not wash everyone clean or cast over his sins the mantle of His infinite satisfactions. That would contradict the doctrine taught here. These in white robes are not passive recipients of the benefits of the Great Sacrifice. Thy have been active; they have themselves washed their own robes in the blood of the Lamb. These are not the baptismal robes, though Baptism also clothes with a white robe (XXII.16); it refers rather with strong persuasiveness to the eucharistic grace. In Baptism the recipient is more passive. He gives his consent, if an adult, but that is all. These Christians were most probably baptized in infancy, gave no active consent to the baptism, and so that sacrament worked ex opere operato entirely. Another fact to be considered is "the blood of the Lamb". The worshippers made their robes white in that blood. They have done the washing themselves, and this could be done only by attending the eucharistic sacrifice and by frequent communion.

Frequent confession was not common in those days of persecution, for the true believers lived almost sinless lives. Sinners do not have the moral courage to suffer and die for their faith. The persecution cleared them out of the Church. So this unnumbered congregation before the throne had been cleansed by the sufferings, fortified in virtue by their co-operation with the graces received in holy communion and had become unwavering in their will and heart's desire to retain the blessed state in which their souls lived and feasted. They had divested themselves of earthly affections, the love of wealth, ease, fame and pleasure and sought their consolation and delight in the blood of Christ, which could not be touched by earthly standards of value, and which flooded their souls in ever new waves of love and spiritual riches.

Common experience in our day shows children of people, who for supernatural motives have suffered and sacrificed much for their religion imbued with a deeper faith and purer morals than those of careless or mediocre Christian parents. The young are purer in those communities where frequent communion is a common practice. Thus the first generation of Christians, after the days of martyrdom had passed, were fervent and pure. They found their peace and joy in the practice of their faith; they attended church where the Holy Sacrifice is renewed and washed their robes ever cleaner and whiter; and they found the yoke of Christ ever sweeter and His burden ever lighter. The heresies of this time of growth for the Church were fostered by those who had apostatized during persecution and had been re-admitted into the Church when the danger was over.

Verse 15

Now that religious liberty was granted, those who remained faithful could serve their Lord without fear or hindrance. They were vividly aware of the divine power that emanated from the eucharistic throne in the Church, for it animated them and had made them unconquerable in the great tribulation. Now they stand before the throne and gaze upon their God with reverential awe, with love and gratitude. They submit with joyful heart to His supreme dominion. They do not find His rule tyrannical or His commandments hard and galling. They find His law a bright and sunny path that leads them onward to full and perfect union with God. To them the teachings and directions of the Church are only an expression of God's ineffable perfections and of His kindly care for His children. His house is their home, whither they betake themselves to seek rest from their labors and refreshment for their hungry hearts. Earthly affairs have small importance for them. The eucharistic Lord is their treasure, and He rules their thoughts and rivets their affections to Himself.

The phrase "day and night in his temple" denotes clearly that this vision is not of the state of the Blessed in Heaven but of the happy state of those who serve God in His Church on earth. There is no night in Heaven, neither is there any temple there. The Greek word λατρεύουσιν used to denominate this service shows this multitude not to be in the sanctuary, not to belong to the priesthood but to the lay Christians. The vision is that of unnumbered congregations worshipping in the temple. They are admitted to greater intimacy with God and the Lamb than were the people of the Old Testament, who could not go into the Temple (Lc. I. 10, 21) but had to worship outside in the court. The worship of this throng is distinguished from that of the elders and four living beings, for the word λειτουργεῖν should be expected, if the official worship of the priesthood were meant. The word used may be intended to convey the idea expressed by Christ at the Last Supper, after He had ordained His apostles priests: "I will not now call you servants . . . But I have called you friends". The laity would be these servants of Christ, while the priests are His friends.

The worship goes on unceasingly "day and night", because those who have consecrated their lives to God are united with Him in grace and lose not a moment of their time. Their work, their sleep, their meals, their pleasures, their every thought, word and deed within the circle of reason is sanctified and is a service and worship accepted by God. Their thoughts and intentions have recourse to Him everywhere and at all times. God promised to walk and dwell with Israel both before and after Captivity, if the people were faithful to Him (Lev. XXVI. 12; Zach. II. 10). Here the promise is renewed unconditionally, for this fultitude has proven itself true and faithful.

When creating man God breathed into him His own divine life, and this made him happy and satisfied the aspirations of his soul. After he lost it, he felt a void in his breast which nothing else could satisfy. When left to his own true self with no external appeals to distract him and no excessive passion prodding his heart and will, he apprehends his need in a vague and hazy yearning, in an involuntary movement of his mind and heart and he will be languid and dull or feverish and restless to seek the lost blessedness in earthly objects. So one centers his affections on this idol which he forms for himself and another on that. The young seek their joy in sensual pleasures or in brave deeds, in physical beauty or feats of strength or even in noble generosities and natural virtues; the mature will strive to rise in the world and become famous and will practice rigid self-denial and self-control to attain their goal. And the old seek to satisfy their hunger for happiness in a peaceful and carefree existence, in reviewing their past accomplishments in an idealized setting and loftier intentions than they ever really possessed. They must have an object for which to live, to think and feel, even if it be unworthy of an immortal spirit. These fortunate ones, however, before the throne of God have found their True Life, the Object in which they may wrap up their devotion without reserve and to which they may surrender themselves securely with full persuasion, unhindered and unrestrained.

Verse 16

The cares of the body do not burden or worry them. They do not seek the choicest and most delicate food or finest wines as did the pagan Romans. Nor do they have any anxiety about the future, for they know that "their heavenly Father feeds them" and supplies their every need. They seek "first the kingdom of God" and know that all else shall be added thereunto. They do not mind the inclemencies of the weather, because they delight in sufferings, that they may be cleansed the more and become more Christ-like. Had St. John been a northerner or written in a northern climate, he would have chosen a different illustration. The sun is a burden to the southerner but a cheering friend to the northerner. In a northern climate, the cold is the enemy of comfort. The Greek has the future tense and repeats the conjunction, ἔτι, emphasizing thereby the happy state of the elect after the persecutions.

Verses 16 and 17 are found in almost identical words in Isaias (XLIX. 10), so that commentators say St. John borrowed them from Isaias. Isaias describes the happy state of that part of Israel that shall be converted to the Church of Christ and faithfully cling to Him. It would hardly seem in keeping with the dignity of an inspired book, if the writer "borrowed" ideas; it seems more logical to suppose this an interpretation of the text of Isaias. Certainly Isaias meant that all who follow Christ shall be in such a state of felicity as he describes in figurative language, and St. John applies this to those who have passed through the horrible era of persecution and preserved their fidelity to Christ un-moved.

Verse 17

The Lamb shall rule them from His eucharistic throne. His standing in the midst of the throne is mentioned again to call attention to His divinity and power in that august mystery. He will "shepherd them" "and lead them". The word "lead" is in the Gospel and is said of the Holy Spirit (Jo. XVI. 13). The leading His faithful ones to the fountains of the waters of life would then mean to teach them all truth and replenish their souls by the holy sacraments. The words are chosen with great care to suggest worlds of thought. The eucharistic Lamb shall be the shepherd over His flock who have braved fire and sword for Him, and He shall tenderly care for each one in particular. He shall be on the lookout for the wolf, so that His sheep may roam about carefree in His pastures from one spiritual delight to another. In guiding them He will teach and feed them. Following Him as their shepherd, they shall be secure against briars and brambles, poisonous and noxius food; and there shall be no draught of bitterness in their daily repast, but all shall be sweet and refreshing. The fountains of the waters of life are not Christ Himself, for He will lead his sheep to them. They are the divine truth, moral law and the sacraments. In chapter twenty-two, where the Church appears in its maturity, full growth and glory, those fountains have become a "river of the water of life" (XXII. 1).

This symbolism would be meaningless, if it were applied to the life in the next world. The blessed in Heaven possess everything and need not be led to fountains of water. No attempt is made in the inspired writings to describe the bliss of Heaven. In reference to it, all terms are negative. St. Paul writes: "Eye has not seen nor ear heard"; and he was not permitted to reveal the secret words he heard in the third heaven. The whole scene idealizes the happy state of the Church after the great tribulation viewed from the lofty spiritual plane on which St. John received these revelations.

"God shall wipe away all tears from their eyes" (See Is. XXV. 8). Those before the throne are the sons and daughters, brothers and sisters of the martyrs who suffered death in most excruciating torments. What wonder that their sympathetic eyes were filled with tears! However, those very torments brought their loved ones inestimable glory, and they are now to be envied. Their names shall be inscribed in the calendar of saints, and their intercession shall be sought by the Church. Those before the throne possess the spiritual heritage of the martyrs. They are in the inner sanctuary of God. They serve Him with a pure intention. And this higher life is derived from the fountains of the eucharistic Lamb, who cheers them in every conflict with evil, cautions them against all allurements of venomous pleasures, refreshes them for every burden and takes the sting out of every sorrow.

CHAPTER VIII.

Westminster Version

And when the Lamb opened the seventh 1. seal, silence reigned in
heaven for about half an hour.

Then I beheld the seven angels that 2. stand before God, and they
were given seven trumpets. And another angel came and stood at the altar
with a golden 3. censer in his hand, and he was given much incense to
mingle with the prayers of all the saints upon the golden altar which
is before the throne.

And the smoke of the incense went up with the prayers of the saints
from the angel's hand before God. 4.

Then the angel took the censer 5. and filled it with the fire of the
altar, and cast it towards the earth; and there followed thunderpeals and
voices and lightnings and an earthquake.

And the seven angels who had the 6. seven trumpets prepared themselves to sound them.

And the first angel sounded the 7. trumpet, and there followed hail
and fire mixed with blood, which fell upon the earth; and the third part
of the earth was burnt up, and the third part of the trees was burnt up,
and all green grass was burnt up.

And the second angel sounded the 8. trumpet, and as it were a great
mountain, burning with fire, was cast into the sea; and the third part
of the sea became blood, and the third part of the creatures in the sea
which have life died, and the third part of the ships was destroyed. 9.
And the third angel 10. sounded the trumpet, and there fell from heaven
a great star burning like a torch, and it fell upon the third part of the
rivers, and upon the fountains of waters. The 11. name of the star
is 'Wormwood'; and the third part of the waters became wormwood, and
many men died of the waters, because they had become bitter. And the
fourth angel 12. sounded the trumpet, and the third part of the sun, of
the moon and of the stars was smitten, so as to darken the third part of
them, and prevent a third of the day from shining, and of the night likewise.

Then I beheld, and I heard an 13. eagle flying in mid-heaven, saying
with a loud voice: 'Woe, woe, woe to them that dwell upon the earth,
at the sounding of the other trumpets which the three angels are about
to sound'.

IV. THE SEVEN TRUMPETS.

A.

PREPARATORY VISIONS.

1. The Seventh Seal. Half Hour's Silence.

Chapter VIII.

Verse 1.

Verse 1

When the Lamb opens the Seventh Seal, silence settles on the scene before the Seer. The half hour's silence is actual time given him to contemplate the vision. The developments in the Church of which nothing is noticed on earth call for contemplation. The progress of history is halted. It is the time before the Four Winds, the same time occupied by the visions of Chapter VII. This may allude to Zacharias (II. 13). But the pause betokens evolutions of wide importance. No one offers St. John an explanation while he reviews and records the visions, for their significance is to remain veiled in mystery. The silence calls for obedience to await in awe the time set by Providence to reveal His decrees. What has been instituted must have time to grow strong and firm to withstand the storms that shall sweep over the earth. The pause presages both good and evil.

2. The Seven Angels With The Seven Trumpets.

Verse 2.

Verse 2

Seven angels are standing in the presence of God. It recalls the words of the angel in Tobias (XII. 15). The Archangel Rafael was one of *those* seven. These are *not* the 'Seven Spirits of God' (IV. 5). The text does not reveal who they might be. Some interpreters aver them to be great saints who shall appear at critical times in the history of the Church and defend her against the forces of evil. They may visibly exemplify the invisible decrees of God, for they later at fore-ordained moments blow the trumpet, which each one receives from an unnamed actor to announce the beginning of scourges that punish infidelity. The seals made mysterious revelations which were not understood, whilst the trumpets announce the advent of judgments. In prophetical language, the prophets call themselves

God's trumpets (Jer. VI. 17), when they announce the coming judgments, wars and enemies. (Osee VIII. 1; Joel II. 1; Mt. XXIV. 31; 1 Cor. XV. 52; 1 Thess. IV. 16).

3. The Second Vision. The Angel With The Golden Censer. Verses 3-5.

Verse 3

During the half hour's silence another scene comes into the field of vision. A golden altar towards which an angel stepped with a golden censer engrossed the Seer's attention. It revealed the preparedness of the Church for the judgments that shall follow the trumpet blasts of the seven angels. In V. 8, the hierarchy have golden bowls filled with incense; whilst here the angel offers the incense upon the golden altar. Under this figure another institution in the Church is shown, and it will have a vast influence in shaping her destiny. This angel may be the protector of this institution. In many passages of the Apocalypse, institutions in the Church are typified by Old Testament regulations.

In the Ancient Covenant, there were several altars in the Tabernacle and Temple. At the entrance stood the altar of holocausts. In the Tabernacle, this altar and the altar of incense were made of the precious setim wood. In Solomon's Temple it was made of cedar. The second Temple was built behind the altar of holocausts, upon which were offered the sacrifices of the highest order, and which was overlaid with brass (Ex. XXXVIII. 1), but the altar of incense was overlaid with pure gold. There may have been a practical reason for the brass covering of the former, but the gold covering of the latter was surely not meaningless. The altar of incense stood next to the Ark of the Covenant separated from the Holy of Holies by only a curtain (Ex. XXX. 1-9). The incense was to be burned upon it in the morning and evening, "an everlasting incense". And the fire upon this altar as also upon the altar of holocausts was never to be extinguished, though the sacrifices were not continuous. The altar of incense must have had in God's intentions a higher typical significance than was expressed by its use in the Old Testament. Incense was not a symbol of prayer in the Old Law, though prayer was imagined in the later psalms to ascend to God like incense.

The future history of the Church revealed to St. John is clothed largely in the symbolism of the Old Testament. Sometimes he takes the external form and appearance of the symbols and attaches a different meaning to them; sometimes he unfolds the fuller inner or typical meaning. The use of the golden altar in the Old Law according to St. Paul's interpretation (Heb. IX. 1-10) would intimate something more than was known in ancient times. St. Paul claims for it a close association with the presence of God. In the Holy of Holies was the throne of God, and the golden altar of incense was nearest to this throne (Ex. XL. 5). Only the high priests had access to this place. Particular manifestations of God's will were made known here from time to time. Here Zachary received the message of the Archangel Gabriel (Luke I. 11).

The golden altar then typifies an institution in the Church which is admitted to most intimate association with God. Methodius says of this altar: "Moreover, it has been handed down that the unbloody altar of God signifies the assembly of the chaste: thus virginity appears to be something great and glorious" ('Banquet of the ten virgins VI). The entire old Covenant typifies the New, prepares the way for its institution and foreshadows the ordinances of the Church of Christ. The golden altar typifies a grand institution in the Church, THE RELIGIOUS ORDERS, especially the CONTEMPLATIVE LIFE, the life of prayer, self-denial and self-sacrifice.

The religious orders were inaugurated during this period. Nothing in the history of the Church has been of greater importance in shaping her destiny and spreading her influence than the religious orders. They appeared in this century between the end of the persecutions and the beginning of the barbarian invasions. They arose almost unperceived in the East and in the West. The father of monastic life was St. Anthony, who died in 356 A. D. St. Pachomius was the first to draw up a monastic rule. St. Ammonius established monasteries in the Nitrian Desert. The monastic life spread to Palestine, Arabia, Mesopotamia, Syria, Persia and Asia Minor. In Asia Minor, St. Basil's rule became the basis for all other monastic institutions. His rule has remained the principal order in the Greek and Eastern churches. He may be the angel before the golden altar, because St. John received these revelations primarily for the churches of Asia Minor. In the same century, all the deserts from Lybia to the Caspian Sea were peopled by monks. St. Pachomius founded eight monasteries in Egypt. And the two Macarii established monasteries in the desert of Scete, which numbered tens of thousands of monks. By 372 A. D. there were 100,000 monks in Egypt. St. Athanasius translated the monastic life to the West in 340 A. D. By the end of the fourth century it had spread throughout the West.

The golden altar, the fire upon it, the incense and the golden censer are all symbols of the religious life, the life of prayer. The gold is the symbol of unselfish and complete immolation to God. It is free from earthly alloy, free from the hope of earthly rewards or glory. The fire is the symbol of both love or hatred. Here it is pure love for God in which the incense, the whole of the religious life with all of its prayers and good works, is consumed as a perfect offering to God. These prayers and good works ascend to God like the perfumed smoke of the incense. Not any part of their life is rubbish, for all is entirely consecrated by obedience. They pray for all the world and by their life of self-denial make the prayers of the faithful acceptable to God.

The text does not state whether the angel received the incense in his hand or in a vessel, for the whole action is symbolic. He puts the incense on the live coals, and from under his hand the smoke arises to the throne of God. In the Greek, "the prayers" are in the dative case indicating that the angel gives to the prayers of the saints some quality lacking them to make them acceptable to God. The word "incense" is plural suggesting clearly its symbolic meaning for it represents the various kinds of good works and virtues. The love of God consumes the lives consecrated to Him for the salvation of the world supernaturalizing the works and prayers of all members of the Church. Prayer is as unceasing in the religious life as the perpetual fire on the golden altar in the Old Dispensation.

The angel fills the censer with fire from the altar but puts in no incense. He casts the censer to the earth reminding us thereby of the words of our Lord: "I have come to cast fire on the earth and what will I, but that it be kindled?" (Lc. XII. 49). The contemplative life is not to expend its force within the Church but is to spread the fire over the earth. The love of God, engendering zeal for the salvation of souls which contemplation kindles in the hearts of its devotees, is to set the heathen world on fire. And in fact, the zeal for converting the barbarian nations was enkindled in the monasteries as the Roman Empire was falling into heresy. The work of conversion was taken up by this new institution and has continued through the ages. The golden altar represents the institution itself and the golden censer the individuals who are sent into the heathen world (See Lam. IV. 1, 2) to spread the fire over the earth, while the smoke of incense keeps ascending from the altar. Each missionary's work was truly unselfish and was offered as golden service to Christ and God.

The thunders that accompany the casting of the censer upon the earth symbolize the preaching of God's word to nations still in barbarism. The lightnings are the charismata in general and the miracles wrought by the missionaries enlightening the minds of the pagans. In IV. 5, the voices came from the throne of God preceded by the lightnings and followed by the thunders. Here the order is reversed. This might signify that in apostolic days, the Holy Spirit conferred the charismata, enlightenment by grace first, and thereafter the Church instructed the miraculously enlightened. Here the thunders are first indicating that the preaching of the Gospel preceded, and its acceptance voiced by the astonishment of those who are convinced followed. They would try to convince others who hardened their hearts against the preaching and would express their belief in words of victory and exultation.

The earthquake again rumbles forth the overthrow of social, political and religious institutions of paganism and barbarism. It recalls the earthquake of chapter VI. which revealed the abolition of the Roman state religion. The missionaries by their preaching, example and miracles cut down the pagan nature-worship of the barbarians and planted the true faith in its place. Monastic centers were founded in Italy, Burgundy, Gaul, Britain and Ireland during this period from which radiated the true faith into lands that were still pagan and barbarian. The monks converted the countries of Europe, which have remained the strongholds of Christendom ever since. The fire has kept on spreading, has radiated continually and is still radiating its light and love chiefly from the monasteries to peoples stupid with unbelief.

THE FOUR WINDS

1. The First Trumpet. The Plague Of Hail.

Verses 6-7.

Verse 6

The seven angels understand that the time to blow the trumpets has arrived. After the establishment of the religious orders throughout the empire, the Church is prepared to take over the direction of world affairs and to save all good fruits of ancient civilization and culture. The empire had been prepared negatively by heresy and schism which weakened it as well as the Church. It had lowered the esteem of pagans for Christianity and had caused much confusion; it had broken down Christian discipline and perverted the moral standards of clergy and people; and although paganism had been officially outlawed in the empire, its corrupting influence still worked, and it fought side by side with heresy to uproot what the Church had so laboriously planted and watered and fertilized with her tears and blood. The time had arrived to purify the world.

Blowing the trumpet is a sensible action heralding the beginning of a judgment, separating one judgment from another and denoting a decree or permission from God for each affliction upon the Church. These actions of blowing the trumpet at each new epoch instead of a mere movement of successive events reveal that each historical event is of vital importance and significance for the Church. In Ezechiel (X. 2), the beginning of God's judgment upon Jerusalem was introduced by a like symbolic action.

Verse 7

The trumpets herald the winds spoken of in the preceding chapter. The first trumpet blast is followed by hail and fire mingled with blood. This scourge has some similarity with the seventh plague of Egypt, but the blood is the extraordinary feature. In the Greek text, the blood is the mass containing the hail and fire. This clearly makes it an allegorical description of something that is not a thunderstorm but has the effect of lightning and hail on inanimate nature. Primarily the storm represents bloodshed. Hail destroys crops. The storm wipes out "all green grass". It sweeps over a third of the empire. It does not destroy everything but leaves two thirds of the trees in the devasted one third of the earth. The fire destroys only one third, whilst the hail wipes out all the crops. This is only an approximate estimate made by the Seer.

The interpretation of this storm can be found in Ezechiel (XIII. 11). Hail is there an instrument of judgment. It is not real hail, but hostile, pillaging, plundering armies. In Exodus (IX. 23), it was real hail, while here the devasting forces do the same work as hail does, flaying the crops to the ground. The lightning strikes one third of the trees or buildings, or possibly all buildings. The figurative hailstorm therefore signifies armies waging cruel warfare. During a protracted war in antiquity, the crops were invariably trodden under foot and agriculture was neglected. Famine always followed in the footsteps of the invading, marauding armies. When in chapter six the wasting of the crops of Palestine was revealed, the order was heard not to touch the olive-trees and vines. Here one third of them shall be destroyed. There the devastation swept over one fourth of the earth, whilst here it is approximately one third.

In Ezechiel, hail came as a punishment for heresy, for the false doctrines of the false prophets. The storm is given the same feature here to indicate the same reasons for this scourge. "The earth", in the Apocalypse, is a stereotyped term for mere temporal affairs. Here it obviously means Europe, because Patmos was close to Europe. The narrative presents a different view of what was already related in VI. 14-17. The sixth seal showed the same judgment as the punishment for the heresies rending the Church. It described the effect of that judgment upon Roman officialdom and the intriguing Arian bishops and the overthrow of the old Roman order. The judgment was executed by the barbarian invaders. They put an end to luxurious living and robbed Arianism of its support in Roman Officialdom, just as the 1st world-war frustrated the great Luther celebration planned to be world-wide. In the barbarian invasions, the just also suffered. They were purified by suffering, restrained from falling again into pagan ways and then became ministers for the conversion of the barbarians and were thus again taken up into the number of those who came through the "great tribulation".

The barbarian invasions are fitly described in this verse. They swept over one third of the empire. They devastated the fairest provinces of western and southern Europe and of northern Africa. Vines and fruit-trees were abundant in those provinces. Agriculture was the main means of support for the inhabitants. Historians relate the ravages of the barbarians. "Everywhere ruin marked the track of the invaders. Towns and villages were burned, fortresses leveled to the ground, and Christian churches, of which there were then many in the Roman colonies, destroyed. Thousands of the inhabitants fell by the sword and thousands were reduced to slavery". St. Gregory writes: "Lights and sounds of war meet us on every side. The cities are destroyed, the military stations broken up; the land devasted; the earth depopulated. No one remains in the country; scarcely any inhabitants in the towns; yet even the poor specimens of humanity that remain are still smitten daily without intermission. Before our eyes some are carried away captives, others mutilated and murdered. Behold how Rome fares; she who was mistress of the world is worn down by manifold and incalculable distresses, by the bereavement of her citizens, the attack of her foes, the reiteration of overthrows. Where is her Senate? Where are her people? We, the few survivors, are still the daily prey of the sword and other innumerable tribulations. Where are they who in former day revelled in her glory? Where is their pomp, their pride, their frequent and immoderate joy? Young men of the world congregating here from every quarter aimed at secular advancement. Now no one hastens to her for preferment; and so it is with other cities also; some places are laid waste by pestilence, others are depopulated by the sword; some are afflicted with famine and others are swallowed up by earthquakes" (Birkhauser, Church History, p. 141.). These words of St. Gregory give only a glimpse of what really happened in those days under the ceaseless incursions of the northern invaders.

All Christian historians agree that the barbarians had a mission from God. It is not claimed in the Apocalypse that they came in punishment for bloodshed as is done in chapter XVI. 5-7. They came to punish the Roman Empire for heresy and schism and moral turpitude, which is always the fruit of heresy; they came to crush out the last vestiges of paganism, which in spite of the closing of its temples, in its circusses, theatres, amphitheaters and baths still continued to exert a corrupting influence even upon the Christians, as the Fathers of that period so loudly lament.

2. The Second Trumpet. The Burning Mountain.

Verses 8-9.

Verses 8-9

The second scourge is somewhat similar to the first plague of Egypt in part of its effects but totally different in others. At the sound of the trumpet, a burning mountain, a volcano, seemed to be hurled into the sea. One third of the sea was turned into blood. This is an allegorical narration of a future historical event. The whole mountain seems to be burning. It would not seem unnatural for a tornado to hurl a mass of red sand and dust out of the desert of Africa and deposit it into the Mediterranean Sea coloring a part of it red. But the description does not permit such an explanation. The mountain is a mass of fire. And it converts the water of the sea into real blood. The allegory forebodes something that is aptly clothed in this figure.

"Blood" is again the outcome of this scourge. It is produced in the sea. So much blood is produced that one third of the living creatures in the sea die. It is obviously another figurative representation of wars. If the sea were actually changed into blood, all living creatures in the sea would die, as in the first plague of Egypt. The fire is the element that converts the third part of the sea into blood. If a mere fire were cast into the sea, it would be extinguished at once. This could then be only a metaphorical fire. In other parts of the Apocalypse, fire represents hatred. Here too it evidently represents hatred or religious fanaticism.

One third of the creatures that "have souls" die in the sea, when the burning mountain turns it into blood. This effect is an allusion to the first plague of Egypt. However, the figurative concept of the whole chapter makes us seek an allegorical interpretation for this passage. These creatures are rational, are human beings, and therefore probably die a spiritual death. The two verses take in view the Mediterranean Sea as the physical embodiment of that "sea" which is the human race (See XVII. 15) or the nations of Asia or Africa bordering on the Mediterranean. This "sea" is opposed to the Crystal Sea.

The huge mass of the burning mountain tumbled into the sea throws it into such convulsions as to sink a third of the ships. This is the result of an earthquake in the bed of the seas. Two thirds of the ships and two thirds of the living creatures escape. The peculiar grammatical construction gives a quasi-personal character to the ships that are "destroyed" as if they had life and to the creatures "that have souls".

In prophetical imagery, it is nothing new to depict a menacing and plundering world-power as a burning mountain, for Jeremias had employed the same figure (LI. 25) to denominate Babylon at the time of the Captivity. After its destruction Babylon was called a "burnt mountain". In our text the Seer describes the coming menace from the south as a "burning mountain", because it would not be an extinct or destroyed world-power but active and full of devastating fire for a long time.

In the history of Christianity, this allegorical figure describes nothing with truer precision than Mohammedanism. Mohammed preached an unceasing and holy war against all unbelievers who would not believe his religion. He inaugurated a world-movement and established a world-power by the edge of the sword, which turned a part of the world into blood. The motive for that bloodshed was religious fanaticism and hatred for all who would not accept his doctrines. With fire and sword he devastated the earth. The barbarians swept over the land in Europe, only the Vandals crossing over into Africa. Those invasions were the north wind. A burning mountain hurled into the "sea" by the south wind aptly represents Mohammedanism. This scourge heralded by the second trumpet punishes another third of the Roman Empire for the perversions of paganism, heresy, schism and luxury. Mohammedanism literally drenched one third of the known world with blood by its unceasing wars of conquest. All countries around the Mediterranean Sea eventually fell victim to it. It gave occasion to the Crusades, which for two hundred years involved all of Europe in apparently offensive but really defensive wars.

The death of a third of the creatures that "have souls" would obviously mean the Christians who were coerced to relinquish their holy faith. They died a spiritual death. Mohammedanism is a religion of crude materialism; it reduced the moral standards of its adherents to animalism; it abolished the Christian standards of self-restraint and self-denial; its spirituality is an affected oriental fanaticism; it upholds thievery, robbery and slavery against all unbelievers, and it promises a heaven of sensual delights. It not only brought spiritual death to the regions it conquered but a bloody death to all who opposed its progress.

In the writings of the early Fathers, the ship has been a symbol of the Church. The idea must have been of apostolic origin. Ships in this verse are churches and places of worship. Mohammedanism destroyed most of the churches in the lands of its aggression. Some of the grander ones, as in Jerusalem and Constantinople, it turned into Mohammedan mosques. They may truly be said to have died, for the life within them, the eucharistic Lamb, perished. Possibly one third of the churches of the world were torn down by the Mohammedans; surely far more than one third of them in the countries conquered by the Musselmen.

In St. Augustine's time, Africa counted six-hundred bishoprics. But Africa was overgrown with heresies. The Vandals conquered it in 450 A. D., and after adopting Arianism persecuted the Catholics almost to extermination. The Greek general, Belisarius, destroyed the Vandal kingdom, but the inhabitants lingered on in heresy and immorality. Mohammedanism wiped out all those African and Asian heresies. In Arabia in spite of six centuries of Christianity, the Khaaba, a meteoric stone, was worshipped. Persia had almost extirpated the Catholic religion. Aided by the remnants of the Jewish nation, who hated Catholics fanatically, the Persian kings invaded Palestine, conquered Jerusalem and put 100,000 Catholics to death. The Jews had equipped an army of 26,000 men to help the Persians. Emperor Heraclius finally defeated the Persians in 614 A. D. But Nestorianism had found a home in Persia, and the Catholic religion almost vanished. Thus had Jews, pagans and heretics nearly rooted out the true faith in Africa and Asia. Bishops, priests, religious and the faithful laity were martyred to establish heresy. Then came Mohammedanism. Within half a century, all of northern Africa, Arabia, Palestine and Persia as far as India were subjected, and before a century passed, all of Spain and Syria had fallen under the sway of the Crescent by the power of the sword. Fully one third of the civilized world fell subject; and everywhere churches were destroyed or turned into mosques. Catholics could remain true only under the direst difficulties and with constant peril of martyrdom or slavery. All attempts to convert the Mohammedans from their degrading religious fanaticism have failed. In Spain, Arianism had been abandoned, but the morals of the nation remained low up to the Saracen conquest. Seven centuries later Spain emerged from Saracen domination stronger and purer in faith and morals.

3. The Third Trumpet. The Star Wormwood. Verses 10-11.

Verses 10 and 11

The scourge announced by the third trumpet comes down from heaven, from the Church. The first two scourges were upon the "earth" and the "sea"; they wrecked *human* institutions and deranged temporal world-order and brought into action God's final decree against heresy and schism. The Church is now aggrieved by a sad loss. A star resembling a meteor falls from heaven; it is a "great star". It is not extinguished in its fall but keeps on burning like a "torch" emitting a stream of light as it falls and still burning brightly when it strikes the earth. It falls upon the rivers or rivulets and wells, the sources of fresh water for mankind. The connotation is probably topographical, pointing to a territory that has many brooks and rivers. The word ἡ πηγὴ means more than just a fountain of water, it denotes the source of anything.

The star is given a name; it is "called" Wormwood. Though not wormwood by its nature, it receives that name because it changes the sweet waters into wormwood. It is not mixed with the water or merely makes them bitter; it transforms them into the very nature of wormwood. Wormwood is not poisonous, but, strange to say, in this case the water thus transformed becomes a deadly poison; and though not fatal to all people in the area upon which the star falls, it brings death to many.

This metaphor contradicts the nature of wormwood and intimates something contradictory of God's order or ordinance. The "star", according to I. 20, is a bishop or a priest. A "great" star would be an eminent bishop, a metropolitan. The name of the star and the effect of the fall contains a perturbation of the natural exigencies of both wormwood and falling stars. It might be called an incongruous, mixed metaphor, which must be employed by the inspired Seer to express a fact in a way best fitted to reveal its strange nature.

Bishops having the divine revelations and fullness of spiritual powers are the light of the world. This bishop does not lose his divine effulgence when falling or apostatizing. Still, falling like a meteor he does not appear to be a genuine "star" like the planets. If he fell into heresy, his fall would be death to all who would drink the effects of the fall, and he would lose the light with which to enlighten the world. But he still beams in the fullness of divine light, therefore holds on to the true doctrines of Jesus Christ, valid ordination and the sacraments. Yet he makes the sources of divine life a bitter and death-bringing draught, which is not in accord with the nature of wormwood. If he lost any part or parcel of revelation, he would no longer burn like a torch to enlighten the world; he would fall like the stars of VI. 13, IX. 1, or XII. 9. He therefore does not fall into heresy or unbelief but schism. And he pollutes the waters of one third of the territories belonging to the Church. If a real meteor were so large that in falling it would cover a wide territory of rivers and rivulets, it would crush out life instantly in that part of the earth and produce a great earthquake by the shock.

In the language of the prophets a figurative use was made of the idea of "wormwood". The name "Wormwood", clearly predicts a great apostasy in the Old Testament meaning of the term as well as in the fall of the star. God threatens wormwood as food to the pseudo-prophets who usurped the right and authority to teach claiming to have received visions and revelations, when they knew they were deceivers and had no mission to speak for God; while here the star itself is called wormwood, because it turns everything it touches into wormwood and poisons those who drink at the sources polluted by it.

1). Wormwood is threatened by God as food for disobedience (Jer. IX. 13-15). The spiritual favors and temporal blessings promised the Israelites for obedience to God's laws and ordinances are milk and honey. When they sever their relationship with Him and become disobedient, He will feed them wormwood.

2). Through the same prophet, God threatens wormwood as food for the perverse priests and false prophets, because they gave the example of injustice and adultery to the people, perverted their naturally true mind and heart by abetting injustice and hindering the return of those who would repent and encouraging the evil-doers in sin (Jer. XXIII. 11-15).

3). Wormwood shall be the food of false prophets for hypocrisy, for pretended visions and for teaching false doctrines which they knew to be false. They were self-appointed prophets, who received no call or vision from God and contradicted the warnings of the true prophets. They misled the people for their own gain. They gave out the revelations of the true prophets as their own, in order to obtain the leadership over the people, to become supreme in authority. They subverted God's order. (Jer. XXIII. 15-40).

4). Wormwood symbolizes perverting the sources of grace and spiritual life into poison and bitterness. The people of Israel became so perverse, that they hated those who defended the oppressed and those who taught them the law as revealed by God. The very truth and justice of God became wormwood to them. (Amos V. 7, 10-13).

The use of the figure by the prophets was surely in the mind of the Seer when he called the falling star "Wormwood". Wormwood is to be given those people, priests, and bishops who refuse to obey the authority of the Church which possesses this authority by divine commission from Christ. This is schism, and formal schism is grievous sin. And many shall die from participation of the fountains, the sacraments, polluted by the star fallen into schism. Schism does not pollute the sacraments. But those who receive them from schismatics, knowing them to be schismatics, will commit sacrilege and thereby imbibe death.

Wormwood will be the spiritual refreshment of all bishops and priests who mislead the people by false standards and practice injustice against zealous and faithful pastors. Selfish ambition and advancement in the Church for earthly gain is the object of their labors. This fallen star changes the sources of spiritual life into "wormwood", into sources of spiritual death by disobedience, pride and ambition. He himself becomes wormwood by his apostasy, because he becomes a self-appointed teacher or prophet. He loses his divine commission. Those who receive their commission from him are also changed into wormwood, because their commission and appointment is unlawful. Their ministrations cannot produce sanctity and the heights of perfection which the ministrations of priests and bishops in the true Church produce.

The fallen star is guilty of pride, hypocrisy and rebellion, when he assumes unlawful authority over others and perverts and refuses submission to the true order established by Christ. It begets pride and rebellion in his followers. They follow a slippery path and must stumble and fall, after they have partaken of this poisonous potion. Sharing in the hypocrisy and rebellion of their schismatic superior, they knowingly partake of his wormwood and become wormwood themselves.

By his assumed authority, he turns truth into falsehood. He is guilty of oppression and injustice when he exercises such authority. The law of God and matters of faith become wormwood to those who partake of them and to the bishops and priests who follow into the schism, for they climb up another way into the sheepfold and not through the door.

The definition and symbolic use made by the prophets of the idea of "WORMWOOD" indicates the Third Scourge to be the GREEK SCHISM. All other schisms in the Church passed away rather quickly, but the Greek Schism has remained. It has carried away from Christendom approximately one third of the membership of the true Church. Schism is not heresy but embodies it in the practical denial of the Church's authority. As disobedience, it perverts the sources of spiritual life into sources of spiritual death, because in formal schism the sacraments are received sacrilegiously.

The Greek Schism began in the first instance with a courtier, Photius, in 857 A. D. Bardas, the uncle of the emperor Michael III., was refused communion by the Patriarch, Ignatius, because of immoral relations with his daughter-in-law. He vowed vengeance for having his sin punished. He prevailed on the emperor to force his mother and sisters into a convent. Ignatius refused to consecrate them because they were unwilling. Ignatius was banished by the emperor for disobedience. Then the learned and crafty Photius, a layman, was consecrated Patriarch contrary to the laws of the Church and appointed by the emperor. The bishops who refused to submit to this injustice were deposed and exiled. Photius sent letters to Rome full of lies, misrepresenting everything to get the Pope's approval of his appointment. The Pope sent legates to investigate and report to him. But the legates were forced by threats of the emperor and enticed by gifts to depose Ignatius and confirm Photius. The Pope, after he learned all the facts from the Abbot Theognostus, excommunicated the legates and Photius. Then Photius threw off the mask and in 876 openly began the schism. The emperor was assassinated that same year, and Photius was deposed. But later he regained the favor of the emperor Basil, who appointed him patriarch on the death of Ignatuis. The Pope, John the VIII., consented to recognize him as patriarch. But he again resorted to fraud and opposition to the pope, and in a synod had the Eighth Ecumenical Council, 869 A. D., condemned. Thereupon the Pope excommunicated him. Photius remained in power till the death of Basil, 886 A. D. The schism was then healed. It was renewed by Patriarch Michael Caerularius, a proud and turbulent man. He refused all communication with the papal delegates, whom the emperor Constantine IX. received graciously. He was thereupon excommunicated together with all his adherents in 1054 A. D. From that time dates the final Greek Schism. The whole Eastern Church of the Greek Rite eventually followed the Patriarch of Constantinople into the schism. Russia was not yet converted when the schism began but was later drawn into it. The Mohammedan Turks subjected all those countries that had fallen into the schism except Russia. This is another evident example of the abhorrence of God for heresy and schism.

The description in the Apocalypse fits the Greek Schism in every detail, even as to the topography of the countries involved. Asia Minor and the Balkan peninsula being mountainous have very many rivers and in the rainy season many more brooks. But the rivers and fountains symbolize the sources of knowledge, the divine truth, and of spiritual life, the sacraments. The star still in effulgence as it falls represents a bishop who has not lost his luster through heresy. It would symbolize a lapse into schism, retention of all true doctrines, ordination and administration of all the sacraments radiating thereby the fullness of divine light. This continued burning of the star may also allude to the teachings and example of the illustrious fathers and doctors of the Church in the East. Not all died of the wormwood waters, only those who knowingly consented to the schism. The disobedience which had been partial in the Iconoclast controversy became complete in the schism. The usurpation by Photius and the unjust banishment of the rightful patriarch and the willing consent of all perverse bishops and priests who followed the self-appointed Photius changed the sources of spiritual life into sources of poison and spiritual death.

This Greek Church once brilliant with many saints produced no more saints after the schism. Many Christians losing their fervor and finally their faith accepted Mohammedanism and died a spiritual death. After the conquest of Constantinople by the Turks, the learned Greeks fled to western Europe bringing with them the culture of the decadent schismatic church and caused a partial return to paganism in the Renaissance period. The Church entered the Renaissance movement to direct it along Christian standards and succeeded fairly well, still many people died spiritually from the wormwood doctrines and culture of the Greeks. And this was one of the causes which brought the greater darkening of the world as described in the next chapter (IX. 2). The final result of the Greek Schism appears in Communism, which is a complete return to unbelief and barbarism.

4. The Fourth Trumpet. The Lights Of Heaven Are Dimmed.

Verse 12.

Verse 12

At the sound of the fourth angel's trumpet the lights of heaven are bedimmed. No star falls, but the sources of light, the sun, moon and stars lose their full power. This scourge neither shortens the day nor brings on an Egyptian darkness as in Exodus (X. 22) but partially eclipses the lights of heaven. Men no longer have the sure and clear vision they had in the full light of day and night. Everything becomes shrouded in gloom; the sun, the source of light and life on earth, shines with reduced brilliance which will allow the earth to cool off. All life must lose its vigor, and decay must set in. Fruits, flowers, grains, vegetables and ornamental plants cultivated for so many centuries with insistent care are in danger of being lost. The beauty and productivity of the earth may be changed into a northern steppe or desert. Glaciers may again creep over the most fertile fields and gardens. The standard of living must be lowered; civilization and culture must give way before the oncoming blight of frigid zones; the teeming population of tropical and subtropical zones must dwindle down to small tribes of northern nomads, and the vigorous health of people in sunny climates must be reduced to that of frigid inhabitants. Men must turn their minds to the procuring of a meagre existence, and there would be too little time for education and progress. Barbarism must reign supreme in the world again.

The scourge bedimming the lights of heaven afflicts the Church, the spiritual order. It shows a strong contrast to what is contained in the prophecy of Isaias (XXX. 26) describing in figurative language the future brilliant illumination of the world by the Messias. The prophecy in our text foreshows a time of trouble for the Church and an obscuration of her splendor and her power to enlighten the world.

The prophets called any misfortune that dimmed the luster of the theocracy a day of darkness. Likewise when they prophesy defeat and humiliation for other nations they predict it by the obscuration of the sun, moon and stars. Isaias speaks thus to Babylon, (XIII. 10) and Ezechiel to Egypt (XXXII. 7). Joel calls the coming war with the Babylonians "a day of darkness and of gloominess" (II. 2); of the temporal extinction of the theocracy in the Babylonian Captivity he says, "the sun and the moon are darkened, and the stars have withdrawn their shining". Ezechiel likewise calls the extinction of the theocracy "a cloudy and dark day" (XXXIV. 12). The darkening of the lights of heaven would then logically mean some calamity befalling the Church and dimming her glory, weakening her authority and ushering in a rapid decline in her influence to direct the destinies of the world.

This dire calamity next to befall the Church was in chronological order the GREAT WESTERN SCHISM. Heresiarchs, such as Wycliffe in England and Huss in Bohemia, darkened the minds of some men by their rebellion against the true doctrines of Christ and the authority of the Church; the Albigensian heresy had caused some turmoil in France, Italy and elsewhere. But their doctrines left no lasting evil results, because men easily recognized them as NOT the teachings of the Church. The Great Western Schism was IN the Church; and in the heat of that controversy, men's vision was so blinded that even the most learned, pious and loyal could not know with certainty who was the rightful head of the Church. The learned rector of the Sorbonne, the greatest seminary of the time, and St. Vincent

Ferrer, the miracle-worker of the age, adhered to the anti-pope, Peter de-Luna, known as Benedict XIII., sincerely believing him to be the legitimate pontiff. Christendom was for a generation hopelessly divided.

The Great Western Schism was not in the literal sense a schism; it was rather a division of opinions as to who was the legitimate successor of St. Peter. But it was a great disaster for the Church. The papal teaching and ruling authority divine in its origin, giving spiritual light and life to the world, no longer shone with the brilliancy with which it had beamed upon the world for a thousand years. For thirty-eight years the voice of authority was lost in a babble of contradicting voices. Neither the faithful nor the clergy could look to the papacy as the source of light and strength but had to deplore the confusion caused by the contentions for the supreme office. Theology, science and culture, which had reached their culmination in the 13th century, decayed; discipline, the changeable laws of the Church, more strictly observed after lay investiture was abolished and the throttling hold of feudalism on the people was broken, relaxed; piety declined. These things are typified by the "moon". The lives of the clergy no longer shone as brilliantly with learning and virtue as during the two preceding centuries. Seeing the ambition, quarrels, envy and vainglory in the members of the episcopate and cardinalate, the clergy became obsequious seekers after episcopal favors instead of sincere pursuers of duty. No doubt bluff and hypocrisy prevailed in obtaining favors. This is represented by the dimming of the stars. Thus the lights of heaven were obscured, and the world was in semi-darkness during this period. There was no apostasy during the schism; no star fell from heaven: But the Church lost much of her influence in directing world-affairs along Christian standards, and she never regained this lost influence.

The four scourges announced by the first four trumpets afflicted the earth, the sea, the rivers and fountains of water and the sun, moon and stars. All phases of life were thus drawn into common misery. These scourges are the four winds of chapter VII. 1. They will eventually call down upon the world the "woes" of the three remaining trumpets.

The darkening of the sun in the Old Dispensation foreboded the nearing of God's judgments. Thus Amos prophesied upon the kingdom of Israel (VIII. 9). They are an omen portending the same here. God's scourges are called forth by the wicked, but the good will always be chastised with them for their correction. The number FOUR signifies a universal application of the scourges for the world that was in contact with the Church.

V. THE WOES

1. The Eagle In Midheaven Announces The Three Woes. Verse 13.

Verse 13

We have heard four of the seven angels with trumpets in succession. Another scene is now inserted denoting a new epoch in history. By this inserted scene, the last three trumpets are separated from the first four, and these last three are closely allied.

The "Eagle" flying through mid-heaven is obviously some great saint with a direct commission from God to preach to the world the impending judgments. The "Woe" is not an uncommon term either in the Old or New Testament to designate the direst judgments of God (Is. V.). Our Lord spoke it both as a threat to hardened sinners and a warning to all who might be prone to grievous sin. The eagle flies through mid-heaven where he can be seen and heard by all who dwell under "heaven". In apocalyptical symbolism, the eagle is the emblem of the contemplative life, and in prophetical imagery the emblem of an independent government.

By a wonderful co-incidence a great saint appears at this stage in the history of the Church. His eminence and influence procured for him the distinction of an eagle flying through mid-heaven. This was the Dominican priest, St. Vincent Ferrer. When in 1398 he lay at death's door with fever, our Lord, St. Francis and St. Dominic appeared to him, miraculously cured him of his fever and commissioned him to preach penance and prepare men for the coming judgments. Preaching in the open space in San Esteban on October 3, 1408 he solemnly declared that he was the angel of the judgment spoken of by St. John in the Apocalypse. The body of a woman was just being carried to St. Paul's church nearby for burial. St. Vincent ordered the bearers to bring the corpse before him. He adjured the dead to testify whether his claim was true or not. The dead woman came to life and in the hearing of all bore witness to the truth of the saint's claim and then slept again in death (Fr. Stanislaus Hogan O. P.). He made his claim before the Dominican Fathers, his superiors, who did not protest, because the miracle convinced them. The bull of canonization compares him to an "angel flying through mid-heaven". The breviary uses similar language. (Hogan). The above testimony is accepted by all biographers of St. Vincent as a proof of his claim. But they make his reference to the Apocalypse indicate chapter XIV. 6, for they say he often chose it as his text, "Fear God, and give Him honor, for the day of His judgment is at hand". They do not prove that he pronounced himself that particular angel. And he seems to have had only the general revelation that he was appointed "the angel of the judgment".

By designating him the angel of chapter XIV. 6, the commentators run into inexplicable difficulties. For St. Vincent emphatically and repeatedly asserted that the Day of Wrath was to come "soon, very soon, within a very short time", *cito, bene cito et valde breviter.* St. John also announced that the judgment was to come very quickly (Apoc. III. 11), which meant that it would *begin* to operate soon. Since St. Vincent uttered these prophecies, five centuries have elapsed, and the end of the world and last judgment have not come. Some try to explain it by saying that the saint meant the particular judgment; but this is meaningless. Others contend that he predicted the approach of the last judgment conditionally, as Jonas predicted the destruction of Niniveh (Hogan). But these are all conjectures of biographers. St Vincent did not aver that he was the angel of chapter XIV. or that the General Judgment was very near. Father Hogan makes a distinction between what was explicitly revealed and what is the conclusion of a secret instinct (p. 54) and he follows the explanation of St. Thomas on the principles of prophetic revelations. He says: "He had received a divine command to preach the approach of the judgment, as legate *a latere Christi;* but he had not received any explicit revelation as to when the judgment was to be". He should have added, "nor as to what *kind* of judgment it was to be", and furthermore, "that he received no revelation that he is the angel of chapter XIV.".

Commentators depend on the biographers of St. Vincent for their explanation of his words. These biographers may not have been careful and exact enough in recording his words, for no one took his sermons down in shorthand. Besides they may have missed the key to his revelations and thus misunderstood the proper role assigned to him in the Apocalypse as well as the meaning of the word "judgment". The language of chapters VIII. 13 and XIV. 6 is the same, "flying through mid-heaven"; only in the first instance it is an eagle and in the last an "angel". The word "angel" in VIII. 13 is found in some ancient manuscripts instead of "eagle", but the word "eagle" is better authenticated and is adopted in the received text. Furthermore the eagle is an omen of judgment (Mt. XXIV. 28). The role of the eagle in chapter VIII. 13 is that of a rational being and the words are spoken by a human mouth. The inspired writer chose the eagle in the symbolism to denote with greater precision the character of the bearer of that message. In the Apocalypse the eagle is the emblem of the contemplative life, and therefore it here points to the religious orders. Now St. Vincent was a Dominican, a member of a contemplative order, and under that guise could strictly be called an eagle.

The near approach of the judgment expressed by St. Vincent in the words "cito, bene cito et valde breviter" is easily explained by seeing it as the next world-wide event without anything else of importance intervening and as identical with the three "woes" announced by the "eagle". These three scourges or "woes" as announced by the last three trumpets are revealed to be the development of the ONE judgment, which begins in chapter IX., reaches its culmination in chapters XVI. to XIX and its end in chapter XX. That the judgment should come very soon can find its meaning in the words "Behold, I come quickly", (III. 11) i.e. it would soon be operative in definite form. St. Vincent could not be the first angel of chapter XIV., because that angel appears in the days of Great Babylon and the "Beast". Now whether this "Beast" is the ancient Roman Empire, the emperor, or the future Antichrist makes no difference as concerns St. Vincent, for he appeared at a time when none of them existed and could not possibly fulfill the role allotted to the angel of chapter XIV. He is therefore evidently the eagle of VIII. 13. The results of his work also demonstrate him to be that eagle. He preached in Spain, France, Flanders, Switzerland and northern Italy. St. Bernardine of Siena took up his work and carried it through the rest of Italy as thoroughly as St. Vincent had done it in western Christendom. The first "woe" of chapter IX. was averted from those countries in which the two saints labored.

For twenty years St. Vincent labored untiringly in western Europe. So many came to hear him that he had to preach in the open places of the cities. The influence he exercised by his austerity, piety and miracles throughout Christendom upon kings, papal claimants and all classes of people, and the revival of piety and religious life which he inaugurated were as true, sincere and far-reaching as those of the greatest saint of any age. He converted large numbers of Moors and 70,000 to 125,000 Jews in Spain. His biographers narrate the vastness of his influence thus during this time of darkness, and they attribute to him the gift of tongues, because knowing only the Limousin language he nevertheless evangelized all the nations of southwestern Europe. He did superhuman penance and was convinced of being the messenger of penance to prepare men for the judgments to come very soon. His work was the real beginning of missions in the Church. He launched this movement, which has gained momentum steadily since that time and is still preparing men for more dreadful judgments to come.

Now that St. Vincent himself might have been mistaken about the place assigned to him in the apocalyptic prophecies need not appear strange. He adhered to the anti-pope, Benedict XIII., and sincerely believed him to be the legitimate pontiff. This was a matter in which his human judgment gave the decision. And this judgment can easily err. So also, since it was not explicitly revealed to him what angel of the Apocalypse he was, he may have drawn the mistaken conclusion that it was the one of chapter XIV. 6. However, it has not been proven that he claimed to be that angel or even thought he was. This latter angel has the commission to preach to EVERY "nation and tribe, and tongue, and people". St. Vincent, even though his fame spread over it all, so that he was like one "flying through mid-heaven", personally reached only a small part of Christendom.

In 1406, while preaching at Alexandria in Piedmont, St. Vincent foretold that his mantle should descend upon one who was then listening to him, and that *he* would evangelize the rest of Italy. This was St. Bernardine of Siena. Paul Thureau-Dangin in his life of St. Bernardine quotes him as having frequently used the words of the eagle, "woe, woe, woe", and of having threatened the sinners with the plague of locusts of chapter IX. in the Apocalypse, if they did not repent of their sins and evil ways and live up to their faith. He may have heard this in the sermon of St. Vincent. That St. Bernardine could be the "eagle" of VIII. 13 is possible and has some plausibility. He was a Franciscan, a member of a contemplative order; his work was in Italy, the headquarters of the Church, and therefore locally in the center of Christendom or "midheaven"; his success in Italy in overcoming vices and abuses of power, luxuries and indifference to the practice of their religion, and the return to penance of sinners and the re-establishment of a vigorous and living faith over all of Italy equals the work of St. Vincent in the countries which he evangelized. He labored from 1417 till 1444, the year of his death. He spread the work of reform of the Franciscan order under the name of Observants and succeeded so well, that the membership of the reform was increased from 130 friars to over 4,000 before his death. One saint would just as fully fill the role assigned in the Apocalypse as the other. But in the light of the special revelation and appointment by our Lord, St. Vincent is more probably the "eagle" of the Apocalypse. If the biographers had taken down verbal copies of his sermons, as some hearer did of St. Bernardine's, they might show the same pertinent words from the Apocalypse spoken by him to threaten the judgment of God upon sinners as St. Bernardine frequently expressed.

CHAPTER IX.

Westminster Version

And the fifth angel sounded the trumpet, and I saw a star which
had fallen from heaven to the earth, and there was given to him the
key of the bottomless pit. And he opened the bottomless 2. pit, and there
went up from the pit a smoke like that of a great furnace; and the sun
was darkened, and the air, by reason of the smoke of the pit. And out
of the smoke locusts 3. went forth upon the earth, and there was given
them a power like that of the scorpions of the earth; and they were told
not to harm the 4. grass of the earth or any green thing or any tree, but
only such men as have not the seal of God upon their foreheads.

And it was given to them, not to kill, 5. but to torture them during
five months; and their torment was like the torment of the scorpion, when
it striketh man.

And in those days men shall seek 6. death, and they shall not find it,
and they shall long to die, and death fleeth from them.

And these locusts were like unto 7. horses arrayed for battle; on their
heads appeared crowns like gold; their faces were like those of men; they 8.
had hair like the hair of women; and their teeth were like those of lions.

They had breastplates like unto 9. iron breastplates, and the noise of
their wings was like that of many horse-chariots rushing to battle.

And they have tails like those of 10. scorpions, and stings, and in their
tails lies their power of harming men during the five months. They have
as 11. king over them the angel of the bottomless pit, whose name in
Hebrew is Abaddon, and in Greek he is called Apollyon. The first woe
has passed 12. behold, hereafter two woes are still to come. And the sixth
angel sounded 13. his trumpet, and I heard a single voice from the four
horns of the golden altar which is before God; and it said to 14. the sixth
angel who had the trumpet: 'Loose the four angels who are bound on
the great river Euphrates'. Then 15. were loosed the four angels who had
been held ready for the hour, and day and month and year, in order
that they should kill the third part of men. And the number of the
troops of the 16. cavalry was twenty thousand times ten thousand; I heard
the number thereof. And this is the manner after which 17. the horses
and they that sat on them appeared in my vision: they wore breastplates the
color of fire, and of hyacinth and of sulphur; and the heads of the
horses were as heads of lions, and out of their mouths issue fire and smoke
and sulphur.

By these three plagues were killed 18. the third part of men, by the
fire, by the smoke, and by the sulphur issuing from their mouths. For
the 19. power of the horses is in their mouth and in their tails; for their
tails are like serpents, with heads, and by means of them they do harm.

And the other men, who were not 20. killed by these plagues, did
not repent of the works of their hands, and cease adoring the devils and
the idols of gold and silver and bronze and stone and wood, which can
neither see nor hear nor walk; and they did not 21. repent of their murders, nor of their enchantments, nor of their impurity nor of their thefts.

2. The Fifth Trumpet. The First Woe. Vision Of The Locusts.

Chapter IX.

Verses 1-11.

Verse 1

At the sound of the fifth trumpet, a scene somewhat similar to, yet essentially different in nature from that of VIII. 10 comes to view. The star in chapter eight is in the act of falling from heaven, whilst here it is already fallen to the earth when the curtain is lifted. This star, as the other one, is some apostate bishop or priest. He does not light up the earth where he has fallen. His falling forebodes calamity and woe to the earth, for in prophetic symbolism falling stars are harbingers of grief and disaster. It is the first woe predicted by the eagle.

A key was given the fallen star. The aorist tense here employed leaves some doubt as to whether St. John saw the act of handing the key to the star, or whether it was in his possession at the beginning of the scene. The latter seems more probable, because the same tense is used in other texts where there is no doubt of its exact meaning (VII. 2). Because the key was "given" him, the star can use it only by divine permission. There is but one key to the "shaft" of the abyss indicated by the definite article, and therefore this star alone is able to open it.

This key alludes to other keys. Our Lord promised Peter: "I will give to thee the keys of the kingdom of heaven". The keys promised Peter for his fearless profession of faith in the divinity of Christ were the emblem of supreme power and authority over the Church. They would convey possession of the whole of divine revelation and of the perpetual privilege of being divinely guided to make unwavering and infallible decisions in matters of faith. The mind of God would be in him always as it was at the time when he made this declaration of faith. It entailed humility, because it required submission of the intellect and will to Christ. And the promise guaranteed purity of morals through the ratification of all his decisions and decrees.

In the significance of the key given the fallen star, we have the antithesis of what was promised Peter. The star is an apostate bishop or priest. The key to the shaft of the abyss is an emblem of rebellion, as the keys promised Peter are an emblem of submission to Christ; it leagues the star with the rebellious angels.

This key of the pit is then also an emblem of error, as Peter's keys are an emblem of truth. As God revealed the truth to Peter enabling him to make a clear declaration of it before Christ and the Apostles, so the "king of the bottomless abyss" (v. 11) infused his errors into the mind of this fallen star inspiring him to teach and spread error and immorality over the world. The mind of the "angel of the bottomless abyss" was filled with pride and hatred and concupiscence. The keys of Peter conveyed to him supreme authority over the Church of Christ, and the power to bring the light of Heaven down to earth; The apostate priest has his key from God. That is to say, the powers of the priesthood perverted by the rebellion of the will enable him to open the pit. Were he a layman, he would not have this power. The priesthood is vested with the power to suppress and subject the satanic forces, but when abused it serves to foster and propagate evil and to open the abyss and envelop the earth in darkness. This fallen star used his power to seduce, enslave and precipitate into damnation vast numbers.

This fallen star is clearly some great leader of revolt against the Church. He is the father or shepherd of apostates from or of rebels against the Church, as Peter is the father or shepherd of Christ's followers. As the followers of Peter accept his doctrines, so the followers of the fallen star will accept his. The latter will extol him as a great leader, as the followers of Peter give him due submission in virtue of his appointment and hail him the Rock of the Church. The possessor of the key of the pit is then the head of Satan's church, as Peter is the head of Christ's Church. But since the key of the pit symbolizes unbelief and rebellion, whilst the keys of Peter symbolize faith, submission and obedience, the followers of the star will go their own ways and repudiate any authority he may want to exercise over them.

Verse 2

"And he opened the pit of the abyss". The abyss is not the "pool of fire" of the nineteenth and twentieth chapters. The bottomless abyss may be the boundless void outside the universe, "the darkness outside", and it may release its prisoners and permit them to enter God's creation again when He so decrees. The Apocalypse seems to reveal that not all the evil spirits are chained down in the lower hell, or "pool of fire". Satan himself will not be cast into it until after the condemnation of Gog and Magog (XX. 9). Before that time he is bound with a great chain and consigned to the bottomless abyss (XX. 3). So this bottomless abyss is some other place of imprisonment for the evil spirits, whilst the pool of fire is the final destiny of all wickedness.

The fallen star opened the pit or shaft leading down into the bottomless abyss. This is only an allegorical figure for some action of the apostate, by which he propagates his errors and turns loose the forces of evil onto the earth. These evil spirits had probably been bound by the Church during the preceding ages. Legions of evil spirits had been driven out of possessed persons and out of the world, oracles and divining spirits had been silenced, and the superstition and stupidity of idolatry had been cleared out of Christendom. Those spirits may have been relegated to the bottomless abyss by the Church through the powers of the priesthood, the spread of truth and the administration of the sacraments; they are now released and permitted to work towards the re-establishment of paganism.

Something streamed out of the pit resembling the smoke of a blast furnace. The pit served as a chimney flue shaft for the abyss. The smoke rose into the sky but did not dissipate as it rose. The sun though not entirely blotted out by it grew dim and dark (Acts II, 19; Joel II. 30), yet men may still be able to see their way through the semi-darkness. The air becomes infected. The air which men inhale is the region of the clouds, the atmosphere (1 Thess. IV. 17), and was according to St. Paul infested with evil spirits in his day (Eph. II. 2)). Everything is tainted with this smoke spreading over the earth, and where it spreads men cannot inhale the life-giving air in its pure state anymore. They lose their health and vigor but are not dazed and are still responsible for their actions.

The obscuration of the sun and sky betokens the darkening of the authority of the Church lowering men's respect for her and showing her less divine or no longer divine at all. It signifies the success of the errors or heresies to such a degree as to bring darkness to men's minds. In appearance it is something like the last scourge in the foregoing chapter but of an entirely different nature. The infection of the air is moral and spiritual and denotes the errors and immorality which the angel turns loose.

The scourges announced by the first four trumpets grew

upon earth, whilst this "woe" comes from hell. The doctrines of Christ taught by His Church enlighten the world; the doctrines of error originating from hell would bring back the pristine darkness of paganism, if they could entirely prevail.

Verse 3

"And out of the smoke there came forth locusts upon the earth". The smoke ascending out of the abyss is not a swarm of locusts, but as it comes in contact with conditions on the surface it produces locusts, it is their efficient cause. How numerous these locusts are, the text does not state, nor does it give any hint of their being very numerous. They are only numerous enough to sting all the wicked who do not have the sign of God on their foreheads. (Ezech. IX. 6). They seem to increase in numbers as long as the smoke ascends out of the pit. The smoke spreads over some parts of the earth for the Seer beholds the locusts coming out of the smoke and over-running regions not enveloped in smoke.

The influence that ascends from the abyss produces the locusts and confers on them a power like that of scorpions. The word "power", ἐξουσία , primarily means regal "authority", the right to exercise some magisterial office over others. The figure of diction used is therefore a condensation of several ideas. These locusts receive permission from God to exercise authority over others, as all men receive liberty to do evil, and that authority is likened to the venomous sting of the scorpion. The scorpion is associated with poisonous snakes and other deadly creatures in Scripture, which represent the spiritual enemies of man. Our Lord associates scorpions with the activity of Satan (Lc. X. 19) (See Ecclus. XXXIX. 36) and He assures His disciples that He has given them authority over all noxious beasts. This figure alludes to Joel (II. 1 ff) where the oncoming Babylonian armies are described as locusts in language similar to our text. They killed all the wicked in Israel who did not have the sign of God on their foreheads (Ez. IX. 6). The effect of this woe will then be somewhat similar to that of the Babylonian war. It will clear out of the Church, as far as it spreads, all the faithless and unregenerate in heart, will purify the faithful, strengthen them and arouse new zeal and activity in the Church.

Verse 4

Common locusts eat the grass, crops, trees and every edible green herb. But these locusts are different. They receive *COMMANDS*, which restrain them from injuring grass, crops and trees. So they are rational beings who have power to destroy vegetation, but are limited in the exercise of their power by a Superior Will. Their power is like that of scorpions, but that power is only the symbol of theirs. Being rational, they are human beings, because nowhere in sacred history do we find angels destroying the vegetation of the earth, and hence they needed no prohibition against such activity. The power of the locusts is from hell, but they can use it only as far as God permits. Their permission is to inflict spiritual chastisement on those who do not have the sign of God on their foreheads, who have lost the graces of Baptism and Confirmation and are living a life of sin. The faithful servants of God are secure against their malevolent authority, as the Israelites were secure against the plague of locusts and other plagues upon the Egyptians.

Verse 5

These locusts are not permitted to kill the sinners nor to drive them into hell but only to torture them for a short time. The test is not to be a bodily one, directly or indirectly, but purely a spiritual torment. All they may do is to inflict anguish of spirit, to torture the conscience by depriving them of the means of spiritual life. The point of resemblance between the torment instilled into their victims by these locusts and the sting of the scorpion is that the venom injected is not ordinarily fatal but causes excruciating physical pain and agonizing fear of death. The anguish inflicted by these locusts is the keenest remorse of conscience and fear of eternal damnation. This intimates apostasy from the true faith, because apostates invariably suffer the pangs of conscience and dread of damnation from the uncertanity of their spiritual status. This dread of damnation generally leaves in them for a while a prospect of conversion.

The word of the Greek text really means 'to apply the touchstone', to put to the test. The Apocalypse was written at a time when persecution was imminent and when this 'test' meant torture, physical, mental or spiritual. Those who are not practical Catholics are spiritually dead. The men represented by the locusts are to torment the indifferent Catholics so as to arouse in them a vivid consciousness of their state.

The torture shall continue for FIVE MONTHS. After a certain lapse of time, the remorse will no longer be felt. The purpose of it is clear; God desires the conversion of the sinner not his damnation. And in the state in which these indifferentists lived, they sinned presumptuously and still consoled themselves with the last chance of conversion and repentance at death. That presumption is the sin against the Holy Ghost. After their apostasy, they are horrified at the condition into which their lukewarmness has brought them, and then the fear of damnation takes possession of them. They are not sure of going to hell but are uncertain in hope, as a man who has been stung by a scorpion is in dread of approaching death. These five months have been interpreted as a reminiscence of the 150 days of the deluge or as an estimate of the duration of locust life (Swete). But it need mean only that it is a judgment of God temporarily urging the sinners to repentance. The figure 5 is frequently used without a special reason to make the narrative more concrete (Mt. XXV. 15, "Five talents", Lc. XII. 6, "Five sparrows", 52, "five in one house"). After some time the apostate will become callous to the sting of conscience, soothe the wounds made by the gnawing worm by lazily submitting to the decrees of fate and grow satisfied with his spiritual status. And then he will even defend his deliberations and actions.

Verse 6

The pangs of conscience torturing these apostates are so keen at times that they bring on the desire of death. Their remorse may be accounted for as follows. Their intellects become confused by the errors of which they are victims; and the false moral standards set up by the leaders of the apostasy deliver them into the torturing tyranny of every vice. Sin can be no real joy. Indulgence in sinful pleasures brings ultimately nothing but pain. The resulting torments become a burning sting, slavery to sin, dissatisfaction, anguish of heart and mortal fear of eternal death. Thus during the five months while the sting is fresh they fall into such despair as at times to make them seek death.

The death such men seek may mean annihilation, because suicide has always been possible. All attempts of infidels to prove that there is no life hereafter only express a desire. Unbelief and doubt in a future existence make men too weak to subdue their passions; and indulged passions bring on disgust with life. Most suicides are of men hopelessly steeped in vice. Not being able to escape the allurements of sin, they wish to die like brutes and be no more. But their wish is no assurance. They are still convinced of immortality. "Such a death as they desire, a death which will end their sufferings, is impossible; physical death is no remedy for the βασανισμὸς of an evil conscience" (H. B. Swete).

Verses 7-11

When the smoke rose from the pit, there was something present on earth, which being touched by the smoke produced these monstrous locusts. The results of their activity are depicted in the first seven verses. The Seer now delineates their character.

The locusts resemble war-horses and are equipped for battle. The head of a locust is oddly shaped like the head of a horse. Cavalry and war-chariots were the most formidable and irresistible forces of offensive warfare in antiquity. Locusts were the most thorough destroyers of the means of life. These two agents of destruction are united in these monsters with the power of scorpions to symbolize the spiritual havoc which the first woe shall spread over the earth. It will demolish the bulwarks against the powers of hell and will consume the means of spiritual life. These monsters are men who have the nature of brutes expressed in the shape of the body and possess the destructive power of both horse and locust. These monsters do not kill but bring men into utmost misery and deter those who are not fortified by the grace of God from daring resistance. The doctrines adopted by these locusts make them bold enough to intimidate those who do not have the "sign of God" on their foreheads and are therefore too indifferent to hold fast to their faith. This description is somewhat like that given by Joel (II. 4 f) of the oncoming army of Babylonian warriors who were God's agents "on the day of the Lord" to destroy the theocracy.

The next words of this verse are a contrast to those of IV. 4. The elders described there wear crowns of pure gold symbolizing legitimate authority, wisdom, prudence, justice, unselfishness and other virtues of true princes and faithful servants of God. The golden crowns confer upon them spiritual dominion in the Empire of the Lamb over those who freely submit to their jurisdiction. The locusts wear something that resembles a crown and is made of imitation gold. This denotes a twofold usurpation: the wearers arrogate to themselves the authority to rule and tyrannize beyond their territorial and hereditary domains and subject people against their will, and they usurp spiritual jurisdiction; they set themselves up as heads or rulers of churches without any divine commission.

These monsters have a man's face. The human face is the symbol of reason. It is another feature revealing how formidable they are. Man if brutally wicked is a greater menace than any beast, for he has a mind and reason to plan evil-doing. When that mind is perverted by falsehood and bent on evil, the most cruel and bloody beasts of prey are weak antagonists.

Verse 8

These locusts have hair like that worn by women. This has since antiquity been the symbol of voluptuousness, effeminacy and vainglory. It is an external trait of the inner character. Though they have the reasoning power of men, their nature is weak, and they are swayed like women by sentimental considerations. The motives of their actions are sensual pleasure and vainglory. They are devoid of the manly strength of character or chivalry of mediaeval knights.

They are cruel yet have not the other qualifications of lions but only the teeth to lacerate defenseless victims. They are bold, self-assertive, malicious and treacherous. This alludes again to Joel (I. 6). These monsters are thus a composite of man and woman, horse and locust, lion and scorpion. Their activity in the spiritual order produces all the havoc which these various creatures can produce in the material order. They meditate and plan evil; they give themselves up to sensuality and vainglory and listen only to sentimental pleas; they destroy the institutions and means of sanctification and terrorize people into subjection, and they lacerate all who do not submit to their tyranny and bring those who do submit into the utmost misery.

Verses 9-10

The monsters wear breastplates like iron. This detail shows them to be obstinate in their baleful intentions and activity and unwilling to listen to reason; and, although clearly convinced of their errors, they will rather die than renounce them (Cor. a Lapide). This figure reveals them to be mailed against attack in debate and unwilling to be won over by reason or persuasion. They are invulnerable, victorious hordes.

Their wings make a noise like war-chariots and a great force of cavalry. Horses and chariots were the swiftest means of transportation and the most irresistible forces of attack, and here they are a portent of the speed and rapidity with which this spiritual scourge shall spread over the earth. In prophetical language, wings are emblems of contemplation and of swift movements. These wings have only the latter quality. The noise of their attack reminds us of savage warfare, and it signifies great power of propaganda. Reason or logic does not rule their speech or manners, and they can win only by their menacing appearance and vehement impetuosity terrorizing into silence all who would assert their right to liberty of conscience and imposing their will upon all by military force. Like war-horses, they trample all opposition under foot. It recalls again the description of Joel (II. 4 f). There as in other parts of prophetic literature the thought constantly prevailing is that the enemies of the theocracy would come from the north. The borrowing of figures from Joel points to the northern regions of the Church as the territory to be afflicted by this scourge.

The locusts have an infernal faculty likened to that of scorpions and symbolized by the tail. In Isaias (IX. 15-17), the tail is the symbol of lying, hypocrisy and false doctrines. The poisonous sting in the tails of these monsters aptly represents sophistry, cunning, deceit and the false conclusions which propagators of heresy draw from Scripture and from the teachings of the Church, by which they mislead their victims and engender in their dupes anguish and pangs of conscience. Death by persecution and martyrdom for the true faith is not meant, for that is not considered a woe in the Apocalypse. These locusts can afflict none but the wicked by injecting the poison of heresy into them and leading them astray. According to the Greek text, the sting of the locusts is the authority to impose "injustice" on their victims. For a short time only, symbolically five months, shall those who lose their faith and surrender to sophistry and heresy feel the injustice and wretchedness of their state, and then their conscience becomes inert. The "five months" could be distorted to mean five centuries, but such a view would be unreal and fantastic.

Verse 11

In the book of Proverbs (XXX. 27), the "locust has no king". But these figurative locusts have a king. He is "the angel of the bottomless abyss" (XX. 3), Satan, and his name is "The Destroyer". These locusts obey him and do his work. He aims at the destruction of the Church, of the faith of his poor victims and of their souls forever in hell. The promoters of heresy, error and immorality, are the subjects of Satan and bring irremediable and final ruin to all his followers.

The ancient Fathers and Doctors of the Church have understood the fallen star to be Arius. That application is plausible, if the army of horsemen appearing after the sixth trumpet is interpreted to be the barbarian invasions of the fifth century. The ancient explanation of some of the Fathers must be set aside, however, for that view has long ago been discarded and been superceded by more up-to-date opinions.

The whole description of the locusts fits down to the last details the kings and princes who established by force the heresy of the 16th century. Prior to the coming of Protestantism, the Church had through great saints whom God raised up always successfully combatted and overcome all heresies. None of the heresiarchs gained any lasting following. Although Arianism seemingly claimed the whole Christian world at the zenith of its power and diffusion, it speedily wasted away and had almost disappeared after three centuries. It was different with Protestantism, which successfully established itself and was victorious from the outset. Luther did truly open the pit and let loose against the Church all the fury of hell. Therefore modern interpreters almost universally see in this fallen star Luther (Cor. a Lapide, p 201, Note 1 ma).

When Luther propounded his heretical and immoral doctrines, the sky became as it were obscured by smoke. It spread very rapidly over some regions of the earth, and it brought forth princes and kings who were eager to despoil the Church of her possessions. They compelled the people of their domains and in the territories robbed from the Church to accept the doctrines of Luther. The proponents of Protestantism made false translations of the Bible and misled the people into their errors by apparently proving from the "Bible" (their own translations) the correctness of their doctrines. It was all deceit, lying and hypocrisy. Bad and weak, lax and lukewarm, indifferent and non-practical Catholics and those who had neglected to get thorough instruction in their religion were thus misled; and these, seeing the Catholic Church now through this smoke of error from the abyss and beholding a distorted caricature of the true Church, began both to fear and hate her.

Luther did everything to instill hatred for the Church into the hearts of his followers. This hatred is alive today in misrepresentations of the Church, in an over-readiness to believe all the evil of which she is accused and in a refusal to believe the truth about her. Protestants often persecuted to death those who disagreed with them. Christ's true followers have suffered martyrdom in all ages somewhere.

The princes of Germany eagerly took up Lutheranism to become the spiritual heads of the churches in their domains and to plunder the Church. Their assumed jurisdiction in spiritual matters was usurpation; it was not pure gold. In Denmark, Norway and Sweden the Kings imposed Lutheranism upon the people by the power of the sword and by lying, deceit and hypocrisy. They left the altars in the churches and had apostate priests use vestments and external trappings of the Catholic Church to mislead the people. They crushed out the Catholic faith by terrorism, by making it a felony and treason to remain a Catholic. Each monarch made himself the spiritual head of the church in his kingdom. They had so-called historians falsify history to arouse hatred against the Church in the hearts of the people. They pretended to prove the truth of Lutheranism by false translations of the Bible made by Luther and others and by still falser interpretations of it. Those princes and kings were the locusts appearing in the vision of St. John. They had the teeth of lions to terrify lukewarm Catholics into submission. They hardened themselves against the truth so as to nullify all efforts to reason with them in various councils and diets. Luther directed them by saying: "sit pro ratione voluntas". He knew that truth and reason were against him, but he would have it as he listed. All intelligent converts to the Catholic Church today admit that Protestantism is based on sentimentality. Voluptuousness and immorality kept step with the progress of Protestantism. Luther himself admitted that there was "a worse Sodom under the Gospel than under the Papacy". "Who would have begun to preach", he writes, "if he had known beforehand that so much unhappiness, tumult, scandal, blasphemy, ingratitude and wickedness would be the result?" In contradiction of the teachings of Christ, Luther permitted the Landgrave of Hesse to have two wives at the same time.

In England, Henry VIII., an adulterer, violated the unity of faith by making himself the head of the church in his kingdom. He acted on the same principle as the princes of Germany and the kings of Scandinavia: "Cuius regio, eius religio", i.e. "whose territory it is, his religion must be accepted." King Henry despoiled 741 monasteries to enrich the newly made 'nobles'. With what bloodshed and persecution of Catholics, Protestantism was established in England, all reliable historians testify. They also testify that only 30% of the English were practical Catholics, 70% having lost the "sign of God". So the locusts soon stung the majority of the English with heresy. They suffered the penalty with which Christ threatened the lukewarm (III. 16).

In earlier defections from the Church, apostate bishops promoted the heresies; in the defection of Protestantism it was the kings and princes who then appointed themselves spiritual heads of the new churches. They usurped spiritual jurisdiction thereby wearing crowns of imitation gold. The voluptuousness of their lives is a noted fact of history. "By their fruits you shall know them", says Christ of the false prophets; and it was borne out in the lives of the "reformers" and their followers. Luther openly taught: "Sin valiantly, only believe more valiantly".

The vainglory of the "reformers" and their intolerance are also well-known. They hated and fought one another, as they contradicted one another's doctrines. Since then the world has been filled with contradictory interpretations of Scripture, with sophistry and intentional deceit to explain away the obvious and true meaning of the sacred text. The solidity of the true Church is in its unity. Protestantism is the antithesis of unity. This bears out what Christ predicted: "He that gathereth not with me scattereth". Peter gathered into one fold, Luther scattered: Peter received the "keys of the kingdom of Heaven"; Luther received the "key of the bottomless abyss", of the kingdom of Satan. As Peter is the Vicar of Christ, so Luther is the vicar of Satan.

That Luther himself suffered great pangs of conscience in the castle of Wartburg for his apostasy is contained in his own confessions. That was no doubt the reason for his fanaticism, for his advice to the princes to kill as mad dogs all who would not obey them and accept his doctrines. The English king and nobles likewise impoverished by robbery and confiscation the Catholics and by torture and threats of death compelled them to share their own wretched state of apostasy from the true faith. All earlier heresies were overcome by zealous saints who converted the erring again to the truth; but such men were barred from Protestant countries. Thus the promoters wore breastplates as of iron; they were hardened against the truth. A majority of their descendants have quit Protestantism; but they have not returned to the Catholic Church; they have on the contrary drifted into agnosticism, unbelief and neo-paganism. This vision is thus in all details verified in Protestantism. The "Destroyer" has used its promoters to destroy divine faith in the hearts of men and to lead them little by little into complete spiritual death, infidelity.

3. The Sixth Trumpet. The Second Woe.
The Vision Of 200,000,000 Horsemen.

Verses 12 to the end.

Verse 12

St. John announces the end of one woe threatened by the eagle. The lukewarm and proud are cleared out of the Church in the countries struck by the first woe. Two more woes are to follow. The next woe will bring calamities upon the whole world the good and bad alike and will separate them more completely in all countries.

Verse 13

At the sound of the sixth trumpet the Seer hears a single voice from the four horns of the golden altar. This reference to the FOUR HORNS may signify the expectation by the Church of a more disastrous woe than the foregoing one. The golden altar represents the religious orders (See VIII. 3). The voice from all four horns is the unanimous declaration of all religious, that the Church is now ready to meet the fiercest onslaught of the enemy in her whole history. So let the woe begin.

Verse 14

After the spread and establishment of Protestantism, the Council of Trent re-iterated the dogmas of the Church and crystallized them in clear language that left no doubt of what is true and what is false. Science, philosophy and theology received a new impetus and went out to explore new fields. The Four Horns of the golden altar include particularly, besides the older orders, the religious congregations, contemplative, missionary, charitable, teaching etc. founded since the appearance of Protestantism. All religious organizations have done efficient work for the spread of faith as well as of charity and education. Through them the Church has actualized more fully her mission upon earth. She has been strengthened and been enabled to contend successfully with all the machinery that Satan has invented to destroy her. And she is speeding up the Christianization of savage and semi-savage peoples year after year. No matter what upheavals will occur in society, what wars or revolutions may scourge the earth, the Church is prepared to fulfill her mission when God permits new calamities to afflict mankind.

The four angels are to be loosed. They are evil spirits, otherwise they would not be bound. They come from the region of the Euphrates, whence come the enemies of God's people. Since the order comes indirectly from God, it is consoling to know that they can do only what God permits. The number four forebodes a woe on the whole world that will rouse hatreds and wars and deluge the world with blood. The second woe culminates in the reign of Antichrist. The release of these four evil spirits may precede a resurgence of Mohommedanism and may lead its religionists to unite with communists in a holy war against all nations who will not join them or submit to their domination.

Verse 15

The four evil spirits have waited a long time for the hour in which they might begin their depradations. The "hour" is mentioned first, then "day, month and year". They cannot begin their murderous work until the predetermined hour. This ascensive order denotes a definite hour set by Providence. They seem to have known for a long time the work of vengeance allotted to them and may have done the same work before (in the days of Genghis Khan) and were then bound again. But they must now bide the time until the golden altar gives the word. Their bloody task is to kill a third of the human race, perhaps the good as well as the wicked.

The text gives no intimation about the interval of time between the first and second woe. It will be a time of wars developing into a world-revolution that will deluge the whole world with carnage and bloodshed. The three-and-a-half years of the reign of the Beast will be its climax. The time of its beginning is wrapped in secrecy, and the duration of this time of slaughter is likewise a deep and dark secret. Verses 20 and 21 presage a time of peace between the first reign of terror in the second woe and the reign of Antichrist. It seems to be a mystery of the future to be brought on by the new menace, militaristic and atheistic communism.

Verse 16

St. John abruptly gives the number of killers appearing in the vision, which is 200,000,000 horsemen. The revelation seems to startle the Seer so much that he forgets to connect this verse with the foregoing and leaves out all conjunctive particles or phrases. The number exceeds the population of the whole Roman Empire of his time. St. John makes it especially emphatic by adding: "I heard the number of them", as if he would suspect skepticism by the reader of so large a number of cavalry in the world. It is, however, a symbolic and approximate number. It is limited and not like that of chapter XX. 7, where the number of enemies is "as the sand of the sea". The number indicates either a long session of wars, in which vast armies are engaged, or a universal revolution and overthrow of governments with incessant guerrilla fighting, when every person carries weapons for self-defense, and rapine and murder become universal.

Verse 17

The Seer describes both the horsemen and the horses upon which they ride. The riders are mailed wearing breastplates that have the color of fire, of flaming smoke and of sulphur showing them to be armed for defense and attack and to be invulnerable and formidable. It is useless for anyone to combat these victorious hordes. The colors seem to forebode the approach of the empire of Antichrist, in which this woe reaches its consummation, for in XIV. 10-11 the followers and adorers of the Beast will be tormented by the same agencies. The colors reveal the character of the riders. Fire is the symbol of hatred, flame-colored smoke of blasphemy and sulphur of rebellion against God and His law. Sulphur denotes immorality and sensuality. Sulphur is the material that is burned in the hatred of God and produces the smoke of blasphemy. The three substances are united in this wise: hatred of God begets disobedience of His law and leads to immorality, and expresses itself against Him in blasphemies. Thus the damned in hell are tortured. They hate God, cling to all evil and give voice to their hatred in blasphemies (XIV. 10-11). The activities of the saints in Heaven are the opposite. Their happiness is in possessing God in love, worshipping and praising Him and harmonizing their will with His.

These horsemen are not the locusts of the first woe. The riders are distinct from the horses they ride. The men have on their armor only the color of the substances emitted from the mouths of the horses. The unearthly power of the horses is from the four evil spirits who inspire or activate them. How long the materials that make up these monsters were on earth before the unbinding of the four spirits can only be conjectured. The horses and riders execute the judgment of God. The horses would then represent the institutions or organizations that are filled with satanic hatred against God and Christ. The riders direct the institutions or forces and through them rule and direct world events. The horses have the heads of lions, which are emblems of royalty. Whether they have the voices of lions is not stated but may be assumed. They have great power of propaganda. This feature alludes to the Beast who has the mouth of a lion. These monsters will preach the overthrow of governments so that *they* have the chance to subjugate and tyrannize the peoples. They are then related to the Beast (XIII. 2) in their power of propaganda and in being the rulers of the world. They are also related to the locusts who had the teeth of lions but could inflict only spiritual injury. Both derive their power of evil-doing from the abyss.

From the mouths of the horses issue fire, smoke and sulphur. In chapter six, War rides a red horse and he receives a *great sword* with which to kill a small nation, while these horses kill *a third* of mankind with other weapons. It uncannily points to modern weapons of war, to missiles hurled by explosives, fire, poison gasses, liquid fire and igniting gasses and atomic bombs. Sulphur, too, is used to compound gunpowder. These destructive secrets might have been revealed to St. John as future inventions. But all through the revelations he deals with spiritual agencies that shape the destiny of the world. So he evidently has those in mind as the real causes of destruction, for sin has always been the ultimate cause of all misery.

Verse 18

The fire, the smoke and the sulphur issuing from the mouths of the lion-headed horses will bring death to one third of mankind. Hatred of God and of fellow-men is the efficient cause. It will voice its sentiments in blasphemous propaganda against God calculated to scare men away from belief in Him and to rob them of all revealed religion. The result will be rebellion against His law, refusal to keep His commandments and a surrender to voluptuousness and immorality. St. John calls the fire, the smoke and the sulphur three distinct plagues and thereby alludes to the plagues of Egypt. He repeats them in this verse to make the narrative more vivid and to emphasize the causes of the carnage. Only the color of these agencies is on the armor of the riders, revealing how deeply imbued they are with these satanic qualities of mind and heart.

Verse 19

The power of the horses is in their mouths, propagating their will and tyrannizing over peoples by promulgating laws against God's ordinances, by emitting hatred and blasphemies against Him and by inciting to rebellion against all authority He has established.

In verse 10, the locusts have the tails of scorpions, while these horses have tails with serpents' heads showing both monsters to be allegorical figures or spiritual forces. They kill with the fire, smoke and sulphur streaming from their mouths, while with their tails they only injure their victims. The tail is the symbol of error, deceit, hypocrisy and false doctrines (Is. IX. 15). In Scripture the serpent is considered the embodiment of deceit, cunning, secret and unexpected treachery. The venom of these tail-serpents does not kill, is therefore of a spiritual nature. They instill doubt, agnosticism, unbelief, rebellion against authority and possibly atheism, as the serpent in Paradise advised unbelief and rebellion against God. The heads of the serpent-tails can devise means and ways of deceiving and misleading people who give ear to the new doctrines of death.

Verse 20

The two-thirds of the human race remaining after the plague of the 200,000,000 horsemen has swept over the earth will continue in sin and unbelief. Verse 20 points specifically to the pagan world, which comprises almost two-thirds of the earth's population today. Devil-worship and idolatry in one form or another prevails in the vast and teeming populations of Asia and Indonesia. In a large part of Europe and the Americas, many so-called civilized peoples do not indeed worship idols but the works of their hands. Man is extolled as the lord of the world, the god who performs technical miracles that grow more stupendous day by day. Some men worship their creations of art, others their literary output, others their adventures, their engineering feats, their inventions, their wealth or their physical prowess. Some scoff at the sovereignty of God and deify the State. Verse 20 gives a synopsis of the sins against God, from which necessarily follows spiritual death. The death of any percentage of mankind is only a consequence of rejecting God. After the slaughter of one third of mankind, the rest will live just as they do today.

Verse 21

As men shall still sin against the sovereignty of God, so they shall sin against the moral order. Verse 21 points to the Christian world. After the slaughter of a third of mankind is ended, the Christian world shall still be given to murders, adulteries, divorce, birth-control, false beliefs, impurities and dishonesty. Large numbers shall be secretly addicted to superstitious practices, such as spiritism, fortune-telling and false doctrines. Deceit and hypocrisy shall be unchecked. Dishonesty and graft in business shall be almost universal. The laborer shall be cheated out of the fruits of his labor through the economic conditions created by the godless manipulators of the financial systems of the world. And the whole moral order of God in the Christian world shall be upset worse than ever, in spite of all former promises of the lords of the world to make it a decent place in which to live. Men shall still be given to self-indulgence and overselfishness, and even Catholics shall begrudge God the little time He demands for worshipping Him. And this state of sin and corruption will go on until the Church is fully prepared to carry through with God's special direction and help the overthrow of the reign of evil and the conquest of the world for Christ.

The prophets of Old have left us the reasons for God's judgments. Isaias foretells judgments upon the whole world, because even God's people sought their happiness in excessive desire for wealth and luxury, adored the works of their hands and felt secure in their armaments and armies (II. 7-9). They did not heed the preaching and warnings of the prophets (VI. 9-10). God wills full freedom for men to do good or evil, that if they scorn the good, evil may grow in them to maturity, and that when God's punishments come, they may be truly merited. (Is. VI. 9-10; Apoc. XXII. 11). The Jews practiced spiritism (Is. VIII. 19); they made treaties of defense with pagan nations; they trusted in the strength of Egypt, which led them into idolatry; and they scoffed at and rejected God's protection (Is. IX. 11; XXX. 2 & 12). They practiced "diplomacy", duplicity, hypocrisy and deceit and respected this diplomacy as an accomplishment. They derided uprightness and sincerity and they punished it (Is. XXXII. 5-7). No one was secure against the slanderer and murderer (LIX. 10). The final reason for God's irrevocable judgments was IDOLATRY (LXV. 7).

Jeremias writes that false teachers bring God's visitations (XIV. 15). Those teachers will admit no guilt in themselves (XVI. 10); they will persecute the true and faithful pastor (XX. 10, 11); they will give a false interpretation to Scripture, one that suits their views (VIII. 8); they are ever-ready with deceit: "with his mouth he speaks peace with his friend, and secretly he lies in wait for him" (IX. 4, 8). God will accept no sacrifices from hardened sinners (VII. 20-21). Some are so steeped in sin that they claim God did not help them when they served Him, but when they turned away from Him, they were prosperous (XLIV.

16). False shepherds led the people so far astray as to make them forget the truth and be no longer willing to believe it when preached to them (L. 6). They put their trust in idols and vain things; this is worse than the sin of Sodom (Lam. IV. 6). If they acknowledge their guilt and repent, forgiveness waits for them. (III. 20-22).

God sent diverse plagues: droughts, storms, pests, pestilences, wars and famines on the wicked, and they were not converted (Amos IV.). Some claimed: "We are not so very bad after all, even if we do some wicked things" (Mal. II. 17). A large number were so far advanced in sin that they brazenly committed it in every kind and form (Soph. III.).

These revelations, depicting the state of religion and morality in Israel just before the judgments struck all countries in communications with Israel, give a true picture of society throughout the world today. Christendom is hopelessly divided by heresy and schism. The rest of mankind are satisfied to live in religious indifference; and they resent any attempt to enlighten them, although they listen eagerly to heretical teachings and to slanders against the Catholic Church.

As the ancient judgments began at the center of the theocracy so they will begin again at the House of God. What amount of evil within the Church will be the measure to call for the beginning of the judgment cannot be known, but surely *that* will determine the day and the hour. If the Church would remain irreproachable, the judgment would be stayed off. By continually tempting Catholics to a compromise with false standards, or even by leading the clergy away from the strictness of virtue into worldliness, the wicked will hasten their own judgment. Finally then they will deserve the full weight of God's wrath, because they have challenged Him to punish them.

The 200,000,000 warriors could have begun to appear three hundred years ago, causing all the carnage and pillage of the past three centuries, and they would then be still operating. The first world-war was the outcome in its time, and it in turn produced the second world-war, and the trouble in the world in 1962 is still the aftereffect of this last war. What future developments will be, no man can foresee. There is growing up and increasing very fast in numbers, strength and influence an enemy of God and man in our day, whose salient traits are exactly those of the horses and riders of this scourge, which is the beginning of the second woe. This enemy is militaristic Communism. The culmination of this second woe will be the reign of Antichrist. These warriors seem to be the proximate preparation for that reign. The reign of the Beast, or Antichrist, is described in a new and very specific revelation given to St. John; yet it is not a distinct woe for itself. The evil institutions that have grown up in Christendom during the past centuries seem to be but a remote preparation for the reign of Antichrist. They all aimed at weakening the influence of the Church. Mercantilism brought disregard for the laws of justice, developed piracy and robbery and produced the inhuman slave traffic, which was engaged in by Protestant and Catholic despots alike in defiance of the condemnation of the popes. The secret societies were a rebellion against the state religions and clash of creeds in Protestantism. They together with mercantilism and autocracy developed the evils of modern capitalism. Communism openly leagues the Church with the evil capitalistic system and in preaching abolition of capitalism also preaches hatred against the Catholic Church. Communism is only one of Satan's inventions and is probably the proximate preparation for the reign of the Beast. Communism was invented by the Jew, Marx. It is a rebirth of many of the ideals of the Kabbala and the Talmud which contains the doctrines of the anti-christian Jews who were the descendants of the crucifiers of Christ. St. Paul writing to the Thessalonians refers to the "Mystery of iniquity" which was already working at that time against Christ. Militaristic and agressive Communism working out its ideals in military aggresson may be the scourge of horsemen through which the four evil spirits from the Euphrates are destined to exterminate a third of the human race.

Communism has all the characteristics of the horses and horsemen. Its promoters are filled with a satanic rage against God and man. They burn with hatred against the Church, the ministers of the Church and the Sacrifice of the Mass. Death and pillage follows them everywhere. Their mission is destruction. To blot out all knowledge of God and to institute the universal sway of sheer atheism is their avowed aim. They scoff at belief in God and Christ and utter blasphemies such as could not be equalled by the worst of ancient paganism. As in their intentions, all belief in God must be abolished, so Christian morality must disappear from the face of the earth. They break through all restraint and promote disregard for all divine moral law. Their moral code is that of the Beast, of the lowest degree of animalism. Their rebellion against all things divine, against faith, law, morality, prompts them to the vilest blasphemies ever spoken by man against the revelations and ordinances of God. It is evidently communism that is destined to wipe out one third of mankind by a universal revolution, anarchy, guerrilla warfare and the propagation of hatred of man for man.

Although verse 20 seems to point out as the field of operation for the 200,000,000 warriors that part of the world that is still in paganism, verse 21 takes in view the perversion of the moral law of God and points to the nations who know the true moral code but do not obey it even after the woe has overwhelmed them. Fully two-thirds of the human race resides in Asia and Europe. Although Europe is free from idolatry, it has turned away from the revelations and moral law of God more and more for centuries; and all efforts century after century to convert Asia from idolatry and unbelief have failed. If the time is at hand for the unbinding of the four evil spirits, Asia and Europe would seem to be their pre-destined battlefield. That these destroyers are bound in the Euphrates may also point to Asia as the continent alloted to their depradations. If communism is introduced there slyly and imposed on an unarmed mass of people, they may be at first subjugated, but when they learn the hatefulness of the yoke, they may rise in rebellion, and the counter-revolution may then put 200,000,000 killers to work. This, however, will wait for the loosing of the four devils in the Euphrates.

Even if left to his human sagacity alone, St. John would have before his mind the true perpective of time in this vision of the 200,000,000 horsemen. He would easily have understood this to be an event of the far distant future, because the whole Roman Empire in his time numbered not much over 120,000,000 people. The barbarians outside the empire were an unnown quantity but were not calculated to be of very extensive populations. The vast number of warriors would easily demand a world-population twenty times as great as it was then. St. John understood this, for the number startled him. The words of chapter IX. 12: "the first woe has passed; behold hereafter two woes are still to come", and the words of chapter XI. 14: "The second woe has passed, behold, the third woe will come quickly" prove the close connection of these chapters and the whole logical and chronological sequence of chapters IX. to XVII. And chapters IX. and XI. prove that the visions and events related are not re-duplications of visions related in chapters VI. to X. St. John did not therefore, mean to represent the Roman Empire of his time as the Beast of chapters XIII. and XVII. And still less could it be a Nero-redivivus, or resurrection of Nero in Domitian. The context of chapters XIII. and XVII. does not agree with so ingenious an explanation, when seen in the light of chapters IX. and XI. Therefore when in this vision, St. John beheld the population of the world grown to such numbers that it could put into the field 200,000,000 warriors, he comprehended it to be in the far distant future. Furthermore, chapter XVII. proves positively that the Roman Empire had passed away, when the Beast appears on the scene, for he comes up out of the abyss (XI. 7; XVII. 8).

The four horns of the golden altar obviously represent all religious congregations, missionary, charitable and teaching and especially those founded since the advent of Protestantism. All, together with the older orders, have done marvelous work for the spread of faith, charity and education, making the Church actualize more fully her mission upon earth. They are preparing the world rapidly for the coming of the "great day of Almighty God" by training a native hierarchy among all nations and tribes of the world and are enabling the Church to cope with all the machinery of Satan, when the day of battle shall arrive. The mission work among Catholics has raised their spiritual standards of living by enlightening their faith, purifying their morals and fanning their piety to remain steadfast in the ordeals of the 200,000,000 warriors and the reign of Antichrist.

The sixth trumpet, which ushers in the second woe, calls our attention to the River Euphrates; and the sixth angel in chapter XVI. 12 pours his bowl upon the same river to summon the oriental nations for the battle on the "Great Day of Almighty God". That co-incidence is surely not meaningless. The second woe may not have begun in 1934 A. D. when this was written. There may be a very violent antichristian movement among the governments of Asia and Europe incited suddenly or gradually. The missionary work well-organized and all-embracing as it is may suddenly be halted by hostile attitude in missionary countries. Japan has in the past almost entirely wiped out the Church again in that country established by the missionaries of three hundred years ago. Communism may overspread Asia and overthrow the existing governments and establish its God-hating reign, may assassinate the missionaries or drive them out, martyr the native clergy as Sovietism has done in Russia and extirpate the missions annihilating everything gained so far. This plague of 200,000,000 warriors is a punishment for hostility to the truth of God and indifference to His law and grace. And therefore it may come upon Europe after antichristian governments have stopped the support of the missions in money and personnel, have suppressed the religious orders, disbanded them and stopped the education and training of candidates. Then all religious congregations may speak with one voice, "loose the four angels" (IX. 14), because all the fruits of their labors have been swept away, and paganism or atheism has gained universal sway. If the whole continent of Asia including Russia were in a state of anarchy and guerrilla warfare, 200,000,000 men might be fighting, and under such conditions, half the population of that vast continent might be wiped out, which would equal a third of the human race. The rest of Europe, the Americas and even Africa need not be touched by this part of the second woe to bring about a literal fulfillment of the prophecy. And such warfare would not convert these peoples, nor the nations of Europe, and therefore verses 20 and 21 would still be true. For these and other reasons, the Second Woe has probably not begun. But the four evil spirits may be turned loose any time.

Book II

CHAPTER X.

Westminster Version

Then I beheld another strong angel coming 1. down from heaven,
wrapt in a cloud, and the rainbow over his head; and his face was as the
sun, and his feet were as columns of fire. In his hand he had a little volume
open; and 2. he placed his right foot on the sea, and his left on the earth,
and cried with a loud 3. voice, as a lion roareth; and when he cried, the
seven thunders uttered their voices. And when the seven thunders had
uttered their 4. voices, I was about to write, when I heard a voice from
heaven saying, 'Seal up the things which the thunders spoke, and write
them not'. Then the angel whom I beheld standing upon 5. the sea and
upon the earth, lifted up his right hand unto heaven and swore by him who
liveth 6. for ever and ever, who created the heaven and all therein, that
there should be no more delay, but in the days of the trumpet-peal of the 7.
seventh angel the mystery of God would be consummated, as he announced
to his servants the prophets.

And the voice which I had heard from heaven 8. again spoke to me
and said, 'Go, take the little volume which is open in the hand of the
angel who standeth upon the sea and upon the earth'.

So I went to the angel, and told him to 9. give me the little volume.
And he saith to me, 'Take and eat it up; it will be bitter in thy stomach,
but in thy mouth it will be sweet as honey'.

And I took the little volume out of the 10. hand of the angel and ate
it up, and it was as sweet as honey in my mouth, and when I had eaten
it up, it was bitter to my stomach.

And I was told, 'Thou must again prophesy 11. touching many peoples
and nations and tongues and kings'.

BOOK TWO

THE OPEN BOOKLET

I. INTRODUCTION

The second natural division of the Apocalypse portrays in symbolic visions together with literal narratives the culmination of the growth of evil upon earth and the most sanguine attack upon the Church jeopardizing her very existence and the salvation of the world. The various evil institutions appearing at the trumpet blasts have grown to maturity by the time the prophecies of the open booklet shall go into fulfillment. Out of these institutions shall grow the enormities predicted in this and the following chapters. That prediction is contained in the first part of this open booklet. In the second part (XIV.-XX.) is contained the overthrow of the reign of evil and the end of wickedness, and in the third part the unending reign of justice, during which the whole world will serve the King of Kings.

Chapter X. is divided into two parts: In the first part verses 1-7, an angel appears and announces with an oath that "the mystery of God" shall be accomplished at an appointed time; in the second part St. John receives the revelations which describe the manner of fulfillment.

1. The Mighty Angel With The Open Booklet. Seven Thunders. Oath.

Chapter X.

Verses 1-7.

Verse 1

This vision presents a powerful angel stepping into the wicked world to make a momentous revelation. He is not a saint of the Church indicated by the nimbus surrounding him, which is the vehicle of celestial spirits, but he resembles Christ (I. 13-17) and bears a message similar to that of Christ. His face shines like the face of Christ and reflects a rainbow from the cloud. The word, ἡ ἶρις "rainbow" is preceded by the definite article probably referring to IV. 3 and signifying a message of mercy, although it forebodes the direst of all God's judgments upon the world. His face shining as the sun beams with divine authority and knowledge to enlighten the Church and the world. And his feet like pillars of fire foreshadow a guidance of the Church in truth and justice and the extermination of the evils in it. It alludes to the pillar of fire that led the children of Israel out of Egypt. The angel is probably St. Michael.

The vision of chapter X. 1-11 is connected with, is the introduction to and the announcement of what chapter XI. 1-14 relates; and the latter narrative is the culmination of evil begun in IX. 15-21. The first WOE ended in IX. 12. Thereafter the sixth trumpet announced the SECOND WOE; this began with IX. 13 and continues through chapter X. and up to XI. 14. All events then predicted in these three chapters, IX. 13 to XI. 14, are continuous. But the vision of chapter X. coming between IX. 21 and XI. 1 reveals a distinct world-event which is to begin at XI. 1. Chapters twelve and thirteen show a different phase of that same event. It is related to chapter IX., because it is part of the sixth trumpet blast and the full development of the SECOND WOE. Chapter X. indicates that a time of preparation is allotted the Church to enable her to face the trials of chapters XI. XII. XIII. and XIV., as chapter VII. showed a time of preparation for VIII. 7-13.

Verse 2

The angel holds a very small scroll in his left hand. In Greek the diminutive of a diminutive is used perhaps to signify the short duration of the events recorded therein, although their being written on a special scroll denotes their importance. The size of the scroll may also signify that it contains a very small fragment of the revelations recorded in the Book of Seven Seals. The contents may be readily understood and explained because the scroll is open. St. John retains the standpoint of I. 9, IV. 1, and VII. 1 before the open door of the Church. The action of the angel setting his right foot upon the sea and his left upon the land manifests his plenipotential authority over all God's creation. The judgments contained in the scroll shall be executed upon all things terrestrial. The sea is as solid a footing for him as the land. This fact and the gigantic stature of the angel would convince the Seer of his irresistible power and authority and his certainty of victory over all enemies.

Verse 3

The angel speaks with a great voice like the deep roar of a lion. The Greek verb employed suggests distant thunder that sends threatening reverberations through the ground. It is a fearless challenge flung at the enemies of God inspiring awe and terror. It is so like Michael's attitude towards the rebellious angels. It is the antithesis of what St. Peter attributes to the devil (1 Pet. V. 8).

The angel did not utter an articulate word, but when the roar of his voice rolled away into the distance, there was an immediate answer. 'The Seven Thunders' utter their own voices. The definite article designates them as well-known voices. They are the supreme voices of authority in the Church not the single voice of the Supreme Pontiff alone but "seven" voices, the totality of sacred authority, the voices of an ecumenical council. The time has arrived for decisions of far-reaching importance. The arrival of the angel uttering that ominous cry shall set the day and the hour. The thunders may mean dogmatic declarations of the Church against infidels expressed in an ecumenical council. In the revelations of St. Brigitt (Book VI. chap. x), when the question is asked what the seven thunders signified, the answer is said to have been, that by divine revelation she learned the seven thunders were threats decreed from heaven on the persecutors of the Church. (Cor. a Lapide, p. 216).

The Seven Thunders might mean the voices of several popes declaring infallible doctrines of the Church, such as that of the Immaculate Conception or of the Infallibility of the Pope by Pius IX. Or they may be wonderful encyclicals, such as the one on the correct relationship of labor and capital by Leo XIII., the condemnation of Modernism by Pius X. and the epoch-making encyclical on the advantage of a native over a foreign clergy by Benedict XV. These doctrines and encyclicals thundered around the world. But these do not seem to fit into the context of the following chapters.

Chapters XI. 1-2 and XII. 7 argue for many and great evils in the Church. And those verses together with XII. 5 suggest a great conflict between the Church and the world-powers and the necessity of drastic measures of reform for the Church to free herself from the danger of contamination by the evils in the world and purify her from the prevalent internal evils. The Seven Thunders may then be declarations of an ecumenical council clearing up all that was left unfinished by the magisterial office of the Church, before God will permit Satan to exert his supreme efforts to destroy her from without. The Seven Thunders will strengthen the faithful and loyal clergy in their belief and practices, expel all who are addicted to corrupt lives and superstitions and manifest the unwavering stand of the Church on the then prevailing maxims of the world.

Verse 4

According to this verse, St. John had been taking notes all the way through the visions and narratives. He is about to dip his pen into the ink and write what the Thunders had spoken. He therefore understood their message clearly and knew its import. But a voice came forth from the Church ordering him to seal up what the thunders had revealed by not writing it. Through the Seven Thunders, God gave him a special revelation of great importance, indicating what would immediately precede the coming of Antichrist, but it was to remain a secret to the Church. It was as with the revelation made to Daniel concerning the most savage persecutor of the Jews, Antiochus. The length of time he would oppress God's people was to be revealed through Daniel, 2300 days, but the time of his arrival was not to be revealed, was to be "sealed up" (Dan. VIII. 26; XII. 4 & 9). St. Paul likewise heard secret revelations which he was not allowed to communicate to the Church. The Thunders do reveal this: there will be special decisions made by the Church and these will complete the work of her magisterial office before the culmination of evil is due to arrive. The decisions may be the "reed" by which the wicked are separated from the good and expelled from the Church. This scene of the Seven Thunders is a scene within a scene leaving the Church at sea as to the *time* of Antichrist but foreshowing her preparedness for the attack.

No creature will know his time until the Church has enacted what the Seven Thunders have spoken.

Verses 5 and 6

The angel lifts up his right hand to Heaven, which is the gesture of an oath. He still holds the little scroll in his left hand. His oath will be the immediate answer to the Seven Thunders. He swears by the "Living God" who has given existence to all creatures and therefore all creatures must bear witness to the truth of his words. The earth, the sea and heaven is a standard division of all creation. All creatures received life from the Source of life, and they are to witness the universal judgment, because men would not adore the true and living God nor serve Him, though He is the Origin of their life, but adored the works of their hands (IX. 20) and subverted the whole moral order of God in the world (IX. 21). All creatures are furthermore evidence of God's irresistible power. The 200,000,000 warriors have wiped out a third of mankind, and men have lost control of human affairs. The world-wars were only a prelude to the great war or revolution in which one third of mankind shall perish. By the time the 200,000,000 killers have done their work, all thinking men will envision nothing but chaos. All ideals will vanish. And therefore the angel calls attention to the power of God, who will be able to direct all life to the end for which He has created it. No power in Heaven, earth or sea can withstand His decrees. If men are no longer able to manage their affairs for their own felicity, the almighty Creator will step in to guide them. When that direct intervention of God is finished, men will acknowledge their inability to get along without Him and will submit to Him willingly.

"There shall be no more delay" in the execution of God's judgments is the angel's oath. St. John mentions again his position upon the earth and the sea, to assert his universal authority and the speedy beginning of divine intervention in human affairs and to put an end to the kind of things that are wrecking the world. Evils have grown so rapidly and to such enormities as to bring to despair the most optimistic. The time has come in which this shall be stopped. The world is not to be destroyed but to be saved. And salvation shall be brought by the Church (See XII. 10). The Church in men's outlook seems doomed. The oath of the angel does not mean that evil shall be overcome at once, but that the end is in sight. It will be a continuous development and a successive growth into the accomplishment of the "mystery of God" when the seventh angel will begin to blow his trumpet. And this comprises the culmination of evil under the Beast and his destruction. So his appearance and reign is at hand. St. Peter predicted a time when scoffers would laugh at the promise of the Parousia made by the apostles, because the delay had been long, and all creation followed its natural course (2 Peter III. 3). The angel therefore assures all that the exact time is pre-determined in divine providence and there is no doubt of its fulfillment. But this oath was not intended to awaken in the minds of the Asiatic Christians an expectation of a speedy Parousia.

Verse 7

The time of fulfillment shall be when the seventh angel shall begin to blow his trumpet. The Christians at the end of the first century were confronted by the "great tribulation", the Roman persecutions, which would soon become universal. And although the predictions of this prophecy could not be realized in their entirety at once, Christ's ultimate triumph must be affirmed time and again in the revelations. The successive events in chapters 8 and 9 if diligently studied would convince anyone of a long lapse of time before the Parousia. So no one could conclude from the angel's oath to its immediate arrival but only to the promise of its certainty. Before the "mystery of God" shall be fulfilled, the "mystery of iniquity" (2 Thess. II. 7) must run its course in XI. 7-13.

The "mystery of God" as foretold by the prophets (Amos. III. 7) will begin to become an actual fact on "the great day of almighty God" (Mal. IV. 5). This will be the conversion of all nations to God and unending peace for the Church and the world (Is. LXII. 1 ff). The powers of evil shall by that time have spent all their fury against the Church; they shall be surfeited with the blood and slaughter of the true believers; their measure of iniquity shall be filled up, and they shall be ripe for the sickle (XIV. 18) and the winepress of God's wrath. (Is. LXIII. 3). After their swift destruction, the golden age shall dawn upon the world. Not the message of woe was sworn to by the angel but as stated in Greek and Latin the joyful message of peace. The evils adhered to and propagated, as IX. 20-21 states, shall hasten the judgment; and this is announced at XI. 14. If the nations would return to God and halt the progress of evil, the judgment would be postponed (Is. XXXVIII. 6-7). It will not wait till the Church has become so much affected by the prevalent evils that only a remnant can be saved.

The EXECUTION OF THE JUDGMENT does not begin at XI. 15 but at XVI. 1. There are many phases in this judgment, and they are minutely narrated in chapters XVI. to XX. The reign and persecution of Antichrist and the False Prophet partly shown in XI. 1-12 must be related first. This is the climax of the "mystery of iniquity". Human language must traverse the same ground several times to depict the many phases of the supreme conflict in separate scenes, before it can unravel the final outcome into which all events of the grand drama converge. The completion of the mystery of God will not come about immediately after the angel's oath, but in future "days" when the seventh angel shall begin to blow the trumpet. That trumpet heralds the end of the mystery of iniquity and at the same time the solution of the mystery of God.

2. St. John Takes And Eats The Scroll.

Verse 8

The same voice that forbade him to write what the Seven Thunders had spoken now commands St. John to take the open scroll from the hand of the angel. The sea and the land are mentioned again to keep before the Seer's mind the universal authority of the angel and the extent of the revelations in the scroll.

Verse 9

St. John rapturously leaves his station at the door of the Church and goes to the mighty angel to ask him for the booklet. The angel invites him to take it, adding that it will be sweet to the taste but bitter to the stomach. This is rather a strange metaphor, because the stomach has no sense of taste. The metaphor is used in the Old Testament to signify the imparting of future secrets to the prophet. He eats the scroll by pondering deeply over its contents to get a clear understanding of the whole scope of the revelations contained in it.

From the angel's words as also from his oath and appearance, we can draw the inference that the wicked shall receive their just retribution. The last words of verse seven, "as he has declared the joyful message by his servants the prophets", assure the preservation of the faithful and the triumphant ascendancy of the Church above the smoke of the great conflagration. The message will fill St. John with mixed feelings. The angel's words convey the fearsome foreboding of persecution and martyrdoms and the uncertanity of what will become of the spiritually lame and sick. Will they be converted or not? And what will the faithful be made to endure? St. John is to ponder the revelations to understand them clearly and then to relate all we need to know to suffer steadfastly for the faith.

Ezechiel was handed a book (II. 9), which was written within and without (Apoc. V. 1). He was ordered to eat it (III. 1-3). When he ate the book, it was "sweet as honey" to the taste. He says nothing of its bitterness, though it contained the final judgment upon Jerusalem and its utter destruction in 586 B. C. Jeremias calls receiving the revelations of God "eating" His words (Jer. XV. 16). In Ezechiel's book, eating the book of God's judgments had the same meaning as here in the Apocalypse. By pondering it deeply St. John would understand its far-reaching application in God's plans and the importance of a clear and true knowledge of it by the Church.

Verse 10

As he absorbed the contents of the scroll with his mind, St. John found the angel's words verified. At first reading, the message seemed sweet and consoling, for it revealed the sweeping triumph of Christ and the Church and the peace and security resultant from the victory for the just. This the prophets had foretold; for this blessed consummation they had yearned and for this the apostles had hoped. But to the Apostle of love, it was a bitter message, when he understood the full price that must be paid for the victory; the direst persecution for the Church; the plagues to be inflicted by God which were to be borne both by the good and the bad; the sacrifices of countless precious lives; the most horrifying chastisements for the wicked, many of whom would be near friends and relatives of the just, and the apostasy and final damnation of many weak and timid souls. So the reception of the revelations was sweet when glanced at for joys, but bitter when pondered for its sorrows; sweet for the prospect of unbroken peace and happiness that shall grow out of the wreckage of the old world, but bitter for the long-felt burden of loss that the world shall bear.

3. He Must Prophesy Again.

Verse 11

St. John is told to prophesy again. The same voice that directed him to ask the great angel for the little scroll speaks to him once more. The new prophecies concern the whole world. Their universality of application is indicated in the four words, "to many nations, and peoples, and tongues, and kings". Many nations and tongues and peoples existed at the time these prophecies were received. But by the time this second prophecy merges into actuality, the Roman Empire and Emperor no longer hold sway. There are then many *kings.* The conjunction "and" indicates a simultaneous judgment upon all nations and kingdoms. The scourges at the opening of the seals and the announcements of the first six trumpets affected only parts of the earth at one time: in the seals only one FOURTH; and in the trumpet blasts each scourge only ONE THIRD; and that was of the then known world. Now the judgments will afflict the whole world. In the Old Dispensation, God's judgments were sometimes inflicted upon the whole world then known or with which the chosen people came in contact. Now the chosen people are scattered over the whole earth; and when His judgments shall begin again, the Church will be established everywhere or will have been rejected by nations which will have had a fair chance to enter it; and therefore will His judgments be fully merited.

These words are very clear in so far as they prepare the reader for prophecies to be enunciated which will not be meant for the Roman Empire but for all nations and peoples and tongues and kings. They point to the passing of the empire and the building of many nations on its ruins. There will be new nations enjoying independence, new peoples working out their destiny, new tongues spoken by millions, new kings and kingdoms all over the earth. If the nations and tongues in St. John's time had been meant, the definite article would have been used. But all articles are left out in this sentence. The message of this little scroll is then to those who shall live while the SECOND WOE is in progress. The words of the angel also contradict the theories of the interpreters who make the Beast of chapter XIII. the Roman Emperor and the Harlot of chapter XVII. ancient pagan Rome.

The first division of the prophecies is concluded with this verse, as the whole chapter is also the introduction to the second division. The first division shows the struggles of the Church throughout the centuries for approximately 2,000 years. During the first part of the trials prophesied by St. John, the Church encountered every device of Satan to destroy her; but she waxed ever stronger in that battle; and Satan lost ever more of his kingdom on earth. The persecutions and oppositions of wicked men of every type and character have only incited the Church to greater efforts in extending the blessed kingdom of Christ. By the time these new prophecies blend into fulfillment, the Church will have succeeded far enough to cope victoriously with the supreme exertions of Satan and his hordes. The prophecies which St. John is now to record will narrate and depict this conflict ending in the utter defeat of the powers of evil.

CHAPTER XI.

Westminster Version

Then I was given a reed like to a rod, and 1. I was told, 'Arise and measure the sanctuary of God, and the altar, and those that adore thereat. As for the court which is without 2. the sanctuary, omit it, measure it not, for it hath been given to the nations, and they will trample on the holy city during forty-two months.

And I will grant unto my two witnesses to 3. prophesy, clothed in sackcloth, during a thousand two hundred and sixty days.

These are the two olive trees and the two 4. lamps which stand before the Lord of the earth.

And if any man is minded to harm them, fire 5. issueth from their mouth, and devoureth their enemies: if any man shall be minded to harm them, thus is he destined to be slain.

These have power to shut the heaven, in 6. order that no rain may fall during the days of their prophesying; and they have power over the waters to turn them into blood, and to smite the earth with every plague as often as they will. And when they have completed 7. their witness, the beast which cometh up from the bottomless pit shall make war against them, and conquer and slay them; and their corpses 8. (shall lie) in the street of the great city, which spiritually is called SODOM and EGYPT, even where their Lord was crucified.

And men from the peoples and tribes and 9. tongues and nations see their corpses for three days and a half, and do not allow them to be put into a tomb.

And the inhabitants of the earth rejoice 10. over them and make merry and shall exchange presents, because these two prophets tormented the inhabitants of the earth.

And after the three days and a half the 11. spirit of life from God entered into them, and they stood upon their feet, and a great fear fell upon those that beheld them.

And they heard a loud voice from heaven, 12. saying to the twain, 'Come up hither!' And they went up to heaven in a cloud, in the sight of their enemies.

And at that very hour there befell a great 13. earthquake, and the tenth part of the city was overthrown, and seven thousand named men were slain in the earthquake, and the rest were terrified, and gave glory to the God of heaven.

The second woe hath passed; behold, the 14, third Woe cometh speedily.

And the seventh angel sounded the trumpet 15. and there followed

loud voices in heaven, which said: 'The kingdom of this world hath
come to our Lord and to his Christ, and he shall reign forever and ever'.

And the twenty-four elders who sit upon 16. their thrones before
God, fell upon their faces and adored God, saying:

'We give thee thanks, O Lord God almighty, 17. who art and who
wast, that thou hast assumed thy great power and entered upon thy
reign. The 18. nations were wroth, but thine own wrath came, and the
time to judge the dead, to give the reward to thy servants – to the prophets
and to the saints, and to those that fear thy name, the small and the
great – and to destroy the destroyers of the earth.'

And God's sanctuary in heaven was opened, 19. and the ark of his
covenant was seen in his temple. And there followed lightnings and voices
and thunder-peals and an earthquake and great hail.

II. CONTINUATION OF THE SECOND WOE.

1. St. John Measures The Temple.

Chapter XI.

Chapter XI. is naturally divided into two parts. The first narrates very tersely the activity of the Two Prophets, who shall appear in Jerusalem to combat the claims of Antichrist until their work is finished and shall prove the truth of their mission by miracles. Slain by Antichrist, they rise from the dead and ascend visibly into Heaven. This ends the Second Woe. The second part of the chapter is taken up with the announcements of the Third Woe, which is to begin quickly. The death of the Two prophets, their resurrection and assumption into Heaven is the pledge of the Third Woe's swift arrival.

Verses 1-2

The Prophet Zacharias (II. 1) saw an angel with a measuring line prepared to measure Jerusalem. Ezechiel beheld a similar vision in which the angel had a reed (XL. 3). These visions presaged a rebuilding of Jerusalem and of the Temple after the Babylonian Captivity. St. John is himself ordered to measure the "sanctuary of God". The measuring unit given him is a "reed", one of those twenty-foot stalks that grow along the Jordan River (Lc. VII. 24), but it is "like to a rod". Ezechiel's reed was six cubits long, which is about 9 feet. Whether any significance attaches to the Seer's measuring unit must be left to speculation. But an ominous revelation is contained in the word "rod". The ROD in prophetic usage is the symbol of severity by which the faithful are separated from the unfaithful (Zach. XI. 7). It is the symbol of authority, which is here of divine origin and right. This measuring the "sanctuary" with a "rod" could mean either the preservation of the faithful or the destruction of the wicked. Since everything except the "sanctuary" is to be "cast out" or omitted, the measuring signifies the preservation of the true believers in the judgments to follow, because they are in the "sanctuary of God", they are "sealed". Since the instrument with which he is to measure the "sanctuary of God" is not a measuring line, an enlargement of the temple or any other building could not be intended. He is not to measure the city nor the outer court nor the whole Temple but only the "sanctuary". The "rod" thus portends a decrease in the size of the Church, a restriction to the altar and to those who adore at that altar and a marked division at the appointed time between the true believers and the world. It forebodes scourges and plagues to be inflicted by the Two Prophets upon the good and bad alike, through which aided by the persecution the just will be segregated from the wicked.

This is not "THE TEMPLE", i.e. the Old Testament Temple, but "the sanctuary of God" (2 Thess. II. 4), the place where God is present, the Church. The old Temple is here the visible representation of the spiritual edifice, the Church. The "altar" is represented by the Altar of Holocausts, where the supreme worship was enacted. Those who adore at the Altar are the faithful bishops, priests and practical Catholics who have the true worship and believe in the Eucharistic Presence. The old Temple is the model for the "sanctuary of God". It contained the priests' court with the "holy" and the "Holy of Holies". The Altar of holocausts was erected at the entrance of the priests' court. Before that altar was the levites' court, then the men's court and behind that the women's court. All who were allowed to enter those various courts represent here the faithful of the Church. The "sanctuary of God" thus embraces all who are actual and true Catholics. These alone shall be preserved in the decisive judgments about to begin. All others shall be ignored. God's graces have been given in a certain measure to those outside the Church who are in invincible error, but when the supreme test shall be applied, grace of perseverance will be given only to those within the fold, because in the light of the miracles then so manifest, those who will not be converted will reject all grace.

There are in the world many who have not actual membership in the true Church, because they have convictions that conflict with her teachings. But not knowing or suspecting such a variance with the true Church of Jesus Christ in their convictions, they, if they are sincere, will accept the truth at all hazards and will in the time of Antichrist be admitted into the sanctuary. Perhaps there shall be many at that time who are actual but wicked members, unwilling to keep the commandments or obey the Church. These will apostatize. Chapter III. 3 and 16 tells us of the casting out of the dead and lukewarm, the lame and half-hearted. All these are in the "outer court", will join with the enemies, shall be subjected to Antichrist and in the last plagues shall be destroyed. Those who will not follow their conscience, who have not desired to hear or know the truth, will all turn against the Church. These will dominate in Jerusalem, and through it in the world forty-two months. Jerusalem under that supposition will be the seat of Antichrist.

If the outer court is understood to mean the apostates from the Church, the "holy city" might mean the heretics, schismatics and infidels. That the "holy city" is Jerusalem is quite certain from both the Old and the New Testaments. (Is. XLVII. 2; LII. 1; Dan. IX. 24; Mt. IV. 5, XXVII. 53; Apoc. XI. 8). The last clause of the verse has a finite verb and is joined to the foregoing clause by the conjunction "and" to denote a simultaneous time for both clauses. The two clauses are really independent sentences. In verse 8, Jerusalem is called the "great city". St. Luke has a sentence that is a very close parallel to the last clause (XXI. 24). But it comprises the whole time from the destruction of Jerusalem till the conversion of the Jews in the days of Antichrist. During their 42 months, the separation of the good from the bad will be completed, and the wicked will dominate the "holy city". The whole context of the chapter up to verse 14 seems to make the "holy city" and the "great city" identical with Jerusalem. Under that assumption, Antichrist will come to the Jews and will be received by them as the Messias and will make Jerusalem his capital. Irenaeus expects the establishment of his empire in Jerusalem (Adv. Haer. book V. xxv. 4).

The nations are the infidels who do not believe in Jesus Christ. They will rule in Jerusalem after the measuring of the sanctuary of God. All who will not worship at the true altar, who do not adore the Eucharistic Christ, will in those days be in danger of submitting to Antichrist. How thorough the work of external subjection of all non-Catholics to the divinity of Antichrist shall be, nobody can foresee. But the measuring of the sanctuary carries the intimation of zealous work on the part of the hierarchy to teach and instruct, and the keenest eagerness on the part of the laity to become fully instructed in the faith so as not to be deceived by the doctrines, the wonders and signs of Antichrist. Those who are indifferent then and lax priests and bishops will be cleared out of the Church. The searching tests of faith will leave in the Church only those who rather lose all than their faith. Such faithfulness will be possible only for all who before this day have lived the teachings of the Church or then join with full conviction and intention to sacrifice everything for it and have been developed, enlightened and strengthened by grace. No one can be a member of the Church and a friend of Antichrist.

2. The Testimony Of The Two Witnesses.

Verses 3-13.

Verse 3

The one who speaks here is Christ or His angel. St. John does not say who gave him the reed, but it must have been the one who is now speaking. What he will give the Two Witnesses is added by the word "and" with the succeeding clause, namely the authority to speak and act in His name for a thousand two-hundred and sixty days. The time is given here in days to denote the unceasing activity of preaching and working miracles day by day. It corresponds to the public life of our Lord. The witnesses shall preach penance and give the example of penance by their austerity and dress.

The definite article designates THE "Two Witnesses" as two definite personages who can easily be known from the books of the Old and New Testaments. The prophecy seems clearly to refer to Malachias (IV. 5), where he says: "Behold, I will send you Elias, the prophet, before the coming of the great and dreadful day of the Lord". Elias was taken up in a fiery chariot alive and is preserved in a secret place, a paradise, for the "great day of Almighty God". Henoch was also transported alive, as says St. Paul (Heb. XI. 5) "Henoch was translated, that he should not see death". His translation similar to that of Elias would logically presage for him a share in the work of Elias. This is the opinion of most interpreters. Those commentators who think the second witness might be Moses, because he appeared on Mt. Tabor with Elias, forget Deuteronomy (XXXIV. 5-6), where the death and burial of Moses is related; and they forget Apocalypse (XI. 7-12) where the Beast kills both witnesses, and where after that they arise from the dead. According to the record in Deuteronomy, Moses died, was buried and went the way of all flesh. Would he now after so many thousand years arise from the dead, be killed once more and again rise from the dead?

In speaking of John the Baptist, our Lord said to His disciples: "And if you will receive it, he is Elias that is to come" (Mt. XI. 14). But John himself said, when the Pharisees sent to ask him: "Art thou Elias?" "I am not" (John I. 21). St. Gregory explains this seeming contradiction by saying that our Lord spoke of the "office" of John, as the angel had said to Zachary (Lc. I. 17): "He shall go before Him in the spirit and power of Elias", while John spoke of the *person* of Elias when he denied that he was Elias. John the Baptist did not usher in the "great and dreadful day of the Lord", as was foretold of Elias. That day will be the destruction of Antichrist and all his hordes and the establishment of the Millennium thereafter. Our Lord clearly predicted the coming of Elias: "Elias indeed shall come, and restore all things". (Mt. XVII. 11; Mc. IX. 11). Those who reject such an interpretation give extremely fantastic explanations. The greatest scholars have held that the Two Witnesses must be Henoch and Elias in person. The coming of Henoch is recorded in the book of Ecclesiasticus (XLIV. 16). "Henoch pleased God, and was translated into paradise, that he may give repentance to the nations". This was quite universally the interpretation of the ancient Fathers, including St. Jerome. These Two Witnesses might be said to embody the traits of Moses, of Jesus the son of Josedech and of Zorobabel. Hippolytus, a disciple of St. Irenaeus, says: "There remain only one week, the last, in which Elias will appear, and Henoch" (II. 22, Exegetical).

Verse 4

There is an allusion in this verse to Zacharias (IV. 14). The prophet's words are: "These are the two sons of oil who stand before the Lord of the whole earth". He relates the vision of the one candlestick with seven lamps and of the two olive trees from whose oil the lamps received their fuel. The two olive trees are Zorobabel, the prince, and Jesus son of Josedech, the highpriest. These two restored the Theocracy after the Babylonian Captivity. The golden candlestick is the newly restored Theocracy, and it receives its nourishment from the two olive trees, the temporal ruler and the spiritual head.

The Two Witnesses in our text have the function of restoring all things. The definite article used before "olive trees" and "lampstands" refers to the prophecy of Zacharias and makes Zorobabel and Jesus types of the Two Witnesses. In both instances they are ANOINTED ones. Perhaps at the time of the Two Witnesses all governments will be hostile to the Church. Elias may then revive the purity, influence and power which the Church possesses in her spiritual endowments, and Henoch may restore the Christian foundation for the governments of the nations.

The olive-tree is the symbol of God's mercy and the oil of the threefold office of prophet, priest and king. In I. 20, the seven lampstands are the seven churches to which the Apocalypse is addressed; and in Zacharias, the golden candlestick was the Theocracy. But here the lampstands are persons who are clothed in sack-cloth. As olive-trees, they do not forebode destruction to the world but mercy. Their office, symbolized by the sevenfold candlestick and the seven golden lampstands, is to enlighten the Church and the world by preaching and example and to restore God's kingdom on earth. As olive-trees they shall convert many, especially of the Jews, who shall then be saved from the deluge of devastation which shall sweep over the world, when Antichrist and his followers meet their doom. They will bring back to the world the peace of Christ.

Verse 5

The Two Witnesses will read men's minds and will strike dead by fire issuing from their mouths anyone who conspires to injure them, before he can carry out his nefarious purpose. Fire fell from Heaven at the command of Elias and killed the soldiers of Ochozias (IV. Kings I. 10-13). The power of the Two Witnesses will be so much augmented that by a word they can slay their enemies as if by lightning (Jer. V. 14). They will mete out death not only to those who would injure their person but also to those who will try to hinder or frustrate their work of conversion. During the three and a half years during which they continue their work, they will testify by word and miracles to the divine origin of the Catholic Church alone, condemn all scandals within it, bear witness to the divinity of Jesus Christ and expose the imposture and blasphemy of Antichrist. Among Christian nations, this would seem quite superfluous, because they have this prophecy of St. John and other prophecies of the Old and New Testaments proclaiming who was the Savior and foretelling the sure advent of false christs and false prophets. But among heathens and Mohammedans it will be necessary to prove the divinity of Jesus Christ, and by that time there may be little belief in Him among some once Christian nations. Russia exemplifies today the possibility of a nation forgetting Christ within a quarter of a century. By their testimony the Two Witnesses will reap for themselves the hatred of Christ's enemies, for they will expose the falsity of heresies and discredit them to absurdity and lead to the truth all who sincerely seek it. The hypocrites will then turn to Antichrist.

Verse 6

With their power of miracles, the Two Witnesses will order a drought, as did Elias for three and a half years during the days of King Achab (3 Kings. XVII. 1); (James V. 17).

Whether the Two Witnesses will remain in Palestine or travel from country to country; and again whether the drought will afflict the whole world, only the country in which they are testifying, or only those peoples that resist their preaching cannot be gathered from the text. The prophets told the unbelieving Jews that drought had scorched and withered some fields only, because their owners had given way to idolatry. The punishment would have been more widespread, if all God's people had followed the sinners. Again, Baruch complains of being ordered to write the prophecies of Jeremias, because the Jews would then persecute him as they did Jeremias. God rebukes him saying, that he should not complain of suffering with the rest, since he would be spared, when the time for the extermination of His chosen nation should have arrived. Most probably during the testimony of the Two Witnesses, the good will suffer with the bad. They will be purified and spiritualized, whilst the wicked shall perish without gain. If the drought would be universal for three and a half years, not a living soul would survive. The text only concedes to the prophets the right and authority to close heaven and says nothing about the manner and extent of their exercising that power.

The Two Witnesses may turn waters into blood and may strike the earth with all the plagues with which Moses struck Egypt. The manifestations of their power will be known among all peoples giving all nations and tribes ample proof of its genuineness and divine character. The plagues will surely not be limited to Palestine, even if the Witnesses would remain within its borders. By that time the missionaries will have carried the Gospel everywhere, and all peoples will know the import of these plagues, because the Church will explain them. Being similar to the plagues of Moses and Aaron should make them impressive to the Jews and convert them.

The authority of the Two Witnesses shall be unrestricted. They shall need no special order to inflict new plagues, as Moses and Aaron did, but shall strike with them whenever and as often as they choose. The one plague of turning water into blood may connote the separation of mankind into two opposing armies, as they accept the miracles of the Two Witnesses as genuine or are captivated by the false prodigies of Antichrist and his prophet. The Christian nations may mobilize for self-defense in as far as they have not been subjugated to Antichrist by stealth and intrigue. He will wage war to subject all nations to himself, but many will surely resist his demands. One powerful independent nation, as XII. 14 indicates, will refuse to submit or join him. So there will be wars and revolutions, persecutions and martyrdoms. Our Lord said: "Unless those days had been shortened, no flesh should be saved", (Mt. XXIV. 22), "but for the sake of the elect those days shall be shortened". So the Witnesses may then to punish the crimes of the wicked turn the rivers, fountains and wells into blood in the countries that accept Antichrist, overthrow Christian governments, abolish Christian civil order, enforce the laws of Antichrist and persecute all faithful bishops, priests, religious and people depriving them of all rights or assassinating them. Other countries may be struck with other plagues such as will suit their particular sins.

How the "great eagle" (XII. 14) will fare is not stated. The miracles of the Two Witnesses will certainly so far disenchant the signs of Antichrist and the False Prophet as to save from being misled all who are sincere.

Verse 7

The Two Witnesses have a definite task to perform, an important message to deliver. They are immune from harm until their task is finished, after which they are no longer protected by supernatural power. Their preaching and example and miracles shall have won many people and particularly the Jews. There will be adherents of Antichrist in Jerusalem who will control the government, but the majority of the Jews shall be won over by the Two Witnesses. These will reject Antichrist, whom they at first accept as the Messias, and under the leadership of the Two Witnesses may arm for defense. Many people from the nations of the world may enlist in the defense of the Holy City. The power of the Two Witnesses will have largely undone the work of Antichrist there. All people who could be converted at this time shall have been converted; the good shall have been separated from the wicked; and thus the work of the Prophets is complete.

The Beast is mentioned here for the first time. Various kinds of creatures have appeared heretofore but no beast. The definite article used in the text seems to presume a knowledge of this beast in the reader. It may be related to the beasts of Daniel (VII. 1 ff). This wild beast is the one described in XIII. 1 ff and XVII. 8 ff, and it may be the one in Daniel (VII. 11). The Beast here ascends out of the abyss, whilst in XIII. 1, he comes out of the sea of peoples and nations. He may be of Asiatic birth and of Jewish blood. The abyss was first mentioned in chapter IX., when the fallen star opened it. The Beast's power and dominion will be satanic in origin. He has Satan's traits. Only by the power with which Satan shall endow him will he be enabled to triumph over the Two Witnesses and their armies and slay them. For that reason his coming out of the abyss is here stated. In chapter IX., the doctrines of the Beast were anticipated and exemplified in the work of the fallen star and in the result of it, the plague of the locusts and the army of horsemen. The human race was shown to be gradually drawn deeper and deeper into the character of the Beast and into the adoption of Satan's principles and ethics, which are diametrically opposed to those of Christ. All began with apostasy from the Church, has been advanced more rapidly by the activity of the secret societies, is speeded up still more by socialism and communism and shall reach its mature growth after the advent of the Beast in person.

The Wild Beast is Antichrist, and he ascends out of the abyss, because his power and strength is from Satan (XIII. 2). His empire will be universal (XIII. 7) very quickly. Although it seems that his military power shall be reduced by the time the testimony of the Two Witnesses is drawing to a close in a war in which the Christian nations shall defend themselves against him, he shall be victorious. His followers shall then exult in their triumph, for no one can resist him. His crimes will reach their full measure in the murder of the Two Witnesses. That event will mark the end of the 1260 days or 42 months during which the Beast is triumphant, and then begins his downfall.

The ancient Fathers identify the Beast with Antichrist. Irenaeus says he will establish his capital at Jerusalem (Adv. Haer. V. xxv. 4); Hippolytus in his treatise on Christ and Antichrist identifies him with the fourth beast of Daniel and also with the Beast of the Apocalypse. Hippolytus was a disciple of Irenaeus, who in turn was well acquainted with Polycarp, a disciple of St. John. Their interpretation of the Apocalypse should therefore have some weight. Modern interpreters largely identify the Beast with the Roman Empire or the Emperor. Such an interpretation is untenable and contradicts itself and the text on many points.

Verse 8

The bodies of the Two Witnesses will not be buried. God would not allow anyone to injure them until their testimony was complete. But now He permits the greatest of all indignities (in the eyes of a Jew) to fall upon them, namely, to lie unburied in the public street of the city like dogs. God will thus prepare the more striking a proof of their glorification at their resurrection.

The city is called the "great city". In XVII. 18, the "great city" is Babylon; but in the vocabulary of a Jew, Jerusalem would naturally be the "great City". Still more eminently would it be the GREAT CITY in the mind of an Apostle of the Lord, because REDEMPTION WAS WROUGHT THERE by the Crucifixion. And it is to be the city of the RESTORATION by the two witnesses, of their resurrection and ascension.

This great city is the capital of Antichrist and will therefore deserve to be called "Sodom", because from it will issue doctrines and practices that lead to the lowest depths of moral depravity. Jerusalem had been called "Sodom" and "Gomorrha" before, when it was full of idolatry and heathen morality. (Is. I. 10; Ezech. XVI. 45-56; Rom. IX. 29). Now it has fallen into the worship of Antichrist, the greatest enemy of Christ, His Church and His morality. In inspired language it is thus fitly called "Sodom". In the same inspired language, it is called "Egypt", because being the capital of Antichrist's empire, it will be what Egypt was before and during the Exodus, the head of the beast's empire, the oppressor of God's people. From this capital emanate the decrees of persecution against God's people.

In verse two, Jerusalem is called the "holy city", and here Sodom and Egypt. This is quite a paradox. It shows two different viewpoints. It was the Holy City to a Jew and the Lord's apostle and in the days of the Two Witnesses will be the scene which stages the most brilliant manifestation of God's Almighty power and holiness. The Church shall have fled from Rome and her headquarters established in the "desert" (XII. 14). The Two Witnesses shall guide the Church. Their followers in Jerusalem shall be the local type of the true believers throughout the world, the local representatives of the "sanctuary" and the "Altar" and be protected by the Two Witnesses during their testimony. Jerusalem would be both the principal scene of their miraculous power and the head of Antichrist's empire, just as ancient Rome in St. John's time was the headquarters of the Church of Christ and also the head of the adversary of Christ. Jerusalem could then be still called the "holy city". Commentators up to modern times have held various theories on the last clause of verse eight. Most of them consider that Jerusalem was designated merely to typify the center of Christianity, as "Babylon" was to typify the city of the False Prophet.

Scholars have found it difficult to reconcile the real Jerusalem as subject to Antichrist and at the same time as the "sanctuary" in which the Two Witnesses shall unfold their miraculous activity, because so few Jews were residents. But Isaias (XI. 11 ff) points to the days after Christ, when the Jews shall be gathered a SECOND time at that city from the dispersion. From 135 A. D. till the end of the first World-War, Jerusalem was a forbidden city to the Jews. But that war has given the Jews again the first right to Jerusalem. The Allied Powers defeating the Turk have brought about a literal fulfillment of the prophecy of Isaias. Might not these same powers be preparing the way for Antichrist by promoting secret societies, communism and injustice towards weaker nations and giving fuller scope and license to every vice? Certainly Russia is laboring successfully to obliterate all vestiges of Christianity.

In the book of Jeremias, we find a prophecy which indicates a re-building of Jerusalem in Messianic times on much larger and grander lines, a freeing it from all curse and reproach and elevating it to metropolitan glory in the Messianic Kingdom (Jer. XXXI. 38-40). That Jerusalem should be trampled under foot for a long time until the times of the nations are fulfilled is foretold by our Lord Himself (Lc. XXI. 24). It may connote the elevation of the city to be the capital of Christ's kingdom. The "mystery" in St. Paul's letter to the Romans (XI. 25) is the conversion of the Jews after the full number of the Gentiles shall have entered the Church. In our own day we see many mysterious prophecies merging into fulfillment. The "mystery of iniquity" seems to be near its culmination and the "mystery of God" to be revealing itself. Many Jews have returned to Palestine and have re-established their nation in the ancient homeland. They are not God's people in a higher sense than the rest of mankind, but to a Jewish seer their destiny holds a more lively interest.

A pertinent question obtrudes itself here. Why should Satan have the Beast establish his empire at Jerusalem, when he knows it will fulfill prophecy? Perhaps because the Church will be gaining ground very fast through the zeal of both priesthood and people after the slaughter of the one-third of mankind; Satan sees his world-dominion slipping out of his hands; no matter what turn events shall take, in the end he shall lose. He knows he will have but a short time to hold his kingdom (Apoc. XII. 12); and by establishing it in Jerusalem, he can mislead Jews and Protestants and Mohammedans – the Jews, because it is their beloved city and the Protestants because it is opposed to Rome. They will both fall ready victims to the signs and prodigies of the False Prophet, not being able to distinguish between real and satanic miracles, for they will not accept the verdict of the Church in these or in any other matters. Therefore Satan will devise the one scheme to make his kingdom as numerically strong as possible while it lasts. And this he thinks to actualize best by having his agent erect his capital at Jerusalem. He desires it out of pride and rebellion against God making the "holy city" in sheer derision the city of his vicar. He will imagine he can also destroy more souls from Jerusalem than from any other center.

Many people from all nations shall be gathered in Jerusalem in those days, because it is Antichrist's capital and the "sanctuary" of the Two Prophets. There will be good and bad people there. The victory over the Prophets will convince the wicked overwhelmingly of Antichrist's divinity. His waning glory will shine forth once more in full brilliancy. But all the well-informed Christians will be patient, knowing how quickly the enemy's exultation will grow silent. For three days and a half unceasing processions will pass by the bodies of those Two Prophets who inflicted so many terrible plagues upon the world and who are now conquered and slain by the "savior of the world", Antichrist.

Verse 10

The wicked feel relieved and gleeful, because those Two Prophets roused their consciences and made them apprehensive of punishments for their freely indulged vices. They will celebrate the victory over the Prophets and the Church. In a few minutes the news will be flashed across the world by cable, radio and television. Their preaching and example tortured a world wallowing in sin, and the plagues they inflicted on their adversaries reaped for themselves and all Christians demoniacal hatred. And the fanatical exultation of the earthly minded will go beyond all bounds. Gleefully Antichrist's adorers will extol the victory of their "god" and congratulate one another for their belief in him and will appoint a universal holiday. The true believers in all countries subject to Antichrist will dread the gory ordeal to follow from the fury of the mobs. Many will suffer martyrdom. The antichristians may still fear, however, that the Christians will defend themselves against attack.

Then will be the time for the execution of the demon's injunction, as expressed in chapter XIII. 15-17. With fiendish satisfaction, the wicked will view the dead bodies of the Two Witnesses as they celebrate their victory by carousing and debauchery. They welcome and promote the persecution against the Church. The prophecy of XIV. 15-16 will become an actual fact. By all they have suffered up to this time, many of the faithful will walk in the light of holiness and will passionately thirst for martyrdom. But as always, it will be everyone's duty to save himself by rightful prudence. There probably shall have been many martyrs before this time during the three and a half years of Antichrist's reign, but these THREE DAYS AND A HALF will bring in the harvest for Heaven. The Catholics will patiently await the resurrection of the Prophets. The weak and sinful who have not kept the commandments or who are converted from fear of the Two Witnesses or from earthly motives may go over to Antichrist. "They that dwell upon the earth," which includes all unbelievers, will hasten the coming of the last plagues as described in chapter XVI. by their redoubled fanatical fury. "For the sake of the elect those days shall be shortened", says our Lord, otherwise the human race would be exterminated.

Verse 11

After three and a half days, the people who have come to Jerusalem to see the corpses of the Prophets and the inhabitants of the city who happen to be present at the place where the bodies lie shall see them arise and stand on their feet. St. John here changes to the past tense to show how unexpectedly the event transpired in the vision. The wicked are struck with deadly fear, because the last thing is worse than the first. If they can arise from the dead, all opposition of their adversaries is undone. "The spirit of life from God" designates the source of animation for the body. The almighty power of God must re-animate a dead body, or the soul must be endowed with much greater power than it possesses in the mortal life. If every soul had the inherent power to keep the body alive, no one would die. The bodies of the Prophets die after Antichrist wounds them mortally, and their souls are compelled to leave them. Perhaps their bodies shall not be corrupted; they may merely be killed and animation cease, but at the appointed time their souls return from God, and He shall re-animate their bodies. They then enter the glorified life. "The spirit of life from God" alludes to Ezechiel (XXXVII. 10) depicting the restoration of the Jewish nation after the Babylonian Captivity.

Verse 12

While the wicked look upon the spectacle rooted to the spot or thrown into a panic and fleeing for safety, a voice heard like a trumpet from one end of the city to the other calls the Two Witnesses up to Heaven. As they look on, the Prophets over whose death they gloated ascend into Heaven on a cloud of glory. The true believers in Jerusalem expecting their hopes to be realized will know that the victory over the Beast is not far off. The great news will be flashed over the world by cable, radio, television and the newspapers, and the Beast will not be able to suppress it. The Prophets are made like Christ in all things, and their miracles will even be greater than His, and so they ascend into Heaven in the sight of their friends and enemies. Christ arose unseen and ascended in the presence of His disciples alone. The Prophets thus anticipate the general resurrection as a reward for their faithfulness during life when most people followed evil and for their labors and penance during this last sojourn on earth. They will be a manifest proof of the resurrection of all men.

Verse 13

While the inhabitants of Jerusalem stand thunderstruck at the glorification and ascension of the Two Prophets, a terrific earthquake jars the city. Walls of buildings tumble down and crush God's enemies. The Seer employs the round number, 7,000. There was an earthquake at the death of Christ and at His Resurrection, but no casualties are reported. Perhaps not each and every enemy of God in Jerusalem shall be struck dead by the earthquake, but those who are left will no longer have a voice in ruling the city. The earthquake and the resurrection and ascension of the Two Prophets will convert many. It will be a conversion from fear. Revolutions and overthrows of governments are also called earthquakes in prophetical diction. The citizens may then at once rebel against Antichrist who will probably be absent and will judge and execute all his officials and those who have helped to kill the Two Prophets and many Catholics. Only one tenth of the city falls, but the throne of Antichrist falls with it.

From the events related in this verse, we may glean that the forty-two months and the 1260 days and the "time and times and half a time" will be the same identical period. The citizens of Jerusalem are converted at the resurrection of the Two witnesses. Now after this conversion, the heathens will surely not trample the city under foot anymore. It is therefore logical to suppose that the empire of Antichrist will be prepared before the beginning of the forty-two months, and that the measuring of the sanctuary as also the "battle in heaven" (XII. 7) will take place during that time. Likewise Babylon has then been built. This would require a longer period of growth and evolution than three years and a half.

Antichrist will be very busy after the death of the Two Prophets to show himself in all his principal cities demonstrating the superiority of his power over theirs and corroborating their death at his hands. In his boasting he will extol the ease with which he triumphed over them and will take pains to justify his act. He will assure the world that it is freed from their malevolent activity by HIS supreme power. In the midst of his boasting will come the terrifying news of their resurrection and ascension into Heaven, of the earthquake that killed 7,000 of his followers and of the revolt against him. At this news, he will probably at the devil's suggestion transfer the seat of his empire to another city, which will thenceforth be called "THE GREAT CITY".

Many prophecies in the Old Testament reveal the ultimate conversion of the Jews to Jesus Christ. And St. Paul confirms that interpretation of the prophecies in the epistle to the Romans (XI. 25-26). Isaias says there will be a SECOND return of the

Jews after their dispersion and their final conversion to the Messias (XI. 11). He describes their return as a triumphant one not from Babylon but from all parts of the world. And he adds: "the enemies of Juda shall perish". He takes up the same theme in chapter XLIX. saying that the Savior will convert Jacob, but that Jacob must bide his time until it is "acceptable" to God. The whole world will then be converted to the glory of Jacob. The prophecy of chapter XLIX. has not been fulfilled in the return from Babylon nor so far in Christian times, though many Jews were converted in the first centuries and many again by St. Vincent Ferrer. The Jews have indeed been "barren" (Verse 21), because they repudiated Christ.

In chapter LIX. Isaias once more speaks of a complete conversion of the Jews, which is connected with the destruction of their enemies (17-20).The first part of the chapter describes very accurately the Jews and their moral standards in Christian times up to present days. Chapter LX. 1-7 has been traditionally applied by the Church to the Epiphany; but the language of the whole chapter argues for a more extensive fulfillment of the prophecy than in the Epiphany. The context reveals a much more conspicuous exaltation of Jerusalem than any so far enacted in its past history. This exaltation shall be everlasting. In verse 11, he says: "And thy gates shall be open continually . . . that the strength of the Gentiles may be brought to thee"; and in verse 14: "the children of them that afflict thee, . . . shall call thee the city of the Lord and the Sion of the Holy One of Israel"; and in verse 15: "I will make thee an everlasting glory"; and in verse 22: "I, the Lord, will *suddenly* do this thing in its time". Sophonias also says of that event: "The Lord has taken away thy judgment . . . Behold I will cut off all that have afflicted thee at that time" (III. 15-20). This points to the 7,000 slain. The prophet combines the days of the Messias and the final conversion of the Jews with the return from the Babylonian Captivity. Isaias lastly confirms the promises of the Lord by an oath, that all these predictions shall be fulfilled, and that Jerusalem shall be "called by a new name" (Apoc. II. 17); and this shall not be at the return from Babylon, for this prophecy of the perfect restoration shall be heard "in the ends of the earth" (Is. LXII. 2, 11 & 12) at a SECOND liberation, which is the final fulfillment of all the hopes of Israel. The people shall thenceforth be called "the holy people", the "redeemed of the Lord". And the city shall be called: "a city sought after and not foresaken". They will be holy because they shall be the property of the Lord. He shall have manifested His glory among them in the works of the Two Prophets and in their glorification. Jerusalem will then again be the center of the Messianic Kingdom, and the nations of the earth shall seek it in unending pilgrimages. According to Revelations (XI. 13), these prophecies can be literally fulfilled after the ascension of the Two Witnesses.

Rationalistic and Modernistic scripturists have put up the principle, that prophecies are always general in terms never specific and always vague in their application. This false principle is tantamount to denying all prophecy. Under that principle the above-quoted prophecies could be explained to be enthusiastic exaggerations describing the present state of the world. Now the prophecies touching the person of Christ were very specific and literal. Why then should not these pointing to His victory over the world be equally specific and literal?

When Irenaeus states (V. xxv. 4) that Antichrist will establish his capital at Jerusalem, he adds: "The Lord also spoke as follows to those who did not believe in Him, 'I am come in the name of my Father, and you received me not; if another shall come in his own name, him you will receive', calling Antichrist 'the other', because he is alienated from the Lord".

3. The Third Woe And The Victory Of Christ Announced. Seventh Trumpet.

Verses 14-end.

Verse 14

The SECOND WOE is completed with the ascension of the Two Witnesses, the consequent death of their enemies and the conversion of Jerusalem. The first woe struck those who did not have the sign of God on their foreheads, while the second one afflicted all people of the world. The Third Woe will descend directly on the followers of the Beast; though indirectly it will also cause the good to suffer. The third woe will begin in chapter XVI. The activity and success of the

Beast and the False Prophet outside of Jerusalem must first be staged, after the judgment upon the Church and her conflict with Satan has been described. Thereupon the prophecy narrates the defeat and annihilation of all evil forces. The Apocalypse is written in a perfect dramatic form, which shows the various acts and scenes of the conflict between the forces of evil and those of good finally converging in the victory of the Lamb.

Verse 15

The Seventh Trumpet is instantly answered by jubilant voices from heaven. The voices anticipate the victory. Jeremias (L. 2) announced the fall of Babylon as if it were a past event. The great voices are evidently the voices of the four living beings and the elders before the throne of God and the Lamb, the voices of the episcopate and the priesthood in the Church. Those who speak know the signs, admonish and instruct the people and confirm them in the expectation of a speedy victory. They are 'great voices", voices that shall be heard far and wide, voices of authority, voices in whom the faithful will trust (Jer. XXV. 30-31). They announce the victory in advance with positive certainty. Those who raise the voices are still threatened with death at the hands of Antichrist and his followers; but forgetting their own peril, they rejoice in the victory of Christ and the Church. They know that Christ's universal kingdom will now become a reality, that it will never end and that all promises made through the prophets shall be fulfilled.

"The kingdom of this world" is the kingdom of Antichrist. The capital city, Jerusalem, has come over to our Lord; and that promises His near and decisive victory over all the rest. The Church will be re-established upon the ruins of unbelief in Antichrist's empire, as it was established upon the ruins of paganism in the Roman Empire. The new establishment of the Old Church will prove for all time that no power on earth can destroy it. The words "our Lord and His Christ's" are taken from Psalm II. 2 The same exultation is expressed in XII. 10 and XIX. 6.

Verses 16-17

The priesthood takes up the hymn begun by the episcopate and offers sacrifices of thanksgiving now for the assured triumph.

The Greek word chosen brings forward again the Holy Eucharist. The Greek construction reveals an extraordinary manifestation of God's power, when it says, "Thy power, Thy great one", signifying not the ordinary sovereignty of God but the super-eminent lordship which rightfully belongs to Him and shall henceforth be unhindered in its boundless expansion. The world-empire has become His own, after Antichrist, the usurper, arrogated it to himself for a short time. The original text has only, "who art and who wast", omitting the future, because the Eternal Kingdom now ruling universally makes all hopes and expectations a reality. God will now convert all nations and rule forever. He will do this because He is the Source of all creatures, the Director of all phenomena and the end of all created beings.

Verse 18

The first words of this verse bring to mind Psalm II. The whole verse is a condensed statement of what is expressed in that psalm. St. John makes the psalm a prophecy pointing to Antichrist and his followers. The nations subject to him were angry with God, which is a most unnatural and blasphemous attitude for a creature to assume towards the Creator. It is satanic. They raged against Him, fought against Him in their blind fury, even denied His existence and put all His goodness and mercy to naught. His wrathful visitations were therefore made inevitable. The last plagues, which begin in chapter XVI., would be averted, if the wicked were converted by the Two Prophets. But they will not and hence their doom is sealed.

The time has arrived for all who are already spiritually dead and beyond redemption to be judged and condemned. With their destruction will come the reward for the labors of God's prophets. Through them God guided His people from the end of patriarchal times to the Babylonian Captivity and then replanted the Theocracy, from the root of which grew the Messianic Kingdom. Their labors and penances seemed all in vain, because the chosen people reverted to idolatry again and again and had adopted a worse hypocrisy and moral depravity in our Lord's time than ever before. The saints of apostolic times and later believed the teachings of Christ and His apostles and preserved the faith for future generations during the "great tribulation".

But Satan, after the beast ceased to exist, labored and schemed incessantly to revive it and at last succeeded. He re-established his empire, and Antichrist, the Beast in person, came to rule over it. The Two Witnesses then appeared to combat his open hostility against the Church now flourishing over the whole earth. The ancient prophets, the Two Witnesses and all the saints of the Church, who have lived and labored for the peace and salvation of the world, and all who have suffered martyrdom shall now see their labors and sacrifices crowned. Their glory will be augmented by the victory about to be won and the rule of justice to follow.

"Those that fear Thy name" are possibly the people who are invincibly in error or ignorance of the true faith or who have been converted by the Two Prophets but have not been formally admitted into the Church. Or they may be the true believers who have lived an ordinary Christian life, refused to submit to Antichrist, have kept the commandments but have not labored to spread the kingdom of Christ. They also shall be rewarded. "Blessed are they that trust in Him" (Ps. II. 13). They shall live in peace and security henceforth and reap respect from all peoples for their constancy in the evil days.

Those who destroy shall be destroyed. Paganism in St. John's time was the destroying agency in the world. It destroyed faith, religion, worship, morality, life, property and freedom through its temples, emperor-worship and tyranny. But the future destroyers are the followers of Antichrist. When the Two Witnesses shall have had their triumphal entry into Heaven, the time will be ripe for the extirpation of all evil growths in the world, whether persons, organizations or institutions. This means primarily Antichrist and all agencies that have paved the way for him and his empire.

Verse 19

This verse is the conclusion to this chapter, is co-incident in time with XV. 5 and points to the end of chapter XIX. giving a glimpse of the final judgments upon the wicked and stating in an epitomized form the THIRD WOE. That woe will have its fulfillment in chapters XVI. to XIX. Chapter XII. depicts the battle of the Church with Satan and chapter XIII. with the Beasts, as chapter XI. described the combat between the Beast and the Two Witnesses.

The "sanctuary of God" is again in view and is opened. This is only a momentary flash revealing the extraordinary divine power, which the Church will now be permitted to manifest and which is more graphically described after XV. 5. God's judgment upon the world shall proceed from the inner sanctuary, after the Church has herself been judged and purified. The ancient "Ark of the Covenant" was lost, and the Temple in the days of our Lord did not contain it, as did the Temple of Solomon. Neither did Ezechiel see the Ark in the ideal temple. The "Ark of the Covenant" in the new "sanctuary of God" is the "place of rest" in the Church, the tabernacle where Christ dwells in the Eucharist. This reveals whence will come the power to execute judgment upon the world. The lightnings, voices, thunder-peals, earthquakes and hail are symbols of judgment.

The opening of the sanctuary indicates the nearness of the judgment upon the wicked who have "corrupted the earth". The judgment will begin at the Church and from thence will break forth upon the world, as Jeremias wrote in reference to Israel (XXV. 30-31): "For behold I begin to bring evil upon the city wherein my name is called upon . . . the Lord shall roar from on high, and shall utter his voice from His holy habitation . . . for the Lord entereth into judgment with the nations". St. Peter stated: "For time is, that judgment should begin at the house of God". Those words presaged the coming persecution under Nero.

The lightnings symbolize miracles and manifest acts of God pouring the last plagues upon the world by saintly men (XVI. 1) who act in God's name and power. The voices are exclamations of astonishment by those who are convinced through the last plagues and who then wish to join the Church. They are probably also the contradictions of antichristians, their blasphemies and counter-anathemas, as the plagues are poured upon them. St. John thus heard a babble of contradictory voices.

In the thunders the Church warns the hardened sinners, the heretics, the schismatics and the followers of Antichrist of their impending peril and his doom and the fall of Babylon. This is more fully announced in chapter fourteen, verses six to eleven. The thunders are uttered by the supreme authority in the Church and by those whom almighty God has chosen to deter the unwary from believing in the signs of Antichrist; and they are repeated by zealous bishops and priests over the earth, who know the nearness of the judgment by the manifest signs.

The earthquake and hail demonstrate the completion of the plagues as mentioned in XVI. 18-21, which may occur at the condemnation of the Beast and his assistants at XIX. 21. The last plagues are probably real earthly phenomena but symbolize the overthrow of kingdoms and empires, after Antichrist and his prophet have met their doom. In Ezechiel (XIII. 9-23) the prophets who had established their authority by lies and hypocrisy were warned that what they had built would be thrown down with "great Hail-stones". There is in that prophecy a caution against deceit and flattery for advancement in the Church and against cringing obsequiousness.

Verse nineteen is therefore not an introduction to chapter twelve but a statement of the theme of chapters fourteen to nineteen inclusive. It also puts the full close to chapter eleven, sums up the main events of the Seventh Trumpet and flashes forth a momentary glimpse of the final judgment upon the wicked.

CHAPTER XII.

Westminster Version

And a great sign was seen in heaven: a 1. woman clothed with the sun, the moon under her feet, and upon her head a crown of twelve stars.

She is with child, and crieth out in her 2. travail, and is in anguish of delivery. And 3. another sign was seen in heaven – behold, a great red dragon, having seven heads and ten horns, and upon his heads seven diadems; his tail draweth after it the third part of 4. the stars of heaven, and it cast them to the earth. And the dragon stood before the woman who was about to bring forth, in order that when she should bring forth he might devour her son.

And she brought forth a male child, who is 5. destined to rule all the nations with a rod of iron; and her child was caught up to God and to his throne.

And the woman fled into the wilderness, 6. where she hath a place prepared by God wherein she is to be nourished during a thousand two hundred and sixty days.

And a battle took place in heaven, Michael 7. and his angels battling with the dragon. And the dragon and his angels battled, and they prevailed not, nor was their place 8. found any more in heaven.

And he was cast down, the great dragon, the 9. ancient serpent, who is called the Devil and Satan, he who seduceth the whole world – he was cast down to the earth, and his angels were cast down with him.

And I heard a loud voice in heaven, saying: 10. 'Now is come the salvation and the might and the kingdom of our God, and the power of his Christ; because the accuser of our brethren hath been cast down, he who accuseth them day and night before our God.

And they have conquered him through the blood of the Lamb, and through the word of their 11. witness, and they loved not their life in face of death.

Wherefore be glad, O ye heavens, and ye that dwell therein! Woe to the earth and to the 12. sea, because the devil hath gone down to you in great fury, knowing that he hath but a little time!'

And when the dragon saw that he was cast 13. down to the earth, he pursued the woman who had brought forth the male child.

And there were given to the woman the two 14. wings of the great eagle, in order that she might fly into the wilderness, to the place where she is to be nourished a time and times and half a time away from the serpent.

Then the serpent cast out of his mouth, after 15. the woman, water like a river, that she might be swept away in its flood.

But the earth came to the help of the woman; 16. the earth opened its mouth, and swallowed the river which the dragon had cast out of his mouth.

And the dragon was wroth at the woman, and departed to make war with the rest of her seed, 17. with them that keep the commandments of God and bear witness to Jesus.

And he stood upon the sand of the sea.

III. THE BATTLE BETWEEN THE CHURCH AND THE DRAGON

1. The Vision Of The Woman.

Chapter XII.

Verses 1-2.

One aspect of the supreme conflict between Christ and Satan, between the Church and Antichrist has been depicted in chapter XI. The present chapter depicts another aspect of the same conflict showing Satan to have been active within the Church and to have won a notable following. But he is expelled, and the Church is purified and freed from all scandals. This struggle in the church is assumed as finished in XI. 1-2. In point of time then, the happenings of the present chapter antedate those of chapter XI. Satan fails to destroy the Church from within, and that leads to the battle with the two beasts in the next chapter, where they, inspired, instigated and endowed by Satan, strive to destroy the Church from without. In chapter XI., the Seer first describes the battle of the Church with her adversaries in Jerusalem and her apparent defeat at their hands, which, however, wins for her a real victory under the leadership of the Two Prophets and which ends in the conversion of Jerusalem; and thereafter he vividly narrates the battle with Satan in chapter XII. and with the two beasts in chapter XIII. Probably because chapter XIII. is a continuation of the theme stated in chapter XII., the events of chapter XI. were narrated before chapter XII.

Verse 1

Before the eyes of the Seer, a great sign, the first of the "signs", a portent of something momentous, appears in the Church. It is of divine origin. "Signs" in prophetical terminology are ominous revelations of what is about to happen. Therefore the apostles asked our Lord for the "sign" of His coming (Mt. XXIV. 3). The pharisees demanded "a sign from Heaven" as a proof of our Lord's claim to divinity (Mc. VIII. 11; Mt. XVI. 1). The word furthermore denotes the wonders wrought by evil powers (Apoc. XIII. 13; XVI. 14; XIX. 20). In the Septuagint, the word is used for celestial phenomena (Gen. I. 14). The sign appearing here is GREAT, because it will indicate the time of the judgment that shall proclaim the "Great Day" of almighty God. It will herald the near approach of the events narrated in chapters eleven and thirteen. Appearing in heaven, it will point to the center of the whole desperate struggle for the possession of the world by Satan and his hordes. When this sign appears in the Church, the advent of Antichrist is near. In chapter eleven a reed, a symbol of judgment, was given St. John; in chapter twelve that symbolic action shall be fully explained. The interpretation of this "sign" is thus very important.

There are many and varied interpretations out, some of which are obviously impossible. One among the many extant seems perfectly logical and agrees with the best interpretations of the ancient Fathers. It is that of Father Gallois, O. P.; but strange to say, it has passed unnoticed. It is, however, adopted here, because it not only fits into the context of the chapter but also of the whole book.

The "sign" that shall appear to announce the arrival of direst judgments for the Church and the world is "a woman clothed with the sun and the moon under her feet and on her head a crown of twelve stars". This is the first "woman" to appear in the Revelations. She dwells in light and her very raiment is light and is thus the antithesis of the powers of darkness whose machinations are dark. She stands in a mass of light, which clothes her entirely, and upon an orb of lesser light. And her head is encircled by a halo of smaller orbs. She thus somewhat resembles Christ (I. 13-16) and God (IV. 3); yet the light is not her own, does not emanate from her person, as it does from Christ and God, but it is given her for raiment and ornament. These orbs of light are of heavenly origin, tokens of divine endowments. She has received light as her dowry, and on that account the prince of darkness persecutes her. This woman is a contrast to the scarlet woman of chapter XVII. 4.

The woman of chapter twelve is not the Blessed Virgin Mary. The ancient interpreters beginning with Hippolytus and Methodius understood this to be a figure of the Church. Since Hippolytus was a disciple of Irenaeus who had associated with Polycarp, a friend and companion of St. John, his exposition should have greater authority than that of later Fathers who identified the woman with the Blessed Virgin. According to the ancient Fathers, the human nature or character of the Church is here delineated, while in chapters four and five her divine nature and prerogatives were depicted. Heaven in the Apocalypse is the Church as to her divine origin, constitution, endowments and prerogatives. In this heaven, the Church now appears in her human character. The human nature of the Church is clothed with divine authority, because the priesthood is endowed with the light and power of Christ. The twelve stars represent the twelve apostles; or they may be God's mystical number symbolizing the Christian nations, that as a contrast to the ten crowned horns of the beast, shall be the glory of the Church when the days of Antichrist approach. If these stars represent the twelve apostles, they allude to Daniel declaring that those who teach many unto justice shall shine as the stars (XII. 3). They would thus aptly typify the exposition and exemplification of the divine truth by the apostles enlightening the mind of the Church. The moon under her feet has ever been understood to symbolize the unchanging and unchangeable character of the Church. Though consisting of frail human beings, she is not changeable like they or like the phenomena of nature. The moon beneath her feet fitly represents her power to make laws of discipline accommodating them to changing conditions in human society; and this power and right is also of divine origin.

Verse 2

The "sign" in heaven is that of a woman with child crying out in her travail and anguish of delivery. This has often been held to mean the constant travail of the Church to beget faithful followers for Christ, the teaching Church ever suffering from the curse of sin. The blame for the sins of her members has persistently been imputed to the priests, who thus suffer the curse pronounced upon Eve. When saving souls the Church suffers the agony or travail in giving them spiritual birth. Hippolytus and Methodius give such applications to this detail of the vision. However, the text demands a more specific application to the definite future event to which the prophecy obviously points, and in which the Church suffers the keenest pangs passing at that time through the greatest crisis of her whole life. In that travail, she gives birth to some definite "person" who is to RULE the Church with a rod of iron (verse 5). It then points to a conflict waged within the Church to elect one who was to "*rule all nations*" in the manner clearly stated. In accord with the text this is unmistakably a PAPAL ELECTION, for only Christ and His Vicar have the divine right to rule ALL NATIONS. Furthermore, the Church does not travail in anguish at EVERY papal election which can be held without trouble or danger. But at this time the great powers may take a menacing attitude to hinder the election of the logical and expected candidate by threats of a general apostasy, assassination or imprisonment of this candidate if elected. This would suppose an extremely hostile mind in the governments of Europe towards the Church and would cause intense anguish to the Church, because an extended interregnum in the papacy is always disastrous and more so in a time of universal persecution. If Satan would contrive to hinder a papal election, the Church would suffer great travail.

Some commentators explain this travail to mean that of the ancient synagogue begetting Christ. Such explanation is impossible, because the event lies in the future. (See IV. 1). Methodius holds and correctly so, that the birth of Christ is past history, while St. John in the Apocalypse writes of things present and future. (Banquet of the ten virgins — discourse VIII. chap. vii). But the explanation Methodius gives that the general travail of the Church is meant begetting children for God through Baptism at all times does not agree with the text, because they are not all destined to RULE the nations with a rod of iron. By his explanation "the enlightened receive the features, and image, and manliness of Christ . . . and the Church travails in birth until Christ is formed in us, so that each of the saints by partaking of Christ has been born a Christ" (Dis. VIII. chap. viii). If this be true in a measure of the ordinary Christians, how much more eminently is it not true of the Vicar of Christ who has the mind of Christ and teaches and RULES the nations in His stead.

2. The Vision Of The Dragon.

Verse 3

A second "sign" appears in heaven having a hostile relationship to the first. It is a blood-red dragon and is a horrible contrast to the first figure of divine beauty. The dragon has seven heads and ten horns. This red dragon it is that brings the Church into great distress at that time. Red is the color of anger and of blood. Commentators have commonly held this to signify the blood of the martyrs with which the dragon became dyed, because he instigated the persecutions that shed the blood of the Christians to satisfy his anger against God and the Church. But it may have another signification. No fiercer enemy of God and man has appeared in Christian times than Communism, and strange to say, RED is its emblematic color. Communism may by that time have gained control of the governments of Europe. It would then erect almost insurmountable difficulties for the holding of a conclave to elect a pope. Burtain says the Greek phrase "is an object infinitive governed by the idea of desire implied in the preceding particle" (parag. 389). Satan knows how extensively an interregnum in the papacy would favor his success in recovering his ancient lordship over the world. (See 2 Thess II. 7).

The dragon wears a diadem on each of the seven heads, while the woman wears only a wreath. The diadem is the emblem of sovereignty; and the wreath of excellency or subordinate regency placed on the head by the supreme authority. The dragon appears as a "sign", just as the woman appears as a "sign". The dragon is therefore in its outward appearance not Satan in person, but is a symbol of him in his political aspect and activity, as the woman is the symbol of the Church in its human character and action. As the Church is the mystical body of Christ, so the evil world-powers constitute the body of Satan, of which he is the soul. As a dragon, Satan through the evil world-powers of that time will enter the Church, interfere with her liberty and perhaps by stealthy suggestions having long before directed the choosing of candidates for the episcopate will now endeavor by threats of force to hinder the election of the worthiest candidate for the papacy. The seven heads may be seven world-powers existing and holding sway over the world at that time. They would then not be the same heads as those of the beast but would become the Ten Horns of his empire. The Beast in the next chapter does not wear diadems on his seven heads indicating that those heads, of whom he is one, serve another than himself. His ten horns, however, bear diadems; for these horns represent the ten kings whom he shall appoint to rule his empire under him. He will thus rule the world through the ten kings, as Satan rules the world through the seven heads or empires.

The seven heads suggest the seven capital sins, from which all other sins and vices flow and through which Satan thwarts the work of saving souls. The ten horns intimate the principal institutions in the world inimical to the kingdom of Christ, namely Judaism, Paganism, Heresy, Schism, Mohammedanism, Atheism, Rationalism, Agnosticism, Indifferentism and Communism. Satan in this chapter and the Beast in the next have the same emblems, seven heads and ten horns, because the Beast will embody all the virtues of the dragon and will exercise his power in the service of Satan.

Verse 4

The tail of the dragon draws in its coils one third of the stars of Heaven and casts them to the earth. This is one third of the clergy. In Arianism (VI. 13), there was great apostasy of bishops and priests; the stars fell from heaven in large numbers. In the Greek schism, a great star, the Patriarch, fell from heaven (VIII. 10); and a star fell from heaven who led the apostasy from the Church into Protestantism (IX. 1). Before the appearance of Antichrist, "one third" of the stars shall follow the dragon. This is a compulsory apostasy shown by the Greek word, σύρει which means "to drag by force". The subsequent phrase, "and cast them to the earth", specifies this meaning with greater precision. Satan will probably through the evil world-powers of the time exercise such tyranny over the church as to leave the clergy the alternative of submission to the government or martyrdom by death or imprisonment and will enforce the acceptance of unchristian morals, false doctrines, compromise with error, or obedience to the civil rulers in violation of conscience. St. John evidently had in mind the world-empires of ancient times, all of which were persecutors of God's people. The text suggests a use of the apostate clergy, after their own defection, in persecuting the Church. Verse nine clearly states that those who will not brave martyrdom will surrender to Satan. The dragon will have them doing his will.

According to Ven. Bede, "Tyconius more suo tertiam partem stellarum quae cecidit falsos fratres interpretatur". Though Tyconius was a Donatist, his interpretation of the Apocalypse was very popular. Origen likewise expresses this opinion (Lom. iv. p. 306) "qui . . . peccatum . . sequitur, trahitur a cauda draconis vadens post eum". They probably followed the lead of Methodius, who says of these stars: "And the stars, which the dragon touched with the end of his tail, and drew them down to the earth, are the bodies of heresies; for we must say that the stars, which are dark, obscure, and falling are the assemblies of the heterodox".

The verse seems to allude to Isaias (IX. 15-16). The tail is a symbol of lying and hypocrisy. Through false doctrines and principles, Satan will mislead the clergy, who will have become worldly-minded, haughty, hypocritical, obsequient avaricious sycophants. It seems to forebode a long period of peace, growth and temporal prosperity for the Church, so that many will enter the priesthood from bad motives. They will look to the Church to satisfy their ambition and avarice and will think it easier to gain an honorable position in the Church than in the world. In Catholic countries pious parents often for pride or other unworthy reasons urge their sons unduly to enter the priesthood for the honor there is in it. Such have not the spirit of sacrifice or mortification in the priesthood, and when persecution shall "sift them as wheat", they shall be found to be chaff. By their lax principles they will infect the laity. They will easily welcome a mitigation or change of doctrine to sanction the lukewarm lives they want to lead. Then will Satan see a rich harvest ripening for himself. The symbolic meaning of the dragon's tail may reveal that the clergy who are ripe for apostasy will hold the influential positions in the Church having won preferment by hypocrisy, deceit and flattery.

In scriptural language, the clergy are stars. Daniel says "And they that instruct many unto justice (shall shine) as stars for all eternity" (XII. 3). And of Antiochus he says: "And it threw down of the strength, and of the stars, and trod upon them" (VIII. 10). This does not mean the martyrdom of pious Jews but rather the forcing of many into idolatry, for he says again, "such as deal wickedly against the covenant shall deceitfully dissemble" (XI. 32), meaning the apostasy of hypocrites. Our

Lord says of the faithful: "Then shall the just shine as the sun" (Mt. XIII. 43).

In Genesis the patriarchs, heads of the twelve tribes of Israel, are also called stars. And the words of Daniel (VIII. 10) cannot be restricted to the priests only of the Antiochean persecution but surely embrace all martyrs of that ordeal. If the chosen people of the Old Testament are called stars, much more appropriately so the true believers of the Church of Jesus Christ. The great apostasy will then most likely include the laity as well as the clergy. The apostasy of the laity is a constant process of elimination of the lukewarm and indifferent in countries strongly Protestant or non-Catholic. But in Catholic countries, these nonpractical members are not expelled from the Church. The voluptuous, the drunkards, the impure who commit crimes and abuses against marriage, the fornicators, the proud and avaricious, the lukewarm and indifferent and all who are not ready to suffer everything the world can inflict on them will certainly be drawn into apostasy by the dragon's power. This may be the "revolt" of which St. Paul writes, complete apostasy from God, as is under way now through the persecution of Communist governments.

The prophets condemning the works of the priests and false seers before the Babylonian Captivity point out the prevalent evils that might cause an extensive apostasy from the Church, if they obtained entrance. In the prophecy of Malachias (I. 7, 8, 12), we find priests and people offering God contemptible gifts that are worthless to themselves. There were priests who neglected to preach the truth (II. 7, 9) or to admonish the sinner by a good example (II. 9) but rather sought popularity by being lax and the slaves of human respect. Spiritual havoc is wrought, if priests and people live in sin boldly yet hold themselves blameless not minding the denunciations of their wickedness by the Church and not willing to understand the true meaning of God's chastisements (II. 17). If there are hypocrites among the priests, when Antichrist appears, they will apostatize as in the days of Antiochus (Dan. XI. 32). All those will apostatize who are "without faith", i.e. unfaithful, unjust and untrustworthy; they desecrate sacred things (Soph. III. 4). Those priests also will follow the dragon who surrender to the wishes of such people as want to hear "pleasant things" (Isa. XXX. 10). And those will fall away who fear for their own interests and will not remonstrate against evil practices in the Church (Amos. V. 13); likewise those who work zealously, preach well and administer the sacraments, but for hire, money and popularity; those, furthermore, who fulfill their duty with external exactness but have no heart or charity in their work (Is. I. 11-15; LVI. 2-3). Ezechiel gives as a principal reason for expulsion from the Church neglect of duty in many ways out of carelessness or fear (III. 18-21). Deceit, pretense and impurity shall be expelled from the Church (Jer. XXIII. 11-17).

If there are bishops who practice favoritism (Mal. II. 9) or who love presents and "take bribes" (Amos V. 12) or who abhor upright priests who dare to tell the truth (V. 10) or who call deceitful and flattering priests "great" (Is. XXXII. 5) or who slander others for their own gain or revenge (XXXII. 7); they are followers of the dragon. If bishops give judgment, favors and honors for bribes, presents, flattery and friendship (Mich. III. 11), abhor candidness, and pervert truth and right (III. 9), they corrupt the priests by rewarding sycophancy and by punishing sincerity and will apostatize (Jer. XXIII. 2). This is expressed more clearly by Ezechiel (XXXIV. 2-6): "Woe to the shepherds of Israel that fed themselves . . . you ruled over them with rigor and with a high hand" . . . fff. If bishops weakly give sanction to false principles, and priests praise them to be in their good graces, and the people love laxity, they will all apostatize (Jer. V. 31).

The above were some of the sins and vices enumerated by the prophets as the causes for which the judgments began at the house of God in the Old Dispensation (Jer. XXV. 29). But God would probably not permit many of such evils to become prevalent very extensively in the Church. This seems to be the promise of the prophet of Jeremias (XXIII. 4). Yet that promise may not be fulfilled until after Antichrist. In the rise of Arianism, the Greek Schism and before Protestantism, many of the above evils did seem to exist. They may therefore become widespread again in some nations in which the Church has not been purged and from them spread to other nations. And certainly, where they do exist at the time the judgment begins, they will cause great apostasy. In His Church, our Lord demands a higher standard than in the Synagogue, and so the principal causes for apostasy of the clergy may be revealed in chapters II. and III., especially in III. 1-6, which shows a state of mortal sin in the bishop, and in III. 15-22, which reveals a state of tepidity, loss of zeal, charity and the spirit of penance and sacrifice. The apostolic democracy founded by our Lord may have given way to an absolute monarchy, in which the episcopate rules with oriental despotism. The priests may be reduced to a state of servility and fawning sycophancy. The rule by reason, justice and love may have been supplanted by the absolute will of the bishop, whose every act and word are to be accepted without question, without recourse to fact, truth or justice. Conscience may have lost its right to guide the actions of priests and may stand ignored or condemned. Diplomacy, expediency and other trickery may be upheld as the greatest virtues. And the honesty and simplicity, straightforwardness and truthfulness exemplified by our Lord and the apostles may be frowned down. Hypocrisy and pretense may become the surest roads to advancement. Nothing can demoralize the Church so fast and so far as the knowledge that faithful work and strict attendance to duty count for little and that studied diplomacy in playing up to the members of the episocpacy gains everything.

Some eminent cardinal may be particularly outstanding in his efforts to stem the tide of demoralization of bishops and priests. Satan will know, and the world-powers will know, that he is the likely choice for the papacy, and that if elected, he will convoke a general council and exercise his supreme jurisdiction to inaugurate measures of reform. Satan knows that his own hopes of a rich harvest of souls will then be dashed to the ground. Hence he must avert the election or have the pope assassinated when elected. The judgment is about to begin "at the house of God" (1 Peter IV. 17). The influence of the dragon will everywhere aim to subject the Church to the state. This persecution is thus a political subjugation, and one third of the bishops and priests will be ripe for apostasy. Satan's intention is to subject the newly-elected pope also to the purposes of the World-powers or to plot his death. He may contrive an assurance of safety and immunity from harm for the cardinals to convene for the election the more easily to take the pope-elect prisoner. The dragon will want to intimidate the new pope into non-interference—to let affairs run and develop as heretofore. In that way would he "devour the son", absorb the papacy and alone direct and rule the world.

3. Delivery Of The Woman. Her Flight.

Verses 5, 6.

Verse 5

She brought forth a male child who is destined to rule all nations with a rod of iron. The pope elected is virile and fearless. He is the one destined by Providence to overthrow the schemes of the dragon. The text in the Vulgate is in the future tense. This is the nearest way of expressing in Latin the force of the Greek μέλλει with the infinitive. The child "was to have ruled", or was on the point of ruling with an "iron rod". The one whom God has destined for the papacy at that time will institute the needed reforms. A general council may decree the reforms, but the pope must enforce them. These decrees will be the "seven thunders" mentioned in chapter ten. The pope cannot be intimidated by the minions of the dragons nor be misled by flattery or sophistry. His vision is clear and his character Christ-like. He goes straight to his object. The lax clergy of that time will extol the conditions then existing and will try to keep out of the Church apostolic purity and virtuous severity and will oppose the decrees of the pope with deliberate fanatcism.

The clause, "that he might devour her son", does not necessarily mean assassination. The dragon is a symbolic form of the evil world-powers, who will resent the existence of a spiritual empire among them and through them and independent of them in its essential functions and will attempt to subject this empire to their will and service. They will try to make the Church a "state church" everywhere. This is possible only if they can subject the pope to their wills and compel him to teach and rule as they direct. That would be literally devouring the papacy. Since they are defeated in this, they have the pope assassinated and "he is taken up to God and to His throne", just as Christ by His death "was taken away from distress" (Is. LIII. 8).

The words of Psalm II. 9: "Thou shalt rule them with a rod of iron" are said of Christ. But in our text they are said of His Viçar. The "rod of iron" is a scriptural symbol of divine chastisement or law-enforcement, by which the good are separated from the wicked. The reference here is to XI. 1, where the "sanctuary of God" is to be measured with a "reed like unto a rod". This one event is thus shown under a different aspect in each of the three chapters. The Church will be purified. The good will accept the enforcement of divine laws; but the wicked will rebel and apostatize.

This "son" is not Christ at His first advent, for he was to rule with a "rod of Iron", and when on the point of doing so he is rapt out of the world. This was not true of Christ. By His own words, He did not come to judge but to save. The last words of the verse, it is true, allude in a way to what Isaias (LIII. 8) said of Christ. He writes of the death of Christ, which took Him away from the power of His enemies. There was no need of His Ascension to escape the persecution of Satan. After his glorious resurrection, Satan and all the power of hell kept out of His way. He was not killed at His birth, nor did He ascend into Heaven immediately after His death, as the text here indicates regarding this "son". And He did not ascend to the throne of God in order to escape from the dragon. Again, as Methodius wrote: "John speaks concerning things present and things to come. But Christ long ago conceived, was not caught up to the throne of God when He was brought forth, from fear of the serpent's injuring Him" (Banq. of 10 virgins; Dis. VIII. chap. vii). But this "son" will hardly have time to purify the Church, before he is persecuted, imprisoned and martyred. He is therefore surely not Christ.

The words, "and to his throne", point to XX. 4 and 6: "and they lived and reigned with Christ a thousand years". This pope will be given the power to rule over the destiny of the Church immediately from Heaven. He carries out the will of God and loses his life in consequence; and immediately as part of his reward, he receives in Heaven patronage over the Church on earth.

Verse 6

Verses 4, 5 and 6 state briefly what is more fully stated from 7 to 15. Verse 5 states the assassination of the pope and verses 7 to 14 explain the reason. Verse 6 relates the flight of the woman and verse 14 the manner of her flight and the place of her exile. The pope is assassinated but the cardinals are rescued. The flight of the woman recalls the words of Isaias (XXVI. 20): "Go my people . . . hide thyself a little for a moment, until the indignation pass away".

The meaning of the word "wilderness" is probably contained in the prophets. Isaias says: "And the wilderness shall rejoice, and shall flourish like the lily" (XXXV. 1). The prophet by these poetic figures names the Gentiles the wilderness, for they are devoid of God's benefits and are a spiritual desert. *Osee* calls the captivity among the heathen Babylonians a dwelling in the wilderness: "Behold I will allure her, and will lead her into the wilderness and will speak to her heart" (II. 4). Ezechiel speaks of the Captivity in the same figurative language: "And I will bring you into the wilderness of people and there will I plead with you face to face" (XX. 35). The Synagogue was thus led into the wilderness and was cleansed of all inclination to idolatry. It appears quite logical therefore to interpret "wilderness" to mean a non-Catholic country rather than a desert proper but a nation that is not an apostate nation. Providence will prepare a place of refuge in that country to protect the Church during the reign of Antichrist. Verse 14 corroborates this conclusion. The Great Eagle protects its citizens; and though a heathen nation, it will receive and protect the Church. It will be independent and powerful enough to maintain its liberty against Antichrist. After it protects the Church during the Great Crisis, it will receive the grace of conversion. The 1260 days co-incide with the same period during which the Two Witnesses are active in Jerusalem (XI. 3) and also with the time and times and half a time of verse fourteen.

4. The Battle In Heaven.

Verses 7-12.

Verse 7

The narration of what the first clause of verse 4 stated begins now in full detail. The newly elected pope, aided by St. Michael and the cardinals and loyal bishops and priests, takes up the combat with the dragon under the assurance of a speedy victory.

Satan weens himself triumphant in the large following he has drawn from the Church and the assistance of the malicious world- powers. But he is due for a crushing defeat. The bishops, priests and religious will everywhere obey the pope and council and accept the decrees of reform and discipline whole-heartedly. The battle is intense but of short duration. The wicked clergy will exercise all their wiles to maintain their positions in the Church, without doing penance or renouncing their heathen mode of living but will pursue their hypocritical, neglectful living and compromise with the doctrines of the dragon. Through such, Satan can lead the greatest number of souls to perdition, therefore he must keep them in the most populous parishes and dioceses in the Church.

This battle into which Michael enters with his might was announced by the oath of the angel in chapter X. 5. That angel was probably St. Michael. The judgment shall be delayed no longer. It has begun at the house of God. And Michael will see it through to a decisive victory. It synchronizes with the measuring of the sanctuary in XI. 1-2.

The battle of Michael and his angels with Satan and his hordes has been understood by many to be the apostasy of the fallen angels and a subsequent battle in Heaven. But St. Peter states that they were "drawn by infernal ropes to the lower hell" (2 Pet. II. 4), they were not cast unto the earth. Some commentors can imagine that the evil spirits re-enter Heaven and attack the angels and saints there. H. B. Swete says: "As the Incarnation called forth a counter-manifestation of diabolic power on earth, so after the Ascension the attack is supposed to be carried into Heaven" (p 153). He says furthermore: "Still less can we accept the interpretation of ἐν τῷ οὐρανῷ proposed by several of the Latin commentators, e. g. Bede: 'coelum ecclesiam significat', a view which throws the symbolism into hopeless confusion" (p. 153). The fact is that H. B. Swete's interpretation is a hopeless confusion, as is that of many interpreters. St. Bede's interpretation causes no confusion, but is the only view that makes a logical interpretation of the Apocalypse possible. If "heaven" is the Church on earth in the Apocalypse, the battle of the evil spirits in heaven can be easily and logically explained. The angels who fight under the leadership of Michael are the loyal bishops and priests of the Church, while the angels of the dragon are the sinful priests and bishops. Perhaps the Two Witnesses will appear at this time before the entrance of Antichrist on the stage and will take part in the battle to expel the wicked clergy from the Church. The mission of Elias will be as Our Lord said, to "restore all things". Above all they must restore in the Church the apostolic spirit of zeal and penance, simplicity and uprightness. In obedience to their admonitions, the loyal bishops may enforce the acceptance of all decrees of a general council and of the martyred pope.

Verse 8

The wicked, not willing to do penance or expose their lives to danger or lose the favor of the world-powers or relinquish a life of worldliness and luxury, will leave the Church. In verse 4 the dragon "cast them to the earth", seduced them into a state of mortal sin. In early times, those who schemed to get the lucrative bishoprics became Arians at the behest of the emperor. The world-powers now will demand a giving up of the rights of the Church and a submission to the governments. The venal bishops by complying will have gone so far that they can no longer be tolerated in the Church. Jeremias (XXVI. 2) relates that the external cult of religion was not neglected but it was mixed with idolatry. (See Ezechiel VIII.).

Verse 9

Thrilled with exultation, St. John announces the happy news of the expulsion of the dragon with all his followers from the Church. He names the same old enemy of God and His people in all his nefarious activities. As a dragon he is the ruler over all Godless and anti-God world-empires that have existed and shall exist including that of Antichrist. These empires shall be SEVEN in number when the last one shall have been established. They all enforce emperor-worship and dynastic or state supremacy in spiritual matters. They all serve the usurper of God's rights, the dragon. As the "old serpent", he is the primaeval seducer of man. He is now straining every nerve and calling upon and using every resource to seduce into worshipping and serving himself the world that would not serve God. He will succeed with the disloyal clergy but not with those who love God truly. He is the "devil" because he is the originator and promoter of all evil in the world; he is the father of lies, hypocrisy, bluff, flattery; through his envy, sin entered into the world that belonged to God. As "satan" he is the adversary of God and man having nothing in view but the ruin of all God's beautiful works and man's happiness; he therefore aims at the overthrow of the kingdom established by the King of kings and to establish his own kingdom of evil in its place.

By the expulsion of the lax and sinful bishops and priests from the Church, Satan is cast out; for by their toleration of sin and lukewarmness the spirituality and virtue of young priests are put in jeopardy and evil is promoted among the believers. Satan can vent more malice against the Church indirectly through bishops and priests than by his own power. Lukewarm, indolent priests condemn activity and zeal and hinder the zealous from saving souls. If they work, they do so for selfish reasons. How can the luke-warm enkindle piety? How can the luxurious lead to self-denial? How can the impure lead youth in purity? How can sinners love God? How can the indolent and lovers of ease improve their mind by serious study? How can hypocrites, slanderers, the dishonest, the diplomatic and revengeful exemplify the teachings of our Lord? When none such are in the Church, renewed life and vigor will grow up in it and will bloom and flourish.

The battle of Michael and the faithful priests and bishops against the attacks of the dragon recalls the scene in Zacharias (III. 1-5), where Satan attempted to frustrate the restoration after the Babylonian Captivity, which Jesus, the high priest, was to achieve. The priests misled by Satan had defiled themselves by mixing idolatry with the true worship and thus shut off the source of spiritual life and strength from the people. Now Satan tried to accuse the highpriest before God of being unfit to bring salvation to the people, because he wore filthy garments. The angel says to him: "is not this a brand plucked out of the fire?", i. e. has he not endured sufferings in the Captivity? That cleansed him from all defilement. He is clothed with clean garments, emblematic of the washing away of all sins, and is invested in grace, which is an impenetrable armor against all reproach. Likewise after the expulsion of the wicked clergy from the Church, there shall be no more matter of reproach against the priesthood. And when the clergy are all on the height of virtue intended by Christ, the Church can withstand every assualt.

Verse 10

Verses 10 to 12 bring the announcements of verses 8 and 9 to a climax, the same thought being repeated with greater jubilation. The Seer hears a voice in heaven, a great voice. It may be the voice of an eminent saint, a cardinal or the pope. It proclaims the actual arrival of the salvation predicted by the prophets of old in glowing terms and brilliant imagery. One third of the Church was unfaithful, the rest will bring salvation to the whole world.

The latent power of the Eucharistic Christ has manifested itself now in the zeal it has inspired to renounce the world and all its promises. It has armed and actuated the Church to face the dragon, to fight him and expel him. In pagan Roman times, only one empire in the service of Satan fought the Church. Now the dragon's power is more far-reaching and irresistible in all the unchristian organizations over-growing the world and in all the unchristian governments and empires leagued against the Church. But the Church has fearlessly faced the dragon and ejected all his followers. Her strength was pitted against his vaunted strength and overthrew him. This strength shall now prevail.

The sovereignty that belongs to God, the Creator and Redeemer, shall be re-assumed, because the way is cleared for it in the purging of all evils from the Church. The definite article is used throughout to indicate the definite and expected results promised by the prophets ages before the coming of Christ. Up to this time there shall have been only a partial fulfillment of these prophecies due solely to the indifference of the people and clergy. But those who frustrated the realization of those prophecies are outside and can no longer hamper the carrying on of God's program.

Inseparably united with the sovereignty of God is the power and authority of Christ. He is divinely appointed King over God's "holy mountain". When this power concealed in His Eucharistic Presence finds no evil in the Church to stem the forces of its love, it will inundate the world with a quickening flood of grace, wash away all malice and plant the everlasting peace, strength and salvation of God's kingdom. When the Church is cured of all weakness, the triumph of the power and authority of Christ is assured. Hence we hear the voice of victory and jubilation from the tabernacle of God.

"The accuser of our brethren has been cast down" alludes to Job (I. 6; II. 1). "Accuser" refers to Satan's boasted success within the Church. He led the clergy to accept his doctrines, the maxims of the world, and through their acceptance crowded out grace and the spirit of sacrifice and penance with its consequent state of hypocrisy, tepidity and spiritual death. With a triumphant sneer he then pointed to the lives of Christ's chosen ones accusing them before the face of God of being his own followers instead of Christ's. He used such to sow heresies in the Church, and he reaped a rich harvest of apostasy. But not satisfied with that much, he throws accusation against the whole Church. He is not logical but draws conclusions wider than the premises. He wants to boast before God of having the larger share of mankind in his service, and God has permitted his ravings to continue in order to prepare a much more far-reaching and decisive victory for His grace and the Church. If Satan could hate anything more than God, it would be the Catholic Church; and he is active day and night to cast opprobrium upon it. But that hatred is finally reduced to impotent rage. The Church is cleansed by the expulsion of his followers, and his accusations are rejected as untruthful and invalid.

Verse 11

The means by which the good overcame the dragon were the blood of the Lamb, the true doctrine and fearless faithfulness to Christ on peril of their lives. The "blood of the Lamb" means here the same as in VII. 14, the blood that flows from the eucharistic Christ in the sacrifice of the Mass and inundates the soul of the individual with grace and strength to make a fearless profession of faith at all times. It cured them of spiritual anemia and fortified them to stand unmoved in the face of death. By their public testimony and by not having "loved their life in the face of death", they conquered the dragon. The last clause intimates that the blood of the martyrs has begun to flow. It refers to the "red dragon" and suggests that the world-powers are "REDS". All fearless true believers are perfecting their sanctification by heroically avoiding all compromise with error and sin. The blood of the Lamb does not call to heaven for vengeance but for mercy and pardon.

Verse 12

The "voice" calls on the heavens to rejoice. The "heavens" are the dwelling places of the blessed. The Church is "heaven" in the singular number. The blessed in the heavens are interested in the victory of the Lamb on earth, because it will bring the universal dominion of Christ. The expulsion of the dragon from the Church, they know, is the "sign" of the approaching complete victory of Christ. They are invited to rejoice in advance in this positively certain victory. The schemes of the dragon to destroy the Church from within have failed.

There seems to be a contradiction in the wording and meaning of the text. (2 Cor. V. 1). St. Paul contrasts the **οἰκία τοῦ σκήνους** the earthly, Temporary dwelling, with the **οἰκία αἰώνιος** the eternal home in Heaven. The word σκηνοῦντες in our text might therefore seem to contradict the word "Heavens", the abode of the blessed, and point to the clergy and faithful in the Church, whose abiding there is only temporary as in a tent. But the seeming contradiction is cleared away by interpreting the word to mean what the context shows, the same as **κατοικοῦντες,** "inhabitants" of the Heavens, even if the later word is commonly used in the Apocalypse to designate the non-Christians dwelling on the earth. The word is thus only a substitute for the commoner word and its meaning is sufficiently clear from the context pointing to the blessed in Heaven.

The words, "woe to the earth", carry an ominous message to the world. Satan will now aim to destroy the Church from without. The world-powers, peoples and nations that are in his service will lend their aid. But this will bring upon them all those plagues related in chapter eleven and in sixteen to nineteen, which constitute the completion of the second woe and the fullness of the third. Yet men are so steeped in sin and captivated by its love, that Satan will easily win them for his work through Antichrist and his Prophet. Prejudice and vice have darkened their minds too much to let them believe they are bringing woes upon themselves by persecuting the Church. The "sea" is composed of the nations subject to Antichrist. These nations will help to wage war on the "Crystal Sea" composed of the Christian Laity.

The dragon's expulsion from the Church is described as a descent to the earth. This represents the Church as a supernatural institution in contrast with the world or those who live mere natural lives. Not being able to subject the Church to himself or infect her with false doctrines or debasing morality or to impute sin to her any longer, Satan will plunge the world as deeply into vice as he can, for he knows that his allotted time for action is short. The defeat has not deprived him of his natural faculties, and he will use them now to wreak vengeance on the Church by mobilizing all antichristian organizations and marshalling all evil forces for a concerted attack on the lay members.

Obviously the original rebellion of the angels and their fall from Heaven is not presented here. According to verse 10, Satan accused "the brethren . . . before our God day and night". "Brethren" was not an appellation for the chosen people of the Old Dispensation. The term began with Christianity, in the sense in which it is employed here. The human race was already existing and Christianity established when Satan is cast out of "heaven" with his angels. This could not have been at the beginning of Christianity either, because verse 12 says that he knows he has but a "short time". It is now nearly two thousand years since he has been going about like a roaring lion seeking to destroy the Church from within and without. A thousand years is not called a short time in apocalyptical language. (See. XX. 2, 3).

5. Malice Of The Dragon Against The Woman And Her Children.

Verses 13 to end.

Verse 13

After Satan and the world-powers have seen the rejection of all their demands by the Church, they start up the persecution in full force. Satan knowing there is no time to lose incites all hostile governments against the Church. There may be a divided opinion and stand for and against the Church in Rome. The cardinals may still be there after the papal election and General Council directing the reform and enforcing the decrees from headquarters. The dragon clamoring for the punishment of those who excommunicated his followers may incite an invasion of the Vatican by military forces and murder the pope. All cardinals present are in danger. The city of Rome, the center of the Messianic Empire, has turned against the Church. If Satan can infuriate a mob to kill all the cardinals, he will wipe out the supreme ruling power conferred upon Peter by our Lord, so he hopes, and achieve an easy victory over the headless Church. But the cardinals appeal for aid to their home governments.

Verses 6 and 14

In chapter eleven we have 42 months and 1260 days. Each period three years and a half, and the periods seem identical. The same holds true for the 1260 days and the time and times and half a time in chapter twelve. They would lead to the conclusion that the cardinals remain at headquarters in the Vatican after the election of the pope and the closing of the General Council to direct the reform and enforcement of disciplinary measures. It will take some time to complete the work of the Council, which clearly expresses the stand of the Church on all burning questions of the day. The Church may re-state and reaffirm all her dogmas and moral tenets against the world and the clergy clamoring for changes. The order of the narrative is probably the same in this chapter as in many other parts of the Apocalypse. Verses 5 and 6 briefly state the main events, and verses 7 to 14 relate the cause of the dragon's anger and of the assassination of the pope. Verse 14 then continues the narrative and states the manner of the woman's flight. The pope is assassinated immediately after the publication of the decrees of the council, before he can enforce their acceptance. All governments of Europe may be so hostile to the Church on account of the election and decrees of the council that the cardinals do not return home. A second assembly of the cardinals if they returned home and a second flight seems improbable.

Verse 14

In both verses 6 and 14 the woman flies to "her place". This argues very persuasively for only *one* flight. She is given "two wings" of a Great Eagle. This intimates a rescue by airplane. An armed band of assassins may invade the Vatican, overpower the guards, murder the pope and some of the cardinals and menace the others, who, however, appeal to their home governments. The "Great Eagle" may send or have present a powerful airplane to bring its citizens home. The other surviving cardinals may be included in that rescue. The government of Rome though also a part of the dragon's force may permit the rescue in deference to the government and citizens of the GREAT EAGLE. They may have been promised safety by the government of Rome to assemble for the papal election. The government may now advise all cardinals who are not assassinated to flee for their own safety. Satan will not be able to hinder this flight.

The "Eagle" is an emblem of an independent government. In Ezechiel (XVII. 3, 7), the kings of Babylon and Egypt are called eagles. In Isaias (XL. 31), God promises that those who trust in Him shall take "wings as eagles".

The "wings" of the great eagle will enable the woman to fly into the wilderness. This wilderness is a heathen nation that has not joined the dragon, is not subject to him and is not an apostate nation either. In prophetical symbolism, the apostate nations of Israel and Juda were called harlots. The great eagle therefore, as a nation, has never been Catholic. The word "eagle" suggests that the nation may have become great by conquest.

This eagle will protect and shelter the Church during the reign of the Beast. The place of safety for the woman is the same as the one in verse 6, for it is called "her place". Probably some of the cardinals are citizens of that great country, and they are safely brought home. The text uses the definite article to designate THE eagle, "the great one". It makes this eagle appear to be the most powerful government on earth, and for this reason it will have the strength to defy the dragon. And later it will refuse to join Antichrist and will protect the Church during his domination of the world.

According to some commentators, the 42 months allude to the 42 generations in St. Matthew's gospel, from Adam to Christ, and this is thought to be a Messianic number. Christ is the new David par excellence; Antichrist is an imitation of Christ, hence he rules 42 months. Under that supposition the number would be only symbolic. Others give it a Babylonian funeral origin. These and many other 'findings' are only accretions to the Apocalypse. The time is stated in three different ways, in years, months and days to make the literal meaning unmistakably certain. Evidently it is three and a half years actual time. The time given in verse 14 is indefinite, similar to that of Daniel (XII. 7); But since in Daniel (XII. 11) it seems to mean 1290 days, so here it evidently synchronizes with the 1260 days of verse 6 and the same period in chapter eleven.

Verse 15

The Great Eagle protects the Church from the "face of the serpent". The serpent casts a great stream of abuse after her likened to a river. This flood with which he now aims to destroy the woman is slander. The idea of the SERPENT is brought to mind to show the source of the propaganda against the Church, for Satan is the arch-liar and archdeceiver of the human race from the beginning. In St. John's day the Church suffered from false accusations by Jews and pagans. At all times this has been one of Satan's methods of attack. It will be only a renewal of the ageworn and long disproven slanders by which Satan will incite the country that rescued the Church to refuse her sanctuary. All evil organizations in that country will aid him in his vile campaign. Some martyrs may be made by the fury of the ignorant, the prejudiced and the criminally inclined. The figure of speech, likening persecution to a flood of bitter waters is frequently employed in the psalms (Ps. XXXI. 6; CXXIII. 5 ff) and the prophecies (Is. XLIII. 2). Satan has always goaded the wicked on to slander and persecute those who want to serve God. When the greatest persecution of all times is getting under way, the world will be wise to the tactics of the serpent, and his propaganda will not sweep it off its feet. The Fathers (Cyprian, Victorinus) see in this flood the decrees of Decius, the fanaticism of the populace or the forces of persecution in general. In the later persecutions of Decius and Diocletian, the very name of Christian was to be wiped from the face of the earth. Thus, the way some commentators expound the Apocalypse, St. John might have written this prophecy during the fourth century, so exactly does it describe the persecution of Decius and Diocletian. St. John was not writing of his own time but of the future, when the Roman Empire should have vanished and when the final preparations for the appearance of Antichrist would be in the making. The serpent will then invent the vilest slanders against the Church and pour them after her to incite the world against her.

Verse 16

The government of the Great Eagle will guard and protect the cardinals. The officials knowing the slanders to be only stock in trade of the enemy will give no heed to them. The people fairmindedly will likewise sympathize with the persecuted. The great nation may also fear the agents of the dragon, for after delivering the other countries into his hands, they might stir up a revolution by the aid of lawless mobs to overthrow the government. It will be more vigilant and will protect those citizens on whose loyalty it can rely. Thus the flood of slanders poured out by the dragon will be swallowed up.

Verse 17

When the dragon sees his campaign of slander unavailing, his rage grows to white heat. If he cannot annihilate the Church, he will start up a war against the nations that have not joined him to crush the faithful members by bloody persecution. He succeeded in having the "son" who was to rule the nations with a rod of iron assassinated. But he did not destroy the work of that "son", which was to purify the Church and drive out Satan. This brings the events up to the appearance of Antichrist and the Two Witnesses (XI. 2-3). The happenings in this chapter chronologically precede those of chapter XI. This last verse gives the reason for the production of Antichrist and connects this chapter directly with the following one in which his character and career are related. The six principal characters of the great conflict will then have been described, the Two Witnesses, the Woman, the Dragon, the Beast and the False Prophet.

"The rest of the offspring" of the Church are the Catholic Nations that are not in the service of the dragon. He will go to wage the war against them. Those against whom he wages the war are the practical Catholics who keep the commandments and have the testimony of Jesus believing all He has revealed and taught. Those also may be included who outside the fold are in invincible ignorance, sincerely believing themselves to be true Christians, only misled by false ministers of the Gospel, whom they trust as reliable. Such ministers, if insincere, shall be punished in the judgments, but the people who have been misled will be spared in God's mercy (Ezech. XIII). Some nations may mobilize their forces quickly to protect themselves against invasion. The Great Eagle, divinely appointed guardian of the Church, will calmly await developments in the world, as Satan starts the war against the Christian nations.

Verse 18

All Satan's attacks on the Church have been for her benefit. Although he will corrupt some within and weaken the defenses, his plans shall fail when the traitors are ousted. After the apostasy of the unfaithful clergy and laity, the Church will stand forth purer and stronger than ever before, and Satan shall be forced to re-organize his whole campaign of attack. And for that purpose he stands "upon the sands of the sea". This sea is composed of the nations and peoples hostile to the Church. He stands there in his own personality, no longer in the form of the world-powers.

Since they are fully imbued with his philosophy, he will as an extra-mundane power direct their attacks upon the Church. The world will by this time be sharply divided into those who adore at the altar (XI. 1) and those who drift on in ignorance and uncertainty or who have given themselves to moral turpitude. Having himself failed again this time by the power-politics of the world-powers as much as by misrepresentation and slander, Satan will call forth out of the "sea" that serves him the champion, who will organize the world for the last effort to undo Christ's work and end the existence of the Church.

CHAPTER XIII.

Westminster Version

And I beheld rising out of the sea a beast 1. which had ten horns and
seven heads, and upon its horns ten diadems, and upon its heads blasphemous names.

And the beast which I saw was like to a 2. leopard, and its feet were
as those of a bear, and its mouth was as the mouth of a lion.

And the dragon gave it his might and his 3. throne, and great power.
One of its heads was as it were wounded unto death; but its deadly wound
was healed. And the whole earth followed the beast, wondering;

And men worshipped the dragon, because he 4. had given authority
to the beast, and they worshipped the beast, saying: 'Who is like to the
beast, and who can battle with it?'

And there was given to it a mouth uttering 5. haughty and blasphemous
words, and there was given to it power to work during forty two months.

And it opened its mouth to utter blasphemies 6. against God, to
blaspheme his name and his dwelling, even them that dwell in heaven.

And it was given to it to make war with the 7. saints and to conquer
them; and there was given to it power over every tribe and people and
tongue and nation.

And all that dwell upon the earth shall 8. adore it, every one whose
name is not written in the book of life of the Lamb that was sacrificed
from the foundation of the world.

If anyone hath an ear, let him hear! 9.

If anyone is for captivity, into captivity 10. he goeth; if anyone shall
slay with the sword, with the sword must he be slain. Herein lie the
patience and the faith of the saints.

And I beheld rising out of the earth another 11. beast, which had
two horns like those of a lamb, and which spoke like a dragon.

And it exercised all the power of the first 12. beast in its presence.
And it maketh the earth and all the dwellers therein to adore the first beast,
whose deadly wound was healed.

And it did great signs, so as even to make 13. fire to come down from
heaven upon earth in the sight of men.

And through the signs which were given it 14. to do in the presence
of the beast, it leadeth astray the dwellers upon the earth. It bade the
dwellers upon the earth to make an image to the beast which had the
wound of the sword, and yet is alive.

And it was given it to put life into the image of the beast, so that
the image of the beast 15. should even speak, and should cause to be
slain all that worship not the image of the beast.

And it causeth all men, small and great, rich 16. and poor, bond and
free, to mark themselves on the right hand or on the forehead, that no one
17. may be able to buy or sell, save he that hath the mark – the name
of the beast or the number of its name.

Herein lieth wisdom: he that hath understanding, 18. let him count
the number of the beast; for it is the number of a man. And its number
is six hundred and sixty-six.

IV. DESCRIPTION OF THE TWO BEASTS

1. The Beast Out Of The Sea.

Chapter XIII.

Verses 1-4.

Verses one to four describe the appearance and personal character of the Beast from the sea. Satan standing on the shores of the sea calls forth someone who will henceforth lead the campaign against the Church. This beast has like the dragon seven heads and ten horns. It at once calls to mind the wild beast which Daniel saw coming out of the sea (VII. 7), which, however, did not have seven heads but had ten horns. This was the fourth beast of Daniel's vision. The first three were a winged lion, a bear and a panther representing the Babylonian, the Medo-Persian and the Grecian Empires. The third beast of Daniel's vision appears again in chapter eight (VIII. 8) as a he-goat. The panther had four heads, while the he-goat grew four horns. The angel explains this to foreshow the division of the empire of Alexander (VIII. 21-22). The fourth beast is evidently the Roman Empire. This fourth empire according to the angel (VII. 23) is to become greater than all the foregoing. That was not true of any of the kingdoms that succeeded Alexander. It could be true only of the Roman Empire. The empire represented by the fourth beast will in the end be divided into ten kingdoms. This is a round number, the world's number of completion. In the description of that beast, the fourth empire blends into another empire of the future, with which the fourth beast has some similarity. The description of the fourth beast does not fit the kingdom of the Seleucidae at all. But it does not fit the Roman Empire either in all details.

A little horn grows up among the ten on the head of the fourth beast, and it brings down three of the ten horns. This little horn is not a kingdom but a man who has eyes and a mouth like a man and speaks blasphemies against God (VII. 8). The kingdom of this little horn shall differ from all other kingdoms, and he shall destroy three of the existing kingdoms (VII. 24).

The ten horns will evidently be the principal kingdoms or

empires that grew out of the ancient Roman empire. And lastly a godless one will subdue three of these ten empires; and his empire will be different from all others. This has not occurred since Roman times, and it can point only to the future empire of Antichrist. The further illustration of his activities show the exposition of the Fathers to be obviously correct. According to the text, judgment shall come upon him after three and a half years, "that his power may be taken away, and be broken in pieces, and perish even to the end. And that the kingdom, and power, and the greatness of the kingdom, under the *whole* heaven, may be given to the saints of the Most High: whose kingdom is an everlasting kingdom, and all kings shall serve and obey him" (Dan. VII. 26-27). The Fathers gave the above interpretation, and it is the only logical one.

Some modernistic scholars try to make chapter VII. of Daniel converge to the same person as chapter VIII., but their conclusion is not logical, because their premises are wrong. The little horn of chapter VII. has an entirely different origin from that of chapter VIII. In chapter VII., it grows up among the ten horns of the fourth beast, while in chapter VIII., it grows on one of the four horns of the he-goat, the third beast, or Grecian empire. In Daniel's chapter VII., the little horn brings down three horns growing out of the head of the fourth beast, while in chapter VIII., it brings down none of the other horns. The last part of chapter VII. clearly reveals the little horn of that chapter to be the future Antichrist, who shall establish the last godless empire ever to exist.

St. John's description of the beast has a great similarity with Daniel's fourth beast. He gives the same time to his beast (XII.14; XIII. 5) as Daniel's (VII. 25) and states it to be 1260 days. In Daniel the little horn speaks blasphemies against God as does the apocalyptic beast against God and the Church. Verse 21 in Daniel reads almost verbally like verse 7, chapter XIII., in the Apocalypse. And lastly, the interference of the coming Messias to judge and condemn the little horn and to establish an everlasting kingdom under the WHOLE heaven points to XIX. 20 and XX. 4 of the Apocalypse.

Verse 1

As in Isaias (LVII 20) the godless world is an agitated sea, so in the Apocalypse the surging sea is unchristian humanity, which brings forth the Beast. This Beast from the sea has like the dragon seven heads and ten horns. It is not taken from Daniel but is the proper description of the Beast at his appearance in the vision of St. John. In chapter XVII., the heads are asserted to be seven empires. The Beast comes up out of the sea here, while in chapter eleven he "ascends out of the abyss". The latter was to indicate the origin of the power by which he kills the Two Witnesses, and the former to specify the source of his world-dominion. The Beast will be a man, "the man of sin". He will be known as Antichrist when he has established his empire. And this will be the seventh and last of the godless world-empires that promoted idolatry, emperor-worship, devil-worship and persecution of God's people. He will be the incarnation or embodiment of the beast which in ancient times engendered every blasphemy. Satan was the soul of those empires, and through them he promoted his world-control. Those empires were the Egyptian, the Assyrian, the Babylonian, the Medo-Persian, the Grecian and the Roman. The ruling dynasties of those empires persecuted the people of God and aimed at destroying the true faith and worship. Hence the character of Antichrist, as it were, pre-existed in those ancient dynasties. When he appears in the world in person, his antichristian character will reach the fullest development of evil man.

The nations will be a seething mass of warring forces by then, raging against God and Christ. Communism may be quite universal. After the horrible war which will have wasted one third of mankind, the remainder will be largely in a blasphemous state of mind. Satan will direct all discontent in society against the Church. After his failure to destroy it from within and his expulsion from it with all the bad clergy, he will exhaust every resource to instigate the world to the most venemous attacks on all faithful members; and as a last resort, he will call some inveterate hater of God and Christ out of the surging sea of humanity and make a pact with him. And this "man of sin" accepts his proposals. He will be naturally gifted, excessively proud and will scorn all restraint of law and superior power. He may become supreme ruler over THREE world-powers that are in existence and through them conquer the rest of the world. One "Great Eagle", however, will maintain its independence.

The Beast appears in the form St. John describes, because he is the incarnation of the ancient beast of the prophets. In the vision of Daniel, the beast representing the Roman Empire had only ten horns not seven heads; he represented only the one empire then; but when he appears again in the person of Antichrist, he will have seven heads and ten horns. The ten horns of this beast are not the ten horns of the Roman Empire, not the kingdoms into which the empire was dissolved, but ten kings appointed by Antichrist to rule under him. His horns are crowned because through them he will rule the world. In this chapter St. John describes the person and character of Antichrist and in chapter XVII. his empire. That empire will have many traits of the pagan Roman empire, and from a political viewpoint it is the same beast. In St. John's time it had not had seven heads but only six. Antichrist appears so monstrous, because he is the seventh head.

Antichrist will proclaim himself the Messias and will be accepted by the Jews as the long expected one. This appears quite clear from our Lord's words: "I am come in the name of my Father, and you receive me not: if another shall come in his own name, him you will receive" (Jo. V. 43). His words might refer to Bar COCHBA or other imposters. But Bar Cochba did not work signs and wonders. St. John also writes: "You have heard that Antichrist cometh, even now there are become many antichrists" (1 Jo. II. 19). These antichrists were apostates, heretics and enemies of Christ and His Church. In the opinion of St. Irenaeus (Book V. 28/2) the beast from the sea is Antichrist.

In the treatise on Christ and Antichrist, Hippolytus writes: "After the manner of the law of Augustus, by whom the empire of Rome was established, he too will rule and govern, sanctioning everything by it, and taking greater glory to himself. For this is the FOURTH BEAST, whose head was wounded and healed again, in its being broken up or even dismembered, and partitioned into ten crowns; and he then (Antichrist) shall with knavish skill heal it, as it were, and restore it" (49). Hippolytus in the fragments from commentaries on Daniel says: "As these things then are destined to come to pass, and as the *toes* of the image turn out to be democracies and the ten horns of the beast are distributed among ten kings, let us look at what is before us more carefully, and scan it, as it were, with open eye" . . . "The 'legs of iron' are the 'dreadful and terrible beast', by which the Romans who now hold the empire are meant" . . . "The 'one other little horn springing up in their midst' is the antichrist" (On Dan. II. 3).

Many speculations have been current about the origin of Antichrist and the time of his appearance. Satan does not know the time. According to verse two and also the foregoing chapter, he will get the permission to choose his man at God's appointed time. From Genesis (XLIX. 1, 7) and Deuteronomy (XXXIII. 22) and Jeremias (VIII. 16), the tradition had arisen that Antichrist will come from the tribe of Dan. This is the view of Irenaeus (V. 30, 2), of Hippolytus and of Victorinus. The tribe of Dan had apostatized so entirely that after the Captivity it is not enumerated any more. The tribes have long ago lost their identity. Antichrist will evidently be of Jewish descent, but from what country he will hail must be left to speculation. Personally he comes up out of the "sea" of the antichristian "peoples and nations and tongues" (XVII. 15). The "Sea" in Old Testament prophecy is the Mediterranean Sea, and this would seem to intimate that a country bordering on that sea shall produce him.

The blasphemous names written on the heads of the beast are divine prerogatives and titles, which Antichrist will assume as did the Roman emperors and the kings of other world-empires. They assumed such titles as "Supreme Lord, God, the Divine, the Savior etc". Antichrist will doubtlessly claim to be the lord of the world or the son of God. Pagan Rome was therefore a living example or model to the Seer for the description of Antichrist. The seven capital sins may also be called virtues by Antichrist. Each of the seven world-empires may be, in the sight of God, the exemplar of one particular vice: Egypt of avarice, Babylon of anger, Assyria of lust, Medo-persia of Sloth, Greece of envy, Rome of gluttony and Antichrist of pride. Each of the seven heads may have the names of all the capital sins, for they were all practiced more or less and worshipped as divinities in the idolatrous empires.

The beast is not the aggregate of infidels, heretics, enemies and persecutors of the people of God but a person. He is Antichrist, who had not yet appeared when St. John wrote his first letter (1 Jo. II. 18). St. Paul speaks of the same person, when he says: "he sits in the temple of God, showing himself as if he were God". This could not be said of a world-power or organization of any kind but only of a person. The phrase "temple of God" does not mean the ancient Temple but a Catholic Church. When this comes to pass, "the mystery of iniquity" will have reached its culmination, which mystery was already developing in apostolic times. The height of iniquity is reached when a man poses as God and demands divine honors for himself. Though this was done by rulers of kingdoms and empires, Antichrist will make the boldest pretensions to the possession of divine prerogatives. And though the rulers of the world-empires allowed temples to be built to their own divinity and demanded the worship of their statues, there is no record of their going personally to the "temple of *God*" to be worshipped.

Verse 2

The aspect of the fourth beast of Daniel terrified the beholder, but it did not have all the features of the apocalyptic beast. The fourth beast of Daniel was an empire, while the Beast of the Apocalypse is a person, who represents an empire. The apocalyptic Beast unites in his person all qualities of the other beasts. It has the ten horns of the fourth beast, the spots of the third, the bear's paws of the second and the lion's mouth of the first. It will have ten kingdoms or powers serving under its supreme dominion, subjecting through their military resources all nations save one. It will be agile, stealthy, treacherous and bloodthirsty as the leopard getting the nations of the world in its power unawares and stifling all opposition by mercilous cruelty and bloodshed. It will have the battering force of a bear's paws. One of its first activities will be to overthrow and demolish everything that does not further its aims. Scarcely an institution in the world will escape its ravages. It will batter down the Christian foundation of our civilization and bring the world back to barbarism. And it will have the voice of a lion to make itself heard throughout the world. Primasius says: "leoni comparatur propter linguae superbiam" (Swete). By its power of propaganda, it will make its doctrines known everywhere and will terrify into submission everyone who does not have the "sign of God" and who is not written in "the book of life of the Lamb".

Did each head have the mouth of a lion, or did the Beast have a head out of which all the other heads had grown? The mouth of the lion is obviously that of the seventh head, otherwise, though the beast is only a symbolic figure, the description would be impossible. The lion is the emblem of the papacy in the Apocalypse; and the pope's voice is like the voice of thunder that is heard around the world. Antichrist, the vicar of Satan, will have traits that are imitations of the vicar of Christ. The lion's mouth of the beast will overrule all opposition by lying propaganda and will broadcast his doctrines and commands over the world.

The three animals may also allude to the three "horns" which the little horn will bring down (Dan. VII. 25) and be the three world-powers having the features of the three animals. These powers may make up the one vast empire of Antichrist. However the description of the Beast in this chapter shows primarily his personal traits and qualifications fusing the exercise of his power very intimately with his empire. This symbolic description is given to show his irresistible might in waging war, his loud and terrifying propaganda and his stealthy, cruel and bloody methods to obtain world-dominion.

The dragon endows the Beast with his own might and throne and great authority. The Douay text follows the Vulgate, which leaves out the second member of the clause, "his throne". The word "power" or might refers to the nature of the possessor embodying all the natural faculties of anyone. St. Paul continually employs it to denote the innate personal ability of Christ to subdue all creation to Himself; it includes the force of grace and of the Gospel and all the endowments of the Church which do not depend on human excellence. Hence it means here whatever personal ability and might the dragon has or can muster, he will confer upon the Beast.

The ἐξουσία or authority and right Satan confers upon Antichrist will be the antithesis of the authority and right which Christ confers and will carry with it the natural gifts of a fiendish resemblance to himself. Our lord said: "ALL POWER is given to me", which means "All authority". As Christ in His Humanity has His divine commission, so Antichrist will have his satanic commission. Every word has been chosen by the Seer with solemn emphasis.

Satan will also concede to the Beast his throne as "prince of the world", so he may in opposition to Christ, who is "the King of kings", be the first and most glorious among the rulers of the earth, the head of the world-empire re-established. The world-empire ceased to exist when paganism in the Roman Empire was abolished, and religious liberty was declared, and with it emperor-worship was banned. Now it will be re-inaugurated, by virtue of which Antichrist will demand and receive from his obsequious subjects the homage which is due to God alone. It was that throne that Satan proffered to Christ, if He would submit to him (Lc. IV. 6). The Beast accepts the throne under the inevitable condition of submission to Satan. With this throne, the Beast will receive irresistible military might freely conceded him by the evil world powers. But no, ONE sovereign government at least will not submit or be subjugated.

The antichristian powers will be so firmly established as to compose an irresistible force. They will think and feel they have the might to do what they will and therefore eagerly welcome as head of their federation someone resolute enough to force their tenets upon the world. Through the powers, the dragon will confer this great might upon the Beast and subject everything to his command. His might will be both of earthly and satanic origin. The powers forming a union or some looser federation may be the "three horns" spoken of by Daniel and may include some lesser nations, all of whom choose Antichrist as their head. This may allude to Apocalypse II. 13 and may have hinted at the Roman empire as the beast and the emperor as Antichrist. St. John uses the Empire for his model of Antichrist's empire.

Antichrist will then use his great authority in defiance of all international law and natural justice and employ all the most deadly weapons of war invented by that time. This is the time of which Christ said: "If those days were not shortened, no flesh would be saved, but for the sake of the elect those days shall be shortened". The exercise of that authority and his designs of subjugating the world will be cut short.

Verse 3

This verse seems to foreshadow a re-establishment of the

pagan Roman empire. That the empire was the sixth head of the beast is clear from chapter XVII. One of the heads has a mortal wound, which is not like that of the Lamb "as if sacrificed", but "as it were wounded unto death". The "deadly wound" was finally healed, and the head has come to life again. In its conflict with the Church, the pagan Roman empire was destroyed. When Constantine proclaimed religious liberty in the empire, official paganism was ended in the civilized world. The mortal wound by the power of the sword points to the war in which Constantine overthrew the other Roman caesars and with them Paganism. The beast received the death-wound and was no more for a time. When Antichrist rules, this wound shall be healed, and the restoration of caesarism will mean the worship of Antichrist. The False Prophet will promote this and will order the worship of his statue and person. People who do not believe in the immortality of the soul and a future life will desire the extermination of the Church and the re-establishment of caesarism or state supremacy. Socialism advocates it, denies immortality, is of Jewish origin, is diametrically opposed to Christ and is living up to its profession in Communism.

Antichrist will work great signs and lying miracles. St. Paul writes of him: "Whose coming is according to the works of Satan, in all might, and signs, and lying wonders" (2 Thess. II. 9). And he adds: "And in all seduction of iniquity to them that perish". It will be easy to recognize him in his doctrines and works, for his doctrines will be vicious and will encourage immorality. St. Paul describes his dupes as they who "receive not the love of truth, that they might be saved. Therefore God shall send them the operation of error, to believe lying: that they may be judged who have not believed the truth, but have consented to iniquity". The Church has preached and has admonished the erring for centuries to listen to the truth and accept it, but most of them have been eager at all times to believe falsehood. And the Two Prophets will offer all men a final choice, after which there will be no more excuse for ignorance. The true believers will heed the warning of our Lord: "For there shall arise false christs and false prophets, and shall show great signs and wonders, insomuch as to deceive (if possible) even the elect" (Mt. XXIV. 24).

This Beast, which all the world will follow with great

admiration, was not the pagan Roman empire, for although all the nations of the West were subjugated, they did not admire it. They bore this yoke of Rome with reluctance and resentment. This admiration can be reaped only by Antichrist, who will win the antichristian and nonchristian world by his signs and lying wonders. Some modern scripturists apply this to the Roman Empire, no matter how it contradicts the text. Victorinus held as possible the fable of a Nero redivivus. Even that Domitian might be Antichrist in the Seer's mind is absurd.

Verse 4

The people who have rebelled against God and His law will find a welcome reason for their rebellion in the signs and wonders of Antichrist. To them, these signs are full proof for the truth of his claims. And they will follow him in everything with enthusiastic fanaticism. They will know that the power and authority of Antichrist proceeds from the dragon, and that devil-worship will be implied in the worship of Antichrist. He will promise his followers riches, temporal prosperity, the full indulgence of their lusts and freedom from all commandments, self-restraints and self-denial. In the doubtful works of Hippolytus are these statements in reference to Antichrist: "behold he will give you corn; and he will bestow upon you wine, and great riches, and lofty honors" . . . "And by reason of the scarcity of food, all will go to him and worship him" (xxviii). The consequences of this are written by Jeremias (XXIII. 11-12): "for the prophet and the priest are defiled: and in my house I have found their wickedness, saith the Lord." Hippolytus thinks that he will walk on the water and remove mountains, turn the day into darkness and the night into day. (xxvi). There shall be no return or repentance, for Antichrist will lead his dupes deeper and deeper into his evil doctrines and immorality. The hardened heretics will likewise scorn the admonitions of the Two Witnesses, who will condemn all heresies and point to the true Church as the only hope of salvation. All who prefer error and sin to truth and virtue will find their desired support in the signs and wonders of the Beast and will scoff at the Church, at Christ and God. Antichrist and the dragon will be their gods whom they will admire, love and adore. They will compose a psalmody and liturgy in their honor and sing hymns of adoration to them, such as David addressed to God. (Ps. XXXIV. 10; LXXXII. 1; LXXXVIII. 9; Exod. XV. 11).

The last words, "who can battle with him", hint at a refusal of some nations to submit to Antichrist, which calls for a destructive war of subjugation, in which his followers and admirers will feel certain of a decisive victory, for he overthrows the foe by diabolical aid. The words are addressed by his followers to those nations who will neither submit nor believe in his signs and wonders.

In this last clause could be an allusion to the Roman Empire and the emperor but no more, for the nations of the civilized world were subjected to it, and the apostles taught submission to the government, as Christ did by His words to Pilate. Emperor-worship was practiced and demanded by the government officials, and in Asia temples had been erected to the divinity of the emperors (Ephesus & Pergamum), but neither emperor nor empire did great signs and wonders for which they were spontaneously worshipped. The empire was the model for the description, which St. John gives of the political power of Antichrist, and in his mind he may have identified the empire with the universal dominion of the beast, but his BEAST is Antichrist not the Roman Empire. If the military power of Rome compelled worship for the emperor, and if that were meant here, the empire would be the all-powerful beast not the emperor, yet the emperor would be the one worshipped. The Beast in this chapter is a living, breathing person, who shall have only three years and a half to conquer and rule the world and then be cast into the pool of fire.

2. The Works Of The Beast.

Verses 5-8.

Verse 5

On the strength of his satanic endowments, Antichrist will open his mouth in blasphemies against God his Creator. The words are those of Daniel attributed to the little horn (VII. 20). The admiration of his followers, their praises and flatteries, the divine cult organized in his honor will elate his pride to consider himself equal to God and prompt him to utter words of blasphemous daring. Domitian was the living example of how pride will induce a man to assume divine titles. Antichrist can act and speak thus only by divine permission, just as all agencies of Satan can do no more than God allows for the fulfillment of His purposes. This permission refers to verse 2, "and the dragon gave it . . . great power". So in every other text in the Apocalypse, the phrase, "it was given to him", means that no one can do good or evil unless God permits.

The permission to continue his satanic activity will last forty-two months, the same time allotted the Two Witnesses to work real miracles and preach penance and conversion to God, and also the time during which the great eagle protects the Church against the serpent. Hippolytus holds two periods of three and a half years each, during the first of which the Two Witnesses shall preach, work miracles and convert the world, and at the end of which Antichrist shall overcome them by a war and kill them and then shall rule supreme for the second period. That interpretation proposes inexplicable difficulties, and it contradicts the text. The whole time allotted him in this verse is "TO DO two and forty months". That seems to be the entire time at his disposal to conquer the world and hold his dominion.

Verse 6

"He opened his mouth" is a stereotyped clause to denote the beginning of a discourse. As the prophets, our Lord and the apostles opened their mouth to speak the praises and revelations of God, so Antichrist will open his mouth to teach the multitudes his lies and blasphemies. He will not be satisfied with assuming divinity and having himself proclaimed God; he will spread and enforce his blasphemous doctrines everywhere. The imperial edicts of the caesars and the laws of the communists in Russia and Mexico foreshadow the work of Antichrist. But his work will be more fundamental, more thorough and more replete with pride and malice. He will jeer and scoff at the divine life of Christ, at His Resurrection and Ascension; he will ridicule the belief in any other god than himself, indicating by specious reasoning, by the evils that override the world, by the bad management of the world, that a God with the perfections attributed to Him could not exist; and he will dare God to punish him, if He exists. His blasphemies against the *name* of God will equal those against His Person. The second commandment must be abolished as necessarily as the first. His followers must honor HIS name not that of a God who does not exist. And therefore he will assume divine titles and will make people swear by his name and by his divinity. The Roman emperors typified Antichrist in this. To abolish belief in God and His law, it will be sufficient to trample upon the first three commandments of the Decalogue. Men who openly dishonor the *name* of God will express their contempt for God Himself and for all His laws.

The hatred and malice of Satan inspiring Antichrist will reserve its most venemous shafts for the Church and especially for the Holy Eucharist. "His tabernacle" is the best translation for σκηνὴν because it fits in a rigid context with "those who dwell in heaven", which as most interpreters admit means the Church; "those who dwell in heaven" would be the episcopate, priesthood and religious orders; and the tabernacle would be the dwelling place of the Lamb. The Sacred Mystery of the Real Presence of Christ has thwarted all the malice of Satan, who will inspire his vicar to exert all his efforts against that "dwelling" and the Indwelling Divinity there. "The tabernacle" and "those who dwell in heaven" stands for the whole Church and all the Church holds sacred – the sacraments, the priesthood and religious life, the Christian family, the infallible dogmas and the moral law. The whole efforts of Antichrist during the forty-two months of his reign will be directed against all that God has planted in the human heart and instituted in the world, because Satan knows it will be his last chance to wreck the work of Christ. If he could drive the Eucharistic Lamb out of the world, he might have the victory, but he cannot do this unless he wipes out the priesthood of Jesus Christ. So Antichrist's blasphemies are only the impotent rage of Satan against God and the Church.

Verse 7

The "war" which Antichrist will wage against all who will not apostatize from the Church, accept his doctrines and submit to his dominion, has been mentioned in XI. 7 and XII. 13 and 17. The texts agree with what Daniel averred (VII. 21) of the "little horn". This verse shows who those are "who dwell in heaven". Antichrist is not satisfied with emitting the satanic venom that is in him against the clergy; he aims to kill them, to root out the people of God. Some nations will not accept him, and he will then use the military power of his empire to subdue them. Evidently it will be a far bloodier war than any so far. Still, along with God's permission to wage such a war is assured the fulfillment of His purposes expressed by the patent phrase "it was allowed". Antichrist's victory will be complete with the death of the Two Witnesses, which seals also his own horrible destiny. Only during the 3½ days until the resurrection of the Witnesses will Antichrist be entirely triumphant. This will be the time of the "harvest" of Christ's elect (XIV. 6), when in all nations in which the Beast shall be victorious, the clergy and religious will be marked for martyrdom. The faithful nations no doubt will fight to the last ditch, knowing that Antichrist shows no mercy to those whom he conquers and subjects.

The completeness of Antichrist's victory will aid his followers in the country of the Great Eagle and bring the struggle between them and the rest of the population to a climax. His propaganda will strive to subject also this country to himself. There are probably many Jews there, who will put forth every effort in his favor especially after the execution of the Two Witnesses. The fury and fanaticism of his agents will make many martyrs. But the Church will be on the alert and will prevail on the wondering people to wait till the three days and a half are over to see the fruitlessness of his victory. Thus he will not gain military control of the Great Eagle. After the prophecies of the Apocalypse have been so far fulfilled to the letter, it will not be difficult to convince the unbiased of what is to follow. No doubt the preaching and miracles of the Two Witnesses have made many converts. But those who have submitted to Antichrist and adored him will be so struck with blindness that no prophecies or true miracles will have any beneficent influence on them.

The four words of the sentence, "And there was given to it authority over every tribe, and people and tongue and nation", shows the universality of the empire and dominion of Antichrist, though it need not mean the submission of every government to him. However, he will probably have followers among all peoples. All the wicked will hail him as their champion. Further statements in the Apocalypse seem to indicate that the inhabitants of the earth shall not yet be divided into Christians and antichristians. Many will probably remain neutral up to this time, neither adoring Antichrist nor joining the Church. But they will aid the Church by remaining aloof from his designs.

Verse 8

"All the inhabitants of the earth" are the willing subjects of Antichrist, whose doctrines, laws and kingdom are of the earth. They adore him. The true believers "dwell in heaven", are in the supernatural order, and their names are written in the Book of Life. All shams and hypocrisy shall be exposed then; false doctrines shall be discredited, and those who adhere to them shall be subjected to Antichrist. How the unbelievers and heretics in the country of the Great Eagle will behave must be left to conjecture. The proud and those who resent the self-restraint imposed by the laws of the Church will adore the Beast. Those who resemble the ones mentioned by Daniel (XI. 32; 1 Macc. I. 55, II. 23) will adore Antichrist and persecute the just; but the faithful and those of good shall be saved. People who have no positive religious belief will easily submit and externally comply with the forced adoration; but in this instance it cannot be done with impunity.

The Book of Life of the Lamb takes in view the Holy Eucharist. Our Lord said: He that eateth my flesh and drinketh my blood hath everlasting life". Those who are nourished by this divine food shall be enlightened to readily understand the falsity of the "signs" of Antichrist and in the strength of that food shall be able to endure persecution, escape all snares and face all threats; Their life is transformed making them eager to suffer martyrdom, and they will adore only the true God.

The phrase, "from the foundation of the world", refers to the Lamb and to His predestination from the beginning to be the Mystical Sacrifice. Through this perpetual Sacrifice He singles out the elect and enters their names into the Book of Life, for their faithfulness to Him wins for them their election.

The words, "foundation of the world", represent God as the Architect of the visible world laying the foundation for the whole superstructure of this creation, at which time the mediatorship of Christ was already decreed.

3. Warning And Consolations.

Verses 9-10.

Verses 9-10

The words of verse 9 are a solemn warning to all, both good and bad, like the warnings to the seven Churches. The words are equivalent to "woe to anyone who is indifferent to the warning". It is a solemn threat to Antichrist and all his followers and a consolation to the faithful who patiently endure persecution and face death.

The Greek wording of verse 10 is quite uncertain in its application. According to some commentators, if a Christian is condemned to exile, as St. John had been, he is to regard exile as his allotted destiny and to go willingly; if he is sentenced to death, he is not to lift his hand against the tyrant – to do so would be to deserve his punishment. If such a view were held rigidly it would be fatalism. It would be equivalent to saying that everyone must accept passively what fate has decreed for him. Verse seven states that Antichrist will make war against the saints and overcome them. In a war there are two opposing sides. Antichrist will be the victor in this war and become the lord of the world. After that it would be folly to fight against him. The thought of it could not enter anyone's mind. The faithful are then to practice passive resistance, because the individual cannot prevail against the world-power. Peter drew his sword in defense of our Lord at His seizure but heard words of warning very similar to those written here. The words recorded here had immediate practical application to the Christians during the Roman persecutions. No one must plot or desire revenge but must oppose patience to violence and accept as a penance the direst persecution remaining confident that God will direct the trend of events to His own glory and the happiness of the elect. The admonition to patience recalls Isaias (LIV. 16-17) and Jeremias (XVII. 5 and 7). Sophonias also sounds the same note of warning to patience and trust in the Lord (II. 3).

The words may, however, be understood in another sense. They seem to be an echo of similar words of Isaias (XXXIII. 1-6) and may be intended to menace with just retribution the agents of Antichrist who rob the faithful of all liberty and possessions not allowing them to engage in business or to exercise the civil or religious rights and compelling them to adore the Beast under threats of torture and death. Those who have gone beyond this and have helped to shed the blood of innocent martyrs will in turn meet a violent death. The power of Antichrist will be quickly broken, and thereafter universal justice will reign. After the end of Antichrist, the rightful governments will bring all murderers to justice, if they have not perished in the seven last plagues. And Antichrist himself, after he has done his utmost to destroy the Church by the execution of all the clergy who fall into his hands, will be cast alive into the pool of fire by the might of the Lamb. The "sword" alludes to the one of XIX. 15.

4. The Beast Out Of The Earth.

Verses 11-15.

Verse 11

In the vision of the Seer now appears a second beast rising out of the earth, having two horns like a lamb but speaking like a dragon. This beast is the prophet of Antichrist. In other places he is called the "False Prophet" (XVI. 13; XIX. 20). Antichrist will have a forerunner or prophet, who will prepare the way for him. It will undoubtedly be someone who has done great work of evil in the world so as to be especially fitted for the position. Many may have developed so evil a character as to be fit for such a job, but this one may be at the head of a strong world-power. Satan will not know long beforehand the time of these events, as he will not know when he shall be cast out of the Church. So choosing the False Prophet will be the work of Antichrist himself after he has made his own pact with Satan. This prophet may re-establish the pagan Roman Empire and build the "Great Harlot", Babylon. He comes out of the earth, which is the term for the Gentile nations from which he springs.

He is briefly described. He has two horns; Antichrist has ten. These two horns might stand for two kings subject to him, if the phrase "like a lamb" were not added. That gives the horns a different significance. He *may* have two world-powers subject to himself; but the added phrase seems to intimate that he is an apostate bishop or cardinal, or he resembles one. The Church having fled from Rome after the murder of the pope leaves the papal chair vacant. This false prophet possibly at the behest of Antichrist usurps the papal supremacy and proposes himself as emperor of Rome. His assumed spiritual authority and supremacy over the Church would make him resemble the Bishop of Rome, and his temporal regency over the re-established empire would make him emperor of Rome. He would be Pontifex Maximus, a title of pagan Roman emperors, having supreme spiritual and temporal authority. Assuming authority without possessing it makes him the False Prophet. Does this allude to what our Lord said?

Though he poses as a lamb, a Christian, his doctrines betray him, for he preaches the doctrines of the dragon. His principles and dogmas to be accepted, his moral and civil law will be of diabolical inspiration. It may be communism or plain idolatrous paganism; it will comprise emperor-worship and devil-worship coupled with persecution of the true believers. They will know him at once as an impostor and will not be misled. He will be in league with the antichristian world-powers and adopt their principles of government and civil law. As spiritual head of his empire, he may declare it treason against the state to accept Christianity or the moral law of God. He will evidently do in his own empire what Antichrist will do in his, who as Daniel writes, "shall think himself able to change times and laws".

Verse 12

Antichrist shall endow the False Prophet with his own satanic might and authority, who will then exercise it in the presence of his master. Seeing Antichrist invest another with his own superhuman power shall win the admiration of the infidels. Satan will hold himself at the service of Antichrist at all moments and also at the beck and call of the False Prophet invisibly working signs and lying wonders in the presence of

Antichrist. Being the constant guardian angel of Antichrist, so that his apparent supernatural powers might seem personal, Satan can be at the service of the False Prophet only in Antichrist's presence. He is present only in one place, and though he can move with swifter than lightning speed, he is not omniscient and could not know when in Pekin with Antichrist, what the False Prophet might have in mind for him to do at Rome, unless the communication were brought him by other devils. Then he would need to leave Antichrist's presence to attend to the wishes of the False Prophet. Antichrist's power would then be suspended, and the charmed life he will possess under the tutelage of Satan would be endangered. The False Prophet will therefore be able to work his signs only in Antichrist's presence, who shall thus easily win the antichristian Jews and be proclaimed the long expected messias by them. His "signs" will gain credence for himself among all infidels who have been or shall become unfaithful to the Church. The False Prophet will exercise his borrowed power for Antichrist's honor and glory and will persuade all infidels, apostates and apostate nations to worship and adore him. And Antichrist will support his prophet and secure him in his empire.

One of the main reasons why people will accept Antichrist is the healing of the "wound to death" of one head of the beast. That one head is ancient Roman paganism, which shall be restored by the False Prophet through the power of Antichrist. This seems to locate the prophet's capital at Rome. It would make possible a literal fulfillment of the prophecies of chapters XVII. and XVIII. In chapter XVII., the beast carries the scarlet woman, showing the re-establishment of the pagan empire made possible by his power. The covenant between Antichrist and his prophet will probably stipulate the submission of all people in the restored empire to the former, the acknowledgement of his divinity and the acceptance of his doctrines and morality. The empire will not be as large as formerly, for the empire of Antichrist shall occupy some of the ancient empire's territory. The influence of the False Prophet shall induce the unchristian and apostate nations to deify Antichrist. His doctrines will be enunciated in a high-sounding literary style and ornamented with an alluring mysticism, the better to fit them for fostering every degree of pride and moral abandonment. They shall then be enthusiastically accepted by all sinners. And these enthusiasts shall proclaim the resurrection of the Roman Empire the miracle of the ages. The Church is defeated. The papacy is abolished.

St. Paul says that Antichrist "sitteth in the temple of God" to receive divine worship as if he were God (2 Thess. II. 4). This is not the ancient Temple of Jerusalem, nor a temple like it built by Antichrist, as some have thought, for then it would be his own temple. In chapter XI. 1 and 19, this temple is shown to be a Catholic Church, possibly one of the churches in Jerusalem or St. Peters in Rome, which is the largest church in the world and is in the full sense "THE temple of God". If Antichrist went in person to that great temple to receive the worship of his followers, the False Prophet would accomplish his mission eminently. The capital of Antichrist will be in Jerusalem until the resurrection of the Two Witnesses. But if he were never seen by the peoples outside his capital, his power and influence would remain very limited. He will surely travel from country to country to show himself, teach his doctrines, work his lying miracles, establish his empire and be worshipped by his votaries. By personally appearing in all the principal cities of his empire, he will persuade the wicked to mobilize great armies enabling him to crush the nations opposed to him.

Verse 13

The False Prophet working his "signs" will even cause lightning from the sky at his command. That Satan can cause lightning seems proven in Scripture (Job I. 16). Satan will use this power to establish his church, his world-dominion. By such signs the False Prophet will gain credence to the claims of divinity for Antichrist. It will be all the more convincing to the wicked, because Antichrist confers this power on another. What will happen if others request the power from him?

Those who claim that these words of the Apocalypse mean the practice of magic can put forward no authority for the claim, especially not for the falling of fire from heaven at the command of any man in history except Elias. St. John writes of a great sign to be wrought by the False Prophet alone, which shall show the true believers who he is, when the "Beast" shall have appeared. This description is no proof of such things having been accomplished in St. John's time. Magic and deceits of various kinds were practiced, as in India today, but this sign was to be beyond the power of the fakirs of that time. And it proved to the reader that the Beast had not yet appeared. It demonstrates too, that the Beast is not the Roman empire nor the emperor, and the False Prophet is not the pagan priesthood of that time. Those who hold such a view and know that the signs were not produced contradict themselves. In the present chapter, the personal traits and satanic gifts of Antichrist are portrayed in apocalyptic imagery as being the soul of the world-empire founded by him to constitute Satan's last obstacle to the progress of the Church. The verbal dictation of this book is not held here, but the visions are true revelations not the Seer's own imaginings. Identifying the jugglery practiced by fakirs in the presence of the imperial officers with the "signs" mentioned in this text is dragging in an explanation by the hair. No historical record proves that a fakir made lightning fall from the sky at his word, or that an emperor possessed such power or conferred it on another. Had it been a fact, the memory of it would not have been lost.

Verse 14

The pagan priesthood ordered statues of the emperor to be made and set up for worship. At Pergamum was a temple dedicated to the emperor, and his statue was worshipped there; and this practice spread to other cities. The cities of Asia really vied with one another in worshipping Caesar. This passage may allude to such practices, but this narration of the False Prophet's work does not state the above idolatry. Whenever in later times persecution was decreed and enforced against the Christians, they were given the choice between worshipping the statue of Caesar and death by torture. But in the vision here, the peoples are "seduced" by the False Prophet through the "signs" he works, and especially through the lightning he causes to spring from the sky. And those who are seduced render the craven worship to Antichrist freely and enthusiastically.

The clause, "which had the wound by the sword and lived", again returns in this verse. This fact will be considered of decisive importance. The opinion that it means the resurrection and return of Nero is absurd. Such a fable was circulated but not as widely as some modern writers imagine. Besides it was an impossibility, and therefore no inspired writer could have entertained the idea. Too many fables have been dragged into the Apocalypse by strenuous interpreters. There is a much easier explanation for this head that had the "death-wound".

The Church claims to have overthrown Judaism and paganism not by military force but by the sword of God's word. The military power of Rome subjected the world. The divinity of the Church was particularly evident in its ability to live and thrive under imperial persecution. Paganism was destroyed indirectly by the Church but directly and finally by the military forces of Constantine. The Roman empire was the sixth head of the beast. By his victory and by his edict of religious liberty and the abolition of official paganism, Constantine gave the beast "the death-wound by the sword". The False Prophet will proclaim the resurrection of the Roman empire and the whole pagan order of affairs with its worship of Antichrist, its laws, its oracles and the pagan religious system the greatest miracle of the ages. Paganism came back and destroyed its destroyer. He will attempt to demonstrate this to be the absolute proof of the divine origin of paganism and of the divinity of Antichrist. He will thus win for the Beast the admiration of all who hate the Church. This is stated in verses 3 and 12. They need not fear the Church any longer, for their champion defies her and all she holds sacred. Their fear of the Church was nothing but the fear of Satan, and he instills this fear in his dupes.

Verse 15

The False Prophet will even outdo the Two Prophets. He will advise his followers to chisel a statue of Antichrist, will animate it and order it to speak. The word "image" is in the singular number, indicating only *one* statue, which he may set up in the great church, St. Peter's. We do not know the limits of Satan's power, but as he can possess persons and animals, he may be able to enter a statue and give it flexibility, motion and speech. We have a demonstration of this in what the magicians of Egypt did (Exod. VII. 12). By this sign of his prophet to apparently give life to a statue of stone, Antichrist will move his followers to believe in his own creative powers. Neither Christ nor his apostles showed off with such power. St. Vincent Ferrer did give life to two boys who had been killed and hacked to pieces, and they lived many years after. But he did not turn a statue of stone into a living being. In the minds of his followers, this power of Antichrist will offset any claims made by the Church or any miracles wrought by the Two Witnesses. The plagues they shall inflict on the earth will not win the anti-christians.

Animating a statue may have been a possibility for the demons in St. John's time, but no historical writers record it. Later commentators on the Apocalypse advance the legends about Appolonius of Tyana and Simon Magus as a proof of these things having been done by the magicians. But they claim no other authority than this verse in the Apocalypse. The Acts of the Apostles record the astonishment of Simon Magus at the miracles worked by the apostles. They were far above his magical trickery. There is no proof in history of anyone animating a statue. This will be a sign shown by Satan in its time at the command of Antichrist's prophet to win the world away from Christ.

Satan speaking through the image of Antichrist, will demand the death of all who refuse to adore the statue. By adoring the statue, they adore Satan who animates it and Antichrist whom it represents. The fanatical worshippers of the Beast ready to obey the oracle will begin the bloody persecution of the true believers at once considering it an honor and a service due their god to put all unbelievers to death.

5. The Mark Of The Beast.

Verses 16 to end.

Verse 16

All classes of people whom the doctrines and signs of Antichrist will captivate and mislead are named in this verse. Those who will not accept the true faith shall then be at the mercy of error. Another idea is contained in this verse: Antichrist will abolish all class distinction and make his followers alone the elite. It points to something like communism. The educated and refined, the uneducated and rude will submit.

The mark of distinction borne by antichristians will be a brand like that seared on the forehead of slaves in Roman times. Those who are steeped in vice, who are enthusiastic about Antichrist and are stupefied by the marvels of his signs will proclaim themselves his slaves and have his stamp put on their foreheads. Others will go still farther and have their right hands dedicated to him becoming his soldiers. This alludes to the signing of the faithful in chapter VII. The foreheads of all Christians are signed in the sacraments, while the hands of the priest are also annointed. The False Prophet may institute secret rites, through which the followers of Antichrist will be advanced by degrees into the deeper mysticism of his cult. A sort of diabolical sacramental system would thus be instituted conferring the graces of Satan and consecrating people to the service of the Beast. They will bear this mark of disgrace openly and thus easily recognize one another and those who do not follow the Beast. The adorers of the Beast will worship the animate statue in awe and reverence. And in the spiritual darkness into which sin has led them they are convinced, because they wish to be, that Antichrist is God.

All commentators who try to force this chapter as fulfilled in St. John's time are constrained to admit that they are confronted with a fact prophesied and not fulfilled, for those provincials who conformed to the caesar-cult were not branded as here stated. Since the preceding part of this chapter only uses the Roman empire existing then as a model for the description of the empire and times of Antichrist, so do these last verses. The Apocalypse is a genuine prophecy and depicts future history, whether we hold verbal dictation or not, and is not a mere poetic embellishment of existing conditions. Those commentators who do not see the foretelling of real future events in this prophecy find no *satisfactory* explanation for anything contained in it.

Verse 17

By the absence of the mark on the hand or forehead, the

followers of the Beast will know those who have not adored him and will deprive them of all rights as far as they can. External submission to the Beast will be enforced wherever he gains control, and economic boycott will be employed against all who refuse. They will not be able to procure the necessities of life. Everyone who would engage in business must have the mark of the Beast on his forehead or right hand or profess belief in his divinity and reverence his name by wearing the number of it. The purpose is to drive out of business all who will not join the wicked, who alone aim to get control of the sources of wealth and exploit the laborers. Catholics will thus lose their property, and Antichrist will have the wealth of the world at his disposal to prosecute the war against the Christian nations and to compel submission to himself.

A very similar thing was done in England after Protestantism was triumphant. Catholics were fined and fined again for not worshipping God in a Protestant way, until they were reduced to utter pauperism. Their property was confiscated, and all political rights were wrested from them. The tactics of the Roman empire were followed.

If such boycott were resorted to in the United States, the whole economic structure of this immense nation would collapse. The economic balance is too exact to admit the imposition of such radical restrictions. Not only the 30,000,000 Catholics (they may be 100,000,000 by that time) would refuse adoration of the Beast, but the big majority even of those who are not friendly to the Catholic Church would spurn any interference with their liberty. Still the domination of Antichrist could be initiated as stealthily as the country was lured into the first world-war in 1917 against the wishes of the majority.

Although at the time of these revelations, those who would not profess their belief in the divinity of the emperor and adore the gods of Rome could not hold an official position, and though emperor-worship had reached its height under Domitian, St. John could not have feared at this point in the revelations a speedy fulfillment of this verse, for the other visions had to become actuality first, and then the 200,000,000 horsemen had to destroy one third of mankind. He therefore did not write of his own time but of what was to come in the reign of Antichrist. During some of the later persecutions, statues of the gods of Rome were placed in the forums, and all customers had to offer incense and bow to them. But nothing such as is narrated in this verse occurred to coerce men to adore a statue of Caesar.

Verse 18

St. John clearly states that the Beast is but a man, for he has the name of a man given him by someone else; and the numerical letters of that name will enable the true believers to know him when he appears. In what language this name must be written to have the number is not stated; but since the Apocalypse was written in Greek, the number will probably be made up of the name written in that language. Explanations of diverse kinds have been proposed, but none of them has been satisfactory. Father Sloet advances the solution that if the name, "king of Israel" be written in Hebrew, it will make up the number 666. But then some violence must be done to Hebrew orthography. No doubt he will style himself king of Israel. St. Irenaeus warns against proposing any name as certain, for he, though he had known Polycarp, a disciple of St. John, would not dare to hold any name. He suggests the name "LATEINOS" or "Nero Caeser" in Greek but prefers "Teitan". Yet he "will not incur the risk of pronouncing positively as to the name".

It might be a mere symbolic number. In a modern explanation, Antichrist may flatter the secret societies by affirming their claim to the derivation of their mystic symbols from Solomon to be historical and thus win them over to become his supporters. They claim that an order or guild was organized among the laborers building Solomon's Temple, and from this order date their symbols. Hence the number 666 (3 kings X. 14; 2 Para. IX. 13) alludes to the income of Solomon, which he is supposed to have spent largely for the erection of the Temple. But this is as fantastic and unreal as other explanations. The number is probably no symbol at all but a mere cryptogram to be deciphered in Antichrist's time.

According to the testimony of St. Irenaeus (V. 30 – 1 ff), all old and good copies had χξϛ, and this reading was attested as being the original by those who had seen St. John. These letters which were probably the cryptogram in the original manuscript, may simply be the initials of the name of Antichrist, of the given name and the surname. Even in the time of St. Irenaeus there were two readings χξς and χις In chapter fifteen, the victors over Antichrist and over "the number of his name" are privileged to sing a new canticle of praise to God for the victory. This intimates a short cryptogram, probably one containing the three letters. And probably the mark worn by his slaves on the forehead or hand will consist of the three Greek letters. As to his name St. Irenaeus says: "If it were necessary that his name should be distinctly revealed in this present time, it would have been announced by him who beheld the apocalyptic vision". "For that was seen no very long time since, but almost in our day, TOWARDS THE END OF DOMITIAN'S REIGN".

CHAPTER XIV.

Westminster Version

Then I beheld, and lo! the Lamb stood on 1. the mountain of Sion,
and with him one hundred and forty-four thousand, who had his name
and his Father's name written on their foreheads.

And I heard a voice from heaven like a 2. voice of many waters and
like a voice of loud thunder; and the voice which I heard seemed as it
were of harpers playing on their harps.

And they sing a new canticle before the 3. throne, and before the four
living beings and the elders; and no one could learn that canticle, except
the one hundred and forty-four thousand who had been redeemed from
the earth.

These are they who have not defiled themselves 4. with women; for
they are virgins. These are they who accompany the Lamb, whithersoever he
goeth. These were redeemed from men, to be first-fruits to God and to
the Lamb; and in their mouth no lie was found, 5. for they are blameless.

And I beheld another angel flying in mid-heaven, 6. with an everlasting gospel to proclaim to them that dwell upon the earth, to every nation,
and tribe and tongue and people.

He said with a loud voice: 'Fear God and give 7. him glory, because
the hour of his judgment is come; worship him who made the heaven and
the earth, the sea and the fountains of waters'.

And another, a second angel followed, 8. saying: 'Fallen, fallen is
Babylon the great, she hath made all nations to drink of the wine of wrath,
because of her impurity'.

And another, a third angel, followed, saying 9. with a loud voice: 'If
anyone worshippeth the beast and its image, and taketh its mark upon
his forehead or upon his hand, he too shall drink of the wine of God's
wrath 10. which is poured unmixed into the cup of his anger, and he
shall be tormented with fire and brimstone, in the sight of the holy angels
and in the sight of the Lamb'.

And the smoke of their torment goeth up forever 11. and ever, and
they have no rest, day or night, even they that worship the beast and its
image and whoso receiveth the mark of its name.

Herein lieth the patience of the saints, 12. that keep the commandments of God and the faith of Jesus.

And I heard a voice from heaven saying: 'Write 13. blessed are the
dead henceforth, that die in the Lord!' 'Yea', saith the Spirit, 'in that they
shall rest from their labors; for their works do follow them'.

Then I beheld, and lo! a white cloud, and upon the cloud one sitting
like to a son of man; he 14. had on his head a golden crown, and in his

hand a sharp sickle. And another angel came forth 15. from the sanctuary,
crying with a loud voice to him who sat upon the cloud: 'Send forth thy
sickle and reap; because the hour is come to reap, for the harvest of the
earth is now ripe'.

Then he who sat upon the cloud cast his sickle 16. upon the earth,
and the earth was reaped.

And another angel came forth from the 18. altar, he who had charge of
with a sharp sickle.

And another angel came from the 18. altar, he who had charge of the
fire; and he cried with a loud voice to him who had the sharp sickle,
saying: 'Send forth thy sharp sickle, and gather the clusters of the vintage
of the earth, for the grapes thereof are ripe'.

And the angel cast his sickle upon the earth, 19. and gathered the
vintage of the earth, and cast it into the great winepress of God's wrath.

And the winepress was trodden outside the 20. city, and there came
forth blood from the winepress rising as high as the bridles of horses, for
a distance of a thousand six hundred furlongs.

V. SOUNDS OF VICTORY.

1. The Vision Of The Virgins.

Chapter XIV.

The time of this vision is the same as that of XI. 15. St. John beholds a choice group of those who have overcome the allurements and terrors of the reign of the Beast. He again hears sounds of victory as in chapter XI.

Verse 1

After the terrifying vision of the Dragon, the Beast and the False Prophet and their persecution of the Church, the Seer beholds a vision of supernatural loveliness. The Little Lamb appears in a new setting. He is still in the midst of the throne. In chapters IV. and V., the throne is erected in the Church, but no hint is given where the location is in the world. Now it is on Mount Sion in Jerusalem fulfilling the prophecies of Old. The vision anticipates the victory of the Lamb, which is going through its final preparations. Mt. Sion allegorically represents the Church. Isaias had written: "The law shall come forth from Sion" (II. 3). These last triumphant days are fast approaching. The seat of the Church shall be in Jerusalem. Christ shall henceforth rule from Mt. Sion. It alludes to the Temple of Solomon, from which God thundered forth His decrees in olden times. Mount Sion also symbolizes the culmination of virtue, perfection and power. The apostles went forth from Sion with power from on high to conquer the world. And the Church shall again sally forth from this stronghold of God to win the victory over Antichrist and to subdue the world to Christ.

The "Little Lamb" is surrounded by 144,000, who have His name and the name of God imprinted on their foreheads. This is contrasted with the name of the Beast on the forehead of his officers and symbolically proclaims the faithfulness of this 144,000 to God and to the Mystic Presence of Christ on earth. Their faith has not wavered and it is evident before the world. Through the supernatural strength with which they were nourished by the Church, they have withstood the attacks of

Antichrist and are now gathered around their Champion from whom is their strength and victory. Their victory is conspicuous before the world, because chastity is a very difficult virtue in its perfection and in the days of the Beast will be put to the most crucial test. None are more faithful to God than the chaste, and none are more ardently attached to the eucharistic Lamb. This 144,000 is not the throng of chapter VII. Those were from the twelve tribes of Israel, while these are from all the nations of the world. The number is only symbolical, and the actual count may be much larger. The Church has grown to immense proportions since the vision of the other 144,000. These are now the chosen imperial guard of the Lamb, and they stood fearless and unmoved against the onslaughts of Antichrist and his black hordes. Because they were unconquerable, they are the first to herald the coming victory of Christ to the world.

Verse 2

St. John hears a great voice from heaven. This again shows "heaven" to be the Church. The "voice" is the canticle of the virgins, and they are not in Heaven but on Mt. Sion. St. John searches for poetical similes to give the reader a faint understanding of the beauty and majesty of the canticle sung by the 144,000 in such perfect accord that it was like a single voice. All language must fail to express what the Seer heard. It was like the babbling, soothing voice of unnumbered waterfalls swelled to the volume of reverberating thunders and mingled with the harmony and inspiring melody of many harps. The sweetness and exquisite harmony of harps that seemed to travel upwards to mystic distances was filled up with the rhythm and melody of rippling waterfalls and supported by the deep undertones of rolling thunders. The canticle was so beautiful and sublime that all sounds of nature and art streaming together in a most perfect symphony would be but a broken echo of its heart-enchanting harmony.

The canticle alludes to Joel. The prophet exults over God's judgment upon the wicked in the Valley of Josaphat. (III. 9-21). He may have heard an echo of the canticle which St. John heard in all its fullness. Joel's invitation to the wicked to assemble for the battle (III. 11) probaly points to what is stated in the

Apocalypse in XVI. 16 and XIX. 19, where the last battle of Antichrist is imminent. Joel in chapter III. 13 obviously has the same event in view, which the Apocalyptist describes in XIV. 18-19. The virgins shall in this new canticle celebrate in advance the victory foreseen by Joel. It is quite common in prophetic announcements to state a future event as past. Jeremias (L. 2) thus announces the fall of Babylon. But this manner of announcing is also partly due to the Hebrew idiom. The announcements in this present chapter and the next are of the same order.

Verse 3

The canticle which St. John heard was *like* a new one. Cornelius a Lapide holds that the ὡς is not used as a simile but is assertive. The context, however, seems to disagree with that explanation. The simile construction is used to express the sound of the voice in the foregoing sentence and in this sentence to explain the nature of the canticle. The canticle voices the jubilation and exultation of the virgins for the preservation of their virginity in the fiercest attacks of the Beast and his followers against it. Perfect virginity has always been found in the Church, having begun to grow in the mortal life of Christ. So in the days of Antichrist, it shall be nothing new. The temptations against it, however, shall reach their climax in those evil days, and therefore the canticle of those who withstood them shall be like a *new* one. In V. 9, the episcopate and the priesthood sang a new canticle because the Lamb had made them His priests and had taken the destiny of the world into His hands. But the canticle of the virgins is *like* a new one. It will possibly be written under the inspiration evoked by the certainty of victory for them, when the Two Prophets have ascended into Heaven. The virgins will sing it before the altar of the Real Presence, before the bishops and the priests and will obtain the approval of the Church to make it official and liturgical.

At less perilous times, earthly motives may be mingled with heavenly ones and may be strong enough to carry virginity safely through the ordinary temptations, but when evil reaches its apex of malice, only the pure motive of perfect love of God and the eucharistic Christ will be able to hold out till victory. Their canticle of jubilation for having preserved this rare privilege shall have greater significance and shall seem to be a new canticle because only those who have passed through that fiery ordeal can learn it. St. John did not hear the real voices of these virgins but only an imaginary or intellectual transmission of them through the vision.

The canticle can be learned only by the 144,000, because it will express the special prerogatives of the singers. Other saints may hear it, be thrilled and entranced by it, but cannot aspire to sing it. The reason is that these have given themselves so unreservedly to God, that the world has no claim on them. They have risked all for Christ without wishing or hoping for any earthly honor or glory for their sacrifice or constancy. They have gained so perfect a purity of body and mind as to lead a heavenly life in the midst of the reign of terror. The blood of Christ will seem to have been shed in a most special intention for them, and He will seem to have labored, prayed and suffered specifically to purchase these finest gems of virtue from the earth for His heavenly Father. They have become super-mundane beings. And for such reasons they alone can sing this canticle.

Verse 4

This throng might include the virginal priesthood, but in chapters IV. and V., the priesthood is shown nearer the throne of God than the virgins here. These are probably the other virgins of both sexes in the religious orders or living in the world. They are, however, not the virgins of all times, but only those who triumph in the days of the Beast. Although the text mentions only those who are "not defiled with women", it means both sexes.

"They will follow the Lamb withersoever He goeth" explains the reason for their eminent virtue. Many and varied explanations have been given of this clause. The following is proposed here. The virgins can preserve their virginity only in the most intimate association with the eucharistic Lamb. Their life is centered around the tabernacle, and they have surrendered all earthly joys and consolations to possess Him and to rest in His presence. The Sacred Species are always in the midst of the virgins. Only if they live in daily communion with the Lamb, could they have the constancy to risk and brave all for Him.

That makes their lives so like a copy of His, that they are almost identified with it, and His victory is theirs. And hence they rejoice in the victory of their Beloved. As the first-fruits are the choicest part of the harvest, so are these virgins the rarest form of virtue on earth; as the first fruits were completely dedicated to God, connoting the dedication of the whole harvest to Him, so the sacrifice of the virgins makes all virtues and all vocations of life acceptable to God. They are the product of a holy, Christian family life and of the zeal and shining example of His Church, which has produced such exquisite lilies of virtue. A great deal of care and watchfulness is necessary on the part of the parents to preserve the virginity of the growing youth from corruption. And above all must they implant the true motive of love of God in the mind of the virgin. Thus in the consecration of this virginity to God, the labors and cares of the parents and the continued education and guidance of the Church is consecrated. Only those who are weaned from all earthly affection will persevere in the days of Antichrist. They have not followed their natural inclinations but the promptings of grace. The first-fruits were always sacrificed to God, but this does not prove these virgins to be martyrs, for they are not in Heaven but on Mt. Sion. The text, however, does not exclude martyrdom.

Verse 5

These virgins have kept themselves free from antichrist-worship. Heresy and idolatry are most pernicious acts against God and the worship due Him. The impure readily fall into heresy or persist in it and will worship Antichrist. The virgins will not apostatize. They will remain true to their vows. During the Reformation, many religious broke their vows, and greater numbers will follow that example in the reign of the Beast. But this 144,000 will speak no lie when they vow themselves forever to God. They seek to please Him alone, and so they shall not fall into the snares of flatterers or sycophants, whose cunning has led many a virgin astray. The ornament of the virgin combined with mental and bodily integrity is sincerity, truthfulness, candor and uprightness.

Because the God-fearing shall be subjected to so many

terrors, the virgins will cleanse every stain of sin from their soul and will be confirmed in the purest virtue; they will be without spot. A stain must be understood to be a grievous one, attachment to grievous sin, impurity, lying, hypocrisy, not mere immodesty. No one would be without some stain of venial sin. If freedom from all stain of sin were meant, they would be martyrs who have entered eternal glory. But such interpretation is against the context. These verses indicate that it will be possible to keep clear of the contamination spread by the followers of the Beast. Only those will be polluted who choose to be. The contrast between the pure and the impure will then reach its clearest distinction.

2. The Three Announcing Angels.

A. Warnings Against Antichrist Worship.

Verse 6

Alcazar imagines the first angel who flies through mid-heaven to be St. John and the next two SS. Peter and Paul. However, such a view is impossible. Others have held that the first angel is St. Vincent Ferrer. This is equally as impossible, because it points to a future event which shall be enacted in the days of the beasts. While the Two Prophets were alive and active, the Church followed their direction, but Antichrist has subjected all nations now except "the great eagle" and has put the Two Prophets to death. Nevertheless the Church comes forward with undaunted courage to preach the Gospel and warn the wicked of the approaching judgment. The true Christians need special encouragement after Antichrist is everywhere triumphant, and his persecution is at its height. Many may be in danger of losing heart and the hope of final victory. This angel may be some saintly member of a religious order or society founded to combat Antichrist and the False Prophet or some eminent priest, bishop or cardinal clothed by the pope with universal authority. Or it is the pope himself, who with wonderful eloquence will preach the Gospel so it will be heard to the ends of the earth. All this presages present-day inventions: radio, television etc.

"In mid-heaven" may mean the Catholic nations, which

would be western Europe and South America. Or it may mean that the message shall come from the then residence of the pope. This message, which is prepared for the unbelievers, will rouse the faithful to death-defying firmness. It will be "an eternal Gospel" to those who sin upon the earth, to the heretics and infidels and worshippers of Antichrist. The Greek text does not use the definite article, denoting this as a special admonition for those who are carried off their feet by the temporary triumph of the Agent of Evil. Even when the persecution is the most violent ever, the Church shall be solicitous for the salvation of all men. This "eternal Gospel" is contrasted with the doctrines and promises of Antichrist, which appear a fraud and imposture, while Christ's promises will be proven true forever. This Gospel will re-assert of how short a duration the earthly felicity promised by Antichrist shall be and on the other hand how certain and everlasting is the life to be derived from faithfulness to Christ, the Savior.

As the empire of Antichrist is universal, indicated by the four terms, so the audience to whom this special Gospel is addressed is universal. The preacher may use the radio. A large percentage of the people of heathen or apostate nations may be inclined to join Antichrist, while he is in the zenith of his glory, and the bodies of the Two Prophets lie unburied in Jerusalem. He may fly to the capitals of his empire, voice his impudence against God by boasting of his victory and convince all his followers of his superior power by showing himself alive after his battle with the prophets. The great preacher who takes the defense of the Church in hand knows the nearness of the judgment and the horrible plight of those who assist Antichrist. He will refer all men to this book of prophecies and the fulfillment so far of everything as foretold, and that will stem the tide of conversion to Antichrist. The Christians will remain firm, and the rest who are not steeped in vice will await the outcome as foretold.

Verse 7

The message of the great angel is: Believe the truth, for judgment is at hand; worship God alone, for He is the Creator and Lord of all things. The words allude to Isaias (VIII. 13).

They are a new and positive announcement of victory. The hour of judgment upon Antichrist is near. It is an ominous warning to his fanatical worshippers and a consolation and encouragement to the faithful. It will confirm all faithful bishops and priests to brave imprisonment and death and with unflinching courage and unflagging energy to teach and spread the truth. No one need fear Antichrist and his short-lived victory, but all must fear God alone, for He will shortly gain an *everlasting* victory for His elect. St. Augustine says that fear and love of God leads to every good work and fear and love of the world leads to every sin.

Only God who is the Creator of heaven and earth, of the sea and the fountains of water, is worthy of honor and adoration. The followers of Antichrist will say of him: "who can fight with him". The world-wide miraculous power of the Two Prophets was experienced for three years and a half, but the lord of the world has killed them. He will receive the worship of his votaries. As stated in XI. 10, they will hold a great carnival, during which the world's measure of sin shall be filled up. Against this unchecked orgy of debauchery the Church will raise her voice.

The mention of the "fountains of water" indicates the suffering of the world from the drought inflicted by the Two Prophets (XI. 6). The "sea" is the symbol of God's power and infinity and the source of rain. The followers of Antichrist will call on him to give them rain once more. After the death of the Two Prophets, he may possibly cause some precipitation by the agency of myriads of evil spirits. The great preacher will, however, show that rain and all blessings come from God, and that Antichrist has a sinister purpose in all he does for the world. The heathens and the obstinate apostates will not be able to comprehend the full import of this message or of God's revelation in general or of the promises of the Savior. Yet the words still hold out a hope of repentance and forgiveness before the judgment is executed.

B. The Second Angel Announces the Fall of Babylon.

Verse 8.

Verse 8

Perhaps the first angel is silenced by martyrdom. But he

has delivered his message and checked the growing success of Antichrist. A second eloquent preacher now raises his voice against the seductive success of the False Prophet in Babylon. He will probably be in Babylon itself. Or he speaks over the radio from outside the city to warn the inhabitants of its impending doom. The False Prophet may be with Antichrist. There shall still be Catholics in the city, and for their sake the preacher predicts her doom. He announces it as al-already fallen, just as Jeremias announced the fall of ancient Babylon as a past event (L. 2) fifty years before it happened, and as Isaias had predicted it long before (XXI. 9). The fall of the city is beginning, because the death of the Two Prophets will shortly be followed by their resurrection and ascension, and this will be the harbinger of the last plagues, which shall cause the nations to turn against Babylon to destroy it. Christians must therefore leave, for the clouds of God's wrath are beginning to gather upon the city.

Several ideas are condensed in the last clause of this verse. The wine of her fornication means the wealth and vices of Babylon which intoxicate all nations. This new Babylon in the days of Antichrist shall induce the world to accept his doctrines. Fornication means infidelity to God, apostasy, idolatry and antichrist-worship, which leads infallibly to impurity. These doctrines are also the wine of "wrath" calling down the judgment of God. In spite of all warnings then having surrendered to them freely, the wicked shall be in a drunken stupor from these doctrines and cannot be converted. The prophets of old spoke to the capitals of the world in similar language and predicted their doom. Nahum spoke of the "fornication of the harlot" (Ninive) (III. 4); Isaias called Tyre a harlot (XXIII. 15 f) and also Sion after her apostasy from God (I. 21).

C. The Third Angel. Dire Threats on Beast-worshippers.

Verses 9-11.

Verses 9-11

The second angel has probably been silenced by martyrdom, because Antichrist's power is now universal. The Church is as courageous as ever and produces another saintly preacher whose voice is heard over the whole empire of Antichrist. No excuse is to be left to the wicked, and the Christians must be warned again of fraud and submission. Events succeed one another quickly. The bodies of the Two Prophets will lie in the street of Jerusalem only three and a half days, and during this time the Church is in the thickest of the fight, while developments ripen in a day that take decades in normal times. The third preacher connects his warnings with the second. He predicts the punishments upon the followers of Antichrist, whether they adore him or his image or only receive his mark on their foreheads or in their right hand, i. e. whether they are only enrolled into his fellowship by his rites or are engaged in winning others to his cause. All who accept the fellowship of Antichrist shall share the fate of the doomed city. It is the last warning to all followers of the Beast and to all persecutors of the Church. In XIII. 15-17, the False Prophet compelled all men who would engage in business to wear the mark of the Beast; the angel threatens a worse fate than loss of business to those yielding to the demands of the False Prophet.

Verse 10

The first punishment for Beast-worshippers is the same as for the inhabitants of Babylon: namely spiritual blindness and a stupor that shall make it impossible for them to see the hand of God in what is to follow. They shall run headlong into destruction, as did Pharoah and his army. Those who ignore or reject this last plea and offer of mercy shall incur condemnation when the judgment arrives. The "wine of God's wrath is poured unmixed into the cup of His anger"; It is the wine in full strength undiluted by water. Wine is the symbol of God's judgments (Jer. XXV. 15 f; Isa. LI. 22). The "wrath" of God is an anthropomorphism used in both the Old and New Testaments (Rom. I. 18, III, 5, XII. 19) to forebode an unmitigated rigor of justice. It is frequently employed in the Apocalypse after Antichrist appears (XI. 18; XIV. 10, 19 etc.). The unmixed wine is a foretaste of hell for apostasy from God. In all human trials and afflictions, there is a consoling note: It is God's mercy working for the conversion of the afflicted. But if after all pleadings, miracles and warnings, the wicked still remain obstinate in sin, the unmixed wine of God's wrath shall bring on spiritual blindness and obduration, foreclose all mercy against the sinner and let the rigors of justice take their course. The threat of the angel is a solemn warning to all who might have a mind to weakly surrender under persecution with the intention of repenting later. Those who worship the Beast shall fall into impenitence, and the gates of mercy shall be shut against them forever. God's hatred of sin becomes a saturating quality of the impenitent after they are forsaken by grace.

The Christians of Roman times were generally treated as criminals, as the outcasts of society, and were executed in the presence of vast crowds in the amphitheaters. But the wicked who worship Antichrist shall be tormented in the sight of the holy angels and the Lamb. They shall hate with satanic hatred, which Antichrist will instill into his followers, the Sacrifice of the Mass and the priesthood of the Lamb, because these brought about the downfall of Satan and the loss of his kingdom on earth.

"In the sight of the holy angels and in the sight of the Lamb" then means that the worshippers of Antichrist shall have vividly before their consciousness at every individual moment for all eternity the mercy of the Lamb offered them through His priesthood. This divine mystery of love would have saved them and brought them to eternal bliss, if they had not deliberately rejected it. "Fire" is the symbol of hatred. It feeds upon the sulphur of sin and produces the smoke of blasphemy. And it smothers the victims of hatred into eternal death and shall be the possession of the followers of the Beast for hating Christ and His priests.

Verse 11

The hatred with which those who submit to Antichrist shall be surfeited in hell shall be so intense that the "smoke of their torment shall ascend for ever and ever". (See Isa. LXV. 5). The torture begotten of their hatred shall drive them to despair and impotent ravings against God and the mystery of the Eucharist and the priesthood. Those blasphemies make up the smoke that ascends unceasingly. For all eternity, they shall never have a fraction of a moment's rest from the prodding of their hatred. It will be a fury that shall totally consume them. The Apocalyptist makes a specific application of the text of Isaias, LXVI. 18-24. This prophetic text is Messianic. It reveals the cycle of feasts in the new Jerusalem succeeding one another in an unbroken series, month after month and year after year. Redeemed mankind shall assemble there from all nations and shall worship before the face of God. Outside of the city is the Gehenna, where the bodies of the enemies of God and Christ are tormented by an unquenchable fire and the worm of self-reproach. The human race shall then be divided into the citizens of the kingdom of God and the outcasts from that kingdom, who are living corpses, spiritually dead. The eminent saint who gives this dramatic warning against submission to Antichrist, repeats the reason for the judgments and torments incurred: "Who have adored the Beast and its image, and anyone who receives the mark of its name". This text, as the whole of the Apocalypse, was of immediate practical use, for the coming persecutions under the caesars were similar to those coming under Antichrist.

3. Consolations For The Martyrs.

Verses 12-13.

Verse 12

After the martyrdom of the last of the three eminent saints, discouragement will naturally seize many a Catholic. And therefore St. John pens the following words to console them. Antichrist and his followers are in a white hot fury, because the three preachers have nullified the success of his efforts to win the world by seeming kindness and lying miracles. He will decree persecution to death for all who will not submit to him. The persecution may be more of a political and economical nature till then (XIII. 17), and that may be the more dangerous because it does not call forth a heroism of the highest type. Many may save themselves from trouble and loss by complying externally with the commands of the False Prophet internally not worshipping Antichrist. The work of the three saints shall stop this kind of success for the Beast and leave him no alternative but persecution to death. His bloody decree is foretold in the consolations of verses 12 and 13 and is the conclusion from the words of the three preachers. The patience of the saints who keep from sin and cling to their holy faith and confidence in Christ is nourished by the thought of the great rewards to follow. They shall win a glorious victory, while those who obey Antichrist shall sink into ignominy and oblivion.

Verse 13

As the Seer pronounces these words, he hears them ratified in Heaven and is ordered to write: "Blessed are the dead who die in the Lord". The Church has always applied these last words to all the faithful departed. They were directly written for the martyrs who give their life for Christ during the persecution of Antichrist but are applicable to all who die in communion with the Church in sanctifying grace. The martyred dead are blessed because they are fortunate for having been taken out of distress; their work is done, and they have gained the highest merits and glory. The thought was of practical value whenever persecution raged against the Church.

St. John then hears the Spirit speak within him affirming the words he had heard from Heaven. And the Spirit adds the reason why the dead who die in the Lord are blessed: "in that they shall rest from their labors; for their works follow them". The "works" are not their mere deeds credited to them when they shall reach their rest, for those works preceded them and are stored up in the treasury of Heaven. The works meant here are the ones enumerated in XI. 18 and XX. 4-6. The results of the sacrifices and labors of the martyrs shall continue to grow during the thousand years of peace. These their works and the example of their constancy shall increase and multiply while they rest in Heaven enjoying the Beatific Vision and ruling with Christ as a reward for their heroism. Only those die in the Lord who have lived in the Lord, who have kept the commandments and the faith of Jesus. These consolations are of the highest importance and shall make all the faithful eager for martyrdom. They must be patient, for as soon as the enemy employs the utmost violence, God will take the same measures to protect His own.

The Greek text seems a little incongruous, for it states that their works "follow with them". The idiom of the language answers for this. The whole passage is intended to bring vividly to the consciousness of all the dire loss to those who prefer the enjoyments offered for antichrist-worship, and the endless gains and joys to those who sacrifice them. St. Augustine says (Hom. 42, chap. 8): "ipsa, inquit, est infelicitas hominum, proper quod peccant, morientes hic dimittunt, et peccata secum portant". On the contrary losing the fruits of their labors will win everything for the saints, and their virtues will accompany them into everlasting glory.

4. The Harvest Of The Good.

Verses 14-16.

Verse 14

The 12th and 13th verses are the introduction to the three that follow. The Seer announces the next vision with the usual "and behold" intimating its decisive importance. A white cloud floats into view, and sitting upon it is someone who has the appearance of Christ. It is not Christ Himself, because he takes an order from the angel who steps out of the Church. This second angel is some bishop or priest of the Church. Clouds in Scriptural language are indicative of a direct intervention from God, as shown in the Transfiguration, Ascension and the giving of the ten commandments.

The angel resembles Christ, because he comes in His name and with his authority. It may have been his voice that St. John heard from Heaven in verse thirteen, for he comes to do the very thing to which that verse is the introduction and prediction; he comes to reap the earth. The golden crown is the emblem of authority from on high to fulfill the purposes of God. The emblem of his office is in his hand; for a scepter he has a sickle. It must be St. Michael, who in the language of the Church has been given dominion over all souls to be saved. The sharp sickle may be the decrees of Antichrist. In chapter twelve St. Michael fought to expel the wicked from the Church, and here he comes to gather in the saints. Our Lord has said that he will send out His angels to gather the harvest on the day appointed.

Verse 15

Another angel comes out of the sanctuary. It recalls XI. 1-2, where the true believers are restricted to the sanctuary. This angel comes with knowledge and supreme authority. It may be a great saint or the pope who was elected before the "great eagle" carried him away to safety. The loud voice indicates him to be a great bishop, and since he comes from the sanctuary possibly a cardinal or the pope. The angels serve the Church. Here the one sitting on the cloud obeys the command of the angel from the sanctuary, who knows the spiritual status of the faithful and how well they are prepared for the bloody ordeal to be enacted by the minions of Antichrist. It recalls the command issued in IX. 14. Only one who has intimate knowledge and special enlightment by grace would be able to decide the hour in which those who are destined for martyrdom are strengthened enough by the preaching and warnings of the three saints and are purified enough by the reception of the holy sacraments and the sufferings thus far endured to be willing to die for Christ. They welcome death as the liberator from the danger of apostasy, and they desire it out of pure love for God. They are ripe for entrance into Heaven.

Verse 16

The bloody decrees of Antichrist or of the False Prophet go into effect, and the angel reaps his harvest of souls. This chapter reaches its climax in this verse. The foregoing visions were the preparation for the harvest. The bulk of the harvest may be gathered in before the Two Prophets ascend into Heaven. Their bodies are still lying in the street of Jerusalem. The harvest cannot be finished with one sweep of the sickle but will continue till the destruction of Babylon or possibly the death of Antichrist. The angel upon the white cloud directs the malice of the wicked to carry out God's will, and he protects and strengthens those who are destined for martyrdom.

5. The Vintage Of The Wicked.

Verses 17 to end.

Verse 17

Still another angel comes forth from the "sanctuary in Heaven". It is another champion of the Church, who shall have power to destroy the wicked. His coming out of the sanctuary in heaven probably refers him to the headquarters of the Church. He may belong to the nation of the Great Eagle that has rescued and is protecting the Church. If a pope was elected, he may reside there, or the remaining cardinals are in exile there, or they are of that nation. This angel may direct the campaign that shall end in the destruction of all followers of Antichrist. He does not come on a cloud, consequently he is not a celestial spirit. But he has a sharp sickle too, which is possibly the power to inflict the seven last plagues. This scene is prophetic and shall be staged during the succeeding chapters up to the end of chapter nineteen. This angel may be the one who gives the seven bowls to the seven angels in chapter fifteen.

The angel comes forth from the sanctuary to order destruction upon all the wicked. From the sanctuary should have come salvation and eternal life, but the followers of Antichrist have vehemently rejected this, and so from the same source shall come death to them. As in Ezechiel (IX. 2), the destroying angels began at the altar of holocausts, from which help and safety should have come, so the destroyers of the wicked come from the same center of sanctity here. Everyone of the angels in Ezechiel's vision has a destroying weapon in his hand. One of the angels is clothed as a priest, and he must mark a "Tav" on the foreheads of the just that they may be spared. The office of the priest is to save not to destroy. In order to save the just from contamination and damnation, the priests must labor to exterminate evil. So this angel from the sanctuary is appointed to reap all evil from the earth and cast it into the winepress of God's wrath.

Verse 18

As soon as the angel appears all prepared to destroy the wicked, a second one steps forth from the altar of holocausts, and he has authority over the fire. The angel is probably a martyr (See VI. 9) who has met his death at the hands of Antichrist's henchmen. This vision is prophetical pointing to the seven last plagues with which the destruction of the wicked begins. This vision is possibly timed for the three days and a half before the resurrection of the Two Witnesses. The soul of

Elias may appear to order just retribution to the wicked. This office would properly belong to Elias, because the Beast silenced him by assassination to end his miraculous power which clearly came from God, by putting the Two Prophets to death the measure of sin has been filled up for Antichrist and his followers. All the wicked consented to this blasphemous act by holding a carnival over their death. The "grapes are ripe", and so the judgment is due. While they celebrate the victory over the Two Prophets, the followers of Antichrist execute his decrees of persecution and dye their hands in the blood of Christians. They will not repent any more; all grace would be wasted on them, and hence they shall receive no more mercy. All martyrs of all times are about to be avenged. The angel having authority of the fire might mean the zealous work of priests and bishops throughout the world converting all who have not surrendered to antichrist-worship, and this angel might be the cardinal at the head of the congregation of missionary activities. But that he stepped forth from the altar of holocausts shows him to be a martyr, who has been slain by Antichrist's agents, and he has experienced the completeness of the measure of iniquity merited by the wicked and therefore pronounces the grapes ripe for the winepress.

Verse 19

In the words of Micheas, God threatened to "execute vengeance in wrath and in indignation among all the nations that have not given ear" (V. 14). The prophecy may mean this day of vengeance now approaching, for in that chapter the prophet foretells the birth and conquests of Christ. The judgment about to begin shall be complete. All without exception who have not assented to the truth but have actively joined the Beast shall be condemned. They no longer shall "drink" of the wine of wrath, through which they have become intoxicated, but shall be cast into the winepress, "the great one". As grapes thrown into the press are destroyed and changed into another substance through a chemical process, so the wicked shall be changed into reprobates. This fruit is not from the "True Vine" but is the fruit of the earth, the fruit of apostasy from God.

Verse 20

The great battle in which Antichrist and his followers and helpers are destroyed shall be fought outside the city of Jerusalem not of the ancient city but of the New Jerusalem of chapter XXI. This place is called in Hebrew Armagedon, "the hill of robbers", as stated in XVI. 16. This may be any place in the world, which will afterwards receive that appellation. In Joel (III. 12 ff) there seems to be a prophecy pointing to this last battle against Jerusalem. Also Isaias (LXVI. 24) points to the valley of destruction, in which the carcasses of God's enemies shall lie. They seem to be living carcasses that shall suffer eternal torments. Isaias may have meant the armies of Gog. Most likely the battle against Antichrist shall be fought not far from Jerusalem, as XIX. 19 indicates.

This last verse of chapter XIV. explains the meaning of the wine-press. It is some battle that produces more bloodshed than ever seen on earth before. The gathering of the armies for that battle is mentioned in XVI. 12. It is more fully described at the end of chapter XIX., making this verse prophetic and giving a glimpse of the slaughter in XIX. 20-21. The slaughter shall follow the plagues in chapter XVI. and the razing of Babylon in chapter XVIII. The plagues and the doom of Babylon shall be the signs to the true believers indicating the time of judgment for the Beast and the False Prophet. The blinded and glutted votaries shall fight to the end for a foredoomed cause, so that they may all be wiped from the face of the earth.

The blood runs in a stream for 1600 furlongs, 200 miles. The distance has been estimated to roughly correspond to the length of Palestine. The number is obtained by squaring 4, the directions of the world, and multiplying it by 100. This would not seem to limit the bloodshed to the vast armies possibly gathered in Palestine but to spread it among all peoples of the earth. When Antichrist meets his doom in this battle, his followers shall be paralyzed by a mortal dread, as they shall be made helpless by the seven plagues (See Isa. XXX. 28).

In the prophecy of Joel the invitation is given to all the nations round about to gather in the valley of Josaphat. The order to end the career of the wicked shall go forth from the Church, for the Church shall be enlightened to know when the time to execute God's will has arrived. St. John's words in verse 18 here and those of Joel in verse 13, chapter III. are almost identical, both texts referring this judgment to the greatest enemy of God's people and his destruction and that of his armies. From verse 16 to the end of his book, Joel predicts the blessings of Sion after this judgment. Jerusalem shall then be the metropolis of the Church. The last sentence of Joel may be literally fulfilled.

Jeremias says that sounds of jubilation shall be heard from the just when the judgment of God comes. (Jer. XXV. 30). Although this may have been meant for the nations after the end of the Babylonian Captivity, the language was similar to that of St. John, who surely alludes to the text of Jeremias.

In Isaias LXIII. 1-6, Christ is seen coming from Bozra in Idumea his garments red with the blood of His enemies. He is sprinkled with blood, because He "trod the winepress alone", and He "trod them down in His wrath". Some scripturists apply this text to the bloody sacrifice of the Cross, during which all His friends left Him, and through which He alone was worthy and able to defeat the enemy. In that sacrifice, however, He was stained with His own blood, and He did not tread the winepress of His wrath; He died for love and mercy. He did not crush his enemies, and His garments were not sprinkled with their blood. The prophecy of Isaias is therefore properly intended to some future event, when Christ shall come in judgment upon His enemies. If we compare the two prophecies of chapter XIV. 20 and XIX. 13 with Isaias, St. John seems to foretell the fulfillment of Isaias' prophecy in the destruction of Antichrist and his followers. The faithful nations are subjugated by Antichrist, and the Church is at his mercy, only Christ can bring deliverance. Of that occasion He can say: "I looked about and there was none to help . . . and my own arm hath saved for me . . . And I have trodden down the people in my wrath, and their blood is sprinkled upon my garments". (See Eyzaguirre, pages 381-385).

CHAPTER XV.

Westminster Version

Then I beheld in heaven another sign, great 1. and wonderful: seven
angels holding seven plagues, which are the last, because with them the
wrath of God is completed.

And I beheld as it were a sea of glass mixed 2. with fire, and the
conquerors of the beast and of its image and of the number of its name
stood by this sea of glass, holding the harps of God.

And they sing the canticle of Moses, the 3. servant of God, and the
canticle of the Lamb; saying: 'Great and wonderful are thy works, O Lord
God almighty! Just and true are thy ways, O king of the nations!

Who shall not fear, O Lord, and glorify thy 4. name? Because thou
alone art holy; Because all the nations shall come and worship before
thee; Because thy judgments have been made manifest.

And after these things I beheld, and the 5. sanctuary of the tent of
witness in heaven was opened, and there came forth from the sanctuary
the 6. seven angels who hold the seven plagues. They were clothed in
linen pure and *bright,* and girt about the breasts with golden girdles.

And one of the four living beings gave 7. to the seven angels seven
golden vials, full of the wrath of God, of him who liveth forever and
ever.

And the sanctuary was filled with smoke 8. from the glory of God and
from his might, and no one was able to enter into the sanctuary, until the
seven plagues of the seven angels should be completed.

VI. THE THIRD WOE

1. Preparations For The Third Woe.

Seven Angels And The Crystal Sea.

Chapter XV.

Verses 1-4.

Verse 1

St. John beholds another "sign" in the Church. The word, SIGN, links this and the succeeding chapters with XII. and XIII. A "sign" brings to the understanding a future event under an allegorical form. The sign appearing now is "great and wonderful". In Greek and Latin the phrase is clearer than in English. It signifies the miraculous power of the Church portending a manifestation of extraordinary miracles about to be wrought. When this sign appears the faithful will understand that it is full of ominous forebodings for the wicked. How soon after the death and ascension of the Two Prophets it shall appear, the text does not indicate, but the context reveals the passing of only a few days.

The sign is seven angels holding the seven last plagues. The angels as the representatives of the hierarchy have these plagues in their possession at their appearance. The Church has at all times the gift of miracles to protect herself, but priests may exercise this power only when necessary and when appointed by rightful authority, or when God gives such sanction manifestly. The number seven denotes the completeness of this miraculous power and its sacred character. All faithful bishops and priests may have in the persecution of Antichrist advanced to such heights of sanctity that all are worthy of being empowered with the gift of miracles, but these appointed ones shall manifest the divinity of the Church sufficiently to convince all peoples of her supernatural origin.

The subject of this and the following chapters is here briefly stated to be the "seven LAST plagues". The plagues began in IX. 18 to destroy many of the wicked who prepare the reign of Antichrist. These "last" plagues shall exterminate his worshippers. Whatever sins shall be committed after that time shall not be punished on earth anymore by such demonstrations of God's wrath. In those evil days the wicked will boldly sin to crush down and wipe out the true faith and its adherents, and for that reason God will through His Church strike them with these plagues. The word "plague" links the subsequent judgments of God with those of the foregoing chapters (IX. 18; XI. 6), but here they have the distinction of being the "last", for in them the punitive hand of God completes its work. This first verse is the antithesis of the first verse of the preceding chapter: There the reward of God to His faithful was revealed; here His wrath upon the infidels is foreshadowed. This vision is synchronized with XI. 15 and is the beginning of the vintage ordered in XIV. 18.

Verse 2

A short interlude is introduced here, before the action indicated in verse one proceeds. St. John beholds again the Crystal Sea which he had described in chapter IV. And those who have overcome the Beast are standing over the sea. The Crystal Sea is the whole body of the true believers who adore "in the sanctuary of God" (XI. 1). The faithful are thus shown separated from that other "sea" (XIII. 1; XVII. 15) which produced the Beast. The latter sea is steeped in darkness, while the Crystal Sea is pellucid with the teachings of the Church, with grace and the presence of God. Those who have risked all to preserve their virtue and their faith in Christ and God have overcome the Beast. It seems to mean the clergy and religious in this chapter. If they were martyrs they would no longer be part of the "Sea" but would be in Heaven, and the symbolism would vanish. The martyrs are elsewhere shown under the altar. It seems necessary for the logic and unity of this verse to consider these singers priests praising God with all their heart and soul for the grace of perseverance and for the coming victory. The "harps of God" are some special gifts of grace or powers of ordination, with which they can give God acceptable adoration and praise. The minds, hearts and wills of the singers are attuned to the charismata and therefore they can serve God acceptably.

"Fire", which is not present in chapter IV., is now mingled with the Crystal Sea. This fire and the singing of the canticle of Moses in the next verse allude to the pillar of cloud and of fire (Exod. XIV.) and to the canticle of thanksgiving for the liberation of the Israelites from the domination of Pharaoh (Exod. XV.). The presence of "fire" in the Crystal Sea intimates a high degree of sanctity in the laity and presages destruction for the Beast and his followers, if not by the Church at least for the sake of the Church. Christ will protect and fight for his own as did Jahve for the Israelites. Those of the clergy who were not brought to sin by the Beast celebrate this victory before his destruction actually begins. They have ·passed through a sea of fire. They are happy because they have heeded the warnings of the angels in the preceding chapter, have not feared the Beast but have risked all rather than submit to him by any sign whatsoever. They overcame "the beast and his image and the number of his name". They did not believe in his false miracles or misleading doctrines. Neither did they go to see the miraculous statue or portrait nor wear the number of his name on their person. They know now that his reign is drawing to a close.

Verse 3

The seven angels sing the canticle of Moses. The recorded words however, are not like the canticle but only a vague illusion to one verse (Exod. XV. 11). Yet the text suggests more than the words express. Moses was "the servant of God", His spokesman and ambassador. The allusion then evidently means that the conquerors are servants of God and Christ and representatives of the people who compose the Crystal Sea. They are the clergy, both religious and secular, a body separate from the faithful, who offer God the prayers and worship of the faithful and are the leaders who have brought them through the fiery ordeal of the persecution. They sing the praises of God not after the destruction of Antichrist, as did Moses after that of Pharaoh, but in anticipation of it positively knowing it to be inevitable. The singing of this canticle is synchronized with that of the elders in XI. 16 and may be just another statement of it. At the ascension of the Two Prophets the victory of Christ has begun. The miraculous power with which God has endowed His Church shall now break the power of the Beast.

These angels also sing the canticle of the Lamb. This cannot be sung by any but virgins. Celestial spirits cannot sing it. Since the name "angel" denotes a bishop or priest as well as a celestial spirit, and since here they are classed with Moses, the servant of God and leader of his people, these angels must be priests and likewise virgins. This clearly reveals that the celibacy of the clergy is divinely approved and is of apostolic origin. These angels are of the virgin priesthood of the Church. They appreciate the privilege of being picked to destroy the powers of evil and save mankind. They call God "Lord God Almighty", because He can communicate his almighty power of miracles to His Church. In the face of this power, the vaunted power of Antichrist shall soon wither away. God is the King of Ages, because the happenings of all ages are subject to Him; He is not dependent on human consent or aid, but can shape every age as He wills and realize His purposes at all times. He is just and true; and the priests glory especially in this, because, although they underwent the most terrifying persecution, they understand the value of the merits gained by their sufferings. They themselves deserved what they suffered to make amends to divine justice for their faults. Above all God is true to His promises and will mete out justice to the persecutors of His faithful. And these judgments and all things foretold by the prophets are about to be made manifest. Though He left men their free will, God knew how to direct all human progress to the fulfillment of prophecy, the sanctification of His children and His own glory.

The received Greek text calls God "O King of ages", while other well-authenticated readings render it "O King of the nations". It is of no consequence whether the first or second rendition is adopted. But the rendition "O King of the nations", is in more rigid verbal logic with the next verse, which reads "all the nations shall come and worship before thee".

Verse 4

This verse alludes to the foregoing chapter, verses 7-11. The words are the same as those in Jeremias (X. 7). (This verse of Jeremias is in the Vulgate but not in the Septuagint). The wicked shall be compelled to fear God with or against their will. The just will praise Him unceasingly for manifesting Himself the protector of those who serve and adore Him. He alone is holy who is Holiness Himself and therefore no one else deserves any honor. This is an acknowledgment by the priests of their own nothingness and is a true expression of their humility before God, who alone deserves the honor and praise for their charismata. God has endowed the Church to glorify her and His own name. Through this manifestation of His power, justice and holiness, He will convert all peoples to adore and serve Him and thereby save them. The last sentence of this text is prophetic, and the fulfillment is shown in chapters XXI. and XXII.

The judgments of God have been manifest in the miracles of the Two Witnesses, in their resurrection and ascension but shall be still more manifest in what is to follow now. In the last words is the introduction to the following chapters and is the proof of the miraculous character of what is to follow.

2. The Open Sanctuary And

The Seven Angels Receiving Seven Bowls.

Verses 5 to the end.

Verse 5

The scene that presents itself to St. John is not a new one. He saw the same one in XI. 19. The different phases of the battle between the Church and Antichrist up to the ascension of the Two Prophets have been shown, and now the action moves forward to the completion of the "mystery of God". St. John heard the seventh trumpet in XI. 15, but all developments that led up to the last trumpet had not been revealed to him. Those developments were depicted in chapters XII-XIV. The onward movement of the drama can now be recorded. The scene from the sanctuary thrown open alludes to Isaias, (LX. 11-12) as does also verse 4.

There is an accumulation of epithets here, each one of which denotes the place of the divine Presence: the sanctuary, the tent of witness, heaven. Heaven is the Church; the sanctuary or temple is the church-building, and the "tabernacle" is the central divine dwelling place. The tabernacle or tent of witness was constructed according to plans divinely dictated and was God's "resting place" in the Old Dispensation. The reference here denotes the sanctuary in which is the Real Presence of

Christ, as the place from which God will roar forth His judgments upon His enemies. The sanctuary here shown is probably at the headquarters of the Church, the church of the pope. The opening of the sanctuary forebodes the manifestation of God's aid in the decisive conflict revealed to both the good and the bad leaving no doubt whence shall come the *last* plagues upon the wicked alone. Under the leadership of the Beast, they blasphemed the Church and ridiculed her impotency in fighting him, and they shall now feel her power. The spiritual might of bishops and priests and of the Lamb shall now be proven to the unbelieving world.

Verse 6

What the seventh trumpet announced is about to be enacted. The seven angels coming out of the sanctuary with the plagues are clothed in white, shining linen, the official vesture of priests, as Ezechiel had foretold (XLIV. 17). According to him, priests of the New Law shall be thus vested when offering sacrifice. The linen robes are clean and white because they are the symbol of purity. By penance and the sufferings endured in the persecution of Antichrist, the priests have atoned for all their sins and faults. White is also the symbol of victory, and it betokens here the victory over sin and attachment to the world making the wearers worthy to share in the sweeping victory of Christ. The glint of divine light on their robes indicates that the motives for remaining true to Christ were pure love of God, whch produced in them the heroic virtues now divinely manifested.

Their cinctures of pure gold are emblems of wisdom and a pure intention, and their being bound over the breast denotes the fullness of Christly power and authority to pour out the plagues (See I. 13). The cinctures over the breast likewise symbolize the perfect control of passion without any thought of resentment or revenge in their actions but with sheer obedience to the command of the Church, when they pour out the penalties upon the wicked. Their office is to preserve not primarily to destroy. They will preserve the faithful from too great dangers to their faith. They act thus with a pure intention and as instruments of God's will to execute His purposes.

Verse 7

When the angels go forth from the sanctuary, they have the plagues, but according to this verse, they are given the golden bowls "full of the wrath of God". It seems to be a contradiction. It only seems so, because these symbolic actions express invisible powers and gifts. The angels at their appearance had the gift of miracles including the power to inflict the plagues but could not exercise that gift until the Church authorized it. Which one of the four living beings gives the bowls to the angels is not stated, but it is evidently the first one who spoke to St. John in VI. 1, the Lion, who comes from the "sanctuary in heaven" in XIV. 17. The Lion is the emblem of royalty and represents supreme authority in the Church. It is the POPE bidding the angels to act. This order is visualized by the giving of the bowls. The bowls are of pure gold to signify that the plagues contained therein are decreed by the justice and wisdom of God. The gold furthermore indicates the preservation of the just. These bowls allude to those held by the elders full of the prayers of the saints (V. 8), but here they contain only the wrath of God. The coals in the first bowls (V. 8) effected to offer God the prayers of the saints, to give Him acceptable worship. Now the coals shall be poured out upon all forces of nature to burn up the evils that polluted God's creation. The plagues called for by the Two Prophets descended upon the good and the bad alike but these last plagues are upon the bad alone; the former were for the sanctification of the just and the conversion of the wicked, while these last are for the preservation of the just and the punishment of the wicked.

The relative phrase, "who liveth forever and ever", attributed to God, must have some pertinent meaning, or it would be a useless addition. It calls to mind the infinite perfections of God, who must punish evil because it generates death, while He, the living God, can only will and give eternal life, although in His justice He does will eternal death for the sinner who cannot be separated from sin. If He did not punish evil, the just might be in too great peril of consenting to sin and incurring the sentence of death in the end. The coming plagues are decreed by God the Giver of life. The phrase calls attention to the "living being" who hands the bowls to the angels, because these living beings possess the sources of spiritual life in the Church. And it is the proper office of the Lion to authorize the pouring out of the plagues which shall preserve the spiritual life of the faithful.

This verse also indicates the reason for fearing only the living God, who alone can punish the infidels. The gods of mythology never had life or existence, and no one needs to fear them. Neither need a Christian fear Antichrist, because he shall not live forever, and his power shall soon end and vanish. The power of real miracles coming from God is directed by the living being in opposition to the might and great authority, which the dragon conferred upon Antichrist (XIII. 2). The power conferred upon the seven angels is a continuation of the same power exercised by the Two Prophets (XI). Satan and Antichrist shall be powerless in the presence of these real miracles, which shall clear away every doubt for all men and shall manifest the divinity of the Church and the imposture of Antichrist and his Prophet.

Verse 8

"And the sanctuary was filled with smoke from the majesty of God and from His might". At the dedication of the Tabernacle and of the Temple, the holy of holies was filled with smoke which betokened the presence of God. But here another event in the Old Testament is alluded to, namely the destruction of Core, Dathan and Abiron and the tumult of the people thereafter. When Moses and Aaron fled to the Tabernacle, the cloud overshadowed it, and the glory of God was seen there, and no one dared to attack them. There is in this verse also an allusion to Isaias (VI. 4), who beheld the Temple filled with smoke signifying the presence of God and of the approaching judgment upon the wicked. In Habakuk (II. 20) the presence of God in His Temple is an indication of the nearing triumph of the Church over her enemies. Ezechiel (XI. 22 ff) saw the glory of God departing from the Temple and abandoning the city to the destroyer. God's glory returns to the Temple later (XLIII. 2 ff) betokening the restoration of the theocracy. This restored theocracy as shown in many prophecies shall not be destroyed again; it shall be superceded by the everlasting covenant, in which God will dwell with His people always. The prophets often couple the glorious reign of Christ after Antichrist with the restoration following the Babylonian Captivity. In Isaias (LIV. 10) God refers the prophet to His oath given to Noe, that He would not execute a judgment again to destroy all flesh. Since judgments follow sin, God's holiness must execute them, but His providence will protect His children who earnestly seek true internal sanctity. He will not abandon His Church; His glory will remain therein.

The majesty of God's presence in the sanctuary shall terrify all who have not heeded the warnings and miracles, so that no nation and possibly no individual shall be admitted into the Church until the plagues have been poured out, and Antichrist is destroyed. The Two Prophets have risen from the dead and ascended into Heaven. The Jews in Palestine are converted and perhaps large numbers outside of Palestine. The separation of the good from the bad is complete for the present; the good are so far advanced in sanctity and the bad so far in wickedness that association of the two is no longer possible. Because the wicked are as confirmed in evil as devils and are impenitent, their end is decreed. What shall become of the indifferent in the last plagues is not revealed in this prophecy, but they may be referred to in XVI. 19; XIX. 9 and XXII. 2.

That the time of mercy passes away is clearly revealed by the threats of Osee over Israel (I. 6) and by those of Jeremias over Juda (XI. 11), who expresses the same thought in the prophecy of the coming darkness (XIII. 16). In the Lamentations, he mourns over the passing of the time of mercy. (Lam. I. 17).

The faithful in the sanctuary shall be shielded by the smoke of God's majesty and power. When the seven plagues begin, the wicked shall not dare to touch them any more. According to the last clause of this verse, the Real Presence may manifest itself in a visible manner; or the worship of the faithful attending solemn services may fill the house of God with smoke, since incense is but a symbol of the prayers of the faithful. No doubt these prayers shall be multiplied during the dreadful days of the persecution. The smoke is a symbol of the miraculous manifestation of God's presence, and it indicates that the plagues shall proceed directly from His almighty power.

In verses 5 to 8, the Real Presence in the Holy Eucharist is without doubt spoken of. St. John beholds this under the form of the ancient tabernacle, in which the tables of the Law were kept. But the holy of Holies was far from being as sacred as the tabernacles of the Catholic Church. As Jahve testified visibly to uphold the authority of Moses and Aaron, so will Christ visibly uphold the authority and teachings of His Church and its belief in His Real Presence. The scoffs against this truth and the desecration practiced by the adherents of Antichrist against this Mystery of Love shall be driven to cover, when the open sanctuary reveals the majesty of Christ to unbelievers and shields the true believers against their enemies and against any more faltering in their faith. Through these revelations, St. John has shown the Church what to do, and she is confident that God will be true to what He has revealed.

CHAPTER XVI.

Westminster Version

And I heard a loud voice out of the sanctuary, 1. saying to the seven angels, 'Go, and pour out upon the earth the seven vials of the wrath of God'.

And the first departed, and poured out his 2. vial upon the earth; and an evil and malignant sore came upon the men that bore the mark of the beast and that adored the image thereof.

And the second poured out his vial upon the 3. sea; and it became as blood of a dead man, and every living creature that was in the sea died.

And the third poured out his vial upon the 4. rivers and the fountains of waters; and they became blood. And I heard the angel of the 5. waters say: 'Just art thou, who art and who wast, O holy one, because of these thy judgments. They shed the blood of saints and prophets, 6. and blood thou hast given them to drink; such is their due.'

And I heard the altar say: 'Yea, O Lord God 7. Almighty, true and just are thy judgments!'

And the fourth poured out his vial upon the 8. sun, and it was given it to scorch men with fire; and men were scorched by the fierce heat, 9. and they blasphemed the name of the God who hath power over these plagues, and they did not repent and give him glory.

And the fifth poured out his vial upon the 10. throne of the beast, and its kingdom was thrown into darkness; men gnawed their tongues through pain, and they blasphemed the God of heaven because 11. of their pains and of their sores, and they repented not of their works.

And the sixth (angel) poured out his vial upon 12. the great river Euphrates, and its water was dried up, in order to prepare the way for the kings that come from the rising of the sun.

And I beheld issuing from the mouth of the 13. dragon, and from the mouth of the beast, and from the mouth of the false prophet, three unclean spirits, like frogs.

For they are spirits of devils, which work 14. signs, and they go forth unto the kings of the whole world, to gather them together for the battle on the great day of God Almighty.

'Behold, I come as a thief. Blessed is he 15. that watcheth and keepeth his garments, that he may not walk naked and let men see his shame.'

And they gathered them together to the 16. place which is called in Hebrew 'Armageddon'.

And the seventh angel poured out his vial 17. upon the air; and a loud voice came forth from the sanctuary, from the throne, saying, 'It is done.'

And there followed lightnings and voices 18. and thunder-peals; and there was a great earthquake, such as never befell since man appeared on earth, so great an earthquake was it.

The great city was rent into three parts, 19. and the cities of the
nations fell; and God remembered Babylon the great, to make her drink
the wine of his fierce wrath.

Every island fled away, and the mountains 20. were not to be found.

And great hailstones, heavy as a hundred-weight, 21. dropped from
heaven upon men; and men blasphemed God because of the plague of
the hail, because the plague thereof was very great.

3. The Seven Last Plagues.

Chapter XVI.

Verse 1

The "loud voice out of the sanctuary" which orders the seven angels to go and pour out the seven bowls is the voice of the one who gave them the bowls, the voice of the Lion, the voice of supreme authority in the Church. These plagues being in the sacred number seven will effect all conditions of life. They are a faint echo of the seven prophecies of Ezechiel against Egypt and also of the ten plagues of Egypt. The second, third, fifth and seventh plagues have some resemblance to the Egyptian plagues. They are for the wicked only, as the Egyptian plagues were for only the Egyptians.

Ezechiel (XXX. 3) and Jeremias (XLVI. 10) refer to the battle of Charkamis, in which the Egyptian army was defeated by the Babylonian, as "the great day of the Lord", making it the beginning of God's judgment upon the beast. Egypt was the first head, and though Assyria had defeated Egypt before this, the judgment against the beast was begun and decisively consolidated by the battle of Charkamis. God's defeat of the first head of the beast was really the beginning of his destruction. The other judgments announced by all the prophets, and which Daniel describes so vividly, culminate in these "last Plagues". These shall end the existence of the beast forever.

There are convincing reasons why these last plagues shall be in the order of nature and be recognized as manifest punishments from God.

The last verse of the foregoing chapter argues emphatically for a visible manifestation of God's presence in the Church through the coming plagues. The Church will so openly inflict these plagues that everyone, learned and unlearned, shall know them as directly coming from the almighty power of God and this shall terrify those outside.

In XV. 4, the Church praises God for making His judgments "manifest". Some deep theologians understood the judgments of the seven seals and the seven trumpets to be from God; Even they did not understand with certainty to what happening the various prophecies in the Apocalypse referred; all the rest understood them to be but natural phenomena produced by natural causes. The siege and destruction of Jerusalem and of the Temple were manifest judgments of God, because Christ had clearly foretold and described them. Only the Christians understood them as such; Jews and Pagans did not understand them. In the seven last plagues, all peoples shall see the hand of God, and for that reason "all nations shall come and shall adore in His sight". This demands a literal fulfillment.

These judgments are called "plagues". The word had a specific meaning in olden times, when they came upon Pharaoh and Egypt and were recognized by both Pharaoh and his people as direct punishments from God. What followed the opening of the seven seals and the blowing of the trumpets were not called plagues. They were developments of human history consequent upon the acts of human wickedness. Very few understand them as judgments of God.

In chapter XI. 6, the Two Witnesses shall have the power to inflict "plagues" of various kinds whatever suits their purpose, to shut heaven so that it does not rain and to turn water into blood. There is no reason for the word "plague" to mean anything different in chapter XVI. than in chapter XI. The conclusion therefore is that the plagues of chapter XV. and XVI. are real physical phenomena and shall resemble those inflicted by the Two Prophets and by Moses and Aaron.

First Plague. The Ulcer On Antichrist-worshippers.

Verse 2.

Verse 2

The first angel goes forth and pours out his bowl upon the earth, upon the countries entirely subject and submissive to Antichrist. He may actually carry a vial filled with blest water or oil or some other matter used in divine service and may visibly pour out the plague upon the earth, as did Moses sprinkling ashes from a chimney upon the air. The effect is similar to that of Moses sprinkling the ashes. The followers of the Beast are afflicted by an incurable ulcer (See Jer. XXX. 12-15). It is "malignant" in the technical sense. They may have disposed their bodies by the corrupt and impure lives they led at the behest of the Beast and the False Prophet. But the angel directly causes the ulcer. It may be like the ulcer with which God struck the Israelites for adoring the golden calf. (Exod. XXXII. 35; Deut. XXVIII. 35). The ulcer shall be extremely painful and bring confusion to the adorers of the Beast, who shall be powerless to relieve them. This is his first serious defeat. It is similar to the 6th plague of Egypt.

Second Plague. The Sea Becomes Blood.

Verse 3.

Verse 3

The second angel pours out his bowl upon the "sea". This could mean only the Mediterranean Sea. All fish and other living creatures in the sea shall die, as they did in the Nile after the first plague of Moses (Ex. VII. 21). If all the oceans were meant, it would mean the destruction of all life in the waters, and this seems altogether unreasonable, even monstrous. It would then be a plague upon all men. It is foul coagulated blood as of a dead man; and if all the seas were thus polluted, the air would be infected and all living beings on earth would die. If the plague is on the Mediterranean Sea alone, it will be a manifest punishment for the countries surrounding it, which may all have submitted to Antichrist constituting the empire of the False Prophet, who will have persecuted and executed most of the faithful clergy. Some countries might escape infection depending on the direction of the wind. Antichrist and his prophet may, like the magicians in Egypt (Ex. VII. 22), turn other waters into the appearance of blood, but they shall not be able to change the nature of water into real blood nor be able to change the blood of the "sea" into water again. They shall be as helpless in freeing their followers from this plague as from the first one. So Antichrist's claims to divinity shall be discredited.

Third Plague. The Rivers And All Waters Become Blood.

Verse 4

Perhaps the Beast and his prophet shall continue to deceive the wicked by their prodigies, and perhaps the image of the

Beast continues to appear alive encouraging his followers to believe in him still; they remain obstinate in sin. Antichrist may have turned a river into the appearance of blood. The third angel steps forward and pours out his bowl upon the rivers turning them, their tributaries, the springs and wells into blood like that of the "sea". This is only an enlargement of the second plague. Possibly only those countries may be struck that have submitted to Antichrist altogether and have murdered, imprisoned or exiled all Catholics. They were not converted by the plagues and miracles of the Two Witnesses, and they rejoiced and made merry over their dead bodies. Now they receive just retribution for their cruelty. Pestilence may be the outcome of this plague. Every additional plague increases their woe. And the Church will inform the world of the approaching end of Antichrist and his followers.

Pronouncement Of The Angel Of The Waters.

Verses 5 and 6

The following interlude separates the first three from the last four plagues. The angel of the waters now speaking may be the guardian angel of those nations that make up the empire of Antichrist. All nations seem to have a special guardian angel (Dan. X. 13; Acts XVI. 9). God is the "Holy One" who must destroy all unholiness. The apostate clergy and all followers of Antichrist adored him as god, preached hatred and death for all unbelievers and shed the pure blood of saints and prophets. Now they deserve to drink foul, coagulated blood, a foretaste of their due hereafter. If they have been deceived by the signs of Antichrist or his prophet, they can no longer be in darkness. They feel, see and taste the power of the Church now.

Verse 7

The altar also approves the plagues and the words of the angel. The personified altar may speak for all martyrs but specifically for those who died in this persecution. Or it is the voice of the first great martyr of chapter XIV. 6-7, who warned all nations of the impending judgment; through him the martyrs pronounce the judgments upon their tormentors fair and just. Their rejoicing does not voice any rejoicing of revengefulness but of exultation for the glory accruing to God in these woes. The Church will not be silent but will explain the justice and logic of these plagues to gain for the world their beneficent results. God's honor is vindicated in avenging those who serve Him.

Fourth Plague. Excessive Heat On Beast-worshippers.

Verses 8-9.

Verse 8

When the fourth angel pours his bowl upon the sun, it radiates unbearable heat. It is easily understood how this could be possible without disturbing the universe. The collision of a heavenly body with the sun would not be necessary, for some radioactivity or extraordinary chemical combination of matter could vastly intensify its radiation of heat. Again temporary atmospheric conditions could account for the whole phenomenon. The Two Prophets during the time of their testimony, which is just ended, shut up heaven, and the consequent drought heated the earth unusually. Mountain snows and glaciers melted away; rivers, brooks, lakes and other small bodies of water dried up. The air became oppressive with humidity intensifying the rays of the sun to a blistering heat. But how this heat would effect only the wicked is the difficulty. It must therefore be miraculous like the darkness which enveloped only the Egyptians (Exod. X. 22-23). This may then be limited to the countries that have voluntarily accepted Antichrist and murdered the Catholics.

Verse 9

The burning heat shall blister and scorch the skin. No one can furnish relief. Excessive thirst from lack of water shall increase the torture, and the ulcer of the first plague shall drive the wicked to frenzy. They have not the consolations of the martyrs, and so like the fallen angels they will rise up in rage against God blaspheming His name and refusing to repent of their sins or bear their pains patiently. They will not concede God the victory of winning their hearts. And they will try to explain the heat in a natural way. Their trust in Anichrist will wane, but pride will not permit them to acknowledge their disappointment or forego their allegiance to him. Such are the shackles of sin when the time of mercy has passed away. Antichrist is powerless to help them. After they spurned the grace of God and clung to sin, they must bear its consequences without any hope. Hell has begun for them on earth. (XIV. 10-11).

Fifth Plague.
Darkness Settles On the Capital Of Antichrist.

Verses 10-11

The Fifth Plague falls upon the capital of Antichrist. The Jews not killed by the earthquake in Jerusalem are converted by the ascension of the Two Prophets. Antichrist is rejected by them, and his capital is transferred to some other great city, possibly to great Babylon. This capital shall be steeped in an Egyptian darkness so dense that business must stop. The text says nothing about his presence in the city. but this may be presumed. The darkness lasts until his followers are famished with hunger. Their pains drive them to gnaw their tongues. Their dispair goads them to impotent ravings against God. The text seems to restrict the darkness to the "seat of the Beast" alone manifesting to the world that the plagues are for him; his followers are still called on to throw off allegiance to him so they may escape his destined doom. Although his standing before the world and his glory will fade and his power crumble away and he be powerless to help the antichristians who are in great distress from the first plague, they will still blaspheme God and refuse to do penance.

Verse 11

Antichrist may at this time hold a convention of his viceroys to adopt ways and means of saving his empire, after the Jews rebelled against him, and the havoc wrought by the plagues threatens to unseat him. The angels who inflict the plagues are probably in Jerusalem. After the ascension of the Prophets, the Church may have quietly established headquarters there and ordered the plagues upon the wicked from the Holy City (See Joel III. 16). Antichrist may be caught in his capital with his ten kings, and they may be all trapped there by the darkness unable to escape. His followers will not repent. They blaspheme the "God of heaven", the Eucharistic Christ, whom they give all credit for these plagues. But they will not submit to Him or believe in Him. Whether the other plagues continue in force is not stated, but the malignant ulcer of the first plague still tortures the wicked. Antichrist is as helpless as any of his followers. The physical pain of the ulcer added to the hunger brought by the darkness and the mental pangs of pride, hatred and rage against Christ and the Church make them continue their blasphemies, and with fiendish malice and deliberation they refuse to repent of their works and of their allegiance to Antichrist.

The darkness alludes to what Jeremias threatened upon the Jews for their obstinacy against his admonitions to repent (XIII. 16). Ezechiel also uses the figure of darkness (XXX. 18) to denote the completeness of God's judgment upon Egypt, the first head of the beast. Joel (II. 31) seems rather to mean a physical darkness like the Egyptian plague, which shall precede the "great and dreadful day of the Lord". The Jews shall thereafter be restored and converted. (Joel III. 16 to end.).

Sixth Plague. The Euphrates Is Dried Up.

Armies From The East.

Verse 12

The sixth plague is upon the River Euphrates, which is the symbol of the regions where the enemies of God's people resided in the Old Covenant. Those regions may be the stronghold of Antichrist, because the governments are Communistic. They would not accept Christianity, and they may have been convinced that their chance of independence and equality with western nations depends on the extirpation of the Church. The armies seem too numerous to cross the river over the bridges or in pontoons or ferryboats, and so the river is dried up for their convenience. The way is thus opened for them to gather for the great day in which Christ will annihilate all his enemies. The leaders of the military forces of Asia and all their antichristian troops will then be exterminated together with those marshalled by Antichrist and his prophet. It all recalls the assembling of the nations for the great day of the Lord as the prophets predict (Joel III. 14), and it refers to XIV. 20. It is significant that the sixth trumpet turns loose the angels bound in the Euphrates to begin the massacre of one third of mankind.

Some take a different view of this sixth plague. They consider it an invitation to the nations of the East to come to the defense of the Church and destroy the power of Antichrist, who has subjected them also. The nations faithful to the Church have fought a hard war against Antichrist, have been defeated and subjugated. The war wasted his resources and military power. All nations have suffered a great deal by now and all understand that the reason for the plagues are the blasphemies of Antichrist. The plagues have destroyed most of Antichrist's power, and the nations may see the time opportune for rebelling against his domination and for overthrowing his empire. The miracles of the Two Prophets and of the Church in the first five plagues have cleared up matters for them, for all people understand that the doctrines of Antichrist promulgated by the False Prophet have brought down upon the world all the plagues it had to suffer. Their hatred shall be roused against the cause of those evils. They may come to the defense of Jerusalem. The Church has been eminently manifested to have power far superior to Antichrist.

The verse alludes obscurely to the drying up of the Red Sea and the Jordan River at the approach of the Israelites. St. John may also have had in mind the capture of Babylon by Cyrus, who had canals dug up above the city to lead the waters of the Euphrates out of its channel and dry up the river. Then he marched his army into the city of Babylon through the empty bed of the river. (See Isaias XI. 16).

The idea of great forces from the East at this time to defend the Church does not seem tenable in the light of prophecy and the rest of this plague as stated in the text. Antichrist will have subjected the nations of the East through their military forces. Those forces are at his beck and call. He orders them to come forward against Jerusalem. He knows the Church is already established there, and he plans to kill the pope and the cardinals as he killed the Two Prophets and so end the power to inflict plagues. Thus he will free the world from the menacing might of the Church. That may be the prime reason for calling the kings of the East to battle. As the servant of the Dragon, he will blindly go into the trap.

The Prophet Joel quite evidently prophesied concerning this gathering of the armies of the world for the "great and dreadful day of the Lord" in the valley of Josaphat (III. 14) after the coming of the Holy Spirit (II. 28-30). Likewise Zacharias gives a vague description of the judgment of God upon the wicked, who shall fight against Jerusalem on the "great day of Almighty God" as depicted in the Apocalypse (XVI. 14; XIX. 19-21). The prophecy of Zacharias seems to indicate a conversion of the Jews and a rejection of Antichrist and thereafter unbroken peace for the Church (XIV. 8-11). The prophecy of Malachias gives a glimpse of the judgment upon the wicked as it is depicted here in the fourth, fifth and sixth plagues. In IV. 1, he seems to point to the fourth plague, IV. 2 to the fifth and IV. 3 to the sixth. But Elias is to appear before these plagues: "Behold I will send you Elias, the prophet, before the coming of the great and dreadful day of the Lord" (IV. 5). The faithful will hide during the height of the persecution but will come forth openly to practice their faith with the fifth plague (IV. 2). The plagues hinted at by Malachias would follow the work of Elias. And that prophecy would give a literal meaning to all that is stated in this chapter. The Fathers, namely Justin, Hippolytus, Tertullian, Origen, Hilary, Ambrose, Augustine, Chrysostom and others understood the prophet Malachias to refer to Elias, the Thesbite.

Evil Spirits Gather All Antichrist's Followers.

Verses 13-16.

Verse 13

While the armies of the East are moving westward across the Euphrates to their predestined doom, Satan realizing the nearness of his own undoing urges Antichrist and the False Prophet not to be idle. St. John sees the agencies by which they will try to persuade the kings and army leaders and rally them to their aid. He sees in the mouths of the dragon, the Beast and the False Prophet three unclean spirits under the appearance of frogs. The mouth is the organ of speech through which the widest public influence is wielded. This presence of the evil spirits denotes how active all agencies of propaganda in the empire of Antichrist will be through the world-powers, Antichrist and his Prophet. Since the dragon is the symbol of the anti-christian world powers, of which Satan is the soul, it will work in harmony with Antichrist and his Prophet to bend the wills of his subjects to his intentions and purposes again. The power of these devils will produce great "signs", as they did before the plagues, and will convince the wicked of his divinity. The spirits appear as frogs because the frog was counted among the unclean animals in the levitical law. (Lev. XL. 10, ff.).

Antichrist and his Prophet speaking with the wisdom of Satan will deceive his blinded dupes again, seduce and win the stricken unbelievers and attribute the plagues to natural causes. Nothing is said of the bloody sea and rivers. They would need to be changed back to natural water and the darkness would need to be ended or men would all die in the countries afflicted. Antichrist succeeds with his viceroys. Those who hold office in his empire obey his summons and draw up their forces for the final battle. All will understand his design to recapture Jerusalem and put an end to the Church. He could hardly transport any armies from the Americas so quickly, so his forces would need to be from Europe, Africa and western Asia. The armies from the East are already on the way. All will meet their doom outside the city. (XIV. 20). Jerusalem shall be overshadowed by the presence of the Lamb. Antichrist will bring his armies, airfleets, war vessels and war machinery of every kind into action, so that all war machinery and modern weapons of destruction might be destroyed with the wicked. Thereafter, disarmament and everlasting peace shall be easily attained.

This is not a war between nations but a war against Almighty God. For that reason it is directed by devils. But as was predicted by David (Ps. II. 2), Christ will be victorious. The battle is described in XIX. 11-21. The vision of it was described in XIV. 20, and the preparation for it is reviewed here at the pouring out of the sixth plague. "The Seer sees the whole process foreshortened . . . and the end, which is not yet, will be the breaking of the day of God" (H. B. Swete ad locum).

The "Great day of Almighty God" holds a very conspicuous

place in prophetic literature. The prophets obviously have the same day in view, the day on which the armies of Antichrist shall be annihilated, and evil shall be crushed. (Isa. XIII. 6, 9; Jer. XXX. 7; Ezech. XXX. 3; Joel. II. 11 & 31; Soph. II. 2; Zach. XII. 3; Mal. IV. 5). The prophets often mean any day on which God began His judgment for the defense of the good and the destruction of the wicked. That "great day" dawned when the first defeat was dealt the empire of Egypt. And every decisive defeat of these world-empires was again "the great day of Almighty God". All those days will converge in that one GREAT DAY on which Christ will win the last complete victory over the forces of Antichrist, in whose reign all evil organizations in the world shall be co-ordinated.

Verse 15

The words of this verse are spoken by Christ Himself. They are a solemn warning to all true believers not to consent to sin or be misled by the last efforts of Satan and his agents to win followers. They may presage death for some, when the forces of Antichrist are annihilated. But they point more likely to that earthquake of verse 18, which shall accompany the last battle. In that earthquake principally the city dwellers shall be killed. It shall be sudden and unexpected, and therefore all must be prepared for death. Perhaps some nations have thrown off the yoke of Antichrist and are re-organizing armies to fight him and regain their independence. The words would be a warning to the soldiers not to give way to the trying temptations of army life, because the wicked are still in the world and may try to seduce the soldiers. Verse fifteen with the solemn warning spoken by our Lord is inserted here while Antichrist and his agents are marshalling his forces for the final battle. It is therefore a last warning to all soldiers and all the faithful. It recalls what our Lord said to the bishop who lives in mortal sin (III. 3) and alludes to 2 Peter III. 10.

Verse 16

The meeting place of the armies is called in Hebrew Harmagedon. This is Mount Magedon. Zacharias (XII.) mentions the "plain of Mageddon", when he describes the supreme battle of the theocracy with the armies of the wicked, because Josias had been mortally wounded there (2 Par. XXXV. 22). The clause, "which in Hebrew is called Armagedon", refers us to the Old Testament for the use of the name. The name, "Magedon" recalls the "Mageddo" of the Septuagint, which was a royal Chaananite city and later belonged to the tribe of Manasses (Jud. I. 27). The canticle of Debbora in the Book of Judges (V. 19) celebrates the victory over Sisera, who had oppressed the chosen people for 20 years. He was slain "by the waters of Mageddo". Debbora sings words that might be applied to the coming victory over Antichrist at Armagedon. It matters little where this battle shall be fought, but perhaps Antichrist shall meet his doom on or near Mt. Mageddo. Or "the field of Mageddo", being near the scene of many ancient battles might have a cryptic meaning. It might mean that the great battle shall become another Mageddo, just as in modern times the scene of a nation's defeat is called its "Waterloo". The place where the forces of Antichrist shall be exterminated may therefore be kept a secret.

When Isaias (VIII. 6-9) foretells the ruin of the ten tribes for rejecting the house of David and leaning upon the kings of Syria, he seems to catch a glimpse of the armies of Antichrist, for he exultingly proclaims the victory of Israel over all enemies.

Verse 16 is connected with verse 12 by the intervening verses, since verses 13 and 14 are only an explanation of the willingness of great masses of the wicked to follow Antichrist, even after the manifest judgment of God in the first five plagues have held out to them every possible reason for withdrawing from his allegiance. And verse 15 is a warning to the faithful to be ready to suffer also, when the finishing stroke is administered to the stubborn votaries of evil.

Seventh Plague.

Final Judgments Of God On The Wicked Reviewed.

Verses 17-end.

If the last five verses of this chapter were taken as written in chronological order, verse after verse and sentence after sentence, the interpretation would be impossible. They mention some of the effects of the seventh trumpet, the great earthquake and the hail stated in XI. 19. The men who blaspheme God in XVI. 21 are evidently the wicked, and therefore the great battle in which they shall be killed is not yet over. Likewise, if the earthquake, in which all the cities of the Gentiles shall fall, came before the destruction of Babylon, this city would also fall, because the catastrophe is world-wide. If the cities of the world, especially the capitals of Antichrist's empire, are razed by an earthquake, would the wicked still assemble for the final battle? And again, the earthquake and hail would not be the finish of God's judgment, as verse 17 states they shall be. Therefore the last sentence in verse 19, relating to the punishment of Babylon, is inserted in that place as an introduction to the following two chapters, in which the destruction of the wicked city is fully described. Its destruction shall not be after the earthquake and hail but be the first part of the seventh plague. The assembled kings of the earth shall see the destruction of the city stated in XVII. 16 and described in chapter XVIII., while the preparations for the final battle are being completed.

Verse 17

When the seventh angel pours out his bowl upon the air, a voice is heard coming from the throne of God in the Church. This is probably the voice of God. It could be the same voice that ordered the plagues. It pronounces them complete. Sufficient punishment shall be inflicted and evil shall be wiped from the earth, when the effects of all the plagues are actuality. For the sake of the just no more plagues shall be poured out. Pouring the contents of the bowl upon the air pollutes the air and deranges the minds of the wicked. Instead of being the life-sustaining element, it will become a death-dealing force. It may instill into the minds of a large force of Antichrist's followers the desire to exterminate Babylon. All the elements are now perturbed by the plagues, and all shall aid in purifying the world of the evils that have so long corrupted it.

Verse 18

The lightnings, as in other parts of the Apocalypse, are the miracles wrought by the Church, and they may be abundant again to counteract the false miracles of the evil spirits at this time (XVI. 13). This may be necessary now to safeguard the faith and loyalty of many who are not well enough instructed to discern between true and false miracles, when confronted with only the false, and might be led astray by the prodigies of Satan. The voices are the preaching and instructions of bishops and priests explaining the falsity of Antichrist's signs and the truth of genuine miracles. The voices may also mean expressions of astonishment and assent from many people at the renewed appearance of true miracles. The thunders are warnings from the headquarters of the Church that the judgments are about to be finished and that all who follow the Beast shall share his fate. They are also anathemas against all lying doctrines, false miracles and persons who promote antichrist-worship. These lightnings, voices and thunders were last mentioned in XI. 19 and which are identical with those heard now. They are taken figuratively here as elsewhere, whilst "earthquake" and "hail" are physical phenomena as the other plagues.

In the Greek text, "earthquake", is in a separate clause modified by additional adjective clauses to emphasize its intensity. It will be greater than any that has occurred since men dwelt upon earth and will evidently be contemporaneous with the seizure of Antichrist and his prophet and their precipitation into the pool of fire (XIX. 20). The earthquake is not a local one like that of XI. 13. It will be more destructive than the greatest earthquakes of history. That such an earthquake is possible and even probable some day is admitted by all scientists. The centrifugal force set up by the earth's rotation can break the shell of the earth's crust around the equator and cause the land masses to slip that way flattening out the poles. In the fourth plague the sun radiates unusual volumes of heat due perhaps to great sunspots. Modern meteorologists connect sun-spots and intense heat on the earth's surface with storms and earthquakes. These phenomena may be brought about by the laws of nature, but be miraculous because they are inflicted at the command of the Church.

Verse 19

The "great city" is the same city distinguished by the same

name in XI. 8, Jerusalem. Yawning chasms shall divide the city into three parts. The cities of the Gentiles shall fall in this earthquake, i. e. the capitals of the nations subject to Antichrist and probably all large cities of his empire and the world. An earthquake of such dimensions will bring about universal misery. Everyone will look out for himself. Wealth, power and influence will vanish, and those who have depended on the service of others will be abandoned to their own helplessness. How will hospitals, insane asylums and orphanages fare? The country dwellers, physically, morally and spiritually rugged and sound will withstand the ravages of the earthquake and will repopulate the earth. God's remembrance of Babylon is inserted here to introduce the topic of the next two chapters. That prophecy will be fulfilled in the first part of the seventh plague, after the armies are mobilized for the last battle (See Jer. XXV. 15). The hatred of the nations against the city that has provoked the anger of God to inflict the first five plagues will be executed by the airforces of Antichrist before the last attack on the Church.

Verse 20

The verse carries the same ideas as VI. 14. There the islands and mountains are moved out of their places, whilst here they cannot be found any more. (See Isa. XIII. 13). St. John has Isaias' description of the desolation of Babylon in mind. Mountains in prophetical imagery are kingdoms and empires, (XVII. 9; Isa. XLI. 15-16) and islands are dependencies or provinces. In chapter VI., the moving of the mountains meant the establishment of new kingdoms by the barbarians after the overthrow of the Roman Empire; and moving the islands out of their places the change of seats of provincial governments to other cities. All kingdoms subject to Antichrist will be overthrown in the revolution that follows his damnation; or they will naturally disappear in the earthquake and death of all his followers. Justice may be meted out to the murderers by popular juries. The armed forces will fall with Antichrist. The moving of the islands and mountains in chapter VI. suggested that something of the Roman Empire would remain, and this had been indicated by the ten horns in the prophecy of Daniel (Dan. VII. 7). But here islands flee away, and mountains cannot be found any more; nothing shall remain of Antichrist's empire because nothing is worth preserving; it shall be utterly annihilated, and its influence shall vanish after all vestiges shall be cleared out of the world. In prophetical language, political revolutions, the overthrow of kingdoms are called an earthquake. (Agg. II. 22; Isa. XXIV. 17-25). Antichrist will complete the de-christianization of the governments which has been on foot for centuries. And when the Church wins the victory over him, and he is buried in hell, all he has established shall be buried in oblivion. Cities are the centers of culture and of vice, and the antichristian order of the world will be centered there. When they all fall at the same time, they can get no relief or outside assistance and will be left to their fate. Then will the Church come forward and take the re-construction of the world in hand.

If the earthquake results from a sliding of the land masses towards the equator, the islands would seem to be fleeing away the smaller ones sinking beneath the waves. The contours of the large islands and the continents would be altered. Climates the world over would be transmuted and living conditions too. In a universal earthquake, the earth's surface would be broken so that well-known mountains could not be found any more. The land masses might rise so much around the equator as to lower the temperature there. And great cracks might be sprung in the ocean floor around the poles raising the ocean temperatures. Rivers might change their course and flow backwards. Climates might be more equalized. There are incalculable possibilities in so world-wide an earthquake. It might bring paradisiac conditions during the thousand years that shall follow the reign of Antichrist. The continental blocks that were so many geological eons in the building shall certainly not be submerged but continue to be the dwelling places of the human race. The heat now received by the earth from the sun's rays would be sufficient to produce sub-tropical climates over the whole earth, if it were equally distributed. Such a climate is best suited to bring out the finest spiritual development of character.

In a very fragmentary prophecy, Zacharias describes a breaking up of the massive hills around Jerusalem and the cutting of a chasm through Mt. Olivet (XIV. 4). The logical sequence of his prophecies seems to be that chapter eleven foretells a temporary rejection of the Jews for their pride and indifference and coupled with it the betrayal of Christ and the subjection of the people to foreign domination; chapter twelve relates the victories in Maccabean times and the revival of the true worship; and the last part of the chapter seems to relate the mourning over the death of Judas Machabeus or of Christ; chapter thirteen predicts the founding of the Church of the Messias in Jerusalem, the death of two thirds of the Jews and the conversion of the other third, which shall suffer in the fire of a persecution and be refined as silver; chapter fourteen in verses one and two narrates the taking and sacking of Jerusalem, and in three to seven a war in which Christ shall defend the city, whilst an earthquake splits Mount Olivet, and darkness enfolds the army of the enemy, "which is that day known to the Lord". The description of "that day" is continued in verses 12 to 15. The verses from 7 to 12 promise days of unclouded happiness and unending peace for Jerusalem and the world; and Jerusalem is the center of God's kingdom. Zacharias' prophecy is very fragmentary and the interpretations of it by the Fathers differ widely.

Verse 21

As the earthquake is a real convulsion of the earth's crust razing cities and mountains, the hail in the same context should also be real. Ezechiel (XIII. 11) writes of a metaphorical hail, whilst Exodus (IX. 23-24) and Josue (X. II) relate the flaying of the enemies of God's people with a real hail. The weight of the stones in our hail is hundred pounds or more. It seems naturally impossible for the air to hold clumps of ice until they freeze to such size and weight. So the hail may be a shower of meteorites or a rain of bombs from an air squadron. The hail will fall upon the kings and armies of Antichrist and kill them all.

The wicked rise up to blaspheme God for the plague of the hail. If it comes down on the armies of Antichrist only, the blaspheming is restricted to them. But if the hail is world-wide like the earthquake, it would need to be a continuous shower of meteorites. The good would then also suffer, but they will not blaspheme God. Verse fifteen really intimates danger in some form or other for the lives of the good as well as the bad. The danger for them, however, seems to be from the earthquake, the hail being unloaded on the armies attacking Jerusalem. The wicked blaspheme because they remain impenitent. They expect an earthly heaven such as Socialism preaches; they placed their trust and confidence in Antichrist, and they will not repent of their vices or their pride. They will ask for no mercy but will defy God to His face. XIV. 20 tells how appalling the massacre will be. And the hail will be the last and finishing stroke. (See Isa. XXX. 30).

CHAPTER XVII.

Westminster Version

And one of the seven angels who had the seven 1. vials came and spoke to me, saying: 'Come, I will show thee the judgment of the great harlot who sitteth upon many waters, with whom the kings of the earth did commit 2. fornication, and the dwellers upon the earth were made drunk with the wine of her fornication'.

And he bore me away in spirit into the wilderness. 3. And I beheld a woman sitting upon a scarlet beast, full of blasphemous names, and having seven heads and ten horns.

The woman was arrayed in purple and scarlet, 4. and glittered with gold and precious stones and pearls. She held in her hand a golden cup, full of abominations and of the impurities of her fornication.

And upon her forehead was written a mystic 5. name, 'BABYLON THE GREAT', the mother of the harlots and of the abominations of the earth.

I saw the woman drunken with the blood of 6. the saints and with the blood of the martyrs of Jesus; and seeing her, I greatly wondered.

And the angel said to me, 'Wherefore dost 7. thou wonder? I will tell thee the mystery of the woman, and of the beast which carrieth her, and hath the seven heads and the ten horns.

The beast which thou sawest, was, and is not; 8. it is about to come up from the bottomless pit, and it goeth to destruction. And the dwellers upon the earth shall wonder – they whose name is not written from the foundation of the world in the book of life – when they see the beast, because it was and is not, and is to come.

Here there is need of an understanding that 9. hath wisdom. The seven heads are seven mountains whereon the woman sitteth.

They are also seven kings: five are fallen, 10. one now is, the other hath not yet come, and when he shall come, he must remain but a little time.

And the beast which was and is not, is itself 11. the eighth, and is of the seven, and goeth to destruction.

And the ten horns which thou sawest, are ten 12. kings that have not yet received a kingdom, but they are to receive authority for one hour as kings, together with the beast.

These have one purpose, and their power and 13. authority they give over to the beast.

These will battle with the Lamb, and they 14. shall be conquered by the Lamb, because he is the Lord of lords, and the King of kings, and those that are with him, called and chosen and faithful, shall conquer them'.

And he said to me, 'The waters which thou 15. sawest, where the harlot sitteth, are peoples and multitudes and nations and tongues.

And the ten horns which thou sawest, and the 16. beast, these shall
hate the harlot, and they shall make her desolate and naked, and they
shall eat her flesh and consume her with fire.

For God hath put it into their hearts to 17. carry out his purpose, and
to be of one mind among themselves, and give their kingdom over to the
beast, until the words of God shall be fulfilled.

And the woman whom thou sawest is the great 18. city which
holdeth sway over the kings of the earth.'

VII. THE GREAT HARLOT AND THE BEAST

1. Description Of Babylon, The Great Harlot.

Chapter XVII.

Verses 1-6.

Verses 1 and 2

The condemnation of Great Babylon is so important that it calls for a special treatise. One of the angels, probably the one who poured out the seventh bowl, reveals her destiny to the Seer enabling him to give a graphic description of her judgment. His word invites St. John to his direction so that he might witness the execution of the judgment from a favorable viewpoint. Her annihilation is decreed.

A harlot is given to fornication. Ezechiel (XXIII.) calls Israel and Juda harlots, because they practiced the idolatry of the pagan nations bordering on Israel. Fornication and adultery in prophetical language mean apostasy from the true faith and from God. Hence this GREAT harlot is a city whose apostasy from the true faith is a monstrous thing. This may point to Rome. Rome is the Holy City of Christ, the center of His eternal kingdom, as Jerusalem was the center of the theocracy. And the apostasy of this city, and her becoming the head of an empire that would lead all possible nations and peoples into antichrist-worship would indeed merit for her the title of THE GREAT HARLOT. The apostles called ancient Rome "Babylon" (1 Peter V. 13). So the conclusion is near that the great harlot of the future shall be Rome. However, in this narration, St. John uses ancient pagan Rome as the model for his portrait of the Babylon of the future. And whichever city it shall be, it will obviously be one that was once entirely Catholic, apostatized from the true faith and became the capital of the kingdom that leads all nations into Antichrist-worship. Primasius says: "meretricem vocans, quia relicto Creatore daemonibus se prostituit". (Swete, p. 213).

The clause, "who sitteth upon many waters", does not point to a great seaport that commands the oceans. The explanation is contained in verse 15, where the waters are stated to be nations that have made common cause with the God-less city and have joined her in sin and vice, in persecution of the Church and the worship of Antichrist, his image and his name. These nations have submitted to the leadership of Babylon during the reign of Antichrist and have been led into the blasphemy of emperor-worship by the False Prophet (See XIII. 15-17; Jer. LI. 13). This clause is filled with a dour foreboding for Babylon. At the appointed time, these many peoples will arise to throw off her corrupting and ruinous hegemony and condemn her for all the crimes of the world.

"The kings of the earth" are the viceroys of Antichrist and are allied with great Babylon. They will follow the leadership of the False Prophet in declaring their final and full independence from God and in worshipping Antichrist, his image and his name. The fornication of which the kings are guilty is a detestable barter of their soul's salvation for the glory of an ephemeral position in the empire of Antichrist and the prostitution of their intellect and their honor for his approval, when they worship him as their god. The consequence will be a life stained with immorality and crime. These kings of the earth are contrasted with the unspotted virgins and all who have led an unsullied life and are followers of the Lamb, the Kings of kings.

"The inhabitants of the earth" are the people who obey the False Prophet, apostatize from Christ and God and willingly submit to the worship of Antichrist. His doctrines intoxicate their brains and deprive them of their true intellectual discernment. Instead of turning their thoughts and hopes to the glorious prospects of immortality, they turn them earthward to the enjoyment of sensual pleasures. They shall not be able to distinguish between true miracles and the false ones wrought by Antichrist and his prophet, because the false principles of Antichrist shall blind and mislead them. Perhaps the reaping of excessive unjust profits shall overwhelm them with wealth and debauch them with luxury. The darkening of the mind and dulling of the conscience shall follow. Their immediate reward for worship of Antichrist is earthly felicity, and for this they surrender themselves like persons hypnotized. The rejection of their fealty to Christ, whose revelations and grace enlighten the mind and sober the will, is the wine of the harlot's fornication, in whose spell they blindly obey the mandates of the

False Prophet and incur a spiritual stupor wherein they desire nothing but the unrestrained indulgence of their appetites.

Verse 3

St. John is transported into the desert as St. Paul was transported into paradise (2 Cor. XII. 4). The same Greek word is in both texts. He may have changed the standpoint from which he began to behold this vision, but he was not therefore carried away from the Island of Patmos. The force of inspiration elevated his sense of sight, so that the angel could bring before his view what God had sent him to reveal.

A "wilderness", as explained in XII. 6 and 14, is a region severed from God, is in spiritual desolation given over to atheism or idolatry. Primasius says: "desertum ponit divinitatis absentiam, cuius praesentia paradisus est". (Swete, p. 214). A desert is a picture of death in the midst of a living world of plant life. This vision of the desert is placed in a future time, when God may be banished from a part of the world, which shall then be spiritually dead, because it is God-less. Even this was not rrue of ancient paganism. And this indicates that the vision was not of Roman times.

The first object noticed by the Seer was a woman riding a scarlet-colored beast. The color is emblematic of a world-wide power that shall appear when the vision becomes actuality. The beast carries the harlot, who is dependent on his power to corrupt the world and lead the kings of the earth into fornication. Its color is the same as that of the dragon (XII. 3), and it has manifested the traits of the dragon and labored to serve his designs. The color has been interpreted to represent royalty, imperial splendor and magnificence or bloodshed and the rule by violence. But like the name of the harlot, it probably contains a mystery to be revealed in its time. It may foreshadow Communism. The beast seems to be the same that appeared in thirteen one (XIII. 1). But then it was not scarlet colored, and only its heads bore names of blasphemy. The present vision reveals a different aspect of the same beast.

At its first mention, the beast came out of the abyss (XI. 7). At its next appearance, it came out of the sea (XIII. 1). In both places it was the person of Antichrist. The origin of his power and authority were there revealed. St. John portrayed his personal traits, intentions, ambitions and success. In the present chapter the Seer presents him in his historical connection with the ancient empires, whose emperors claimed divine attributes and prerogatives and demanded divine worship for an assumed divine descent. He stands forth now in his finished character as a scarlet-colored beast with the same number of heads and horns as in chapter XIII. He will not only claim divine descent but will claim divinity for himself, as St. Paul stated, "showing himself as if he were God" (2 Thess. 11. 4). His whole body is now covered with names of blasphemy, of which his career and character are a personification. The few condensed clauses show his demerits when the time of his condemnation is at hand. The seven heads are explained in verse 9 and 10 and the ten horns in verse 12.

Verse 4

The description of the woman alludes to the description of Tyre by Ezechiel (XXVIII. 13). She is arrayed in all earthly ornaments and splendor in strong contrast with the woman of XII. 1, who is clothed in heavenly simplicity and beauty. Her robe is of purple and scarlet. Purple is the color of royalty, but its combination with scarlet makes it a mystic symbol. (See Isa. I. 18). Her royalty and power to rule shall therefore have some dependence on the scarlet beast and shall be derived from the same source, ultimately the dragon. A part of her ostentatious adornment is glittering gold, jewels and pearls. She is decked in all these proofs of unlimited wealth. The masses of gold proclaim her power to command the trade of the world. The choicest possessions of the exceedingly rich are precious stones and exquisite pearls. Pearls are obtained from the sea, stones from the earth. She is thus portrayed as mistress of land and sea. And all departments of the world yield up their wealth to her. By this wealth and splendor, she glorifies her corruption and vices so that her boon companions and paramours, the apostate nations of the world, feel no repugnance for the abominations into which she leads them. The gilded debauchery of upper society appears alluring and enjoyable. It is free from the sordidness with which vice enwraps the poor. Savages experience this sordidness of paganism, idolatry and superstition but not so the inhabitants of rich Babylon.

She has a golden cup in her hand. In Jeremias (LI. 7), ancient Babylon is itself the golden cup with which Almighty God brought all idolatrous nations into a drunken stagger. New Babylon will drink the cup of pleasure after leading the nations into apostasy from Christ and God (See Ezech. XXIII. 35-37). The golden cup calls to mind the libations in honor of the gods, through which the votaries of paganism communicated with the demons, and contrasts it thus with the chalice of the eucharistic Sacrifice. The sacrificial feast of New Babylon will be the worship of Antichrist and his statue, which will bring untold wealth to the city and furnish the means of unrestricted indulgence in every sensual pleasure and vice. Her philosophy will be diametrically opposed to Christianity; and to those who submit to Antichrist, it will permit the throwing off of all restraints. The "abomination" of her fornication is ritual impurity, which compels all who would dwell in Babylon and reap the golden harvest to worship the statue of Antichrist (XIII. 15-17). Phallic worship may be added and may flaunt a ceaseless carnival of debauchery.

This verse alludes to the Church of Pergamus, which was situated where the "seat of Satan" was, because it was the principal metropolis of emperor-worship in Asia and of the worship of Dionysus and the serpent. In alluding to Pergamus, the verse recalls the power of ancient Rome to enforce emperor-worship and the worship of the deities of Rome. If a victorious general returned to the imperial city, he had to offer sacrifice to the divinity of the emperor and to the gods of Rome. The False Prophet will also through the influence of his capital city, Babylon, enforce idolatrous worship and through it lead the world into the depth of Satan's filthiness.

Verse 5

The name of the harlot was written on her forehead. Seneca ("Contro. V. i") says that Roman harlots wore a label with their name on their foreheads. That would make this verse point to Rome, since this woman is the figure of the great city. St. Peter (I Peter, V. 13) writes from Babylon, by which he surely means Rome. In the second century "Babylon" commonly meant Rome in Christian circles. "Rome does not, of course, exhaust St. John's conception of Babylon" (H. B. Swete. p. 223). In St. John's description of Babylon, the conspicuous traits of ancient pagan Rome appear as the most prominent features. Babylon is not ancient Rome, but a new Rome that has a resemblance to the ancient center of idolatry and Godlessness. This new Rome is entirely cut off from God, is in a spiritual desert.

The name, BABYLON THE GREAT, is a mystery. The woman is a symbol of Babylon, yet the name itself is a mystery, implying something different from what it commonly conveyed. After the catholic epistle of St. Peter was published in all the churches, everyone understood the application of the name, Babylon. But this time the readers must consider the mystery contained in the name. The city is not the same city then understood to be Rome under that mysterious name. The name designated the character of the city alluding to the prophecies in which the city of that name is doomed to destruction, because all the enemies of God shall congregate there (Zach V. 11). The name shall remain a mystery until the prophecy merges into fulfillment.

With her name St. John gives her most conspicuous traits. She is the "mother of the harlots", of apostasy from Christ and God. She begot this apostasy by her doctrines and influence leading and compelling other leading cities to become her daughters in apostasy and their ruling citizens to consent to her religious cult and become drunk out of her golden cup of abominations. God's enemies have ever demanded the right to tyrannize over the true believers but have never tolerated being ruled by them. The worshippers of Antichrist may be by far the minority in the world but by the power of New Babylon and that of Antichrist may easily dominate the world for the time allotted.

Verse 6

Added to the sins of apostasy and idolatry is cruelty. Babylon is glutted with the blood of Christians. The image of the Beast speaking demands the death of all who will not adore it. When the beast-image speaks, the edicts of persecution shall be promulgated from Babylon and urged on all kings who rule under Antichrist. Babylon will then revel in an orgy of bloodshed exceeding everything heretofore witnessed by the world. It is the blood of saints who have endured all the years of Antichrist's oppression and have atoned for all their faults. They are the martyrs of Jesus whose belief in His divinity has stood firm and unflinching in the face of all false miracles and attained sanctity by shedding their blood for Him. St. John was also a witness (I. 2). In Greek the same word stands for "witness", "testimony" and "martyr" (XI. 3, 7 and I. 2). After the lapse of many centuries, the faith of Jesus is as strong as it was in the days of St. John. Cornelius a Lapide says of this vision: "idem fiet in fine mundi cum Roma, ad paganismum rediens, Christum et Christianos, ac maxime Pontificem persequetur, expellet vel occidet". The title of the harlot city, BABYLON THE GREAT, leads us to the conclusion that it shall be Rome. This verse certainly alludes to the edicts of persecution under Nero and Domitian. St. John must have turned his thoughts to Rome, when he understood this woman to be the symbol of a city. But the name must have perplexed him, because Babylon was long before a heap of ruins, and it had not shed the blood of our Lord's martyrs. He knew for sure that he was dealing with future history. Therefore the name, the guilt and the woman's character did not seem to agree.

2. Symbolic Meaning Of The Beast.

Verses 7-17.

Verse 7

The angel saw the amazement that clouded the mind of the Seer. He asks him why he wonders but does not wait for his answer. St. John had no doubt expected to see a city in ruins after the vision of the great earthquake. That there was a change in the viewpoint of time, he possibly had not noticed. He could not surmise what this woman full of vigor, splendor and power might represent. The angel tells, as an introduction to his explanation, the salient features of this vision, namely: 'the mystery of the woman' . . . 'the beast which carried her' . . . 'the seven heads and the ten horns'. When these are clearly expounded, the vision may be understood.

Verse 8

The first words of the angel reveal the non-existence of the beast when this vision would become actuality. The time is shortly before the beast "shall come up from the bottomless abyss". The balance of this chapter gives evidence of the existence of the harlot city before the beast appears again having wealth and influence. But the world-wide dominion and might shall be given her by the Beast. Perhaps the city persecuted the Church before Antichrist appears having possibly taken the leadership in some atheistic movement that had long grown in the world. The movement may have developed independently of the city, which espoused its cause and became its leading center and fiercest promoter.

This chapter can be explained reasonably only if the beast is considered under a twofold aspect, as Antichrist himself and as his empire. This verse avers that it was, and it is not, and yet it shall be. Those who hold that the beast was merely the Roman empire are sadly illogical, for this was in existence while St. John received the revelations. This vision is therefore of some future time when the empire no longer exists, but just before the beast-empire re-appears. As a political entity, the beast existed in the days of St. John embodied in the Roman Empire. Satan was the animus of that beast, and it served his purposes, just as Antichrist shall in future. As a religious organization it received its inspiration from Satan. He animated it to oppose all that is God by subjecting the nations and peoples of the earth to Roman idolatry and emperor-worship through the military and civil power of Rome. The last form of its political existence was thus the Roman Empire.

The beast does not exist as an organized world-empire when Antichrist is born. It shall come up out of the bottomless abyss into its final short-lived existence when Satan gives him "his might and his throne and great authority" (XIII. 2). This demonstrates that it could not be re-born except through Satan's power and under God's permission. It shall then have its fully developed satanic character and might. And this beast as a world-empire shall be of satanic birth in a twofold way. His might, throne and authority shall be derived directly from Satan, on whom his passing success shall depend. And again, Antichrist as a human being shall come up "out of the sea" (XIII. 1), i. e. he shall be a product of the antichristian world of his time. His environment and education shall make him love everything evil and opposed to Christ and God and hate everything true, good and virtuous. The character of Antichrist shall give fullest expression to the spirit of infidelity.

The present chapter alludes obscurely to Nero and Domitian as types of the Beast. But the beast of this chapter is primarily the *empire* of Antichrist, which shall come into existence at the time of this vision. The beast is the God-less world-empire, identified with the Roman Empire, personified in the first two persecuting emperors, and is the same that existed in the world-empires of past ages and shall come to fullness of life again in the empire of Antichrist.

The explanation that the assassination of Domitian is meant by the phrase, "was, and is not", is impossible in the light of the whole context of the prophecy. This vèrse clearly refers to XI. 7, where the beast ascending out of the abyss is identified with the beast of this chapter. The event in chapter XI. is the climax of the second woe, which began with the 200,000,000 horsemen. St. John in the light of divine inspiration or even by his knowledge of current history would place that event into the far distant future. He would not have made the mistake of placing this chapter in his own times or even in the near future of Roman times. And the myth of a "Nero redivivus" is equally as impossible. The "mystery" of the woman shall remain forever unintelligible if interpreters insist on making St. John responsible for the belief in the fulfillment of an impossible legend, such as the Nero redivivus. We would have an inspired prophecy that was not fulfilled and was impossible of fulfillment. If interpreters want to insist on putting the fulfillment of this chapter in the times of the Roman Empire, they will entangle themselves in inexplicable riddles. If, however, the context of the whole Apocalypse is kept in view and applied to the course of history, an explanation is not impossible or contradictory.

The empire of Antichrist is foredoomed to complete annihilation, never to re-appear in the world. After the world has become drunk with the wine of apostasy from Christ and experienced the full consequence of this debauch, it will nevermore wish for the return of paganism and the penalties God inflicts for its enjoyment. The Greek word used to express the destruction of the beast in this verse carries the equivalence of annihilation; when the beast means Antichrist personally, it shows his end in the pool of fire (XIX. 20), where he shall be tormented forever. When St. John saw this beast earlier in the revelations, it was the person of Antichrist (XI. 7; XIII. 1-8).

The wicked whose names are not written in the Book of Life will be filled with wondering awe and with happy glee over the re-appearance of the beast in the world. This last part of the verse is a repetition of XIII. 3 and 8, proving that this beast is inseparable from the one of chapter XIII. The present reference to the former identical statement also elucidates the significance of the wound to death borne by the sixth head. The wound was truly a death-wound, which ended the existence of the beast until its resurrection from the abyss. All admirers of the beast will welcome its advent, because under its dominion they can enjoy vice without restraint. They will admire its resurrection after the Church destroyed it. And all enemies of the Church will admire it for being her powerful and deadly enemy. All materials for the political composition of the beast are prepared in the world, and Antichrist at his appearance need only to organize all evil agencies to his purpose to establish the political power of the erstwhile beast.

Those who want to see in this beast the Roman Empire only and in its heads the emperors will lose their way in a maze of contradictions. Tradition accepted by the Church affirms positively that the Apocalypse was written at the end of the 1st century, during the reign of Domitian, who was the eleventh emperor. Galba would be the sixth. Those who ignore the verdict of tradition want to put the composition of the book in the reign of Vespasian. But then we have nine emperors. Again they want to exclude from the list Galba, Otho and Vitellius. This arbitrary way of solving the difficulties leaves the short reign, the reign of Antichrist to Titus. He would be the Beast, who will according to the Apocalypse rule three years and a half. Now Titus reigned less than two years. So the text as well as historical facts must be contradicted right and left, if the fulfillment of this vision is timed during the existence of the Roman empire. As has been stated before, the Roman empire was only the historical background upon which the vision of the beast is depicted.

In the prophecy of Daniel (VII. 7-23-25), the Roman empire shall be dissolved into ten principal kingdoms or empires, or as Hippolytus explains, into ten democracies. Since the Roman empire was antichristian, the horns would also be non-christian. When Antichrist is due, the dechristianization of the governments grown out of the Roman empire shall be complete. The elements of which the beast shall be composed shall then be on earth but shall not take form until Antichrist by his infernal power shall give it actual existence. The admiration of the wicked will then be elicited by the ten horns promulgating and enforcing antichristian and atheistic legislation.

The last clause of the original text amounts to "it will arrive". St. John writes of the time in which it has not yet arrived, but he points forward to the arrival and the consequent admiration it shall receive. St. Jerome left this last clause out of the Vulgate, possibly because it appeared a contradiction to him, probably because he identified the beast with the Roman empire. The clause in the original, however, is important, for it shows that the Roman empire is only one of the heads of the beast, and that empire shall pass away leaving the beast without actual existence to be re-born out of the bottomless abyss.

Verse 9

According to the suggestion in the first sentence of this verse, more than human sagacity is needed to understand the mystery of the beast, even after the interpretation is given. It may be understood only in the light of divine revelation. The description is allegorical and could be intelligible by the aid of Old and New Testament prophecies. The fourth beast of Daniel had some similarity with this beast, but the differences are very marked. Daniel's beast has only one head but ten horns; this beast has seven heads and ten horns. The seven heads are kings as well as the ten horns. The head uses the horns for its needs and purposes. The allegory is very mystifying, yet there is surely a difference between the kings represented by the heads and those represented by the horns. To escape the difficulty involved in the different kind of kings, some English translations have "there are seven kings". Such a translation, however, is not from the Greek approved text. The correct translation is, "they are seven kings".

The seven heads represent mountains which again mean kings and in turn symbolize dynasties or empires. The mountains allude to the seven hills upon which ancient Rome was built but are symbols of kings and kingdoms. The very exposition given by the angel is thus clothed in mystery. In prophetical terms, a mountain stood for a powerful kingdom and especially a world-empire. Jeremias says to Babylon: "Behold I come against thee, thou destroying mountain, saith the Lord, which corruptest the whole world" (LI. 25; See also Zach. IV. 7 and Isa. XLI. 15). Babylon was not built upon a mountain. The word here evidently is the symbol of world-empires. The stability of these empires depended upon the ruling dynasties, and hence the emperors are identified with the empires themselves. The seven heads stand for the dynasties of the seven world-empires. They do not, as verse 10 clearly states, exist at the same time, as do the ten horns, but successively.

The woman "sitteth" upon these seven mountains but also upon many nations and peoples and lastly upon the beast. To picture it graphically, the mountains are established upon the waters, the beast stands upon those mountains and the woman rides the beast. Otherwise the description would be absurd, for the woman would be sitting upon the beast at the same time upon seven mountains and also upon many waters. The figure is somewhat grotesque, for the beast has seven heads and these are mountains. All this dissuades us from giving a literal interpretation to the vision as the Seer describes it. The woman, the beast and the heads are symbols of other things, of future historical facts that shall be bound up with the past. The language reveals the following: the antichristian world-power shall evolve out of seven successive world-empires and shall subject the unbelieving and pagan peoples and nations of the world; the world-controlling *empire* of Antichrist shall be established through the political influence of Babylon but shall be vastly augmented by the satanic power of false miracles derived from Antichrist and exercised by the False Prophet; the empire shall reproduce and unite in itself all that the other world-empires possessed, shall rule the same and vastly more territory and shall be the fullest development of political evil that Satan could produce; the empire shall support the city and kingdom of the False Prophet, which shall be the re-constructed pagan Roman empire; this city shall contrive to subject the peoples and nations to Antichrist by his aid and shall maintain a suzerainty over the governments of those nations; she shall lead them into the lowest depths of moral depravity into which mankind could be led and will therefore be the mother of all evils; she shall have for her foundation the seven world-empires, because she and her kingdom are carried by Antichrist. The woman is not part of the beast but is a being distinct from it. The relation of Rome to the empire was such, that Rome was the head of the empire, which had its support from the ruling dynasty. Here the woman is supported by the beast and depends on it not the beast on the woman. The impossibility of holding this woman to be Ancient Rome, the beast the empire and the heads the emperors can be clearly and easily comprehended by anyone.

Verse 10

In verse ten, St. John turns his attention from the beast to the heads; to the whole series of successive world-dynasties. He therefore changes his viewpoint from the future to the present. In explaining the significance of the heads this verse clears up the meaning of verse nine. The seven heads are seven anti-God empires. Five of them have passed away. One of the world-empires exists; this is Rome, the sixth head. The seventh empire has not yet come, and when it appears, it shall exist only a short time. That is the empire of Antichrist.

The beast existed in and through all the ancient world-empires and shall show fullest development and expression in the empire and person of Antichrist. His empire shall embody, promote and propagate much more extensively idolatry, caesarism or state supremacy, immorality and devil-worship and persecution of God's people than the ancient empires did. The beast existed unceasingly from the ascendancy of Egypt as a world-empire until the end of the pagan Roman dominion. Each empire grew up in the shadow of its predecessor and attacked, crushed and ended the world-dominion of that predecessor. But the beast has ceased to exist since pagan Rome fell and shall come back to life when Antichrist resurrects it by satanic power. Yet it exists potentially in the *ten horns* (Dan. VII. 24) into which the sixth, the Roman empire was dissolved. Some of the ten horns seen by Daniel may be existing in our times.

Verse 11

In this verse St. John returns to the time in which the beast does not exist. This verse is complicated in English; in Greek it is clear. The clause, "the same is also the eighth", refers to the person of Antichrist. The rest of the verse points to his empire. The English translation, "is itself the eighth" is misleading, because the pronoun "itself" modifies "beast". In Greek "τὸ θηρίον", "the beast", is neuter gender, while the pronoun αὐτὸς is masculine, showing that not the "beast" is the "eighth", but Antichrist considered as a person apart from his empire is the EIGHTH. His power, which is of satanic origin, is personal and is the means by which he establishes the seventh empire. This power is independent of the empire, is not conferred by it, because it is from the throne of Satan. Therefore he is something above and distinct from his empire as a ruling power. This chapter treats of Antichrist only in relation to his empire. Chapter XIII. treats directly of his person and indirectly of his empire. In Greek the clause clearly refers to Antichrist, while in some English translations it cannot be discerned unless it be translated, as some have it, "he himself is also the eighth".

Antichrist himself as a human being endowed with satanic might and authority is the Beast and the EIGHTH something, because he is the culmination and personification, the head and most complete expression of all evil that shall ever exist on earth. He has thus another reason and mode of existence in being the embodiment of sin fully developed in a human being, as Christ was the embodiment of virtue and perfection. Thus the text does not say that he is the eighth head, but his empire is one of the seven heads. He is himself something distinct from those empires, pre-existed, as it were, in the great sin of emperor-worship throughout the whole series of empires, which altogether constituted the empire of Satan, and whereof his own shall be the highest development. Likewise his authority being of satanic origin and personal is something above and distinct from his empire and constitutes an EIGHTH or spiritual empire directing all military and civil resources in his empire and that of Babylon. That the Beast is foredoomed to a speedy end and complete annihilation is repeated for a purpose. It shall come out of the abyss to fulfill its destiny and then be annihilated. The faithful need not fear the beast exceedingly.

Verse 12

The TEN HORNS of the beast may stand for exactly ten governments, states or kingdoms, but they may stand for a larger number. They begin to exist when Antichrist appoints the kings as his viceroys. The time of this verse is just before the ascendance of Antichrist, for the kings have not been appointed. The nations evidently exist long before this time. They will submit to Antichrist, or he will subdue them and appoint his own rulers. This shall be his empire and "great strength". By his satanic authority, he will not be able to injure any faithful member of the Church, since the Two Witnesses will punish those who will try to injure them in this way. But Antichrist will be able to persecute and kill the Catholics by his military and civil authority and might. As a beast uses ITS horns for defense and attack, so will Antichrist attack his opponents by the help of his viceroys, armies, police-courts and henchmen in the kingdoms subject to him.

The term "one hour" may denote the brevity of their reign signifying perhaps the three and a half years of Antichrist's dominion. But it may signify, "at a certain hour", i. e. the hour definitely fixed in God's foreknowledge. The ten horns are simultaneously present on the head of the beast holding their position as long as the Beast is permitted to dominate the world. The crowns which the horns wore in XIII. 1 are not mentioned here, possibly to indicate that these kings are not independent monarchs but subjects of Antichrist.

If the horns are taken to be the barbarian nations that destroyed and occupied the Roman empire, the "mystery" is greater than ever. For with the destruction of Rome the empire was dissolved. The text says that the horns shall receive a kingdom "WITH the beast". The barbarians did not rule *with* the Roman government but destroyed it. The Vulgate translation using "post" is not grammatical. St. Jerome in translating the Greek text into Latin wove his own interpretation into it by this grammatical error, for he may have considered the barbarian nations which overran the empire in his time the ten horns. But the Beast still exists after Babylon falls in chapter XVIII., for he is cast into the pool of fire in chapter XIX. while making war on Christ. The kings are gathered with him there and are all slain. In the present verse therefore "kings" does not mean kingdoms but persons appointed by Antichrist to rule under him. And Beast means Antichrist in person.

The antichristian empire is thus viewed under a threefold aspect: The first is under the aspect of the seventh head, the last world-empire created by the dragon to oppose God; the second is the form of the ten kingdoms through which Antichrist and the dragon will work out their designs: the third is the whole beast embodying all phases of the antichristian and anti-God empires throughout the ages as revealed in prophecy including therefore the seven heads and ten horns.

Verse 13

The ten kings have a common cause with the Beast. The next verse states the nature of that cause, namely, to destroy the Church. Satan uses them for this purpose, as XII. 17-18 indicates. They place their authority, political influence, wealth and military strength and resources at the disposal of Antichrist. During the period of time defined as "one hour", they will unite their forces; and Satan will direct them in one last desperate attempt to wipe out the Church and drive Christ out of His world.

Verse 14

The joining of the kings' forces and resources with Antichrist to fight against the Lamb creates the last world-war. The first so-called world war was only a preparation for others of greater violence and wider scope and destructive power and the final supreme conflict to come. Verse seven in chapter XIII. predicts the victory for Antichrist in his war against the saints. There he defeated them and tyrannized for a short time, but now the Lamb wins the decisive victory. This victory of the Lamb alludes to Daniel (VII. 14, 18, 26, 27). Antichrist will win the victory against the Catholic Nations, subject the true believers and oppress the Church wherever he wins and will kill the Two Witnesses. But the Lamb will finally take up the combat with him for His elect and win the decisive victory. The victory is predicted before the destruction of Babylon to hearten and console the faithful in all their trials and sufferings. Antichrist will no doubt pronounce the Church the greatest curse of the earth, as judaism, heresy, atheism, anarchism, liberalism, agnosticism and communism have always done. The kings will readily accept his views, because they are burning with hatred of the Church. But when the fall of Babylon is nearing, the world in general will have grown cool towards the doctrines of the antichristians.

The titles of the Lamb are the same as those given the Father by St. Paul (1 Tim. VI. 15). He may have caught a glimpse of the judgment against Antichrist and his followers. Antichrist will delight in having himself styled king of kings and overlord over the rulers of the world. But the Lamb is rightfully the King of kings and the Lord of lords, because He is the Creator and Redeemer and rules the souls and consciences of kings and emperors. Jeremias said: "cursed be the man who trusteth in man" (XVII. 5), when condemning the alliances of Juda with Assyria and Egypt. But the blinded kings serving under Antichrist will think their salvation and happiness rest on their alliance with him. So they deliver the man-power and resources of their kingdoms to him.

The saints shall win the victory with Christ, though Antichrist overcomes them (XIII. 7). Daniel heard of this victory (VII. 27). They are the "called" and also the "elect". Our Lord spoke of the many who are called and few who are the elect (Mt. XXII. 14). St. John goes beyond that and grants the victory only to those who are "faithful". The elect will surely remain faithful, if they respond to the graces given them. Their election comes from God through grace, but their faithfulness is their own response to the call and election and gains for them the glorification with Christ in the victory.

This verse points an obscure threat at the ruling emperor, Domitian, who was openly styled, 'dominus et deus noster' and assumed such titles for himself (Suet. Domit. 13—Swete), and it again places the writing of the Apocalypse in the reign of the divinely worshipped Domitian.

Verse 15

The waters in this vision are the nations subject to Antichrist and directed by the wicked city. They are contrasted with the Crystal Sea, on which stood those who had overcome the Beast and chanted the canticle of Moses and of the Lamb. Babylon is the metropolis of the wicked. The viewpoint taken in this verse until the end of the chapter is shortly before the fall of Babylon. The Greek text uses four terms to denote the worldwide dominion of Antichrist, "peoples and mobs and nations and tongues". The universality is not complete, however. The empire of Antichrist has only TEN horns. This number intimates that not all nations shall be subject to Antichrist, because the real number of completeness is TWELVE. SEVEN is the sacred number of perfection, and it also signifies the fullest development of evil, because evil is only the absence of good. The word "mobs" suggests the character of the peoples controlled by the wicked city and points to communism or such like.

Verse 16

This and the next verse are the introduction to the following chapter. They point out the destroyers of the city. These ten horns together with the Beast will hate it, but the cause of their hatred is not revealed. The seven plagues have driven the ten kings to desperation, and they may fasten the blame for those plagues upon Antichrist, and he directs their hatred against the city. They still suffer excruciating pains from the effects of plagues, and they desire revenge against those who led them into their present misery, and they may blame the False Prophet for leading them into idolatry through the city's influence and thus incurring the plagues. They hope to destroy him with the city. Their first act will be a rebellion against her leadership and the declaration of an economic boycott. This was stated in general in XVI. 19. No more pilgrimages to worship the statue of Antichrist shall come to the city. Her revenues and incomes shall cease. The plagues shall no doubt make travel impossible, because only the worshippers of Antichrist travelled to see the miraculous statue, and they are all stricken with the ulcer of the first plague. They and Antichrist have carried the city through the term of her prosperity, but now they will abandon her.

Not satisfied with this humiliation of the city, the loss of prestige and her reduction to poverty, the kings and Antichrist will plot her annihilation. To "eat her flesh" means to depopulate her, to kill her inhabitants. The inhabitants, fanatical followers of the False Prophet and worshippers of Antichrist's statue, haughty, overbearing and cruel will merit the hatred of all peoples. Hence the kings by Antichrist's direction will plan the extermination of the city by incendiary and atomic bombs and leave nothing but the dead bodies of its inhabitants lying buried beneath the ruins until Judgment Day. Antichrist is not consistent in ordering the destruction of the city, but his development in evil is nearly finished, and normally the more anyone's character has grown in evil the less consistent is he in his decisions. Not all inhabitants shall be killed, however, – only those who worshipped and promoted the worship of the Beast's image (XVIII. 4).

Interpreters who see in the ten horns the barbarian nations who finally sacked the city of Rome contradict the text. The Beast as well as the horns hate the woman. It is not historically true that the empire (the beast?) leagued with the barbarians to destroy Rome. Neither did the barbarians rule with the empire while the city of Rome was in its glory and power. If, as some interpreters hold, the emperors were the Beast, it is certain that they never used the barbarian nations to destroy the city. Neither did the governors appointed by the emperors league together to wipe out this city, in the way the prophecy foretells. And the plagues of chapter XVI. were never inflicted upon the empire and the world. The city of Rome indeed lost her power and world-dominion, but she was not annihilated in the way the next chapter describes, and neither were the empire or emperors cast visibly and alive into the pool of fire. So this prophecy is not a past event but a future one. The capital of the empire was moved from Rome to Constantinople by Constantine, but Rome was left undestroyed. If the whole prophecy is taken in review, it seems unlikely that St. John could have imagined the empire to be in existence when Antichrist appears.

Verse 17

The hatred of the kings against the city is infused into their hearts by Almighty God. He is the ultimate Cause of the plagues which shall instill this hatred into them. Though their faith in Antichrist be shaken, the kings still cling to him, because they want to continue in their career of sin and their positions to tyrannize over the world; and hence it is in their hearts to "give their kingdom to the Beast" to do whatever pleases him. Antichrist being jealous of the power and influence of Babylon, because he desires to be sole ruler of the world, is bent on the destruction of the city, and therefore he directs the hatred of the kings against the city. The plagues came forth from Jerusalem. When marshalling his vassal kings and their armies to recover that city and exterminate the Church, Antichrist will soothe their discontent over the terrible plagues which he was unable to ward off by promising them the satisfaction of their revenge against the Church after the destruction of the city of Babylon. They shall trust in his power still, because he was able to kill the Two Prophets, and it should be much easier to destroy the Church. So the kings will lend their military power and resources to the Beast, first to destroy the city of Babylon and then the Church. They shall hold everything at his disposal until "the words of God are accomplished". This clause refers to the "mystery of God" in X. 7. This mystery will go into fulfillment when Antichrist and his prophet are cast into the pool of fire and all his followers and helpers perish in the last decisive battle. The fall of Babylon shall seal the fate of Antichrist.

3. The Symbolic Meaning Of The Harlot.

Verse 18

The woman appeared first in this vision, but her symbolic

meaning is given last. It is the secondary capital of Antichrist's empire and becomes the first after Jerusalem turns against him. It then is the metropolis of his empire for a short time and rules and directs his viceroys, or it may have been conceded this leadership before.

The name of the city is not given, but verse one, "the great harlot", which means the great apostate, and verse five, "Babylon, the mother of fornications", again the great apostate, point to Rome as the city spoken of. Rome has been the center and headquarters of the messianic kingdom throughout New Testament times. If that city should apostatize and become the center of all antichristian activity, it would merit the titles of adulteress and harlot given to Jerusalem by the prophets for its apostasy from God and its practice of idolatry and superstition.

This chapter refutes the whole contention that the "beast" is the emperor of Rome, Nero or Domitian. The empire procured worship for the emperor. In that way the empire would be the false prophet, who shall be cast alive into the pool of fire (XIX. 20). Again the horns lend their power to the beast to destroy the city. Neither an emperor or the empire ever did or desired this. The beast shall be cast alive into the pool of fire, hence it could not be the empire; only the emperor could be thus punished. And there is no record of any emperor having been seized alive and visibly hurled into hell. It is therefore plainly absurd to apply this chapter to Roman times, if anyone expects a reasonable explanation for it. It plainly concerns itself with an unfulfilled prophecy that is waiting for the time appointed by Almighty God.

CHAPTER XVIII.

Westminster Version

After these things, I beheld another angel 1. coming down from
heaven, invested with great power; and the earth was lighted up by his
glory.

And he cried with a mighty voice, saying: 2. 'Fallen, fallen is
Babylon the great, and she is become a habitation of devils, a stronghold
of every unclean spirit, a stronghold of every unclean and hated bird,
because all the nations have drunk of the wine of wrath because of her
impurity, and the kings 3. of the earth have committed fornication with
her, and the merchants of the earth have waxed rich through the excess
of her licentiousness.

And I heard another voice out of heaven, saying 4. 'Come out of her,
my people, in order that ye share not in her sins, and partake not of her
plagues; for her sins are heaped up to heaven, and God 5. hath remembered her iniquities.

Render to her even as herself hath rendered, 6. and give her double
according to her works: in the cup which she hath mixed, mix for her
as much again: as much as she hath glorified herself and wantoned 7. in
luxury, so much give her of torment and mourning. Because she saith in her
heart, "A queen I sit, no widow am I, and mourning I shall not see";
therefore in one day her plagues 8. shall come, death and mourning and
famine, and with fire she shall be consumed; for the Lord God is strong,
who judgeth her.'

The kings of the earth who committed fornication 9. and wantoned
in luxury with her shall weep and wail over her, when they see the smoke
of her burning.

They shall stand afar off, through the fear 10. of her torment, and shall
say, 'Woe, woe, the great city, Babylon the strong city, in one hour hath
thy judgment come!'

And the merchants of the earth weep and 11. mourn over her, because no one buyeth her cargo any more, a cargo of gold and silver and of
precious 12. stones and of pearls and of fine linen and of purple and of
scarlet; all manner of scented wood, and all manner of work in ivory,
and all manner of work in costly wood, and in bronze and iron and
marble; cinnamon and balsam and incense and myrrh, 13. and frankincense and wine and fine flour and oil and wheat and cattle and sheep, with
horses and carriages and slaves—and souls of men.

The ripe fruit for which thy soul longed hath 14. departed from thee;
all things dainty and splendid are lost to thee never to be found again.

The merchants of these things, who gained 15. wealth by her, shall
stand afar off through the fear of her torment, weeping and mourning, and
they shall say, 'Woe, woe, the great city 16. which was clothed in fine
linen and purple and scarlet, and glittered with gold and precious stones
and pearls; in one hour hath all that wealth been laid waste. And all

the shipmasters, and all that sail to 17. any part, the mariners, and all
that work upon the sea, stood afar off, and cried out when 18. they beheld
the smoke of her burning, saying, 'What city is like to the great city?'

And they cast dust upon their heads, and 19. cried out, weeping and
mourning, 'Woe, woe, the great city, wherein all that had ships upon the
sea became rich out of her wealth; in one hour hath she been laid waste!'

Be glad over her and rejoice, thou heaven, and 20. ye saints and
apostles and prophets; because God hath judged your cause upon her!

And a strong angel took up a stone like a 21. great millstone, and
cast it into the sea, saying, 'Even thus shall Babylon the great city be
cast down headlong, and shall be found no more.

No more shall the sound of harpers and minstrels 22. and flute-
players and trumpeters be heard in thee, and no more shall every crafts-
man of every craft be found in thee, and no more shall the sound of the
millstone be heard in thee, and no more shall the light of a 23. lamp shine
in thee, and no more shall the voice of the bridegroom and bride be
heard in thee; because thy merchants were the great men of the earth,
because by thy witchery all the nations of the earth have been led astray.

And in her was found the blood of prophets 24. and saints and of
all that have been slain upon earth.'

VIII. THE FALL OF BABYLON

1. Announcement Of Her Fall.

Chapter XVIII.

Verses 1-3.

This chapter deals with the judgment upon New Babylon. It is divided into four parts: The first part is the pronouncement of the judgment, briefly foretold in XIV. 8, and joined to that pronouncement is a warning to the faithful to flee (1-5); the second part is the command to Antichrist and his forces to execute the judgment (6-8); the third part is the lamentation and rejoicing over her fall (9-20); and the fourth part is a graphic demonstration of the suddenness and completeness of her everlasting ruin.

The language describing the judgment resembles that of the prophets describing the judgments upon the heads of the ancient world-empires. Nahum thus relates the end of Niniveh (III.); Isaias (XIII.) and Jeremias (LII.) vividly narrate the fall of ancient Babylon. The lamentation of the world over New Babylon is not cast in the sweetly mournful threnody of Jeremias over the ruins of Jerusalem, which has flashes of a new dawn and coming future glories, nor in the sublime and solemn measures of a Christian funeral dirge, which is pervaded and transfigured by the hope of immortality and calls up visions of love and forgiveness – it is cast in the language of a lost hope, of the abandonment of all ideals and the forced acceptance of an everlasting doom in the wail of despair uttered by the damned.

Verse 1

The angel who now appears is not the same one who showed St. John the city and the beast. He seems to be another great saint of the Church invested with the power of miracles and the gift of prophecy. His virtues and sanctity, his talents and other natural and supernatural gifts enlighten the infidel and heathen nations as well as the Church. His glory are the gifts with which God has distinguished him; it will bring the dawn of the world's conversion after the condemnation of Antichrist and his prophet. The word "glory" alludes to the vision of God seen by Ezechiel when the divine presence would return to the future Temple of God (XLIII. 2 ff) and remain there forever. The glory of God there also enlightened the world.

Verse 2

The "mighty voice" of the angel is not necessarily the Pope's, because his voice is a "great voice" or a "voice of thunder". The renown for sanctity of this angel is what shall gain world-wide belief for him. He speaks in anticipation of what is sure to follow, so sure that he avers it as an accomplished fact. Isaias (XXI. 9) and likewise Jeremias (LI. 8) make the same statements as regards ancient Babylon, though the fall of the city was still a distant future event. The angel repeats the announcement of the downfall in tones that ring with exultation, praise and thanksgiving.

In the prophecy of Baruch (IV. 35), ancient Babylon was destined to become the habitation of devils. Isaias makes it the habitation of lizards and owls and other creatures of evil omen. Such shall be the destiny of New Babylon. During the days of Antichrist, the power of hell shall sally forth from this stronghold of sin. When Satan exerts his might there through the image of the Beast, myriads of devils shall wait on his command. It shall be the visible metropolis of the kingdom of Satan. The ruins of the city shall then become the prison of the unclean spirits who were active during its evil glory. When Babylon is destroyed those evil spirits shall probably be bound there as Satan shall be bound in the bottomless abyss (XX. 3). Evil spirits can be bound to some place on earth (Tob. VIII. 3; Apoc. IX. 14).

The next clause alludes to various passages of the prophets, but it may have a different meaning here. According to the predictions of Isaias, ancient Babylon shall be inhabited by beasts of prey, poisonous reptiles and birds of night and evil omen (XIII. 21-22). Jeremias repeats the same prediction (L. 39), and Sophonias speaks similar woes upon Assyria (II. 14-15). In the prophecy against Idumea, Isaias uses the same figures (XXXIV. 13, 15). So shall ferocious beasts and birds of evil omen inhabit the ruins of New Babylon undisturbed and shall make it uninhabitable forever. However, the phrase, "a stronghold of every unclean and hateful bird" may be figurative and stand for something else. The souls of the wicked, whose bodies lie buried beneath the charred ruins of the city, may be imprisoned there to be tortured by the demons till the Day of Judgment. This was the scene of all their enormities, their apostasy, idolatry and immorality and their hatred against the Church and their christian fellowmen. They executed the edicts of persecution against all dissenters. If the evil spirits shall be imprisoned there by the power of the Church, in all justice the souls of their servants should also be imprisoned there and be united in the commission of sins and crimes. The ruins of the city shall thenceforth be avoided, for it shall be a historic monument of God's punishment for apostasy.

Verse 3

This verse gives the reasons for the withering sentence upon the wicked city. All nations have accepted the doctrines of Antichrist propagated by the city. In the Old Covenant, God expressed His wrath against these doctrines. And the Babylonians shall reap the consequences of their apostasy and idolatry. They were weary of serving God, and they freely gave themselves to the service of the Beast and Satan. The kings held their authority and office under the condition of propagating the teachings of Antichrist or promoting hatred against Christ and His Church and of shedding the innocent blood of martyrs. Now they shall *see* the wages of sin.

The merchants of the city were the greatest promoters of immorality and debauchery. They owned theaters and other places of amusement with which they satiated the voluptuous pilgrims who came to see and hear the miraculous statue of Antichrist. They made enormous profits out of the souvenirs sold to pilgrims. The city became a city of merchants as ancient Babylon was. Antichrist abolished all restraints for his followers and allowed every kind of traffic to enrich themselves. They were resourceful originators of immodest styles of dress. Luxury became general, and the time was pleasantly spent by both citizens and pilgrims in voluptuousness. The Greek text suggests that the merchants waxed rich and reaped a golden harvest from the lawless excesses of the city's licentiousness. (See Jer. XXV. 15; Ezech.

XXIII. 31-35; XXVI; XXVIII.)

Verse 4

St. John hears another voice from heaven warning the faithful residents to depart. There shall be Catholics in the doomed city up to the day of her destruction. They are warned by their pastor. As God sent angels to lead Lot out of Sodom, and as He warned the Jews to flee from ancient Babylon (Jer. LI. 6: Zach. II. 6-8), so He warns the true believers to depart lest they be punished with the city. The life of sin is a community affair to which all wholly surrender. And the Christians are exposed to giving way to the public temptations and are urged to cease being a part of the city's life before the sentence is executed.

2. Reasons For Her Fall.

Verses 5-8.

Verse 5

This verse reads like the words of Jeremias (LI. 9) spoken against Babylon. The sins of New Babylon have grown to such enormities that they cry for vengeance before the throne of God. All her iniquities are written in the book of God's remembrance; her cup of vice is filled to overflowing; and therefore God has decided to end her career of crime. The crimes of ancient Rome shedding the blood of millions of martyrs shall be imputed to this new metropolis of evil, because it has incurred responsibility for them all. Ancient Rome tried to extirpate the Church; Egypt, Assyria, Babylon and Antiochus tried to exterminate God's people: But none was dyed so red in the blood of saints as New Babylon. Because the inhabitants of New Babylon have outdone all ancients in cruelty, Gods remembrance will lay upon them all crimes committed against His people in all ages. According to the Greek text, the sins of Babylon have been 'fastened' on to heaven. Heaven is the Church, and the clause may mean that the wicked inhabitants of the city have imputed their own sins to the Church and have accused her of every perversity of which they are guilty themselves or have blamed her for the punishment received, just as the ancient pagans blamed the Christians for every calamity. A greater guilt than merely committing sin, no matter how wholeheartedly, is to impute one's own sins or mistakes to another and treat him as the culprit. They call sin virtue, and virtue sin. Such meaning would fit better into the context, and the succeeding verse would follow logically from this meaning. (See Zach. XIV. 5).

Verse 6

The first clause of this verse decrees just retribution for Babylon. As she has imputed wickedness wrongfully to others, so others shall rightfully and justly impute it to her. This is a direct command or encouragement from God to the kings and Antichrist to render to the Godless city an 'eye for an eye and a tooth for a tooth'. In spite of their rebellion against God, they shall be the instruments of His will. Babylon led others into disaster, sin and damnation; now she must receive the reward of her merits. Although the kings desire to wreak vengeance on the city for drawing upon themselves the plagues of God, they shall execute God's decree.

Her retribution is to be double of what she has inflicted upon others. Her citizens are all murderers having obeyed the advice given through the statue of the Beast and deserving now a violent death. They lived in luxurious pleasures and sensuality, arrogance and self-complacency and in the gratification of all their lusts and passions. They contemptuously threw aside all restraints and recognized no law or master. By their advice, the kings and all who chafed under law and restraint gladly drank of the cup of corruption, gladly accepted the license to sin; now they must drink the cup to the dregs, which is the consequence of spurning the law of God and scoffing at His power. The evil they promulgated with all the accumulated sins committed by their boon companions throughout the world and the wrath merited by it shall now fall back upon them to crush and annihilate the city forever. Thus she shall receive double punishment for her crimes, her unbelief, arrogance, hypocrisy, idolatry and debauchery. This divine command follows the law of Moses (Exod. XXII. 4, 7, 9,). Jeremias prophesied in terms very similar to these of St. John (L. 29; Sept. XXVII. 29).

Verse 7

The personification of the City of Evil is made lifelike in this verse. She is made to reveal her arrogance. Her wanton luxury shall call for double measures of shame, degradation and deprivation. The inhabitants have scorned God and deified their own might and ingenuity. In their elation they think themselves gods, (Acts. XII. 22), because they are the lords of the earth. All other nations are leagued with them, and nations that would not submit to the Beast are broken and subjugated. The inhabitants have one mind and heart, so the city may speak as one being for all. Her pride like that of the ancient capitals of the world will laugh to scorn any thought of giving glory to God. This pride is the supreme sin, and the living in luxuries and licentiousness without restraint is the accompanying sin. And all the innocent blood they have caused to be shed fills their measure of iniquity to overflowing. In her pride and security founded on the imagined divine might of Antichrist, she considers herself the queen of the earth. She is no widow but the wife of the Beast and can therefore give herself up to all earthly enjoyments and felicity. She smiles at the possibility of sorrow for her, because new riches and power are daily accumulating. Nothing can cloud her serenity.

Ezechiel (XXVII. 3) makes Tyre indulge in the same self-adulation and complacency in which New Babylon indulges here. Her words are likewise almost identical with those of ancient Babylon quoted by Isaias. (XLVII. 7-8).

Verse 8

The Seer seems to follow the words of Isaias as he continues to write. All the most dreaded calamities that can befall a besieged city shall come upon Babylon in ONE day. No world-capital had ever been punished like this, because all cities of antiquity experienced the force of the siege by degrees, none felt it instantaneously. "Death . . . mourning . . . famine . . . fire" shall descend upon her at one and the same time. Death by the most efficient modern military machines shall be sudden and unexpected. Lamentation for the slain shall follow the first wave of death. Famine was another terror of the besieged, and this is mentioned to indicate the excess of their self-indulgence in all luxuries, their voluptuousness and licentiousness. If the city is annihilated in ONE day, famine could not set in. Yet, if all business is broken off during the plagues and not resumed, famine might have begun before the day of doom. Flight shall not be possible, because in one HOUR the city shall be a heap of smoking ruins. Atomic bombs dropped by a powerful air squadron could annihilate any modern city in so short a time and kill every living soul within it. At the time these revelations were written, it naturally seemed a sheer impossibility for the military forces of ten kings to annihilate a city like Rome of four million inhabitants in one day, or rather in ONE HOUR. This thought would arise in the mind of the reader, and therefore St. John adds the reason why it is possible –, because God the Judge is ALMIGHTY. They have thought, spoken and lived their scorn of God, and therefore their almighty Creator shall let them be crushed in their pride.

3. Lamentations Over Her Fall.

Verses 9-19.

Verse 9

The language of verses nine to nineteen contains in general the ideas of Ezechiel in the lamentation over Tyre (XXVI. to XXVIII.), although St. John is original in his style and terminology. All people who have taken part in the destruction of the city lament her fate: The kings who serve under Antichrist, the merchants of his dominion and the navy and shipowners of the merchant marine. Perhaps only the air forces of Antichrist, enroute to the gathering of all the armies in Palestine, shall be dispatched to destroy the city. This could easily be done while the armies and navies are on their way to attack Jerusalem. The annihilation of the city could then be partially intended to intimidate the inhabitants of Jerusalem and all Christians of the world. It would demonstrate the military might of Antichrist to be still terrific in spite of all plagues. But the true believers know the signs and realize what they portend. The inhabitants of the city would surely be informed of the coming bombardment and utter destruction, if it were an open campaign. But since

Antichrist shall assemble his armies and the kings of his empire for the final battle against the Church now located in Jerusalem, he shall have his vessels transport them to Palestine in one great fleet and have his navy accompany them. His airfleets shall darken the sky. He may take a final review of them near the city of Babylon keeping his purpose a secret until he gives orders to his officers to enact the bombardment. After the end of the city, his forces shall move onwards to their doom near Jerusalem.

Verse 10

The kings will weep and wail over the short-lived glory of earth and the passing pleasure of all its enjoyments. No doubt they shall have friends buried beneath the ruins, but their grief is selfish, and their own possible fate comes up before their consciousness, as they behold from afar the smoking ruins of the wealthiest, the most powerful and most magnificent capital in the world. Their cries and wails are of no benefit to the city they have helped to destroy. They shall not dare to approach the ruins of the once magnificent city but shall look at it from a safe distance or hear it over the radio. Their lamentation might be idle hypocrisy, if the sudden end of the world's most splendid metropolis did not awaken an uneasy foreboding in their own minds. Verse eight foretold the coming of every destructive force upon the city in one day, while now its destruction is finished in one HOUR. It took nineteen hundred years to wipe out Tyre completely as described by Ezechiel, but New Babylon shall have ceased to exist forever ONE HOUR after the forces of judgment shower their vengeance upon her. This must have seemed impossible to all students of these verses before modern times. The kings weep and lament, because after the five plagues upon the world they suspect a judgment of God in the destruction of the city.

Verse 11

The businessmen in Antichrist's empire next take up the hymn of mourning. Their grief is even more plainly selfish than that of the kings, for all they regret is the loss of their profitable trade. The excess profits they realized out of their articles of luxury enabled them to lead a voluptuous life. That prosperity came to an end as suddenly as it flared up. And these merchants shall suffer heavy losses, because no one will buy their goods any more. They have no regrets for the death of the city's inhabitants.

Verse 12

St. John enumerates articles that made up the luxuries of his day and that moved in a steady stream from all directions to the capital of the empire, Rome. The articles are not of the necessities of life but the niceties in which the idle rich indulge and delight. He enumerates seven classes of goods: (1) articles of personal adornment; (2) furniture, works of art and various decorations for the houses; (3) spices and perfumes; (4) delicatessen, the choicest and finest drinks and desserts; (5) the richest and most expensive bread and viands for daily sustenance; (6) richly caparisoned vehicles for pomp and external show of wealth; (7) servants and human souls.

The text does not indicate that any deep symbolic meaning is attached to any of the articles of trade mentioned. Gold and silver are the standard medium of exchange of all ages and the measure of wealth. Linen and fine clothes, precious stones and pearls compose the wearing apparel and articles of adornment. Silk was very common in Rome in the days of her glory. The gold and silver goods are not coins, however, but works of art, statues, jewelry, drinking vessels, lamps etc. The thyine wood was agreeably odoriferous and was much used for tables, mantelpieces, niches and veneering, because it was mottled and veined and took on a high polish. There were many varieties of it, hence St. John says "all thyine wood". Ivory was very largely used in Rome to decorate furniture and was carved into exquisite works of art; whole battle scenes were skillfully and perfectly rendered in ivory as now found in the museums of Europe. Small works of art were carved out of costly wood; and all sizes of statues and busts, scenes from all conditions life were cast in bronze and iron. Marble was the common stone for external decorations of buildings; monuments were often of solid marble, and the houses were cluttered with small and large marble statues.

Verse 13

The cinnamon was not the modern article of this name; it was an odoriferous spice used for a cosmetic or perfume. Incense was burned in a brazier before the statue of an idol in worship. Myrrh was an ointment used to perfume the body, and frankincense was a gum from the tree and was burnt to perfume the air. These were all costly luxuries in Roman times bought and used by the wealthy.

Wine, oil and wheat comprised the abundance and overflow of blessings which God promised His chosen people through the prophets for faithful service. St. John writes in the light of prophecy and also from experience and sums up the choicest delicacies under these three terms. The Romans sought the most mellow wines, purest olive oil and finest wheat flour. A large amount of wheat was imported from Egypt. But Sardinia was the granary of Rome. Cattle and sheep furnished the ordinary viands for the tables of the Romans. The rarest birds and fish were sought for the most exquisite banquets. Horses and chariots were the swiftest and most aristocratic means of transportation. The chariots mentioned are probably the four-wheeled carriages called 'rheda'. They expressed elegance and pomp. The slave-marts of Rome were always a great source of wealth to the brutal traffickers in human flesh. The last item of sale mentioned suggests that there shall be a horrifying white-slave traffic in the world of Antichrist promoted by the wicked merchants and inhabitants of New Babylon.

This whole enumeration of merchants creating the wealth of New Babylon was taken by St. John from his own observation of the business coming to ancient Rome. Without a special revelation, he could not know how much the principal articles of world-trade would change especially articles of luxury. Neither could he know without special revelations that the tables of the common people would be more richly furnished in our day than the tables of the richest Romans. Everyone now indulges in fruits, vegetables, viands and spices from the most distant climes. And the variety of our diet in this modern age exceeds by far what satisfied the most fastidious tastes of the ancients. But St. John models the life of New Babylon after that of Rome in his day. At the destruction of the city these luxuries shall be unsalable and the profits made out of them shall suddenly stop.

Verse 14

The merchants bewail the shortlived pleasure of sensual enjoyments. They name the most refined fruits of material culture in "the fruits of the soul's desire". These fruits were ripened through the ages and are the fine arts with an appeal to a refined lust: music, sculpture, painting, shows of exquisite bodily beauty in form and movement, feats of skill and strength in athletics and acrobatics, daring feats of aeronauts; electrical displays in color, forms and brilliancy; magic, natural and preternatural and everything the idle rich can crave. The excessive wealth of the Babylonians could call for the best the earth and the human race produced, making the earth a vast paradise for them, producing fruits for every kind of earthly enjoyment and satisfaction. When it was all ripened and ready for their use, their earthly existence ended. Dainty apparel and delicious food are of no value for the dead. All the most splendid accomplishments of the world are lost to them, are like trees stripped of their fruit in autumn, after which there shall never be another summer. Their lives travelled towards a phantom which vanished when they were just reaching it. Such lamentations are voiced by the merchants. Their brand of sympathy is that of materialists, unbelievers and atheists.

Verse 15

Verse fifteen resumes the theme of verse eleven. The merchants like the kings mourn the passing of a city that made them rich but will keep at a safe distance from the dead city. Their sympathy is without charity or offer of help for survivors, if any could escape bombs, fire and poison gasses. They only regret that the market for their goods collapses and their ill-gotten gains dwindle to small proportions. Both the merchants and the kings tremble at the displeasure of the great tyrant, Antichrist, for fear of his ruthless cruelty. The words of the prophet might come to their minds: "Woe to a man who trusteth in a man".

Verse 16

The kings regret the fall of "so great" and "so strong" a city, while the merchants deplore the passing of so much gold and jewels and fine merchandise. The lamentation is not a real and true commiseration for the fate of the inhabitants, because both kings and merchants are unbelievers who set their hopes on this world. All the owners of the diamonds and pearls have perished in the city, and these merchants might recover a lot of this wealth later, but they are aware of a divine judgment, and they would never dare to explore the ruins for buried treasure. They consider it a total loss and also the loss of any more profits. Only the loss of business and profits gives expression to their wails and woes. In ONE hour all the wealth that astonished the world was turned to dust and ashes.

Verse 17

The third class of men who bewail the passing of the city are the shipowners, heads of transportation companies, officers and ship crews, stewards and accountants, pilots, sailors from the captains to the deck boy; it includes also in modern times all transportation managers, railroad officials, engineers, conductors, air-pilots. Those who sail to various places are travelling representatives who sell goods for their business firms. The shipmasters are the owners of common carriers by land sea and air, of steamships, railroads and airplanes. The longshoremen, dock-laborers, deck-hands and all who load cargoes or freight cars and by their bodily labor make a living and profits from the transportation of goods are included in those "who work upon the sea". In Greek it is "all who belabor the sea", a very graphic description of plowing up the seas with ships that exchange goods from all over the globe. Both merchant ships and passenger lines are scheduled for this city.

Thus FOUR distinct classes of men are named by St. John to show the universal mourning in the various transportation systems over the world for the loss of a city that by her wealth and opulence furnished immense profits out of the trade she engaged in with the whole world. Since St. John modelled New Babylon after ancient Rome, the trade and prosperity of Rome stood vividly before his consciousness. Transportation by sea was the principal method or route by which goods were shipped to Rome.

Verse 18

The seamen, beholding the smoke of her burning from afar, add their lamentation to that of the kings, merchants and ship-owners to express their astonishment at the sudden end of he city. No city was ever like it in magnificence or in the suddenness and depth of its degradation. In verse nine the future tense indicates that destruction was impending, in verse eleven the merchants mourn during the time of her bombardment in the present tense, and in verses 17 and 18 the sailors mourn in the past tense. When the news reaches them the city is no more. It must then be some distance from the sea, but not too far, for the seamen see the smoke of her conflagration.

Verse 19

Casting dust on the head was an ancient token of the keenest grief. The seamen cry out in anguish and weep for the city, but their grief, too, is selfish. They may be stockholders in the transportation companies. Their mourning excludes the probability of their families living in the city. They bewail the loss of profits nothing more. The prices paid for merchandise by this city were exhorbitant and made all cargo owners and transportation companies rich. The whole city is likened to a priceless jewel in the Greek word, τιμιότητος which denotes her wealth to be without limit or bounds. Many citizens have become millionaires very quickly by speculation in real estate. And they care little about the price of goods or materials desired. The demand for speedy delivery raised prices of building materials manifold. From many places works of art were shipped to supply the demand. The sailors, ship and dock workers commanded fabulous wages, and they spent it in luxury and licentiousness as lavishly as they earned it easily, and therefore they lament when the city is ended in one crash. All who received their wages out of the profits made by the corporation owners lost their jobs, and this elicits from them so much sympathy and commiseration. They repeat the unbelievable fact that in ONE hour the city was laid waste.

4. Rejoicing Over Her Fall.

Verse 20.

Verse 20

The time of rejoicing has come for the Church. The metropolis of evil exists no more, and this puts the seal upon the fate of Antichrist and the domination of sin and Satan. The words are addressed to the universal Church, because as all faithful members suffered the persecution that issued from the evil city, so all deserve a word of cheer to keep up their courage a little longer. The persecution is now dormant. All attention is fixed upon the expedition into Palestine, where the issue shall be settled whether Antichrist and his prophet shall retake Jerusalem, destroy the Church and make himself lord and god of the world, or whether he shall meet his doom. The Church will calmly and confidently await the final outcome of his rashness sure of a victory and of the everlasting peace and security that is about to dawn upon a torn and chaotic world.

The faithful are now truly "saints" having kept aloof from the company of those who were contaminated with the doctrines of Antichrist. They are the first ones called on to rejoice, for they shall now be able to lead a life of sanctity without hindrance. Persecution and hatred of their saintliness shall be dead.

The apostles are the next ones encouraged to rejoice. That probably means apostolic men who fearlessly and zealously propagated the true faith during the horrors of persecution and promoted love of God and the Eucharistic Lamb in the midst of the storm and in defiance of Antichrist's orders. They were especially marked and singled out for death by the powers of evil, and they bore the brunt of the attack on the Church.

The 'prophets' may be a special class invested with charismatic gifts and enlightened to predict near future happenings to preserve the true doctrine, after the death of the Two Witnesses, and expose in their true light the false philosophies, false doctrines and false miracles that threaten to lead astray the whole world. All bishops and priests are prophets, God's spokesmen. They fearlessly warned the world against all falsehood, and God has ratified their doctrines, their zeal and penance by His judgment upon the city of evil.

This verse may refer to the prophets of old, who foretold the consummation of God's judgment against the wicked and the universal establishment of His kingdom upon earth. The labors of the apostles of the Lord can now bear most abundant fruit, after the world has been cleared of all weeds, leaving the whole field to the winnowed wheat of the Lord. And the example of heroic constancy given by the saints of all ages shall after this judgment be universally followed. The reward promised the prophets and saints in XI. 18 will now became apparent, when they shall no longer be condemned and despised by the world but honored and imitated. All shall be avenged, and the wicked shall receive according to their works.

The rejoicing over Bablyon alludes to Isaias (XXV. 1-2). In verse six of the same chapter the Holy Eucharist is foreshadowed (Cyrill, Eusebius, Thomas), and this is of special significance here, because the followers of Antichrist will make this sacred mystery the target of their hatred and derision. (XIII. 6). God's judgment upon the city will confirm the faithful in their fidelity to their hidden Lord.

5. Demonstration Of Her Fall.

Verse 21

The symbolic action of the angel in this verse is borrowed from Jeremias (LI. 63-64). The prophet represents the fall of ancient Babylon, St. John of New Babylon. The prophecy of Isaias (XXV. 2) is interpreted to be Messianic and may point to New Babylon. St. John, however, did not draw this vision from Isaias but from the revelations made to himself. Dropping a millstone from a great height demonstrates with what violence the city shall be demolished. The fall of the city would be a crash like the splash of a great millstone dropped flatly on the water from the sky. It expressed faintly the explosion of a modern bomb especially an atomic one. As a stone dropped into the sea never rises again, so shall the end of the city be final never to be rebuilt. St. John probably did not see an airforce dropping bombs upon the city demonstrating to him the possibility of demolishing the most powerful and populous city of the world in ONE hour, but he draws from the almighty power of God saying by way of explanation, "God is strong" (8).

Verses 22 and 23

The language of these verses is similar to that of the prophets depicting the punishments upon those who apostatize and live in luxury and licentiousness. (Ezech. XXVI. 13; Jer. VII. 34; XVI. 9; XXV. 10, etc.). The text seems to say that not one of the inhabitants shall escape, and not one diamond of the vast wealth of the city shall be saved. The sound of the harp and all instruments playing an accompaniment to idolatrous worship, choirs and choruses and all harmonious symphonies, the flute and all open air bands and orchestras that enliven revelry, feasting, games and dances shall suddenly be silent, after the thunder of the explosions dies away and never be heard again. St. John names four different kinds of music that shall tremble away into a mournful, deathlike silence. Likewise the mallet of the builder, the chisel of the sculptor and the anvil of the smith shall instantly be silent. The factories shall be tumbled down, and the whirr of the wheels shall be hushed forever. Death shall breathe on them all in that fatal hour, and their work and ambitions shall shrivel up. The artisans and mechanics who fashioned a multiplicity of articles of every price to be sold to the pilgrims who brought the wealth of the world into the city shall sink into their last sleep beneath the ruins of earthly magnificence.

Verse 23

In the days of her power and glory, the city shall be brilliantly illumined and be visible all the nights at great distances, but when the wrath of God descends upon her, she shall become as dark as the tomb. While her glory lasts, she shall turn the nights into day, but when the judgment falls upon her, her days shall become an everlasting night, and darkness shall enshroud her ruins.

The quintessence of earthly felicity is expressed by the voice of the bride and bridegroom. The silvery voice of the carefree bride and the light-hearted laughter of the newly made wife answering to the solemn and soulful compliments of the proud bridegroom died amidst the deafening detonations of the exploding bombs and was smothered in the stifling vapors of the poison gasses never to be heard again in this unhappy city. A baleful silence and solitude mourning till the end of time for the lost souls that grovel beneath the ruins shall bury the erstwhile festivities and frivolities forever in oblivion.

Verses 23 and 24

The reason for her degradation and demolition is threefold: (1). The merchants of the city were the rulers of the world by their enormous profits and wealth. The international high-financiers and bankers flocked there and by their money manipulations controlled the world and made all nations dependent on them. (2). The influence of her doctrines, philosophy and idolatry led the whole world astray and into the most finished immorality. This was pointed out in XIV. 8 showing the nations drunk with the false teachings of the city and unable anymore to see what was reasonable and right or would draw down the wrath of God. In XVII. 2, the kings are said to have submitted to the leadership of the city making her the mother of all idolatry and abominations, because she led astray all earthly minded men to worship the divinity of Antichrist and accept his morality. (3). The final and principal reason for her violent end was the bloody persecution she set on foot against the Church by her far-reaching influence. The change of grammatical construction brings out this last reason with special prominence. The prophets are the official teachers of the Church, the pope, the bishops and priests. The inhabitants of the city hated them, because they incessantly condemned their wickedness and preserved the faithful from being misled by their philosophy. The saints are the faithful, who remained unwavering in their faith. The city caused their blood to flow in streams. It was also responsible for the death of all who were struck by the seven last plagues and those inflicted by the Two Prophets. As all the blood of the just, from Abel to Christ, was to come upon Jerusalem (Mt. XXIII. 35) for the rejection of the Savior and the persecution of the Church, so upon this city came the vengeance for all the just and innocent blood shed to exterminate the Church and the penalty for all the apostasies from Christ and God. Her inhabitants filled up her measure of iniquity by developing evil to full maturity and by reaching perfection in evil-doing: Therefore full retribution for all evil there ever was in the world was meted out to the city. And there was no mercy in that vengeance, because the inhabitants had laughed repentance to scorn.

CHAPTER XIX.

Westminster Version

After these things, I heard as it were a mighty 1. voice of a large multitude in heaven, saying: 'Alleluia! Salvation and glory and power belong to our God, because his judgments are true and just; 2. because he hath judged the great harlot who corrupted the earth with her fornication, and hath avenged the blood of his servants at her hands'.

And they said a second time: 'Alleluia! 3. And the smoke of her goeth up for ever and ever'.

And the twenty-four elders and the four living 4. beings fell down and worshipped God who sitteth upon the throne, saying, 'Amen, Alleluia!'

And a voice came forth from the throne, saying, 5. 'Praise our God, all ye his servants, ye that fear him, the small and the great!'

And I heard as it were the voice of a large 6. multitude, as the voice of many waters, and as the voice of strong thunders, saying: 'Alleluia! our God the Lord Almighty hath entered upon his reign'.

Let us rejoice and exult, and let us give him 7. glory; because the marriage of the Lamb is come, and his spouse hath prepared herself; and there hath been given her, to clothe 8. herself withal, fine linen, bright and pure; the fine linen being the righteous deeds of the saints.

And the angel saith to me, 'Write, Blessed 9. are they that are bidden to the marriage supper of the Lamb!' And he saith to me, 'These words are the true words of God'.

And I fell down before his feet to worship him, 10. and he saith to me, 'Forbear! I am a fellow-servant with thee and with thy brethren, who bear witness to Jesus: God shalt thou worship!' For the witness to Jesus is the spirit of prophecy.

And I beheld heaven opened, and lo! a white 11. horse, and he who sitteth thereon is called faithful and true, and he judgeth with justice and giveth battle.

His eyes are as a flame of fire; upon his head 12. are many diadems, and he hath a name written which no one knoweth, save himself; he is clothed in a cloak sprinkled with blood 13. and the name whereby he is called is, 'The Word of God'.

The armies of heaven followed him upon white 14. horses, clothed in fine linen, white and pure.

Out of his mouth goeth forth a sharp sword 15. wherewith to smite the nations, and himself ruleth them with a rod of iron, and himself treadeth the wine-press of the fierce wrath of God Almighty, and upon his cloak and upon his thigh he hath 16. a name written: KING OF KINGS AND LORD OF LORDS.

And I beheld a single angel standing on the 17. sun, and he cried out with a loud voice, and said to all the birds that flew in mid-heaven: 'Come gather yourselves together to the great supper of God, that ye may eat the

**flesh of kings, the flesh 18. of captains, the flesh of strong men, the flesh
of horses and their riders, the flesh of all men, free and slaves, great and
small!'**

**And I beheld the beast and the kings of the 19. earth and their armies
gathered together to make war against him who sitteth upon the horse
and against his army.**

**And the beast was captured, and with it the 20. false prophet, who
performed in its sight the signs whereby he led astray those that accepted the mark of the beast and those that worshipped its image.**

**They were both cast alive into the fiery 21. lake of burning brim-
stone; the rest were killed by the sword of him who sat upon the horse—
the sword which issued out of his mouth—and all the birds were glutted
with their flesh.**

IX. THE LAST BATTLE

1. General Rejoicings: Thanksgiving For The Fall Of Babylon.

Chapter XIX.

Verses 1-6.

The true believers know the signs and therefore rejoice everywhere, because the fall of the Evil City is the prelude to the final judgment upon all the wicked and upon Antichrist and his prophet. His end is at hand; The Church celebrates the victory as achieved; so certain is she of its realization.

Verse 1

"The mighty voice of a large multitude" is expressed with much more suggestive force in the original Greek than in any translation. The redundancy of Greek words used reads: "I heard, as it were, the mighty voice of many multitudinous crowds". It was the rejoicing of the universal Church vast as it will be. It intimates a growth instead of a diminution in numbers. He hears only the voice of those who are in "heaven" not of those still outside the fold, although many peoples and nations may be whole-heartedly on the side of the Church by this time. The universal voice of the faithful expressed the same theme as in IV. 8-11 and V. 8-14: There it was a petition to God, while here it is the continuation of XI. 15-19 and XII. 10-12, a spontaneous *thanksgiving* for the victory of God and the Eucharistic Christ. The God of the Christians has won safety for His believers by manifesting His power in the eucharistic mystery. And therefore the whole glory for the finished victory shortly to be won is conceded to Him.

The "Alleluia" is the liturgical word sung by the Church on Easter to express her exultation over the resurrection of Christ, and it is re-echoed throughout the year on all occassions not of mourning or penitence. The word was taken from the Hebrew language by the Apostolic Church, and as St. Augustine says:

"in hoc quidem tempore peregrinationis nostrae ad solatium viatici dicimus ALLELUIA" (pascal sermon cclv.). On no occasion shall the Alleluia more appropriately express the mind of the Church than after all opposition to Christ shall have been put down in the victory over Antichrist. It is the answer to the command given in XVIII. 20.

Verse 2

The first words of this verse repeat what was expressed in XV. 3 and XVI. 7. The peoples of the world pronounce God's judgment eminently true and just. His judgments are always true and just but are not always acknowledged as such. The judgment of the wicked city, however, is so strikingly deserved that all men will acknowledge it. Two reasons are given for that verdict: The FIRST is misleading and corrupting the whole world; and the SECOND is unjustly shedding the best and most innocent blood of the world. God gave free reins to the wicked to satiate their lusts for sin, to grow to maturity in wickedness and fill up their measure of iniquity. If they had stopped at this, their punishment would not have come as speedily, and it would have begun only in hell. But since they strove to coerce the whole world by every means at their disposal to join in their vices, they advanced to satanic depths of malignity and swiftly completed the "mystery of iniquity". The culmination of their malice was reached when they murdered all who loathed their vices and corruption. This last was the chief reason for the annihilation of the city.

In VI. 10, the martyrs voiced a petition to God to avenge their blood upon the wicked who at that time corrupted the earth. They were admonished to have patience, and they soon saw the reward of their sacrifice in the victory of Christ over the Roman persecutors. But now the Church has tasted a far more bitter persecution from the new Babylon than did the primitive Church from the ancient one. And the gratitude of all her children is here voiced in the word ALLELUIA. God has at the most opportune time heard and granted the prayer of the early martyrs; and the prophecy of the ONE FOLD AND ONE SHEPHERD shall be a reality. (See Isaias XXV. to XXX).

Verse 3

The second alleluia is added by the faithful multitudes exulting over the end of the City of Evil. The smoke ascending from the ruins of Babylon is but the visible pledge of God's justice and faithfulness fulfilling His promises to end the tyranny of sin and to establish His kingdom of truth, justice and liberty. This smoke not only signalizes the final defeat of the powers of evil in the world but also alludes to XIV. 11 and symbolizes the torments and impotent rage of the wicked incessantly hurling blasphemies in the face of God for subduing and condemning them.

The smoke of the burning city will be an everlasting testimony to the elect, to the martyrs of the Lamb, of God's eminent justice and of the horrible consequences of sin, which they have escaped by their sacrifice. The smoke therefore elicits the second alleluia, for it is not like the smoke of a mere material fire that evaporates quickly but is an eternally ascending column of incense to the justice of God. This verse recalls the thirty-fourth chapter of Isaias and especially verse 9 predicting the final destruction of Edom.

Verse 4

After the multitudes of faithful have voiced their exultation and thanksgiving for the judgment upon the mother of evils, the priesthood and episcopate express their approval of the sentiments of the people with a grand AMEN. This order is quite proper and to be expected, because priests and bishops will have been hunted down, and could not publicly lead the faithful in divine service in those days of peril. They will be obliged to save their precious lives when it is reasonably possible. In the countries in which Antichrist is supreme, the clergy will be martyred, imprisoned or in hiding. After the destruction of the city, the people will dare to assert their rights and will give public thanksgiving to God for having condemned the city. The followers of Antichrist will have been subdued and terrified by the seven last plagues and the sudden and un-looked-for end of Babylon. The rest of the people of the world will bring priests and bishops out of hiding and liberate them from prison. Priests will be the first to offer the Holy Sacrifice in thanksgiving for the judgments of God, and then the bishops will offer solemn pontifical Masses in jubilation and anticipation of the complete victory over Antichrist. Thus they pronounce the AMEN and ALLELUIA in the grand and solemn liturgy of the Church. The order of divine service is therefore the reverse of what it was in V. 8 and normally is, when the bishops take the lead, and priests and people follow. The bishops must first gather the priests around before they can carry through the pontifical sevices, but before that the priests can offer solemn Masses of praise and thanksgiving.

Verse 5

After the episcopate has given its approval to the rejoicing of the faithful and priesthood, the pope gives the final orders to worship. The voice from the throne is the voice of one of the four living beings, the lion, the Head of the Church. He may have gone to Jerusalem incognito after the ascension of the Two Prophets and ordered the seven plagues. Now his first act will be to appoint a new holyday. Not only the faithful but all who fear God though not yet members of the Church are invited to participate in this feast of joyful thanksgiving. The text reads, "you who fear Him, the small and the great". This calls on those who have till now not been "servants" of God but have feared Him enough to remain reverent and have not joined the blasphemers. All these are invited to join in worship and thereafter to become members of the Church. The "little" ones have done and suffered little for the cause of God during the reign of terror, have not had the courage to openly denounce Antichrist and his followers but have not denied their faith. It numbers the children and those of lesser spiritual advancement, who have not polluted themselves with the vices of the antichristians. The "great ones" will have risen to lofty spiritual heights by their fearlessness in the path of danger, strengthening and confirming the faith of others, suffering torture or imprisonment, the loss of property and civil rights and the grief over the death of loved ones. Among the great ones will be the seven angels who have poured out the seven last plagues upon the wicked and all bishops and priests who have fearlessly encouraged the faithful, have risked everything and borne the brunt of the persecution. Those who fear God are also rulers of countries that have not joined Antichrist and have aided the Church by secretly upholding the rights of all.

Verse 6

No sooner has the Head of the Church spoken, than the vociferous answer awakens and soars heavenward from every nation under the sun. St. John like a true poet searches from heaven to earth for illustrations to adequately express what he heard. It was again the voice of many tumultuous multitudes but vastly more voluminous than in verse one; it was like the rumbling of enumerable cataracts, of pouring cloudbursts and of the battering waves of oceans and the diapason voice of many vehement thunders reverberating through the skies in a tremendous roar. In VII. 9, the Seer beheld a multitude that no man could number serving God in the Church; but here are many vast multitudes, and their utterings of adoration and thanksgiving surpasses the expressive power of all human language. It alludes by contrast to XI. 10, to the victory of Antichrist over the Two Prophets, and foretells how much greater will be the number of those who shall rejoice over the victory of the Church. Those who feared to join the leaders in verse one now contribute their share to the hymn of thanksgiving.

The rejoicing of all who fear God exceeds all bounds, because all have the most undeniable proof of His benevolent providence, His almighty power having manifestly crushed the pride and defiance of man. The false miracles of the False Prophet and of the statue of Antichrist are exposed to be diabolical fraud. Those who controlled the world by financial manipulations are wiped out, and the world is delivered from their greed. And the faithful know that the destruction of the evil city forebodes the speedy doom of Antichrist. Thereafter war is banned and peace shall weep no more. The church stands glorified before the whole world, and there shall be no more way to deny the truth of her claims or suppress her beneficent activity and universal sway. Through her, Christ will reign. What was announced in X. 7 and expected confidently in XI. 17 and XII. 10 is becoming reality.

The praise and thanksgiving ordered by the supreme

authority are given for a reason that is worthy of the supreme authority. The theme of the note of praise is not the destruction of the enemy, but "Our God the Lord almighty has entered upon his reign". The Godless world-powers are shaken to their foundations and shall pass out of existence, and the King of ages will rule unhindered and forever. The Pope as the Vicar of Christ and representative of God's right to rule the world through the centuries claims the kingdom for OUR God, the God of the Christians, who is Jesus Christ, the King of kings. Antichrist and all other false gods shall wither before the fierce onslaughts of His power. All Christians will see the power of the One in whom they trusted, for whom they lived, suffered and risked all, supreme over all enemies, and hence they join in the alleluia of praise uttered by the supreme voice to OUR God.

2. The Wedding Feast Of The Lamb.

Verses 7-10.

Verse 7

The reason for the world-wide rejoicing as expressed by the Supreme Voice is the approaching marriage feast of the Lamb and the worthiness of the Spouse. The wedding feast is briefly mentioned to be taken up again and described at length in chapters XXI. and XXII. Just as chapters XVII., XVIII. and XIX. give a detailed description of the judgment upon the wicked mentioned in XIV. 8, 9 and XVI. 16, so the glorious career of the Church for the next 1,000 years indicated in XIX. 7-10 and XX. 6 is set forth in an idealized portrait in chapters XXI. and XXII. The faithful most intimately united with Christ through all they have suffered for His sake find their only solace in the eucharistic mystery and utter their joy and jubilation over the sweeping victory that will make Him King of kings in truth. The faithful amplify and swell the alleluia intoned by the supreme pastor and give the eucharistic Lord the glory and homage due Him for the divine strength and life throbbing in their veins which enabled them to hold out to a final victory.

The Spouse is the Church. In chapter twelve she appeared as the mother of the regenerated human race and here as the

Bride of the Lamb. In chapter seventeen another woman appears, the Harlot, the rival and enemy of the Bride and Mother. In the Old Covenant God was the Bridegroom of the Synagogue, and in the New, Jesus Christ is the Bridegroom of the Church. The marriage feast of the Lamb is the conversion of all nations to the Church. At that wedding they will be feasted by Christ in the Eucharist, and He becomes the Bridegroom of every individual soul. The Spouse was purified in the fires of persecution and freed from all faults and made worthy to be the wife of the spotless Lamb and to beget and rear uncounted multitudes of souls for Heaven. This wedding of the Lamb ushers in the predicted golden age in which Heaven shall be peopled with sanctified souls. The Church has labored for ages past to prepare for the feast appointed in divine foreknowledge. She shall be mature in every faculty when the time of the wedding feast has arrived. She has successfully solved every modern problem and will thereafter have the solution for every enigma and the true answer for every perplexing question. Such are the reasons for the jubilation of the faithful when they understand that the realization of God's purposes in the establishment of His universal dominion is at hand. The Bride is ready and is waiting for the arrival of the Bridegroom. A new viewpoint of the old truth is brought before us here. According to St. Paul, Christ prepared for Himself a bride "holy and without blemish" (Eph. V. 27), but here the Bride has prepared herself by her own efforts. In St. Paul's words the divine endowments of the Church are shown, while the faithful co-operation of the Church with these graces and endowments to grow spiritually rich and mature is here presented.

Verse 8

The materials of her wedding gown are pure and shining linen. White linen is the emblem of sanctifying grace in the Apocalypse and in the liturgical usage of the Church. It is made white and fine only by a great deal of labor and sacrifice, self-denial and patience. The harlot of chapter seventeen was arrayed in purple and jewels. Those are the ornaments of the world. The Church is arrayed in white, the color of God's elect. Her children will be saints in those days. The wedding gown of the Church will then be more than white and pure made of sinlessness and sanctifying grace, it will glitter with the righteous deeds and heroic virtues of the saints. This shining splendor is given her bridal attire specifically by her miraculous power manifested so brilliantly before the world in the pouring out of the seven bowls. Besides this, the faithful and especially the priesthood and religious have suffered much and with heroic fortitude have borne the persecution of Antichrist patiently. So now their virtues shine before the world and elicit the admiration of all. The Church will be beautiful to the beholder in those days, and this spiritual beauty and nobility will attract all peoples to her doors to be taught the ways of God (Isa. II. 3). The Bride of the Lamb will command the reverence of all peoples and all will pronounce her worthy to be their Queen.

The bearer of the voice from the throne appears to St. John in person and addresses him. The sentence he verbally dictated is: "Blessed are they who are called to the marriage supper of the Lamb". These memorable words are to be committed to writing at once. This marriage supper is the invitation and reception of all peoples and nations into the Church. It shall be celebrated shortly when the victory over the wicked is complete and final in the defeat of Antichrist. The vision of the Bride is thus exchanged for the vision of the feast to which all people are invited; the metaphor of the Bride recedes from the scene and the conversion of all nations appears in the blessed fruit of membership in the Church.

No one can be pronounced truly blessed unless his happiness is everlasting. All true blessedness grows out of membership in the Church, because it is the earnest of everlasting felicity in Heaven. Probably the chief reason why membership in the Church is now true felicity is the certainty that all who heed the invitation are foreknown to continue in unwavering fidelity, because the miracles of this time shall bring an almost irresistible force to bear upon the will. And the guests are the survivors of the universal cataclysm that shall wreck the old world at Antichrist's condemnation, on which wreckage the new Christian world shall be built. According to the words of Our Lord, the marriage supper had begun in His day. (Mt. XXII. 2; Lc. XIV. 16). The Church was called the Bride in the Gospel. (Jo. III. 29). The Old Covenant of God with His people was also called a marriage feast, and the spiritual favors God granted His people were the ornaments of the Bride, the Synagogue (Ezech. XVI. 8).

Verse 10

The last words of verse nine may have led St. John to mistake the speaker for Christ, when he pronounced the dictated words the "true words of God". Or because he was the vicar of Christ, the pope, he resembled Christ so much that the seer fell down to worship him. He, however, tells him to forebear. He might have been a celestial spirit, but for his words, "I am a fellow-servant of thine and thy brethren who have the testimony of Jesus", he reveals himself a member of the hierarchy, yea the head of the Church, who in the foregoing verses ordered all peoples of the world to offer praise and thanksgiving to God. Although he may hold a higher position in the Church as successor of the prince of the apostles, he is only a fellow-servant of Christ with St. John being divinely directed to reveal these truths to him and having like him "the testimony of Jesus", which is "the spirit of prophecy". The last words of the verse are still the words of the angel (Bede).

The angel is like the other angels of the Apocalypse who act and speak for some future saint, a celestial representative of that pope who shall reign as the first pope of Jerusalem. St. Vincent Ferrer acts in the Apocalypse long before he was created and is beheld in a vision delivering his message to the world. All this is possible in the perfect foreknowledge of God, or prophecy would be impossible. A prophecy which relates mere future happenings is of much simpler nature than one in which persons appear, speak and act, who will not exist until thousands of years after the revelation. Such creations represent the highest achievements of the spirit of prophecy and reveal the foreknowledge of God as concrete and perfect and the revelations to His prophets not general and vague but specific. The action of St. John recalls that of Daniel before the angel (VIII. 17; X. 9, 17).

"The testimony of Jesus is the spirit of prophecy". St. John was a witness of Jesus by his apostolic office by his preaching and exemplification of the Lord's life and also by his martyrdom.

The angel who appears to him is also a martyr of Jesus, having suffered a great deal though not death through the presence of Antichrist. He is like St. John endowed with the spirit of prophecy. The spirit of prophecy is the spirit of Jesus (Acts XVI. 7), which gave testimony of His coming in the Old Testament and of His appearance and future parousia in the New. The angel and St. John are therefore prophets of the new order instituted by Christ, and they are equals.

3. The Warrior On The White Horse. Armies Of Heaven.

Verses 11-17.

Verse 11

A door in heaven was opened in IV. 1, and the tabernacle of God in heaven was opened in XI. 19 and in XV. 5, but heaven itself is opened wide now, and a Victor rides forth on a white horse. The beast in the guise of a victor rode forth on a white horse in chapter VI. It was the emperor and the ancient Roman Empire victorious over the Church. Here the role is reversed. Christ is now the Victor. At his triumphal entry into Jerusalem on Palm Sunday, He rode upon an ass. But then He came as Savior (Mt. XXI. 2). Now He comes to judge "with justice".

The rider is called "Faithful and True". These same titles were given our Lord several times before (I. 5; III. 7, 14). It alludes to Isaias (XI. 5), where justice and truth are the cincture of the Messias. Garments in Scriptural language frequently symbolize traits of character or the attributes of God. Christ is called Faithful, because He will fulfill all prophecy and will prove the reliabiity of His own prophecy, that the gates of hell shall not prevail against His Church. The true believers were often admonished to patiently await the fulfillment of His threats and promises in God's own time. And at last they shall reap the reward of their trust in Him. The golden promises of the prophets shall be fulfilled (Is. XI. 6), and the millennium shall be ushered in. Christ will take no unfair advantage of His enemies but will judge all in justice and will fight a fair fight against them. Justice will make Him invulnerable. And He will mete out to them what they have earned and will liberate the Church from their oppression.

Verse 12

His eyes flashing like a flame manifest the approach of the judgment. They remind us of what He said to the Bishop of Thyatira (II. 18), whom He threatened with judgment for his lack of principle in tolerating wickedness in his congregation. He comes this time to burn all the weeds that have grown in His field and to enlighten the faithful by His power and glory. In Daniel the throne of God coming in judgment is like a fire, and a stream of fire flows before it (VII. 9-10). Fire cleanses, and Christ will cleanse the world with fire to make it a fit dwelling place for His elect.

The rider wears many diadems. The diadem is the emblem of supreme dominion. The enemy of the Church in VI. 2 wore only a wreath, while the dragon wore seven diadems on his seven heads, and the beast wears ten on his ten horns. Those world-powers wear a limited number of diadems, while Christ wears unnumbered ones emblematic of unrestricted dominion over all kingdoms and empires. He refused the kingdom of this world offered Him by Satan in the desert, and now He has won a kingdom that transcends all kingdoms and empires.

He will have a new name, which is a mystery, and which no man knows but Himself. The name may be expressive of His nature and personality, which is an impenetrable mystery and cannot be comprehensively understood by any created mind. The name will have a direct relationship to this victory and will be known but not fully comprehended after the victory. Isaias (LXII. 2) promised Israel a new name given it by the Messias at the time of its future conversion. The followers of Our Lord shall all have a new name in the new Jerusalem (II. 17). Christ may here appear bearing the new name in letters of fire upon His forehead.

Verse 13

The garment of Christ is sprinkled with blood. Isaias beheld the same vision (LXIII. 1-6) but does not give the detailed description given here. The visions of the prophets were more or less glimpses of the future glorious career of Christ. So Isaias sees Him coming from Bozra His garments dyed with the blood of His enemies. Interpreters of Isaias openly admit the blood to be that of the enemies but with strange inconsistency will then consider it His own blood shed in His passion and death. The similarity of the description given by Isaias emphatically argues for the same event. Since in Isaias the blood upon the garments of the victorious warrior is that of the enemy, it must be considered the same here. Edom represented the enemy of God's people, and Bozra was situated between Petra and the Red Sea in the direction of Egypt. Egypt was the first world-empire, the first incarnation of the beast, which Christ comes to destroy. The comparison with Isaias (LXIII) leads with compelling logic to the conclusion that Isaias narrates the judgment on Antichrist by the Messias. In verse four, Isaias calls this treading the wine-press "the day of vengeance". Verse fifteen here is the completed revelation of what was stated in XIV. 20.

The rider upon the white horse leading the armies of heaven is given a name that all knew; His name is "THE WORD OF GOD". He bears that name because in the intentions and decrees of God foretold by His prophets, He is to make the "day of vengeance", which is the Great Day of Almighty God, historical reality. The text seems to carry an allusion to the death of the first-born in Egypt as stated in Wisdom. (XVIII. 15).

Verse 14

The armies that are in heaven follow Christ. These may be the nations that belong to the Church. But Isaias called the heathen Cyrus the anointed of the Lord (XLV. 1), because he was to liberate the Jews from the Babylonian Captivity. So here, many nations not yet Catholic may furnish military forces for the defense of the Church and the defeat of Antichrist. But these warriors would needs be converted by the convincing miracles the whole world shall witness in those days and be baptized and in sanctifying grace, for the text says they are "clothed in fine linen, white and clean". They are in heaven, they are members of the Church. The armies of Christ are the army of the Great Eagle who rescued (XII. 14) and protected the Church and maintained his independence against Antichrist during his domination of the world. Perhaps many others from the nations subjugated by Antichrist shall have joined the standard of the Great Eagle. In Hebrew, the armies of Israel are also called the army of heaven (Dan. VIII. 10). The garments of Christ's army are not sprinkled with blood, because Christ will tread the wine-press of the wrath of God alone (Isa. LXIII. 3).

The army that follows Christ might be the priests of the Church, for these warriors are clothed as priests are elsewhere (IV. 4; XV. 6). Perhaps under divine guidance the pope or some other eminent saint will bear the Sacred Species aloft in an airplane followed by the bishops and priests who are present in Jerusalem and fly out unarmed to meet the hosts of Antichrist. Such interpretation would seem to put the armies from the East (XVI. 12) into the army of Antichrist. The time will reveal the manner of fulfillment. The most stupendous miracle would be, if Christ in the Sacred Host would then appear in human form in the sight of all and give the command that ends Antichrist and his followers. After such a victory the tabernacle of His eucharistic presence would be more glorious than ever fulfilling the prediction of Isaias in a new way (XI. 10). The prophet seems to say that the Sacred Species shall be the ensign around which the faithful shall assemble and be led into battle, as the Ark of the Covenant was frequently carried in the vanguard against the enemies of Israel (Josue VI. 6; 1 Kings IV. 4; Isa. XI. 10). The Eucharistic Christ may give at this time one manifest and unforgettable flash of His hidden power as a warrior to destroy all that is deliberately unholy.

Verse 15

Out of His mouth proceeded a sharp, two-edged sword. The warrior on the white horse in chapter VI. had only a bow with which to single out victims for death, but Christ will annihilate the enemy with the sweep of a double-edged sword. Isaias had foretold (XLIX. 2): "And he made my mouth like a sharp sword". But St. John designates the sword of Christ the instrument of extermination when he calls it the large Thracian, double-edged battle-sword. Christ appeared thus in the first vision (I. 16) to pronounce His verdicts upon the seven churches. He comes now to execute the judgment, to offer no more mercy to the godless armies opposing His Church, to give the sword the right of way without restraint. The followers of Antichrist are surfeited with iniquity, for they have ridiculed and derided all manifest miracles wrought for their conversion and have become impenitent, which leaves nothing for them but condemnation.

In His role as Judge, Christ will not act as the "good shepherd", but for His shepherd's staff He shall have a rod of iron, the rod of justice to punish every transgression. It shall be the rod of death for all followers of Antichrist, for they are all murderers. The sentence, "He ruleth them with a rod of iron", is supplemented by the subsequent sentence, "he treadeth the wine-press of the fierce wrath of God almighty", making the meaning of the first sentence unmistakable. This is language borrowed from Isaias (LXIII. 3), or otherwise the vision was so vividly revealed to both prophets, that both described it in similar phraseology. Isaias also says: "the nation and the kingdom that shall not serve thee shall perish" (LX. 12). Christ uses the rod of iron upon Antichrist and his followers, who have scoffed at the eucharistic mystery (XIII. 6), the hidden power and glory of which shall now manifest themselves. (Isa. XI. 4). The language of this verse refers us to the vintage of XIV. 19-20.

Verse 16

In prophetic imagery, garments symbolize traits of character, rights and dignities of the wearer. Upon all His vestments, Christ bears the title: "KING OF KINGS AND LORD OF LORDS". The many diadems proclaim Him divinely appointed Ruler of creation and the words Lord of all things. Having the name on His thigh signifies His authority to enforce recognition of His rightful title and the submission of all nations. In the eucharistic mystery Christ rules the Church and He will reveal His right by defending her against her persecutors and ending their depradations.

4. The Invitation To The Supper Of The Beast.

Verses 17-18.

Verses 17-18

An angel standing in the sun invites all birds and beasts of prey to come together for a feast. The language used is similar to that dictated to the prophet Ezechiel (XXXIX. 17-20), when he is to invite all beasts to feast on the fallen hosts of Gog. The vision of an angel standing on the sun is a new way of predicting the quick and complete end of Antichrist and all his followers. The sun is the emblem of the all-seeing eye of God, which not only beholds in review all present happenings but all the future as clearly. Hence the outcome of the battle is announced from the sun before it begins. The brilliance of the victory is likewise betokened by the brilliance of the celestial body from which the announcement is made. The invitation alludes to the words of our Lord in the Gospel (Mt. XXIV. 28). Vultures fly very high, and from the viewpoint of the ancients, the sun was just a little above those birds of highest flight. The army is too vast to make burial of all the fallen possible before man shall be devoured by birds and beasts of prey. The battle shall be fought in a tropical or subtropical climate where there are large numbers of vultures. What a horrible contrast is this supper of the Beast to the marriage supper of the Lamb!

This invitation of the angel to so gruesome a feast recalls the words of Jeremias (Lam. I. 15), when the prophet mourns over the feast that God proclaimed for the enemies of Juda. It likewise recalls the vision of Isaias (VIII. 9-10) foretelling the concourse of the nations against Juda, which three times impels the prophet to repeat the exultant words, “and be overcome”. The angel appearing here may be like the one in XIV. 6 an eminent saint of the Church or the same one or the founder of a new religious society or a saintly bishop, cardinal or the pope. His standing on the sun may body forth the supreme authority and the certainty with which he predicts the immediate end of Antichrist. He is deeply versed in prophecy and divinely enlightened to foreknow the moment of victory. The inference may be drawn from this prophetic gift, that all peoples will freely concede to the Church as the spoils of victory for overthrowing Antichrist the right and authority of directing all governments thenceforth. Until the Church has healed the nations (XXII. 2) from the wounds and corruption of Antichrist's reign, the clergy may be elected to direct and guide national affairs.

The detailed portrayal of the army reveals to what vast height the might of Antichrist shall grow in so short a time as he shall have to rule the world. The angel enumerates all classes of men from the Ten Kings down to the common people. Yet with all his ostensible power, he is only the "son of perdition" (2 Thess. II. 3), and "goeth into destruction" (Apoc. XVII. 11). These are the armies he is seen arraying for the last battle in XVI. 16 at Armageddon. The angel announces the complete annihilation of these vast armies.

5. The Defeat Of The Beast.

Verses 19-end.

Verse 19

What was announced in XVI. 14-16 is now an accomplished fact; the mobilization of the armies is completed. The battle array is drawn up. It will be outside the city of Jerusalem, as XIV. 20 suggests, probably along the shore of the Mediterranean Sea the line of battle being 200 miles long. It will be the most stupendous review of military power the world has ever seen. All up-to-date war machinery will be there. And Antichrist will lead his war powers in person. Burning with pride and arrogance, he will eagerly begin the insane battle with the King of kings, as Daniel has foretold (VII. 22, 25, 26)). He has no doubt or misgivings about the outcome, because his self-conceit makes him sure of victory. The kings of his empire shall be there with all the armies and military equipment they can muster, because on the outcome of this battle shall depend the continuance or non-continuance of his reign and their regency. They have many armies. Perhaps the army of Christ will be the priests of the Church gathered in Jerusalem, who are borne aloft in airplanes to meet Antichrist and are led by a plane that carries the Sacred Species. Thus will the "Great Day of Almighty God" (Mal. IV. 5; Jer. XXX. 7; Apoc. XVI. 14) dawn upon the world.

At last appearance, the Beast had his vassal kings assembled to destroy Babylon (XVII. 6), whereupon he was minded to turn against the Lamb, the "Lord of lords and King of kings". The titles given Christ in this chapter, verse 16, are the same, in order to call attention to chapter XVII. The designs are no longer a secret. Babylon has been razed, but the Beast survives. This again shows that ancient Rome was not the Babylon of the Apocalypse and that the empire or the emperor were not the Beast. The city of Rome was not entirely destroyed, but the empire and emperors passed away. Antichrist knows of the return of the pope and cardinals from the "wilderness", and he is determined to end the existence of the Church by this last campaign. But his allotted time has been used up and his fate is sealed in God's decrees.

Verse 20

Although the line of battle is described as drawn up and ready for instantaneous action, no battle is reported. Antichrist is suddenly captured and together with his prophet dropped alive into the pool or lake of fire burning with brimstone. This is a miraculous intervention of Christ. He may utter a command from the Eucharist in words that are heard by both armies like the voice of a trumpet. Angels may execute the command. St. Paul says of this event: "whom the Lord Jesus shall kill with the breath of His mouth" (2 Thess. II. 8); and Isaias says: "and with the breath of His lips He shall slay the wicked one" (XI. 4). Without the aid of his prophet, Antichrist would not have established so vast and vicious an empire as he did or so quickly, hence the False Prophet shares fully in his guilt and must share in his destiny. There is even reason for meting out severer punishment to him, because it was he who seduced the peoples and nations by the signs he wrought in the name of Antichrist, and it was he who set on foot the persecution in which so much innocent blood was spilt. Therefore these two do not deserve to die a natural death but are cast alive into eternal death.

Probably at this moment the "great earthquake" predicted in XI. 19 and XVI. 18, 20, 21 will occur. The sword that proceeds from the mouth of Christ is His command and may appear in visible form, in a beam of lightning shaped like a sword. It may strike the earth at the moment in which the great earthquake is due. The earthquake may open wide fissures in the earth directly beneath the airplane of Antichrist, and a flame may shoot out miles high and envelop him and his prophet. In the sight of all the armies gathered for battle he thus visibly descends into the pool of fire, a visible model of hell.

Jerusalem shall be divided by deep chasms; the cities of the Gentiles shall fall; Antichrist's empire shall disappear forever (See XVI. 19-20). Although Jerusalem is converted to Christ since the ascension of the Two Prophets, the city must be altered and planned anew on a more extensive scale. Isaias intimates a rebuilding of the city on new and expanding lines, after it has been torn asunder by an earthquake. It shall not fall as do the cities of the infidels, although according to XVI. 15 some of the faithful here and elsewhere shall be killed in the earthquake.

Verse 21

The whole army of Antichrist shall be slain, not one shall escape. The chapter ends rather strangely and abruptly. In chapter XVI. 14-16 and in XIX. 19, the preparation for the last battle is briefly stated, but before the battle begins, the leader is cast alive into hell, and the battle is lost sight of altogether. By the sword from the mouth of Christ, the whole army of Antichrist is wiped out. Quite likely at this moment the earthquake together with the "great hail" (XI. 19; XVI. 18-21) shall be the answer to the command. The hail shall be of 50 to 100 pound weights and may consist of bombs. Or the airplanes collide with one another after the pilots become panic-stricken at the fate of Antichrist or burst into flame at the command of Christ. Dust and smoke may shoot into the air and instantly produce impenetrable darkness and a storm of such intensity after the earthquake that the airplanes tumble down with their loads of poison gasses and atomic bombs upon their own army below. All may explode then and open the fissures in the earth to the molten rock below on which water from the sea will run and cause explosions of steam that will throw stones of crushing weight into the air and hail them down on the army. The breaking of the earth's crust will make all war machinery immovable. Fear will paralyze everyone and hold them to be wiped out. The prophecy of Zacharias goes into fulfillment (XIV. 12-14). In the darkness, the army becomes helpless, as rocks and bombs hail upon them. Their strength wastes away; their eyes become inflamed; their tongues swell; panic siezes them and drives each man to frenzy and to fight for his own safety against anyone in his way whilst he stumbles into the great cracks and chasms in the earth's crust. The whole battle-line turns into an inferno; and as from hell itself, a howl of blasphemies mingles with the explosions of war munitions (XIV. 20). The kings and officers of Antichrist's army may be largely Jews (Zach. XIV. 14), who want to fight against Jerusalem and those who are converted to Christ. The instruments and implements of war with which they intended to raze Jerusalem as they razed Babylon shall destroy themselves (See Wisdom V. 22-24).

The last verses of Zacharias (XIV. 12-15) seem to be an afterthought added to what was said in verses 3 to 7 completing the description begun in verse three of the end to the world of sin and the man of sin and of the beginning of the new world, on the day that is known to the Lord called the "great day of almighty God" by other prophets. Commentators hesitate to give a definite time to the prophecies of these chapters of Zacharias. Chapter XII. seems to relate the Maccabean wars and the death of Christ. Chapter XIII. probably foretells the institution of the Sacraments, the final abolition of idolatry in Judea and the appearance of false prophets, who misled the people after the Crucifixion to rebel against Rome and thereby bring on the destruction of Jerusalem and still more complete destruction of the nation from 131 to 135 A. D. After this a small part of the nation shall remain, most of whom shall be converted, as chapter VII. of the Apocalypse reveals. Some apply the first part of chapter XIV. to the destruction of Jerusalem by Titus. (Eusebius, Cyrill, Theodotius or Theodatus). The text seems to be literally fulfilled in that destruction in verses 1 and 2. Thereupon the prophet seems to pass over to the death of Antichrist. In verses 4 and 5 the great earthquake is taken in review and the panic that shall seize the people still jittery from former quakes. From verse 8 to 11, the blessedness of the ages that follow Antichrist seems clearly set forth to be interrupted again by the afterthought on the end of Antichrist and his followers in verses 12 to 15. All in all the prophecy of Zacharias is so obscure and fragmentary that the Fathers are not agreed on a definite application of the chapters and verses to any future event or fact of history.

How large a part of mankind shall be wiped out by the seven last plagues, the persecution of Antichrist and the final earthquake remains a deep secret. Probably the material progress of the world, transportation and communication, culture and the inventions of science shall remain to be inherited by those who shall be saved from the universal cataclysm. Less time will be needed then to provide for the material wants of man, which will leave more for the acquisition of eternal riches. All who have witnessed the miracles and supernatural power of the Church will be thoroughly converted and will strive for spiritual advancement. The marriage supper of the Lamb shall begin. Sin and wickedness shall not be cleared out of the world altogether; however, it shall no longer be the controlling force. Truth and grace shall be triumphant, and error together with vice, irreligion and infidelity shall be discredited and despised and shall slink away from respectability, which in our time clothes it and allows it to parade boldly before the world. With the end of Antichrist and his reign, the third and final "Woe" is finished. The darkness related by Zacharias is told in private prophecies not only to enshroud the armies of Antichrist but to cover the whole earth and to be of three days duration. The great earthquake, if world-wide, would cause an eruption of possibly all old volcanoes and many new ones scattered over the earth everywhere and could throw up so much dust that the predicted darkness would result.

Those who contend, contrary to all conclusions which must necessarily follow from the last nine chapters, that the Beast is the Roman Empire, will have to explain how the empire could be seized or captured while it is leading an army and be hurled bodily into the pool of fire, into which Satan is also hurled later, and be *tormented* there with the False Prophet and Antichrist (XX. 9-10). Death and hell too are cast into the pool of fire (XX. 14), but they are not *tormented.* Only persons and evil spirits can be tortured, not systems, organizations or empires. The underworld and death, being only abstract existences, will continue to exist in the pool of fire, when all the wicked are finally consigned there, but they are not tormented.

CHAPTER XX.

Westminster Version

And I beheld an angel coming down from heaven, 1. holding in his hand the key of the bottomless pit, and a great chain. And he seized the dragon, the 2. ancient serpent, who is the Devil and Satan, and bound him for a thousand years, and cast him into 3. the bottomless pit, which he locked and sealed over him, that he might no more lead the nations astray until the thousand years should have elapsed. After that he must be loosed for a little time.

And I saw thrones, and those sat thereon to 4. whom was committed judgment, and I saw the souls of those that had been beheaded because of the witness to Jesus and because of the word of God, because they had not worshipped the beast or its image, and had not taken its mark upon their forehead and upon their hand. They came to life again, and reigned with Christ for a thousand years.

The rest of the dead came not to life until the 5. thousand years were accomplished. This is the first 6. resurrection. Blessed and holy is he that hath part in the first resurrection! Over these the second death hath no power, but they shall be priests of God and of Christ, and they shall reign with him for a thousand years.

And when the thousand years are accomplished, 7. Satan shall be loosed from his prison, and he shall come forth to lead astray the nations which are in 8. the four corners of the earth, Gog and Magog, in order to gather them together for the battle; their number shall be as the sand of sea. And they 9. came up over the breadth of the earth, and encompassed the camp of the saints and the beloved city.

And fire came down from heaven and devoured 10. them, and the devil, who led them astray, was cast into the lake of fire and brimstone where are the beast and false prophet, and they shall be tormented day and night for ever and ever. And I beheld 11. a great white throne, and him who sitteth upon it: from his face the earth and the heaven fled away, and no place was found for them. And I saw the dead the great and the small, standing before the throne, 12. and books were opened. And another book was opened which is the book of life; and the dead were judged from the things written in the books, according to their works. And the sea gave up the dead from her 13. midst, and death and hell gave up the dead from their midst; and they were judged each according to their works. 14. And Death and Hell were cast into the lake of fire. This is the second death, the lake of fire. 15. Whoever was not found written in the book of life, he was cast into the lake of fire.

X. LAST JUDGMENTS

1. The Fruits Of The Victory.

Chapter XX.

A. Satan Is Bound a Thousand Years.

Verse 1

In chapter IX., a star to whom the key of the bottomless abyss was given was seen fallen from Heaven. Now an angel comes from heaven with the key of the abyss in his possession. In chapter IX., the star was an apostate priest, who was empowered with the key to open the abyss permitting its inmates to lead into error and wickedness those who did not have a living faith. These errors and the resultant wickedness were transmitted to posterity until they culminated in the reign of Antichrist. After this impostor has been dethroned and cast into hell, some saintly bishop or priest having obtained possession of the key by his sufferings, fearlessness and sanctity during the reign of terror comes with the chain in his hand to undo the work of the apostate priest. The action of the angel links the apostasy of the star of chapter IX. with the reign of Antichrist indirectly, since it wipes out the consequences of that apostasy. That partial apostasy from Christ becomes complete in the submission to Antichrist. Mohammedanism, the Greek Schism, the Great Western Schism, and Protestantism estranged the Christian world from Christ and produced secret societies, which plotted everywhere to de-christianize the governments of Europe. Socialism was invented by an antichristian Jew and was an opponent from the beginning of the evil Capitalism sponsored by Freemasonry. Militant Communism boldly compels all where it gets control to apostatize completely from Christ and God. Communism is the final preparation for the reign of Antichrist. And communism was invented by a descendant of the Jews who were left over from the destruction of their nation.

The angel is possibly the one who invited the birds of the air to the gruesome feast of fallen warriors. He will kick Satan into the abyss. If men are left to the beneficent influence of the Church, they will of their own accord join in large numbers, because the grace of God leads them and works with everything the Church officially does. But as long as the powers of darkness have free rein to counteract the work of the Church and to deaden the effect of grace, the work will be laborious and slow; though if the clergy would all have apostolic zeal, the conversion of the world would be accomplished. Why then did God permit the powers of evil to be turned loose from the abyss? In order to punish the wicked in the Church who lolled in indifference and lukewarmness, and to let the Church win the victory not only over the world but over the powers of hell, gaining thus the greater glory for Christ and the greater influence for herself and the more perfect a restoration of all Godliness. The key of the abyss was given to the apostate priest to turn loose the powers of evil against the tepid in the Church, but she has wrested the key again from the forces of evil by her faithfulness in utmost dangers and trials. The key is the emblem of her *authority* over the abyss, and the chain of her *power* to bind Satan and check the activity of his forces. Because she alone has the power to subdue the source of evil, the Church alone can bring peace and security to the world.

According to all signs, the activity of Satan and his hordes in the Church and in the world are making swift and final preparations for the advent of Antichrist. The Church, however, is better organized than ever employing both clergy and laity with fuller force to convert the world and is making a million converts a year. But the gates of hell are sending forth every available force to thwart her work and to destroy the ripening harvest. If there is peace for the Church in some regions, it may be the lull before the storm and is full of woesome forebodings.

Verse 2

The angel seizes the dragon, the ancient serpent, who is the devil and satan, and binds him with the chain for a thousand years. The Seer uses the same names as in XII. 9 to designate the one who tried to wreck the Church from within. After his expulsion, he engaged Antichrist and placed at his disposal all evil forces of earth and hell to accomplish THE SAME results from without. But as in the first, so he failed in the second plan;

and now, after the death of his agent and all co-laborers, he shall be bound for a thousand years, so he may no more interfere with the salutary activity of the Church. He is whisked out of the way, bound and kicked into the abyss, and his baleful influence is at an end. He may no longer as a dragon pervade all world-developments, control and direct them to worship him; nor as the ancient serpent mislead the world into error and sin, from which follows death; nor as the devil overwhelm the world with evils; nor as satan oppose Christ and God and accuse the faithful falsely. He appeared as a dragon in XII. 9 cast to the earth, and in XII. 18 he stood upon the sands of the sea watching and directing the trend of human affairs until he succeeded in uniting his servants under Antichrist to assemble for the world-battle, in which they all met their Armageddon in XIX. 17-21. That ends and seals his influence and activity for a thousand years.

All evil institutions are feverishly active to check the progress of the Church in heathen lands. The hour has not arrived for the supreme conflict, because on the one hand the clergy has not sunk to such a depth of tepidity and torpor as to make an apostasy of ONE THIRD their number possible by bloody persecution, and on the other hand the missions are not far enough developed to enable them to stand on their own feet and to derive for those peoples the benefits of the miracles by the Two Prophets and saints and of the supernatural power of the Church in those days of terror. There is a foreboding of the imminent supreme conflict in the activity of the enemy to bring about a complete revolt from Christ and God which must come before the victory is won. But the conflict will be held off a little while for the benefit of the missions. If governments persist in their persecutions, so as nearly to destroy the Church in some countries, so much the smaller a part of those countries will be saved from the wreckage of Antichrist's reign; while if they aid the work of the Church, so much the greater a part will be saved and so much more glorious will those countries be in the future millennium, when the Church shall be universally obeyed, and her faithful members shall pre-dominate in numbers and influence and shall control the destinies of all nations.

In Zacharias (II. 4, 5, 10, 11) is a prophecy promising the re-establishment of the theocracy in Jerusalem, which shall then lie secure without walls. The prophecy was not fulfilled after the

Babylonian Captivity, for the walls of Jerusalem were ordered rebuilt. The prophets often place the Messianic blessings in juxtaposition to the beginning of God's favors on the return from the Captivity. The re-establishment of the theocracy was the foundation upon which the kingdom of Christ was to be built, which would finally win the victory over evil, whereupon would begin the blessed epoch of which the restoration after the Captivity was the earnest and remote preparation. Isaias relates the attributes of the Savior and the glory of His reign and then passes over to His complete victory over the forces of evil and depicts the millennium. (Isa. II. 2; XI; LXII; LXV. 17-25; Osee I. 10, 11; III. 4-5; XIV. 5-10. See Aug. de civitate Dei. XVIII. 28).

The angel kicks Satan into the bottomless abyss. Antichrist and his prophet were cast into the "pool of fire". The bottomless abyss and the "pool of fire" are obviously not identical. Satan and his hordes shall be shut up in the bottomless abyss, so they may not seduce the world during the epoch of grace, virtue and bountiful blessings. At the end of that time Satan shall be released to seduce the wicked and then be hurled into the "pool of fire and brimstone". Antichrist and his agent filled up their measure of iniquity and received the full penalty. But Satan shall merit still more punishment, after which he is finished.

The angel not only kicks Satan into the abyss and closes it, but he puts the seal of the Church upon the lock, so that the arch-enemy can be released only by permission or action of the Church. He shall no more develop organized anti-Catholic societies to mislead the Christian world, puzzle the heathens and hamper the Church. Individual malice can avail nothing against the Church. No doubt lesser evil spirits will tempt souls, but they will only strengthen them in virtue in this combat. After the decisive battle in which Satan's power has been paralyzed, that host of devils that has developed the evils culminating in the reign of Antichrist will be sealed up with their king not all evil spirits (Thomas).

The judgment upon Satan was stated by our Lord Himself as imminent (Jo. XII. 31), when He said: "Now shall the prince of this world be cast out". And the judgment was spoken, when He instituted the Holy Eucharist, for then He said: "the prince of this world is already judged" (Jo. XVI. 11). The judgment was executed at His death or resurrection, and Satan was bound for the first time. The next binding shall be when Christ shall destroy Antichrist. The first time *Christ* bound him, the next time the *Church* will do it. The smoke in IX. 2 streamed out of the abyss and produced the locusts on earth; Their king, Appollyon, came from the abyss (IX. 11); the mission of Antichrist is from the abyss (XI. 7): therefore all those creatures and forces are related, and the organizations they fostered were hostile to the Church and furthered Satan's plans; and they shall disappear from the earth with the binding of Satan for a thousand years.

B. The Martyrs Shall Reign A Thousand Years.

Verses 4-6.

Verse 4

Verse four is impossible of logical interpretation for those who place the thousand years chronologically ahead of the reign of Antichrist, because its contents are a positive contradiction of that theory.

The sight of the thrones catching the attention of the Seer recalls the manner of description in IV. 4, except that here he does not say who occupies them. They are evidently there as in the former vision for the Four Living Beings and the Twenty Four Elders. The Church sits in judgment on the life and deeds of the martyrs. Antichrist and his bloodthirsty followers are slain. He added many martyrs to the former lists. The Church in solemn session canonizes them. This judgment is therefore not that of Daniel (VII. 9-22) for that is a past event in XIX. 19-21 of the Apocalypse. The court now in session was predicted in XI. 18. These martyrs have encouraged and strengthened the weak to remain faithful to the end; they have given up all share in the earthly millennium and therefore merit the highest recognition and honor from the Church. And the Church now gives it.

These martyrs have died for the "testimony of Jesus and for the word of God". "Beheaded" is metonymy for every kind of violent death. St. John still has in mind the martyrs of his time, who if they were Romans, were most commonly beheaded, although many were tormented to death in other ways. In the days of Antichrist, they shall most probably be shot, for even he and his followers will not want to bring upon themselves the scorn and opprobrium of the world for unnecessary cruelty. Many may die in prison or from the effects of imprisonment. These martyrs have steadfastly professed and practiced their belief in Christ and contradicted the claims of Antichrist to the Messiasship, and for that testimony they died. They did not worship Antichrist, when divine worship was decreed him in the kingdoms of his empire, on the non-conformity with which rested the penalty of death. Neither did they adore his image, which appeared alive in Babylon and spoke. This would be the citizens and tourists who for mere curiosity went to see the statue but did not adore it. These refusing adoration may be arrested, tried and condemned. It will be considered sufficient submission to Antichrist to wear the initials of his name on the forehead or the back of the hand. The Church will sit in judgment, and the judgment will be strict, so that, even if anyone has died for other reasons but has worn the insignia of Antichrist on his head or hand, he cannot be canonized.

The martyrs who shed their blood under Antichrist shall rule the world with Christ for a thousand years. They saved the world from utter destruction by their heroism; so they shall be specially honored by their own nation. They may receive control over the elements and whatever else influences human life, as many saints have had power of intercession against diseases, misfortunes and calamities. The name "Christ" is written here and in three other places of the Apocalypse, XI. 15, XII. 10 and XX. 6, and in each instance it alludes to Psalm II. 2. Christ is now victorious over those enemies about whom David wrote. His champions shall be victorious with Him and share in His unperturbed dominion in the world.

During the thousand years also those shall rule with Christ who have faithfully held to the teachings of the Church, kept the commandments and practiced their religion in defiance of all danger, though they may have died from other causes. The language of verse 4 permits such interpretation. They have not submitted to Antichrist nor adored him nor received the imprint of his insignia on their foreheads or hands. They will protect the virtuous, God-fearing and innocent against the attacks of the vicious, who will still be in the world but will not have the right-of-way as in our evil day. Each nation shall then have many martyr-saints whose power shall be united with Christ and in union with Him shall direct human affairs during the millennium. They will reign from Antichrist till the end of time. This places the THOUSAND YEARS after the advent and domination of Antichrist whom their courage and constancy defeats and overthrows.

Verse 5

"The rest of the dead" may mean only the reprobate. Besides the martyrs, a large number of other people will remain faithful to Christ, but they die from natural causes—diseases or old age or the scourges inflicted by the Two Prophets. They may rule with Christ and the martyrs during the thousand years. And the text does not hold out the enjoyment of eternal life after the thousand years to the "rest of the dead" but only what it says no share in the glory and bliss of the elect, who reject the Beast and all his alluring promises.

The entrance of the souls of the just into eternal bliss after death is called "the first resurrection". Christ and His Blessed Mother have anticipated the general resurrection, because they were not subject to the universal law of death through sin. The Two Prophets shall also anticipate the general resurrection, because they share eminently in the redemption of the world. But apparently the bodies of the martyrs shall not rise from the dead now, for then verse four would not attribute to the "souls" of the martyrs the reward of their faithfulness. When the body dies, the soul lapses into a state of unconsciousness of short duration like a complete cessation of life. On leaving the body, it is roused from this unconscious state, and if it is in sanctifying grace, its entering into everlasting life can be truly called a resurrection. The resurrection of the bodies of all the martyrs at this time seems to contradict other parts of the New Testament. Yet private expositions claim a resurrection of the bodies of the martyrs of Antichrist. Likewise some interpreters reason this resurrection from the text.

Verse 6

The days of the millennium as described more fully in chapters XXI. and XXII. have begun. Perhaps the Christians who have survived the gory ordeal of persecution grieve over their martyred dead and other loved ones who have been carried off by the plagues or calamities of that time. The inspired Seer therefore pens a word of consolation for the bereaved, assuring them that those who have died loving Christ have an enviable glory and happiness which vastly excels the peace and measureless bounties of God during the millennium. The survivors are rather to be pitied. The beatification of the martyrs is also a cheering exhortation to all who shall be brought to trial to be condemned for their faith not to faint or falter, for such a death is the dawn of a glorious morning.

As the reprobate enter eternal death immediately after the body dies, and as that is the completion of the first death, since sin causes the death of both body and soul; so the entrance into eternal life is the first resurrection, because the soul then receives fruition of that life in which the body shall participate after the General Judgment. By a peculiar figure of diction, St. John extols the glories and blessed fruits of the first resurrection and then merely mentions the second death. He does not write of the first death nor of the second resurrection, for we are all familiar enough with the death of the body, which visualizes the death of the souls of the sinners. St. John only teaches positively here an eternal bliss for those who have no more faults to expiate. And they have no more judgment to fear. The resurrection of all the dead, the good and the wicked, is related in verses 12 and 13 being for the wicked only a resurrection to judgment and the second death in the pool of fire at the end of the thousand years.

St. Augustine writes that there are two regenerations, the one according to faith by Baptism, the other according to the flesh in the immortality and incorruptibility it shall assume at the Last Judgment. So there are two resurrections: the first is now for the souls that shall not be subject to the second death; and the second is not yet but shall come to reality before the Last Judgment at the end of time and is the resurrection of the bodies, of whom some shall enter the second death and others the life that knows no death. When at the end of the millennium God's plans are all finished, the souls of those who have ruled with Christ during the epoch of continuous triumph for Him shall be re-united with their bodies, vivify them and appear without apprehension before the Great White Throne and in that final Judgment receive the full reward for their faithfulness, their labors and sufferings.

The only things said of their reward during the millennium is that "they shall be priests of God and of Christ". This represents the priesthood of Jesus Christ as the highest office of honor and merit on earth and in Heaven. Through the priesthood Christ directs the individual souls, sanctifies them, distributes the fruits of His sacrificial death and extends its victory over the powers of evil. These souls shall then have extensive power during the thousand years for the sanctification, security and happiness of the good and the chastisement and suppression of the wicked, so that virtue may be honored and vice despised and abhorred. As the prophet has foretold, the time shall be so holy and blessed that anyone shall hardly have asked for anything before it is granted. The martyrs shall be the protectors of their own people, shall be endowed with divine wisdom and in union with Christ shall guide the destinies of nations clear of all wars and calamities. Miracles may then be plentiful at the shrines of the martyr saints, and faith shall be kept at its highest vitality. And the prophecy in the book of Daniel may be fulfilled in the literal sense. (Dan. VII. 18-27). That prophecy seems to demand a resurrection of the bodies of the martyrs and their visible residence on earth during the millennium. Such a fulfillment of the prophecy may be meant, but it seems to contradict verse 4.

During these thousand years, all prophecies shall have eminent fulfillment. Zacharias writes of the plagues that shall fall upon those who break the unity of the Church (XIV. 16-21). Isaias in chapter LXII. describes God's protection upon the Church and the blessedness of the times after the destruction of Antichrist (LXIII. 1-6), when all nations including the Jews shall be converted and worship God in the way He desires to be worshipped. There shall be no limit to God's bounties (LXV. and LXVI.). All articles used by the Church and every tool, machine and domestic beast shall receive the blessing of the Church. The place where Antichrist and his followers meet their doom shall be a place of pilgrimage, where all peoples shall see with horror the punishments upon God's adversaries. (Isa. LXVI. 24).

2. The Last War Of Gog And Magog.

Verses 7-8.

Verse 7

A by-product of the thousand years of peace will be lukewarmness and indifference in the practice of religion. During times of peace and prosperity, evils have sometimes arisen within the Church. There will always be the good and bad in the world as Isaias foretells (LXV. 20), and the number of wicked shall grow larger as time goes on. These THOUSAND YEARS are stated in round numbers to denote a period of peace for the Church from Antichrist till the rise of Gog and Magog, and they may be two thousand or several thousand. According to the words of Isaias (LXV. 20), a period of only ONE thousand years would seem far too short to bring into actuality in a literal sense what is promised there. Near paradisiac conditions will prevail. Men will live to a great age; the danger to grow lax in the service of God and loyalty to the Church will appear, and evils will multiply as before the Reformation; finally Satan shall be released from his prison to punish the wicked.

The Greek word, δεῖ denotes a necessity for the loosing of Satan, because it is demanded by the will of God to further the working out of His plans. It is an insoluble mystery. Satan will be allowed to lead the wicked and indifferent Catholics into every sin and depravity, to surfeit them with iniquity and vice, which they have chosen, just as through grace God perfects the good in virtue. In chapter XII. 12, the Greek phrase used intimates only a short opportunity for Satan to accomplish his designs, and that time is three-and-a-half years. At or near the end of time, Satan will be released again "a little time". From the text it cannot be determined whether the little space of time is longer than three years and a half or not, but the word χρόνον could designate a longer time than the reign of Antichrist. However, it will not be a century or more, as from the opening of the abyss (IX. 1) till Antichrist, nor long enough for Satan to devise and construct such machinery of evil as will produce the acceptance of his ideas and doctrines in the way he has done during the past four hundred years. He shall only be allowed to lead the torpid from vice to vice, to punish their contempt for God's spiritual bounties and to direct them to their extermination in a war against the Church.

The leaders of the nations are Gog and Magog, and Satan shall assemble them for a battle against Jerusalem, the center of the Messianic kingdom during the thousand years, as he gathered the armies through Antichrist in XVI. 16. The numbers of men in these armies streaming together from the four quarters of the globe are countless. All the wicked will enlist and go forth to rob the Church of the riches reputed to be stored in Jerusalem.

St. John refers us by his silence to the prophecy of Ezechiel, who had given the geneology of the leaders and a detailed description of the armies. According to both prophecies, the army of Gog comes together from the four quarters of the earth and encompasses the Holy City. By human calculations the Church is then doomed to annihilation. They surround the camp of the saints. The Church is not entirely without defense, even if it is without walls. By surrounding the city they hinder anyone from escaping with treasure.

Ezechiel names Gog as the leader or ruler of the land of Magog, the chief prince of Mosoch and Thubal. Now Magog, Thubal and Mosoch are sons of Japeth. Gog will be the leader of nations that are descendants of Japeth and will rise in rebellion against the Church. Perhaps the Church shall then be ruled in large part by the descendants of Sem as it now is by the Italians. The nations may then in part foresake the path of virtue and give way to envy and imagine they can find great riches stored up by the Church in Jerusalem. As the enemies of the Church have thought and done in the past 400 years, so Gog and his millions will think they can get rich by robbing the Church. If many of the Old Testament prophecies are literally fulfilled, choice treasures of art and many precious possessions shall find their way to the center of the Church for its embellishment and glory. Satan shall goad them on to make another attempt to destroy the Church and lure these followers of Gog to damnation.

Ezechiel relates the coming of Gog in chapters XXXVIII. and XXXIX. as due near the end of time: "And the word of the

Lord came to me, saying: 2. Son of man, set thy face aginst Gog, the land of Magog, the chief prince of Mosoch and Thubal: and prophesy of him, 3. And say to him: Thus saith the Lord God: Behold I come against thee, O Gog, the chief prince of Mosoch and Thubal. 4. And I will turn thee about, and will put a bit in thy jaws: and I will bring thee forth, and all thy army, horses and horsemen all clothed with coats of mail, a great multitude, armed with spears and shields and swords. 5. The Persians, Ethiopians, and Libyans with them, all with shields and helmets. 6. Gomer, and all his bands, the house of Thogorma, the northern parts and all his strength, and many peoples with thee. 7. Prepare and make thyself ready, and all thy multitude that is assembled about thee, and be thou commander over them. 8. After many days thou shalt be visited" (By Satan and seduced) "at the *end of years* thou shalt come to the land that is returned from the sword, and is gathered out of many nations, to the mountains of Israel which have been continually waste" (since the destruction of the Jewish nation, and especially since Mohammedanism has held it) "but it hath been brought forth out of the nations, and they shall all of them dwell securely in it. 9. And thou shalt go up and come like a storm, and like a cloud to cover the land" (air forces), "thou and all thy bands, and many people with thee. 10. Thus saith the Lord God: In that day projects shall enter into thy heart, and thou shalt conceive a mischievous design. 11. And thou shalt say: I will go up to the land which is without a wall, I will come to them that are at rest, and dwell securely: all these dwell without a wall, they have no bars nor gates: 12. To take spoils, and lay hold on the prey, to lay thy hand upon them that had been wasted, and afterwards restored, and upon the people that is gathered together out of the nations, which hath begun to possess and to dwell in the midst of the earth". (The Church will have been the center of all human thought and aspirations for 1000 years). 13. "Saba, and Dedan, and the merchants of Tharis, and all the lions thereof shall say to thee: Art thou come to take spoils? behold, thou hast gathered thy multitude to take prey, to take silver and gold, and to carry away goods and substance, and to take rich spoils. 14. Therefore thou son of man, prophesy and say to Gog: Thus saith the Lord God: Shalt thou not know in that day, when my people of Israel shall dwell securely? 15. And thou shalt come out of thy place from the northern parts, thou and many people with thee, all of them riding upon horses, a great company and a mighty army. 16. And thou shalt come upon my people Israel like a cloud, to cover the earth. Thou shalt be in the *latter days*, and I will bring thee upon my land: that the nations may know me, when I shall be sanctified in thee, O Gog, before their eyes. 17. Thus saith the Lord God: Thou then art he, of whom I have spoken in the days of old, by my servants the prophets of Israel, who prophesied in the days of those times that I would bring thee upon them. 18. And it shall come to pass in that day, in the day of the coming of Gog upon the land of Israel, saith the Lord God, that my indignation shall come up in my wrath. 19. And I have spoken in my zeal, and in the fire of my anger, that in that day there shall be a great commotion upon the land of Israel: 20. so that the fishes of the sea and the birds of the air, and the beasts of the field, and every creeping thing that creepeth upon the ground, and all men that are upon the face of the earth, shall be moved at my presence: and the mountains shall be thrown down, and the hedges shall fall, and every wall shall fall to the ground. 21. And I will call in the sword against him in all my mountains, saith the Lord God: every man's sword shall be pointed against his brother. 22. And I will judge him with pestilence, and with blood, and with violent rain, and vast hailstones: I will rain fire and brimstone upon him, and upon his army, and upon the many nations that are with him. 23. And I will be magnified, and I will be sanctified: and I will be known in the eyes of many nations: and they shall know that I am the Lord." Chapter XXXIX. 3. "And I will break thy bow in thy left hand, and I will cause thy arrows to fall out of thy right hand. 4. Thou shalt fall upon the mountains of Isreal, thou and all thy bands, and thy nations that are with thee: I have given thee to the wild beasts, to the birds, and to every fowl, and to the beasts of the earth to be devoured. 5. Thou shalt fall upon the face of the field: for I have spoken it, saith the Lord God. 6. And I will send a fire upon Magog, and on them that dwell confidently in the islands: and they shall know that I am the Lord. 7. And I will make my holy name known in the midst of my people Israel, and my holy name shall be profaned no more: and the Gentiles shall know that I am the Lord, the Holy One of Israel. 8. Behold it cometh, and it is done, saith the Lord God: this is the day whereof I have spoken. 9. And the inhabitants shall go forth of the cities of Israel, and shall set on fire and burn the weapons, the shields, and the spears, and the bows and the arrows, and the handstaves and the pikes: and they shall burn them with fire seven years. 10. And they shall not bring wood out of the countries, nor cut down out of the forests: for they shall burn the weapons with fire, and shall make a prey of them to whom they had been a prey, and they shall rob those that robbed them, saith the Lord God. 11. And it shall come to pass in that day, that I will give Gog a noted place for a sepulchre in Israel: the valley of the passengers on the east side of the sea, which shall cause astonishment in them that pass by: and there shall they bury Gog, and all his multitude, and it shall be called the valley of the multitude of Gog. 12. And the house of Israel shall bury them for seven months to cleanse the land. 13. And all the people of the land shall bury him, and it shall be unto them a noted day, wherein I was glorified, saith the Lord God. 14. And they shall appoint men to go continually about the land, to bury and to seek out them that were remaining upon the face of the earth, that they may cleanse it: and after seven months they shall begin to seek."

Perhaps St. Paul means this revolt of Gog against the Church, when he writes that a revolt must come first before the end of the world and the Last Judgment (2 Thess. II. 3). The prophecy by Ezechiel reveals a return of the Jews to Palestine and a long period of residence there in peace and security. Their cities shall not be walled as they were in all past times as also after the Babylonian Captivity up to the destruction of the nation in the war of 131-135 A. D. The long period of peace and security for them and the world is still in the future. The last part of the prophecy, the invitation to the victim is similar to that given by St. John after the death of Antichrist and his armies. This is necessitated by the similarity of the event. In both instances great armies are destroyed. Ezechiel states that the destruction of Gog is at "the end of years" (XXXVIII. 8), near the end of the world. St. John leaves no doubt in his revelation that the THOUSAND YEARS shall follow Antichrist, and at the end of that time Gog shall some up against the Church. The agreement of St. John's prophecy with Ezechiel's is unmistakable. Some interpreters have erroneously called Gog in Ezechiel's prophecy the Antichrist.

Verse 8

According to St. John, fire comes out of heaven and consumes the hosts of Gog. In Ezechiel the punishments upon Gog shall be pestilence, blood, violent rain, vast hailstones, fire and brimstone. In the next chapter (XXXIX. 6), Ezechiel states that *God* shall send a fire on Magog and on those who dwell in the islands. This all agrees perfectly with what St. John avers about the fate of Gog. Perhaps the Church shall defend herself through a small army by some destructive electric ray. But in the text the fire comes from God. It may therefore be a direct divine chastisement.

How long a period of years shall elapse from the end of Gog till the consummation of the world must be left to speculation. Ezechiel writes that Israel shall gather up and burn the war machinery of Gog SEVEN YEARS (XXXIX. 9). From that day forward, Israel shall trust in God as their protector and Lord not in their inventions and armies. This realization may have grown dim in the minds of men during the thousand years of peace and plenty. There may be another long period of peace for the world after this last manifest intervention of God against the attackers of the Church. Neither Ezechiel nor St. John shows it conclusively, but Ezechiel (XXXIX. 22-29) intimates it.

3. Satan's Final Destiny.

Verses 9-10.

Verse 9

After the defeat of Gog and his armies, Satan is cast into the pool of fire and brimstone, hell proper, into which Antichrist and his prophet were cast alive with body and soul. They may not appear at the Last Judgment. Satan was confined to the bottomless abyss during the millennium and then released to seduce Gog and his followers, whose number is as the sands of the sea. Thereby he fills up his measure of iniquity and merits to be sunk into the deepest chasm of the pool of fire. The final judgment is pronounced and executed upon him as on his two principal agents and with them he is locked up in the burning pool.

Verse 10

This verse suggests another epoch of peace between the destruction of Gog and the end of the world. Perhaps the signs of the approaching end foretold by our Lord will then gradually appear. There is no "day and night" in eternity after the Last Judgment. According to the Greek text, the "day and night" seems not to be identified with the "forever and ever" of eternity. Hence if Satan is tormented together with the Beast and False Prophet day and night, it must be while day and night still continue on earth. Those who shall have forgotten God's judgments upon Antichrist or view them as doubtful legends and have drifted into indifference at the end of the THOUSAND YEARS shall in the destruction of Gog come face to face with the truth of the Church's teachings and a manifest proof of the everlasting punishments on the wicked. As in the Old Testament, so at all times men discount and underestimate in the course of ages the value of God's revelations and treat the Gospel today as fairy tales, deny the reality of the miracles of Christ and even doubt His existence. Many will estimate the history of Antichrist and the miraculous manifestation of Christ's power in the Church and particularly in the Holy Eucharist as far distant fables and will imagine in their overweening pride that men were deceived in those days of ignorance.

Verse 10 refutes with striking clearness all explanations that the Beast and the False Prophet are institutions or organizations, for they are not only cast into the same pool of fire with Satan, whose personal existence no one tries to torture into an institution but are also "tormented" together with him. No institution, organization, kingdom or empire is "tormented" in hell. But even brilliant minds after taking an impossible view will try to hold on to it.

4. The Last Judgment.

Verses 11-end.

Verse 11

This verse follows the foregoing without any connecting particle and without any introduction to the succeeding vision. The One sitting upon the Great White Throne before whose face heaven and earth flee away is Christ coming in the clouds to judge the world. He comes for the Last Judgment. No place is found for heaven and earth any more. The world and all its glory shall pass away, and the Church shall exist on earth no longer.

Between this verse and the foregoing a period of time is obviously passed over, during which the wicked may repent and do penance. Verse eleven following the final judgment upon Satan without the insertion of a connecting word proves nothing about the proximity of the judgment to his condemnation. The "seven years" of Ezechiel may be and probably are a symbolic number. Ezechiel indicates (XXXIX. 22-29) some lapse of time from Gog to the end of the world and likewise a speedy arrival of the end after the last war of Gog (XXXVIII. 8). The prophets commonly write new prophecies verse after verse without any conjunctions and without any indication of long spaces of time between the verses. In one verse they promise the end of the Babylonian Captivity and in the next the glories of Christ's reign, as if the coming of Christ were simultaneous with the return from Captivity. And they connect His Coming immediately with the glorious future days in terms of the millennium, although another couple of thousand years must pass away added to the five hundred from the end of the Captivity to His Coming. Christ steadfastly refused to reveal the nearness of the end of the world, although the apostles evinced the keenest desire to know this. He said to them that the Father had kept this knowledge in His control (Mt. XXIV. 36; Mc. XIII. 32). The time for the career of Antichrist shall be known when the signs appear and also that of the last enemy of the Church, Gog; there is nothing in the Apocalypse, however, to indicate the nearness or remoteness of the end of the world after these other prophecies have been past history. The wisdom of God withholds this knowledge from the human race.

Verse 12

Verse 13 mentions the resurrection of the dead, but the word "resurrection" is avoided here, perhaps because the reprobate have no real resurrection being revived only to enter eternal death. The years intervening between the judgment of Satan and the coming of Christ upon the Great White Throne are passed over and so is the description of the resurrection. St. John immediately directs the reader's attention to the gathering of the risen before the Judgment Seat. They all stand. No other classes are mentioned any more but the "great and the small". All class distinction vanishes before the divine Tribunal. The "great" may be the just and the "small" the reprobate. The separation of the good from the bad takes place when the books are opened. Everyone has written his own book and shall be judged by what he has written therein. Every thought word and deed is recorded and nothing is forgotten making the judgment accurate and just.

The Book of Life is also opened. The names of all the elect are registered there. In the order in which St. John relates it, the record of each one's own book is revealed, and if it shows him worthy of having his name in the Book of Life, his name is entered therein or already found written there. This is all an allegorical portrayal of the revelation of each one's fate as recorded in the book of God's Knowledge or Memory. Each one is judged according to his works, good or evil, which during life are indelibly impressed on his character finishing that character in good or evil and shaping it for its everlasting destiny. And when this character stands revealed before the Tribunal of Justice, its true qualifications are known to itself and all rational creatures as also its fitness and worthiness to be or not to be in the Book of Life. This order of thought is not an order of time, for at the General Judgment no time shall be required for the revelation of each character before all the world; all will be instantaneous.

The conclusion drawn by some interpreters from the many books in which the names of the wicked are recorded and only one Book of Life, that the number of the reprobate far exceeds that of the elect is false. Perhaps up to the time of Antichrist, the bulk of the human race is lost, because so many more have adhered to error than to truth. But during the millennium the population of the world may be five or ten times what it was before. If those shall nearly all serve God faithfully, as seems to be foretold by the prophets, Heaven shall be peopled by the elect during those ages, and at the Last Judgment the elect shall be the vastly greater number. It surely would be a small victory for Christ, if ultimately Satan shall have the larger share of the human race.

Verse 13

This verse supplements the foregoing and completes the description of the arrival of the dead before the Judgment Seat. The sea is mentioned first, because Romans, Greeks and Jews alike recoiled with horror from the thought of burial at sea fearing that the souls of such unfortunates would have no resting place in the hereafter. Our Lord evidently alluded to that dread when he said that it were better to be sunk in the middle of the sea with a millstone around the neck than to give scandal. Christians have lost their horror of burial at sea, because the hope of resurrection is held out to the remains of those resting there as well as to those buried on land.

"Hades" and "Death" are personified as two monsters who have devoured all past generations. Hades is the region of the dead, the region of gloom into which all past ages have entered, and Death is the king of this region. Death possibly appeared in some demoniac form in the vision. The fate of the dead is decided according to their works. This explains the meaning of the "books" from which each of the dead is judged.

Verse 14

Hades and Death appearing in some visible form are cast into the pool of fire. The human race shall increase no more, no more men shall be born, and hence the region of death and death itself will no longer exist. All results of sin shall be expurgated from God's creation and locked up forever in the pool of fire. This is the second death and is the final penalty for apostasy from the Creator and for adherence to sin. Sin and death adhere to the sinner and are cast into hell with the sinner. The death of the body was only a warning. It is swallowed up by the second death. The casting of Hades and Death into the pool of fire is only a symbolic action representing the banishment of all effects of sin from God's perfected creation. It is not like the condemnation of the Beast, the False Prophet and Satan, who are consigned to the pool of fire and brimstone to be "tormented" forever.

Verse 15

When the final sentence of the Judge is obeyed, all those who are not worthy of having their names recorded in the Book of Life shall share in the fate of Death and Hades, i. e. of all Evil and the representatives of Evil. The judgments of God are now complete. All creatures who have opposed His vivifying and beatifying will have been cast into the pool of fire and brimstone. The Beast and the False Prophet, Satan, all Godless people, Death and Hades have vanished from the vocabulary of the elect and are buried in eternal oblivion.

CHAPTER XXI.

Westminster Version

And I beheld a new heaven and a new earth; 1. for the first heaven and the first earth were departed, and the sea is no more.

And I saw the holy city, the new Jerusalem, 2. coming down out of heaven from God, prepared as a bride adorned for her husband.

And I heard a loud voice from the throne, 3. saying, 'Behold the dwelling of God with men, and he shall dwell with them and they shall be his peoples, and God himself shall be with them.

And he shall wipe away every tear from their 4. eyes, and death shall be no more, neither shall mourning or wailing or pain be any more, because the first things are passed away.

And he who sitteth upon the throne saith, 5. 'Behold, I make all things new'. And he saith, 'Write: for these words are faithful and true'.

And he said to me, 'It is done! I am the Alpha 6. and the Omega, the beginning and the end. To him that thirsteth, I will give of the fountain, of the water of life, freely.

He that conquereth shall inherit these things; 7. I shall be his God and he shall be my son.

But as for the cowards, the unbelievers, the 8. abominable, the murderers, the fornicators, the sorcerers, the idolaters, and all liars, their part shall be in the lake of burning fire and brimstone, which is the second death.'

And there came one of the seven angels who 9. had the seven vials full of the seven last plagues, and he spoke with me, saying, 'Come, I will show thee the bride, the spouse of the Lamb'.

And he bore me away in spirit to a great and 10. high mountain, and he showed me the holy city Jerusalem, coming down from heaven in the glory of God.

The radiance thereof was like to a stone 11. most precious, to a jasper stone, crystal clear.

It had a great and high wall, with twelve gates; at the twelve gates were twelve angels, and 12. names were inscribed thereon, the names of the twelve tribes of Israel.

On the east were three gates; and on the north 13. three gates; and on the south, three gates; and on the west, three gates.

And the wall of the city had twelve foundation 14. stones, and on them were the twelve names of the twelve apostles of the Lamb.

And he that spoke to me had for a measure a 15. golden rod, wherewith to measure the city and its gates and its walls.

The city lieth in a foursquare, and the length 16. thereof is as great as the breadth. He measured the city with his rod, twelve thousand furlongs; the length and breadth and height thereof are equal.

He measured also the wall, one hundred and forty-four 17. feet, by man's measure, which is angel's measure.

And the material of the wall was jasper; and 18. the city was pure
gold, like unto pure glass.

The foundation stones of the wall of the city 19. were adorned with
every kind of precious stone. The first was a jasper; the second, a lapis
lazuli; the third, an agate; the fourth, an emerald; the fifth, a sardonyx;
the sixth, a cornelian; 20. the seventh, a chrysolite; the eighth, a beryl; the
ninth, a topaz; the tenth, a chrysoprase; the eleventh, a jacinth; the twelfth,
an amethyst.

The twelve gates were twelve pearls; each gate 21. was formed of a
single pearl. And the street of the city was pure gold, transparent as
glass.

I saw no sanctuary therein, for the Lord God 22. almighty is the
sanctuary thereof, and the Lamb.

And the city hath no need of the sun or of 23. the moon to shine
upon it, for the glory of God enlighteneth it, and the lamp thereof is the
Lamb.

And the nations shall walk by the light 24. thereof, and the kings of
the earth shall bring their glory thereto, and the gates thereof shall never
be shut 25. by day – for night shall not be there – and they shall bring
thereto the glory and 26. the honor of the nations.

And there shall not enter therein aught 27. unclean, nor he that
practiseth abomination and falsehood, but only they that are written in
the book of life of the Lamb.

XI. THE NEW CITY AND THE NEW WORLD

1. The New Jerusalem.

Chapter XXI.

Verses 1-2.

The last two chapters of the Revelations supplement and explain what was briefly stated or only suggested in chapters XIX. and XX. Chapter twenty narrates the succession of events from the condemnation of Antichrist till the end of the world. Chapters XXI. and XII. take up the theme indicated in XX. 6, the blessedness of the times that shall follow the destruction of all agencies of evil on earth. The Apocalyptist always takes up in a later chapter and develops fully a theme only mentioned in its proper chronological setting and order. These last two chapters, furthermore, in describing the triumphs of the Eucharistic Lamb and their happy results for the world give the final interpretation to many prophecies of the Old Testament.

Verse 1

The prediction voiced at the blowing of the seventh trumpet (XI. 15) has at last become actuality: "the kingdom of this world is become our Lord's and His Christ's". A new heaven and a new earth appear. The promise of a new heaven and a new earth was not new in the New Testament; it had been enunciated in the Old. Isaias wrote: "For behold I create new heavens and a new earth: and the former things shall not be in remembrance, and they shall not come upon the heart" (Is. LXV. 17). To this is added the promise of the conversion and restoration of the Jews: "For as the new heavens and the new earth, which I shall make to stand before me, saith the Lord: so shall your seed stand and your name" (Is. LXVI. 22). St. John obviously had the text of Isaias in mind, for his own is verbally almost identical with it. Exegetes interpret this passage in Isaias to mean the happy state of the faithful under the dispensation of the Messias, for they shall be free from the dangers and anxieties of former times, and those who wish to live a Godly life in the world shall find no hindrance to their desires. Since the text is so nearly identical with that of Isaias, St. John surely expresses a fulfillment of the prophecy. By restating it so closely, he applies it to the new state of the world after Antichrist. Isaias, moreover, states that this new heaven and new earth means the changed condition of all things during the millennium (LXVI. 20-23). After the conversion of the heathens, who were ritually impure, and of the obstinate Jews, the Church shall be further embellished by the elevation of the Jews to the priestly dignity and the office of advocates between God and man. Their nation made the coming of the Messias possible; after they are all converted, they shall reap the delectable fruits of that distinction. Thus, after Elias has purified the Church of all hypocrisy, she shall stand in imperishable beauty before the Lord. The new EARTH is the changed state of society, which before and during the days of Antichrist was antichristian and anti-God. It is now entirely submissive to Christ and willing to have all relatons of man regulated and directed by the Church.

The antagonism against the Church is no more. Hence the "sea" has vanished. This "sea" produced all evil in the world, The Church was herself purified and perfected, as far as this is possible on earth, and now this new heaven will radiate benedictions everywhere. The dogmas and moral law of the Church shall suffer no change, but the evils within her at times: the worldliness, lack of fervor, hypocrisy, scheming for control instead of faithfulness to duty, lack of adherence to principle, and above all — lukewarmness in people and clergy — these evils shall be expurgated from the Church in the supreme struggle.

The true spiritual Israel comes forth transformed from the judgment under Antichrist; and transfused with grace it is united in one brotherhood with the remnants of converted heathen nations and stands before the Lord as did the first converts in VII. 9. The NEW HEAVEN is the Church after the conflict with Antichrist mature and transfigured with grace and adorned with all virtues the triumphal achievement of the Lamb. In her earthly form, she reflects the image of the Triumphant Church in Heaven: divine beauty, holiness, immutability, infallibility and indefectibility; and pervaded by the Spirit of God she bears the pledge and germs of divine glory and yearns with inexpressible longing for the pouring out of the messianic benedictions upon all flesh and for the transfiguration and ineffable bliss of the elect in the life beyond.

Verse 2

As the new heaven is the purer survival of the old, and the new earth arises out of the wreckage and decay of the old: So The New Jerusalem is created to be the metropolis of the new earth. The Church cannot exist on earth without a local center, and this will be established at Jerusalem, since Rome is a heap of Ruins and shall never be rebuilt. The Jerusalem of the Old Covenant has been in ruins since the war of Titus, and this fact must have set the Christian mind a-questioning, even in St. John's time, whether and when a new Jerusalem would arise. This new Jerusalem would be of another order and would be the fulfillment of Christian hopes expressed by St. Paul in several letters (Gal. IV. 26). The Apostle clearly designates it to be the Jerusalem of the Gentiles as well as of the Jews. His prophecy has been fulfilled in a spiritual way since the change of pagan into Christian Rome, which has become the Holy City of the New Testament as Jerusalem had been of the Old. Jewish tradition and literature looked for an ideal, a new and greater Jerusalem. They understood this in an earthly sense only, and it remained an indetermined hope until the apostles defined it in a spiritual sense. Yet Jewish traditions were based on the prophecies. When the Church shall establish headquarters at Jerusalem, the prophecies will have literal fulfillment, the blessed visions of peace become true and Jerusalem becomes the Celestial City (Isa. LXVI. 20; LXV. 19; LXII. 6-7; IX. 13-14, etc.). Most modern interpreters have discarded a literal fulfillment of the prophecies of a greater city to be built on the site of ancient Jerusalem and of the Church making this her metropolis. Yet why should not this be contained in the scope of the prophecies along with the spiritual sense?

The New Jerusalem coming from God may be called into existence by Almighty Power, as the prophets intimate, or the city may be rebuilt for earthly purposes and made glorious by the Church. If the Church rebuilt Christian Jerusalem as she rebuilt Christian Rome, it would literally come "out of heaven".

Since the Church derives her divine life from the eucharistic Lamb and the indwelling of the Holy Spirit, whatever city she should select for her headquarters or build to suit her needs would come forth from God and would be the Holy City coming down from heaven and elevated to the place of glory intended in the divine plans. The New Jerusalem thus becomes identified with the Church. (Gal. IV. 26).

The sciences have been developed and been proven to harmonize with divine revelation and to call for a Suprme Cause, God, as the origin and end of creation. The true principles of education have been accepted from the Church, because all educational systems that varied with the principles of the Church have to the extent in which they differed been proven failures. Art has been made the servant of truth and morality. Theology has been perfected and philosophy been made to serve theology. Medical science has been transfused with charity. The true and just relation of Labor and Capital and the rights of each have been proclaimed. The moral laws of the Church have leavened all governments to aim at justice for all and privileges for none. All civil laws are tested by the revealed law and interpreted to conform with it. The source of all contentment and felicity in the world is admitted to be a virtuous life, which receives its inspiration and strength from the eucharistic Lamb. And finally the Church possesses the principles long ago clearly taught that shall insure lasting peace on earth between nations. The Church is worthy to be the Queen of the Lamb and with Him graciously to rule the nations of the world. And she shall people heaven with the souls she begets and rears for Christ, the "Father of the world to come". She is thus prepared for the Great Consummation.

2. Diverse Promises To The Faithful.

Verses 3-8.

Verse 3

The Seer hears a voice from the throne of God. This "great

voice" is probably that of the Lion, the head of the Church. It is not the voice of Christ, for He does not speak until in verse 5. The voice expounds the ancient prophets and this new vision. He announces the Millennium during which God will dwell in the midst of His peoples. The definite article "THE tabernacle", refers to the same dwelling or throne of God in the Old Covenant in the Tabernacle or Temple. Then His dwelling was only in Israel, while now it is "with men". He will make His abode with all who are united to Him in faith and grace. He expresses the same thought again in the words: "and He will dwell with them". The other idea molded into the foundation of the Holy City is also added: "and they shall be His peoples", and the New Jerusalem will make all nations one fold over which will rule the one Shepherd. The plural number employed makes the text differ from the ancient prophecies. In the ancient covenant God claimed only "one people" for His own, while here He claims many "peoples", but they all constitute one brotherhood.

The word σκηνὴ reminds us of the temporary sojourn of God among the chosen people in the Tabernacle or Temple. Not in Heaven is this abode of God with His many peoples established but in the Church on earth. The national existence of peoples will not be carried into the next world. God condescends to dwell with the faithful of all nations as it were in tents thus drawing them more closely to Himself. He will be the God of all watching over all and insuring peace and concord among all nations.

The dwelling of God with His people was first expressed in Leviticus (XXVI. 11-12) and repeated many times by the prophets. Jeremias (XXIV. 7) writes the promises of God to His people at the return from Babylon but uses almost identical words used here by St. John. At the beginning of the millennium they shall have a more complete fulfillment. Zacharias has the same prophecy, when he offers encouragement for the finishing of the Temple after the Captivity. (VIII. 1-8). Ezechiel foretells the appointment of ONE SHEPHERD who will dwell in the midst of his flock (XXXIV. 23-31) and abide there for all times thenceforth (XXXVII. 21-28) and He will watch over them and keep all harm away. In the last sentence of verse 3, St. John combines the two ideas again of their dwelling in God and God's indwelling in them.

Verse 4

The language of this verse is again like that of the ancient prophecies. (Isa. XXV. 8: XLIX. 10; LXV. 19-20). The prophets did not have the life of the blessed after the end of the world in view but the blessed state of the world under the Messias. The Apocalyptist uses the same language in chapter VII. 16-17, where he draws a picture of the happy state of the faithful who have survived the persecutions. No grief could crush them any more, so were they permeated and inspired by their holy faith, for they could look forward confidently to the endless joys of Heaven. During the millennium, unbelief and doubt have passed away. The great miracles wrought by the Two Witnesses and the saints of the Church and finally the destruction of great Babylon and of Antichrist as foretold cleared away all doubt concerning the teachings of the Church. And this impossibility of doubt and the firm will of all, young and old, to serve God shall end all disconsolate grief.

All tears shall be wiped from the eyes of the survivors of the great cataclysm because they are perfectly submissive to the will of God. The first reason given for it is "death shall be no more". If taken in the literal sense, this statement is the most difficult one in the two chapters. If it means only violent and untimely death, it would entail not only the end of all hatred, which produces murders and wars, but also all other sins that lead to hatred and murder and all accidents and all diseases and other causes of death with which the world is inundated now. The imminent danger of death is necessary in the present order of the world to deter sinners from complete abandonment to sin. If these dangers would remain during the millennium, and there should then be no more untimely death, God would need to exercise an extraordinary protection over the lives of all, and men would need to be of a much higher mentality and have keener foresight and have greater will-power and self-control to avoid dangers. If the prophecies are to be literally fulfilled, men shall live to a great age. (Is. LXV. 20). The farther the world receded from Paradise, the shorter did the age of man become, until in Roman times 40 years was a ripe old age. The Patriarchs who lived nearest the days of Adam lived longest possibly because the effects of eating from the Tree of Life were still operative in Adam's posterity. Justin the martyr referring to this sentence in the Apocalypse and the millennium quotes Isaias (LXV. to end) (Dial. with Trypho lxxxi) and draws the conclusion that Adam did not complete a thousand years because he ate of the forbidden tree, but that during the millennium men shall live till the end of that period without dying. St. Justin's conclusion is: "Now we have understood that the expression used among these words, 'according to the words of the tree shall be the days of my people; the works of their toil shall abound', he obscurely predicts a thousand years". In quoting Isaias, Justin has: "For according to the days of the tree of life shall be the days of my people"; and when he draws the conclusion above-stated, he leaves out the two words, "of life". The Vulgate has: "secundum enim dies ligni, erunt dies populi mei". The Septuagint reads: "for as the days of the tree of life shall be the days of my people". The Vulgate leaves out the words "of life" in the passage from Isaias which are contained in the Septuagint. Justin's is a free translation but is close to the Septuagint. In quoting it, he expresses his opinion of the meaning of our text, "and death shall be no more". According to Isaias as the Vulgate renders it, there shall be death during the millennium, though men shall live to a great age. He says: "There shall no more be an infant of days there, nor an old man that shall not fill up his days: for the child shall die a hundred years old, and the sinner being a hundred old shall be accursed". (LXV. 20). The Septuagint differs slightly from this but has the same sense. St. Justin does not put this millennium after the General Judgment, as the Chiliasts do, but before and draws the conclusion from his own rendition of the Septuagint that there shall be no death except that of the sinner during the millenium.

The sentence is probably to be taken in a more spiritual sense, that there is no death for the saint. The day of his departure is his eternal birthday. From a spiritual viewpoint, a saint, as Aloysius, the Little Flower, Francis of Assisi and thousands of others has reached maturity far beyond that of the greatest prophets. Though young in years, they were ripe in sanctity. During the millennium all common Christians may progress to high degrees of sanctity. The sentence, "death shall be no more", may then mean what St. Paul says: "O Death, where is the victory? O Death, where is thy sting?" In apostolic days death was looked upon as a repose. So the Acts say of St. Stephen: "He fell asleep in the Lord". In the catacombs of Rome, that inscription is found quite generally. During the millennium faith may be so lively and intense that men will consider death a transition into a happier life. Sinners may live to grow mature in sinfulness and receive their punishment not in this life but in Hell. Even now the greater anyone's faith, the less does he dread death; and those true Christians who live to a ripe old age often desire the day of death, as did St. John and St. Paul. The bereaved ones will not grieve over the death of one who lived to maturity in years and sanctity nor express it by mourning.

"The former things have passed away" means in the context and by comparison with the ancient prophecies that the chief causes of grief have passed away. All doubt about the future life of bliss has vanished. Those who depart from this life go to the Father's House. They die in hope and love and submission to the will of God. Men are of good will. The old spirit of disobedience and rebellion against God is no more, and no more are violent punishments inflicted by Almighty God. Then death is not what it was in the Old Law nor what it is to the sinner. Death ends all hopes of earthly felicity promised for virtue in the Old Covenant, but it opens the gates of eternal joys. St. Paul expresses very similar thoughts in similar language for the individual (2 Cor. V. 17-19). If people are fully conformed to the ideals of Christ, this renewal of the whole world and with it the passing of grief, pain and mourning will become a reality.

There is a bare possibility that St. John used the future tense of the verb ἕννυμι in this sentence instead of εἶναι. The future passive of the former is spelled the same as the future of the latter. The meaning of the sentence would then be: "death shall no more be shrouded in mourning nor wailing nor pain". There are many variants among the old extant texts of the Apocalypse, and the critics have found no book of the New Testament more uncertain about the original text. However, the above suggestion would seem to be against the context of this verse and cannot be well adopted as an explanation. St. Justin, who was nearest the days of St. John and must have had the original rendition of the text, holds the other meaning and explains it in that sense. Still even he could have misunderstood the word.

Verses 5-8

St. John does not say who sits on the throne. Referring to chapter IV., it should be God the Father, but the words He addresses to St. John are those of our Lord in chapter I., when He ordered him to write to the Seven Churches. It may be the Deity. He orders St. John to write the revelations and without delay the one sentence: "Behold I make all things new". This is the task of the Lamb. The words, "It is done", re-assert the fulfillment of all revelations just as they have been shown. We have now arrived at the final visions and the finishing of the judgments promised in the first chapter of the Apocalypse.

Verse 5

In chapter XLI., Isaias promises from God a deliverer to lead back Israel from the Babylonian Captivity; The deliverer is Cyrus. From that delivery, the prophet goes over to the more complete delivery of Israel under the Messias in chapter XLII. Again in chapter XLIII., he speaks of the rewards God will give Cyrus for delivering His people. Then in verse 6, he passes over from the Babylonian to the general messianic deliverance not from ONE land but from all the countries of the globe. The release from the Babylonian Captivity would be the prelude to the deliverance from all nations. In verse 19 he says: "Remember not former things, and look not on things of old. Behold I do new things, and now they shall spring forth, verily you shall know them: I will make a way in the wilderness, and rivers in the desert". St. John's words written at the command of Christ: "Behold, I make all things new", are then not a mere allusion to the words of Isaias but an interpretation. St. Paul may also have had the text of Isaias in mind when he wrote: "The old things are passed away, behold all things are made new" (2 Cor. V. 17). It predicts especially in the Jews a new standard of valuation. They measured the value of keeping God's laws by the amount of temporal gain, reward and felicity they would win. During the millennium, their standard of valuation shall have entirely changed; they will appreciate all values according to their spiritual, eternal, supernatural worth. Tremendous as is this message, it is "most faithful and true", because all men will have changed their way of thinking and evaluating everything, when Christ shall have His standards accepted by the world. And this happy state at the beginning of the millennium shall become universal reality.

Verse 6

"It is done". These words state more then the foregoing. The regeneration promised is already a reality in the Church; the victory of Christ which St. John beheld in visions is achieved in divine foreknowledge, and the prophecies are in fulfillment. But how shall it be brought to a finished actuality as the Seer has beheld it? It can become actuality because God is the Alpha and the Omega, the First Cause, the Source and Origin of creation and the Accomplisher of all His plans. Now in what manner will He accomplish it? He is the Giver of life unlimited in His bounty, and He, the Source, has created a fountain of eternal life and from it will give everyone gratis all he wills. Thus He will heal all from the corruption of sin and ward off the death which it entailed. But only those who remain faithful and drink of the fountain of life shall share in the renewal of all things. During the millennium the great majority of the peoples will drink of this fountain and carry out in an eminent degree the will and intentions of God to renew the face of the earth without coercion.

Verse 7

He who will overcome the carnal man and the carnal way of thinking and the earthly standards of valuation shall inherit everything. It recalls the promises made in chapters II. and III. The conqueror of self shall drink of the fountain of life, be renewed in mind and heart and view all things in life from a new viewpoint. Thus will the new human race be created to inherit the world. This race of men has been reared since the day of Redemption; more are added to it daily; and when its number is complete enough to satisfy God's intentions, the judgment of the world under Antichrist shall begin. The remnants of the nations who adhere to Christ shall then inherit all achievements of the world. All conquests of material creation, all inventions, education, culture, art and refinement shall be theirs. But they must be ready to forego everything that sin proffers and not fear for their life, possessions, friends or any earthly thing. As a reward for such victory, God will be a Father to them, and they shall be His sons. The last clause is in the future tense pointing to the future life possibly after the first resurrection. This promise of inheritance of eternal possessions with God is above all earthly promises and is the reward of victory over earthly attachments, which retain their attractiveness even during the millennium. The spiritual blessings showered upon those who cling to Christ in this life shall be the pledge of the sonship and eternal inheritance in the kingdom of God.

Verse 8

The destiny of those who sin against the moral law is in the pool of fire. At the head of the list of reprobates are the craven cowards, the apostate Catholics, who deny their faith for fear of the sacrifices entailed in the practice of it. During the reign of Antichrist, they lost heart and fear a glorious death by martyrdom. Next in order are the unbelievers who will not believe the revealed truth, even when in the supreme struggle undeniable miracles prove the claims of the Church clearly and persuasively. Among the "abominable" are numbered all the following who persistently break the law of God but in particular the morons whose character is saturated with the monstrous vices of heathenism, which will come out in the open under Antichrist. The first of the abominable are the murderers, who have comitted sins against the 5th and 7th commandments. Perhaps murder shall not entirely disappear in the millennium, or perhaps those are pointed out who have crimsoned their hands in the innocent blood of martyrs under Antichrist. The other impure, abominable ones are the adulterers and fornicators, who sin against the 6th and 9th commandments; the sorcerers are those who sin against the 1st and 2nd commandments and seek gains through the aid of evil spirits and place their trust in money; the idolaters who sin against the first three commandments and adore the works of their hands, the works of art and machinery come next;

and lastly all liars, slanderers, perjurers, hypocrites and heretics who sin against the 4th and 8th commandments merit condemnation: all who break any or all of God's commandments are threatened not with punishment in this life during the millennium but with the pool of fire. (Is. LXV. 20). The sins enumerated are the same as those the heathens shall commit before Antichrist (IX. 21).

Perhaps, these threats are intended for all grades and shades of sinners who shall live before the beginning of the millennium, to show them that they shall not share in the blessed times awaiting the courageous, the just and the true, the pure and the faithful but shall attain their destiny in the pool of fire. The nations shall not all be converted at the beginning of the millennium, as XII. 14 and XV. 8 clearly reveal. And according to Isaias (LXV. 20), there shall be sinners at all times, although their number shall become comparatively small, and the Church can easily neutralize their baleful influence and example. So the exact meaning and scope of this verse cannot as yet be discerned.

3. The New Jerusalem Described.

Verses 9 to end.

Verses 9-27

The vision of the New Jerusalem becomes more vivid, and St. John remembers and gives the description of the city in all essential details, as did Ezechiel of the New Temple (XL.-XLIV.). The Temple was never built, neither shall be. The description is purely symbolical of the higher life of virtue after the Captivity, which was to culminate in the reign of the Messias. The revelations about the millennium are imparted to Ezechiel, the priestly prophet, under the figure of a perfect Temple; to St. John, the priest of Christ, under the figure of a city without a temple: In Ezechiel's way of thinking the Temple was the center of the theocracy; In St. John's higher knowledge, the eucharistic Lamb is the center of thought and aspirations in the new theocracy. Both represent the millennium but each one from the plane of his own spiritual elevation: Ezechiel depicted the great consummation in an obscure way, which no one could comprehend, if new revelations did not clear it up; St. John in a few verses draws the same picture showing the unchangeable and everlasting worship of the Lamb in clearest allegory and of the happy state of the faithful in the new covenant: Ezechiel could attain to no loftier height of thought unless the whole New Dispensation and worship had been revealed to him; St. John needed only an apt allegorical illustration of the Church to embody in it the full revelations he knew and possessed: Ezechiel relates the earthly felicity, which shall inundate Israel, in language that was intelligible to the people of the Old Covenant – the perpetual sacrifice, the healing of nature from the curse and the establishing of the nation in unperturbed peace; St. John gives the exposition of a spiritual empire ruled by the Lamb, who enlightens, inspires and transfuses the minds and hearts not of Israel alone but of all men by His grace transforming and elevating them to sonship of God to participate in His own divine life: In Ezechiel's view the apirations of men are still earthly; in St. John's earthly cares are forgotten, earthly hopes and aspirations are overcome, and the minds and hearts of men are weaned from inordinate attachment to earth and are raised heavenward, where alone the longings of the heart ennobled and deified by grace can be satisfied.

Verse 9

One of the seven angels who poured out the seven last plagues upon Antichrist and his followers comes to show St. John the "Bride, the wife of the Lamb". The word "bride" is a reference to verse 2 and the word "wife" to XIX. 7. Both words are contrasted with that of "Harlot" of chapter XVII. The Holy City is the "Bride" of the Lamb, because it is chosen to become the mother of the New Earth. The marriage will be solemnized when the nations that are not yet converted shall enter the Church in the first epoch of the millennium. The prophets called the Synagogue the rightful wife of God and when Juda and Israel fell into idolatry termed them harlots. Likewise was the city which was constituted center of the messianic empire termed a harlot after her apostasy from Christ. The Church has now found a new home on earth and from the new home will rule as Queen with the King of kings. As Babylon was the metropolis of the evil earth directing the kings and capitals of Antichrist, so the New Jerusalem is the metropolis of the holy earth and capital of the Kingdom of Christ. The prophet Osee (II. 16-19) uses the same figure of speech to characterize the relationship of God with the Synagogue, and he speaks of the restoration after the Captivity in terms of the millennium.

Verse 10

The angel takes St. John in spirit on a high mountain, as he had taken him in spirit into the desert (XVII. 3), and as the hand of the Lord led Ezechiel in spirit into Juda and up on a high mountain (Ez. XL. 2), while his body remained in Babylon. The mountain is both broad and high and enables the Seer to look down upon the city and view its interior. The scene upon which his gaze rests is one of utmost loveliness and a contrast to that of chapter XVII. The angel may be the same one who showed St. John the Great Harlot. The angel showed St. John in chapter XVII. the "condemnation" of the City of Evil, and now he shows him the exaltation of the Holy City. That condemnation of the Evil City was the effect of one of the seven plagues intended ultimately to restore all primeval blessings to the world. From the Holy City will emanate these blessings. The coming of the Holy City out of heaven reflects its origin and true nature. The Church will create the New Jerusalem. From men it could not procure the power of establishing itself and of attaining the glory it shall possess in the millennium, if the Imperishable Church of Christ did not make and appoint the city what it is destined to be, her metropolis and capital. God giving the Church the victory over her enemies and directing her to Jerusalem as her new home is the ultimate Cause and Creator of the New Jerusalem. It then comes forth from the Church through God's almighty power.

Verse 11

The Holy City is clothed with the glory of God as the Church was clothed with the sun in XII. 1, and as in XV. 8 the sanctuary was filled with God's majesty. In IV. 3 the color of the jasper was blended with that of the sardine stone, which is the color of anger and of judgment. God appeared in that color when He began His judgments upon the world and the Church. Now he appears in the whitest ray of pure crystal, of the diamond, the purest of all stones and the most precious. His judgments are suspended and He appears only in His Holiness to His children. He comes to delight them and draw them to His fatherly heart by love, since fear is no longer necessary to keep them faithful. In this description is contained a demand of a higher holiness during the millennium. His glory is no longer veiled by a cloud as in Ezechiel but shines forth with crystal clearness both in His manner of guiding the Church and in the lives of the faithful. The New Jerusalem is the lightbearer of God's glory and reflects His holiness in its whole constitution. Then will become reality what Isaias predicted: "O House of Jacob, come ye, and let us walk in the light of the Lord" (II. 5).

Verse 12

The New Jerusalem is fortified by a wall so high that it cannot be penetrated by any war machinery. It has twelve gates, three on each side. The gates are open wide, but each one is guarded by an angel against wicked intruders. The number TWELVE is God's number of perfection and is obtained by the number of the Blessed Trinity multiplied by that of universality. One name of the twelve tribes of Israel is on each gate.

The "great and high wall" would contradict the prophecies, in which the New Jerusalem is stated to be "without walls", if this were not an allegory. In antiquity a city could not be imagined without a protective wall. The great high wall is the emblem of security against attack and might be understood to be the wall of Truth. The organization of the Church symbolized by the city will be so perfected that all imputations of error, ignorance, stupidity, indolence or corruption shall recoil harmlessly. Through the open gates communication with the new earth shall be unrestricted. The Church will invite all nations to receive salvation within her gates and will extend her influence and activity equally to the four parts of the earth. No nation or people shall be specially favored, but all, white and colored, rich and poor, little and great shall be equal. Though communication with the new earth will be free and unrestricted through the open gates, the watchful angels will allow no error or corruption to enter the Church. They will keep her immune from whatever she and the world were contaminated with formerly. Converts will enter the Church in vast throngs until the world is converted, but no one shall be permitted to retain false principles or vicious practices. These angels are the priests of the Church, who shall without exception be faithful and will receive none without thorough instruction and a willingness to reject all error and superstition. It is a clear allusion to Isaias (LXII. 6-7) who places guards on the walls. The number twelve indicates that the whole priesthood of the Church will be zealous and faithful.

On each gate is the name of one of the twelve tribes. This agrees with the description of the Holy City given by Ezechiel (XLVIII. 31 etc). According to Ezechiel, the old disposition of the Temple, land and city was not to be followed, because everything differs from precaptivity order, though the individual features of the new order bear the impress of the old. Thus is Ezechiel's new Jerusalem. A hint of this new and entirely different order is XLVIII. 19, where the guardians of the city shall be taken from all tribes and by extension from all nations on earth. Ezechiel enumerates the names of the tribes and has the name of Dan on one of the gates, while St. John does not name the tribes here having done this in VII. 6 and there he substitutes the name of Manasses for Dan.

The names of the twelve tribes symbolize their office in God's plan to preserve and spread over the whole earth the knowledge of the true God and His revelation. They were God's chosen nations in the Old Covenant, which prepared the way for the coming of Christ and the universal sway of His truth. They were thus the gates of salvation for the world through which the nations shall be gathered into the Church. Perhaps during the millennium those of Jewish blood will have the leadership in the Church, because Christ who has opened the eternal gates to the world is of that nation.

Verse 13

The city has three gates on each of the four sides. Besides

having its symbolic meaning, this is a mathematical necessity, for the only proper symmetry would be three gates on each side of a four-square wall. This is quite a contrast to the cities of antiquity which had only one or two main gates to make them less vulnerable to hostile attack. During the millennium, the Church fears no danger, never closes her gates but receives people from the four quarters of the globe and sends forth her blessings to all the world. In naming the gates St. John follows a different order from that of Ezechiel. Ezechiel has North, East, South, West; and St. John has East, North, South, West.

Verse 14

The twelve foundations of the wall are likewise a mathematical necessity. If the city is four-square and has three gates on each side, there will be twelve segments of wall around the city, four of which are the corners. A massive foundation-stone upholds each of the segments so high above the ground that its precious material can be seen and the inscription read by the Seer. The foundation stones bear the names of the twelve apostles. St. John does not specify or assign any single stone to a particular apostle. He holds to the perfect number twelve and surely does not include Judas in the number nor exclude St. Paul. The names of all may be on each stone, for the college of apostles is the foundation of the Church. St. Paul writes: "Built upon the foundation of the apostles and prophets, Jesus Himself being the chief cornerstone". The stones are not the foundation for the city but only for the wall. And the stones are not the apostles but are only adorned by their names. The wall fortifying the city so securely is then probably the truths of divine revelation. The names of the apostles vouch for the truth of the revelations they propagated, and their teaching authority assisted by the Holy Spirit makes the wall firm and adamantine in solidity. All materials of the wall are cemented together with the foundation stones so solidly that the city is secure and invulnerable against all attacks. The names of the apostles on the foundations then probably means that they interpreted correctly and under divine inspiration the revelations of the Old and New Testaments, and that all worldly knowledge must conform itself to and harmonize with their doctrines.

Verse 15

Ezechiel (XL. 3) in spirit accompanied a man who measured the new city that was to take the place of the old Sion. St. John himself (XI. 1) was told to measure the sanctuary with a reed, which had the force of a rod. The rod was the symbol of judgment to purify the Church and to drive all the wicked into the exterior darkness. An angel who directed him thus far now produces a GOLDEN reed to measure the heavenly city. The city is pure, and there is no one within who should be excommunicated. Gold is the most precious of metals and is the emblem of unselfish service of God. Since the whole Church is now devoted to God with unreserved devotion, her capital city is worthy of being measured by standards that are emblematic of her perfection. The angel will first measure the city to make the Seer familiar with its size and the number of its inhabitants. Then he will measure the gates to show how correctly proportioned they are with the size and population of the city, and what easy communication they afford with the world, and whether they will admit the throngs from out of the whole world which the expanse within the city is capable of receiving. And lastly he will measure the walls to show their height and width and the perfect protection and the proper lines of beauty they lend the city. This measuring of the city is a symbolic action to impress upon the mind of St. John its details and unblemished perfection.

Verse 16

Before the angel begins to measure the city, St. John notices that "it lieth in a four-square". The symmetry of its size symbolizes ideal beauty. It measures twelve thousand furlongs. This might mean so much in length, but according to the Greek text, it means so much in circumference making it three thousand furlongs on each side. The Greek furlong is 606¾ feet, while the English is 660 feet. This would make the city 345 miles square. It would cover the length and breadth of Palestine from the Arabian Desert into Syria and from the Mediterranean Sea across the Jordan into the ancient territory of Edom, Moab and Ammon. Compared with this size, all other cities of antiquity were but miniature villages. Its vast size is the most striking example in all literature of the power and influence of the future empire of Christ. Rome had four million inhabitants. Modern cities equal and exceed the size of ancient Rome. Yet no city will ever stand comparison with the New Jerusalem. If the length alone were 12,000 stadia, about 1500 miles the description would be ridiculous, because it would begin with the southern edge of the Arabian peninsula and run north into the Caucusus. The twelve thousand furlongs are, of course, symbolic figures signifying the inimitable perfection of the New Jerusalem.

The height of the city also 345 miles recalls the prophecy of Isaias (II. 2): "And in the last days the mountain of the house of the Lord shall be prepared on the top of mountains, and it shall be exalted above the hills". These symbolic words of the prophet foreshow the conspicuous renown of the Church when she shall have reached full development. Even now the Church is known by all nations, although large parts of some heathen nations are still in ignorance of her existence. During the millenium all shall know her.

The shape of the city is a perfect cube. It seems to be modelled after the Holy of Holies in the ancient Temple, which measured 20 cubits wide, long and high. The shape corresponds to various measurements in Ezechiel's temple and city. The foursquare of ancient cities was in general indicative of perfect construction. Historians report this of the city of Babylon and Niniveh. And it was probably the fundamental idea in Egyptian and Grecian architecture. Later pagan Roman architecture had more of the rotunda for the ground plan. But the rectangle gained predominance in Church architecture. The above figures in the Apocalypse have captivated the imagination of many commentators and have elicited many and varied allegorical explanations.

Verse 17

After the angel measured the city round about, he measured the wall. This was found to be 144 cubits high, the square of the perfect number 12. It shows the Truth with which the city is surrounded and fortified to be of the highest perfection. The height of the wall is rather insignificant, if compared with the height of the city. Yet from a human standpoint the wall was "great and high". The height of the wall, 216 feet, would make the city impregnable at the time of these visions; no war machinery could make any impression on it. "The walls of the city are not for defense, for there is no enemy at large any more, but serve for delineation, marking the external form of the civitas Dei. And the order and organization of the Church, necessary as they are, fall infinitely below the elevation of its spiritual life" (H. B. Swete).

The last two clauses make the measurement appear realistic, since St. John actually saw the angel measuring the walls and city by such measure as were in use among men. The angels accomodate themselves to human intelligence and standards when they reveal to men any message from God.

Verse 18

The *COMPOSITION* of the wall next catches the attention of the Seer. It was rather not a composition but was of pure jasper, pure diamond. The wall reflected the lustre of the city. Now the city is 345 miles high. Its lustrous walls pervaded by the divine light radiated from the presence of the Lamb within and its buildings like burnished, transparent gold, light up the world to the farthest blue distances. The city shall then be the light of the world. The allegorical language calls attention to the brilliant victory of the Church over Antichrist, to the extraordinary miracles performed during the days of darkness, humiliation and oppression and to the corroboration of her claims by the fulfillment of all prophecies of the Old and New Testaments. These achievements shall radiate her fame and renown to the farthest horizons of future generations. During the evil days of Antichrist, the world was sick at heart, and for this incurable disease the Church will have the cure, and the world shall the better learn its total dependence for health and happiness on her beneficent power. All peoples will then admire her unblemished perfection and divine beauty. And it will be the actualization of what St. Paul said of her: "that she shall be holy and without blemish" (Eph. V. 27).

The city itself is of pure gold, a symbol of disinterested and unselfish devotion to the service of God and man. In the Church of the early ages, the religious orders are shown to give such service to God under the symbol of the golden altar and golden censer (VIII. 3-5). After Antichrist, the whole Church will practice unselfish CHARITY and live up to the ideals of the religious orders. It does not mean that no one will own private property or that no one will marry, but that each one in his own state of life will live up fully to the Christian standards of that state. The wicked shall be so much in the minority that their influence shall not lower the high spirituality of the Church.

The pure gold is as transparent as glass, the emblem of sincerity. There will be no bluff, trickery or hypocrisy in the service of God or man. The lives of the clergy shall be pure gold, the motive of their work and sacrifices pure love of God, and their record shall have no dark pages. No suspicion shall be cast upon them any more. No one will seek advancement by skillful flattery or sycophancy or beyond his deserts or begrudge it to the deserving. And those who rule and direct the Church will direct according to divine standards of truth, justice and reason guided by the grace of God. The doctrines of the Church, her moral law, laws of discipline, liturgy and administration of spiritual and temporal matters will be transparent in sincerity. There will be no hidden motives of temper or revenge in the management and no secret discipline in any part of the Church. And the faithful shall live open and sincere lives of true piety, which is free from fear or worldly motives.

Isaias, after he narrates the sufferings and death of the Savior in chapter LIII., reviews the result of His death as it reaches its culmination in the establishment of the New Jerusalem. In chapter after chapter, he takes up some phase of the theme stated in LIII. 10 of Christ's triumph in the world. What St. John depicts here in detail of the construction and material of the Holy City, Isaias briefly mentions (LIV. 11-12). The theocratic Sion is to be rebuilt into the messianic Sion. Sapphires shall be the groundwork of the city making it immovable as the heavens. Diamonds and all precious stones shall adorn it. The messianic re-establishment of Sion, in the variegated splendor in which Isaias saw it, shall put upon it the unmistakable seal of God, and all the world shall recognize it as His work, for it shall excel anything the world has seen. St. John beholds the city in a much higher degree of perfection than Isaias did;

to him its walls appear as pure diamond and the city itself as pure transparent gold.

Verses 19 and 20

St. John next takes notice of the precious stones that compose the foundations of the wall. Isaias also noticed this, but he does not give a detailed description of it. As verse 14 stated, each segment of wall had a precious stone for its foundation. The twelve foundations are twelve different stones. It alludes to the Rational, the breast-plate of the highpriest, which had the name of a tribe inscribed on each of its twelve stones. In the Septuagint, four of those stones have a different name from those given by St. John (Exod. XXVIII. 17-21). But they may be different names for the same stones. In the New Jerusalem, not the names of the twelve tribes are on the foundations but those of the Twelve Apostles.

To give a definite meaning to each foundation stone would be the sheerest speculation and be untrue. It is evidently a figure of diction according to Old Testament models. St. John uses mystic symbols to denote the inestimable price of the offices in the Church. In verse fourteen the twelve foundation stones were said to bear the names of the twelve apostles, but now the Seer is more specific and enumerates twelve assorted stones and every one a gem. No two are alike, which may signify an attribute of God conspicuously exemplified in each apostle, or what St. Paul says: "Star differs from star in glory". Four colors or shades of colors are shown in the stones, yellow, red, blue and green. Whether any symbolism is blended in the colors cannot be known, but the details reveal the inestimable wealth of the city and the spiritual riches embodied in the apostolic college. If the city is 345 miles square, and the wall of each side divided into three segments, and each segment supported by a precious stone, all the riches of the world would bear no comparison with the value of one foundation stone of that wall. The Great Harlot was shown in chapter XVII. clothed in gold, precious stones and pearls, but her wealth is poverty compared with that of the Holy City. This is all spiritual wealth, symbolic of how far in value above all earthly wealth and splendor are spiritual riches, so that all comparison is lost, and all the wealth of the world could not purchase one block of truth possessed by the Church. Ezechiel (XXVIII. 13) recounts for the king of Tyre the riches with which he is surrounded in order to make his humiliation appear the greater by contrast, when he shall be stripped of all his wealth. And he there mentions nearly all the precious stones that are in the foundations of the New Jerusalem.

Verse 21

The Twelve gates each bearing a name of the twelve tribes are pearls. If so large a pearl and one so pure could be commercialized, what would be its price? In all these details, the spiritual riches of the New Jerusalem would exceed the wildest dreams of all poets. Our Lord made this clear when He used the pearl to illustrate the value of spiritual things (Mt. XIII.). St. Bede finds the pearly gates to signify the "lux vera" of the saints. Whether the arched gate-towers or the open gates are the pearls, the text does not state. But if the open gates are pearls, they would be rolled back inwards, and this would make the view difficult from the top of the high mountain.

The streets of the city are of pure gold transparent like glass as are also the buildings. The streets are the channels of communication and transportation and the avenues of social and business life. The streets connect with the gates and the outside world. Charity will be the universal law of the Holy City and will radiate it out into the world during the millennium, will actuate all inhabitants and draw crowds of pilgrims year by year.

The clear transparency of the golden streets signifies sincerity. There will be no hypocrisy in the dealings of men with men, and no one need distrust anyone. No one will defraud another or seek undue advantage for himself. Pilgrims will be safe in their possessions and their virtue, because vice will be unknown. All will live in the state of sanctifying grace and will avoid all that may endanger that blissful state of the soul. St. Bede says of the symbolism of the pure gold: "nihil simulatum est et non perspicuum in sanctis ecclesiae". The New Jerusalem will be a conspicuous model to the Christian nations and will reflect the golden age of the millennium in the new earth.

Verse 22

After describing the Holy City in detail as viewed from the outside, St. John returns to the statement of verse eleven, "having the glory of God". There is no Temple in the New Jerusalem. The old Jerusalem was incomplete without it. It was the emblem of God's sanctuary, where He dwelt and at times manifested His presence under a significant mystery. The chosen people felt the presence of God in the Temple; their consciousness of His omnipresence was rather vague and uncertain. When they entered the courts of the Temple, the dread of the divine presence settled on them, and when without but still in the sight of His Holy Temple the spell of His Presence was still upon them. In the New Jerusalem it shall be different. The presence of God will no longer be hidden under a Shekhina or shadowy form in a temple, but will be really, truly and substantially present there not in symbol, or figure, or power, or virtue. St. John's revelations make it clear that a Temple of the Old Covenant type with its ceremonial and symbolic rites, although the Holy City should be rebuilt, should remain abolished forever. For the "Lord God Almighty will be the temple, and the Lamb". The Eucharistic Lamb will be perpetually present in the Holy City in His humanity and divinity and as it were sacrificed (V. 6). Therefore a temple with its symbolic rites and sacrifices and a shadowy presence of God would be out of place and a profanation.

This by no means excludes the presence of churches from the Holy City. There shall no doubt be numerous beautiful sanctuaries there, in which the Eucharistic Lamb shall be given the highest honor that human skill and devotion in art and architecture can fashion. But there shall not be the profanation of heretical houses of worship or idolatrous shrines in it. The whole city shall be of pure gold, with nothing in it that cannot bear the light. Everything shall be pervaded by the healing and sanctifying presence of God. Such a consummation must have seemed, when St. John received these revelations, the porch of Heaven if not Heaven itself. Yet who will hold such a victory impossible?

Verse 23

St. John repeats the revelation of Isaias (LX. 19) in this verse, but expresses it in his own original manner and interprets Isaias in a definite literal sense. The Church applies this chapter of Isaias to the coming of the Wise Men to the cradle of the infant Savior, but the prophecy quite clearly presages a greater coming of the whole world to Christ, although the coming of the Wise Men was typical of the great advent of the nations during the millennium. The sun and moon shall not be a necessity to the city, because God's glory enlightens it; and the eucharistic Christ is the visible luminary from which radiates the light of God's glory throughout the city. The allegory shows how human wisdom, prudence and providence are supplied by the divine Presence in the Holy City. The consciousness of God's presence transfuses and directs all conditions of life, and the inhabitants do not strive for the glimmerings of transient felicity. As does Isaias (LX. 19-20), so does St. John blend time and eternity in this verse to show what unending bliss shall flow from the presence of God in the Church during the millennium. According to Isaias: "Thy sun shall go down no more, and thy moon shall not decrease" promising an unchanging new covenant in the New Jerusalem which shall not be suppressed by any foe but shall be perpetual. This shall not be a gradual growth but due to a sudden act of Omnipotence to re-establish the city in indestructible security, as the prophet again says: "I the Lord will suddenly do this thing in its time".

"The glory of God" is the divine Presence, the divine nature of Christ, with which is united in a necessary, inseparable union the Father and the Holy Ghost. This Presence makes earthly glory, power and wisdom superfluous, for It manifests Itself in the blessed gains It achieves for the city and through it for the world. Perhaps something extraordinary is meant here. Perhaps in the battle with Antichrist, the Sacred Species carried in an airplane will execute judgment upon Antichrist and his attacking legions. And thereafter the miraculous Host is worshipped for all time in a special shrine in the Holy City. At all events, "the Glory of God", which is the light of the Holy City, will be the Real Presence of Christ.

"The Lamb is the lamp thereof" reiterates the fact of the eucharistic presence of Christ, for through His Sacred Humanity it is possible for the "Glory of God" to be really, truly and substantially present in the city. The eucharistic humanity of Christ is thus the vessel by which the light of God enlightens the city and the world.

Verse 24

The Greek text reads: "And the nations shall wend their way through her light". In the vision, the light of God beams forth from the Holy City into the world in every direction guiding all nations on their march of progress. All nations shall be willingly directed by the dogmas and moral law of the Church during the millennium, and their politics, business, professions, social life, arts, sciences, culture, education and every achievement shall be submitted to her moral and spiritual standards. The residue of the nations not destroyed by the plagues inflicted during the reign of Antichrist will united with the converted Jews constitute the true Israel spoken of by the prophets and apostles. "So far history has verified the Seer's forecast, and the fulfillment continues to this day . . . The words may havę reference only to the present order, or they indicate some gracious purpose of God towards humanity which has not yet been revealed" (H. B. Swete).

The first sentence of this verse alludes very clearly to Isaias (II. 3-5) and to Micheas (IV. 1-4). The conversion of the Gentiles is foreseen by Osee (I. 10-11) and also the conversion of the Jews to Christ (III. 4-5; XIV. 5-10). Jeremias shows that there will be no distinction any more between Jews and Gentiles and that Jerusalem shall no longer be called the "ark of the covenant", the resting place of the Lord, but shall be called "the throne of the Lord" (III. 15-19).

Everything that honors kings and constitutes their glory, the best the rulers of the world have, they shall bring into the city for her adornment, because the light and glory of God is there and is the center and source of life and felicity. This intercourse of the Christian kings of the millennium with the Holy City is thus contrasted with the intercourse which the kings of Antichrist maintained with the Evil City (XVII. 2). That city encouraged and led those kings into sin and temporal and eternal disaster, while the Holy City encourages to spiritual life, leads people and rulers alike onward in virtue and secures for them temporal blessings and eternal happiness.

Verse 25

This verse expresses the exact ideas of Isaias, but the wording is different from the Septuagint (Is. LX. 11 ff), yet it clearly interprets Isaias. The gates shall not be shut day or night, says Isaias, but St. John leaves out "night". He must then give the reason for this omission, and so he explains that there shall be no night there. This has a deeper significance than Isaias revealed. The Old Covenant was a religion which promised earthly rewards for faithful service, was a religion of the earth: The Covenant God made with His sons in the New Order entails spiritual and eternal rewards and happiness for faithful love of Him. In the Old Order, wars ever threatened the peace and security of God's people, and the gates of Jerusalem had to be closed against the enemy frequently; in the New Order war shall be unknown, and therefore no day of darkness and no night of terror threatens. The Old Dispensation takes in view the natural order in which darkness follows light; in the New, night disappears, and it is forever day. The perpetual sacrifice of the Old Law was offered only in the Tabernacle or Temple in one place on earth, and at a certain hour in the morning and in the evening; under the New Law the Holy Sacrifice is offered without ceasing from the rising of the sun till the going down, because the Church embraces the whole world making the sacrifice of the spotless Lamb continuous. Since His becoming present and His being present is continuous, no night intervenes; since the Eucharistic Lamb is the lamp of the Holy City, there is no need of the sun or moon, which divide the day and night in the natural order: There is just ONE UNENDING DAY during the blessed years of the millennium, because God's Presence illumines the world with unbroken continuity. This verse alludes by contrast to the "days of darkness" under Antichrist, during which the Lamb shall be banished from many tabernacles especially from Babylon. And perhaps in St. John's mind lingered the conditions of his own times, in which the Sacred Species for fear of desecration could not be reserved in the churches.

Verse 26

Not only the glory of the kings but also that of the peoples shall be brought to the New Jerusalem. The nations shall give their best, unselfish devotion. The highest achievements of human endeavor shall deck the sanctuary of the living God. Isaias avers this in a poetic figure: "The glory of Libanus shall come to thee, the fir-tree, and the box-tree, and the pine-tree together, to beautify the place of my sanctuary: and I will glorify the place of my feet. And the children of them that afflict thee, shall come bowing down to thee, and all that slandered thee shall worship the steps of thy feet, and shall call thee the city of the Lord, the Sion of the Holy One of Israel" (LX. 13). The trees mentioned are evergreens foreshadowing the unending life that the Church of the Messias shall create and nourish. And the figure probably means that most exquisite examples of virtue shall flourish in abundance and adorn the Church universally. The "place of my feet" and "the place of my sanctuary" was the Holy of Holies pointing this prophecy of Isaias to the Holy Eucharist.

Verse 27

This verse is made up of two negative and one positive statements. No one can enter the Holy City, if he be defiled by original sin. During the Millennium, the angels of the gates will be so watchful as to keep out of the Church all the abominations that have in the past found entrance at times of wholesale conversions. The Church will no longer make concessions to princes and rulers, which have often endangered her liberty in the past. The City of Evil reeked with abominations (XVII. 4). But that city is no more; and with its passing, vice was stripped of its gold, precious stones and scarlet raiment and shall appear in all its hideousness thenceforth. The lives of the true believers shall not be tainted by moral turpitude, for the morally corrupt world with its insistent urge to evil has passed away, and people vie with one another to live up perfectly to the ideals of the Church.

The Church has never compromised with heresy or moral errors. Protestantism has experienced this. The Church will never surrender any of her divine prerogatives or truths and will never change one dot or tittle of the revelations of God to please anyone. No error or false doctrine can enter the infallible Church. But individual members of the episcopate have sometimes held erroneous views, have exemplified heresy in action or for policy sake have connived with it or have practiced the greatest of all abominations, hypocrisy, shown vainglory and loved flattery and pleasantries and hated and punished uprightness. In the New Jerusalem, all things that are based on lies and falsehood are scorned. And no one will be tolerated in the Church who holds questionable views. Those of low-grade mentality, who are petty, mean and resentful for slights to their feigned dignity, who are weak in upholding principle, whose word is unreliable and worthless and who take revenge on those whom they have in their power will not hold high positions in the Church during the millennium. St. John had knowledge enough of the insincerity of the pagans, but his condemnation in this verse strikes those who are knowingly and deliberately insincere.

Only those may enter the Holy City whose names are written in the Book of Life. Christ is in possession of the Book of Life, because through Him alone can men be saved. All saving power emanates from the Eucharistic Lamb, and He will enter in the book the names of those who procure this right for themselves by being His devoted servants and seeking their refreshment, strength, inspiration and perseverance in the eucharistic mystery. This was His own promise: "He who eats my flesh and drinks my blood has life everlasting and I will raise him up on the last day" (Jo. VI. 55). Some names may possibly be entered in the Book of Life and be later blotted out. (III. 5). But during the millennium, no one who is hostile to the Church shall dare to enter the Holy City.

CHAPTER XXII.

Westminster Version

And he showed me a river of the water of 1. life, clear as crystal,
issuing forth from the throne of God and of the Lamb, in the midst of the
street of the city. On 2. either side of the river was the tree of life, which
beareth fruit twelve times, yielding every month its own fruit, and the
leaves of the tree are for the healing of the nations.

And there shall no more be aught accursed. 3. And the throne of God
and of the Lamb shall be in the city, and his servants shall minister before
him, and they shall behold his face, and his name shall be on their foreheads, and night shall be no more, and they shall 5. have no need of
the light of a lamp or of the light of the sun, because the Lord God shall
be their light; and they shall reign for ever and ever. And the angel said to
me, 'These words 6. are faithful and true; and the Lord, the God of the
spirits of the prophets, hath sent his angel to show his servants what
must speedily befall. And behold, I come quickly. Blessed is 7. he that
keepeth the words of the prophecy of this book!' I John am he who heard
and saw 8. these things; and when I had heard and seen them, I fell
down to worship before the feet of the angel who showed them to me.

And he saith to me, 'Forbear! I am a fellow-servant 9. with thee, with
thy brethren the prophets, and with them that keep the words of this book.
God shalt thou worship!'

And he said to me, 'Seal not the words of 10. the prophecy of this
book; for the time is near.

Let wrong-doers do wrong as yet, and let 11. the filthy be defiled
as yet, and let the just do justness as yet, and let the holy be hallowed
as yet.'

'Behold, I come quickly, and my reward is 12. with me, to render
to each according to his work.

I am the Alpha and the Omega, the first 13. and the last, the
beginning and the end.

Blessed are they that wash their robes, in 14. order that they may
have a right to the tree of life, and may enter by the gates into the city.

Outside are the dogs and the sorcerers 15. and the fornicators and
the murderers and the idolaters and everyone that loveth and worketh
falsehood.'

'I Jesus have sent mine angel to testify 16. to you thus touching the
churches. I am the root and the son of David, the bright star of the
morning.

And the spirit and the spouse say 'Come!' 17. And let him that
heareth say, 'Come!' And let him that thirsteth come! Let him that willeth
take the water of life freely!

I testify to everyone that heareth the 18. words of the prophecy of
this book: if any one add to them, God shall add to him the plagues

described in this book; and if any 19. one take away from the words of
the book of this prophecy, God shall take away his part from the tree
of life and from the holy city, which are described in this book.'

He who testifieth these things, saith, 20. 'Yea, I come quickly!' –
Amen! Come, Lord Jesus!

The grace of the Lord Jesus be with the saints.

4. Paradise Restored.

Chapter XXII.

A. The Water of Life.

Verses 1-2.

Verse 1

The same angel who showed St. John the outside and construction of the city leads him to the sources of contentment and felicity within. The text forgets to take notice of his leaving the high mountain to enter the city. Arriving here the angel points out "a river of the water of life". According to Jeremias, God is the water of life (II. 13). Isaias holds the same view (XXXIII. 20-21), and he promises an overflow of waters for the new Sion of the Messias, when God shall surround Jerusalem as mighty rivers. It may allude to ancient Babylon. The prophet Joel, after relating the judgment of God upon Antichrist and all the wicked, paints the picture of the New Jerusalem with the river of life; "And a fountain shall come forth from the house of the Lord" (III. 18). Ezechiel beholds the river of life issuing from under the east entrance of the Temple and flowing eastward into the Dead Sea curing its waters and nurturing fruit trees on its banks as it flows, which produce fruit every month and leaves for medicine. Likewise Zacharias promises that living waters shall flow from Jerusalem after the destruction of Antichrist. (XIV. 8) St. John's description of the same vision is very near to that of Ezechiel, and it alludes vaguely to the rivers of Paradise. The revelation seems to promise near-paradisiac conditions in the world, when the Church has gained the ascendancy over the powers of evil and finds all men willing and eager to be instructed in the truth. When men shall have given up all deliberate perversity, the living conditions of the earth shall have a different operation. Atmospheric forces may be changed; death and destruction by the elements may be unknown; vicissitudes of life now necessary to deter men from complete abandonment to vice may no longer be needed: Then will God's blessings flow forth upon all life without measure.

"The Water of Life" is evidently grace which will now be abused no more but be eagerly sought after and prized at its real value. This water more than clear and transparent, free from all impurities shines like a diamond, which signifies its divine origin and power as a supernatural gift. It has in this respect the same quality as the walls, which are the divine truth revealed through the prophets and apostles. In the early times of the Church, the water of life flowed only from the fountains (VII. 17), but they have now grown into mighty rivers that are impassable to man (See Ezech. XLIII. 6). And these mighty rivers flowing down the millennium shall bring back paradisiac conditions. The language of this whole chapter intimates that God's revelation to man shall end in the condition in which it began.

B. The Tree Of Life.

Verse 2

The "street" is the principal boulevard, and the river of life seems to flow down the middle of it. Along this street on both sides of the river are rows of the Tree of Life. The description takes us to the sub-tropical countries of the orient where trees are necessarily attached to a river and depend on it for sufficient moisture. Both the River of Life and the Tree of Life are supernatural creations but are transplanted into this natural world to sustain supernatural life here. The spiritual, invisible sustenance of the divine life of the world becomes visible under the natural necessities of life – food and drink. The name and idea of the tree is taken from Genesis (II. 9; III. 22). What mankind lost in Paradise is re-instated in the world with more lavish munificence by the restoration of original integrity in the untainted Human Nature of Jesus Christ, which secures for man the constant Real Presence of God, the exhaustless Source of life.

Verses 3-5

The tree of life bears twelve different kinds of fruit and yields them regularly every month. This may mean the twelve fruits of the Holy Spirit (Gal. V. 22). But the number TWELVE is probably again used as the number of perfection to denote the adequate fruits derived from membership in the Church which satisfy man's spiritual needs and restore human nature to the perfection lost by sin. There shall now be nothing wanting to replace the spiritual life of the beginning. The tree is not in a place difficult of access, not enclosed in anyone's domain but is in the public street and is public property. No one shall be deprived of its fruits or leaves but may freely take all he desires.

The leaves of the tree are for the healing of the nations. It alludes to the "evil and malignant sore" (XVI. 2) but does not suggest a cure for it, because those who were afflicted have evidently perished. This verse demonstrates emphatically that these last chapters do not describe Heaven or the happiness of the Elect in a paradise to be planted on earth after the resurrection and Last Judgment. The nations still exist; the end of the world has not arrived. In the next world the nations do not exist as nations, and no nations need healing. According to St. Paul, no one can attempt to describe the next life: "Eye has not seen, nor ear heard, neither has it entered into the heart of man what things God has prepared for them that love Him". How then will the leaves of the tree heal the nations? This healing may be wrought by the theological conclusions from divine revelation, the application of the moral law of the Church to the fundamental principles of government and the fruits of the grace of God in the social and moral virtues regulating the relationships of man to man. The nations were sick at heart, because they had under Antichrist imbibed false standards of government by human wisdom alone ignoring the rights of God. They will now give public acknowledgment and worship to God and conform the constitutions and laws to the moral law and the direction of the Church. The Church in her own organization and life will be purified of all despotism and hypocrisy and will be perfected to do the will of Christ faithfully. The Church has elaborated and enunciated the right principles of government long ago, but the world would not listen. The Church has the remedy to heal the ills of society in the laws of justice and charity. She can establish the true relationship between Labor and Capital. So can she direct science to true progress and achievement and save it loss of time incurred by setting up theories which contradict Revelation and always prove untenable. And she can cure Education and the Arts of all vagaries and guide them along the path of true culture and refinement. Such leaves protect the fruits of virtue.

Osee says: "I will heal their wounds, I will love them freely: for my wrath is turned away from them" (XIV. 5). Although this points to the restoration after the Captivity, it takes in view the ultimate triumph in the millennium, for at the end of the chapter he says: "Who is wise and shall understand these things?" The complete restoration shall be in the New Jerusalem after Christ has won the victory.

Verse 3

The curse also shall be banned. When the sin of Adam merited death for all mankind, God said: "Cursed is the earth in thy work" (Gen. III. 17). This curse settled upon all conditions of life and was part of the punishment for DISOBEDIENCE. Original sin, the supreme penalty for disobedience, is taken away by Baptism. After the millennium begins, the original disobedience will have been amended by obedience to Christ, and most of the penalty shall be removed. Death has lost its sting; diseases and plagues shall ravage mankind no more. The war between man and the lower creation shall cease, and universal peace shall reign. This may not be the literal meaning of Isaias (XI. 6-9), but this verse suggests it. When the curse shall depart, grief and bitter tears, mourning and despair shall vanish from the earth.

The fundamental virtues of a happy social life are justice and truthfulness, the opposite of hypocrisy (Zach. VIII. 16-17). Zacharias speaking of the millennium after the final victory of Christ says: "And people shall dwell in it, and there shall be no more a curse: but Jerusalem shall sit secure" (XIV. 11). Isaias likewise says that the effects of the curse shall be taken away. Jeremias gives the reason for the happy state of the messianic Jerusalem, the same as St. John gives when he says: "At that time Jerusalem shall be called the throne of the Lord" (III. 17).

The throne of God and the Lamb shall be in the city. In the strength of this divine Presence, the Church shall bless all things banishing the curse. The Church has ever blessed all things used in the service of God and all labors and possessions of her children. The curse still rests on the earth, because the human race will not submit to Christ. The power of the Church is thus restricted by the DISOBEDIENCE of men. If the evils of the first six trumpets had not appeared, Christ might long ago have been triumphant in the world. But they have continued the evil of disobedience and promoted the curse. The seventh trumpet has brobably not been sounded in our time (1936). And the world has yet to experience the climax of evil and the consequent judgment of God. After that, Christ will win the decisive and final victory in winning the obedience and submission of all men, and then the curse shall be lifted. The second reason for the end of the curse is, "and His servants shall serve Him".

All bishops and priests shall, after Antichrist, be on the high spiritual plane of the apostles and saints. They will not serve their selfish and worldly desires but will strive only for the glory of God and the salvation of souls. The cares and pleasures of this life will not enslave them; laziness and hypocrisy will be unknown among them; their lives will be pure, transparent gold exemplifying the teachings of the Church consistently and thereby winning the world for Christ. Grand results will follow.

Verse 4

The first sentence of this verse, "And they shall see His face", may again be used to prove the vision of the New Jerusalem to reveal the state of the Elect after the resurrection and their enjoyment of the Beatific Vision. But another explanation is possible. Our Lord said: "Blessed are the clean of heart, for they shall see God" (Mt. V. 8). This shall indeed be true in a perfect way in the Beatific Vision, but all the elect shall see Him then. Even in this life, the pure have a more enlightened and vivid faith and a keener love of God and see His ways in everything. In the Old Dispensation, only the ceremonially clean, who had purified themselves levitically, might enter the Temple. David expresses this: "Who shall ascend into the mountain of the Lord: Or who shall stand in His holy place? The innocent of hand and clean of heart" (Ps. XXIII. 3-4).

Those who see His face may be all who deal most intimately with the eucharistic Christ. They actually see Him hidden beneath the sacramental veil. The sentence referring to "His servants" means first the bishops and priests and may include the religious and faithful laity who have a vivid faith, and impelled by love receive daily communion, anxiously keep the commandments and keep their hearts clean and free from impurity, hypocrisy and self-interest.

"His name shall be on their foreheads" alludes to III. 12. It expresses the sincerity of their devotion to our Lord and the unselfish charity of their hearts. As has been written in the biographies of many saints, their true love of God and of their neighbor beamed from their countenance. This was said of the virgins (XIV. 1), because they had consecrated themselves to the Lamb with sincerity and without reservations, had overcome the Beast by refusing submission to him and had kept themselves unspotted from the world. St. John still has the Beast in mind. The name of God and of the Lamb on the foreheads of His servants is stated as an antithesis to the name of the Beast on the foreheads of his votaries. And these servants of the Lamb are thus marked as true priests of God and are His property.

Verse 5

What was said of the city in the foregoing chapter (23-25) is here said of its inhabitants. There shall be no more night for the world. This alludes to the darkness that came upon Egypt in the Ten Plagues and figuratively pronounces the end to all plagues and punishments for the world. The judgment upon Antichrist and his followers is called darkness and evening and his end the breaking of day for the world, because there shall be no more judgments upon the world until the resurrection of the dead (Zach. XIV. 6-7). When the millennium has begun, and all peoples eagerly seek God, fear of God shall have passed away, and in its place filial love shall abide and tingle in every heart.

This verse is still predicated of the "servants". The light of the lamp may mean human artifices which men have invented to find truth. Those who have not the fullness of truth wander around seeking it by the erring light of reason or science. This was the light of the heathen world in the time of St. John. When divine revelation is accepted without reserve or doubt, the flickering light of philosophy or of science or the aspirations of the heart are no longer needed to light men through this life to their eternal destiny. The knowledge of God shall solve all problems of life and direct men through all difficulties and perplexities.

The light of the sun is not artificial light but the symbol of God's visible creation, which conveys to the mind a positive knowledge of Him. But even that will not be needed during the millennium. This may have a varied explanation. Miracles may be plentiful, or the direction of human life by clearly supernatural power so visible or the answer to prayer so instantaneous, that the phenomena of nature are not relied on by men, for the hand of God is plainly visible. It may have another meaning. Since the covenant of an earthly order bearing a promise of earthly reward for faithful observance has passed away; and since a new covenant of a supernatural order and spiritual enlightenment has arisen in its perfection, earthly promises are superfluous to move men to faithfulness, because God enlightens their minds with such an effulgence of grace, that they understand the vastly greater value of eternal gains and are moved more forcefully by them than by earthly promises. "Behold I make all things new" shall have reached its fulfillment, when men think as St. Paul (2 Cor. V. 15-18), who evaluated all things by their eternal worth.

The reward for these servants is, "they shall reign forever and ever". The elders expressed this: "Thou hast made us to our God a kingdom and priests, and we shall reign on the earth." (V. 10). St. Gregory says: "cui servire regnare est". Those who serve Christ shall become masters of themselves and shall lead their fellowmen to like victories. How deplorable it is if laymen have more earthly than divine motives for faithfulness to the Church and would apostatize if God gave them no earthly prosperity. It might be feared that some enter the priesthood for temporal gains or are active and busy when they see temporal rewards for their labors. When all his servants shall serve Him, they shall gain an eternal empire. Perhaps the meaning is still more idealized. Perhaps during the millennium, priests and bishops will live so spiritual and unworldly a life as to make all natural gifts superfluous. Natural excellencies of mind and character may be lost sight of in the divine light and power that radiates from their example of unblemished virtues. The Holy Spirit may deal out His charismata to supplement the lack of studies, for which there is no time immediately after the end of Antichrist, when his persecution has caused a dearth of priests in the world.

St. John evidently indulges in a very refined idealism in these two chapters as he did in chapter VII. The New Jerusalem is the ideal Church, which shall become a very near reality, when the power of the enemy is bound in the abyss. To some extent the ideals have been realized in the lives of individual saints during past ages of the Church. But when the new age has been inaugurated, the ideal may become quite universal reality. St. Augustine rejects the application of this vision to his own time and to the status of the Church and the world then (de civ. Dei. xx. 17). His was the true conception of that time as it would be of the present time, but it may become reality in the world during a millennium to begin when Satan can no longer mislead mankind. St. Augustine pushes his opinion too far, however, when he supposes that such an ideal state cannot be attained until after the end of the world. His ideas contradict St. Justine's and that of the most ancient Fathers.

XII. CONCLUSION

1. The Testimony Of The Angel.

Verses 6-11.

Verse 6

The first words are a repetition of words in the foregoing chapter but have a different application. St. John has received richer promises and prospects of vaster triumphs than before, and they too shall be fulfilled as the former little by little at the beginning of the millennium and that shall be the pledge of the complete fulfillment of all revelations, the coming of Gog and the Last Judgment. Although the range of the visions seems to compass the highest idealism, there is nothing meaningless or extravagant in the promises, and not a superfluous word has been used in recording them. God who is the Lord and Inspirer of the prophets is the source of these revelations, and they are therefore truthful and trustworthy. Here again the book is clearly averred to be a prophecy and not a book of consolations alone. The same Lord who inspired and instructed the prophets of Old has revealed these facts. The angel here is not the same one who showed St. John the city but the one of chapter I. 1.

The prophetical part of the Apocalypse is now complete in the detailed description of the New Jerusalem and the New World. St. John then speaks as an apostle to the Church and with divine authority utters his last admonitions. The style of the last part of the book is broken and disconnected. He may have added it later, when he added the introduction.

The Apostle voices a practical warning to the Christians by repeating the words of our Lord (III. 11): "Behold I come quickly". The recorded judgments shall not be long delayed. If the Seer wrote them about the year 96 A. D., as is universally held by all orthodox Scripture scholars, the judgment upon the Church was in operation and would soon be intensified under Trajan. The judgment upon the first persecutors of Christ, the Jews, was also soon to begin and was to end with the extermination of their nation.

Verse 7

"The words of this prophecy" are all the words of the book including the first three chapters. The admonitions in those first chapters are highly important, for those who will not hear them shall be in grave danger of not bearing patiently the trials foretold. He who keeps in mind the words of warning to the churches and conforms his life to them will keep all the other admonitions, for God will supplement his intentions and will-power with efficient grace to endure. He is felicitated for his good will.

Verse 8

The witnesses of these revelations are the ones named in the first chapter, the angel, Jesus and St. John himself. All three testify to the truth of everything recorded. St. John possibly dictated the whole book to several secretaries, and before them he attests the veracity of all he has dictated. The awareness of the extraordinary favor conferred by the momentous revelations entrusted to him so overpowered the Seer, that in spite of the admonitions of the other angel (XIX. 10), he falls down in obeisance at this angel's feet. He relates this incident when making the attestation to denote that neither he nor the angel are the source of the revelations. As he did in XIX. 10, St. John again expressed his gratitude in this manner to the angel for pronouncing those blessed who receive and accept the revelations and are called to membership in the Church.

Verse 9

The angel refuses to accept the obeisance of the Seer, because he is himself a fellow-servant of God with the Apostle and a fellow-prophet. They are equal before God. The angel as a prophet has believed in this prophecy and is a brother of those who reverently accept it now. He thus restrains St. John from giving him any glory for the revelations, because God is their Cause and Origin and the Accomplisher of the facts revealed. The angel acted only as a messenger to deliver the message, of which St. John is the recipient and recorder for the enlightenment of the faithful and the glory of God. Therefore God alone must be adored for having drawn it from the depths of His Foreknowledge and alone must receive thanksgiving for pronouncing those blessed who hear and accept it.

The angel being one of the prophets is possibly Isaias, who wrote in his own book a great deal of what is contained in this book. From the very first chapter, the titles Christ assumes are those given Him by Isaias. Although many scenes in the book are contained in the other prophecies, Isaias has the key to the visions throughout. The angel may therefore be Isaias. The prophecies recorded by Isaias are somewhat obscure but are expounded and cleared up in these new revelations, so that the future Church might know their import and especially at the time of greatest peril, the reign of Antichrist, might be enlightened and guided by them.

Verse 10

As in chapter one (I. 9-11) St. John received the injunction to make known the revelations without delay, so here he is not to seal up the knowledge imparted, but to report it at once because the fulfillment is at hand. He probably noted down the visions at the time of their reception and dictated them as soon as possible. The Holy Spirit then watched over his dictation to state without error all details of the revelations including the interpretation of the unintelligible ancient prophecies. Only once was the Seer forbidden to write what he had seen and heard (X. 4). The revelations were of immediate use, because the judgments were to begin shortly at the house of God. This puts the date of composition at about 96 A. D. Domitian had exiled St. John in 95 at the beginning of his persecution which did not last long, since he was assassinated in 96 A. D. His successor, the gentle Nerva, forbade any molestation of the Christians. Long before the composition of the Apocalypse, persecution had been known in Asia Minor (II. 13), and this was probably under Nero.

St. John may have had Domitian in mind when writing many statements in the book. But the whole book is the revelation of the Holy Spirit and conveys God's own meaning. The persecutions became general under Trajan after the year 98 A. D. From that time on there were always many martyrs, because the decrees were never erased from the statute-books until 311 A. D. There was a lull in the storm at times, during which the emperors did not enforce the decrees against the Christians, but even then popular fury made martyrs. So the clause "the time is at hand" probably means the persecution of Trajan.

Verse 11

The first words of this verse are linked to the last thought recorded and refer to the cruel persecutors. Those who injure others shall have full liberty to grow more cruel until they are confirmed in injustice and are worthy of damnation, for their downward course is rapid and sure and it becomes a single act in its consequences to fix the character in evil until finally there is no more change or repentance possible. The pure and blameless lives of the Christians excited the envy and hatred of the degraded pagans and the malice of the devil and thus called forth the persecutions. The Christians too needed a warning, for some had given way to sin, and if they still chose evil after hearing these revelations, they would ripen in wickedness and would be cast out of the congregation of the just. Also the filthy shall be given perfect liberty to wallow in moral filth, if they prefer this to virtue. The evil consequences are recorded in this book, but beyond a sufficient admonition the Holy Spirit will not interfere with anyone's free will. These statements are not an encouragement to sin but reveal the will of God to give every rational being liberty to choose what he lists. The persecution brings the opportunity to develop in virtue or vice, sanctity or filthiness, cruelty or charity.

As the cruel and filthy shall become finished in evil through the persecutions, so the just shall have the grandest occasion to ripen in virtue. By bearing patiently the loss of all civil rights, all property and security, the just elicit the grace of God and rise swiftly and surely to higher heights of virtue and to closer and more intimate union with Him. The consequence of this is an advance from holiness to holiness accelerated as graces become more abundant and intense. The Christians who are enlightened by the Holy Spirit will make no mistake, will choose aright and will then be fortified against the danger of apostasy.

2. The Warning Of Our Lord.

Verses 12-15.

Verse 12

Our Lord repeats the words of verse seven that He will come to begin a rigorously just judgment. Although he said: "The last shall be first and the first last", He will strictly reward everyone according to his deserts. His words in the Gospel may hint at rewards meted out in the Church according to human standards. Many may have been "firsts" or been advanced above others more deserving, but when the Rewarder comes, these firsts shall be last, and those who were shoved aside shall be first. But all this will depend on their merits. And only those can look forward to the judgment confidently who have sincerely labored for higher virtue and purer holiness. This is a terrible warning for those who wait for extraordinary manifestations of God's truth. If they will not accept it until He comes in judgment, it will be too late, because He will then render to everyone according to his works. Even then they would not be ready to sacrifice everything for eternal life. When Antichrist arrives, the enemies of the Church and all who have stood aloof and scorned the call of grace and all bad Catholics will not be converted by the plagues of the time but will fall into the snares of Satan. This sentence is not contained in the same way elsewhere in the Apocalypse but is made up of what is said in II. 23, XI. 18, XX. 12. The verse alludes to Isaias. (XL. 10; LXII. 11).

Verse 13

Our Lord repeats what he said in chapter I. 8, 17, 28. The Alpha and Omega are the first and last letters of the Greek alphabet. He pronounces Himself the source of revelation, the last letter of it and the finisher of God's purposes. The words allude to the Gospel (Jo I. 1), where St. John develops this truth showing Christ to be the beginning of creation. In the book of Isaias, God says: "I God the first, and to futurity I am" (XLI. 4 Sept.). "I am the first and I am hereafter" (XLIV. 6). "I am the first and I am forever" (XLIII. 12 Sept.). Christ is the beginning of creation, the one for whose sake it was called into existence, since through Him and by Him all would be brought to the feet of the Father to glorify and praise Him. He, the Mover and Motive, induced Almighty Power to begin creation and subject it all to Him that He, the divine Captain, might lead it to its final destiny and triumph. He finished revelation to give every rational creature the knowledge and means to get to his destiny. He is thus the first and last letter of revelation showing the reason for the existence of all creatures and impelling them gently and reasonably to attain their last end. Then

He will mete out the awards deserved by all.

Verse 14

The Lord adds the condition here for those whom He pronounces blessed, which an elder in chapter VII. 14 expressed. However, the Greek text leaves out the phrase "in the blood of the Lamb". The Vulgate contains it, and the association of ideas calls for it. Perhaps for that reason St. Jerome added it. But our Lord is speaking, and therefore the phrase is out of place. These who washed their robes have not retained their sins, have not had them covered by the merits of Christ as by a mantle, but have themselves washed them by works of penance and piety. They are in a blessed state, are actually clean and are clothed in wedding garments. The purity acquired by penance or piety gives them the right to the tree of life. Adam was driven from the tree of life for his disobedience, and those who accept the revelations of Christ with unreserved submission of mind and will repair that disobedience, are restored to original grace and purity and may then partake of the tree. The fruits confer spiritual immortality, sanctity, virtue and perfection. The tree of life in Paradise conferred only immortality of the body. Those who continually wear the robes of innocence and are free from all willful attachment to sin are citizens of the spiritual kingdom of Christ and may enter the Holy City through the open gates whenever they choose. They have free access to the holy sacraments, the right to instruction and enlightment in the religion and protection against errors and vices, so they may know God's ways and be enabled to walk in His paths.

Verse 15

Seven classes of sinners are enumerated here, and among them are included all sinners as in the enumeration of XXI. 8 and 27. St. John under divine enlightenment probably understood that as the Church grew in numbers she would lose in purity, and so he rejoices in the final triumph, when all who are impure in any manner are outside the communion of the faithful. To the oriental mind, dogs are contemptible creatures, and they symbolize moral filth and spiritual and moral cowardice. Sorcerers sin against the first and second commandments seeking gain through the aid of evil spirits. The unchaste sin against the 6th and 9th commandments, murderers against the 5th, 7th and 10th and servers of idols against the 1st commandment. The beginning and end of a sentence are the strongest grammatical positions, and hence St. John puts at the end of the sentence those who love and act a lie, which was probably the order in which our Lord spoke. He who acts a lie, a pretender, a hypocrite, who evades his duty will eventually love a lie considering it skill and adroitness to trick others or to dodge the acceptance of a serious decision thus getting around a difficulty by 'diplomacy'. By putting this class of sinners in the strongest grammatical position, our Lord expresses His strongest condemnation for the insincere and hypocrites, as He did in the Gospel. They sin against the 1st and 8th commandments. In their number is not only included the unbelievers, scoffers and heretics, but all the falsehearted slanderers who are quick with rash judgments. The lover of falsehood is akin to Satan who is the father of lies. During the millennium, such shall not be admitted into the Holy City nor be permitted to partake of the tree of life. Apostolic simplicity and sincerity shall rigidly rule.

3. Final Attestation.

Verses 16-end.

Verse 16

For the first time, Jesus mentions His personal name here. By this He places His seal upon the whole book. And because it is the last book and completion of all written revelation, it is His seal upon the whole written word of God. It is the signature of the King of Ages at the foot of this divine document. Our Lord Himself now mentions the angel, whom St. John first mentioned in I. 1 and again in verse 6 above. In verse 6 above, the angel testified to his mission and office in the delivery of these revelations, and our Lord now corroborates this testimony. It attaches to the revelations the highest test of credibility, for no one will doubt them, if our Lord confirms their veracity and authenticity. The churches to which these last revelations were addressed by name are the type of the universal or Catholic Church. Our Lord makes that wider application here. St. Ignatius used the term 'Catholic Church' some ten years later (Smyr. viii).

In Isaias (XI. 10), Christ is called the "root of Jesse" and in the Apocalypse (V. 5) the "root of David". Now He presents Himself as "the root and offspring of David". The word "root" is used figuratively and "offspring" literally; the latter is clearer and leaves no room for doubt. He is the true descendant of David, whom God promised an everlasting kingdom. And the archangel Gabriel reiterated that promise when he said to the Virgin Mary: "The Lord God shall give unto him the throne of David his Father; and he shall rule in the house of Jacob forever". The reference to the titles given Him by Isaias opens up before the Seer's mind the vistas of all those prophecies and confirms the promises in them. The churches may build safely upon His promises, because the kingdom of David cannot be shaken, when the noblest Scion of that house holds the scepter and as the predestined Victor overthrows the powers of evil. All who enlist in His ranks shall be victors with Him. And because He is the offspring of David, He is the hope of the Gentiles and the morning star of the eternal day which shall not be followed by night. He is the bearer of light, which is the gift of faith driving away the darkness in which the soul of the unbeliever is enveloped. And thereafter darkness cannot overtake him any more.

Verse 17

St. John hears the Spirit under whose guidance he wrote this prophecy declaring the time opportune for the coming of the Judge. And he likewise hears the voice of the Church pronouncing herself sufficiently schooled and prepared to invite the divine Judge to begin judgment upon her. This brings us back to the time of the first vision (I. 11), in which the Seer reviewing all the judgments and their blessed results under the impulse of the Spirit's enlightenment avers opportune any time in which the Judge shall decide to come. Every faithful lover should also eagerly desire the coming of the Lord, for He will not come to destroy but to purify and sanctify the Church and to cleanse the world of the evils in it and make it a fit dwelling place for His children. The Spirit and the Church acknowledge His right to be the Judge of the world knowing He will judge in truth and justice and judgment. And therefore they both yearn for this vindication of the truth, for the establishment of everlasting justice and the universal kingdom of love. The individual Christians shall share in the triumph and reward of the Bride, if they yearn and pray for the fulfillment of the divine will.

The next sentence is rather difficult. It seems to be a promise to the halfhearted or partially enlightened. If they dispose themselves to participate in the yearning of the Church, they too shall receive the promised gift. It seems to be an echo of the words of our Lord: "No man can come to me, except the Father who hath sent me draw him" (Jo. VI. 44). He must first receive the grace to desire the coming of Christ and His justice, and thereafter he shall receive the greater gift of desiring Him as does the Bride, who keeps no reservations in mind but gladly accepts the bitter with the sweet (See X. 10). If he will be amenable to the gift of faith, he shall freely receive gifts of ever increasing value, until he becomes perfected enough in virtue to desire without fear the coming of the Judge. It seems to allude to Isaias (LV. 1, ff) deploring the wanton waste of effort and sacrifices to procure pleasures that do not satisfy the aspirations of the soul.

Verse 18

It is impossible to determine with certainty whether the words of warning in the next two verses are the Lord's or St. John's. Verse 20 seems to make them our Lord's, whilst the two verses themselves are against such a view. They warn against every willful subversion of the teachings in the book not against a mere inadvertant mistake of copying or interpretation. They threaten to 'lay' the plagues described in the prophecy on the culprit like the lashes of the whip. He may never dare to falsify or mutilate the prophecies about the development and completion of the kingdom of God or add anything arbitrarily to their content. If he does, he shall not escape the penalty for his blasphemous endeavors. He shall suffer a part of the penalty here and be hereafter condemned with the followers of Antichrist and of Gog. Just as the falsifier attaches falsifications to the true prophecies, so will God attach to his very being whatever is repulsive and hateful.

Verse 19

If anyone deliberately mutilates the words of this prophecy, ignores their teaching or elides any of them in order the easier to use the rest for a vicious purpose, God will take away his share in the tree of life. The Vulgate has "out of the book of life", whilst the Greek text has "his share from the wood of life". The Greek text fits into the logic of the context. If we read "book of life", we ought to have "his name" instead of "his share". The reading "tree of life" is moreover consistent with "holy city" in the same sentence, because the two chapters deal with the holy city, the tree of life and the water of life almost exclusively. The Greek text is therefore preferable. The culprit who perverts the text shall not partake of the fruits from the tree of life which confer eternal life. The prophecy is inspired, and every word proceeded from the mouth of God. If anyone would be presumptuous enough to amend the inspired word, he would sin grievously by pride and blasphemy and then advance no more in sanctity and virtue but starve spiritually. If he will nullify this prophecy or even deny it to be a prophecy, he shall lose his membership in the Church, which protects by its great high wall the faith and morality of its citizens against the approach of all danger. These prophecies shall support, console and enlighten the Church in the days of her dourest tribulations. Anyone daring to falsify the promises of the prophecies would weaken the hopes of the whole Church.

The warnings of these two verses are like those of Moses (Deut. IV. 2) and allude to those of St. Paul (Gal. I. 8) pronouncing his anathema against all who should dare teach anything at variance with his gospel or try to improve upon the teachings of the Church or to detract from them. The verbal order of verse 19 is aptly transposed from that of verse 18 possibly to ward off a falsification of the sense by attachment of a particular import to the very order of the words. The first sentence emphasizes the necessity of taking to heart the prophecies in their full integrity, and the second pronounces the whole book a book of prophecies, which is to remain intact. The first verse refers to all plagues and menaces with them the falsifier who adds to it or reads into it what is not there and with the consequent eternal punishments; the second verse threatens those who mutilate the book and ignore the admonitions in it with the loss of the promised consolations and rewards.

The words are a withering threat to those Protestant sectaries who have interpreted the prophecies in accordance with their prejudices and their own private purposes. They have ever represented the Pope as the Antichrist, although such an interpretation is an open contradiction of the text and of the whole New Testament. Many of these sects have ignored the teachings of parts of the Sacred Text or misconstrued other parts to suit their evil intentions and have torn sentences from the context and used them to contradict other portions of the New Testament. The Apocalypse and the book of Daniel have been distorted into many kinds of contradictory meanings by those who will not hear or believe the truth but want to follow their own prejudices and impose them upon others. The Apocalypse is full of consolation and inspiration for those who receive the revelations in the sense in which the Infallible Church, the authentic Interpreter, explains them, i. e. to harmonize with and supplement the whole body of revelations in both the Old and the New Testament. Protestantism has rejected the Interpreter and appointed the judgment of every individual reader, no matter how ignorant, as the INFALLIBLE INTERPRETER of Scripture. The result of such a principle had to be what it is. Hence the learned Scripture scholars, such as H. B. Swete, were forced to contradict the absurd and vicious use of the Apocalypse and other prophetical books by the wild and bigoted sectaries. Protestantism itself contradicts the principle of a free interpretation of Scripture by having Bible Schools in which it teaches definite views of interpretation. Everyone who interprets this or any text of Scripture in accordance with his prejudices is out of harmony with the divine Will, is unworthy of his divine inheritance and cannot share in the bounties of the Spirit of God.

Verse 20

Our Lord Himself answers the invitation of the Spirit, the

Church and the faithful reader and promises to come soon. He has given His solemn testimony to the veracity of all the revelations in this book, and He will come to fulfill all promises contained therein and will direct the destiny of the Church through the ages. It is a final admonition to every Christian to stand ready for the supreme test of his loyalty to his Lord.

St. John addresses the last invitation to our Lord by the words "Amen, Come Lord Jesus". The "Amen" means more than 'so be it'; it is the solemn close to the written word of God and an acknowledgement of a perfect rendition of Revelation by the Son of God. All shall be well with the world, if God's will has its sweet and benign way without hindrance. The "Amen" is the fitting response to our Lord's promise given a devoted soul eagerly awaiting His coming to direct the forces of destiny to the goal set for them in the divine Plan. The last words, "Come Lord Jesus", are a restrained outburst of the feelings pent up in the heart of the inspired Seer. After his great mind reviewed the whole panorama of revelations from the first vision to the last, grace alone made it possible to control the intensity of feelings evoked. When he spoke the words, he had in mind the final triumph as depicted in the visions of the New World and the New Jerusalem, and he saw the realization of it pushed away into the distant future, and therefore he all the more desired the coming of our Lord to bring about this realization as speedily as the divine Plan and Will permitted. But above all, he desired the triumph of his beloved Master over the many enemies who now ignored, despised and derided Him. His triumphs would bring the revealed joys to a world in which only the ruling lords revelled in an earthly felicity. God alone could know the depth of feelings expressed by the beloved disciple in those parting words.

Verse 21

The ending of this prophecy is not like the ending of the prophetical books of the Old Testament nor like the gospels but like the epistles of St. Paul. It has the form of an epistle in its beginning and end but the contents of a prophecy. The seven letters are a real epistle, and probably for their sake, St. John put the whole book in an epistolary form beginning and ending it according to the models of St. Paul. The closing words are a pious wish and a prayer for the faithful. Only by the grace of God would they have the strength and courage to face all weapons and attacks of the powers of evil and triumph with the Lord, their Captain and Leader. The old world that served Satan was to be wrecked and demolished, and the faithful were destined to survive its demolition. When the old earthly empires and kingdoms had passed away and the curse of God with them, and their vices and corruption had been buried beneath the wreckage and the dust of the ages, the faithful were to inherit the good that was in them and to rebuild another world and under divine guidance model it according to God's own plans and specifications and to dominate this new world. The whole course of history was to be directed for God's honor and glory and the benefit of those who give Him his glory, who shall inherit all bounties of God, complete the divine plans and satisfy the desire of the Creator, the Redeemer and Sanctifier.

THE END